Praise for **Mash Up**

"Klingler's new thriller is a ride into the dark side of computers and comedy. Klingler's plot definitely has a Quentin Tarantino-feel to it. Cleverly designed, *Mash Up* is the perfect detective read, as well as a classic addition to the noir genre."—***San Francisco Book Review (5 of 5 Stars)***

"Klingler is skilled at writing action scenes. He puts the reader directly in the line of fire, and he doesn't let up…Anyone interested in thrillers or police procedurals will find much to appreciate in this newest Qigiq installment."—***Foreword Clarion Reviews (4Star ✷✷✷✷)***

"Klingler makes supreme use of his tech knowledge in a grisly mystery that strives to address the ethics of content ownership. His effortlessly clever prose makes the subject thoroughly entertaining …a thoughtful, well-constructed tale."—***Kirkus Reviews***

"[Klingler] has fantastic talent for imbuing wit into situations that normally wouldn't be witty...almost every character offers some sort of unique perspective and really great moments where I laughed aloud. If you can make me laugh while simultaneously making me wonder what the hell is going on, then I'll read any book you have to write. The author's writing style actually reminds me a little of Dean Koontz, if you take out Koontz's supernatural leanings."—**Literature Typeface**

ALSO BY JOE KLINGLER

RATS
Missing Mona

To occasionally receive news on book releases, previews, discount
promotions and more, please join *Joe's Readers* at
www.joeklingler.com

J O E
KLINGLER

Mash Up

A KANDY & QIGIQ NOVEL

Published by
Cartosi LLC

ISBN: 1941156037
ISBN-13: 978-1-941156-03-2

Cover design by Ansel Niner
Violinist image copyright Katarzyna Wojtasik.
Knife image copyright indigolotos.
Both used under license from Shutterstock.com.

Designed in the United States of America

www.joeklingler.com

DEDICATED TO ROBERT J.

Bending stainless steel was never so much fun

Acknowlededements

While writing is a solitary effort, feedback is indispensable as the course from opening sentence to the ideal The End is charted. The author would like to thank Amy Brekeller and Jim Elliott who helped navigate these waters by providing commentary on early versions of this work. Robyn Russell, editor extraordinaire, again contributed her time, keen eye and unique perspective to help refine this story. Thanks also to Catherine Kuchers and Michele Bighouse who proofread, corrected, and asked insightful questions of the penultimate draft. Finally, a big thank you to R., whose persistant support and belief continues unabated.

Five inches of duct tape stilled the air. This hadn't been the plan—but the softness of her bare body flopping on the deck like fresh flounder had insisted. And why not? Why not use it before it was gone?

The Velcro strap of the headband opened with a quick tear and closed to affix a tiny camera to forehead. Both hands in front, rotated palms up, showed off smooth supple rubber gloves like a player in Blue Man Group. Tap the keys of a laptop, adjust camera position, and wait for the exact moment. Closer now, her flopping stopped, gazes met. Her wide blue-crystal eyes screamed a fear that didn't seem so different from desire.

Kneeling; smiling; nakedness lowered towards nakedness.

The rocking of ocean waves superimposed on the floating softness of her belly felt like bathing in heroin. This should happen more often—escape drudgery, follow the calling. Closed eyes and long slow breaths, holding back like the dam built by Hoover. Holding. Holding.

Crashing in a long, long spasm. Again, again...fading.

Sweating face dropped to bare chest. She had stopped moving, but the soft warmth of her breast caressed a cheek. Eyes closed and mind drifting in the aftermath of a simple biological function. Yet the effect was beyond description.

And anything but simple.

Resting now. Resting. It was time. There was work to do.

Qigiq woke to the rumble of a V-twin. He dragged the phone to his face and touched the *Answer Call* button to his nose.

"Qigiq here."

"Morning, Qu. We have fingers," Kandy said.

"Hi, partner. McDonald's for breakfast?"

"Nope. From a hand."

Qigiq rolled to his back and sat up. He blinked hard.

"Go ahead, Kandy. I'm awake."

"We have the middle finger and thumb of a left hand. Nail length and purple polish says female. A guess from the skin puts the age at sixteen to twenty-two. No lab work yet."

"Uh-huh."

"One thing."

"Only one?" Qigiq said.

"Yeah. There's no hand. The base of the finger has been stitched to the thumb to make one long digit. Looks likes a pale Cuban cigar."

"And?" He waited for the punch line.

"And...the fingers showed up in a bag. At least that's what Robina is telling us."

Robina.

"Came in a cardboard Amazon box bigger than a book. Inside she found a Ziploc. And the fingers."

"Was there a packing slip, Kandy? Amazon always sends a packing slip." He tried to laugh but failed.

"I'm humorless before seven. There's a sticker on the outside of the baggie."

A pause. She was going to make him ask.

"And the sticker says..."

"Under a crude Apple logo there's lawyer mumbo: 'This device is for legal or rights-holder copying only.' Then it says in big letters, 'Don't Steal Music.'"

"Don't steal music. On the sticker."

"Right."

"Is the baggie special?"

He heard crumpling plastic. "Not that I can see."

"Would you check if that's an official Apple sticker, and if they ship products in a baggie like the one you're crumpling even though it's evidence in—" he hesitated. In what?

"Got it," she said.

His new partner was quick. He was lucky.

"I'm on my way," he said.

"I'll start checking...if anyone's awake down in Cupertino. And I'll locate some real Amazon boxes."

He swung his feet to the hardwood floor and padded barefoot to the head. A tiny window over the sink let him see the sun's warm red rays reflect from the water of San Francisco Bay. Kandy had been right, living on a houseboat in Marin County was indeed a new experience for a man from Alaska.

He dressed quickly.

As he ducked out the main door from the cabin—a small rectangular house that covered almost the entire hull beneath it—he noticed tall buildings across the bay protruding through floating gray mist. For a brief moment he imagined the piano harmonies of Debussy's *Sunken Cathedral*, wondering if he could ever grow accustomed to blue water, fog and concrete after decades of snow?

He crossed a weathered wooden dock supported by pillars the size of telephone poles. Ten steps up a bank brought him to a white and green Moto Guzzi motorcycle, police edition, missing its protective plastic fairing. He strapped on a helmet, swung a leg over the machine and instantly felt at home, though Fairbanks was three thousand miles to the north.

On the third try the sensual rumble of the Italian twin greeted the bay. Traffic on the Golden Gate was barely keeping up with tourists strolling the sidewalk, but California law allowed him to ride over the white Botts' dots embedded in the pavement between lanes. Eighteen and a half minutes later he circled to the back of an eighty-year-old brick building. His parking spot between a green trash bin and the steel railing for the basement stairs was empty, except for a wrapper from a Mucho Grande burrito.

"About time," Kandy said to his reflection in the two-way mirror where she stood watching a girl alone in the interrogation room sip from a big beige mug, her shoulders rolling in giant sobs.

He stopped beside her. "Traffic. Even with a bike and those fancy FasTrak toll booths you have down here."

She turned to face him.

"Her name's Robina. Came in less than an hour ago with the package. She was in hysterics then, swears she knows whose fingers they are. Want to see them?"

"Before breakfast?"

She twisted her right cheek into a smile and cocked her head. "This way."

Kandy led him to a cubbyhole makeshift kitchen: drip machine, microwave, fridge. The fridge had yellow strips of "Crime Scene Do Not Cross" tape wrapped across the door. She started to peel them off.

"Lab's on the way over, but I thought you would want to see this."

"Thanks."

She slipped on rubber gloves, withdrew an SFPD evidence bag from the top shelf, and tilted her head up to face him. Her auburn hair dropped left.

"Robina says this was in her mail yesterday, that would be Wednesday in case you're not paying attention. Like I said on the phone, Amazon.com box, packed with dry ice, and this."

Without opening the evidence bag she held back the flap of the box with the fingertip of her right hand. Qigiq peeked in at another plastic bag half covered with a white sticker. Protruding from behind the sticker he could see a fingertip with metallic purple polish. The polish was chipped. He wondered if they might be able to find that chip someplace. He sighed. Someplace in a city of over half a million if he didn't count the sprawl. The finger looked like a very real mannequin pointing him in the right direction for good pancakes.

He visualized a girl's hand missing two digits. Turned his eyes away from the mannequin, but it didn't help. He swallowed hard, unclenched his jaw, pointed at the bag.

"Robina thinks she knows this person?"

"Yeah. Swears it's a girl named Sally Bellowi. They play...um, played in a string quartet together. Call themselves Fourtunate: F-O-U-R."

Qigiq glanced at Kandy's face. No grin.

"Dusted?"

"First pass. We've only been touching it with these." She produced a set of forceps about as long as his hand.

He clamped on the edge of the bag and lifted it from the box. He twisted his wrist so he could see the digits from the other side of the baggie. They were indeed stitched together base to base, creating an alien looking object that a humanoid robot might use as a gripping tool. Blood that had oozed through the stitching before freezing formed a rusty red glue where the two digits were joined. He noticed the same purple polish on the thumb, this time no chips, just a smooth shiny finish like a hot rod at a car show.

He took a deep breath, tried to detach himself, think objectively, but his chest stayed tight.

"What's that on the side of the thumb?" he asked.

"The lump? Yeah, we noticed that, too. It looks like a skin eruption of some sort. Robina says it's called a cellist's callus, apparently an occupational hazard. If she's right, that's the left thumb. Sally bowed right-handed."

"Motive?"

"Nothing."

"Leads?"

"Robina says Sally was dating a couple of guys: an angry rock musician studying composition at the San Francisco Conservatory, and..."

Qigiq looked up. Kandy's eyes were searching the room.

"It's just a rumor."

"Robina said it's a rumor?" he asked.

"No. She claims to know."

"Know what?"

"Sally is having an affair with a college professor."

"Ground breaking. I've never heard of that happening before." He managed a wry smile.

"He's married."

"I'm so shocked," he said. "Anything else?"

"Not really. Figured you might want to talk with our new friend Robina."

Qigiq glanced at Kandy's deep blue sleeveless shirt stretched tight across her breasts: no markings—not even a designer logo pressed into the cloth. Black jeans and black leather boots that he would be comfortable riding around the world in implied business.

"You think I look less intimidating?"

"Nope. I figured you could try the father-figure thing." She laughed, returned the evidence to its makeshift locker, and replaced the Do-Not-Cross tape.

© © ©

Qigiq turned the doorknob to the interrogation room slowly with only his fingertips, so as not to startle the young girl. She was sitting with her back to him, still holding the ceramic coffee mug with both hands. He walked in, tapping the floor with his riding boots. She didn't move. He stepped around the table, pulled out a scratched wooden chair, and sat down to face her.

She watched him from behind strands of pale yellow hair.

"Hello. I'm Detective Qigiq."

Her deep brown eyes were wet under an eye shadow that looked like gray ash from a fireplace.

"Could we talk about the package you brought in?"

She lowered the mug. Looked up.

"Ki-jeek? Sort of weird. Where's the woman detective?"

He met her gaze. "Taking a break. I'm from Alaska."

"You mean you're not a European import like the rest of us?" She tried to smile.

"Never been to Europe."

"How do you spell it?"

He figured she could spell Europe.

"Q-i-g-i-q. Like kickstart, soft g, eke...as in eking out a living as a detective."

"Retrograde," she said, lifting the index finger of her left hand and wiggling it back and forth like a human metronome.

He raised his eyebrows.

"The retrograde is the same as the theme. You know, the same forward and backwards. There's a word for it."

He smiled. "Palindrome."

"Yeah...yeah, that's it. Funny."

At least she was talking. She looked thin inside a loose black T-shirt that bore a musical score. She wore blue jeans cut off mid-thigh and soft fur-lined boots that rose to mid-calf, the knee between looking like it couldn't support a small grasshopper. He wondered if she was one of those anorexic college girls who starved themselves trying to be attractive. He glanced at his wrist, almost eight.

"I know you've been through this, I've seen the report." He fibbed, he had only heard Kandy's summary. "Do you think you could go through it once more so I can hear you tell it?"

She squeezed the mug. Her eyes weren't focused.

He guessed where her mind was. Had an idea. "Have you had breakfast?"

Her response was instantaneous.

"God no, I'm starving. Do you have anything decent in this place? Your coffee is the worst."

Qigiq straightened. Surprise number one.

"No, there's nothing decent here, but Peggy's Pancakes has good food. Would that be okay?"

"Sure." A hesitation. "If you're buying. Music students don't have much in the way of discretionary funds." She looked up. "Is it close? I don't have a car."

Qigiq stood. "Sure, on me. About a mile, we can get there fast."

~ 3 ~

Eddy Blake looked past the board members on either side of the polished ash conference table and out through the plate glass fourth-floor window. His eyes landed briefly on his black SL550 Mercedes in the far corner of the lot, parked diagonally in two spaces to prevent door dings, then beyond the car and across the boulevard to the building that housed Apple's headquarters.

He suppressed a smile.

Everyone had insisted he couldn't run a music company in northern California. He had insisted music was now a technology business about distribution at a profit, not making records in the City of Angels. Hell, anyone could record a hit song in their bedroom with a Korean guitar and a smartphone. And the best technology and the money to fund it was up north—in Silicon Valley.

He had been right.

It was easy to find funding up here, and he liked being across the street from the big shiny music machine of Apple Inc that sold songs the way McDonald's sells hamburgers: billions every year. His eyes dropped back to the black shine of the SL. What a fantastic vehicle, and only six months old. He would hate to have to give it back because the people around this table didn't have the cranium power to see his vision.

The other three men in the room were still all talking at the same time.

"Wait, wait, wait!" Eddy shouted. "Please guys. One at a time."

They grumbled into silence, slowly deferring to the CEO. They didn't work for him, he worked for them. But if he failed, it was their money that would vaporize.

"Yes, there is a problem in the media business, especially the music business," he said.

Terry McTyme, a tall wiry guy who ran marathons for fun, said, "Yeah, customers have decided stealing product is the American Way." With his right hand he pushed back loose more salt than pepper hair that had fallen forward during the shouting match.

Terry's firm, ALL-CAPS Partners, had provided the first round of funding for Eddy's start-up: Silver Platter LLC. Eddy owed him.

"Correct, Terry. Music, movies, e-books; anything digital is at risk. Which is precisely the problem that Silver Platter has set for itself. You've seen the specification for our Full Disclosure project?"

"But when does it release?" Terry said.

"And is it legal?" Greg Simmons asked.

In Eddy's experience, the lawyers were always the worst. And Greg had minored in math, which gave him a weird quiet demeanor that Eddy found hard to predict. But at least he didn't waste hours exercising like crazy Terry.

"We're trying to stop theft here," Eddy said.

"Yes, but your Disclosure technology invades computers like a virus," Roberts offered.

Eddy sighed. He didn't like an investor saying *your* instead of *our*. Hugh Roberts had followed Terry's lead on investing, but Roberts was short, probably rated as obese by his doctor's BMI chart, and hated to take risks. Eddy wondered how he had ever made big money.

"More of a worm than virus. And it does no harm."

"Invasion of privacy," Simmons interjected.

"That has yet to be proven. And second, it removes itself after sending us the information."

"Reaching into a customer's computer and analyzing their music files? Sounds like invasion to me," said Roberts.

"And it isn't ready anyway," Terry added.

Eddy held up both hands like he was giving himself up. "It'll be ready this month. We're beta testing right now. Results are positive."

"Eddy, utter real facts will you please?" asked Roberts.

Eddy tried not to glare at him, since the guy had an eight figure investment on the line.

"I'll bring our young expert in shortly to go through details, but here's what we have. Our farm has two hundred computers working day and night to substitute our music files for ones circulating on the Internet from the peer-to-peer sites that use BitTorrent and similar technology. We've already infiltrated several popular download sites and more than one digital vault."

"Could you please not say infiltrated?" Simmons said.

Eddy watched Simmons scribble on a long legal pad without looking at his hand, knowing the man was recording like a court stenographer. Claimed he learned to do it in law school so he could stare at coeds without missing anything in the lecture.

"OK, we've *contacted* music sites." Eddy studied Simmons' smile for signs of sarcasm but couldn't find any. Lawyers were only helpful in takeovers. "Which means, when someone steals a song over the Internet, they get our tagged music file instead of the original. Ours sound identical to most people and contain the exact number of bytes as the originals. But we can recognize them wherever we find them."

"This is in place and working?" asked Terry.

"Yes. How well it's working will be part of the demonstration."

The room grew quiet for the first time in almost an hour. Eddy sipped cold coffee from a ceramic mug with a silver logo, biting the edge, admiring his reflection in the big glass behind his colleagues. George Clooney should play me in a movie, he thought. Hmm, too old? Maybe DiCaprio, he did a good job with Howard Hughes.

Roberts said, "Then?"

"Then," Eddy echoed, "we say go, Full Disclosure starts roaming and feeding back to us the location of offenders. We work with the RIAA to go after them in court, confiscating machines to analyze whenever possible."

"The court system has been tried," Simmons added.

"Yeah," Eddy replied. "But only twenty, maybe thirty thousand lawsuits. Wimpy. That's not enough to get on everyone's radar. I'm hoping for ten times that, once we know we have the worst offenders so the Recording Industry Association is likely to win. We need all these kids to hear about friends paying huge fines, or better yet, going to jail. Hell, they steal ten thousand songs worth ten thousand dollars and don't even get their fingers smacked. If they stole a ten thousand dollar car it'd be grand theft auto and they'd do time. We need fear instilled in enough people so they return to buying product like they should have been all along."

"What if the courts turn against us?" Simmons asked.

"Good question," Eddy said. "If the courts won't help us enforce justice, then we have a decision to make."

Terry sipped water from a metal bottle containing a special filter and a blue light that was supposed to kill bacteria. Simmons looked down at his yellow legal pad, causing hair to flop across his forehead, and scribbled small blue circles with a Mont Blanc fountain pen. Roberts glanced around the room as if looking for a fly.

"If the courts won't bring thieves to justice we have several options. We could sell the technology or the company to someone who is in a position to make it widely available. Say a Microsoft or Google who might want to use our delivery method to remove illicit material from computers. Imagine parents who want to ensure that they don't see an RIAA lawsuit, so they run software on all of their computers that automatically removes offending files. Microsoft delivers the software, licensed from us, and we stay in business tagging files, since they change every time new music is released. Much better than a digital watermark, more like a watermark factory."

"At least Microsoft would get sued along with us," Simmons said, without looking up.

"But that depends on cutting a deal with a big gorilla. Those are hard to make happen," Roberts said. "Other options?"

Eddy looked to Roberts directly. "Yes. We let Disclosure remove files and report back to us. Or maybe not. We might just want it to run and then remove itself and not have any connection to us."

"And that would?"

"That, Hugh, would scare the bejesus out of anyone downloading files because their music would keep disappearing. And the more they download to replace it, the more likely they would get the virus, I mean Disclosure, again."

"There would be public outcry."

"True. But people who steal can't call too much attention to themselves," Eddy replied. "Especially if the courts are working even a little bit."

The room fell silent. Eddy guessed they were considering how much risk they wanted to take to protect their money. Maybe even make a little more.

"There are two keys and we have to turn one," Eddy said. "Either people have to be afraid to download stolen music because they believe something bad will happen to them." He looked around the room. "Or stealing has to be so damn annoying that we exceed their tolerance level and they start buying just to end the hassle. Either of these can work."

"Fear?" Terry said. "I like that. Fear keeps people in line."

Simmons stopped scribbling. His eyes danced, but didn't land on anyone.

Eddy waited, he knew Simmons was thinking. Even a lawyer had a good idea once in awhile. He rubbed his upper lip with his lower teeth and forced himself not to talk.

"Eddy," Simmons finally said, eyes still darting around the room, "How come you don't speed in your flashy car?"

"What do you mean, Greg, I speed all the time? Well, not *all* the time. There are too many cops."

"Exactly," Simmons said. "This is game theory. Non-cooperative opponents who know each others strategy. I bet there's even a Nash equilibrium."

Eddy waited. Roberts and Terry looked from Eddy to Greg and back.

"You don't speed because you could get a ticket," Greg said. "Enough tickets and you lose your license. There goes your right to use the highway."

"You're saying we should give people tickets for stealing music?" Eddy asked. He didn't get where Greg was headed, but he hadn't thought of this angle before.

"Not us. We're going to be the traffic-light camera company."

Hugh Roberts leaned far back in his chair. "What the hell are you guys talking about?"

"Yeah," Terry said. "Those companies install camera equipment and take a percentage of—" Terry stopped. He looked from Eddy to Greg to Hugh and back to Greg. "You think we could pull it off?"

"It's the Information Superhighway, right? Al Gore said so." Greg smiled, his pen now scratching across the writing pad. "We tag people who harbor illegal files, the local cops send a ticket. Too many tickets, you lose your right to drive." Greg took a deep breath and dragged a finger across his throat. "The local ISP cuts them off." He looked down as his hand-scribbled numbers. "We take a couple percent off the top for installing the virtual red-light cameras."

Eddy dropped his chin into his hand for three full seconds before speaking.

"We run this just like the traffic cameras. Hide under the same surveillance legislation, same local laws. Maybe even get the same percentage of ticket revenue."

Hugh leaned forward. Terry nodded. Greg's hand stopped moving.

"We have some good options. Let's take a break, " Eddy said. "I'll call Engineering."

He pushed away from the table and tapped digits that were special to him. It unlocked.

~ 4 ~

Harold Zeto placed bare elbows on his black desk and stared at two flat displays that blocked his view out the window. The office door was behind him, but a mirror from the door of a candy-apple red '69 Mustang clamped to the right monitor gave him a view into the hall by moving only his eyes.

His chair creaked as he leaned back, studying the rows of symbols that were hieroglyphics to most people, but precise instructions to a computer. He yawned. A stupid demo. Why did execs insist on having board meetings before noon?

Besides, he was behind schedule.

He rocked the chair with one foot and thought hard. If his audio driver was properly identifying the tags as it played music, why wasn't it also lighting up the warning? There was a bug...and he had written it. He had written most of Full Disclosure—including a few hidden bits he never talked about. He worked like a dog so the company could get to an initial public offering, the sacred IPO, and make the worthless paper options Blake had given him over two years ago magically become life-changing money: a mountain of lead turned instantly to gold.

There. He was incorrectly accessing the screen handler. His hands reached for the keyboard as soft tapping drew his eyes to the rearview mirror. The tiny reflected image was Lili wearing a maroon blouse and tight blue jeans, open toe heels, long dark hair flowing free to her shoulders. And those square gold-rimmed glasses sliding down her nose no matter how many times he told her to go to the optometrist to have them adjusted.

"C'mon in, Lili," he said.

"Sorry to bother you, Harold, I know how you hate interruptions. I was just so surprised to see you here early." She stepped through the open doorway. "I brought you a donut."

He spun his chair to face her as she walked in with two cups of coffee and two donuts stacked on a napkin balanced atop the cup in her right hand. He'd bet she was stuck again.

"Thanks Lil," he motioned for her to sit. "What's up?"

She sat in his guest chair, a chunk of woven green cloth and a few steel bars, and pulled her knees together so she could place a napkin and donut on her lap. She sipped at her paper cup; the company having abandoned Styrofoam for employees as not green enough, even though the paper leaked.

She leaned forward to hand him a coffee with a donut on top and grinned. "Harold are you sunburned? I didn't know you ever went outside."

He rubbed the back of his neck. "I don't normally. But my last physical showed elevated cholesterol even though I'm in the normal weight range on the BMI tables. Doc says I should exercise, so I tried hiking."

She shook her head. "My my, Harold Zeto, super-geek, actually goes outdoors."

"You want me to help you, right?" he said.

"Okay, Okay. I'm working on the module that will auto-post to blogs. You remember, we talked a few weeks ago. Give it a list of blogs and some text, and it does the entry for you. So the user doesn't have to post the same thing manually over and over, which would be...well, kind of a yucky job."

"I remember," he said. "Why would anyone want to do this? Blogs are unique and the postings more like a conversation."

"True. But imagine you want to get information out fast. Why not post it a bunch of times: blogs, forums, comments on YouTube, everywhere?"

He watched her take a bite from a chocolate-covered chocolate donut and marveled that she could maintain her slender five-foot-five frame while eating the way he liked to eat.

"Why not just build a website?"

He knew the answer, but wanted to know if she did.

"If you build a website, you have to wait for Google to index it, and then it's only in one place. You would have to build many websites, and host them all, and wait for them all to be indexed."

"Yes..."

She licked the middle finger of her left hand.

"But if you post to a hundred blogs, people who regularly read those blogs will see it right away, and they'll comment, creating more entries to be indexed."

He smiled.

"It's a much faster way to get the word out," she concluded, and took another bite.

"Correct. And it's something else too."

Her perfectly plucked eyebrows frowned beneath a smooth, tanned forehead. "I give, what?"

"Who hosts those blogs?"

"Uh, lots of people," she said through a gooey mess of chocolate.

"Right. Lots of people. Meaning, *not us*. So if your program runs from an anonymous location—"

"Oh. Oh," she brought her hand up to cover her mouth. "They can't find us. Um, I mean, the postings couldn't easily be traced. At least not as easy as looking up a website."

"Bingo, Lili. How's your donut?"

"Great. Aren't you going to eat yours?"

"Sure am. While you tell me what your problem is."

Halfway through her explanation of how she was looping the blog list and mapping her generic blog posting procedure to the vagaries of each individual blog his phone vibrated. He held up a finger to pause her in mid-sentence.

"Hello Mr. Blake...Yes sir, I'm ready." He looked at the floor to concentrate. "I'll tell Lili...Thank you."

He ended the call and met Lili's round blue eyes. "They're ready for the demo, will you bring them to the lab?"

She vibrated off her chair. "Oh yes, for sure." She washed the donut down with coffee. "When do you want them?"

He turned around to face his code. He really wanted to fix this while it was fresh in his head. "Give me ten minutes."

She stood and walked over behind him, admiring the hieroglyphics on his screen. "They're going to love it, Harold, I just know it."

"Hope you're right, Lili."

He watched the denim stretched across her bottom disappear in the rearview mirror then turned his attention to the troublesome line of code. He had nine minutes to finish a donut and get this thing running.

~ 5 ~

The dark lab hummed with the steady sound of four hundred cooling fans inside two hundred computing machines stacked like small black skyscrapers with beady green eyes. Harold pressed the projector button and waited for it to light a screen on the side wall so he could align the image, then dragged the three chairs in the room into a theater viewing row. Though he hadn't presented a live demo to the board before, he had confidence in his software. Less than sixty seconds later Lili walked in leading Blake and three other men.

"It's cold in here," one of them said.

"Helps keep the processors at operating temperature," Harold answered, even though it hadn't been a question.

Blake motioned for the men to be seated. He and Lili stood behind them.

"What have we got today, Mr. Zeto?"

Harold touched the laptop driving the projector. The screen changed from the shiny circle logo of Silver Platter LLC to the desktop of his Windows machine.

"You're familiar with the architecture of Silver Platter technology so I'll skip the diagrams that everyone ignores anyway and show you how it works."

No one moved, but the guy he knew as Terry had his arms wrapped around his body like he was in a meat locker. Harold glanced at Lili to see if she was cold too, but nothing showed under her maroon blouse.

"Our goal is to sell digital assets, beginning with music. The Internet has made the old empire of paper and plastic obsolete, and a new world order is evolving. Toward that end we want to identify people who are stealing assets, though few call it that. Terms like file-sharing and the fair-use clause of copyright law are generally bantered about. But essentially, people are deriving the benefit of listening to the work of an artist without compensating that artist according to the laws of the land."

He started a music player on the screen and let punk-rap rattle the room, then lowered the volume.

"As you know, the free market can only operate if there is competition between suppliers, with the market making its choice when consumers purchase the products they feel provide good value, and rejecting those they feel are overpriced. They reject it by not buying it, thus depriving themselves of its benefit, and its maker the benefit of their dollars. Those suppliers— musicians, record companies, distributors—who cannot provide benefit at the desired price will, therefore, perish economically and cease being suppliers."

Harold watched the older men nod, and Blake smile.

"However. When a high percentage of product is stolen, the portion of the market that is paying for product must bear the cost of all creation and distribution. If theft is rampant, as it is now on the Internet, the free market cannot operate."

"Why is that exactly?" asked Simmons, who was watching the screen carefully while taking notes on a large pad on his lap.

"Because prices aren't set by consumers paying for the merchandise they prefer to listen to. Stealing forces the price to zero, so the means of production will struggle and eventually collapse. Musicians provide benefit, the joy of listening to music, but receive no financial benefit for having done so."

He turned and faced the screen. "This software player is an example of how a customer might listen to their music. They might also copy it to a mobile device like an iPod or an Android phone. The principles I am about to demonstrate apply whenever digital audio passes through this computer, and therefore through the low-level portion of Full Disclosure. We can, of course, eventually build versions for devices other than Windows and the Mac OS, though each one is a new technical challenge."

All eyes were focused on the screen.

"I have set up this machine to be ninety-nine percent complete by letting it play music over several weeks. Naturally, most of this music has been tagged with our dynamic digital watermark technology we call Ink Stain."

They nodded.

Simmons muttered, "Ink Stain?" as he wrote.

Blake looked like a proud papa about to pass out cigars. Lili stood motionless.

"As the music plays, the tags are removed and assembled into a program, like puzzle pieces being locked together. The individual pieces are scattered around the hard disk, so if anyone finds a file, they only have a tiny portion of the whole. Once all the pieces have passed through our driver, a complete copy of the Invisible Hand will exist on the machine. The driver randomizes a delay so we can't be traced to a particular song, then runs IH. Once it starts, we can have it do anything we want."

"Such as," Terry asked, visibly shivering.

A new window popped up on the projector.

"Such as open a window to warn that this machine contains pirated copies of music and is at risk of a lawsuit by the RIAA. Maybe not the scariest thing it could do, but an example."

He saw Blake's lips twitch toward a smile.

Roberts asked, "But what about the argument that all recorded music should be free and artists can make their living by performing live and selling merchandise like T-shirts?"

Harold looked at Blake, wondering if he wanted to take the question. Blake nodded ever so slightly.

Harold said, "My first reaction is simple, bullshit. Artists should be able to benefit from their creations however they wish. If they want to operate under a business model of free recordings and charging for their concerts, that's fine, the technology of the distribution channel should be able to support that. But what if they want to give free concerts and charge for recordings of their music? Why shouldn't they have the freedom to operate under that business model as well?"

"No one uses that model," said Simmons.

"Not yet," Harold said. "But if so-called 'file sharing' were to cease, then some bands might choose to operate that way. Or anywhere in between, adjusting the prices of their concerts and recordings in whatever way works best for them. Perhaps an artist would choose not to tour at all, like Janik down in Texas who prefers to remain obscure, and only make records. Others might only tour, and not make recordings so people would be drawn to their live shows as the only way to hear their music. The options are many, but Silver Platter's position is that the choice should be made by the creators, the artists—not dishonest listeners who have no clue why copyright laws even exist—because it is the artists who are in competition with each other for the listening dollar."

Roberts's cleared his throat.

"You're talking about the artist who records, but doesn't have the health to travel. Why shouldn't that artist be able to sell her work? And symphony orchestras that are fading to museum pieces. Why should a recording by an eighty-piece orchestra using violins that cost five million dollars sell for the same price as something done in the garage by a couple of tone-deaf teenagers? In my opinion, it shouldn't. Each should be able to sell their work for what they choose and let the market decide who profits."

Harold smiled for the first time. "Exactly. And our Full Disclosure suite of technology will help make that possible. Remember, pirates raided the high seas for decades, and Jesse James robbed trains? Whenever assets move, someone tries to go in and grab them. The Internet makes digital grabbing easy. But these people remain pirates and outlaws, and if we want to profit from selling digital assets, we have to stop them."

He tapped keys on his laptop. "Notice that as the Invisible Hand runs it deletes from storage all pirated copies of music, which in this demo is over ninety percent of the library."

Heads nodded all around the room.

"And if we wish," he let the program continue, "the Hand will transmit back to the machines behind you the Internet address of the customer, the number of pirated files it identified, the names of those files, and...the date they were downloaded."

"Bravo," Terry said.

"And." Harold paused to be sure he had their attention. "Now the Hand does it's magic trick. It removes any record of itself from the machine registry including the fact that it ever ran, then securely overwrites itself in memory so it can't be identified from what it leaves behind. No footprints. Gone without a trace. It will even replace our driver, that we insert via a mock software update, with the original one from Microsoft or Apple."

Harold smiled a second time.

Terry stood and stomped his feet in an effort to warm up.

"Looks good Mr. Zeto; very good. Eddy, can we get out of this igloo and discuss how to use this?"

~ 6 ~

Robina's arms squeezed Qigiq as the motorcycle glided between rows of stopped cars, her borrowed black and white helmet tucked up against his left ear. He rumbled the bike to the front of the line and waited for the green light. They were across the intersection before the cars beside them started moving, and backing into a slice of pavement between a black Cadillac SUV and a green Toyota fifty feet from Peggy's three minutes later. He flicked the kill switch with his thumb.

"Wow," Robina said, "I thought you would have a smelly cop car."

Qigiq stifled a grin.

"Do you always ride like that?"

He twisted around in the seat to catch her gray-shadowed eyes. "No, I am much more conservative when I have a pillion rider."

"Wow."

He held the bike while she fumbled her way off and stood staring at the machine like it was something good to eat.

"Wow—uh, thanks for the ride."

"You're quite welcome. I'm sorry I didn't have a smelly cop car."

She grinned, and for the first time he saw worry lift from her face. But only for the briefest moment.

They joined a dozen others hustling toward buildings whose shadows darkened the street. She walked close by his right side, brushing against his arm occasionally, as if the closeness from the ride had carried over.

The entrance to Peggy's was a single brown door beside a window painted on the inside with pictures of eggs and waffles on huge blue and red plates. Robina looked through the glass and wrinkled her nose.

"You eat here?"

"Better than it looks."

Her nose remained wrinkled, but she stepped through the door he held open for her.

The café was long and narrow; an ice-cream-style counter along the right wall featured chrome stools and torn red vinyl seats. Crammed against the left were wooden tables with mismatched chairs. The place looked full, not even a stool was available.

"Hello, Qigiq," called a round woman from behind the counter. She wore a calf-length dress the color of a banana milkshake with the name Betty embroidered in red over a large left breast.

Qigiq waved.

"Not alone today?" Betty said, raising her right eyebrow beneath unruly hair that was once naturally red.

"Betty, this is Robina. She's helping us on a case."

Her face sagged. "A case? We're never going to find you a girl. You want the back table then?"

Qigiq nodded.

"Give me a minute."

Betty disappeared and Qigiq grabbed a menu from behind a chrome box of napkins.

"What are you hungry for?" he asked.

"An exit," Robina said.

Qigiq grinned. "It's not so bad. Almost as good as the bike ride."

Her look remained dubious. "Okay, I'll try it. But only because I'm starving." She hugged herself and her body shivered like a small dog too long in air conditioning.

He wondered if the vision of her friend's fingers had passed through her mind.

"Back here."

Qigiq turned to see Betty waving menus in a big circle. He led Robina toward the last table in the row.

"What are you drinking, Miss?" Betty asked.

"Orange juice, please."

Betty disappeared, leaving the menus on the table.

Robina flipped one open and buried her face in it.

"When did you first see the box?" he asked.

She spoke through the menu. "It was below our mail slot when I got home last night, about eight. But I left it there because I was carrying my violin case, backpack and groceries."

"When did you open it?"

She flipped the menu on top of the one that Qigiq hadn't touched. "Six twenty-two this morning. I remember because the radio guy said the time as I was cutting the tape with a kitchen knife. His voice is stuck in my head like a bad song. I opened the box a minute later."

"And?"

"And...don't you have all this in the report?"

"I have Detective Dreeson's summary of what you said earlier today. Much as I like Kandy, it's not the same as hearing you tell it."

She pressed her lips together so tightly they turned white before speaking again.

"And I saw a tube packed in what I thought were those little foam peanut things they use to protect stuff. But when I reached in, they were cold. I mean really really like hurt my skin cold."

18

Qigiq nodded. "Dry ice. Frozen carbon dioxide. One hundred and nine degrees below zero."

"A hundred and nine?" Her gray-shadow eyes opened wide. "Isn't that like the dark side of the moon?"

"Not quite. It's cold enough to damage your skin, though. So?"

"So I grabbed an oven mitt and pulled out the white tube. I'm thinking, hmm, maybe something good to eat." She choked and turned silent.

"Sorry," she said. "But that's what I was thinking. Like a friend had sent me some kind of gourmet delight."

Betty waddled up to the table. "The usual Qu?"

He nodded.

"And for the lady?"

"Um. Two eggs scrambled, whites only, wheat toast, jam no butter. And a side of fruit. And a double order of bacon, crispy."

Betty's eyes danced over the girls body, then sliced toward Qigiq and back to the girl.

"Double bacon?" Betty asked.

"Yes please. Crispy; like almost burnt. And coffee. Black, if it's good. Have you ever tasted the stuff he drinks?" She pointed across the table.

Betty smiled. "Coming right up," and she turned away.

The crowd's voices filled the narrow space. He heard someone say, "Have you seen YouTube? It's totally not possible," but didn't catch the topic of disbelief.

He met her soft brown eyes and waited, thinking he understood why Van wrote that song about a brown-eyed girl.

"So, I opened it, and at first I thought it was a weird prank, like they were made of rubber or something and one of the guys was trying to freak me out. They know how squeamish I am about stuff like spiders and gooey insects. So I dropped it back onto the ice nuts."

She stopped. He knew she was seeing it all over again.

"That's when I noticed."

"You noticed the thumb?" he asked.

"Yeah. That callus. Sally and I are roommates, we talk about everything. Especially how musical instruments screw up our girlie-girl good looks." She tilted her head back and to the right.

"See this?" She pointed to a red mark on her neck with her left index finger. "Violin hickey. I've tried all kinds of changes to my technique and it never gets any better. Sally complained she couldn't grow long nails because they interfered with fingering her cello." She wiggled her fingers. "And the side of her thumb always had that lump."

"Cellist's callus?" he asked.

She nodded.

"You recognized it as hers?"

"Not at first. I thought it was part of the joke. Then I looked closer. And I started shaking. So I ran. I ran into her bedroom and looked for nail polish. Right in front was Very Berry. I grabbed the bottle and stumbled back to the kitchen and held it next to the finger."

Tears rolled down her cheeks, but her shoulders were still.

"Yes, that would be enough," he said softly.

"And she hadn't been home for a couple of days."

Betty showed up with plates stacked up her arm.

"Here we go honey," she said, as she placed a bright green plate holding scrambled egg whites and fruit in front of Robina, a yellow plate with slices of wheat toast, and another yellow plate with a stack of blackened bacon as high as the coffee cup.

Robina smiled. "Thanks."

"And for you Mr. Qigiq," Betty said, dropping a big bowl of oatmeal with brown sugar and cinnamon sprinkled thick enough to draw in with a stick, a bowl of fresh fruit and black coffee.

"Bonjour," Betty said as she walked away.

"Excuse me, orange juice?"

"Oh yes, one fresh coming up," Betty called without turning.

Robina stared at Qigiq. "Bonjour?"

"Classy place," he answered.

Robina crunched into a three-inch piece of charred pig.

"Gone," Qigiq said. "Sally had been gone?"

Robina chewed while nodding.

"Yeah. She's a free spirit, disappears for days all the time. Usually with...um, a friend, but..."

Qigiq tested the coffee with his tongue. Too hot. The girl was quiet, forking eggs into her mouth, her eyes staring at the wall behind him. He waited, feeling her silence despite the rough cackle of the crowd.

Robina twisted her head around, apparently seeking the fate of her orange juice. When she turned to face him, their eyes met.

"But she always took her cello. And it was in her room. In fact, it was out of the case like she had been practicing and just stepped out for a, um, a quickie of some type."

"You mean like a cappuccino with a friend?"

The girl's lips turned up slightly at the corners.

"I've never heard it called a cappuccino before."

Qigiq looked down at his cereal.

"Did she have many friends?" he asked the cinnamon.

"Sally's an experience junkie. She has friends everywhere."

"Anyone special?"

"You mean sex? Sure. Danny Meckel. He plays guitar. A rock addict actually, which isn't like Sally at all, she's more Grieg and Shostakovich. But Danny's here studying composition. That was cool with Sally. She worships anyone who can write music."

The girl's use of the present tense struck Qigiq. He swallowed coffee even though it was still a bit too hot, hoping Sally was still alive. Wondering what life would be like for a cellist missing a finger and a thumb.

"Anyone else close to her?"

"You still mean like sex, right? Well, there's Professor Walters. He's a technology geek, teaches computer music and sound manipulation. It's kind of fun, but makes a lot of crappy music if you ask me. I know Sally dug him though, something about the way his hair waves." She found a slight smile. "Sally likes lot of things."

"Should I keep asking?"

"Well, uh, sure. Sally had, like, a few girlfriends too. Violet, she's a flutist, and Veronica, clarinet." Robina met his eyes. "Need I say more?"

Qigiq stared at his half-eaten oatmeal again, wondering if his college classmates in Fairbanks had been anything like Sally and he just hadn't known. He thought not. From his brief experience so far, it seemed San Francisco's aura attracted adventurers.

"Oh yeah, and that lawyer. He was so uptight he squeaked coming through the door. But he adored Sally. Bought her outrageous gowns and took her to symphony concerts I'd have to usher at just to hear the music."

"Do you know his name?"

Her lips twisted.

"She called him Mony, you know the song," she sang with a soft sweet voice, right on key, "You make me feel, Mony Mony...So, Mony Mony...Good, Mony Mony...some kind of joke. Danny might know his name."

Robina crunched into another black strip.

Qigiq toyed with his fruit wondering why Danny would know the name of a guy dating his girlfriend.

"And..."

He waited, chewing so he wouldn't ask a question. This girl didn't really need questions, just an audience. He watched her eyes; she appeared calm. He wondered if the shock would hit later.

Robina's orange juice arrived, delivered by a Latino boy who said nothing. She drank half of it without breathing and placed the glass down with a thud.

21

She looked at him straight on with an orange mustache.

He stopped chewing.

"Me," she said.

He didn't react; at least, he tried not to.

"You and Sally?" he asked gently.

"Yeah. Stuck home practicing, we're pretty regular. But like I said, she's a free spirit."

He ate his oatmeal, trying to form the right next question.

"Don't be too surprised. This is San Francisco. And we're musicians," she said.

"And lesbians?"

"Oh hell no. We're broad thinkers on that topic. Sally's bi- for sure, you know, I gave you the list. Me too. It's more fun, like that old Doublemint gum commercial I saw on YouTube." Her lips twitched. "Those twins were hot."

He still didn't have the right question, but he tried.

"Would any of these people want to hurt Sally?"

She grabbed for the last piece of bacon from the mound as he marveled at how it had all gone into that tiny body.

"I suppose they love her in their way...but like I said, she's into absolute freedom." She met his eyes. "They probably all want to hurt her some days."

He shook his head. Qigiq knew he would never understand criminals, but now he was losing his grip on normal people. Love her and hurt her? Maybe there were no normal people.

"Not me though. I understand her."

He nodded and pulled out a folded sheet of paper, scribbling all the names she had told him with the stub of a pencil like the ones used to keep score in a golf game. But he didn't play golf; he had lifted it from a casino in Vegas after playing Keno.

"All of these people live in the city?" he asked.

She frowned. "The students live near campus, you know the Conservatory and Davies Symphony Hall. Professor Walters lives in the city I think, he complains about traffic when he's late for class. I don't know about Mony."

He felt his pocket vibrate and pulled out his phone. The screen said he had a new text message.

"Excuse me for a moment." He held the phone below the table and read.

Got a call. Another finger, and an ear. Could be Van Gogh. Please call. —KD

He took a deep breath. Robina was poking fruit with a spoon, but didn't look like she wanted to eat it.

He keyed a reply to the message while speaking to Robina.

"Do you have a car at the station?"

She huffed a single laugh. "A car? You imagine a music student with a car in San Francisco? Parking costs more than my rent."

"Would you like me to take you home?"

"I can walk," she said.

"I thought you liked the bike."

"I do. But if you take me home, you're going to come in and examine Sally's room."

"Not unless you invite me. We don't have a search warrant yet." He thought for a moment. "It might be best if no one touched her room before we got a look at it."

"Yeah, I figured that. I locked her door before I left. But it won't stop anyone who really wants in."

He was quiet.

"We got good locks to protect our instruments. My violin is why I don't have a car."

He stood and his chair screeched backwards.

"Let's do it by the book. You leave it locked, and I'll ask Kandy to get the warrant and meet us there. Deal?"

She looked down at her boots.

"Can we take the long way through the Presidio? I bet the park is fabulous on your motorcycle."

"Glad to," he said, and dialed Kandy's number.

~ 7 ~

Blake, you are out of your fucking mind," Greg Simmons said loudly, which was as good as a shout for a lawyer.

Blake held back a smile. He had them engaged now.

Terry stood. "Wait a minute, Greg, Blake may be crazy, but what option do we have? We're out of cash. It will take months if not years to get the municipalities on board with that virtual-camera ticketing idea you had. We either need another round of financing, which means the guys in this room get diluted, or we need more revenue. This Invisible Hand thing is ready now. So if I understand Eddy, we can release it at no cost and maybe frighten enough people that sales of our audio recordings will improve. Since they're all digital and sold online, the revenue is pure profit. We've already paid for those two hundred black monoliths back there to serve the stuff."

Simmons frowned and leaned back, making his roller chair squawk.

"If you call releasing a virus onto the Internet no cost. Read the tech news. These virus things always, always, get out of hand."

"But this isn't destructive. It just reports information," Terry countered.

Simmons sighed. "Yeah, private information that we don't have a right to access."

"If they have our driver," Eddy said.

"Yeah. Like they even know they have it. You think that 'Please click to Accept' license will stand up in court as agreeing to have their music files analyzed?"

"That's what it says. Is it our fault if they don't read it?" Eddy said.

The room grew quiet. Everyone took a drink of sugar, caffeine, or both; except Terry, he drank purified water. Eddy studied the wet rings on the polished wood where their glasses had been.

"Let's be clear," Eddy said. "We can leak this to the Internet from an anonymous café's Wi-Fi system. That part is easy. But I'm suggesting that we not only capture the music file count, we also pull personal information."

"Like what?" Terry asked, and sat down.

Eddy stood and crossed to a white board on the long side of the room. He pulled the green cap off a marker.

"Consider this." He crudely sketched a column of computers.

"A bunch of people who aren't yet our customers get the Invisible Hand. We have it send the file counts back to us here, or better, post them to a web site in the Cayman Islands, somewhere that isn't connected to us."

He drew an island with a palm tree and a rack of machines on it.

"But more important. We have the Hand pull the machine's address, and the owner's name and address if we can get it. And get this, Zeto tells me that if the computer has a webcam, we might be able to grab a picture of the thief as he sits there listening to music."

Simmons groaned. "Please tell me you're not going to do this?"

"*We're* going to do this Greg, we, as in the board of directors of Silver Platter LLC," Eddy corrected him.

Simmons groaned again.

"And what would we do with the data? It even sounds like violation of privacy to me, and I'm no lawyer," Terry said.

Hugh Roberts remained silent, as he had been since their return from the demo.

"We could sneak in a fake license agreement that covers our actions," Eddy said. "No one reads it anyway; then we make the data public."

"Oh my God," Simmons moaned, dropping his forehead into his hands.

"It's not so hard. We have something in development, not done but close, called Blabbermouth."

"Where do you get these crazy code names?" Terry asked.

"The programmers make them up. But when you hear what it does, you'll agree the name is pretty damn descriptive."

Roberts reached for his soda. "Okay Eddy, I'm interested. What the hell is a Blabbermouth?"

Eddy drew lines from the box representing the non-customer's machine.

"As Invisible Hand runs it gathers knowledge about the host machine. It can send that data anywhere we want. For example, it could email the information directly to the RIAA, or send it to an address we control at an offshore location, so the U.S. Government can't subpoena it easily."

He drew a box for the RIAA, and one labeled *Cayman Islands*.

"That much is interesting and might get us the attention we want. But what if the Hand also sent the critical information: name, age, a picture, number of stolen songs, maybe even some info it could pull from a Facebook page...what if it sent all this data to..."

He paused to let them imagine what could be done with information on a large number of pirates.

Terry said, "Pressure."

Roberts tilted his head to see what Terry was on about. "You mean make the information available?"

"Yeah," Terry said. "Widely available somehow. So the whole world would know who the pirates are. Parents could see their kid's names in big letters."

"And see their picture posted," added Eddy.

"This is a violation of privacy," Simmons said. "Clearly."

"C'mon Greg," Eddy said. "You see someone rob a 7-Eleven, maybe they get a few hundred bucks and a carton of cigarettes, what do you do? You report them. They were observed in the act of committing a crime— just like here."

Roberts chewed his lower lip. "Meaning we could send this data directly from the pirate's machine to a police station?"

"Sure could," said Eddy with a big smile, while drawing a box with bars to represent a jailhouse and connecting it to the customer machines. "Remember John Lennon's Instant Karma?" Eddy said, "behold Instant Justice."

"But they'll find us," Simmons complained.

"Us? We're not in the picture. Remember, the Hand is *Invisible*," Eddy said, showing gleaming white teeth.

Roberts looked to Terry. "You said widely available. You weren't thinking police station."

"No," Terry replied. "I was thinking peer pressure. Post information online where it can do some real damage. Make people afraid they'll be found out and publicly humiliated if they steal."

Eddy elaborated as he drew. "Imagine that our pirate's particulars are posted to a hundred blogs, along with his playlist, and photo, and maybe the dollar value of what he's stolen. What happens when people start seeing themselves online for illegally copying songs?"

Roberts sipped his Coke. "We remove the anonymity of the Internet that people hide behind to break the law."

"Exactly," Eddy agreed.

"Where do we post this info?" asked Terry.

"Depends. We could search the thief's own machine and find the blogs she reads and the RSS feeds she likes and try to post to those locations. That would put the Wanted message out directly into the online communities that the thief frequents," Eddy said. "And of course Facebook and Twitter, where things can spread fast."

"Or," Roberts began. He coughed. "Or, we post to hundreds of websites focused on file sharing in an effort to deter the greatest number of potential pirates."

Simmons sighed. "Beyond our dubious legal position, this could backfire. The kids might figure a high file count is a badge of honor and start stealing to see if they can get to the top of the list."

"Their parents and the law won't agree," Eddy said. He drew a starburst of lines fanning outward and wrote BLOGS across the top. "And we begin working on your traffic light idea as back up. When these people start getting fined, we will have their attention."

Roberts looked at Terry.

Terry nodded slightly.

Roberts looked to Simmons.

Simmons froze, not indicating yes or no.

Roberts turned to Eddy, who was still standing by the big white board nailed to the side wall. He drank the rest of his Coke without taking his eyes from Eddy's face.

Finally he said, "When?"

~ 8 ~

Robina was off the bike before he could get it fully stopped.

"Oh my god, that is so cool. A cop bike even, from Italy. I've never had so much fun going someplace in my life."

He killed the engine.

"Happy you liked it. Next time it'll be safer if you wait for me to stop. Would you like to take your helmet off?"

She grinned and reached up to fiddle with the strap.

They were squeezed in behind a green Lexus three doors past the apartment Robina had pointed to on Arcadia Lane. The street rose slightly going west, jammed with cars parked end to end like colored stones on a huge necklace. The sidewalk reached from the curb to the six steps leading up to the first of three stories. Qigiq felt compression, the closeness of buildings squeezing his lungs. It had been over a month, but San Francisco still felt like a shoebox.

He clipped the helmets to the bike and followed Robina toward her apartment. He had placed his right foot on the first step when he heard Kandy whistle—a single short shriek that was good at getting attention. He turned and sat on the second step. She approached from his left, alone.

As she walked up she said, "Got it."

Qigiq stood. "Thanks. Was it hard?"

Kandy smiled. "Just have to know the right judge. And explain that the missing persons report included only ninety percent of the body."

He nodded, and watched Robina fumble with the key in a door that was twice her age.

He whispered to Kandy, "An ear?"

She pulled a document out of her back pocket and handed it to him. Handwritten notes. He scanned it, trying to decode the scribbles until he heard the scrape of Robina pushing the big door inward, then handed it back.

"Didn't bring the evidence in?"

"Nope. Doesn't want anything to do with cops."

"Then why call?"

"Claims the Post Office wouldn't take the package back and he didn't know what else to do with it. He was going to throw it away until he realized he might get in trouble if someone found a finger in his garbage. That's when he called us."

Qigiq frowned.

"Who is he?"

"Don't know much—"

"Are you coming?" Robina called from inside the hallway.

They both turned to face the open door five steps above them.

"Be right there," Qigiq said.

Kandy finished her sentence. "Said his name was Merkel. Danny

Merkel." She turned to head up the stairs.

Qigiq reached out and gently touched her biceps. Kandy froze.

"Robina gave me that name over breakfast. He's one of Sally's boyfriends."

Kandy turned from two steps above.

"One of?"

"It's complicated."

Robina had disappeared.

He followed Kandy up the steps.

Qigiq checked the row of brass colored mailbox doors embedded in the wall just inside the main door. Below them was a tray for holding deliveries that wouldn't fit through the mail slot. Not particularly secure, but common.

He read the names on the boxes until he saw #3: R. Kidner & S. Bellowi.

He followed Kandy up one flight where faded brown doors faced each other across a hallway carpeted in golf-course green. He tapped his knuckles below a golden 3, its edges oxidized to bluish gray.

The door swung open to a barefoot Robina holding a glass of what he hoped was water.

"Come in," she said, leaving the door ajar as she disappeared behind a wall that held a picture of a jumble of people, tables, a topless woman and what looked to be a horse. It had been put up with pink thumbtacks.

He noticed Kandy watching him.

"Salvador Dali's *Cabaret Scene*," he said.

"They make cops study art in Fairbanks?" She laughed.

"Elective."

They stepped into a tiny room with a partial wall that separated the kitchen. A dark hallway led toward the back. Qigiq could see three doors.

"You want something to drink?" Robina called out.

Kandy shook her head.

"No thanks, we're fine," Qigig said.

Robina padded out from behind the wall. The clear liquid in her glass now a pale orange.

"Oh, hi," she said to Kandy.

"Hello again. Just to put your mind at ease, we have a search warrant." Kandy handed a paper to Robina who glanced at it and dropped it on a square end table next to a yellow love seat.

"So you want to see Sally's room," she said flatly.

"That's a good place to start."

Robina led them toward the back of the apartment. The dark hall held pictures of huge halls with orchestra concerts in progress. The only one he recognized was Davies' from right there in San Francisco.

She caught him looking. "That's Tokyo on your left. And Carnegie of course next to Davies."

"Ever been to them?" Kandy asked.

"Oh yeah. I've played them all. Sally too. Youth orchestra concerts usually held like on a Monday afternoon. Wow, do they sound great."

Qigiq looked at the glorious golds on the inside of Davies' Hall and wondered what it would feel like to sit in front of thousands of people and perform what little he knew about playing the piano. His knees felt funny.

Robina stopped in front of the second door on the right. It was closed and someone had put an 'X' of blue tape across the door jamb.

"I didn't want anyone to walk in by accident," she said.

"When did you put this up?" Kandy asked, making an 'X' motion with her hand.

Robina sipped and pulled the glass away from her lips.

"Before I left for the police station." She swallowed hard. "After I recognized Sally's thumb." Her face went blank and she blinked twice. Hard.

"Is the door locked?" Qigiq asked.

"Oh yeah." Robina padded away on the bare carpet and returned holding a silver key.

The door swung open to reveal the living space of someone who was organized. Not more than ten by twelve feet, it magically contained a single bed, nightstand, laptop computer on a table, sliding doors in front of a closet, and a music stand holding a thick book opened to Mozart's String Quartet No. 4 beside a cello leaning into the corner. A hard cello case lay sideways on the floor, its back pressed against the wall, the front covered with stickers from France, Prague, Colorado, Utah.

"I think she left in a hurry," Robina offered.

Qigiq glanced her way.

"The cello. Sally would never leave her instrument out of the case."

"Even in the apartment?" Kandy asked.

"Especially in our apartment," Robina replied. "Parties get out of hand." Her eyes found Qigiq, "Even if there are only two in attendance." She smiled, her teeth shiny white, and a damp mustache over her lip.

Qigiq grinned and shook his head.

Kandy slipped on surgical gloves and started in the far corner of the room.

"Are you going to search?" Robina asked.

"That's what detectives do, Robina," Qigiq said. "We'll look for clues that might tell us where Sally went, or how, or with whom. Then we'll send in a team to take fingerprints and samples of any odd materials they can find."

"Odd?" she asked.

"Things that don't belong here. A blade of grass, bit of sand, even a single hair. We need to know when and why Sally left."

Robina fell silent while Kandy opened drawers and looked through clothing Qigiq had only ever seen in a catalog.

"I know we covered most of this, but when was the last time you saw Sally?" Kandy asked.

Robina looked like she was thinking hard.

"She wasn't here last night or the night before. I saw her Tuesday morning before I left for class, around eight-thirty. She was supposed to be at rehearsal at two in the afternoon, but she didn't show."

"Does she do that often?" Kandy asked.

"Uh, yeah, sort of." Robina's eyes flicked to meet Qigiq's. "If she gets a better offer and feels like she has her part covered, she'll skip practice. So I wasn't worried. More pissed than worried. It's hard to practice without the cello."

"How about Wednesday night, when she wasn't home and her cello was sitting out."

"That was weird. I almost put it away, but then I thought maybe she had it worked on and it was supposed to sit out to dry or something. So I left it alone."

"Does she do that too?" Kandy asked. "Disappear for a night or two."

"We're college girls," Robina said.

Kandy nodded.

Qigiq thumbed slowly through an appointment calendar touching only the edges of the pages. It had pencil markings for quartet, orchestra, choir, a cello lesson, and big black blocks with *Practice* scribbled inside. A dinner time entry for the following Monday read: *Mony@Yoshi's*.

"When did the box arrive?" Kandy asked, even though Robina had already answered the question at the station.

"I'm not sure. I saw it last night and noticed it was for me, but my hands were full. That was around nine. I went down and got it first thing this morning to open before breakfast. Thought it might be something nice."

Qigiq looked for names and addresses in the appointment book, but found nothing.

"Do you know how to contact Mony?"

"Me? Nope. But Sally's super organized. Everything you need is probably in that computer."

Qigig walked around the bed so he could stand next to Kandy in front of the machine. She touched it carefully with a gloved fingertip.

They heard a slight mechanical sound and the screen faded up.

Qigiq saw a desktop full of colored icons that felt like staring into a bowl of Trix. They floated over a picture of an empty concert hall.

"Do these all mean something?" he asked.

"Only to Sally," Robina said. "No one else can find anything on her machine. She has everything color-coded and laid out on some sort of matrix that makes sense to her. She has that kind of brain."

"What's the blue?" Kandy asked.

"Blue is music. She told me once. Not because of the blues, Sally doesn't listen to the blues much, except during...well, not much. She said she used blue because music is universal, like the sea and the sky."

No one spoke.

"Double-click a blue one," Robina said.

Kandy positioned the arrow over a blue triangle and double-tapped.

Apple iTunes opened and the room filled with the opening lilt of violins dancing in moonlight.

"Tchaikovsky," Robina said. "Serenade for Strings."

Qigiq looked for speakers that could be making such a full sound.

Robina laughed. She stepped across to the side of the bed and removed a painting that looked like a man with a guitar after falling down the stairs. She saw him watching. "Picasso," she said. Behind it, bolted into a hole in the wall was a shiny speaker with the word Genelec along the bottom. Robina held the painting between them and looked through it. It had been printed on light-colored grill cloth.

"Sally doesn't like to see speakers," Robina said. "So the sound appears to be arriving from the cosmos."

Kandy clicked a button.

The room fell into silence.

~ 9 ~

Harold saw only a blue flash in his rearview mirror before Lili rushed into his office carrying a box with a ribbon. No knock...no hello.

She swung the door closed.

She whispered, "Harold, you've got to help me."

"Whoa, slow down. You okay?"

"No, I'm not okay. Mr. Blake has gone insane. I can't believe it. I just can't believe it."

Harold frowned, wondering if Blake had propositioned her. She certainly transformed the deep blue Blabbermouth project T-shirt into a fine set of hyperbolic curves. He grinned at the big double lips over her breasts, and wondered what had happened to her maroon shirt. Maybe that had been dress up for the demo.

"Believe what?"

She continued to whisper, "He wants the fucking project done this week. Says we're going live on Monday. It's already *Thursday*. And I have tickets for my friend's recital in San Francisco. Shit...er, shoot."

"I wonder what happened after the demo?" Harold said. His lips curled. They must have been impressed to be pulling the release date forward. Or the company was out of cash and they were grasping at straws to save it. Which meant his stock options—

"He didn't say anything about the demo," she said. "But if they think we're going live on Monday, *this* fucking Monday—" Her eyes darted around the room and landed on his calendar of great mathematicians. "That's like...like...oh my God, four days. I can't finish this in four days even if I don't sleep. He's fucking nuts."

She had ceased whispering.

"You might want to keep it down a little."

"Oh Christ, you're right. Thanks," she whispered. "You have to help me." She smiled and held out a gold box with a Green ribbon. "These are for you. A bribe."

He took the box and untied the bow with one pull. Inside were two layers of chocolates, six to a layer. He held the box out toward her.

She looked them over like they were glittering gemstones, and finally took a round dark one.

"Thanks," she said, and bit.

He picked a square milk chocolate and placed the box next to his monitor.

"We'll need these if we're going to make Monday," he said.

"We?"

She was adorable when those lashes batted over her blue eyes.

"So you'll help me?"

"Lili, Lili, of course I'll help you. When haven't I helped you?"

She crossed her arms. "Well..."

"OK. Sometimes I'm busy," Harold said. "But this weekend I can help."

She hopped up and down and clapped her hands, making him wonder if she was really old enough to have a Master's degree in computer science from Michigan like her resumé claimed.

"Easy Lil, show me what you've got."

She danced over to the wall and grabbed a big red marker. "As engineering manager I usually get specifications from Marketing, but this time Mr. Blake stopped by my office and described what he wants directly. Maybe there wasn't time to consult Marketing." She shrugged and met Harold's eyes.

Or maybe Blake hadn't told Marketing. He knew what else she was thinking: Why hadn't Blake talked to Harold? But Harold knew that answer. As lead engineer Blake was afraid of him. Eddy Blake didn't tell Harold about deadlines, he *asked* about them. So Blake told Lili, knowing Lili would run to Harold: simple corporate politics. Didn't bother Harold. In fact, he liked knowing he was in a power position. He had no doubt he would be able to use it someday.

"Don't worry about it, Lili. You're cuter than I am," Harold said.

She frowned.

He knew she wanted to be a real engineer, not get ahead because she was cute. She'd talk about that when she didn't feel appreciated by management.

"Did Blake say anything about an IPO?" Harold asked.

Her frown deepened. "I don't know that project. Is it part of Full Disclosure?"

Harold laughed outright. "Sorry Lili, you're out of context. Think business."

"Oh yeah, Public Offering, when we can sell our stock. No, he never mentioned it."

He wouldn't, thought Harold. The boys in the boardroom only take care of the boys in the boardroom. "Show me what you've got, Lili," he said, which made him think about what was under her blouse.

She ignored his eyes.

"Remember I talked to you about Blabbermouth auto-posting to blogs? He wants to do that." She paused. "And Facebook and Twitter."

She drew a series of boxes on the far right and labeled them B1, B2...BN.

"That much is cool. I can do that by Monday. But get this. He wants Invisible Hand to pull what he calls *non-customer* information from the user's computer. This is so bold. He wants the person's name, city and state. And he wants me to put it on the blogs. Can you believe we're going to do that?" Her voice was rising again.

Harold smiled inwardly. About fucking time we did something.

"The board must have really liked the demo," he said. "Thanks for helping me set it up."

She blushed. They both knew it was mostly Harold's work. Her primary job was to keep the team organized, which she did well. His was to invent technology, which he did in his sleep.

"You're welcome, Harold."

"So what's the problem?"

"Well. I don't have code to search the host machine's address book to identify the owner."

"Problem one: grab owner information. I can help with that."

She sighed. "That's great. But it gets worse. He wants the owner's picture to be posted too."

Harold nodded. "Things might get weird if we put the street address and phone numbers up so strangers could contact them. But that wouldn't be hard either, assuming the info is in their address book. Most people keep it there, in case they need it for a return address."

"But Harold, a picture? How are we going to get a picture?"

"Blake wants to destroy their anonymity. Clever. You're right Lili, I didn't think the board had cojones this big."

She scowled at him.

"Sorry. That's a technical term. Didn't they teach you that at Michigan?"

"Men," she huffed. "Always so disgusting."

He laughed and offered her another chocolate. After some deliberation, she went with the white-chocolate coating before continuing.

"Most people have a picture of themselves on their computer someplace because they store digital photos on the hard drive. But how will we ever find it?" she asked.

Harold was quiet.

"He's going to fire me if I can't figure this out," she said.

Harold popped out of reverie.

"Who?"

"Blake. He's going to fire me," she said.

Harold sat up. "Did he say that?"

"No. But I can tell. He needs this, and if I can't deliver, he'll go find someone else who can."

Harold shook his head. "You need more confidence, Lili. Blake isn't going to fire anyone. Now that the board has seen the light, we'll show them real progress by Monday and get this company moving."

She finished her white chocolate.

"But how? There might be a thousand pictures on a hard drive. And we have to find one of the owner."

"Maybe," Harold said.

She backed across the room and slumped into the plush guest chair he kept in the far corner. It didn't get much use, but he liked the geometric diagrams on the material.

"Maybe? What do you mean, maybe?"

"I mean maybe. As in maybe we have to find one of the owner. What if we just scan through the pics and grab the first one that we analyze to be of a single person. We'll use facial recognition software to guess that there's an adult in the pic, so we don't post dogs or babies."

She straightened.

"Will that work?"

"Of course. Blake isn't going to know if the pictures we upload are of the real owner or not. Besides, that's not the point."

She slumped back. "But that's what he said he wanted."

Harold stood. "If we're going to get this done, I need caffeine."

As he fed dollar bills into the machine down the hall from his office Lili looked around to be sure they were alone and whispered, "But he wants the owner's picture."

"No he doesn't."

"Darn you, Harold. That's what he said."

"Lili, you know people always ask for stuff off the top of their head. As an engineer you have to look past what they say they want to their underlying desires—to what they *really* want. Like in this case. Maybe Blake just wants to get into your pants." He smiled as a Coke can rumbled through the machine.

"Will you stop it? He's married for heaven's sake."

"Yeah. That stops men all the time."

"OK. What does he really want?"

"He really wants our software to post names and pictures to blogs to draw attention to the music piracy problem in the hope of shifting more people to buying."

"And it doesn't matter whose pictures we post?"

"Precisely. Michigan must not be as bad as they say."

"Go Blue," she said, punching him in the arm.

"So how about we do this? When the Hand runs, we take a picture if there's an attached webcam. There's a fair chance the user will be sitting in front of the camera. If our analysis says we have a pic of a person, we just use that. If not, we try to find one in the address book, it's a common place to store pics of friends."

"Love it," she said, feeding her own dollar bills into the vending machine. "And if we don't get a person?"

"Plan B: we search for pics on the hard drive until we find one that meets our person criteria. Then we use that one, regardless of who it is."

A Dr. Pepper can rumbled and stopped.

"So either way," she said, "we have a fair chance of posting a picture of the owner. And a really good chance of at least posting a person's face."

He poured cold sugared salt water down his throat.

"Man that's good."

"All we need," she went on, "is the code to find the name in the address book, the code to take the picture, the code to analyze if it's a person, the code to search for pics on the hard disk. Oh yeah, and Blabbermouth, of course, to post the results to the blog list, which we also have to assemble. All by Monday. Did I miss anything?" she asked.

"Yes, one thing."

She lowered her Dr. Pepper and frowned. "Damn. What?"

"We'll need pizza starting right now if we're going to get this done."

She smiled sadly. "It's impossible, Harold. I really appreciate your help, but this is a huge project for only four days."

He chugged his Coke and enjoyed the buzzy feeling in his throat.

"I agree."

She leaned her back against the big vending machine and sagged.

"Then he's going to fire me."

"I agree it's a big project. But you almost have Blabbermouth done. And I just happen to have code to read an address book, and to operate a webcam. So that reduces things down to scanning the disk for pics. Easy. And recognizing a face. Hard."

"Hard? Well if you think it's hard, he's going to fire me for sure."

"Hard if you start from scratch. Let's go search university sites for a face recognition project that has some open-source code posted. I'll bet what we need already exists, and we just have to massage it into the Hand. Won't take but half the night."

She started to smile. "I like it. But aren't there licensing issues around using that kind of code? Like we have to give them our code or something?"

He started back towards his office.

"Depends on which license the code is under. We want the one where if we modify their stuff we have to give them the changes, but using their code doesn't contaminate ours with their open license. We'll be happy to give them the changes, right, if it helps us pull off this Monday deadline?"

He stopped abruptly and spun around. She walked into him, but managed not to spill her soda.

"So you don't get fired," he said, and winked.

~ 10 ~

Eddy floored his 550 to blast around a dogging driver in a piss-green

Prius. What was it with people who bought Toyotas? That move put him in the HOV lane so he checked for the hours. It didn't activate until 3:00 pm, so he was still okay. He dialed with the thumb of his right hand and steered with his left index finger. By the time the phone was ringing through the stereo the speedo passed ninety-five. He lifted his foot, another ticket would mean another stupid traffic school—and being late. He hated to be late.

He loved I-280, a road someone claimed was the most beautiful highway in the U.S. No way. But the absence of billboards let the beauty of the undulating hills show through. He thought of a see-through blouse on Alicia, smiled and tapped the control to pop to the next satellite radio channel. Technology was cool, gave him more control. The new channel filled the car with the bopping rhythm of a Stray Cats song. No, it wasn't the Cats, someone else playing rockabilly. He looked down at the radio: Hell Leopards. What the hell was a Hell Leopard? Maybe he should sign them for distribution through Silver Platter.

Stacy's voice mail answered so he dictated to his phone.

"Hi Stacy. Got another one. See what you can find on a band calling themselves Hell Leopards. Don't dig too deep; I only heard one song. Thanks." He had wanted to find out if that bitch Helen had called, but no way was he leaving voice mail for some frigging divorce lawyer to find.

He watched the road with one eye and fumbled his phone away. He loved the way technology could get things done without all the chitchat humans craved.

You've been beaten, I've been beaten, now we're gonna do the beaten together...

What were the Hell Leopards beating?

The quiet German car flowed across seamed cement.

The Leopards were interrupted by a loop of the Beatles singing, "I want money, I want money, I want mo-ah- uu-ney, *that's what I want*—"

He looked at his phone and groaned at the ID. He took a deep breath, eased himself deeper into 12-way adjustable black leather and thought about letting it go to voice mail, but the Beatles were right—he wanted money.

"Hi, Honey."

"What 'Honey' Eddy?"

"Just trying to be nice. I know I usually rant when you call me at work."

"A little late to start being nice, Eddy. I need those papers back. Signed."

Breathe, he told himself. Breathe.

"I told you, Helen. They're with my lawyer. You're being awfully demanding about the house."

"Damn right, Eddy. I demand you give it to me. It's the least you can do, you fuck."

"C'mon Helen. I was trying to be nice and you have to—"

"You're only nice to other women, Eddy. Stop pretending. What is your problem? Those papers should have been signed last week. Let's get on with this thing."

Finally, she was growing anxious to sign. This he could use.

"I want the boat. It's a hassle to sell it and split the money and then find another one. Plus, I might lose my slip at Pier 38. I'd rather just keep *Bullet*. Besides, it reminds me of our time together."

Her laughter filled the car.

"You can keep your damn boat...if and only if I get the house and everything else on that list you've had for over a week. And Eddy. The house means the whole house, no liens, no mortgage, and everything in it except your sorry ass."

"I'll talk to my lawyer, Helen."

"Do that Eddy. And do it right away, before I change my mind and decide not to divorce you. Sometimes I think I'm letting you off too easy."

He couldn't let that happen.

"I'll call Markay and get those papers to you."

"Tomorrow Eddy. Tomorrow."

"Yes, Helen."

The phone went dead in his ear. He smiled because negotiating was the most fun he ever had with his clothes on. He dialed Markay, who answered on the second ring.

"She didn't go for it," Eddy said. "Wants the house all right. Even gave me the boat." He watched the road slide under his hood. "Yeah, I'm fine with giving it to her but *with* the mortgage...I know what it's worth and I'm not paying it off...and I want to keep everything else. Everything, and she's trying to get the contents. That means the record collection, jewelry, guns. All the artwork. Not acceptable. She might even want her Jaguar if she thinks because it's in the garage it counts as contents." He accelerated slightly, preferring to move fast when thinking. "By tomorrow. Is that possible?" He noticed a dark car in his rearview, but it didn't look like a cop. "Excellent. Talk soon."

He whistled along with another song that sounded like the Stray Cats but wasn't. He wished for the transporter from Star Trek. That was back in the 60's, engineers should have figured out how to build one by now. Waiting sucked. And riding in a car, except for the tunes, was nothing but waiting for his body to be where he wanted it to be next.

Thirty minutes later the highway abruptly became Embarcadero Boulevard with condos dozens of stories high lining the bay side of the wide street like the wall of a fort. He turned right at 5th Street, waved a plastic card at the parking gate, and was standing in front of a huge window on the twenty-eighth floor holding Jim Beam on the rocks less than two minutes later.

"God, what a view. Blue sky, AT&T Park, flower-petal yachts strewn on a blue floor. I love San Francisco."

He draped his suit coat across the maroon sofa and loosened a red and gray striped tie without taking his eyes away from the vista that cost him over three-quarters of a million dollars of a bank's money.

He sighed and tried not to think about Helen grabbing his assets.

A tubular bell bonged three descending tones.

He crossed the shag carpet and pressed a black button surrounded by a bit of polished nickel while drinking with his other hand.

He unlocked the door and let it stand open an inch, returned to the window for a last look at the Bay, then stretched out on the sofa.

He was wondering if he should change the color of the ceiling when the door moved silently inward and a slender Asian woman in black slacks and four-inch heeled mules glided through. Her black hair was chopped just below her earlobes and hidden under a teal beret tilted like a sunflower facing the sun. She wore a black jacket of a smooth leather that looked soft enough to sleep on, no make-up, and a pink iPod with matching pink earbuds.

She pressed the door closed behind her and turned to twist one lock, then a second. Her hand drifted to the wall. The lights flicked off and a motorized curtain hummed across the tall glass wall whose view had held Eddy's attention.

Eddy didn't move.

She sauntered across to the left wall and unclipped the iPod from her waist, sliding it into a slot in a large black amplifier. Her right fingertips stroked a round knob, rotating it as her teal and black fingernails scraped along the face of the amp.

Sound filled the room. Not quite music, but a wash of frequencies like a mass of violins on amphetamines, floating over a deep moan of rhythm.

She turned.

"Hello, Eddy."

Eddy didn't move from the couch. But he smiled.

She smiled back, and began to dance.

Her hips rolled like a ship in a storm and her face showed the relaxed smile of a hypnotic. She interlaced her fingers below soft full lips and rocked them in concert with her hips.

Wearing black she appeared as a silhouette against the sunlit curtains, like the dancers in those original iPod commercials, only much more fluid.

The CEO would get arrested if Apple ran commercials like this on prime time TV. He brought his Beam to his lips. They were dry.

With each step she moved a tiny bit closer to the sofa. He wanted to jump up and grab her, but he had learned to wait. She liked to control the pacing.

She hadn't removed the earbuds, so they were swaying along with her hips and arms throwing little pink flashes against her black clothing.

"Hello, Alicia."

She smiled without looking at him, her tongue darting out to caress her teeth. When she reached the sofa, she unzipped the jacket and let it slide off her arms as hot fudge slips over ice cream. Both her nipples were standing full and hard.

He had learned it would be best if he did not move.

She draped herself over his body and continued flowing to the music. He relished the softness of her breasts through his shirt, the smell of flowers from her hair, the taut tone of her legs intertwined with his.

He still didn't move.

"Well, baby?" she asked, dancing on him like he was a floor she was trying to clean with her bottom. "Do I get more of you soon?"

"Papers go back tomorrow for the next round," he said.

She smiled with her tongue between her teeth.

He felt a hand move between their bodies…and the strength of her grip.

~ 11 ~

The gang from Crime Scene had dusted and bagged most of Sally's room, including the computer and the cello, before Kandy got an answer at the number in Sally's address book for Danny Merkel (guitar, comp, dreamboat). Robina suggested he might be in a group rehearsal, but Qigiq thought the usual reason a cellphone went unanswered was because the owner didn't care to be reached. Why that changed around 12:30 that afternoon he could only guess.

Kandy talked for less than a minute, hung up and said, "Tired, or stoned. But agreed to let us come over if we promise to take away the Amazon box."

Qigiq slipped into the shotgun seat of Kandy's black Mini with checkered-flag rearview mirrors. She was moving into traffic before he clicked his seatbelt.

"What do you think?" he asked.

She dug into her pants, squirming to get her fingers into the front pocket of tight jeans while strapped into a bucket seat, and withdrew a single stick of gum in a yellow wrapper.

"Juicy Fruit?"

"No thanks."

She expertly removed the wrapper and foil with one hand and popped the stick into her mouth. Through the big chews needed for a fresh stick of gum she answered, "Random grab. Rape. Serial killer. Revenge. Jealousy. All of the above."

"Bothers me," Qigiq said.

She turned left through a yellow light onto Third Street.

"There's a lot to be bothered about."

"Why an Amazon box?" he asked.

"Anonymity."

"Body parts to friends?"

She stopped behind a lifted Cadillac Escalade that the Mini could have used for a tunnel.

"Perp knows the friends, so someone close to Sally did this. Or is still doing it. We don't have a body; we have a finger and a thumb…maybe an ear. The girl could still be alive."

"Hmm."

She passed the stilt machine on its right and tucked in between a Corolla that was moving along well, and a Porsche that wasn't.

"The sticker bothers me," Qigiq said.

"Maybe it was handy, or the doer's trying to be clever."

Kandy cracked her gum. Qigiq had learned that was the thinking sound.

"Sally's a musician." He knew they should assume she was alive, but his gut was struggling with the thought. "Maybe something to do with musicians?"

"Don't steal music? Profound. *Thou shalt not steal* put it better a couple of thousand years ago. Along with thou shalt not kill…or dismember."

"The bag was sealed with the sticker," he said. "Like a warning. You know, *Contents under pressure.*"

"Or a threat. Steal, you end up in the bag."

Kandy swerved to miss a steel construction plate on Market Street, the sharp corner pointing at her tire like a dagger.

Qigiq raised his right hand to the handle over the window.

"A deterrent?"

"Just a thought," she said, braking at a stop sign.

"So, a warning to Robina? And this guy Merkel we're going to see. Extravagant packaging for such a simple message."

She gunned the Mini, gluing Qigiq's back onto smooth gray leather.

41

He pondered the closeness of the parked cars and the speed at which they were passing. "Doesn't add up. Why a *musician's* hand? They're the ones hurt the most by music theft."

"And record companies. They complain about piracy destroying profit. CD sales down, revenue down, the courts won't help, the law has no teeth, and all that jazz."

Qigiq scratched the short-cropped hair at the back of his neck.

"Do you have an iPod?" Kandy asked.

"I buy CD's and put them on a little tray. They sound great."

"Not portable." She reached across his knees and popped the glove box. "Take a look."

Qigiq extracted white wires with tiny disks on the ends and something the size of a matchbook, only metallic green. He had transferred to San Francisco to learn more about computer crime. He hadn't expected an education from a glove box.

"This tiny thing plays music?"

"Something like ten thousand songs in there."

He turned the device over. There was a clip on the back.

"You could use it on your motorcycle."

He wasn't sure he wanted the distraction of music while riding. But he would try it. He shook the device. "Wouldn't the vibration bother it?"

She wagged her head, screeched to a stop and reversed in a single S-motion that placed them six inches from the curb.

© © ©

The door was green, not painted recently, and once held a number 6 where an outline of grit remained. Qigiq rapped three times.

They waited.

He rapped again, a bit louder.

"He said he was home?" Qigiq asked.

"Said he'd be here all afternoon."

Qigig placed his ear to the door. Nothing. He pulled his hand back to knock louder and heard a bang from inside the apartment. The door vibrated.

"Door sticks," a male voice shouted from inside.

Qigiq stepped back.

Kandy kicked the middle of the door with the sole of her boot and followed its swing into the apartment. Qigiq walked behind her, shaking his head.

A waist-high skateboard leaned against the far wall. A young man with his back to them wearing baggy blue jeans and a white sweatshirt with no sleeves stood beside it, strapping on a gold guitar. Loose hair that he combed perhaps once a day, and hadn't gotten to that once yet, reached to his collar. He pushed a disk attached to a wire into his left ear and started playing scales like he was in a hurry.

"We're detectives Dreeson and Qigiq," Kandy said. "Are you Danny Merkel?"

He nodded without turning around, fingers still flying.

Qigiq's eyes roamed the room: Future Shock, Spook Country, Lolita; a two-foot high stack of Guitar Player magazine; army green helmet older than the kid; Formica table in dark blue holding a laptop between a pair of speakers each about the size of a human head. Across from the computer a single unmade bed with light green sheets and a blue blanket sat beside a futon chair. The sole door probably led to the bathroom.

He listened to the un-amplified sound of the electric guitar as his eyes moved right into a makeshift kitchen and a mini-fridge under a microwave next to a sink half-full of cream-colored dishes. One long stem wine glass stood on the counter.

An Amazon box with a flap standing open sat on top of the microwave.

The kid turned around, head hanging down like his neck couldn't support so much weight. The fingers never slowed.

"Yeah, I'm Danny. Thanks for coming over, saved me time."

Qigiq noticed Kandy noticing him noticing the box.

"Is that the box you called about?" she said, pointing towards the microwave.

He nodded, in rhythm, like he was beating a drum with his head.

Kandy slipped on rubber gloves while crossing to the kitchen. She studied the box and spoke as if dictating a report. "Amazon printing on box, same size as the first. Addressed to Danny Merkel, return address is the same non-existent P.O. Box, number 5488, South San Francisco, California. Subject has cut the tape on one flap only." Without touching the box Kandy peered inside. "One-inch bubble wrap used to contain a dry ice med-pack. The pack has been split open to reveal a Ziplock baggie. Sticker on top, "Don't steal music." Baggie is closed and contains an ear with a finger inserted into it...as if it's trying to stop sound. Finger appears to be glued into ear based on visible clear fluid around fingertip. No ID of the victim at present."

Kandy turned around. Danny was watching her but hadn't stopped playing.

"When did you get this?" she said loud enough for him to hear with one ear.

"Yesterday."

"When did you open it."

"Yesterday."

"And you called us this morning?"

He nodded his drum-beating nod.

"Why the delay?" she asked.

"Didn't know what to do."

"So you just let it sit here?"

"Nope. Put it in the fridge. Got it out when you called."

She frowned.

"Do you know whose finger that is?" she asked.

Qigiq watched the young man concentrate deeply on the sound of his guitar. His reaction to the question, which would have sent Robina into fits, was a shrug of the shoulder not supporting the guitar and a barely perceptible shake of his head.

Kandy met Qigiq's eyes, so he walked to the kitchen and stood close to her.

"He doesn't seem curious," he said softly. "Does he know they're real?"

Her eyes flicked into the box. "I'm not sure either. Could be something else. I mean, an ear?"

Qigiq turned to face Danny. "Have you seen Sally?"

His eyes lifted slowly to look at Qigiq. His lips barely moved.

"Sally who?"

"Sally the cellist you're bonking," Kandy said.

The hands stopped moving. His lips curved into a smile.

"You're looking for Sally? What did she do now?"

Kandy crossed the midget apartment and sat on the dusty futon. The boy's eyes followed her.

She said, "Sally didn't do anything. But she's missing."

He slipped the guitar off and leaned it in the corner, draping the wire from the single earbud over the headstock. He leaned against the wall himself, and crossed his arms, long and slender—like his fingers.

"I saw Sally Sunday night. We went to the Infinite Loop concert at Bimbo's, over on Columbus."

Kandy held her eyes on him.

"Dropped her off about midnight," he met her gaze, "and left. We both have early classes on Monday."

Kandy nodded.

Danny's eyes flicked between Kandy on the couch and the Amazon box.

"What does Sally have to do with that stupid box?"

Qigiq watched Kandy. She remained silent, was going to let him do it. He cleared his throat.

"Robina received a box too. Except hers had a finger and a thumb."

"Fucking weird," Danny said, shaking his head. "Sick sense of humor, even for California. I figure they don't like my music, and this is their unique way of letting me know."

Kandy said, "Robina believes the thumb in her Amazon box is Sally's."

A contortion spread across Danny's thin face. His brow frowned and rested, frowned and rested, like it was exercising.

"They're real?" He coughed.

Kandy nodded. "And are probably Sally's."

Danny's face whitened, almost matching his sweatshirt. His body melted down the wall until his knees touched his chin.

"Sally," he whispered. "No way. I just saw her. Sunday, like I said. We were dancing. She's so beautiful when she moves." He looked up. "We drank Mai Tai's." His eyes defocused to a detached glaze. Fifteen seconds passed before he spoke again.

"She had three. I remember, because she said her limit was two on a school night and if she drank three she wasn't sure she'd be able to play on Monday. So we each had a third as a sort of experiment to see if it would trash our musical memory. We walked home, thinking it might help process the alcohol away. And I kissed her goodnight right on the steps going up to her...."

Kandy got up and sat on the floor next to him, shoulder to shoulder.

Neither spoke.

"Sally," he sighed.

He turned to face Kandy, their noses less than a foot apart. "This can't be real."

"Robina thinks the thumb is Sally's because of a callus and the nail polish. We have to run tests against the prints in her apartment. We'll have the results soon." She paused. "Did you go in?"

He blinked. "Sunday? No, we said goodnight on the steps. We both needed some sleep." He managed half a smile staring at the floor.

"We should do the same thing with yours. See if we can get a print."

He didn't move. "Sally."

"Okay if we take the box?" Kandy asked.

He pulled his feet under him and stood straight up from a deep squat. He shuffled across the carpet to the box and peered inside. He moved his hands toward the opening, like he wanted to touch her.

"I shouldn't touch it should I?" he said toward the box.

"Probably better if it's not handled more than necessary," Qigiq said, leaving it to Danny to decide if it was necessary for him to touch her.

Danny picked up the box with two hands and held it out for Qigiq.

Qigiq took it and closed the lid with his coat sleeve, everything happening in slow motion.

Danny stared into Qigiq, his dark gray eyes like stones under water.

"Get the motherfucker." Danny said. "Please?"

Qigiq cleared his throat.

Kandy moved across the room until she stood close to Danny.

"We'll do our best, Danny. Our very best. If you think of anything that might help us, call this number." She pressed a business card into his left hand—the one with the fast fingers.

~ 12 ~

McDonald's chicken fingers in greasy paper bowls glided down a stainless steel counter. A deep-fried purple finger was draped across the top of every fifth container, like anchovies on a Caesar salad. The bowls came fast as he bagged and bagged and handed them out the drive-thru window to a customer who grinned with a missing eyetooth and three-day stubble and tossed them into a huge Amazon box in the back of a black pickup truck that had a vinyl roof like a hearse. Robina stood to his left in a white dress with golden arches over her breasts, taking cash and tossing change at the customers while shouting, "Hurry Qigiq, hurry," her register ca-chang'ing with each sale to the rhythm of the *Mony Mony* chorus being played by a pounding audio system in the truck...

His eyes opened. Sweat had beaded on his forehead. He was breathing through his mouth and the phone was ringing.

He rolled onto his side. 3:18 am.

He reached. "Qigiq here."

"Good morning, partner. You weren't sleeping were you?" Kandy called into the phone.

"No, of course not," he moaned. "I was up working the case. We should check McDonald's."

"McDon—? You must be hungry."

"Dreaming. You're up early."

"Got a call from our friend Danny. Wants to show us something. Said it can't wait."

Qigiq swung upright, the wood floor was smooth and cool on his bare feet. He rubbed both temples with one hand.

"What's that?" he asked.

"Don't know, he won't say. Just picked him up, we're on our way to your place. He refused to go to the station with me."

Qigiq dropped back against the pillow.

"You're on your way here to show me something at three in the morning, but you don't know what it is? Am I hearing right?"

"Right as rain, Detective. ETA in fourteen minutes."

He slowly placed the receiver back in place. Kandy must have tried his cellphone and he slept through it.

He urged his body up to slip on a long-sleeve black shirt and a pair of gray sweat pants he used for hanging around the boat. Fourteen minutes was enough time to get coffee, and maybe a muffin.

He heard a clunk-clunk outside and opened the door to see Kandy on the dock, her red-brown hair blowing in the night breeze looking blue gray under the mercury vapor lights of the harbor. She stepped aside. Danny was still wearing his white sweatshirt and jeans, had a bag slung over his shoulder that looked to be made for carrying large sheet music, and a skateboard in his left hand painted with fiery explosions bursting from guitars.

"Hi," he said, so softly Qigiq wouldn't have heard him if he hadn't seen his mouth move.

"Welcome aboard."

He lead them to the main cabin. No fireplace, but a flat panel TV, teakwood stereo speakers, electric piano, and a few places to sit without using the floor. They settled in and stared at each other in silence, each holding a mug of coffee.

"Danny called me about a half-hour ago. Said there was something we had to see that couldn't wait," Kandy said.

Danny reached into the black bag he had dropped at his feet. It had a red circle-slash symbol on the side but nothing beneath it. He removed a laptop computer. A small white light on the edge glowed up and down like the machine was breathing.

"Do you have Wi-Fi?" Danny asked.

Qigiq rubbed his eyes with fists. "The marina does, they include it in the dock fee."

Danny carried the machine across the room and held it towards Qigiq. The screen said *Would you like to join network Houseboats?* and was waiting for a password.

Qigiq typed with one finger.

Danny returned to sitting cross-legged in the center of the room on his skateboard and worked the keyboard.

"I was up late worrying about Sally, contacting her friends online to see if anyone had heard from her. You know, forums, Twitter, Facebook type stuff. And when I went to YouTube, this video popped up as one of the top viewed in the past hour."

He looked down at the screen. "It's been viewed 965,341 times."

"This has something to do with Sally?" Qigiq asked.

Danny held up a finger.

They waited.

"It's called Fear of Fibonocci. Posted by someone using the name F12358. Those are the first five Fibonocci numbers, in case you don't recognize them, I used them for a composition once in Dr. Walters class."

Qigiq looked at Kandy, who shrugged.

Danny turned the machine around so they could watch.

"This is in a category tagged *EmoSim,* which I presume is short for Emotion Simulation, because it also includes a tag for*Fear.*"

Numbers flew through the video starting with the same ones Danny had just listed. A low distorted voiceover said, "Growing, uncontrolled, spreading from one to another like fear before the blitzkrieg. Know thy fear."

Kandy mouthed, "Who is that?" toward Qigiq, who shrugged.

A girl's face filled the screen.

Qigiq jumped off the sofa to be closer.

Kandy arrived next to him.

She was blonde and the camera was close. She had a strip of silver duct tape across her mouth and was struggling, her head whipping from side to side, hair flying.

"Fear," the voice said. "It's why you do. And why you don't."

They didn't need to hear it because Robina had shown them pictures at the apartment, but Danny said, "That's Sally."

The girl twisted left, right, left. Qigiq guessed she was tied at the wrist and ankles, allowing her little movement. The camera moved closer. Her eyes grew wider, wilder, like blue buttons about to pop off a suit.

"Think you won't get caught?" the voice said.

The camera moved in a rhythmic pattern, her face coming closer and receding every few seconds like it was bobbing in a pool.

"Think we can't find you?"

She struggled and then stopped fighting, apparently resigned to what was happening. Her face was red and looked hot, but she wasn't crying.

"You have what is ours."

The camera stopped moving and the girl lay still, her blue eyes closed. Then it shifted, the image becoming dark and blurry with an ear to the left and moving not at all.

"And we will take it back..."

There was an abrupt edit and the warning label from the baggies and its message *Don't Steal Music* filled the screen for five seconds. The camera zoomed toward the label and froze on the three words.

"Now," the voice said.

And the three words started trembling before they exploded into thousands of tiny bits.

Qigiq blinked. He was wide awake.

"This is on YouTube?" Kandy asked.

Danny nodded. "Posted yesterday. The bastard wore a headcam while fucking her, and put it on YouTube. The mother-fucking bastard..."

Qigiq rolled onto his back and stared at the fine varnished beams of the cabin's ceiling, trying to understand the electronic world. "Won't they remove it?"

"Not unless people complain," Kandy said. "It's had almost a million views in less than a day."

"But she's being *raped*," Danny yelled, his voice echoing across the quiet bay.

"That's what we think," said Kandy. "But it could easily have been simulated. And there's not any real violence. No blood, no weapons."

"Get it to the forensics guys?" Qigiq asked.

"I'll send an email, but who knows what time they'll show up for work," she said.

"I recorded it," Danny said. "If you need it."

Kandy nodded.

"Thanks for not waiting until morning," Qigiq said.

Danny nodded once, a slight movement that could be easily missed. "What the fuck is going on?" he whispered.

Qigiq hated not having answers when people needed truth. He sighed and sat up.

"We don't know yet, Danny. Let's find out."

They played the video again, six eyes watching for any clue of where it was taken or who took it.

"What are those tiny blocks?" Qigiq asked.

"From the compression, like crackles and hiss in a vinyl record," Danny said. Reacting to the look on Qigiq's face, he added, "The way the data is made smaller so it can be sent across the Internet."

"I see."

"What time of day?" Kandy asked.

Qigiq studied the moving images. "Late. There's very little color. The floor, assuming she's on her back, is gray. Maybe it was shot by moonlight."

Kandy worked her gum over. Her eyes sliced to the kid, and back to Qigiq.

"Maybe we should do this when we're fresh," Qigiq said. "The last eighteen hours have been nuts."

Danny looked up. "How much time do we have?"

Another question Qigiq wished he could answer. He had left Fairbanks to get away from answers hidden too deep for a lowly detective to unravel.

"Can't tell. That's why we move as fast as possible." He watched Danny's face. "But no faster."

Danny handed Qigiq a flat bar not much bigger than a pack of Kandy's gum.

"Here's a copy of the movie. I'll look for others when I get home."

Qigiq walked them to the door.

"Try to get some sleep, Danny," he suggested, knowing none of them would.

Danny turned. Dark eyes stared at Qigiq from a sunken face for a good ten seconds that felt like an hour. Then he nodded and stepped into the night.

Qigiq closed the door behind Kandy. It was 4:11. He lifted the stick the kid had given him, wondering how exactly a movie could be in it? He looked east between open curtains at the bay. The water rolled with a light wind, no whitecaps, just sparkles from moonlight. He saw nothing move on the docks save the swaying shadows of masts stuck into million dollar sailing yachts. He turned. A calendar of Italian motorcycles held to his fridge by a white bear magnet showed six more days to a full moon.

He flicked the lights off in the kitchen and went to a low table at the end of his couch to retrieve the computer Kandy had arranged for him. He touched the smooth metal thinking about how complex things are manufactured, dimmed the lights and carried it to the bedroom. Sitting with his back against pillows, he inserted the stick and found the video. He watched, listening carefully to the way the voice said, "Fear." Perhaps they could do something with voice matching when they found the person who would sever a young woman's fingers. He wished for a federal registry of voices like the fingerprint database.

He watched the girl named Sally struggle. He studied the tension in her triceps and forearms. If that was an act, she was well rehearsed. He studied her eyes. If he had to guess, and he was guessing like crazy, she knew the attacker. All too true in the majority of cases: friends raping friends.

He noticed the floor. It was gray, had stripes and looked hard: kitchen, or maybe a bathroom. The movement of her head left no impression like it would in a carpet. The tape over her mouth was folded at the corner. So the attacker planned to pull off the tape?

He leaned toward his nightstand drawer and lifted out a huge pair of black headphones with cracked ear cushions. With the headphones on, he heard soft sounds, maybe from the camera itself. The girl was moaning or trying to speak because the little mounds of sound were in sync with the movement of her cheeks and throat. It was the same over and over again. Two syllables. Maybe the lab guys could do something with it.

He listened to the entire movie with his eyes closed, focusing on the moan. And something under the moan. A pounding. Her elbows on the floor? He opened his eyes. Not synchronized. Something else. He watched the rhythmic movement of the camera. Yes. The attacker was pounding on the floor. Maybe his shoes. The only parts of the attacker in the shot were hands wearing blue gloves and the sleeves of a black shirt with elastic wrist bands.

His?

Qigiq wondered for a moment. Not a shred of skin was showing. He would check out the gloves and shirt, but would bet they were generic and would lead nowhere. *Was the attacker male?* That would be the obvious conclusion if this were rape, and not some bizarre form of performance art.

San Francisco, he reminded himself. Not Fairbanks.

He sat with his knees apart and the computer halfway down the bed and watched again, ignoring the girl's face and looking for clues. Very light gray patterns shifted across the screen. His last thought before falling asleep was to wonder if the camera might be auto-adjusting to changes in light.

~ 13 ~

Sunlight reflecting from water colored his bedroom the gold of a pharaoh's tomb. Not a refreshing thought. He rolled over and kicked his laptop, still sitting on the bed, now with a black screen. Sally's face flashed through his mind, twisting side to side. He opened his eyes.

It was 9:14 Friday morning. No call from Kandy. No news.

He showered and started eggs frying. He watched the bay through the kitchen window—thought about glaciers, and permafrost. The American flag at the end of the double row of houseboats, twenty in all, hung limp. Colors reflected from the languid surface: whites, yellows, even one red hull. Reflected masts twisted and bent on the ripples, reminding him of movie special effects.

He sipped black coffee Kandy had given him from a place called Peet's, like Lance Armstrong if interviews can be believed. He'd be happy if it gave him a fraction of Armstrong's superhero endurance. His eye caught a round white blob that grew and shrank as the water moved—like a giant soap bubble trying to stay alive.

He blinked and stared. The bubble was the reflection of the flying bridge of a power boat. He watched the shape undulate and felt his tired mind wanting to suggest something. He turned to check on the eggs, flipped them over, and walked back to the window.

The white blob moved like an animal inside was trying to get out.

An animal.

He turned the heat off under his eggs and picked up his cellphone, stopped, placed the device on the counter and trotted bare foot back to the bedroom. He dug in the drawer of the nightstand. The phone's camera wasn't bad, but he wanted a zoom lens. He found the Canon point-and-shoot that fit in the palm of his hand, saw 9:48 on the clock, and headed outside.

He had to go back to shore and jog along the gravel past three docks, then out the fourth until he found the source of the reflection: a thirty-foot Grady-White with flybridge, and above that, a marine radar unit. He walked backwards on the dock watching the angle of the unit relative to the sun. When the shadow of the bulb landed on the dock it lulled back and forth, painting a gray patch on the weatherworn slats. He raised his little camera and started shooting. Nothing happened. He lowered it and studied the tiny icons all over the back, found one that looked like a movie camera, pressed and held the power button. The lens whirred. He brought the camera to his right eye, took a deep breath, held it, stood statue still and pressed the shutter. A red light came on in the upper right corner of the viewfinder. He let his breath out slowly.

© © ©

Thirty minutes later Qigiq was in the break room thankful someone had made fresh coffee. He pressed his hips against the counter and leaned backwards to stretch his lower back, trying to shake the ache from interrupted sleep. He carried his black mug bearing the spread wings of a silver eagle back to the office he shared with Kandy. Two gray desks sat face to face, each holding a black laptop. Both were off. He walked to the corner where a combination printer-scanner-copy-FAX machine sat on a stool and banged around in its back until it gave up a single fresh sheet of 8 1/2 x 11 paper.

He dug down in the outer pocket of his dark green cargo pants and came up with a short pencil with half an eraser. He placed the coffee next to the laptop, the paper next to that, and sat down. He reminded himself it was

Friday morning. Thinking back to the previous Sunday, the last known sighting of Sally, he started a list:

SUN: Danny saw Sally at a concert. Left her about midnight.

MON: ??

TUE: Robina saw Sally at breakfast, 8:30 am.

TUE: No Sally at afternoon practice per Robina.

WED: Robina and Danny both receive packages.

THU: Robina shows up with package No. 1 at the station.

THU: Danny calls the station. Detectives pick up second package.

FRI: 3:00 am Danny finds YouTube video of Sally. A million views.

FRI: 10:00am, Qigiq shoots video of radar shadow.

He flipped the pencil around and erased the last line. The shadow was less than a hunch. He would wait until he knew more. He replaced it with:

FRI: No sign of Sally.

He left white space and made a list of names: *Robina, Danny, Veronica, Violet.* His pencil hesitated then wrote: *Sally*...followed by *Mony* and *Professor Walters.* He sat up and stared at the paper. They didn't have much. No body, no crime scene, just a missing person.

Well, most of her was missing.

He now wished he hadn't left the eggs in the pan in his excitement to take pictures. He glanced at Kandy's Elvis desk clock, the King's leather-clad hips gyrating slowly back and forth. Just after eleven. He added to the paper:

FRI: Rape video on YouTube—Fear. Possible voice ID.

He was thinking about lunch when Kandy flew into the room waving a folder. She tossed it on his desk with just enough force to slide it across the smooth top, across his paper and into his coffee mug, where it stopped like a puck in the net.

"Print results," she said, as she kicked her chair out of the way and started tapping keys on her laptop.

"Want me to guess?" Qigiq asked.

Without looking up she said, "Sure, but for low points. The questions are only Category 4."

He picked up the folder and tapped it against the edge of his desk without opening it. Cat 4: the easiest climbs in the big Tour de France bicycle race.

"The thumb and index finger stitched together that Robina brought in match prints from Sally's room on Arcadia."

"Qigiq, you're a genius," she said.

He noticed her leaned over the laptop, breasts pushing against a long-sleeved black shirt that hugged her everywhere. He looked back at the folder in his hand as if it could speak to him.

"Can't get a print off the Finger-in-Ear art piece."

"Too much superglue," she said.

"Can't trace the glue, generic."

"You're batting a thousand, too bad I'm slow-pitching soft balls." She pulled the chair back with her toe and sat down to watch him.

"But you have a DNA match and all four body parts are Sally's."

"Bzzzt! Overconfidence in our lab. No DNA results until Monday at the earliest," she said, laughing.

"Operating assumption?" he asked.

"Don't have to assume much. Even without Danny's package, we know we have a girl kidnapped, possibly sexually assaulted, with a mutilated hand, who may or may not be alive," Kandy said.

"I hope you have a pleasant weekend, too," Qigiq said.

Kandy yanked her desk drawer open and a stick of gum appeared. She held it up.

When in Rome. He nodded. She flicked it across the desk and scored another goal against his coffee mug.

"Forensics have anything?" he asked.

"No report beyond the prints. Not even a preliminary."

"Want to go see Pillar?" Qigiq asked, still tapping the spine of the folder against the edge of his desk, like it was a giant redwood tree and he was chopping it down with a hatchet.

"You go see him. He's still mad at me about the case of the black Porsche."

Qigiq grinned. "He'll forgive you. Let's give it a try." He got up. "I'll go alone if you want."

She shrugged. "You're right. He'll get over it."

He motioned toward her computer.

She pulled her lips to one side. "I had an idea."

"That video is bothering you, isn't it?"

She nodded.

"Me too," he said.

"Think it's just glory-mongering?" she asked. "A sociopath getting kicks in public?"

Qigiq picked up his cup and downed the rest of the coffee. It was cold.

"If I committed a crime," he said, "I wouldn't show a million people on YouTube."

She sat back down and tapped keys. "Three and half-million."

He walked around the desk and saw the video start playing.

"It's still up there?"

She leaned out of the way. "Popular too. Amazing what some people think is art."

He watched the video play silently. At the end he folded his single sheet of paper once in each direction and slipped it into his back pocket.

She watched his face.

He headed to the door, stopped and turned around.

"I can't shake the feeling that Sally's alive and in terrible pain."

He watched her take a deep breath, the black shirt following the movement of her body.

"That's hard to think about. Let's go see Pillar."

She popped out of the chair like it was an ejection seat and went through the door before him.

~ 14 ~

Qigiq knocked on the words painted in smaller black letters on frosted glass below DIGITAL FORENSICS. The glass rattled in the oak door. The rattle was followed by approaching footsteps. The door swung inward to reveal a short, heavy set man in glasses wearing a white lab coat that had EER stitched above the left breast pocket. The pocket contained a plastic protector and enough pens to write all of Shakespeare without a refill.

"Hello, Qigiq." A balding head nodded. "Kandy, welcome."

They entered a room that could have been a Chinese sweatshop for manufacturing computer hardware except there were no workers present. Machines in various stages of disassembly sat side by side on long tables interrupted occasionally by an office divider. Most were not on, but all had pink, green and yellow tags attached to their components.

"So, you come to Ferdinand for help. Pillar has nothing for you?" the round man asked.

"Pillar had a little," Qigiq said. "The finger was sealed into the ear with Krazy Glue, the instant kind, not the skin guard formula. And the sticker with the message was stuck on with the same adhesive that Apple used on early iPod packaging. But, that glue is used a thousand times a minute in China."

"Is that the best Mr. Pillar can do?" He kept walking, leading them toward the back of the open room.

She said, "Pillar confirmed the Amazon boxes are authentic, and the postage was printed by a real postal meter—the red ink matched what's sold by the US Postal Service."

"Ah, I see," said Ferdinand. "But how was it cancelled? By a machine?

By hand? Was it cancelled at all?"

Qigig turned around to look at Kandy, who shrugged. He didn't remember Pillar saying anything about the cancellation of the postage.

"Your silence tells me you haven't checked the cancellation. We must be thorough," Ferdinand said. "Always thorough."

Kandy's mouth opened, then dropped shut.

They walked another twenty meters.

"You do not yet have DNA?" Ferdinand asked.

"Lab isn't finished," Qigiq said. "They promised Monday."

Ferdinand nodded knowingly and pressed round black frames up to the bridge of his nose. He stopped in front of a gray machine that had a note taped to the divider next to it. A case number was printed in black above a handwritten red scribble that said

"This is her machine?" Qigiq asked.

"Most of it. We have duplicated the disk drive and removed the original and placed it in the safe. The hard drive is the heart and soul of the computer where all information is stored. So we protect it first," Ferdinand said. "Thorough."

Kandy tried not to smirk but only partially succeeded.

"We also found this machine sleeping." Ferdinand looked up. "You know this state, sleeping?"

Kandy nodded. Qigiq shook his head.

"The power is on, the operating system is in memory along with many other things—network software, active programs—just sitting waiting. That is how we found your Sally's machine. So we analyzed memory also, before bringing little Sally here to our center."

"Anything?" Kandy asked. She hesitated. "We played a song on our first visit."

He shrugged. "Your Sally likes music. She doesn't shut her computer off, the iTunes player had been running for three weeks. She uses the Firefox browser, favored by some who believe it offers superior security. She visits many websites, social places where musicians gather. She also—"

He cleared his throat.

"She enjoys the human form. Has many pictures, male and female."

Qigiq nodded and watched Kandy for a reaction that didn't come.

Ferdinand pointed to the flat display.

"We are running the programs we found active on her machine to see if Sally was doing anything that might help us." He tapped the keyboard and synthetic rhythm bumped out of a pair of six-inch speakers accompanied by a singer that was halfway between a whisper and heavy breathing. Ferdinand leaned forward to read the display.

Kandy said, "Elektrokardiogram by Kraftwerk."

Qigiq glanced her way.

She smiled. "I bicycle."

Qigiq and Ferdinand stared.

"That's from the collection," she said.

"Ah," Ferdinand sighed. "Yes. The big race. So maybe Sally too has a bicycle?"

Qigiq pulled the slip of paper from his back pocket, and the half-pencil from the front and wrote *bicycle,* and below it *postage cancellation?* without unfolding it. Ferdinand tapped the screen with the fingernail of his middle finger, like he was insulting the computer.

"Sally has quite a music library. Very big."

"How big is big?" Kandy asked.

Ferdinand consulted a clipboard hanging from the computer table the way a patient's chart hangs at the end of the bed. He flipped two pages.

"Fifty-three thousand, four hundred and nineteen entries. Most represent songs. But there is also much Classical music with multiple movements, poetry readings, political podcasts and instructional material for cello." He looked over his round spectacles. "The poetry readings are not PG-13."

"Erotica?" Kandy asked.

Ferdinand nodded. His lips hinted toward a smile.

"How old is this Sally?" Ferdinand asked.

"Twenty-one two months ago," Qigiq said.

"Quite a girl."

"Anything else?" Qigiq asked.

"Fingerprints."

"Pillar's team already dusted before you picked up the machine. They found dozens of partials, mostly Sally's." Kandy said.

Ferdinand pushed his black circles back up his nose.

"Thorough." He flipped through the clipboard. "Here." He held it up. The page showed six prints down the left side, two full and four partial. Ferdinand pointed. "These three were on the inside of the main case, perhaps when hardware was installed or repaired. The other three we found on a circuit board that was added. I have never seen this board, but it has its own processor. If you turn the page, you will—"

"Who makes it?" Kandy asked.

Ferdinand frowned and turned the page himself. "You will see pictures of the board. It lacks the markings required by law for such a unit: country of manufacture, serial number, FCC and CE certification for use in consumer products, corporation, often patent numbers. None are present."

Qigiq examined the pictures. It looked like a flat piece of green plastic with Legos stuck to it. Tiny lines squirmed across the plastic, connecting the Legos.

"What does it do?" he asked.

"Ah," Ferdinand said. "So very interesting. We are monitoring this board while running the programs that Sally had active: music, browser, mail. We are not yet sure, but it appears that this device," he lowered the clipboard. "It is watching."

"Watching?" Qigiq said without thinking first.

Kandy flipped the pages of the report like she was taking a speed reading test.

Ferdinand watched Kandy.

Qigiq figured he wanted to ask if she was being thorough.

Without taking his eyes from Kandy's face, Ferdinand said, "We think this unusual board is analyzing what happens on this machine. We are watching it to see what data it collects. And what it does with it."

"Do you have a hypothesis yet?" Qigiq asked, attempting to mirror Ferdinand's formality.

"I have what you detectives call hunches."

Kandy perked up.

"What kind of hunches, Ferd? Maybe they'll lead somewhere."

The round man's thick eyebrows rose. Qigiq suppressed a grin.

"Indeed," Ferd said. "My *hunch* is that this board is a stand alone computer. The chips are available at your local electronics store: standard memory and CPU. What is most interesting are the network chips. My hunch is that this little machine is setting up a secure network connection locally and then asking the main machine what it's up to by masquerading as a trusted peer."

"Seems like a lot of trouble," Kandy said.

Ferd examined her like she was a test machine and he was trying to uncover evidence.

"Much trouble, yes. But such a configuration has unique advantages. There is nothing running on the main machine to be detected by a virus scanner or security software. And it is hidden out of sight."

"Hard to find, huh?" Kandy said.

"The network activity could be detected if one knew what to look for. But most machines use their networks a great deal. It would be like trying to find a drop of blood in the Mississippi River."

"So someone was spying on our innocent blonde cellist?" Qigiq asked.

"That would be my hunch," Ferd said, and smiled.

Qigiq stared at the machine. It stepped to a song entitled *Spellbound* by someone named Yngwie J. Malmsteen.

"What's next?"

Ferdinand swung a mechanical arm toward them that had two fingers on the end, like the arm in a dentist's office that holds a drill. He positioned one finger over the 'J' on the keyboard.

"Now we feed her computer input. Our test machine in the back sends information to this mechanical hand, which operates the keys as if someone were sitting at the keyboard. It can also move and click the mouse. We will start with the sequence we found stored in memory when the machine arrived. Thankfully, the acquisition team kept the machine on power."

"And then?" Kandy asked.

"Then we see what Sally's machine does, and what the mystery board does, and write a report."

"Thorough," Qigiq said, while looking at Kandy.

Ferdinand smiled.

Kandy shook her head.

"YouTube?" she asked.

"An interesting social phenomenon," Ferd replied. "Millions of people watching poor video quality just to see what other people find interesting. And no one paying much attention to Copyright laws. Intriguing. Anarchy in TV land. Free speech in an electronic world."

"You pay attention to this stuff?" Kandy asked.

"I work with computers. I pay attention to anything that might be relevant to," he tapped his chest, "Electronic Evidence Recovery."

Qigiq nodded at Kandy as if to say, *see how thorough he is.*

"Must keep you busy," Kandy said in a voice that said she meant it. "Anything you can tell us about the video of Sally?"

Ferd motioned with his index finger and led them to the far corner of the room where a Mac laptop sat alone on a black metal desk. Its screen showed a picture of an empty Carnegie Hall taken from the stage, the same picture Qigiq had seen on Sally's desktop. He held up his hand to stop and pointed at the machine.

It was doing nothing near as Qigiq could tell. He turned to Kandy. She shrugged.

They waited.

"In a moment," Ferd said.

Qigiq listened to soft pop's from Kandy's gum and wondered if Ferd ever trimmed his caterpillar eyebrows. He slipped his left hand deep into a front pocket and rubbed the smooth back of his camera like a worry stone.

The machine launched a web browser, navigated to YouTube and showed the video of Sally. The sound was low, but Qigiq remembered the mutters of *Fear* from the first time he had heard them float through his houseboat.

"This machine verifies once per minute that the video is still available. It also maintains a total count of views, subtracting its own plays, of course."

Qigiq nodded.

"Thorough," Kandy said with a wide grin.

Ferdinand continued, "We have only been working on this video since this morning, but it has several unusual features. Look at the dark bottom of the frame and watch carefully."

Qigiq stared. He saw what looked like static on a TV set, but only at the very bottom.

"I believe the flickering is a form of data. Its frequency spectrum doesn't match standard noise patterns that occur in video transmission or wireless data transfer."

Blank looks faced Ferdinand.

He said, "We're assuming for the moment that this was recorded with a wireless camera."

They nodded.

"In any case. I believe there is data in that last row, and will work to decode it today."

"Thanks," said Qigiq.

"And thank you," said Ferdinand. "This is the most interesting project we've seen for a long time. It feels good to flex our digital muscles."

Kandy smiled. Qigiq guessed she was imagining the rotund Ferdinand in spandex at the gym.

Ferdinand crossed to the opposite corner of his laboratory. He sat down in front of a huge flat display that sat on a desk with, Qigiq counted, four towers side by side beneath it, and started typing.

Kandy walked with long purposeful steps to peer over Ferd's shoulder. Qigiq followed, his thumb continuing to stroke the camera in his pocket as its images and what they might mean intruded on his mind.

A large version of Sally's video filled the big screen.

"There is something rotten in the Denmark of this movie," Ferd said. "I need more time for analysis, but let me show you what I have. I know you detectives work many angles on a case simultaneously, and this might have meaning for you."

Ferd spoke flatly, like he was teaching a class of freshmen.

"We are assuming this girl is being raped, which would create motion along this plane. Though there is no direct evidence of rape."

A grid pattern of lime green lines appeared almost vertical over the video.

"That's fine," he continued. "But notice her spine." A red line parallel to

Sally's spine joined the green grid. "It's moving not only in the plane of motion one would normally associate with the sex act, but also dipping and rotating. What does that tell us?"

"The camera is moving," Kandy said.

"Precisely. So we ask, how is the attacker holding the camera, and why is it moving in this particular pattern. A pattern that, in fact, repeats once every five point eight seconds. Or I might ask, is the attacker holding the camera, or is there another person and he or she is not holding it steady?"

Qigiq stared at the moving lines. "Can you separate the two?"

Ferd smiled. Next to the video two line drawings appeared. One showed a green circle moving in an up-down motion. Then a blue square sketched a figure eight at an oblique angle.

"There are two kinds of motion?" Qigiq asked.

"At least two," Ferd replied.

"Any idea what's going on?" Kandy asked.

Qigiq's thumb stroked his camera.

"I have only guesses," Ferdinand said. "Educated ones."

"Do any of those guesses involve a boat?" said Qigiq.

Ferd's caterpillars crawled high up his forehead. "Yes, Detective, they do."

Qigiq pointed at the video. "I think the attacker is wearing the camera."

Ferd nodded.

"And even though it's dark, there's a shadow moving right through here," Qigiq pointed at the area above Sally's right shoulder, "that sometimes crosses her face."

"A shadow?" Ferd repeated. "But how?"

"I don't know. But I think I know what it might be a shadow of. Would that help?"

"A great deal."

Qigiq pulled his camera out and fumbled with the door that covered the battery and memory chip. He handed the chip to Ferdinand.

"A movie I took this morning."

Ferd nodded and brought the movie up on screen. They watched a shadow pass back and forth across a wooden dock that needed paint. It looked like a giant gray lollipop swaying in the wind.

"What is this?" Ferdinand asked.

Kandy answered. "It's the shadow of the radar tower on a sport fishing boat." She turned to Qigiq. "Am I close?"

He nodded.

"A fishing boat," Ferd said softly. "Assume that Sally is lying on the deck of a boat. Constrain the analysis to possible wave motions. Yes yes, let me work on this."

"Can you extract that shadow?" Qigiq asked.

Ferdinand frowned. "It is barely there. Why so faint? Yes, I will try to extract it. You wish me to tell you what model of radar it is a shadow of?"

Kandy smiled.

Qigiq said, "You sure are thorough, Ferdinand."

~ 15 ~

Lili hated it when her body spoke things she wanted to hide, so she tried not to let her knees shake as she met his eyes.

"But Mr. Blake, we're rushing to make Monday. Do you really want to release this vir..., um, tracking software *today?* We won't be able to test." She pressed her lower teeth against her upper lip. "That's very dangerous."

He watched her closely. "What do you mean by dangerous?"

"Unpredictable. When the Hand is released, it will have no connection to us. If something goes wrong with the replication algorithm, well...." She swallowed hard and tried to pull her shoulders up and back. "Anything could happen, Sir."

"Anything? That's awfully broad."

Her eyes dropped automatically. She was standing a meter in front of his desk like a private taking orders. She forced them back up to his face.

"Harold says—"

"Please don't tell me about Mr. Zeto, Miss Volker. We both know he errs on the side of perfection."

She froze. Harold knew more about the software than the rest of the the team combined. She tried hard to remember what he had said about IH failures.

"There is a risk that IH will replicate in ways we haven't tested. And since it's extracting data from the host machine, and posting it to multiple target locations on the Internet, a lot could happen. Sir. It could infect machines that aren't stealing music, it could post inappropriate information that would put us in violation of right to privacy laws and—" She blinked and cleared her throat. "The most dangerous business issue is that it will implicate Silver Platter by connecting to our domain."

"Goddam software. Can't anyone write this stuff? Miss Volker, I want it to go out over the weekend. It'll make us front page news on Monday when the market opens."

She felt like she was standing in a sandstorm naked. She reached into her back pocket and pressed speed dial number one, hoping Harold would see the ID and answer right away. She waited in silence.

Blake sighed, "So you're telling me there is no way to release over the weekend and get that Invisible thing working for us? You're aware that—

A hundred meters away in Harold's office a cellphone rang. He glanced and saw Lili's name, finished the line of code he was writing, then picked up his phone and said, "Hello." He heard a distant voice say, "...every day wasted puts us one day closer to failure, Miss Volker? I thought you were one of us: the people who hate to fail?"

Harold heard, "I am, Sir. One of those people. But spending the weekend testing is crucial. If we release...and it leads back to us—"

She stopped mid-sentence. He didn't know what would happen either. But his bet was on bad voodoo.

"If you lead the authorities to us..." Blake began.

Blake was grilling poor Lili. The jerk didn't even deserve to look at her tits lift the purple stripes of the shirt Harold had seen when she went by to get her TGIF coffee.

Blake continued. "Just make sure there is no connection between us and any part of IH. None. Test that part."

"Mr. Blake—"

Blake waved a hand at her. "Sit down, Volker, let's examine our options. I know you can't make this stuff appear by magic. But we need it, and we need it now. Timing is everything."

Lili let out her breath as she took two steps back and sat down slowly in a blue cloth chair meant for visitors—not too comfortable, not too large—so they wouldn't stay long or feel important.

"We would have to go with only one testing phase. In my opinion, that's far too risky for a replicating module."

"Isn't there some way? We're nearing the end of the month, *and* the end of our quarter. Even a tiny up-tick in revenue would do great things for us."

She cast her eyes at the carpet. She represented Engineering, she wasn't supposed to ask financial questions—as if engineers couldn't do math.

"Our only option is to bring in more testers, but there's no time to train them. Everyone we have is already working the entire weekend."

She stopped and lifted her head up. She wanted to ask a question.

"What is it?" Blake asked.

Harold had moved to the lobby and was pacing back and forth with his cellphone pasted to his ear. Pacing was one of his three default modes, the other two being eating anywhere there was food, and sitting, staring at his computer monitor. He listened intently to the conversation.

"I know you handle this, Mr. Blake. But what great things could an up-tick do for us?"

Blake pushed out his lower lip until it hid his upper.

"Great financial things, Miss Volker. We must show revenue growth at a rate that our investors can sell to Wall Street. You know our objective is to IPO. Once the public starts buying our stock, the sky's the limit. But every day we are late now, is a day we delay the IPO."

His eyes held her in the chair. She tried to show she was a relaxed professional taking everything in stride even though an IPO and price run-up would make her a millionaire three or four times over. She could finally buy something besides a used Subaru.

"The sky?" she said, sounding like a secretary.

Blake smiled. "A hundred dollars a share is within our reach, Lili. But we need to start now."

Her eyes widened against her will. Would twenty million feel different from three or four?

"But we can't, Mr. Blake. There is just no way to insure quality and be ready before close of business on Monday. Meaning 11:59 pm." She smiled her best please believe me because I'm telling the truth smile.

"God damn it. That's another three days, four counting today. Haven't we been working on this for months? We must have *something* that will do the job. Come on, Miss Volker, you engineers are creative. Innovate something."

Lili shifted in her chair and crossed her legs in an effort to relax. And buy time.

Harold chanted into the phone, "Change the spec, change the spec. C'mon Lili, make the problem smaller so we can handle it faster."

Lili said, "Posting comments to blogs is risky, because we might make a mistake and accuse someone who hasn't stolen anything. And posting pictures is doubly risky, because we haven't been doing images for very long. I'm afraid there isn't—"

She was interrupted by a buzzing sound that felt like she was being pulled off stage in a game show for failing to answer the question. Eddy Blake held up a finger of his right hand and pressed the intercom button with his left.

"Yes?"

Stacy's voice, thinned by the speaker phone, filled the room. "Mr. Zeto is here, says he needs to talk to Lili about the Invisible Hand software. It's urgent."

Eddy's eyes flicked up at Lili, but he spoke to Stacy. "Fine, I'll send her out in a minute." He released the intercom. "Looks like something's up, your star programmer is hunting for you. You better find out what's wrong." He groaned. "How come urgent stuff is never good?"

She assumed he was being rhetorical.

"Would you like me to come back?" she asked.

"Yes, soon as you can. We have to find a way."

Lili nodded and let herself out of Blake's office. She saw Harold pacing next to Stacy's desk holding a cellphone to his ear. She fought back a grin.

"Hi, Harold, got something important?" she asked, loud enough for Stacy to overhear clearly.

"Yeah, a new problem with the identification module. The false positive rate tripled on the last build. With the release scheduled for Monday, I thought you should know right away."

Lili's eyes widened. Three times the rate, that was an awful lot of people being fingered by the Hand that didn't have stolen music on their systems.

"What went wrong?"

Harold glanced at Stacy, who was reading email. He spoke quickly. "The first round of tests on today's build 6503 showed the increase. I think we're not initializing the counter array at the right time and we end up with a positive file count when it should be zero."

"But our ID module has been working for weeks," she said.

"I know, I know. That's why I came to get you right away." He pointed to his cellphone and led her away from Stacy's desk.

As they walked Lili said, "I was just warning Mr. Blake that if we ID people who aren't in violation, we'll have a mess on our hands."

"Yeah. And a bunch of lawsuits," Harold said.

He stepped sideways into an inside conference room with no windows and pulled her elbow in after him."

"What—"

"Shhh," he said, flicking on the lights and closing the door.

"We're in huge trouble," she whispered. "Blake is pushing for a release today."

Harold sat down at the far end of the conference table where he could see the door.

"I know. That's why I came to get you."

"I thought the ID module—"

"Lili, the ID module is fine."

She pulled out a rolling chair and dropped herself into it.

"You made that up?"

"Of course. You know I wrote the ID module. I figured you would smell the set up."

She grinned, which made her cheeks puff out.

"No matter," he said. "There's no way we can go with the full version today."

"I agree. But Eddy——" she jammed her thumb in the direction of Blake's office like she was hitchhiking, "wants to examine options. The financials are in the pressure cooker."

Now he was even more convinced Platter was almost out of money. "That's the other reason I came to get you. I have a suggestion."

She slumped down in the chair, a move Harold found highly erotic, almost as if she were lying on the floor for him. She lifted her eyes.

"Like you said," he continued, "the ID module has been working for weeks. And is still working. How about we release a version one-point-oh that ID's the system, but instead of auto-posting to blogs like Blake wants, just have it delete the offending files. Hell, we know they're stolen, we tagged them."

"And report nothing?"

"Exactly. The file deletion module has been stable for months. Postpone your blogging module, and release the two we know work. We could do it today if we had to, though tomorrow would give us more time to assemble the distribution package."

"And how does that help us?" she asked, sliding even lower in the chair.

"Tell Blake that when people realize their music files are disappearing, they'll post to the blogs and social networks themselves, wanting to know who is getting attacked and why. It will appear more real than our auto-posts. Might get more media attention."

She dropped her head into her hands and spoke just above a whisper. "You know how I hate changing specs. It gives Marketing an excuse to blame Engineering for everything."

"Screw Marketing. When this works, we won't even need them writing stupid copy to misrepresent our products."

She shook her head. "People have to know about us."

"They'll know about us when the Invisible Hand slaps them. Might even buy our protected music files so they can feel safe."

Lili stood and walked backwards until her shoulder blades pressed against the hard surface of the closed door.

"We're not doing this so customers need us to protect them. We're doing it to stop thieves. And protect the investments made by honest people. Why should people who understand that artists have to make a living like everyone else have to carry the losers who think they have a divine birthright to listen to any music ever recorded just because technology built by hardworking engineers makes it possible? It's like they think they should be able to print money for themselves because Gutenberg invented the printing press."

Harold gave her a wide smile. "We could sell lots of those."

She shook her head, but grinned. "Harold, I'm serious. You're suggesting a huge change that has to go through review meetings and be approved by Product Management, not to mention actually changing the software. I'll have to file an engineering change order that will make it look like we're slipping the project. And it's not us, Mr. Blake keeps moving the target dates."

Harold got up and walked over to face her. He liked being close, her body radiated some kind of aura that made him feel good all over.

"There won't be any meetings. Just put the option on the table for Blake, and tell him we can only do it if we're allowed to focus and stay out of meetings. He'll take care of the drones and we can get the job done."

She looked into his eyes, both hands behind her on the doorknob.

"You don't like the Marketing department, do you?"

"I don't like anyone between me and getting the job done." He smiled, enjoying being close to her in a closed room. "Usually that's Marketing, when it's not Finance telling me I can't have the new equipment I want."

She stepped sideways away from the door. "No wonder everyone loves engineers so much," she said with a wink, and turned the knob. "I'll give it a try. Maybe we can at least drop scanning for pictures and identifying faces and stuff. That's all new. We can always add it in a later version."

A triple rap on the door froze her in place.

Harold leapt over the table and dropped into a chair on the far side.

She stared at him. "I hate changing specs, there are always unforeseen side effects." She pulled the door open.

Stacy looked at Lili, then past her at Harold scratching notes on a small pad of paper.

"Mr. Blake is ready for you any time."

"Meaning, he wants me back there now?" Lili asked.

Stacy whispered, "He said, 'Get that engineering bitch back here. We need to get moving.'"

Lili smiled. "He only called me a 'bitch'? No fucking or useless adjectives?"

Stacy blushed. "No, only bitch. But I didn't tell you."

~ 16 ~

Qigiq watched Kandy's face through the gap between his black boots propped on his desk and the back of her laptop. She was pushing the last of a fish taco into her mouth with an index finger. When she finished chewing she reached for an extra-large iced tea and caught his look.

"What made you think of a boat?" she asked.

"I was staring at the bay this morning over coffee, being thankful it's Friday, when a reflection moved on the water. It clicked with something I had seen in Sally's video without knowing I had seen it. That's why I recorded the movie of the water, so I could show it to you and see if I was hallucinating."

Kandy unwrapped another taco and squeezed white goop from a packet across the top. She grinned. "Digital cameras come in handy."

"Our perp agrees," he said.

She nodded, or was chewing, he wasn't sure.

Qigiq forked through the edible bowl of his taco into beans.

The phone rang.

Kandy gestured for him to take it. He shook his head and pointed at her. They both chewed.

It rang again.

He forked more beans into his mouth. She took another bite of the taco.

It rang again.

Qigiq lifted his right foot and swung it at the phone. The heel banged the face in its lower right corner.

Kandy brought her hand over her mouth and shook with laughter, though no sound came out.

"Don't choke," he said. Then louder, "Hello."

The speakerphone emitted a male voice.

"Hello? Qigiq? Did you say choke? Are you ok?"

Qigiq swallowed. "Yes, this is Qigiq."

"This is Ferdinand. I've analyzed your boat idea. I believe it has merit."

Qigiq met Kandy's eyes.

"Thanks, Ferdinand," he said.

Kandy reached for her oversized tea and wrapped her lips around the straw.

"It was difficult. I have sent you a report in email. You may wish to watch while I explain. But I have high confidence in this result. Yes, very high."

Kandy tapped keys on her laptop and motioned Qigiq over.

"I'm here with Kandy. We have two movies."

"Good, good. Open the one named TheCrime."

Kandy clicked.

"This is the original Sally movie, but note the improved stability. I've taken away the motion of the camera that I estimate was induced by the boat, so what remains is the camera motion from the attacker's movements."

Qigiq said softly, "It looks like they're lying on a living room floor."
Kandy nodded.

"Now open TheWaves."

As the second video played Sally's body rocked back and forth like she was lying on the deck of a boat.

"The motion of the attacker has been removed, what you see is the motion of the boat as it affected the attacker's body. Naturally, there are many assumptions that lead to this interpretation."

"Very nice, Ferd," Kandy said.

"Hello, Kandy," Ferd said.

"Does the motion tell us anything?" Qigiq asked.

"Motion reveals much," Ferd replied. "For example, I estimate the height of the attacker between five feet ten inches and six feet."

Qigiq met Kandy's eyes. "His height?" she asked the speakerphone.

"Yes. Assuming a male was wearing the camera, which I base on the relation of the video image to Sally's face. Assuming, of course, that he was raping her. We still do not have independent corroboration of this assumption."

Qigiq reached across the back-to-back desks and grabbed a legal pad lying beside his sleeping laptop. He started drawing stick figures.

"We know from your witness that Sally is five foot five. We used average ratio of torso to legs and put the position of the camera on his forehead like a miner's light. Far from perfect. I can send you the drawings we made if you like."

Qigiq pulled the single page from his back pocket and wrote the estimates down. Next to them he wrote *miner's light*.

"We'll stop by and take a look," Kandy said. "Better to have you explain them to us."

"I agree," Ferdinand said. "I have much more, is now a good time?"

Qigiq looked at his half eaten taco salad and thought now was a great time; he might be able to finish lunch. "We'll make the time, go ahead."

Ferd's voice from the speaker phone said, "After I isolated the motion of the craft, I began to wonder what would cause that motion, so I back calculated to wave height and frequency. I can show you the calculations if you like."

"Later, Ferd," Kandy said, smiling. "How about the executive summary?"

They heard a gruff chuckle from the phone.

"Once I had wave height and frequency estimates I made a few careful assumptions. First, the boat was in open water, maybe out in the bay, or perhaps offshore in the Pacific. I realize it's not necessary that the rape took place close to San Francisco, but I am making that assumption."

"We're with you," Qigiq managed, while continuing to eat.

"I called a colleague in the Coast Guard and the general conditions needed to generate the necessary motion existed offshore Monday through Wednesday of this past week. Tuesday matches best. The surfers also track wave action. Their measurements are consistent with mine."

"You're kidding," Kandy said. "You can be that accurate?"

"The boat is like an instrument, transmitting the motion of the waves directly to the video camera as position and lighting changes. Shadows. It is quite accurate. But there are the assumptions I've mentioned. And we don't yet know the exact characteristics of the boat."

"Where does this lead?" Qigiq asked.

"If you'll allow me to place the radar pole above the bridge and forward of the wheel, where it is located on the majority of pleasure craft, this leads to a thirty to thirty-six foot motor yacht with a Pendum radar system."

"You're amazing," Kandy said.

"Just doing my job," Ferdinand replied, "to help you fine Detectives."

Kandy smirked and punched Qigiq's arm. Pointing at her chest with both index fingers she mouthed *fine Detective*.

"Given the assumptions I've outlined, position of the moon, shadow angles, I believe that video was recorded early this week between 11:00 pm and 3:30 am. If we could know the precise dimensions of the craft, and the location of the radar, I might be able to narrow the time window for you. Of course, if Mr. Pillar could provide a more precise estimate of when the fingers were removed, that might also be helpful."

"But she——" Kandy began, stopping when she saw Qigiq pointing at the screen.

Sally's hands never appeared. She could have been raped before or after they were severed from her body.

Kandy breathed out a heavy sigh. "Amazing, Ferd," she said.

Qigiq added. "Thanks, your analysis is brilliant."

Through the speaker Ferdinand said, "I'll have more on this unusual line of noise soon. I was curious about the boat idea and pursued it first."

Kandy scribbled on a pad How do we find the boat?

"Ferdinand. Any idea how we find this boat you're hypothesizing?" Qigiq said.

"Of course. Find any yacht that is carrying a model of the Pendum Marine radar system that matches the shadow profile in the movie. Check the cruising range from their last known refueling location to see if they could reach the area I have marked based on wave action. That would give you a list of all possible yachts that could have been used."

Kandy jumped in. "Then check their whereabouts for your time window."

"Exactly."

"We're going to be busy," Qigiq said.

"That depends on how popular Pendum radar systems are in this area," Ferdinand said.

"Thanks for your help, Ferdinand," Qigiq said.

"Yeah, thanks Ferd," Kandy added.

"You're both quite welcome. An interesting problem I am enjoying immensely. I will call again when I understand this static."

Qigiq ended the call with a finger instead of his boot heel, and sat down to face Kandy. He stuck a fork into his taco salad and left it.

"What do we know about the person who put the videos up?"

Kandy turned to her machine. "It's still there, over twelve hundred comments from viewers, and three point five million views. Originally posted by someone calling himself Conscire using that F123 whatever account Danny told us about."

"Conscire?"

"What?" Kandy asked.

"Latin." Qigiq spun around in his chair and pulled Webster off a four-shelf mahogany stand behind him. "Con, cons, conscience. Yes, con, as in with, and scire, know."

Kandy twisted her mouth. "Could be con with and science. Something about *with science* rather than conscience."

Qigiq nodded. "How do we find Conscire?"

Kandy tossed black ankle high boots up on her desk and leaned back. Her chair gave way so her spine tilted to a forty-five degree angle.

"You ever going to get that chair fixed?" Qigiq asked.

"I like the feeling of falling backwards. We have to get the courts to order YouTube, or its owner Google, to give up the IP address of Mr. Conscire. If we're lucky it will lead us to an Internet Service Provider who can lead us to a name or maybe a street address."

"And how long will that take?"

"If we rush, a week at least, especially since we don't have a body. I'll rush it, but Google has to protect their customers' privacy."

"What about Sally?"

"How much are you willing to tell Google? It might hurry them up."

"Can we keep this quiet if we show pictures around?" he asked.

Kandy grinned. "If we have enough lawyers in the room." She laughed and popped to her feet.

~ 17 ~

Forty-five minutes later Qigiq was riding with Kandy on a five-lane-wide interstate at what couldn't possibly have been the legal speed limit, listening to her turbo kick in and out as she passed reasonable people using the highway system as intended. A half-hour after that he was in the Google cafeteria sipping a free soda following a ten-minute meeting with two lawyers and a security Vice President. After learning the details of Sally's case they had been cooperative and provided an IP address that had been used at Café Joe on Blummit street: one of dozens of cafés in San Francisco that provided free Wi-Fi. The only thing concrete they had learned was that the movie had been posted at 2:12 am Friday from a machine running Windows that was one version obsolete. Since it typically took years for users to update to the latest version of Windows, this narrowed their search down to perhaps a hundred million people in the U.S. who had a laptop they could carry into Joe's.

"It was a nice drive along the coast," Kandy said.

"Be more fun with fewer wheels," Qigiq said.

"Or more horsepower."

Qigiq chugged his free Mr. Pibb and tapped a finger against the Google report.

"Can't we learn anything from this?"

"Sure," Kandy said. "Our criminal is smart enough to use anonymous connections. This was his first posting under the name Conscire, and he uses Google's own gmail with bogus information. Pure smokescreen."

"We have two packages in San Francisco."

"Could have been mailed from anywhere," Kandy said.

"Not if Ferdinand is right about Tuesday afternoon."

"We don't know if Sally still had fingers then," she said.

He nodded. "She was okay Tuesday morning at breakfast. Can we trace the packages?"

"Already working on it while you slept in. Post Office has nothing. No record of either package, but they're triple checking. I'll have Pillar analyze the cancellation ink, but I don't think the Post Office ever saw these packages."

Qigiq's cellphone emitted its engine rumble.

"Qigiq here...yes...high Robina...what...when...OK OK, stay calm. Do you want us to come over?"

He pressed the glass screen with his thumb and looked up at Kandy.

"Remember Violet and Veronica, Sally's, um, friends?"

Kandy nodded once.

"Veronica didn't come home last night. Violet just called Robina. Robina told her about Sally. They're both 'freaking out.' Robina's words."

Qigiq glanced at the dash. It was 2:12 pm, precisely twelve hours since the video of Sally had been posted from account F12358.

© © ©

Robina was sitting on the couch with her arm around a thin girl whose long blonde wispy hair looked like a TV commercial for a revolutionary hair product. The girl wore maroon suede boots to just below her knees and a jean mini-skirt that failed to conceal lime green panties. A sleeveless top of a pink cloth as wispy as her hair revealed her braless state. Her red face framed puffy eyes while both hands massaged a giant wad of Kleenex.

"Hi," Robina said. "This is Violet. She's a little upset. Vi, this is Kandy and Qigiq. They're detectives."

"Where's Roni?" Violet demanded, as if they should have already found her.

Qigiq looked at Kandy, who stepped in front of the girls and sat down on the other side of Violet.

"How long has Veronica been gone?" Kandy asked.

Vi sniffled. "She didn't come home last night."

"Is this the first time?"

Another sniffle. "What do you mean?"

"Is this the first time Veronica hasn't come home?"

"Oh no. Roni stays out all the time. But usually with Sally. And she tells me when she's going to do it. This is the first time she hasn't called." Her shoulders heaved. "Well, almost the first time."

"Almost?" Kandy urged.

"The first time this year. She did it a couple of times last year, but promised me she would never do it again."

"Any idea where she might be?" Qigiq interjected.

Vi coughed and started crying again. "I've called everyone, no one's seen her."

"Since when?" Kandy asked.

"Since choir yesterday," Vi replied through tears.

"Choir is at two o'clock on Thursdays," Robina added.

"Sorry to be obvious, but she doesn't answer her cellphone?" Qigiq asked.

"I just get a stupid message," Vi said. "The party you are dialing can not be located."

"Where do you think she is?" Kandy asked.

73

Violet started sobbing and didn't answer.

Robina said, "Vi thinks whoever has Sally now has Veronica too."

"Why?" Qigiq said.

Robina looked him up and down like she thought his suit was out of style. "Two girls disappear in the same week and you wonder why we think they're related? You are a detective, aren't you?"

"Sorry, I should be more specific. Other than the fact that Sally is missing, is there another reason that Veronica might not have come home? Could she have gone to see her parents for the weekend? Has she met anyone new? A friend she might have gone off with? Anything like that?"

"She teased she might have dinner out," Vi managed. "But she didn't say who. She knows I get jealous."

"Did she mention where?" Kandy asked.

"Bimbo's" Vi said, and frowned. "Yeah, she said Bimbo's. A swing band was playing."

"Swing? Like from the 1940's?" Qigiq asked.

"Yeah, real old stuff," Robina said. Sensing his confusion she added, "She plays clarinet."

He nodded, understanding that a clarinet player might enjoy hearing other clarinet players.

"Would you like protection?" Kandy asked the girls.

Vi bobbed her head up and down without removing the wad of Kleenex from her nose.

Robina asked, "Do you think we need it?"

Qigiq raised an eyebrow, but remained quiet.

She had seen his expression. "What I really mean," she continued, "is, do you think it will do any good?"

"Where are you from, Robina?" Qigiq asked.

Her eyes swung at him, then softened. "Detroit."

He nodded. "Heard of it." He smiled. "Tough place."

"All places are tough," she said.

He wondered how she had come to this city to study something as gentle as the violin. Maybe she was seeking a kind of balance to a rough childhood.

"I think officers sitting out front might help," Kandy said. "We'll get some to watch over you."

Qigiq watched Robina's slender fingers comfort Vi. He was still thinking about her and a violin.

"Why did you take up the violin?" he asked.

Robina's face retreated with a slender smile, like she was lying in a field of wild flowers daydreaming in spring sunshine for a movie about lost innocence.

"People ask me that all the time," she said softly.

He noticed Kandy studying him. He waited, watching Robina's face. It remained soft as she turned to face him.

"Anger management. I love to rape the motherfucker. Nothing screams like a violin, not even heavy metal guitar. They're just louder." A big smile filled her face. "That's why I love Beethoven so much."

Qigiq coughed and tried to remember what he knew about Detroit. "I see," he managed. "I'd like to hear you play sometime."

She smirked, "Sure you would."

Kandy pulled out a cellphone and requested a surveillance team.

Vi sobbed. Robina held her shoulders.

Qigiq thought he should be somewhere else taking action.

"Really," he said.

Robina's pupil tracked to the corner of her eye nearest him. Her head didn't move. She nodded so slightly he doubted Vi even felt it.

~ 18 ~

Qigiq stood under a tall narrow sign that read BIMBO's from top to bottom in huge red letters. He began to wonder why anyone would name a club after an empty-headed woman but caught himself; he recalled Bimbo meant something in Italian. He stepped up into an alcove to a dark gray door that had been painted a dozen times, though not recently. He knocked. Nothing. His smartphone showed 3:03 pm. Since it was linked to a super clock somewhere on the Internet he assumed it was correct. He stood on his toes, stretching to peek through a six-by-six inch glass window in the door. He saw lights on inside but no movement. This was probably a bad time to visit a nightclub, but the big Bimbo sign said Food and Liquor. If they were open for supper, there might be people here preparing.

He knocked again.

Still nothing.

He pressed his thumb against a large bronze lever and it moved. He pushed the door in. In? It wasn't legal for a door to open inward in a public building; it must have slipped through a grandfather clause for historic structures. He stuck his head through the opening.

"Hello."

Lights, no movement. And no answer.

He stepped inside and scrubbed the door across red carpet to close it behind him.

He waited. His eyes revealed large round tables of dark wood surrounded by high-back red chairs as they became accustomed to the low indoor light in the middle of a sunny afternoon. To his right was a hardwood dance floor with more scratches than a cat post and beyond it a stage at eye level.

"Anyone here?"

He heard a scuffle, hard sole shoes on tile.

A body appeared down a hallway far in the back that he hadn't noticed in the darkness. It was thin, moving inside of baggy pants and an oversize dress shirt with the sleeves rolled up. The shirt was light blue in the low light. The pants were very dark.

"We're closed," the body called out in an alto voice that could be a woman or young man.

"Sorry to bother you. I have a few questions."

The thin body moved closer but stopped halfway across the dance floor.

"No answers here," it said.

Qigiq guessed male. "San Francisco Police. Do you work here?"

He held up his hands like he was being mugged. "I don't know anything." He turned and started back for the dark hall.

"I'm looking for someone who was here last night."

He stopped and turned around. "There were over a thousand people here last night."

Qigiq was glad he was talking, he felt too tired to chase someone down just now.

"Girl. College age. I have a picture."

He laughed. "You looking for dirt on a naughty girl. Going to get her in trouble with her partner."

Qigiq noted the use of the word partner.

"The police don't do that kind of work. She's missing."

He walked across the dance floor and stopped. Lights came up.

"Missing?"

In the light he saw a young man in baggy black jeans and a dress shirt with dirt on both sleeves and a long stain on the breast pocket.

"Didn't come home last night. Roommate is worried. Wanted to hear swing music."

"Thursday night, The Red Hot Skillet Lickers with Lavay. They were great." He started dancing with an invisible partner. From what Qigiq remembered of swing dancing in the movies, the kid was okay.

Qigiq pulled out his phone and tapped it until the picture Kandy had sent him of Veronica displayed. When the kid stopped dancing, he held it up.

The boy walked over and stared. Squinted. Then tilted his head sideways, never taking his eyes from the small screen.

"Veronica is missing?" he said.

Qigiq blinked hard. "You know her?"

"Sure. She's a fun girl." The guy gave Qigiq a look he didn't understand: sort of an exercise in eye twinkling.

"You work nights?" Qigiq asked.

"Afternoons to clean the place up. Waiter for supper. And a bartender until we close."

"Doesn't leave much time for a social life."

The kid smiled. "This *is* my social life. Bimbo's is the cat's pajamas."

Qigiq pocketed his phone. "Are you in school?"

"Everyone in San Francisco is in school. Life is an education." His smiled broadened.

"I mean formal education, like a university."

"I take classes here and there. Want to get a business degree." He spread his hands wide like a preacher. "Own a club like this someday."

Qigiq nodded. He had heard lower aspirations.

"Was Veronica here last night?"

The kid answered instantly. "Oh yeah, she digs swing." He spun 360 degrees on his left toe.

"Mind if we sit down."

The kid looked left and right. "I gotta get this place cleaned up. Can we talk while I work?"

Not Qigiq's first choice because it was hard to watch the kid's face, but he appreciated the cooperation. "Sure, lead the way."

They walked down the dark hallway that Qigiq hadn't seen earlier. At the end the kid yanked on a door that screeched as it scraped the floor revealing a mop bucket and wash basin. He tossed a short hose into the bucket and turned on the water.

"How late was she here?"

The kid leaned over and stuck two fingers under the water. He fiddled with the left tap and looked up like there was a spider on the ceiling.

"Let's see. I didn't see her in the dance contest. That was midnight. She could have been here though, the place was jammed."

He turned to face Qigiq. "Wait, I think I saw her leave. No no, that was Cassie. She and Veronica had the exact same dress on. White, with fringe of all things."

He turned off the tap. Qigiq waited, knowing witnesses remembered all kinds of things if there was enough silence for them to think.

"No wait. Cassie and Belinda had the same dress. That wasn't Veronica." He snapped the fingers of his left hand three time, like he was setting the beat for a big band to start. "I know. Veronica was in the corner with that guy. Yeah, they were still here during the dance contest, because the bastard wouldn't let her dance with me."

"That was midnight?" Qigiq asked, trying to keep the kid on track.

"Yeah, well, it's supposed to start at midnight, but we're never on time. It was probably about twenty after when I asked her to dance."

"And she said no?"

"*He* said no. Veronica dances with me all the time."

"Was she still there after the contest?"

"Don't know." The kid stuck a string mop into the bucket and used the handle to push it into the hallway. He struggled when the wheels hit carpeting. "I don't think I saw her after that. But I wasn't looking, I was pissed at her date."

Qigiq followed the kid to the dance floor where he swung the mop around and danced with it. He wasn't Gene Kelly, but he was smooth.

"Could you identify him?"

"The guy?" The kid frowned in thought as the mop sloshed back and forth. "Maybe. If you had pictures, you know, like the cop shows on TV."

Qigiq sighed, wondering how he was supposed to get a picture of a guy who had arrived from thin air.

"Sorry, no pictures. I don't even have a suspect."

"I suspect," the kid smiled, "someone who likes Veronica."

"How much did he like her?"

The kid stopped swabbing the dance floor. "A lot. He'd push her down on the bench in our big booth like it was the back seat of a '57 Chevy," he motioned to the corner furthest from the stage. "The cushions are nice and soft. But she kept sitting him back up."

He stopped talking and stared toward the back booth.

"She was laughing the whole time. So I don't think it was, you know, like date rape or anything."

Qigiq pulled out his phone and started tapping.

The kid gave him a confused look and went back to washing the floor.

It took him over a minute, but Qigiq came up with a picture.

"Is this the guy?"

The kid examined the picture from a dozen angles, like it was a priceless vase found in the Mayan ruins.

"Maybe...maybe not. I'm remembering something." He tapped his finger on his head. "It was dark you know."

"Try to be sure."

"Veronica's guy was a little bald. He combed his hair carefully, but I could tell. Hmm, am I thinking of the right guy or was he with Cassie? Did you know there's a patent on combing hair over a bald spot? Yeah really. I lost a bet with a customer. He pulled the patent up on his laptop using our Wi-Fi. Cost me ten bucks."

Qigiq examined the picture of Professor Walters he had found on the Conservatory's website. He was lean and muscular. And had close curly brown hair just beginning to gray.

"Did she leave with him?"

The kid shrugged.

"What would you guess?"

Without stopping the motion of the mop he said, "I'd guess she left with him to make sure he paid the bill. Party girls know how to work that."

Qigiq nodded. He wasn't sure what San Francisco party girls did, but he knew Veronica was a student and might need money. He would ask Vi.

"Anything else you can tell me about him?"

"Suit. Soft hands, we shook. Probably office stuff: management, something professional. Courteous to me, but hung all over Veronica like a zoot suit from Wal-mart. Drank plenty by the look of the empties on the table. Something in an Old-Fashioned glass, maybe Manhattans."

"Think you could describe him well enough for an artist to build a picture?"

The kid closed his eyes hard and squeezed. "I can't see him, just his back when he had Veronica down on the bench. Oh wait, wait. He did something in the music business, kept telling Veronica he was going to make her a star. Can you imagine, a star clarinetist? Now's there's something they don't have on *American Idol.*"

"If his face comes back to you, please call me." Qigiq handed him a card. "And thanks for taking the time to chat. I wish you luck with your business degree."

"Hey, is Veronica in trouble? Like, are you going to arrest her?"

"No, she's not in that kind of trouble. But we need to find her. To protect her."

The kid dropped the mop back into the bucket. He looked like he was going to ask a question, but just lowered his eyes to Qigiq's card.

"Okay, man. I'll call."

© © ©

Qigiq returned to his Moto Guzzi parked facing Bimbo's front door with its rear wheel backed against the curb. A white and black helmet hung from the grip by its chinstrap. He swung a leg over the bike and pulled out his phone.

"Hello Kandy. I'm at Bimbo's. There's a kid here."

"A kid?"

"A college kid I mean. Bartender and clean-up guy. He was here last night and claims to know Veronica as a regular customer."

"Did he see her?"

"Shortly after midnight. She was with a male caucasian, late 30's early 40's, what hair he had was light colored, at least under bar lights. Business suit type. The kid claims he never saw the guy before."

"Want me to send an artist over?"

"Kid claims he doesn't remember the guy except for his hair. It was dark in the club; he was focused on Veronica. Apparently she's a good swing partner."

"Do you believe him?"

"Yeah, I think she can dance." He chuckled. She was quiet. "Okay, he seemed helpful and honest. Is he hiding something? Not sure. We can circle back in a few days and see if his story changes."

"Should we put her on missing persons?"

Qigiq thought for a minute. Normally a young girl not coming home wouldn't be sufficient cause to set the authorities looking for her. But she was close to Sally. And they didn't know if Sally was even alive.

"Seems early," he said. "But this is a strange situation, even as strange situations go."

"I agree. I think she's out with a guy she doesn't want Vi to know about."

"Which means we waste the taxpayers' money finding someone who doesn't want to be found?"

"Right."

He could hear Kandy chewing.

"On the other hand..." he began.

"This could be our man and Veronica is the second target. Next we'll see her fingers showing up at the station."

He swallowed. "Sounds like enough to me...but we're a bit conservative in Alaska."

"I'll call it in," she said.

"Thanks. Meet you at the office."

"Wait, Pendum came through. They provided a list of boats that had radar systems installed in the past five years. They can go back further if we want, but the system shaped like our shadow was introduced about then. By the way, they have a patent on that shape, claims it improves radar reception."

"Do you think it's true?" he asked.

"No, I think the shape is a marketing ploy because that big bulb sticks up in the air and everyone can tell what kind of radar a boat has. They wanted to prevent copying by the overseas cloners, so they protected the shape with a technical patent."

"Clever," he said, his eyes on the front door of Bimbo's in case the kid decided he needed to be somewhere.

"Reminds me of the *Don't Steal Music* message. Makes no sense if this is a rapist."

"Maybe the perp is a rock musician," he said.

"Or classical," she said, laughing.

"Point taken. Could be a serial killer and the Don't Steal meaning will be revealed to us in time. Maybe the next one will be Don't Kill or Don't Covet Thy Neighbor's Wife. Remember that Brad Pitt movie about the deadly sins?"

"Now you're freaking me out," she said. "I'll send the boat list to your phone. In some cases we have the boat name, in others the owner. Sometimes both. Most have the yacht club where the boat was docked when the radar was installed."

Qigiq wanted to lower his phone and read the list, but he asked, "How many are we talking about, Kandy?"

"In San Francisco only, about three hundred. More if you include Oakland and Berkeley. Lots more if you extend south to Monterey. There are more than a thousand boats with the Pendum radar system within a day's run of the Golden Gate."

Qigiq chewed his upper lip. "Any idea how we narrow this down?"

"Two," she said. "We run the owner's names, see if we can find anyone with priors. And look at their occupations, maybe find a crazed surgeon or something."

He nodded, then remembered he was on the phone. "Was that two?"

"No. The other idea is to get pictures of all the boats."

"You think one of Sally's friends might recognize a boat?"

"I was thinking we give the pics to Ferd, so he can narrow it down to the boats that could cast the shadow we're seeing."

"Beautiful, Kandy. He'll need orthogonal shots, like an engineering drawing. How are we going to get the pictures?"

He was sorry he had asked before finishing the question.

"Your cellphone will take nice digital pictures if you don't have your camera with you."

She was right. He knew she was right. He didn't want to spend the day snapping yachts, but he could do that and wander the marinas and listen and maybe ask a few questions. Taken together, it was a reasonable next step.

"What can you tell me about the list?"

"Sorted into power boats and sailboats. I'm guessing what we saw in the video is the deck of a powerboat, maybe one focused on fishing. That deck looks like an easy-wash surface for cleaning up fish guts."

Qigiq saw the kid slip out the front door and light a cigarette. He stood in the alcove, didn't even step to the sidewalk.

"The kid just came out of the club. Grabbing a smoke," he said.

The line was quiet. He watched.

"He's poking at his cellphone."

Qigiq saw the kid look up and down the street, talking with the cigarette in his mouth and gesturing with his free hand.

"Maybe waiting for a ride. I'll give him ten minutes. If no one shows, I'm heading to the marina district."

~ 19 ~

Qigiq idled the bike along the rightmost lane of Marina Boulevard admiring the multi-million dollar condos on his left and rows of white fiberglass hulls lined up like Hollywood orthodontia on his right. He turned right into the South Beach Yacht Club, passed through the unmanned security gate, and parked beside a sleek slate car advertising Aston Martin across the rear panel.

Kandy's list contained over a thousand boats, fifty of them at this yacht club. He used the phone to sort the South Beach boats to the top with the most recent installation first, figuring these had the best chance of still being here. He started reading the list to put names in his head: Firebird, Sweet 16, Undercover, CanCan, With a Bullet, IPO Two, Delicious, Ramsey, Carousel...and headed for the row of docks, glancing back once to check on the bike.

The first boat was a long red streak of sleekness with a girl lying on the deck wearing a matching red shoestring around her bottom, and nothing else. It had *Delicious* written in large gold script across the stern. He lifted his camera and clicked. The radar unit was mounted ten feet above her slender ankles at the end of a tapered fiberglass pole shaped like a wing. He moved quietly out the dock to the port side of the yacht while she soaked in the afternoon sun close to the starboard rail. He raised his camera and zoomed fully out to get the full length of the boat in the frame. He stepped back carefully and clicked just as she turned her face in his direction. He lowered the camera fast and slipped it into his front pocket.

"Hey," she said.

He waved and turned to walk away.

"Did you just take my picture?"

"No, I was shooting the boat. For our records," he said.

She frowned. "Whose records?"

"I'm collecting pictures of boats in the area that use Pendum radar." He motioned toward the bullet shaped pod hovering over her. The truth so far. He liked to stick to it, keep things from getting complicated.

She lifted herself to her elbows and twisted toward him to look up. He tried to look up too.

"Radar? Are we going to win something?"

How could anyone who could afford such a craft want to win something?

"I don't think it's a contest."

She sat up and crossed her legs yoga style. He tried not to stare at the evenness of her tan.

"Can I see my picture?"

He reached in his pocket and fumbled with the camera until her picture was displayed on the tiny screen. She was too far away to hand it to her and she didn't appear to be about to move, so he walked down the port dock and up the starboard one until he was behind her. She spun around on her bottom, her skin squeaking against the fiberglass deck. His self-control failed and his eyes dropped to bare breasts like he hadn't seen in a long while before he could yank them back up to her face.

She reached for the camera. "Don't worry, all the guys do that. I don't mind."

He felt his face flush and forced a smile.

She held the camera in two hands and frowned. "My butt's too big."

He looked up at the radar pod like he had just noticed it sprout from the deck. She remained silent. When he lowered his eyes to meet hers she was staring at him.

"Well?" she said.

"Uh. It looks like you have the Architect-3 model."

She shook her head and tapped the picture with a long fingernail painted to match her boat.

He cleared his throat. "I can't imagine anyone would find your body anything except perfectly proportioned," he ventured.

Her mouth became the kind of smile that made men do stupid things.

"Thanks," she said. "What's your name?"

"Qigiq."

"Hi, Qigiq. Mine's Karen. Will you send me the picture?"

"Sure. Do you want me to send it here to the boat?"

She shook her head. "No no. Email the file. Delicious34 at hotmail dot com.

He smiled. "Are you Delicious?"

She laughed.

He realized his error.

"My boyfriend says I am, especially when I shave. But it's thirty-four feet long. The boat I mean. And we think this life is delicious."

"Yes. Sun and water can be wonderful," he said. "I'll be glad to send you the picture."

She leaned forward to hand him the camera. His eyes dropped before he could stop them and his breath caught. He wondered vaguely what being a college student in San Francisco must be like.

She whispered, "What are you really doing here, Qigiq? Are you looking for hot babes for your camera so you can, you know, wank later?"

He choked and coughed. "Heavens no."

"What then? You're young and in shape. You must be looking for something on that motorbike of yours." Her green eyes twinkled at him.

The truth, he reminded himself.

He turned and sat on the deck of Delicious with his feet on the dock so she would be next to him and he wouldn't have to hogtie his eyeballs to keep them off her chest.

"I'm a detective with the San Francisco Police Department pursuing an investigation."

He felt her eyes sizing him up.

He reached inside the leather jacket he was still wearing and flipped open his ID. With his eyes glued on a sailboat plying the bay in the distance, he held it out for her.

He felt her hand wrap around his as she pulled the ID closer to read it. Her body moved toward the badge and he felt her press against his jacket. He fought off thoughts of which body part was doing the pressing.

"This looks real," she said.

He nodded.

"Wow fucking wow. An investigation. Is it a murder?" she asked, breathless.

"You've been watching too much cable TV."

"And you're trying to find him?" she whispered.

"Do you know many owners down here?"

She moved closer. "A few. We only got our slip last year. Do you think it's someone here? Oh my god!"

"No no. We're looking for a particular boat is all."

"The radar," she gasped. "It has something to do with the radar."

He smiled, continuing to watch the sailboat. "You should be a detective."

She pressed closer. He could feel heat from her body through his jacket. He hoped she wasn't coated with lotion, he'd have to clean the jacket.

"Any thirty, maybe forty-something guys, light hair, maybe bald, maybe not, about six footish come here?" he asked.

She laughed. "You just described *every* boat owner in the entire marina."

He nodded, wishing he had a better description of the Bimbo man and that he hadn't mentioned the hair. Nightclub light would look totally different in outdoor sunshine.

He put his ID away and briefly missed the warmth of her hand on his. He pulled his phone out and tapped around for a picture.

"Do you happen to know him?" he asked.

"Barry? Yeah, he's down here a lot. Somehow has free afternoons. He brings me drinks."

He thought she probably sat up to take the drink, two good reasons for Barry to bring her one.

"Do you know which boat is his?"

"Oh yeah. It's over there," she pointed southeast and two slips over. "It's called *Firebird*. I asked him why he named his boat after an old muscle car, but he just laughed."

Qigiq turned to look and smiled. "Do you know what he does for a living?"

"Works at that stuffy conservatory."

"Ever hear of Stravinsky?" he asked.

Her perfectly tanned features crunched into a thinking frown. She shook her head.

"Dead Russian guy. Wrote some music. You might even like it. One piece is called *The Rite of Spring*. Made a big commotion at its premier."

She smiled.

"Another is called, *The Firebird Suite.*"

"He named it after music? That's pretty cool. Too bad no one gets it."

Qigiq nodded. Maybe that was why Barry did it.

"You don't think Barry has anything to do with your investigation, do you?" she gasped, like it was her favorite way to talk.

"No, not at all," he lied, knowing that Barry was likely banging Sally the week she disappeared. But he didn't want Karen gasping to the neighbors. "I hope he might know some of the people down here, help us find the right boat."

Someone started singing about a house rockin' and Karen reached for a black pack of gum hanging from a little red string. She looked at the side and pressed it to her ear. "Hi Daddy, how are you? I'm sunbathing...yes in the middle of the day. Do you sunbathe at night?"

She waved goodbye, which he took as a clue that there was about to be a conversation he wasn't supposed to hear. He waved back and strolled down the dock toward *Firebird* tapping Delicious34@ hotmail.com into a notepad on his cellphone so he would remember to send Karen the picture of her big bottom.

He crossed a grassy park along the docks to the third row and turned up toward *Firebird*. As he approached a white sailing yacht with a large wheel, he heard booming bass float across the water. *Firebird* was smaller than *Delicious*, but still quite a boat for a college professor. He took the two pictures he needed and wished he had a search warrant. He tried to imagine the angle of the sun required to create the video he had seen and guesstimate if the radar was mounted in the right place. He couldn't be sure by eyeballing; Ferdinand would have to help.

He followed the booming bass past three boats to a thirty-foot power cruiser named *With a Bullet*. Two college-age guys were on their knees scrubbing the deck with brushes to booming music from the cruiser's built-in sound system.

He scrolled down Kandy's list until he found *With a Bullet*. The radar system had been installed four months ago. No owner was listed.

He rapped his knuckles against the gunwale. The boys looked up but didn't stop scrubbing.

"Hello. Got a second?" he asked.

Both young men were blond, muscular and tan. He wondered how well they knew Delicious Karen.

They both stood. The shorter one, at about six foot, walked forward and killed the stereo. No one spoke.

"Sorry to interrupt you guys, can I ask you a few questions," he said, flipping open his badge.

The tall guy in back opened his eyes wide, dropped his scrub brush, took two barefoot steps and leapt over the gunwale, hitting the dock in a full sprint. He was gone around the corner of the main marina building by the time Qigiq could slip his badge back in his pocket.

"Must have a date," Qigiq said.

The remaining guy snickered. "He doesn't like cops much."

"Should I be concerned about why?" Qigiq asked.

"If I had to guess, there's something he doesn't want you to see and he's gone to put it in a safe place. My name's Bob."

Qigiq thought briefly about chasing down a college kid with a drug possession charge. It took no effort to decide Sally was more important.

"Hi, Bob. My name is Qigiq. I'm trying to track down a particular boat without knowing much about it other than that it has a late model Pendum radar."

"Like that one," Bob said, pointing to the oblong canister above him on the deck.

"Yeah, just like that one. Seems to be a lot of them around."

"Good radar," Bob said, "especially for the money. C'mon aboard, I'll grab a Coke and take a break. You want anything?"

"A Coke would be appreciated."

Qigiq peeled off his leather boots and placed them on the dock. He stuck his socks inside and stepped onto *With a Bullet* barefoot, not wanting to mar the pristine surface the boys were creating. Moments later he was leaning against the gunwale and sipping iced Coke from a can.

"Thanks for your time. How often does a boat like this get washed?"

Bob spun the captain's chair around and hopped up into it. "Depends entirely on the owner. Most of the people here can afford to be nitpicking neat-nicks. This one gets washed every two weeks. It wasn't due, but we got a call today to scrub her down. No surprise on a Friday, owner probably has a hot date over the weekend and wants the boat to be shipshape." He pointed down a hatchway that ducked below the windshield. "Floating paradise: fridge, bar, bed. With the right girl..." he lifted his can and toasted.

Qigiq nodded even though he had never owned a boat bigger than a kayak.

"Do you know the owner?"

Bob walked aft and looked over the stern. "*With a Bullet.* No, don't know this guy, but I've seen him."

"Don't tell me, forties, business suit, about six foot, thinning blond hair, paunch."

Bob's face screwed up. "You got the suit right. He's one of the few guys who steps on deck in Prada shoes and Armani. He must change clothes at sea, or maybe just gets naked for all I know. But he's taller, curly dark hair. Mid-thirties I'd say. Stay's in okay shape, leaps over the gunwale from the dock, that kind of stuff. Like a kid jumping a fence, just to show he can do it."

This was new. "Do you see him often?"

"Yeah. Takes her out probably once a week."

"Her?"

Bob frowned, pointed down. "Her. The boat. *With a Bullet.*"

Qigiq nodded. "Does he go alone?"

Bob laughed. "Guys don't own boats like this to go out alone, unless they're fishing. And even then it's usually with a bunch of buddies and a keg. Or around here, a case of some flashy wine worth more than my truck."

Qigiq felt the Coke's coldness slide down his throat as the bay breeze on his face told him it was turning onshore and cooling. He was glad for his riding jacket, which moved his mind to Karen's assets, wondering how they were doing with the drop in temperature. He nudged it back to the task at hand.

"Anyone special our Mr. Armani likes to take out?"

He shrugged. "Don't pay much attention. There are so many folks chasing tail around here, especially on the weekends. Money attracts them." He gave Qigiq a half smile. "But this guy gets around, or has a whole bunch of good looking female clients." He chugged the last of his soda and fired the can into the hold where a thud indicated it had found a plastic waste can. "One of 'em might be special. She's part hot Asian. Comes out here in an orange bikini that glows so bright you'd think it had batteries. And heels. She walks on this boat in heels."

"Does she have a name?"

"Never been introduced. I just clean boats."

"A guy like you, the girls ignore you, huh?" Qigiq said.

Bob smiled. "They get tired of the money on occasion and look for a man. You know, someone who can carry them with one arm and keep it going without throwing out his back. I'm not complaining."

Bob picked up his scrub brush and dipped it into a bucket.

"Do you know Delicious Karen?" Qigiq asked.

"Oh yeah. She gets tired of the money sometimes."

Qigiq choked on his Coke. He pulled Sally's picture up on his cellphone. "Ever seen her?"

Bob studied the face carefully. "Pretty girl. Don't think so. Do you have a body shot?"

Must be an occupational hazard of working around bikinis. Qigiq flipped through the pictures Robina had supplied, nothing more than waist up.

"I'll try to locate one. I know you need to get back to work, but do you happen to know what *With a Bullet* means?"

Bob contemplated his brush, like he just realized he was holding it. "I see what you mean, like get rid of her with a bullet, or I brought that bear down with a bullet. That kind of thing?"

Qigiq nodded and made his way across the deck to the opposite side, noting that the floor had parallel lines embossed in the vinyl. Just like Delicious.

Bob said, "I don't think that's it. Has something to do with music. I've heard rappers use it."

Rappers made Qigiq wonder if it had something to do with gangs.

"Thanks, Bob. Appreciate your time. Mind if I take a couple of pictures?"

Bob shrugged his big shoulders. "Not my boat."

Qigiq took his orthogonal shots and headed back through the marina.

Karen was stretched out on her belly precisely as before despite the wind shift, her face now turned toward starboard.

"Hello, Karen. Could I ask you a question?"

Her upper eye opened and a slow smile spread across her lips. He took that as a yes.

"There's a boat over there named *With a Bullet*. Do you have any idea what that means?"

She closed her eye, which made her look like she was sleeping. "Billboard magazine. You know, the guys who rate the Top-40 songs every week. If a song is number nine with a bullet, it means that it got there by going up the charts. All bullet songs went up from the week before."

He'd have to pick up a copy of Billboard magazine.

She continued, her eyes closed, her bare back glowing in the warm sun. "So number one with a bullet means it's a new number one from the week before. Fall Out Boy sang about being number one with a bullet, meaning he wanted to be some babe's new number one. Used the Billboard rating system on himself. Figure that."

"You listen to a lot of music?" Qigiq asked.

"Oh yeah. Everyone does, now that it's free." Her eyes remained closed.

He noticed she was lying on the deck with a red object in her upper ear. He wondered where the music came from.

As if she had heard his thoughts she said, "Like now. Bluetooth wireless earbud to my cellphone music player."

His eyes roamed down her body to the gum pack clipped to the red shoestring around her waist.

"What do you mean free?" he asked.

"You know, file sharing on the Internet. Everything is out there somewhere. No charge. You can get lots just by stripping the music from YouTube videos."

He remembered Ferdinand saying Sally's machine had fifty thousand songs.

"Would you mind looking at a picture and telling me if you've seen this girl around the marina?"

She opened her upper eye again, the lower remained pressed against her red towel.

"Sure."

He held up the phone with Sally's face.

Karen's one eye squinted.

"Hmm. Maybe. Do you have a body shot?"

Qigiq stepped back. "Sorry, not with me."

"I might have seen her earlier this week."

Qigiq's heart pumped a little faster. "Yes?"

"If she owns a yellow bikini. Passed *Delicious* on her way somewhere."

"Who was she with?"

"She was alone when she went past."

He slipped his phone away. She closed her eye.

"Any idea where she went?

"Past *Delicious* toward the docks."

He looked back the way he had just come. She could have been going to any boat in the entire marina. He blinked. But then, if it had been Sally, he knew this was the right marina.

"Thanks Karen. It's been great talking with you."

She smiled without opening her eyes.

He moved briskly down the dock, anxious now to shoot the remaining boats and get the data back to Ferdinand.

~ 20 ~

As the door to Room 114 of The Whale View Inn swung softly closed the sun cast a passing shadow across drawn shades. The inn was attached to the Whale View Restaurant and Lounge. It sported only seven rooms, despite the three digit room numbers, and sat on a rise a quarter mile east and a hundred feet above California Highway 1. Waves lulled up and down a beach an additional three hundred feet on the opposite side of the road. When no traffic was present, the small concrete porch in front of Room 114 had a peaceful, uninterrupted view of the Pacific Ocean; and, in some months, whales could be seen migrating north from their spawning grounds.

Two blue whales blew water and air into the sky less than a mile offshore, but no one from Room 114 saw them. The remaining occupant was stretched out naked under a rumpled sheet and light summer blanket. One slender ankle and foot protruded from the covers and hovered over the brown-crimson carpet. Straight dark hair lay matted to her forehead as if she had been running and collapsed across the finish line onto the bed. Her right arm twisted under her head and lay palm up, the curled fingers showing off bright red nails with silver trim.

A heating and cooling system built into the wall kicked on. A fan bearing rattled as its motor came up to speed and settled into a soft high-pitched whine as it blew warm air into the room. The thin screech penetrated an ear drum and one eye cracked open. The girl reached her left hand across the bed. She sighed. Her right arm cramped near her shoulder. She eased over onto her back and forced the other eye open. The ceiling wasn't interesting.

She rotated her right ankle, making it crack twice. She turned her head toward the bathroom. The door was open and it was empty. She sighed again.

Fucking men, she thought.

Then she smiled. She felt that good kind of ache front and back that only a night of long and intense sexual antics could give her. He hadn't just been good for an older guy with money; he had been good period. Taking his time. Especially that. Taking his time, as if she were the only woman in the whole world he had ever wanted, or ever would want. Now he was gone, and she was in a motel room somewhere on the road to Los Angeles. She sighed and licked her lips.

And smiled again.

She swung both feet to the floor and padded to the bathroom. The seat was cold. She shivered and reached for a white terry cloth towel with blue Whale View embroidery. Now she remembered. She had been teasing him about wanting to see a whale while running her fingernails along his thigh. So he had driven his shiny black car down the coast where they sat up watching the ocean in the moonlight. And she had seen a whale. Well, not the whale, but a spout of water bursting into the air. He had made a lewd comment, she had laughed and pulled his zipper down. It hadn't taken long for him to spout too; she didn't practice the clarinet four hours a day just to make music.

She wrapped the towel around her waist like a skirt and looked in the mirror. The girl that stared back had had a lot of fun last night (and most of the day, as she remembered). She looked around the bathroom, found the complimentary comb and worked it through the tangled mess on her head.

She frowned.

Turning her head as far around as possible, she studied her hair in the mirror. Combed. Lifted. Frowned again. A section an inch wide no longer reached to her shoulders. In fact, it barely made it to her ear and was chopped off—.

He hadn't?

She studied the ends. A single cut at a slight angle, clean and straight. Scissors.

A smile crept onto her face. She loved being an obsession.

She went to the nightstand and bent forward: 6:18. Light through the curtain told her it must be late afternoon. She blew a stream of air between thin lips—a long party even by her standards.

But how could a guy who had been so nice and so...*satisfying*...leave her in a motel room hundreds of miles from her apartment? Did he have an inner bastard that she had missed? Not that *that* had ever happened before. She returned to the bathroom, started the shower and stepped in to let hot water soothe the sore spots while she soaped away Bimbo's, and alcohol, and sweat. Oh so much sweat. She smiled and shivered, though this time she wasn't cold. Glow, he had said. Princesses didn't sweat; they glowed. Well, she had been a thousand-watt light bulb if he called that glowing.

Dry, she dug in her tiny purse for the spare pink thong. She felt better with clean panties even if her sweater and skirt had been worn. She fiddled with the adjustment on her bra. He had been a little tough on it, but at least it wasn't broken. She looked around the room for something she could take, but there wasn't even a fridge to lift vodka from. She pouted at the room and raised the shade.

Breath caught in her throat like an errant ice cube.

Brilliant red flames raced across the sky Roman-chariot style.

"Wow!" she whispered to the window pane. She stared as the huge orange ball of sun sank behind darkening waves, rubbed her eyes with two fists, then stared some more.

A rap at the door jarred her from communing with the gorgeous beams of light in the sky.

"Housekeeping," a female voice said.

"Come back later," she said.

"No, cannot. You checkout," the voice said. "Must clean room."

Checkout? That bastard had even checked her out. He could have at least paid for another night so she could sleep off their bacchanalian love fest. Men just didn't show enough gratitude.

She flipped the door open and let it slam against the wall.

"Do I have to leave now?" she asked a middle-aged Hispanic woman.

The woman nodded and fumbled into the room dragging an upright vacuum cleaner.

"Checkout six o'clock," she said. "You overstay."

The women's eyes met.

"For this room only. Extended by a man," the maid said, her entire face registering disapproval.

The girl grabbed her lavender leather jacket and stomped out of the room with no destination in mind. She clicked open her tiny purse and reached into the pocket where the panties had been. She found her hundred dollar bill right where it belonged. She hadn't spent a dime the night before, but she didn't really want to spend it now. In fact, she never wanted to spend her own money, it was way too much fun spending other people's.

Her black heels with the ankle straps still undone clicked across the rust-brown stones winding between the motel and the restaurant. As she passed under the wooden canopy outside the registration desk that protected guests unloading their cars from sun and rain, she noticed a dark gray town car. It was low and sleek, like a wannabe gangster boy would own. She checked to see if it had those wheels that kept spinning when the car stopped, but it didn't. Its windows were darker than the paint and showed nothing of the interior.

She stopped walking. Leaning against the right rear passenger's door was a tall man with a gray beard and black suit that included a thin blue tie. He was holding a sign like the limo drivers at airports when they're picking up important people who can't find the limo by themselves.

The sign had her name on it.

She hesitated. She was alone, a little lightheaded from the liquor and the sex and the lack of sleep, and now this. She looked at the man and stepped a bit further from the car. She fished around inside her purse until she found her razor thin cellphone. She could call Vi, she would tell her what to do. She flipped the phone open but the screen was dark. She turned it over in her hand and realized it was turned off. She tried to remember how and when it had been bugging her, because that was the only time she ever shut it off. She couldn't recall, and flicked it on.

It buzzed in her hand and a text message appeared.

V. You are the most amazing woman I have ever met. It was sheer pain to tear myself away today, but I must be at a meeting. I have sent a car for you. Think of me while you ride up the coast in comfort. There should be food and drink for you in the back. Raise the privacy partition and enjoy. Sincerely, Your new boy.

She smiled from her toes on up, and reached back to touch her missing hair. He hadn't forgotten or bugged out on her; he had to go do whatever it was he did to make money. She squealed a joyful giggle and mentally took back all the bad things she had thought about him since waking up. Then she ran as best she could on unstrapped heels across cracked pavement toward the man with the dark car wondering if a privacy partition was soundproof.

~ 21 ~

"Have you got Greg yet?" Eddy yelled through his office door.

The door swung open. Stacy's face and long blond hair poked through the opening. "He's not answering at home or his cellphone. I've left messages that you want to talk to him right away."

Eddy growled low. "Lawyers. Are the engineers ready yet?"

Stacy's eyes averted. "They'd like another half-hour, Mr. Blake."

He looked at the clock built into the wheel of the square rigger model on the corner of his desk.

"Sure. I'm already late for dinner. Let Helen know." He looked up and waited for Stacy's eyes to meet his. Helen wanted to keep up appearances for her country club friends, he should try to do his part...at least as a strategic move. "And please try to make her believe that I'm really working. Have her call my office direct if she wants to verify."

Stacy nodded. "She'll want to know what time you'll be home."

"Depends on Engineering. They can't predict anything, how the hell can I?" He sighed, knowing she hated it when he swore. "Sorry, Stacy. Tell her I'll probably be quite late. We're waiting for Engineering to demo so I can give them the go, no go decision. She's been around long enough to know how this software stuff works."

"Will do, Mr. Blake. I'll let you know when Ms. Volker is ready."

His wife would be furious. Either that, or relieved she didn't have to eat another meal sitting across from his mug. He tapped a finger on his desk. The divorce was important. He would have to pay more attention.

He picked up his phone and dialed Simmons' number. If the guy was around, he would answer when he recognized Eddy was calling personally. One ring and he was listening to Greg's voice message, "Hello, This is Greg Simmons, Chief Legal Officer for Silver—"

Eddy hung up. Greg's phone was off, or out of range.

Eddy pressed the button to get Stacy on the intercom.

"Yes, Sir."

"Why isn't Greg here again?"

"The message he left for me said he was taking a day's vacation to have a three-day weekend after that last board meeting. You must have been tough on him."

He could hear the smile in her voice. Eddy was tough on everybody.

"He's on vacation and we're trying to launch a product?" he said, somewhat rhetorically.

"I believe Mr. Simmons is under the impression that the product was to launch on Monday."

Eddy sighed. "Yeah, right. I just moved it up this morning didn't I? Thanks, Stacy."

How could a CEO function if his people weren't at his beck and call?

He pulled an Excel document up on his computer and stared at a graph. The penetration curves from Engineering made one thing super clear: the earlier he launched Invisible Hand the better his chances of getting revenue into the current quarter. The first few days might not amount to much, but the last few, after it had spread, could affect a million customers. That would make a difference.

He heard a knock.

He closed the file. "Come in."

A guy in a white outfit carrying a pizza box entered. Eddy motioned at the conference table in the corner. The guy dropped it and left. Stacy was okay, she knew he'd need to eat to get through this meeting. He walked over and flipped open the lid. Pepperoni and anchovies, smothered in cheese. He breathed in deeply through his nose.

Friday night.

He really wanted that software to go now, so it could work its magic on all those people playing with their computers over the weekend. Volker and that crazy Zeto had to deliver. He laughed. Too bad he couldn't order up software like pizza.

Now *that* would be great.

~ 22 ~

Lili sat at a small table in Blake's office next to a half-gone pizza in a greasy box that smelled like fish. Blake was behind his desk alternating his attention between software on his computer and Harold's scribbles on the white board.

"To be ready by tonight we had to streamline the interface requirements," Harold said.

Eddy frowned. "You mean drop features?"

"Sort of," Lili chimed in.

"We still meet all requirements for posting information from the client computer. But the customer has fewer choices," Harold said, motioning to Eddy's machine. "If you'll click the start button."

Eddy clicked. Internet Explorer opened to a page that said Bootleg music has been found on your machine. You have been reported. The offending music has been deleted. Cancel and OK buttons sat in the lower corner.

"This looks like any other page," Eddy said.

"That's right. But it's not," Harold replied. "It's a picture. A click anywhere in the frame will dismiss it. Invisible Hand has already deleted itself. The only thing that remains is that one picture, and even it has been removed from permanent storage. With this approach, we can release IH with any message we want, simply by providing a whendone.jpg file." He paused. "This lets us try different messages with no additional programming."

Eddy nodded. "Very nice. And how do we make these 'whendone' files?"

Lili jumped in. "With anything that will make a JPEG: camera, PhotoShop, 3D modeling program."

"This one was made in something called Interface Builder, then snapped from the screen," Harold said. "There are lots of ways to do it though. All easy." He smiled.

"Easy is good," Eddy said. "And fast. Nice work. If this goes out tonight, those option grants we talked about for you two," He paused. "I'll double them on Monday."

Lili smiled. Harold nodded.

"Should we talk about how you want to launch this?" Harold asked.

"Yes. And when," Eddy said.

"The software is ready, and if you're satisfied with that message," he tilted his head toward Eddy's screen, "we can go tonight. The real question is *how*. Naturally, we have to prevent any possibility of the injection being traced back to Silver Platter."

Harold drew rectangles interconnected by arcs. "We have been sneaking our driver into users' machines for five months via fake updates. Current count is over twenty million in the U.S. and twice that worldwide, Mac and Windows combined. Our driver will scan all audio played by its host system, looking for our encrypted music streams. We stopped sending out those drivers forty-five days ago and all remnants, except for the golden masters you have Mr. Blake, have been removed from the premises. Silver Platter never heard of audio drivers. It's not something we know how to do."

Harold smiled.

"But to slip the Invisible Hand," he pointed with a red marker, "into the user's machine, it has to be inserted in audio files. It could all go into one file, or it could all go into a hundred files, or it can be broken into small pieces and delivered across many different music files, making it harder to detect, but also slower to propagate. The marketing decision here is the hard part. My encryption software can work with as many or as few files as we like."

Blake asked, "What do you like, Mr. Zeto?"

Harold shot a surprised glance at Lili.

"Multiple approaches, Mr. Blake. Send IH complete in a dozen different songs. Anyone downloading those specific songs will be targeted. But also spread it over ten, fifty, a hundred—maybe even a thousand songs. Make it extremely difficult for anyone who identifies our technology, however unlikely we think that is, to stop them all."

"Sounds thorough, but complicated," Eddy said.

Lili frowned. Harold thought she looked like she wanted to say something. He waited. She remained silent. He kept going.

"There are two tricky parts. Which songs do we pick? If we guess wrong and the files aren't downloaded, IH won't happen. We have statistics on the songs that have been downloaded most often. But like the stock market, past performance is no guarantee of future results."

Eddy grinned.

"The insertion is sensitive. The machine that loads the songs carrying our technology must connect to the Internet and push those files onto sharing and digital vault sites."

"But we have hundreds of machines in the back room. Aren't they connected?" Eddy asked.

Harold nodded. "But they simply download and upload music files like any user; though ours carry a hidden watermark. If they uploaded a toxic program, and that upload was ever traced, it would lead directly to Silver Platter."

"Not good," Eddy agreed. "But your face tells me you already have a solution."

Harold allowed himself a smile. "Wi-Fi. Specifically, public Wi-Fi: Starbucks, the train station, airport, walking down the street passing people's houses that don't protect their networks. There are many places where we could insert."

"And these aren't traceable?" Eddy asked.

"A good trace could find the Wi-Fi node, which means someone might find out it was Starbucks in San Jose. And they might be able to tag the computer itself, so we'll...dispose of it."

"What's the safest way to do this?" Eddy asked. He glanced out the window. "To protect the company."

Harold felt Blake's impatience. "The same way we handle the song files: multiple insertions, in multiple ways, from multiple locations. No one location uploads all the files. We'll want locations with heavy foot traffic, thousands of people per day signing in and out of the network."

Eddy tapped his chin with an index finger.

"Where?"

Harold reached into the back pocket of his jeans and pulled out a Silver Platter Travel Request form #54-P.

"I need to go to New York City to visit family, Mr. Blake. If you approve this now, I can make the red-eye flight tonight and arrive by morning."

Eddy took the form and signed it, then noticed a petty cash request for $5000.

"What's this cash for?"

"I'll need a computer. Thought I might buy one in New York. And I'll pay cash for everything."

Eddy nodded and handed the form across his desk.

"Have a successful trip, Mr. Zeto."

Lili stood, her face showed nothing, but her blue eyes were smiling.

As the door clicked closed behind them Harold heard Eddy's voice through Stacy's intercom.

"Try to get Simmons again."

~ 23 ~

The cylinders had cooled on the Moto Guzzi parked beside the dock so the rising sun would dry morning dew from the seat. And the chili dog he had eaten as a late supper had finally settled and let him drift off when the quiet lapping of waves against his houseboat was pierced by a telephone jangle. As he shifted toward consciousness, he vowed to never sleep again with it plugged in.

"Qigiq here."

"It's Ferdinand. Come quickly. I have...it is unbelieve...I cannot...hurry."

"Hurry where?" Qigiq asked, as the phone went dead in his hand.

He dropped his head back against the pillow and fought his body's urge to sleep as his mind raced to images that would cause the ever-dignified Ferdinand to place such a call. Personal crisis? Break-in?

This last thought threw his legs into action. In four minutes he was riding Highway 1 South onto the Golden Gate Bridge, blue lights flashing, speedo needle inching towards triple digits through light midnight traffic. Damp ocean air floating across the bridge penetrated his jacket. He felt his fingers going numb by the time he slowed for the electronic tollbooths at the bridge exit. City streets slowed him below fifty and he welcomed the heat from the tall concrete buildings of San Francisco.

He arrived at the curb in twelve minutes.

He knocked on the EER door ninety seconds later. No answer. He twisted the knob and burst into the room with his gun drawn and held close to his body. He dropped to the floor. Saw no one. The overhead fluorescent lights were in night mode: every third one lit. He held his breath and listened. The hum of fans inside computer skins was evident.

He crawled along the wall, hiding behind the rows of metal desks holding the current collection of partially disassembled computers. Ferdinand's call echoed in his head. At the last desk he hesitated. He inhaled, then stuck his head out and drew it back in one motion. He closed his eyes to better recall the scene. Another long row of computers and Ferdinand slumped in an office chair at the far end, his legs out with the toes of black shoes sticking straight up like a wooden marionette.

He eased his head around the corner, staying low to the floor, gun ready.

Ferdinand's body shifted. Then his right arm came up, a brown bottle in the large hand. He tilted the bottle and drank.

Qigiq watched, saw no other movement in the room.

"Ferdinand?" he called out.

The man's head swiveled, his eyes scanning the room. He frowned.

"Hello, Ferdinand."

"Hello?" Ferdinand said. "Who is it?"

"It's Qigiq."

The head swiveled more quickly.

"Where are you?"

"Are you alone?" Qigiq called.

"Alone? Of course I am alone. Who else would be in the Recovery lab after midnight on a Friday? We don't pay overtime for general case work on weekends. It just has to wait."

Qigiq slid from under the desk and stood slowly, his eyes working the room, finding nothing.

Ferdinand's eyes opened wider. "Is that a gun?"

Qigiq walked slowly toward Ferdinand, still watching the room.

"Please put that away my friend, before someone gets hurt. What are you thinking?"

"I'm thinking I got a strange call in the middle of the night from someone named Ferdinand who hung up before telling me what was happening. So I approached with caution, thinking you might be in danger."

"Oh my, I am sorry. I was just so...I thought nothing in this business could shock me anymore. I've seen...well...many things...murderers often photograph their handiwork. But this. I've never..."

His arm swung up again and Qigiq recognized the red and white logo of Red Stripe beer. He lowered his revolver and stared at the bottle.

Ferdinand's eyes turned toward him while he swallowed.

"Sorry, my good man. I was flustered and this was all we had in the fridge. Would you care for one?"

Qigiq saw three empties standing in a row next to Ferdinand's chair.

"Did you call, Kandy?" Qigiq asked.

"No. I drank two and called you." He struggled to sit up. "Then continued," he motioned toward the empty bottles. "I had to calm myself. It's so..."

Qigiq put the gun back in his jacket and stood watching Ferdinand. He had never seen the man unglued. Steaming angry, yes, he had seen that. But not this.

"What happened?"

Ferdinand shook his head. "It is what I've found. God only knows what makes sick people tick." He swigged again, his fourth bottle close to empty.

Qigiq waited, trying to guess.

Ferdinand began to stand, wobbled, and dropped back into the office chair, sending it rolling backwards until it bumped the wall. He didn't try a second time, but gestured toward the second computer in the row.

"That one," he said, pointing with a curved finger. "I was working on the signal along the bottom of the Sally video, the one we think was taken on a boat. I'm sorry, I haven't started on the pictures you took. I had planned to stay late...but this? Once the idea formed in my mind, I had to reconstruct it. Now...I wish I hadn't." The big man shook his head. "No, that's not right. I hope it helps you find this asshole. I just wish I had never seen it."

Qigiq stiffened at a word he hadn't thought Ferdinand would admit to the lexicon of the English language.

"What do you mean *reconstruct?*" Qigiq asked, crossing to the second machine.

Ferdinand sank into the chair and stared at the ceiling.

"That flickering along the bottom isn't noise at all. It's a row of data. I had to find an ordering. This took much trial and error. By applying the same math to the noise in the next frame, I got another row. The video is over four minutes long, that's more than 7,200 rows. But each row actually represents two lines of a smaller video. It took much patience to determine how to place the rows together. It's as if the criminal assembled this by hand, putting the data wherever he wanted. So reconstruction required piecing together a huge puzzle."

"Sounds difficult."

"Quite frustrating. I finally had the computer assemble all possible combinations until I found one that didn't look like a Jackson Pollack painting. When I did, I called you."

"Is this it?" Qigiq said, pointing to an open window on the computer screen showing a black frame.

"No. That's a test movie. I closed it after I saw...I almost deleted the damn thing."

Ferdinand finished his fourth bottle and belched.

"Open Recon8776. That is the correct reconstruction of the data. It couldn't possibly be a coincidence."

Qigiq scrolled the window until he found 8776 and double-clicked it. A movie player opened and sat at the first frame: a close-up of the *Don't Steal Music* label that had been used to seal the plastic bags containing Sally's fingers. His stomach contracted strangely around his hot dog.

"Go ahead, play it," Ferdinand said. "You might as well get it over with."

Qigiq wished he'd had more sleep, and clicked the play button. A smallish frame opened, not much bigger than a business card.

Don't Steal showed for a few seconds then cross-faded to what Qigiq guessed was a girl's arm taped to a table or floor. Something smooth. A dozen two-foot sections of duct tape crossed perpendicular to her arm from above the elbow to her wrist. The hand was clenched into a fist. Qigiq immediately recognized the purple polish they had found on Sally's fingernails. As the movie played he leaned forward and placed both palms flat on the desktop.

He took slow, deep breaths.

A left hand wearing a thin black leather glove pulled up over a long-sleeve black sweatshirt entered the frame and grabbed the taped arm just below the elbow. Qigiq tried to see a swatch of skin below the shirt, but everything was covered. The right hand, similarly clad, entered the frame holding a serrated knife of the kind used to clean fish. The tip of the knife pressed into the palm. The fist grew tighter, the wrist twisted and fought and finally opened as the knife cut a small circle in the palm.

Qigiq swallowed hard and fought the desire to stop the movie. He placed more weight on his hands.

The knife moved to the base of the pinky finger and began sawing like a lumberjack removing a tree limb. Blood poured onto the floor around the tape, the hand twitched wildly, and the smallest finger fell away. The knife pushed it to the side, like someone chopping vegetables, before moving on to the ring finger.

Qigiq exhaled hard in an effort to avoid vomiting. He had seen mutilations after the fact, but never one in progress. He forced himself to see. And to think. The perp was right-handed. At least he had learned something.

After the ring finger the screen flashed to *Keep Your Fingers. Don't Steal Music.* Then switched back to the knife working on the middle finger.

Qigiq stood frozen, forcing himself to watch. Forcing himself to believe.

After the remaining fingers and the thumb had been removed like unneeded carrot tops, and the floor was a puddle of blood, the gloved hands disappeared. The camera swept up the arm until it was pointed at the screaming face of Sally Bellowi. There was no sound and the sight of streaming tears and wailing lips struck Qigiq as a living Dali painting, something far far removed from reality.

The left gloved hand grabbed her neck. Her red wet eyes widened to

JOE KLINGLER

whiteness. The right glove flashed into the frame and out. Sally's left ear flopped to the floor beside her head as blood spurted into her blonde hair. She struggled to scream against the hand gripping her throat.

Qigiq tried to analyze the motion, the arm, the strength. The loose sleeves hid much.

The frame cut to *Don't Listen to Stolen Music, Your Ears Will Thank You* and cross-faded to a screen that read only *The End* over a bloody ear suspended and spinning, perhaps by a fishing line or some other support that didn't show clearly in the tiny video frame.

Qigiq realized he was on his knees and leaning against the desk on his elbows. He estimated the size of the hands inside the gloves. Sally was five-foot-four according to her driver's license registration, though Robina had said five-five. The hands with the knife were inside rubber gloves, a size 9, maybe 10. The perp could be anywhere from Sally's height to over six feet. He hoped Ferdinand could produce more accuracy.

A thought flashed through his mind: *A woman?* Did they have anything definite?

No.

Qigiq blinked hard but the images wouldn't leave his mind. He would return with a clearer head and watch the video over and over, searching for clues the perpetrator had failed to hide. Maybe find the source of those gloves, or the shirt. Duct tape was awfully generic, but there might be something—maybe residue from the glue, if they could find the right floor. *Or deck*, he reminded himself. And the knife.

He had to find that knife.

~ 24 ~

Harold was dreaming of Lili presenting an impossible time line for the next development project wearing only a mint green bra and matching thong above black heels with double straps around the ankle while yelling that he needed to get on board with the delivery date and show leadership when a flight attendant closing an overhead compartment nudged him awake.

He heard a voice say "...landing in New York's LaGuardia airport in twenty minutes. The local time is 6:15 am." Harold pressed two buttons on the side of his electronic Casio simultaneously and the hands began chasing each other in circles. He let them stop at 6:16.

Waking up at 3:15 am Pacific time made his bones ache like evil interrogators had injected him with pain-producing drugs. He rolled his

102

head in slow circles to the right, then to the left, glad he had put in for a first class ticket—having guessed correctly that Blake would focus on the cash advance and barely glance at the flight info. But even with the lounge seat and iced shrimp, flying all night was low on his list of fun things to do.

Twenty-eight minutes later he deplaned through a tube-shaped corridor into the expanse of LaGuardia. Needing just a single day, hours really, to release the monitoring software—he hesitated to use the word *virus* even in his own head—he carried only a small green backpack as luggage. It contained a Dopp kit, two changes of clothes, and the USB thumb drive with the magic software to perform the insertion. Believing in the power of redundancy to prevent errors, he also carried an SD flash chip, now taped to the inside of his right shoe although it had been inserted in his portable camera while passing through security at SFO. He also had a copy of the software on his music player, which was safely tucked into the outside left pocket of his black cargo pant.s.

He was the tenth person off the plane and turned left from Gate 51 toward baggage claim. The midnight fog in his head made the Saturday-morning buzz of the airport feel like watching a foreign movie in 3D without the glasses. He stepped onto a people mover and noticed a girl walking in the opposite direction: straight red hair, tight brown boots up to her knees. The lenses of silver-framed glasses looked like photo-optics that hadn't lightened, giving her a movie star hiding from fans aura. Then he saw the skirt: a tiny swath of blue protruding below a short brown leather jacket. He longed to follow her up a portable stairway into a huge jet.

He turned to face the side of the moving belt. He placed a hand on the rail and let his eyes rove up to the cathedral-high ceiling and take in the expanse of the airport, then lower surreptitiously until they landed on her rear end. His breath caught. She was passing by too fast. He longed to stop time and drink in the erotic energy of her motion. He tried to think of an airport approach that would end in wine over dinner. And more. But his left brain reminded him of an important job—important in the way stock options transmogrify into mountains of cash—and that the probability of success for a blue mini-skirt mission was point zero zero one. He cursed women, the world and a society that made it impossible to meet strangers.

As she faded into the crowd and his heart rate slowed he caught a glimpse of a profile crossing toward the restroom. He stood on the balls of his feet. He would swear that guy was the lawyer he had seen on board meetings days. But he was wearing a parrot shirt, khaki shorts and carrying a backpack with random white lines that didn't look like anything. Even on vacation Harold didn't think a stuffed shirt—what was his name? Simon? Samuel?—would be without his three-piece and gold watch. Not that anyone at Platter was on vacation in the current crisis; Blake had stopped approving time off months ago.

He saw the head disappear into the restroom opening and began turning to face forward just as the belt ended. The outside of his running shoe stopped at the little metal teeth where the belt disappeared under the floor. Momentum tossed him sideways where his left knee smacked tile before he rolled onto his back, taking the impact with his shoulder and backpack. Passengers spewed off the belt behind him and parted with barely a look down. No one even muttered, "Are you OK?"

He scrambled to his feet and joined the mass of walkers moving toward baggage claim. He walked slowly and looked back three times to see if the lawyer was coming his way, an odd feeling that Blake was having him followed building in his gut. Which made no sense at all—a lawyer could be sitting beside him while he inserted the payloads and the guy wouldn't have a clue what Harold was doing.

He stopped and looked back one last time, his eyes scanning hundreds of faces. He shrugged, tried to let go of the being-tailed feeling, and headed for the directory to figure out how to walk to the Airport Marriott and a few hours of sleep.

© © ©

Harold woke without an alarm at 7:05 am Pacific time, the excitement of the task ahead pushing him out of bed. A hot shower, two Danishes from the built-in fridge and an orange juice powered him to the Apple Store at 767 Fifth Avenue where he purchased a small laptop with hundred dollar bills. He wanted to use one for insertion, and had gone to the trouble to test the uploader scripts on the Mac at his apartment, because nowhere within the Silver Platter building was there a single Apple computer.

He studied the sharp cheekbones of the slender cashier who looked like she used white flour for makeup.

"Any good Wi-Fi spots close by?"

Her eyes, surrounded by black crayon marks, met his.

"This is New York City," she said, lip piercing dancing, "They're all good."

He nodded, realizing he had just given her a memory to pass on to the FBI about a guy in black cargo pants who paid cash for a computer and asked about Wi-Fi hookups.

He had to force himself to stop looking at girls—they messed with his mind.

He walked up a transparent spiral staircase, passed through glass doors and stopped on the sidewalk to orient himself. Bodies moved around him like he was a lamp pole. He went left, simply because more people were headed in that direction. He walked down Fifth Avenue until the wild-haired goddess logo of Starbucks gazed down at him. He stepped inside, waited for a mocha, and found a corner table strewn with coffee-stained pages of the New York Times.

And a nearby power outlet.

He kicked the chair out, slipped his bag between it and the wall, collected the papers, and set them across the table like he was waiting for a friend who enjoyed the Times.

He sipped the mocha but it burned his upper lip. He hated that sensation of fried nerve endings and silently cursed a company that couldn't deliver its product at a consumable temperature.

The shiny plastic wrappings of the famous Apple out-of-box experience came off quickly and the Mac was ready on the table just as the mocha became drinkable. He slipped the iPod from the pocket of his cargo pants and pushed the connector into the waiting slot of the machine, trying to stop the action from conjuring images of the blue skirt at the airport. He drank half the mocha while his custom scripts and pre-treated music files copied to the new machine.

The sensation of being followed, eyes on his back, returned.

He forced himself not to turn around.

Instead, he slowly lowered the cup to the table, moved his right hand to the computer, and started the video chat software. His face came up on the screen. He leaned slightly to the right to pick up his cup and studied the image the camera saw over his left shoulder.

A short girl was standing next to the counter holding with both hands the largest Starbucks cup he had ever seen. Her eyes moved from his computer to the back of his head, then back to the computer, over and over. Thankfully, the machine was only copying a long list of files with meaningless names, not yet doing anything private.

He brought up a text editor and typed *The quick brown fox jumps over the lazy dog*, just to put something on the screen while watching her eyes as seen by the webcam.

She continued gazing at him between rises of the big cup, apparently unaware of the camera.

So he studied her. Straight black hair, parted in the middle, stopping halfway down her ears. He guessed about five-foot and Vietnamese. Or Thai. Or Chinese. He'd bet she was in New York studying at a hot college like Columbia on Daddy's dime, even though she could pass for fifteen. She wore a tiny pink scarf tied tight around her neck and black: a tight black shirt, skintight black jeans, black boots over her ankles and a black leather jacket that reached to mid-thigh. A gold chain slung over her left shoulder was attached to a black purse no bigger than a paperback novel.

He was thinking about how to get rid of her, remembering his stupid comment to the flour-faced clerk, when their eyes met through the video cam and a jolt immobilized him. They were very dark, like the deep wells poets blathered on about. And they held him.

He blinked himself awake. Eyes can't meet through a cam, the geometry doesn't line up. It had to be his imagination.

But those eyes.

He turned slowly around in his chair. She was gazing at the floor. He picked up his mocha and stood. She sipped at her giant cup without looking up. He walked over near her, placed his mocha on the counter and found the cinnamon shaker. She didn't leave, so as he tapped the fine powder onto his drink he took a slow breath in and said: "Hi, that's a big drink."

She looked up and their eyes really did meet. The jolt was much stronger this time.

She dropped her gaze to the Apple bag now stuffed with packing material on the floor next to his chair.

"Did you get a new computer?"

"Picked it up today. Trying to get connected."

"I love Macs," she said. "They're so smooth." Her eyes didn't come back to his. Instead, they moved to the Mac. "Can I touch it?"

He swallowed with some difficulty. "Sure."

She floated past him to the far side of the table and stroked the side of the laptop with her fingertips like it was a molten-glass Chihuly sculpture.

He watched her fingers. Something about their frailty motivated him into a lie.

"I like them too." He tried to think of a reason. "The people at the store are really helpful."

She smiled with lips pressed together and dark eyes dancing over her giant mug.

He noticed the copy operation had finished, and realized she was too pretty to be present while he worked. He would make a mistake for sure.

"What's your name?" he asked.

"Sarlin. I study violin."

"At Juilliard?" he asked, knowing it was the hottest music school in New York.

Her entire body sagged. "No, I couldn't get in. I'm at Manhattan." She lifted herself slightly. "Juilliard is too stuffy anyway."

He nodded, kicking himself for asking a question with an answer. He knew it was the best way to sound stupid.

"My name's Ha...rvey," he lied. "I'm a tourist."

She looked at him. "A tourist with a new computer?"

He was leaving a data trail. More stupid. Maybe he should just stop talking to people.

"I want info about the city; figured this was as good a place to get a new computer as any. This is my first laptop." He was getting plenty of lying practice.

She nodded.

"I was about to hook up to Wi-Fi," he said, figuring he couldn't screw up something that easy just because those wet eyes in smooth dark skin were watching him.

She lowered her mug. "Oh my gosh, Harvey, have you seen the rape everyone's talking about?"

He choked, grabbed his mocha and took a long swallow. He blew out to cool his mouth.

"What?"

"Oh, you must see."

In two steps she slipped around the table until she was so close he felt warmth against his arm. It couldn't be her, he reasoned, not through a leather jacket.

She pointed at his new computer. "Go to YouTube. Type *simulation*."

"Simulation? That's weird."

"Actors simulate death and birth. It's fucking amazing." Her pupils leapt to the corner of her eyes and she brought a hand up to cover her mouth.

He assumed she hadn't meant to say that in front of a guy she just met, but excitement got the better of her. Why the hell couldn't he find excitable girls in California?

Maybe he should move.

He sat down, connected to the network, then typed *simulation* into the YouTube searcher. Over a hundred items listed. He scrolled slowly past death, sex, more sex, birthing...

"There, that one," she said, hopping up and down slightly.

He looked up so he could see her face and enjoy her enthusiasm. It was then he noticed a dark mark under her chin, like someone had a good time giving her a hickey. He started to speak, but caught himself, figuring it might be a birthmark she would rather not have noticed. Then he felt jealous of the guy she would let do that. He faced the computer and opened the video, reminding himself he had a big job to do today. and this girl was a distraction. The title read: *Simulate + Emo = (Don't * Rape)/Music.*

He glanced at a dozen people milling around Starbucks.

"Uh, Sarlin, have you seen this?" Saying her name for the first time tingled his tongue.

She nodded vigorously. "Lots of times."

"Okay to play in public?" he asked. "I don't want to draw attention." He gritted his teeth. He might as well tell her he's about to inject a virus into the Internet and invite her to watch. Maybe bring along a police officer.

Her head spun to take in the crowd.

"Turn sound down," she said.

He slid the audio low and clicked the play arrow.

Sarlin was right; the blonde girl was good. Maybe she would be discovered on YouTube and get a big Hollywood contract.

"Such amazing energy and passion." Sarlin said softly. "I get goosebumps watching her."

Harold suddenly wanted to give this girl goosebumps himself, but he only said, "Yeah, she sure is professional. Didn't look like she was acting at all." He frowned. "But what's this *Don't Steal* crap?"

Sarlin stood straight, placing her *Breasts Under Black Spandex* works of art just above eye level.

"Silly corporate don't fuck owner by stealing music metaphor. Ignore it."

Harold read the comments below the video. Most showered praise on the nameless actress. Some questioned whether a rape scene was appropriate for YouTube; no one ranted that it should be taken down. Someone calling himself hangDawg wrote: *Record companies suck, they rob artists and music lovers. Steal all the music you can and put them out of business.*

Harold thought Dawg possessed a limited knowledge of economics. But there were four more postings echoing the *Steal from The Man</i* > message. Then someone posting as itsthelaw had submitted:

You towering midgets of the mind have no idea what copyright is for. It *protects* the owners of the songs; the record company only gets a piece of the action if the artist *sells* it to them. The people you're ripping off are the very artists you listen to, and admire, and emulate. And that you want to write more music for you.

"Have you read these?" he asked.

"A few." She shrugged her tiny shoulders, making her artwork move. "I play classical music; it doesn't matter."

Harold looked at her like she had just said the sun revolved around the earth.

"You want to get a job someday?"

"Sure. In a symphony orchestra." Her eyes lit up. "They're so powerful."

He would swear her body shuddered.

"And you want to get paid?"

She frowned. "How else can I live?"

He sighed. "How can an orchestra pay you if they don't make money from their recordings because everyone steals them on the Internet? Don't you think that a person who hears you play has received some benefit and should therefore remunerate you fairly for your work?"

Her frown didn't go away.

"They should pay you if they're listening to you play."

"Of course," she said, lifting her giant mug.

"But they don't. They steal it from YouTube with apps that hide in cracks in copyright law. That's this guy's point." He tilted his thumb toward the laptop.

Her frown hadn't moved, even though she was drinking.

"You mean I won't get paid?" she asked.

"I mean you won't get paid as much if the orchestra can't generate money by selling recordings. In fact, why make them? It's not free to make a recording. And maybe more people would go see orchestras if there were no recordings of them."

"How do I get paid the most?" she asked, her frown unchanged.

"By being able to control your assets." His mind drifted to the back of that leather jacket. "If violins were free, how much would you pay to buy one?"

Her frown deepened. "I wouldn't pay anything if I had a free one. So long as it was good."

"Let's say it's exactly as good as the ones that are for sale."

"Then I wouldn't buy one. I would already have what I wanted."

He smiled. "Exactly."

Her face softened. "This video mean stop screwing people who play music and pay for their work?"

He nodded.

"Wild," she said. "I did not get it. I thought was some guy making dramatic video. You know, screw the record companies before they screw us."

"It goes deeper than that," he said, and felt himself blush. He looked down and shook the image of her tight black jeans out of his mind. He took a breath and looked up to her face.

"Do you have any concerts coming up?"

She smiled. "My quartet plays the first Sunday concert every month at the conservatory. Is week from tomorrow." She lowered her eyes. "Will you be here?" she asked softly.

Of course not. He was leaving today.

"Maybe," he said.

He thought about the doubled stock options Blake had promised for

Monday. He thought about them becoming stacks and stacks of crisp hundred dollar bills. His mind drifted to her artwork. And assets. The image of the hundreds faded.

"Sarlin, are you free for a few hours? I need to visit some cafés, and I'd be pleased if you would join me for lunch."

"Well...I really should practice." She blinked twice. "But I could do that this afternoon." The deep wells fixed on his face. "No classes on Saturday."

"I'm working, so it's really not fair to ask you to help me. But it's easy work."

Her frown returned. "I thought you were tourist, Harvey?"

He motioned her closer with his index finger, and whispered, "That's my cover story."

Her mouth formed the letter "O." He pushed thoughts of an Asian blow-up doll away.

"I work for a company evaluating Wi-Fi networks in New York. I have to travel to a bunch of locations and upload test files to measure speed. Mostly I just sit and wait for the computer; it does all the work."

"That's why you bought new computer. To do tests?" She was whispering.

He nodded, wondering if her pressing the key to start the uploads would provide a level of legal insulation if they got caught, since she wasn't a Silver Platter employee. He decided it certainly couldn't hurt if he never touched the computer.

"Sarlin, please join me. You know the city, it would save me lots of time." He paused and met her eyes. "And it'd be a lot more fun to be with you."

He thought maybe she blushed.

"Let me show you," he said.

He slid his chair back and put an arm around her waist and pulled her toward him until the backside of those black jeans was sitting on the lap of his cargo pants.

~ 25 ~

At the first two stops she released fifty songs, each containing the entire payload for the Invisible Hand. Her job was to double-click the scripts he had coded and watch them upload to pre-selected sharing sites: kazuu, lime, getmp3, yourmp3, itutoo, p2pnet, megaloader, thepirate and others, all of which supported some form of file sharing. He had chosen songs that ran the gamut from Adele to Zunksters, pop candy to electronic thrash metal, with the goal of spreading the Hand fast and deep into the music community.

Now they were sitting in the Backers Deli on 53rd Street waiting for sandwiches and nursing a Dr. Pepper and a Hires root beer. Sarin was staring at the computer and sitting to his left, her slender thigh occasionally touching his leg.

"I see BackerNet. Should I do the same thing?" Sarin asked.

"Let's eat here, and run a longer test." He pointed to the screen. "Fiftyfifty would be a good one."

He watched the nail of her index finger painted with a black eighth note over metallic pink glide across the trackpad to position the cursor. In seconds she had the script running and the names of song files flew by as they uploaded: *Come to me, It's now, Don't Stop Stopping, Can't it be Forever, Forever is far too Long, Stomp Stomp.*

"Lots of songs," she said.

"Over five thousand. Let's see how long this takes."

She was captivated by the idea that they could measure how quickly the network moved data, and the realization that there were real people making the Internet go.

He knew that each one of those 5,050 songs carried a tiny bit of technology. And when taken together in combinations of 1024, the Invisible Hand would magically appear on a thief's machine. He smiled at a warm feeling inside his chest; technology he had been working on for almost two years was finally being unleashed. And he was doing it personally with a beautiful Asian violinist. Lili was wrong. Programmers didn't have to lead boring lives.

"What do we do next?" Sarlin asked.

"Eat," he said, as a waitress clad in a dark blue uniform that made her look like a surgical nurse plopped down a basket containing a corned beef and swiss cheese on a plain bagel the size of a Frisbee, beside a pile of homemade potato chips, and an iceberg of cole slaw. He held the basket out for Sarlin to sample a chip, after which she sucked on the straw stuck through the plastic lid on her soda, and he watched carefully.

© © ©

Six stops later he could see her beautiful eyes beginning to take on the glazed look of a programmer striving to finish a product on the Marketing Department's schedule. But her mood was light, and at each stop she sat a little closer to him, making him wish he was staying for her concert. Every insert worked without a single upload failure; flour-face girl had been right, they were all good.

"This is my stop," Sarlin said, pointing to the stairs leading to the subway train that would deliver her to West 145th.

The soft look in her eyes gave him an odd feeling in his stomach. She was slender and sexy in her black outfit, and made him feel tall and strong. Everything really was relative, just like Einstein had said. He suddenly wanted to do something special for her. He wanted to strip her naked on the sidewalk too, but this was different, strange, possessive.

"Are you online?"

She shook her head. "No computer."

His eyebrows lifted. "Really? But you're so skilled."

"School. And back home in Thailand." She made a fiddling motion with her arms. "Violins are expensive." She raised a hand above her head. "Daddy makes big payment."

He tried to calculate the risk, then doubled it because he knew his brain muddled when a girl was close. He asked her to wait, ran to the nearest building, pulled the laptop he had been planning to crush into a dumpster from his bag and sat down on the sidewalk. The shredding program had installed along with everything else back at Starbucks, which seemed a millennium ago. While it worked its way through thousands of files he typed a note, and named it *Sarlin-Plz Read Me.*

He looked up. She was standing at the stairs watching with those lovely dark eyes, a blank expression on her face. He noticed the toe of her left boot tapping; but couldn't tell if she was growing impatient, or just practicing music in her head.

He closed the computer and stood, brushing dust off his butt and slipping the machine back into the bag. He rushed back.

Her eyes watched him closely, but she didn't speak.

His mind struggled to sort what he wanted to happen into the right order.

"Sarlin, thank you for spending the morning with me. You are wonderful."

She stared.

He put his left arm around her waist and drew her towards him slowly, being super sensitive to resistance from her but enjoying the electric feeling on his palm. She turned her face up to watch his eyes. He lowered his head to meet her five-foot frame and pressed his lips to hers slowly. To his surprise, her mouth welcomed him more with each passing second until he thought his knees were going to turn to water and collapse like the snake alien in the Abyss movie. He didn't want to stop, and he didn't want her to stop. Then he realized, since he had started it, he should end it while sending the message he wanted it to last forever.

He smiled, and she smiled back.

Without releasing her he held up the shopping bag flour-face girl had given him that morning.

She frowned.

"My job is done, Sarlin. Please take this as a thank you for your help today."

Her frown faded as she reached up with her left hand and took the bag.

She leaned towards him and his knees shook.

"Thank you, Harvey. Please come to my concert," she whispered.

She hugged him hard, twisted out of his grip and danced down the stairs, her black clad figure blending into the darkness of the underground. At the bottom she turned and blew a kiss with her free hand.

~ 26 ~

Marie Minnel tried again to play through the minuet movement of the second Bach Suite, and again her right and left hands wouldn't stay together. She let out a mini-roar of frustration at the room and leaned back. She rested her eyes by gazing out the second-floor window of her puny apartment six blocks from Juilliard's campus on West 65th Street. The street was filling with lunch hour walkers, mostly women whose spandex-squeezed pounds of fat they would never lose by walking with a grande latte and a donut yakking with friends. Her eyes drifted down at her own thighs protruding from black cotton shorts wrapped around her wonderful Mnatzaganian cello.

She forced her attention back to Bach's score. Why couldn't she handle this rising run? Sally had shown her how last year when they performed that eight cello music together. She had played it fine then. But for reasons known only to the gods of musicians' hands, she couldn't get through it now at the proper tempo. What had slender sexy Sally said? *If you can hear the music in your head, your fingers will find their way.* It had worked then, but now her fingers couldn't find concert A.

She sang the line slowly and thought about Sally, and why she had left New York for San Francisco, of all places. That city was so tiny; it couldn't be fun. Yes, the weather was better, but not by much. She sighed. She missed playing together and wondered if Sally could teach her the Bach trick over the phone.

She tried to play the phrase twice more and decided to take a break to avoid practicing bad habits. Her tummy was thinking about lunch anyway, which meant the mail. She hardly ever got mail; her friends were addicted to texting. But Daddy sent checks from Texas. If one arrived, she could have a big fresh lunch at the deli instead of reheating leftovers.

Marie placed her precious cello on its stand, knowing she had a minimum of two more hours with the beast today. But she didn't mind. She loved the beast and the sounds it could sing. And it never ever teased her for being overweight.

She padded across a brown shag throw rug and slipped into a pair of lime green Crocs she wore every day, unless she had a performance—no one would let her wear green Crocs on stage. She had thought about trying to wear black ones, but the black looked like a worn out tire so she stayed with traditional leather. It wasn't as if a cellist's shoes made much difference, though, mostly no one ever saw them.

In the upper right drawer of a roll top desk that had come with the apartment she found her mailbox key ring that also held an apartment key so she wouldn't lock herself out. That happened twice before she hit on the idea of putting a spare door key on the ring with the mailbox key. Little things mattered. She hated being locked out and having to go use a neighbor's phone. When she had stopped at Mrs. Ganther's apartment one floor down, she thought the look in the woman's eye might mean she would prefer for Marie to be locked out of her apartment so she couldn't play that damn cello. Yet she had let Marie use the phone after a cup of coffee and two cookies.

Over a pale blue Victoria's Secret bra whose lace made her feel sexy, Marie pulled a maroon sweatshirt that said *Pull Some Strings* on the front below a picture of a string quartet. The quartet members were all plucking pizzicato, but no one ever noticed. She clogged down wooden stairs that had little metal strips over the edge. Most of the strips were dented, and three were missing. At the bottom she turned one-eighty to backtrack to a row of brass mailboxes under the stairwell.

The fifth box from the far end was hers. She inserted the key and visualized the check from her dad tilted inside before turning her wrist, trying to attract it with that *Secret* thing she had heard about—*believe and you shall receive,* or something like that. She wiggled the key because the lock wasn't very good and the door swung open. No check...but there was something. She smiled. It was fun to get surprises in the mail. She bent down to examine a brown cardboard box almost as thick as her mailbox, but shorter. She managed to wiggle two plump fingers in and drag it forward. Even in the dim light beneath the stairwell she could read big black letters printed on the side: *Amazon.* She frowned and thought hard. It wasn't her birthday. She hadn't done any recitals recently. And she didn't have the money to order anything.

She worked her other hand into the mailbox and slid the package slowly toward the front edge until it slipped out into her hand. It felt heavy. Maybe someone had sent her a book.

Back in her kitchen she slit the clear tape with a kitchen knife. Inside was a white block that looked like Styrofoam. She tried to lift it out but it was so cold she dropped it. It slid off the counter onto the red Formica floor and shattered. But it was inside a plastic bag, so the pieces didn't scatter. She stared down at the fragments hoping it hadn't been a sculpture.

Inside the box she found a cylinder wrapped in bubbles, and below that, another white block. She pulled out the bubble wrap and started unwinding it. She saw an L shape made from two brown rods. She lifted the L up in front of her eyes. It looked liked fingers touching at the tips. Was someone trying to tell her she was a loser? With rubber fingers? People had done some cruel things to her, but this would be new.

The thing was cold, and the ends of the rods were leaking. Her stomach rumbled. She turned it over slowly. Oh God, it was so gross. How could they make plastic look so real? She dropped it onto the counter and was looking for a return address on the package when a flash of purple caught her eye. She ran into her bathroom and opened the medicine cabinet. She pushed bottles out of the way—Oxycontin for pain, Prozac for a different kind of pain, three kinds of sleeping pills and a big container of NyQuil—until she found a tall thin bottle. She moved as close to a run as she could back to the kitchen and held up the bottle of Very Berry that Sally had spontaneously given her when she said she liked it. Who else would know what kind of nail polish Sally wore? She lifted the thing up, her hand shaking and felt the rubber carefully.

Maybe it wasn't rubber?

She bent over and vomited into the sink telling herself it couldn't possibly be what she was thinking, no no her imagination was wrong, and should shut up. With her head down she reached out and found a glass on the cabinet. She rinsed her mouth and spit. Three times. Then stood up straight very slowly.

She looked at the thing on the counter, and touched the white block still in the box with her finger: very cold. She picked up the thing between two fingers like it was a dead spider and opened her fridge with the other hand, pulled down the thin plastic door in front of the freezer and then laid it down on a chunk of frost off to the right side. She let the freezer door slam and swung the main door closed. She stared at her hand and shivered, then washed it with hot water and soap at the sink. Three times.

Marie found the red sling bag she used as a purse and dug for her address book and the AT&T calling card she used to call home. She thought about running down to Mrs. Ganther, but decided the woman would ask too many questions. She wished she could afford her own phone, then had a second thought: if she did, her Mom would call all the time and she wouldn't have time to practice. Her Dad had reminded her of that when he refused to pay for a cell phone even though all her friends had one, telling her, *I'm paying for you to be in New York to practice, not talk to people.*

It took her almost five minutes to reach the Walgreens drugstore that still had a pay phone in a back corner. She was glad it wasn't raining.

"Hello," a sleepy voiced answered. Marie remembered California was on a different time, but she could never remember if it was earlier or later. The drugstore clock showed ten minutes to twelve, and SAT in the face.

"Hi, is Sally in?" Marie asked.

She heard static sizzle on the line. A girl's voice said, "Who's calling?"

"This is Marie Minnel from New York. I performed with Sally last year at a cello conference. We played a suite for Eight Cellos by Villa-Lobos."

Marie wondered why she had said that. It didn't matter what they had played.

"I remember Sally talking about that performance. She loved New York."

"We had loads of fun. She helped me practice," Marie said.

Another pause of static.

"Sally's, um, not in. She's been away. I'm Robina, her roommate."

"Hi Robina. Do you know when she'll be back...something weird has happened and I need to ask her about it."

The static was gone.

"Weird?" Robina asked.

"Yeah. Do you know if Sally still wears purple nail polish, well, not purple, it's really Very Berry."

"Oh fuck," Robina said. "You didn't get a package did you?"

"Yes, from Amazon. Did you get one too?" Marie asked.

"Oh my God...oh my God. Marie, I can't believe what's happening."

Marie listened to the girl who called herself Robina start crying.

"What is it?" Marie asked. "Can I help?"

"Marie. Those are Sally's fingers."

Marie blinked repeatedly. The pay phone swirled before her eyes into a melted mess. Her body tilted against the wall, her big bosom heaving from running up three flights of stairs.

"Fingers?" she managed.

"Marie. Sally's been missing since Tuesday. We're not sure..."

Marie listened to sobbing on the phone, her mind picturing Sally's fingers flying over her cello, demonstrating the Villa-Lobos after helping

Marie with the Bach.

"I have to call Qigiq. Where can I reach you?" Robina said.

"I, uh, don't have a phone. But I have email. Do you want to write it down? It's cello minnel at yahoo dot com. Please, tell me what's happening."

Robina's voice grew firm. "Marie. Put the package in your freezer and don't touch it anymore. Someone will contact you."

The line went dead.

Marie tried hard to lift the receiver back to its little chrome cradle, but her arm was too heavy.

~ 27 ~

The low-profile tires of Kandy's coupe carved across three lanes of concrete onto the Monte Mar exit toward Sausilito, drifting easily on the sport-tuned suspension in spite of the speedometer hovering over ninety. She braked hard, downshifted the six-speed transmission and took the sharp right onto Currey Avenue. On the passengers seat, five typewritten pages flapped softly from the swirling air created by a two-inch opening in the passenger window. The pages contained the transcript of a long chat session she had just finished with a girl named Marie Minnel. A third Amazon package had arrived, this one in New York City, which blew a huge hole in their theory that the perp was local and hand delivering the boxes.

Beneath the transcript were pictures Marie had taken with her webcam between sobs of, "I can't do this, I can't do this." Those pictures convinced Kandy that the MO in New York was identical to the two packages in San Francisco. If this wasn't the same psycho, she'd promise to drive the speed limit for the rest of her life.

She skidded up next to Qigiq's Guzzi, grabbed the transcript and jogged down the dock. The sky was clear and the water placid enough to reflect the side of his boat. She ducked to peek through a window: empty. She leapt onto the rear deck and pounded on the door.

© © ©

Qigiq was turning off the shower after using the heat to drive the aftereffects of Ferdinand's midnight beers from his head when the kitchen door started hopping like a jackhammer. He grabbed a pair of jeans hanging over a flat-backed chair and slipped them on sans underwear while hopping toward the kitchen.

The door erupted again.

He yanked it open and was about to yell at the intruder when he recognized Kandy's tan leather driving jacket. She pulled open the screen door, walked past him and tossed a folded newspaper on the kitchen table that now sported a red and white checkered cloth.

"Steal that tablecloth from Firenze's?" she asked.

His head still throbbed, but he smiled.

"No. They gave it to me."

She dropped documents on the table.

"Got coffee?"

He crossed the kitchen to his machine.

"How many?" he asked.

"Fill it up; we've got a serious new problem. But before I forget, Veronica texted Violet from a limousine, who called Robina, who let me know that Veronica is no longer a missing person."

He turned and studied at her. She had peeled off the jacket and wore a plain green sleeveless top, almost the color of money. Or an army tank. Her biceps were cut like those guys in commercials for home gym equipment. She crossed black-jeaned legs and his eyes popped open.

"No boots? Are you feeling OK?"

She wiggled the toe of a white running shoe with green webbing.

"It's Saturday. I'm relaxing."

He turned toward the coffee maker and yawned in an effort to relax, but Ferdinand's movie forced images into his consciousness. How was he going to describe it for Kandy?

"You look tired," she said to his back.

He pulled the machine apart, poured water into it.

"Not getting much sleep on this case." He hesitated. He had to tell her. "Ferdinand called me last night."

"And Robina called me this morning."

He pushed the machine together, flicked its on switch.

"Good news?" he asked, hoping against logic Sally had been found alive.

"More fingers."

He leaned against the counter to face her. The machine gurgled.

"Two," he said. "Amazon box. Today's mail. Same MO," guessing the obvious but hoping it wasn't true.

She crunched her lips and shook her head. "Almost. This box showed up in New York City."

"Ever more strange, isn't it?"

"Worse." She held her fists up with her fifth fingers extended. "The two pinky fingers were glued in the shape of the letter L."

Qigiq frowned. "How does an L play?"

118

"Don't know," she replied. "Might not be an L, could be a reference to ninety degrees."

"Or an arrowhead," he suggested.

"Or a gang's secret hand sign," she added.

"Or the hand of God touching man." He saw her face. "You know, Michelangelo."

"With pinkies?" She huffed her low chuckle.

He shrugged. "So why Robina?"

"Marie, that's the girl who got the package, called to talk to Sally. Robina guessed. Called you at home, but your line didn't answer."

"Went to see Ferdinand. Stayed most of the night."

She nodded. "So Robina called me."

"What do New York's finest think about fingers in an Amazon box?"

"Don't know...meaning, they don't know. Robina told Marie to sit tight until someone contacted her."

Qigiq pulled the coffee pot out, poured two cups.

"You really think Marie sat tight with human fingers in her fridge?"

"Freezer. Robina told her to freeze them. Yeah, she sat tight. I just finished chatting with her."

"Old friends over coffee?" He placed a tall mug with a silver eagle logo on the checkered cloth next to her papers.

"As in session on her computer. She doesn't have a telephone, but her apartment building has Wi-Fi." Kandy tapped the papers with a finger. "Transcript of our conversation."

Qigiq pushed back a chair and sat adjacent to Kandy.

"We used video, and text when she was too scared to talk."

"New York. Not a local like we thought."

"It disturbs me that the package was inside her mailbox. One of those brass swinging door numbers in a row of twenty."

"And it was locked?"

"It was locked."

"You think it went through the mail?"

Her mouth shifted toward her right ear.

"Marie says it's been cancelled." Kandy shuffled through the papers. "Sent this."

Qigiq looked at a pleasant face with big brown curls holding an Amazon box in front of her.

"Taken with her webcam," Kandy said. "I think the cancellation is fake. Ink. Squiggles. Not that hard. Little metal door with a crappy lock."

"And?"

"And someone is, or was, in New York, hand delivering a package." Her eyes rolled up and met his. "No pun."

"Traveled to New York? Big place, throw us off the trail."

"Gut feel," she said, picking up her black mug. "Possibly he's *from* New York, and came here."

"How'd he find Marie?"

Kandy sipped. "I bet we find her address on Sally's computer. Remember Ferd's spy board?"

Qigiq leaned his head back and stared at the seven-foot ceiling of his rented house boat. It felt very close.

"So our perp had access to Sally's computer."

"Right. He, *or she,* has been spying on Sally for a long time."

"Long?" Qigiq asked, one eyebrow raised.

"More than a couple of days. Weeks, months even."

"Okay, so he has her address book. Why New York?"

"It's far away. Designed to distract us."

"And brings in more cops," he said. "Maybe slow us down."

Kandy dug in her pocket and came up with a stick of gum. She unwrapped it with one hand.

"Only if we tell them."

"A package like that arrives in their jurisdiction and you're not going to tell them?" He picked up the papers and browsed the transcript.

"Have Marie ship the box back here; we're already examining the other two. Makes more sense than another lab starting from scratch."

"How about scouring Marie's apartment and mailbox for clues and prints? They could do that for us," he said.

"Or I could fly out and do it myself."

Qigiq thought about losing Kandy for days. And about Ferd's movie.

"Big distraction, perhaps what he wants us to do. Let's decide after I tell you why Ferdinand called me."

"All ears," she said, working on her coffee. "You have any donuts? Cops are supposed to have donuts."

"We're not cops. We're detectives."

"Splitting hairs," she said.

"And I'm not even that; just a visitor on sabbatical assigned to Special Operations. I'm only here because Fairbanks is paying my salary to learn super techno-sleuth techniques from the big city gal." He paused, couldn't stop a little laugh. "Baker's Dozen delivers."

She pulled a phone from the pocket of her jacket. In less than sixty seconds a dozen mixed were on the way.

"We can't eat a dozen donuts," Qigiq said. "Not healthy."

"We'll freeze them." Half-grin.

He shook his head and found a pencil stub in the pocket of his jeans. He turned the transcript over.

"Okay to write on this?"

She nodded. "Just a printout."

He drew a rectangle and a sketch of where Sally's face had been in the YouTube video. He scribbled a line across the bottom.

"Do you remember Ferdinand telling us he wanted to look at this line?" He drew a hash mark near the middle of the line. "He split it in two, then figured out how to shuffle the dots in each line, and the order of the lines themselves."

"Shuffle? Why shuffle them?"

"He was convinced that what looked like interference would mean something if he could only figure out how to put it together. He had been burning midnight oil when his computer hit on the correct method."

"That crap is data?"

Qigiq hesitated as the video fast-forwarded through his mind.

"Ferdinand is convinced," he said.

Kandy waited, watching Qigiq's eyes stare into space.

"And you're not?"

He nodded slowly. "Yes. Fully." He sat entranced, as if watching the climax of a Hitchcock movie, unable to move his mind from the images.

"What? What did he find?"

A knock at the door broke his concentration. Kandy hopped up and returned with a pink box containing thirteen donuts.

"A movie," he said.

"Was Sally in it?"

He nodded.

"Did you get a look at the him?" she asked.

He shook his head.

"Did you bring it?"

She grabbed a chocolate donut.

"No, Ferdinand played it on a computer."

She held up her phone. "This can store movies and play them back." She turned it to face him and he watched a trailer for a movie in which martial artists attacked exploding automobiles.

"Can mine do that?" he asked.

She nodded.

He handed her his phone and she navigated to the movie section. "What's Recon8776?" she asked. "It was added early today."

He bent forward and looked over her shoulder. "How did that get there?"

"You didn't do it?"

He shook his head. "Ferdinand must have while I was in his lab, knowing I would want to show it to you."

She pushed the rest of her donut in and tapped the screen. A movie began to play.

Qigiq leaned away. He wasn't prepared to see it again. Not yet.

She watched intently, her face changing not at all as the video progressed. After almost two minutes, Kandy placed Qigiq's phone gently on the table and stretched back until her entire body was in a straight line and she was sitting on the edge of the seat. She blew a long breath through tight lips like she was trying to extinguish a really big candle.

"She was alive," she said.

He didn't disagree.

"This one is twisted," she added.

He didn't move.

The fingers of her left hand opened and closed like she was limbering them up for use.

He reached into the box, placed a white frosted ring on a napkin and stared at it.

"Even admitting his extensive skill, with all due modesty of course and the fact that he was actively looking, Ferd thinks someone else is going to figure out the decoding."

"Then what?" she asked.

"He thinks the perpetrator wants it found."

She shook her head. "Then why hide it like the Enigma Code?"

The donut won.

They were silent for half a donut.

"He wants it found. But not right away," she said.

"How will we know when someone decodes it?"

"Won't. Unless they tell the world." Kandy tapped at her phone, smudging it with chocolate. "Sent Ferd an email asking how we'll know if anyone else cracks it. He'll figure something out."

Qigiq finished his coffee.

Kandy unfolded the morning Chronicle, bent forward, and glued her eyes to the front page.

~ 28 ~

Kandy read in earnest.

Qigiq crossed wood slats to refill their mugs, watching as she shuffled pages to a middle section without looking up.

Eventually she tossed the paper aside, sat back, and blew another long stream of air.

"Are our intrepid reporters doing their job this fine Saturday morning?" he asked, trying to move past the darkness of that second video and get his brain back to work.

"Someone got to Robina. There's an article here about a missing girl that *may have been raped* for stealing music. The writer suggests the culprit could be a maniac musician pissed about file sharing. The story is used as a centerpiece to talk about file sharing and the future of digital everything more than the unnamed girl. But he digs at the victim, implying a musician should know better than to steal artistic creations."

Qigiq sipped slowly, watching Kandy.

"And—" she said.

He waited.

"Somehow, they got a picture of Robina's package. They didn't have the guts to print the whole thing, they only show Sally's finger from the second knuckle to the tip. They make a big deal about the nail polish."

"We didn't release pictures."

Kandy stared into her coffee. "Robina could have taken a dozen with her cellphone before she even called us."

"And you think she gave one to the Chronicle?"

"I think she *sold* one to the Chronicle. Maybe more than one."

Qigiq frowned. "She would sell them?"

"We don't actually know much about Robina, do we? And Robina knows a whole lot about Sally."

Qigiq stared through the window at orange specks of morning sun reflecting from tiny stones in the gray siding tacked to the houseboat across the dock. He imagined Robina attacking her roommate, remembering how often sex was at the core of a homicide. *Homicide?* He thought of the sisters in Fairbanks who killed a tall fisherman, then each other; and the Eskimo wife with the Glock 17 under her anorak.

"Robina mentioned anger management," he said.

Kandy nodded. "Or maybe she founded a *Help Find Sally* fund and is using the money to get it started."

He sat down across from her. "So what does the journalist detective think?"

"Sex crime. Someone punishing this girl. Crazed artist who caught her with a bootleg. Conjecture mania."

Qigiq leaned back and folded his hands as he thought about their interpretation.

"Why make it look like a sex crime?"

"Bob McGreen likes the punishment hypothesis. Check this." She reached for the paper. *Rape is one of the most feared crimes among young women today. By recording it, I think a message is being sent to those who would violate the rights of musicians.*

"Does he always write with so little supporting evidence?" Qigiq asked.

She tapped the page with the back of her hand. "Newsprint. Op-ed page. Hype sells papers. It's our job to find the truth."

Qigiq eyed a flat square pastry with tan frosting. Reached for it.

"What do you think?"

"I think our criminal has a hard-on for something."

"Poetic."

"Not sure what though. This *Don't Steal* thing is vague. And if that's what he's really about, why harm a musician, even if she does have, what did Ferd say, fifty thousand songs?"

"And the second video," he said, waving at the screen of his phone.

"Sadistic. I can think of two reasons—plus a nut case who forgot to take his meds."

Qigiq chewed the spongy sweetness, knowing he should be having eggs, or oatmeal.

"One, he wants to scare people," he said. "Violence has been working since before fire was discovered."

"Two, he wanted to hurt Sally," she finished for him.

"But if he just wanted to hurt Sally, why make movies? He's leaving a trail for us."

She stared at the article in the paper. "Don't know. I'm missing something."

Qigiq stood. "Our problem is finding the person capable of making the second video. But that article," he paused. "More pressure, less time." He dug in the back pocket of his jeans and pulled out a crumpled sheet of paper folded in quarters.

Kandy shook her head and reached for a donut.

"What?" He smiled. "I just like to see things in one place, helps me make connections."

"Take your time," she said, "I'm still eating."

He unfolded the paper and smoothed it onto the checkered tablecloth.

"How about we make a new one?" she suggested.

He leaned toward the cabinet to his left, opened the second drawer down and came back with a sheet of blank paper and a golf pencil.

"You ever write with a real implement? You know Bic pens are nineteen cents."

"I like the way pencils sound."

She shook her head. A lock of hair drifted over her right eye.

Qigiq copied the timeline he had started earlier, and added info about Marie and Veronica and what he thought of as the *Chop* movie, because he couldn't shake the images of a hand with no fingers from his mind. He saw his note about a bicycle because of the soundtrack on the video, and another about postage cancellation, which Kandy now thought was fake.

He held the finished page up and examined it.

"A penny for your thoughts, Detective Dreeson."

Kandy rubbed her palms together. "We need a body."

His eyes widened. "Any idea where we get one?"

"If I were following hunches, I'd say you're right about a boat. The perp dumped the body in the ocean."

"Should we dredge for it?"

She frowned. "In the San Francisco Bay? The tides have her in Bali by now."

They sat listening to the dribble of the coffee maker.

"No chance it will wash up on a beach down the coast?"

She grinned. "This is real life, my friend. Anything is possible."

"But you wouldn't count on it."

"Nope."

He took a deep breath. "So still pending we have," he held up his right thumb, "DNA results from Pillar," index finger, "geometric analysis of the boat list from Ferdinand," middle finger, "examination of the boats once we have the list—"

Kandy held up the middle finger of her left hand, "And one fucking psycho-perp I want to pop."

"Kandy, Kandy. Such violence in a young woman."

She laughed. "That wasn't violence, that was comic relief." Her eyes grew dark with concentration. "Qu, we have to find him. If this isn't an isolated case..."

"Suggestions?"

"I call New York and have them send a forensics team to Marie's place. We might get lucky."

He nodded. "It'll get complicated."

"We can handle it." She grinned. "I want to go hang around that marina. It's the weekend, maybe someone will go boating."

"Did you bring your bikini?"

She smirked. "No, but I can always use a new one. I'll stop in Sausilito."

"Something besides black?" he teased.

"I'll get pink, with sketches of water lilies," she twirled her finger over the front of her jeans, drawing flowers. "So no one will recognize me."

He laughed and reached for his cup. "I'd like to talk to the intrepid reporter from the Chronicle."

"Won't say anything, protecting his sources and all. He'll claim he's entitled to his opinion, especially because we're not making official statements. He'll also be out, because it's Saturday." She took a huge bite of a double-chocolate donut. "Although you could track him down at home and really bug him," she mumbled. "Then he might write an article about how the police are harassing him instead of out catching criminals."

"You're suggesting that Mr. McGreen isn't worth the trouble?"

"I think he only knows what Robina knows."

He sipped cold coffee and eyed the pot on the counter five steps away.

"No one in Sally's apartment heard anything on Tuesday?" he asked.

"Nope," she said.

"There are too many boats to visit individually unless we shorten the list. I got some pictures."

She nodded.

He tapped his left fingers with the index finger of his right hand. "No way to trace *The Chopper?*"

"Nope."

"Nothing I can do right now?"

"There's one thing," she said.

He slid his chair back and rose slowly. Once to the counter he filled his mug and turned to Kandy and held up the pot.

She shook her head.

"That would be?" he asked.

"I think our guy is a show-off, posting videos, making his actions widely known."

"No argument."

"Find out everything you can about F112358. Keep an eye on the posts to YouTube to see who shows up to comment on the rape video. Monday, let's ask Ferd how he can image search for that video he constructed. Maybe he can match frames and find out if anyone else has done what he did. And if so, what they're doing about it."

He pointed at his chest. "You want Mr. Technically Challenged to monitor the Internet?"

"In a nutshell," she smiled. "Besides, that's why you came to California right? To understand how criminals are using technology to commit crimes that weren't even possible ten years ago."

"Wouldn't we be more effective if I hung out at the marina and you watched the Internet?" he asked.

"How do you look in a bikini?"

~ 29 ~

A black Mercedes convertible turned off Marina Boulevard and cruised along the approach road twenty over the posted fifteen mph limit. It sliced into the second handicap spot at the end of the lot, closest to the boats. Eddy Blake reached into its glove box, pulled out a blue handicap card and hooked it over the rearview mirror post.

"Well, my dear sweet bitch wife, at least your mother is good for something."

He popped the door open with one finger and slid across two-tone leather. His marine Rolex read quarter past twelve, which didn't leave much time to prepare the boat before Alicia showed up. The thought of her slender body and the things she could make it do made his loins ached as he prayed she wouldn't flake out. She wasn't controllable like most women. He glanced up at the summer sun, hoping the fog wouldn't roll in. Alicia hated cold and gray—ruined her mood.

Which wrecked everything.

He pressed his key fob and the trunk lifted silently. He grabbed a blue bag with Yale stenciled across the side and pushed the trunk closed. Still wearing the light gray pinstripe suit he had worn to breakfast with Terry to talk about Platter's finances, off the record as usual, he strolled out the dock toward *Delicious.* Karen was on her belly in a red bikini sunning herself beside a tight-bodied babe Eddy had never seen.

"Hello, Karen. Hogging the sunshine again?"

She turned her head to face Eddy and lifted an arm to wave.

"Going fishing?"

No, if he was lucky he was going muff diving.

"Sure am. They don't bite so well midday, but work comes first." He shrugged.

She closed her eyes and spoke to the air. "A guy like you, why do you bother to work?"

Because my soon to be ex-wife is raping me to get rid of her; and keeping up the payments on all this shit with Silver Platter fading to a puddle of red ink is like tap dancing on a rolling log.

"I love it. Wouldn't want to stop." He flashed his all-purpose smile, and glanced past Karen's round ass to see if Alicia's orange 4x4 had pulled in the lot. He didn't see it so he walked up the dock beside *Delicious,* put one black-soled street shoe on the boat's white gunwale and leaned an elbow on his knee.

"So Karen, who's the new addition to your tanning club?"

Without shifting her body or opening her eyes Karen answered, "Kandy, this is Eddy. He goes fishing on *With a Bullet* over there. For some reason, he knows a lot of girls who like to fish, don't ya Eddy?"

Eddy guffawed like an engine trying to start before saying, "My pleasure."

"Nice to meet you," Kandy said, imitating Karen's belly down stillness, and not bothering to turn to face him.

"I don't mean to be rude," Eddy said. "But you look strong, like you're a yoga instructor or something."

"Or something," Kandy said.

Karen laughed through her nose.

"I don't know, a girl named Kandy in a pink bikini with little white dots—"

"Good enough to eat, Eddy?" Kandy asked.

Eddy was quiet for about two seconds, then his guffaw returned.

"I bet you've heard that a hundred times."

"Nope. Never," Kandy said.

"Do you like to fish?" Eddy asked.

Karen laughed through her nose again.

"For what?" Kandy said.

Eddy grinned, though both girls had their eyes closed.

"Is your boat fast?" Kandy asked, not waiting for an answer to her first question.

"Oh yeah, over six hundred horse power. Twin screws," he said, leaning on the last word.

"Eddy's a master of metaphor," Karen said without moving.

Kandy rolled over and sat up, her arms around her lifted knees. Her eyes swept over his body like a warm breeze.

He smiled.

"A boat could take a real pounding with that kind of power," Kandy said.

Eddy took his foot off the rail and stood tall.

"Not if you know how to handle it." He lifted his empty hand like he was holding the wheel of *With a Bullet*. "Takes finesse and a *slow* hand, as Mr. Clapton would say."

Kandy wrinkled her forehead. "Is Eric a fisherman?"

Eddy shook his head and held his laugh.

"If you want to go for a ride sometime, pink would look great on the foredeck."

"Sometime..." She let her voice drift off as she lowered her back to the deck to let the sun soak the front of her bikini.

Eddy whistled softly. He was about to speak when his eyes caught sight of an orange truck. He hated that color, way too gaudy. He was a black or silver man himself. But its high visibility served him well.

"G'day ladies," he said, in a terrible imitation of an Australian accent. "Hope you decide to go for that ride, Kandy."

"Thanks for the sweet invitation, Eddy," she said, without opening her eyes.

Eddy ducked low and heel-toed down the dock. When he was well past the stern of *Delicious* he stood and headed toward *Bullet* without looking back. He was below deck and changing into blue surfer shorts with yellow dragons stitched into the material, his suit hanging in a small closet like airlines have for their first class customers, when he heard a knock on the gunwale.

He finished stepping into the long shorts and grabbed a sleeveless white T-shirt that Alicia liked because it showed off his biceps: the last muscle on his body that hadn't gone soft since his days as an also-ran athlete. He put on a broad smile and climbed the three-step ladder to the rear deck.

His smile collapsed. It wasn't Alicia; it was a muscle-bound kid.

"Hello, Mr. Blake. I'm Bob. I work here at the marina."

Eddy remembered. One of the college kids hired to keep the boats clean so owners, like him, never had to lift a mop. It was a good setup.

"Hi, Bob," Eddy said, his eyes scanning for Alicia. "What can I do for you?"

"Well, Mr. Blake. This isn't my business, I'm just hired help, working my way through school so I can coach full time."

Eddy was still holding the white shirt in his hand, and noticed gray in the bushy hair on his chest above where his belly pushed against the front of his blue shorts. He felt old facing this young stud, and was suddenly worried that he would lose Alicia. Maybe he should start working out.

"You getting an education degree?" Eddy asked.

The blond-haired, blue-eyed Apollo looked up in surprise.

"Uh, yes." He nodded. "I want to teach mathematics and coach wrestling."

Eddy patted his stomach. "I had better do some training before we hit the mat."

Bob stood on the dock, looking up. "Did you wrestle, Mr. Blake?"

"Long time ago. High school back in Pennsylvania." He paused, remembering the sweat during a match. "Never won State. Then a bit in college."

Bob's head was bobbing like Blake told him he had just won the lottery.

"Lots of competition in wrestling," he said. "What a great sport."

"But you came to tell me something," Blake said, pushing the conversation back on track. He still didn't see Alicia.

"Uh, yeah. I understand you owners here lead very private lives. And this is none of my business, like I said."

Eddy watched him closely, but said nothing.

Bob licked his lips. "It's just that, well, someone came by yesterday and I thought maybe you'd like to know; since *With a Bullet* is your boat, I mean."

Eddy frowned. He didn't like people surprising him.

His peripheral vision caught movement and he glanced over Bob's shoulder. Alicia had just stepped onto the dock from the parking lot. Eddy's heart thumped harder.

Bob turned to look over his shoulder, following Eddy's gaze.

"Wow," Bob said. "Who's that?"

"A friend of mine," Eddy said. "We're going fishing."

Bob laughed. "Some friend."

Alicia was wearing a leopard-print bikini that he hoped had a thong bottom, though he couldn't see from this angle, black heels with straps that encircled her leg, and a light blue sheer top waving in the wind. She moved like a big cat, calm and arrogant, as she glided across the concrete dock towards his boat.

Eddy said, "Who was this person who came by?"

"Don't remember his name, but he said he was a detective. I figured a detective asking questions about your boat might be something you'd want to know about."

Eddy slipped his shirt over his head to gain a moment to think. A detective anywhere near his life could only mean something bad. He stepped over the gunwale onto the dock and positioned himself where he could face the kid and still keep an eye on Alicia. The concrete was hot under his bare feet.

"What did he want to know about my boat?"

"He asked me about the name."

Eddy tried not to frown. Why would a detective care about the name of his boat?

"What did you tell him?"

"I told him I thought it had something to do with music and sent him to Karen, who happened to be topless on *Delicious*."

Eddy nodded. He saw Karen often, made sense she was there.

"He ask anything else?"

"Yeah. Wanted to know how the marina ran. You know, stuff like how often people take the boats out."

"What did you tell him?" Eddy asked. Alicia was swinging her fine ass near *Delicious*. He wondered if one of the girls had spoken to her, because she turned to walk up beside them.

"I said it was all over the place. Some people went out a couple times a week, and some only go out once a month. Hell, some of these boats, I don't think they ever go out. They're just party palaces on the weekends."

Eddy wondered what the hell Alicia was talking with Karen and Kandy about. All he needed was hassle from her interfering with his plans for the day.

"What did you say about *Bullet?*"

Bob hesitated. Eddy met his eyes. Bob looked down.

"Well, I'm not sure. I might have told him that your boat goes out regularly and that we clean it sometimes a couple of times in a week. Because of the fish blood and all."

"Is that all?"

Bob nodded.

Alicia had started to move again. How he loved to watch her walk.

"The guy say anything else? Did he ask about me?"

Bob's big neck shook his head. "No, never asked about you by name. Only wondered about the owner of the boat."

"Wait a second, Bob," Eddy said. He put one hand on the gunwale and leapt over, catching his toe on the rail and almost landing face first on the rear deck. He hobbled toward the hatch, favoring the stubbed toe. He went below and dug around until he found his black calf-skin wallet. He flipped it open and thought about what the information was worth. Then he thought about what it was worth for the kid to keep his eyes open and report to him.

Back on deck he leaned over the rail and held out his hand to shake.

"Thanks for telling me about the detective. I'd appreciate your keeping an eye on *Bullet*, let me know if anyone else comes around asking questions."

Bob shook hands with the firm grip of a young man accustomed to being physical. Eddy saw his eyes shift when he felt the bills in Eddy's palm. But he didn't hesitate.

"Sure will, Mr. Blake. Glad to."

As the young man walked away, Eddy watched him slip his right hand into the pocket of his shorts and whistle what sounded like *Sunshine of Your Love*, but that song was old before the kid was out of diapers. To Bob's credit, he never looked down to see that his hand held a pair of hundred dollar bills: cheap insurance in Eddy's book.

Eddy saw Alicia's eyes scan the kid's muscles like a laser, and watched as the kid couldn't resist the opportunity to twist his big neck around and ogle Alicia's rear as he passed. He saw Eddy watching him, waved, and jogged away. Eddy didn't much care if the kid looked, he was just jealous he wasn't getting that view.

Her heels tapped concrete. Eddy waited. He had thought he would be tired of her beauty after a few months, like all the rest, but the thrill of just looking at her hadn't waned a single drop. He wanted her full-time. But the hip-hop boyfriend she wouldn't leave because they were some kind of stupid soulmates was in the way.

He watched Alicia's smooth dark features broaden into a smile as she approached *With a Bullet*.

"Hello, Eddy. Isn't sunshine wonderful?"

The sound of her voice softened his knees. Something about the way Asian chicks rounded the English language made him go gaga like the high school jock he had been. A stupid and dangerous reaction for a CEO, he reminded himself.

"Just fantastic, Ally. I can't wait to watch it glisten off your wet skin."

She smiled. "Oh, Eddy. Is that all you ever think about?"

He reached his hand over the rail to help her step through the opening in the side of the boat that he should have used instead of jamming his toe on the rail.

"It's all your beauty lets me think about," he said.

She tipped her head right and he would have sworn her eyes shimmered like those fake stars in actor's eyes from special effects computers.

"Did you see that girl with Karen?" Alicia asked.

Play dumb or be honest. He made an executive decision.

"Met her briefly. Do you know her?"

"I wish," she gushed. "Her body is so hard. She must be into something tough, like Taekwondo or ballet."

Eddy huffed through his nose trying not to laugh. Ballet?

"You think?"

"Oh yeah. It's really hard to do that at the gym." She tossed her shirt down the hatch and rotated to show him the bikini top, her brown body golden in the sun. "I know, I've tried for years."

He held out his hand for her. "You look better than she does any day."

"That's only because you have a fetish for the Asian half of my flesh, Eddy. She's much stronger than I am."

"Strong isn't everything." He pulled her towards him, but she spun away.

"Now now, big guy. At sea you said."

Yes, he had said that because he didn't want Helen's photographers catching him. He was getting sloppy.

"God she is so sexy," Alicia said. "I would love to touch her."

This was a line of reasoning he couldn't compete with.

"When do you have to be back?" he asked. "I've got all day, but I know your Saturdays are a little tight."

She frowned. "You know dancers live a disciplined life. Every morsel I eat, every step I take, is to make me better. Except Saturday. That's when I relax. Are you going to criticize me again because I like to party to fuel my psyche?"

He shook his head. No, he wanted to fuck her brains out. And to do that, she had to be in the right mood.

"No way, Ally. I was just trying to be sensitive to your schedule."

She laughed, a gentle wispy sound that grew louder the longer she did it. She turned away from him, faced *Delicious,* and reached into the boat's glove compartment. She pulled out a pair of black-framed sunglasses with gold trim on the temples; their sharp rectangles made her already perfect features appear slimmer.

"What a body," she said. "Do you have binoculars on *Bullet,* honey?"

He ducked below and flipped open a narrow oak door while seeing her body in his mind. On the second shelf he found a vinyl case that should have held his field glasses, but it was empty. He couldn't remember using them; but then, he drank a lot while boating and didn't always remember docking the boat. He knelt, reached into the compartment and dragged his tool box to the door. It was dark inside the narrow compartment, so he flipped the latch by feel and tipped the lid of the plastic box to the right. He squinted, reached in and fumbled around. He found a hammer handle, a flare gun...

"Shit!"

He yanked his hand away from piercing pain. The middle finger of his left hand was bleeding. He shook it a couple of times; droplets of blood flew. He grabbed the tool chest and dragged it out of the compartment, realizing he should have done that in the first place if he hadn't been thinking about Ally's ass.

The culprit stared at him; the serrated knife he used for beheading fish was lying in the tool chest with its sharp edge up. Damn, he had to cut back on the booze. He found the first-aid kit and dug out the largest Band-Aid he could find.

"Yoo-hoo, Eddy. Where are my bin-oc-u-lars?"

He looked into the tool chest, then tossed the kit in and pushed the box into the compartment with his toe. No glasses.

He yelled up the companionway, "Can't find them. They're not in the case."

He checked the second shelf but found only spare towels shoved in the back. The one above that was full of CDs he used to put girls in the mood.

Included were a couple of porn DVDs he liked to watch to get things started, or when he failed to persuade a woman to go boating and went out alone to feel the power of the ocean...and get away from Helen's complaining that he never paid attention to her.

He slammed the closet door shut and rotated one-eighty to check the storage on the starboard side. As he turned toward the stern, hoping to catch a glimpse of Ally, he saw that she was holding something to her face with both hands.

He worked his way up the ladder, holding his throbbing left finger inside his right hand. On deck, it became clear she was staring through the 8x40 waterproof, fog-resistant sport binoculars he used to watch sailboat races, and scan for the Fish and Wildlife cops when he was over the limit.

"You found them?" he asked.

"No," she said. "A tall black man with a French accent and a fleur-de-lis tattoo came by and offered to sell them to me for ten dollars. I figured that was a good deal and we could use a new pair, even though they were likely hot. I mean, since you couldn't find yours."

He shook his head. "Where were they?"

"Probably where you left them." She spun her left hand behind her and pointed to the glove box on the port side of the boat's dash.

He thought back, but couldn't remember tossing them there. It would be odd that he wouldn't put them back in the case; he hated scratched lenses more than stubbly pussy hair.

"You really like her?" Eddy asked, trying to hide his concern over her obvious thrill.

"Oh, I don't know if I like *her;* but I sure like looking."

He stood away so he wouldn't touch her, forcing himself to think of Helen and a lawyer in a courtroom showing photos of him and Alicia embracing on his yacht. It shouldn't matter according to the law. But the law was interpreted by judges: mere humans whose decisions would very much depend on what they thought about the matter at hand. Besides, he was fifteen minutes from bliss; he could be that patient.

"What did you talk about?" he asked.

"Men," she said.

He elevated his eyebrows, but she was looking through the glasses ignoring him.

"Any brilliant insight?" he asked, trying to keep it light.

"Karen says they're wusses, ruled by the needs of their bodies."

Eddy thought about the needs of his body and lowered his eyes to the back of Alicia's bikini, following the leopard string down from her lower back until it disappeared between her cheeks.

"Me, I think they're toys," she said. "They add huge fun to life so long as you don't get attached. Because like most toys, they break." She paused. "They can also be pretty money trees in my back yard." The binoculars shook as she laughed.

Eddy drew a mental line connecting wuss and toy. He thought he preferred toy.

Alicia ran the tip of her tongue counterclockwise around her lips.

Eddy's eyes flashed between her backside and her mouth. Without losing visual focus he reached over with his right hand and flipped on the blowers to clear the bilge of fumes.

"What did K——," he caught himself, "—aren's friend have to say."

"Oh, Kandy? Can you believe that name? I would *so* like to taste her."

Eddy swallowed hard.

"She said that men are challenging."

He liked that the best so far.

"Did she say why?" he asked, as casually as he could.

"Yeah," Alicia said, still studying *Delicious*.

Eddy waited.

Alicia lowered the binoculars and handed them to Eddy. She walked aft and sat on the big white cushion padding the twin V8s that produced the 600 hp he had told Kandy about. She crossed her legs and started unbuckling a high heel.

"She said men have two features. That's funny, features, like on a car...or a cellphone."

Eddy listened carefully. Maybe Kandy was about to give him something he could work with to get her in bed. Now there was a wrestling match he would welcome. He said: "Yeah, funny."

She studied him over her sunglasses. "First, they don't know what they want. So after they expend all their energy getting it, they're not satisfied."

Eddy thought of expending energy on Alicia's body, but an image of Kandy's forced its way in. Either way, he thought it would be quite satisfying.

She dropped one slinky black shoe on the deck. Eddy stepped forward to pick it up.

"And second," she said, while he was down on one knee retrieving the shoe because he knew this was the beginning of the game she liked to play before taking him for a ride on heaven's chariot. "They lie to get what they want."

"I would never lie to you, Ally. You know I just want to be with you."

"You just want to fuck me, you mean."

"That's only part of it."

"Which part, Eddy? The front half, or the back half?" She laughed her wispy sound.

"I can't help it you're so beautiful you make me blind."

She smiled. "Okay, Eddy, this is a test. Would you like to do Kandy?"

He swallowed, and coughed a little into his left hand, her shoe dangling from his right. He thought about starting the engines to buy time.

"Hurry up, Eddy, or I'll think you're lying to me." She almost sang the words.

"If I didn't have you, Ally, yes I would like to do Kandy."

Her mouth opened in a wide smile.

"Well Eddy Blake, I believe for once you have spoken the truth. Let's start those big thumping steel pistons you have down there." She slapped the pad she was sitting on.

He smiled and turned the key to ignite the port engine. He waited until it was idling at 800 rpm before starting the starboard engine. The underwater exhausts rumbled and vibrations from the engines tuned by the Ski and Speed Racing Shop resonated through the entire boat. He turned around. Ally was sitting over the corner of the engine compartment, her legs wrapped around it horseback riding style, her head back, body swaying like she was dancing to an invisible rock band.

Eddy moved to the foredeck, tossed off dock lines, and returned to the cockpit to ease the transmission into reverse. He knew what was coming next, and wanted to be anchored far away from any form of interruption when it hit.

~ 30 ~

Qigiq sat under a blue umbrella at a metal table on a concrete slab jutting out of the Appathal building being used for outdoor seating at the Blue Water Café—staying close in case Kandy needed back up. The South Beach Marina was directly across the street. He saw *With a Bullet* back out of its slip with two people aboard, a hairy guy in surfer shorts who had probably never touched a board, and a tall lean Asian girl who looked like the dancers he saw when Kandy dragged him to the San Francisco ballet because she thought it would help him understand the city. He was watching them leave, the girl sitting on the engine compartment, the guy piloting the slender craft that had the profile of something fast, when he heard the waiter clear his throat.

Qigiq lowered the ancient Leica field glasses he used to watch motorcycle races and looked up at the thin young man. He wore all black: shoes, socks, tight pants, tight shirt. Except for his glasses. They had a brilliant metallic-blue frame. He spoke softly.

"Excuse me." He looked over his shoulder toward a man at the bar in a brown three-piece suit. "I'm sorry to interrupt. But the owner is, um, he's, well, he would like to know what you're doing."

"Send him over, I'll be happy to fill him in," Qigiq said.

"Well, uh, Sir. He asked me to find out for him."

"Do you know what he's concerned about..." Qigiq leaned closer to the young man's shirt, "David?"

David stood tall. "This is an upright establishment, Sir. He just doesn't want anything fishy going on."

Qigiq smiled. "You mean like, boys picking up boys, or the drug exchange that took place about five minutes ago in the far corner," he pointed with his left thumb. "Or maybe that some of these boys maybe aren't really over twenty-one, but are here drinking anyway? That kind of fishy?"

David put his weight on one foot and then the other, like he wanted to dance but couldn't find the beat.

"Uh, well, I don't know about those things. He's more concerned that, well, perhaps you're violating someone's privacy."

"You mean with these?" Qigiq asked, tilting the glasses in his right hand.

The young man nodded.

"David," Qigiq began. "There's a marina across the street, and in the first row of slips is a boat that cost more than you and I make in a couple of years."

David smiled. "There's lots of money in The City. I just don't have it."

"And on that boat are two women lying in the afternoon sun wearing less material than is in your napkins."

David held his smile. "So, you're watching girls?" he said softly, like he had caught Qigiq in a secret lie.

"Not girls, David. *A girl.*"

He handed the binoculars to David and gestured toward the marina.

David swiveled his head around and the guy in the suit nodded. He lifted the glasses to his eyes and swept them back and forth. He stopped.

"Do you mean *Delicious?*" he asked.

Qigiq hid his surprise that David knew the boat by name.

"That's the one."

"Wow, who is that in the pink? Pink's not my color, but for her..."

"That's the woman I'm watching."

"I can't blame you, but the owner, he—"

"You mean the guy who didn't have the guts to walk over here and talk to me? That owner? Let's ignore him for a moment."

"I'd better not—"

"How do you know *Delicious?*" Qigiq asked.

David smiled. "Everyone knows that boat. The owner, Mr. McTyme, comes in here a lot. Throws money around."

"He likes your food?" Qigiq asked.

David paused. "I don't really know what he likes. But he comes in to drink on occasion and buys for the whole bar. He always has a girl on his boat."

"Do you know how he comes by his money?"

David scoffed. "He's one of those Internet-bubble babies down in Silicon Valley that made a bundle of dollars from vapor products. You know how that works. They start a company and sell it before the stock market figures out it's bogus."

Qigiq nodded and took notes on a slip of paper.

"So he has money, drinks here and likes girls."

"Just one girl at a time. Right now that red bikini is on the deck almost every day. He's, um, the jealous type."

"And right now, my partner is with his girl," Qigiq said.

David took a half-step back, but said nothing.

"While I've been watching, a burly guy stopped by and talked to them, and then a young Asian woman who looks like a dancer. I'd sure like to know what they talked about."

"Your partner?" David echoed.

Qigiq nodded. "And I'd like to know what she's doing on *Delicious* with a girl in a red bikini that I've never met."

David took another half step away from the table.

"So, this is, uh, personal?" David asked.

"Oh yes. Quite personal. Can you tell me anything about Miss Red Bikini down there?"

David nodded. "She comes in with Mr. McTyme sometimes. She's—"

David stopped and stared at Qigiq.

Qigiq guessed he was wondering how to describe what he needed to say to a 30-something guy who would sit in a restaurant and spy on his woman.

"Do you know Joan Jett?" David asked.

Qigiq ran the name through his brain. Nothing. He shook his head.

"She paved the way for women in rock-and-roll. I love her music. The stuff she does with the Blackhearts."

"Sounds like a nice person," Qigiq said, adding a smile because he wanted information.

"Oh, she's the best. Has this great tatt—" He stopped and seemed to push a reset button inside his head. "I mean, she's a great rock singer, and did this album called Sinner and on it she has a song called ACDC, just like that, four capital letters in a row." He pointed to the air with his index finger and tapped four times like a hammer flying in an antique typewriter.

"A C D C," Qigiq repeated.

David smiled. "Yeah, like that."

Qigiq nodded and hoped he was getting the drift of the conversation.

"So I had better keep my eye on that pink bikini?"

It was David's turn to nod. "Oh yeah. With the red one? Oh yeah, yeah. Or it might come off." David smiled. His teeth stood in perfect rows.

"Will you talk to the owner for me?" Qigiq asked. "I'll only be here a few more minutes."

"Sure. I'll let you know if there's a problem."

David turned and headed straight to the bar. Qigiq watched them chat, David gesturing wildly and the owner sneaking looks at Qigiq. Eventually the head above the three-piece suit nodded and they both lost interest in Qigiq and his binoculars.

Qigiq opened the browser on his cellphone to the YouTube page of the rape video where he had been reading comments. The most recent post was now four hours old. He played the video with the sound off looking for clues.

His phone played two bars of Number 4 in C-sharp minor from Bach's *Well-Tempered Clavier*. Kandy had shown him just this morning how to attach a custom ring tone to a particular caller. He checked the phone.

"Hello Captain, Qigiq here."

"How are you today?" Jasik said.

Qigiq concentrated, knowing that a captain in homicide did not spend his Saturday calling detectives to ask about their health.

"Finishing a late lunch. What can I do for you?"

"Have you seen today's Chronicle?"

Qigiq let his eyes drift back to the marina. Without the Leica's he couldn't make out Karen and Kandy very well, but he could tell they were still there.

"Detective Dreeson and I reviewed the article this morning."

"And?"

"It appears that McGreen talked to the missing girl's roommate."

"Where did he get the picture?" Jasik asked.

"We're not sure, Captain. I wanted to talk to McGreen, but Kandy advised that we wait until Monday rather than trouble him over the weekend."

"Thoughtful, but he's making us look bad," Jasik said.

"Do you think so, Sir?" Qigiq asked.

"As much as called us bumbling fools."

"But if we look at the knowns, all we have is a missing girl, a frantic roommate and three packages with no DNA analysis."

"We don't know if they're hers? I thought that was verified."

"Only based on purple nail polish, Captain, and the opinion of the roommate. The thumb had a callus that cellists get, and the missing girl is a cellist." Qigiq heard himself use the present tense. He was still hoping. "We won't have DNA results until Monday, but we're proceeding on the assumption that the fingers belong to Bellowi. And I should mention that McGreen has implicitly buried Ms. Bellowi, when there isn't evidence to confirm her death."

"What about this video he mentions? The guy filmed himself raping her."

"Ferdinand is handling the analysis, Captain. All it shows is Bellowi's face, as identified by her roommate. We haven't been able to reach her parents. They don't return phone calls placed to their last known address in New Hampshire."

Qigiq listened to seconds of silence.

"Do you think she's alive?"

He saw the mutilation video in his mind.

"I'm hoping. We feel it's best to operate on that assumption until we learn otherwise."

"Motive?"

The one word question stung. He had been thinking about it for almost three days, and was still coming up empty.

"The obvious, rape, and destruction of the evidence. But the *Don't Steal Music* stickers make no sense. However, mutilation of her hand suggests a hate crime. She was apparently bi-sexual, so gay bashing is a possibility."

Another silence. Qigiq stole a glance at the owner, who was ignoring him, and turned to check on Kandy.

"So McGreen has it all wrong?"

"Opinion is running ahead of evidence, Captain. This could be a murder. It could even be one of many. We only know she was last seen on Tuesday morning." He paused. "And we have no body, or DNA connection."

Qigiq listened to the Captain inhale and sigh three times.

"What can I do to help?"

"Rush the DNA. And he would never ask this, but the more Ferdinand is free to concentrate on this case, the better for Dreeson and me."

"I'll see what I can do," Jasik said. "If you need anything, call me. And keep me informed; the city is going to run crazy with McGreen implying we have a serial killer."

"Even though we don't have the first body?" Qigiq asked politely.

"Yeah. Not like this in Alaska?"

"We have newspapers in Alaska. They don't always spell correctly either."

"This could be politics. If it turns out to be someone wanting a new police commissioner..." He didn't finish.

One more reason he'd come to San Francisco—to learn from a city that had existed for over two hundred years.

"We don't need to sell papers." Qigiq hesitated because he was far from expert, but knew something deeper was changing. The electronically connected world was different; information flowed so fast it actually became part of the story. And accuracy was not always a priority.

"Good point, Qigiq. Maybe I'll go see McGreen myself. Let's speak Monday. Enjoy your weekend."

Qigiq ended the call with a touch on the flat glass of his new phone and wondered what Jasik would say to McGreen, and vice versa, wishing he could be there to eavesdrop.

He picked up his binoculars and found Karen and Kandy both on their backs, but otherwise unchanged. He wondered what lying on a fiberglass deck must feel like with a bikini for padding. A little shift registered in his peripheral vision that wasn't blocked by the eyepiece

He looked down and saw a posting one minute old from someone called mitmiss. He scanned the message and froze when he read: We fed this video into our learning noise reduction system and it stripped the last line off and to our amazement reconstructed a very unusual movie from the stripped information. In the interest of research, we are presently hosting the reconstruction at www.noiselab.mit.edu along with a paper describing the method used by our software. The result is quite surprising. We assume that the creator of this clip inserted the noise algorithmically and intended for someone to reconstruct it. If F112358 would please let us know if our reconstruction is correct, we would be grateful...

There was no mention of the content of the video, though what Ferdinand had shown him would qualify as *quite surprising*. He touched the noiselab link. A window opened welcoming him to *Noise Lab—Where Reduction is a Science*. He read down the list of *Recent News* until he found a reference to YouTube F112358 post. He pulled out his slip of paper and scribbled a note to remind him to look up that Fibo-number. He clicked the link and was taken to a page of mathematics explaining how the movie had been reconstructed. Off to the right was a small frame, less than half the size of what Ferdinand had shown him.

He clicked play.

It took only seconds to convince him the MIT lab had indeed hit upon the same arcane method Ferdinand had found. Sally, her hand, the knife.

He closed the page and stared at the mitmiss posting on YouTube. The rush of guilt and anger he had felt the first time he saw the video of Sally being mutilated returned in full force. He pressed both eyes shut and breathed deeply through his nose for a full minute.

He lifted his binoculars, and dialed Kandy's cell.

He couldn't see it, but he knew a phone was vibrating on the pink bikini string around her waist. As he watched, her right hand lifted off the deck and drifted toward her hip. He heard the connection complete.

She said nothing, but he could hear her breathing. Her right hand moved slowly to the ear opposite Karen. She made an adjustment.

"Hi Kandy, Qigiq."

She said nothing, and didn't move.

"If you can hear me, touch your nose."

He watched through the glasses as she moved her right hand to her nose and scratched an itch she didn't have.

"We have a new problem."

His phone beeped. He took it away from his ear and stared at it. He put it back to his ear.

"Kandy. Ferdinand is calling me. I'll be right back."

He switched calls with a single touch.

"Hello, Qigiq. Yes, before you ask, I am working on Saturday. We must move quickly to stop this fool who is hurting the young women. There is no time to waste."

"I'm with you, Ferdinand."

"I called to tell you I have eight boats that match my model of radar motion. Five are in the marina in San Francisco where you met the girl in red. Now why didn't you send her picture? You detectives keep all the fun for yourselves. Here are the names."

Qigiq grabbed a pencil.

"Firebird, Pimp Squeak, With a Bullet, Master Plan, Barefoot, Delicious, CanCan and Later Gator. These match with ninety-five percent confidence. I recommend we start with Firebird. Don't bother to remember this, I have emailed a report with movies of the original motion overlaid by the geometry of each boat."

Qigiq stopped writing.

"Thanks." He closed his eyes and images of Sally's one-ear face flashed behind them. "Ferdinand, we have a new development."

"Yes?" he said softly.

"There's been a new posting on YouTube."

"There has? And you must tell me? I should be telling you."

Qigiq heard keys clicking in the background.

"MIT is a fine university. Although, NYU of course has much to offer."

"They have the reconstruction you showed me," Qigiq said.

"Actually, no. They are only part way through the analysis, which is why their movie is so small. Perhaps I will help them."

Qigiq rolled both lips between his teeth.

"Do you think we should do that?" he asked.

"Why not?" Ferdinand said. "They might have figured out something that I missed. This is unlikely, but still there is a chance they could help us."

"But they'll post what they know to the Internet," Qigiq said.

"This is true, unless perhaps we ask them not to because there is an ongoing murder investigation."

"We don't have a murder."

"But if we imply that we do, they are more likely to cooperate."

Qigiq shifted in the wooden chair he had occupied for the better part of two hours and moved his phone to his right ear, noting that the connection to Kandy was still in place.

"Whatever you decide, Ferdinand. Thanks for the names. I'll start working them right away."

"Please be careful. One of these boats may be the crime scene and I would hate for you to pollute it before forensics arrives."

"I'll sterilize my feet and board barefoot."

"Ah, you jest. But our killer has left a trail. We must find it."

Qigiq switched back to his call to Kandy and listened to her breathing.

"Sorry, Kandy. It was Ferdinand with the names of the boats that fit his math. He has eight for us."

His field glasses revealed her head bobbing up and down in slow motion.

"Five are in this marina. Including the boat you're on."

She rotated her head, her right cheek flat on the deck so she was facing him. She mouthed "OK," in his direction.

"*With a Bullet* left twelve minutes ago. The two people you talked to were the only ones I saw board."

She nodded slightly, scratching her temple on the deck.

"Something new. MIT reconstructed the YouTube video. Same result as Ferdinand's, well, almost. They posted a notice to YouTube, and linked to their university website."

He saw her lithe body tighten, like she was chilled. She reached her arms overhead and yawned.

He said, "Thousands of people are going to see that video. And

McGreen might be one of them."

He watched Kandy turn to Karen and ask where the restrooms were. Karen pointed without opening her eyes and Qigiq heard her voice in the background.

Kandy hopped off the boat and padded down the dock barefoot. When she was inside the bathhouse she said, "Is the poster our perp?"

"You mean someone at MIT?"

"It fits. The guy chops Sally, posts a video to YouTube to attract attention to how great he is. Then he mysteriously decodes the noise thing and looks like a hero."

"Ferdinand was considering helping them. Thought maybe they found something he missed."

"Better stop him. We don't know anything about the poster. Could be our man."

"*Miss* MIT?" he said.

"Or woman."

He heard water trickle in the background.

"I'll call him back," Qigiq said.

"Hold a sec."

Qigiq waited. Heard a rushing sound.

"OK, back. I sent an email asking him to wait before contacting Miss Mit." She pronounced it like a baseball glove. "You sure this website is really at the Massachusetts Institute of Technology?"

"That's above my pay grade. I saw mit.edu. Isn't that the school?"

"Maybe. Have Ferd check. Boston isn't all that far from New York."

The brutality of the crime had made him think male. "A woman raping a woman?" he asked, his voice not as steady as usual.

"Check the stats," she said. "Sexual violence between women happens all the time. Keep an open mind."

Qigiq's intuition didn't scream female, but it had been built in Alaska, in the snow, on permafrost.

An urge rifled through him.

"Is there any way to impound all eight boats?"

"Impound? You mean like take them downtown and lock them up?" She laughed.

"I want to see if Ferdinand can match the deck surfaces to the first video." He paused. "And maybe even the second."

"We could have forensics go over them as crime scenes. But that'll take days and cost a fortune."

"The owner of *Delicious* likes to change girlfriends," Qigiq said.

"Kandy laughed. "We can't impound a guy's boat because he likes girls.

Have to grab the whole marina."

"We have the radar match."

"But there are eight. You think the same thing I do. One of those eight is our crime scene. Let's narrow it down."

He tapped a finger against the binoculars as he watched Karen on the deck. She hadn't moved.

"Check out the owners?" he suggested.

"Seems like our best shot. We find something, we can get a court order to declare the boat a crime scene."

He looked at the list of boat names he had scribbled before Ferdinand told him about the email.

"We'll have to get the registrations. But we know *Firebird* belongs to Walters via our friend Karen. We need to go see him anyway."

"He hasn't returned my calls," Kandy said. "Probably thinks I'm a student."

"He thinks you worship him," Qigiq said. "Afraid to be alone with you, sexual harassment cases being what they are."

"Clever. What about New York?"

He saw Karen walk along the deck towards the stern.

"Wait. What do we do about our friend Karen?"

"She couldn't tell me much about McTyme's investment business, other than it keeps him away too much for her needs," Kandy said.

"Think she saw anything at the marina?"

Karen jumped into the cockpit and ducked behind the windshield.

"Nothing so far," she said. "If anything even happened at the marina. No one would pull a noisy job with people around. Beyond insane."

"Unless…"

"Unless he wants to be caught? Get famous? Yeah, there are people like that. And they revel in making the chase hard for us."

Karen stood at the back of *Delicious* and lit a cigarette. He wondered if she knew she was inches above a hundred gallons of gasoline that held the explosive power of a modern bomb.

"She's smoking on the boat," Qigiq said.

"I told her smoking would wrinkle her pretty face," Kandy said. "She was clear on one thing."

"What's that?"

"*With a Bullet* is a busy boat. Two, three times a week."

"Maybe the owner likes fishing," he said.

"Yeah, if bikinis work as bait."

"Anyone in particular?"

"The burly guy you saw today," she said. "We still need a photo of

Sally's body, preferably from the back. Karen claims she can recognize anyone she's seen in a bikini."

"So we go see Robina, then the professor?"

"Soon as I change," Kandy said.

Qigiq finished his coffee and used his phone to access Ferdinand's email. It listed the name of the eight boats beside eight tiny videos. He played the first one and recognized the original video of Sally's rape. It cut to a replay with the image dimmed and orange outlining the shadows he had seen in the video. He assumed this was Ferd's model. Then he saw the two stills he had taken of Firebird and a video of a teal-colored outline. Text along the bottom read *Shadow projected by Firebird.* Then he saw all three together, the dim image of Sally, the orange outline and the teal outline. The orange and teal lined up. Midway through, the teal went forward while the orange backed up. But they were close. Then the movie became thin black wedges that widened and narrowed. He guessed this was the difference between the orange and teal lines showing the amount Firebird's projection varied from the model.

Qigiq watched the other seven videos while sipping cold coffee. All were close, yet each was off in a slightly different way. He scanned the message. The order. Ferdinand said to check the boats in the order the model rated them. Ever-thorough Ferdinand had already accessed the California boat registration records and listed the owners names and addresses. His eyes went directly to *With a Bullet,* registered to an Edward G. Blake. Address in Palo Alto. Qigiq asked Google the distance from San Francisco to Palo Alto: thirty-two point three miles and forty-minute driving time.

Not far.

Delicious was registered to Terry M. McTyme, with an address in Atherton, 30.4 miles from the city.

His eyes landed on Firebird at the top of the list. He had skipped it, his mind on *Bullet.* They scanned across.

Owner: Earnest Barry Walters. Residence: San Francisco.

~ 31 ~

Qigiq half-sat on his bike, pressing the back tire deeper into the curb. He studied his orange-banded watch, souvenir of an American winning the world MotoGP title, enjoying the tiny imitation motorcycle parts on its face.

It was 3:17 pm.

He considered the size of the apartment at the corner of Franklin and Lily. Nice. Maybe too nice for a college professor; he would have to find out what music professors were paid. No one had gone in or out since his arrival at 3:02, mirroring the inactivity of the entire street. No one had walked past, and only three cars had whizzed by: a red Ford Mustang fastback almost as old as the one used in *Bullet,* reminding him that McQueen's movie had been shot right here in San Francisco. The Ford had been followed by a silver Honda minivan, and behind it, a black Cadillac SUV with tires bigger than his houseboat. None of the drivers had so much as glanced at him.

Waiting often made him nervous, especially without a cigarette—clocks ticking, unseen things happening—but right now he needed the time to mull over radar systems. He had given up smoking when he left Alaska, new leaf and all that, so he busied his fingers scrolling back and forth through the list of eight boats, imagining how he was going to get his sterilized feet onto each one.

He heard an engine whining a crescendo, punctuated by the squeal of rubber. A car flashed past him going uphill and disappeared over the crest. He touched his wrist to trigger the stopwatch function. He guessed a broken U-turn on the narrow road and back in fifteen seconds. The squeal of stopping tires brought his eyes up to see it backing down the road fast. He touched his watch as it passed.

Six seconds.

Kandy swerved into a perfect parallel park. The car bounced slightly as the angled front wheel touched the curb and stopped at the same time. She hopped out. No bikini.

"Hey, Qu. Sorry I'm late."

"You're not late, I was early."

She stuffed both hands into the pockets of tight black jeans.

"Qigiq, if you ever arrive first, I'm late." She smiled. "Anyone home?"

He shook his head. "No one in or out in the last fifteen. No movement visible through the curtains."

"Which one is his?" she asked.

He pointed his finger right, and up.

They crossed the street to the south of Walters' place, staying in the shadow of the building. Eight concrete steps, chipped on the front edges, led to a landing and a large door painted black.

"Don't read their Feng Shui books do they?" Kandy said.

He tried the door. The knob turned but it bumped against a lock when he pushed.

He watched Kandy run a finger down a list of four names with a faded yellow button next to each one. At #4 E. B. Walters, she pressed and waited.

She pressed again. "He might be at the conservatory."

He shrugged and pressed it himself, holding the button for a count of five.

"Think he expects us?" she asked.

"Or avoiding us," he answered.

The black door vibrated. Qigiq grabbed it. They stepped into a small foyer with light green stripes in an otherwise beige tile floor. Four tin-doored mailboxes lined the wall behind them. The big door clunked shut.

Qigiq poked his head around the stairs and read 1 and 2 on the lower apartment doors. Kandy was already five steps up when he started to follow. At the top, she tapped lightly with her knuckles on a pale door with a numeral 4 drawn carefully with wide black calligraphy strokes.

"Not upscale," Qigiq said.

"Wait until we get inside. Lots of places don't upgrade the access. If his apartment extends all the way to the back, maybe a million plus in this neighborhood."

Qigiq had occasionally tried to imagine a million dollars: winning the lottery, finding a rich uncle from the old tribe who owned thousands of acres with oil under it, meeting a Hollywood actress that loved his motorbike and wanted to take him home with her. But an apartment in San Francisco worth a million dollars? He didn't think it even had a garage.

She was staring at him, apparently reading his thoughts. "Location."

The pale door opened two inches.

They waited; no eye appeared in the crack; no one said, "Who is it?"

Kandy peeked through the opening. "Living room," she said. "A very nice living room, about the size of your houseboat."

Qigiq tried to see over her head, but her almost six feet height didn't give him much view.

She stepped backwards, pushing him away from the door. She looked over her shoulder and he read alarm in he eyes.

"Empty," she said.

She reached into her jeans at the small of her back with her left hand and came out with a small gun whose barrel bore said it was not to be messed with. He stepped to the other side of the doorway and pressed his back against the wall. He had only wished for a gun twice in his life. But this and Ferdinand's call? He would talk to Kandy.

He bent forward and reached into his boot for the seal tusk handle of a six-inch blade. This he had carried in Alaska—for a long long time.

Kandy called out. "Hello. Mr. Walters? Are you home?"

Silence.

She swung the door inward with the toe of her left boot, eyes scanning the interior of the room.

Empty.

She glanced at him.

He shrugged. "It's open."

He watched Kandy step carefully into a living room decorated by a wild man who had a lot of airline miles. A pair of four-foot high teakwood tribal masks hung on the far wall with crossed spears beneath them, an oxblood leather couch below. A woven rug depicting the dance of a dozen warriors wearing mostly paint for clothing covered the hardwood floor. To her left was a mahogany four-top table beside an upright piano that would have been at home in a saloon in Virginia City, Nevada during the 1859 Silver rush.

"Hallway," he whispered from behind.

She blocked the kitchen door and examined the room while he moved silently down the corridor. He passed a sitting room with a huge TV to his right, and continued toward the room at the far corner. Its door was ajar and the soft music of a solo flute seeped out. The portion he could see through the opening was bare, as if it had been vacated. A sunbeam streamed across polished wood floor through a window whose bamboo blinds had been pulled all the way up.

He felt Kandy behind him rather than saw her. He stepped passed the open door and pressed his shoulder against the wall, keeping one eye pointed into the room. She pushed the door open silently with her right boot.

Qigiq couldn't remember ever seeing a naked man upside down before. He was strong in a lean way, and tanned, except where a small swimsuit must have been. He looked late thirties, or maybe older and fit.

Kandy said. "You left the door open."

"Yes I did," the man said. "I assume you two rang my doorbell?"

The guy was supported by his arms and the top of his head. He hadn't looked their way. Qigiq wondered how he knew there were two of them.

"Yes," Kandy said. "We're looking for Professor Walters."

"You have found me. How may I help you?"

Qigiq and Kandy's eyes met. Apparently Kandy hadn't ever done an interview with an inverted man either.

"May we come in?" Qigiq asked.

"Certainly my good man. I regret there are no seating surfaces. But please, take any portion of the floor you wish."

Qigiq didn't want to talk to the man's back, so he sat beside the door and looked at his left side. Kandy took the right wall, directly in front of Walters.

"We're detectives, Mr. Walters," she said. "We're here about Sally Bellowi."

"Sally. A sweet girl. Colossal talent. But please, call me Barry."

"Okay, Barry," Kandy said. "Would you mind if we asked a few questions?"

"Surely no," Barry said. "I have seven more minutes with my yoga practice, if you would care to wait. Or we may continue now if you prefer."

Qigiq wanted to wait until the guy got dressed and they could sit down— so he could watch Barry's eyes.

"When was the last you saw her?" Kandy asked.

"The last time I saw Sally? Let me try to recall. Today is Saturday, correct? I sometimes lose track of the days, my schedule changes so often. Ah yes, I teach a course each Friday called Electronica Fantastique. Sally is taking it this semester. She wasn't there yesterday, which surprised me, because she missed a class before."

"What time does the class meet?" Qigiq asked.

"Three in the afternoon."

"Why would Sally take your class?" Kandy asked.

"Because Sally is a Renaissance girl. She absorbs information like a huge computer, and seems to enjoy doing it."

"What's it about?" asked Qigiq.

"It surveys electronic music from its birth using manual tape splicing techniques, to its ubiquitous presence in the computer age, in both serious music and so-called popular culture."

"You teach pop music at the conservatory?" Kandy asked.

"Heavens no. We only discuss how experimental work in the art world ultimately influences culture. Movie soundtracks and rock music in particular, like the tape loops Paul McCartney did for *Tomorrow Never Knows* having been influenced by Stockhausen's work. Highly advanced. Stockhausen influenced composers for decades, in many genres. You'd be surprised how much ends up in airports and grocery stores."

Kandy said. "And this interests Sally."

"Everything interests Sally," Barry said. "The wind, the sea, sound, love. You name it, she pursues it with every ounce of her being."

Qigiq wondered how long Barry could stand on his head before passing out.

"Are you speaking from experience, Barry?" Kandy asked.

The room was silent except for a sort of canyon wind through a giant straw sound made by Barry's breathing.

"You said you are detectives?" Barry asked.

"San Francisco police department," Kandy said.

"So this is serious?" Barry asked. "Has something happened to Sally?"

Kandy looked at Qigiq before she said, "We think so."

Barry bent his legs until his knees almost touched his chin, then rolled onto his back and sat up with one foot over each thigh, staring out the window.

"I know Sally as an excellent student. And I've also known her in the Biblical sense. She is a soaring spirit, full of boundless love."

Kandy caught Qigiq's eye before she said, "And the last time you saw her?"

His eyes didn't leave the window.

Qigiq wished he could see them.

Barry said, "She was in class a week ago. We discussed Ussachevsky's work in the 1960's with tape recorders and his creation of the ADSR envelope still in use today. Amazing sounds he made with only magnetic tape and a razor blade."

"Have you seen her since?" Kandy said.

Barry sat motionless, save for the rise and fall of his chest.

"We exchanged texts after Friday's class about a tentative dinner on Tuesday. Student recital is every Tuesday night during the term. The performance quality varies, but there is fun to be had."

"Was she scheduled to play?" Qigiq asked.

"No, she was going to see her friend. I believe her friend's name is Violet. Yes, yes. Violet on the viola, or perhaps the flute."

"What happened?"

"I went to the concert as always, part of my faculty duties."

"And she never showed?" Kandy said.

Barry lifted himself onto his hands and performed a strange twisting turn, never touching the ground with his feet, then lowered himself facing Kandy, back in the cross-legged position. Qigiq had only ever seen anything like it at the Cirque de Soleil in Vegas during a law enforcement conference he attended because he wanted to see the moto-cop exhibition.

"You are quite right," Walters said. "She wasn't at the concert, or Park Chow's, our favorite restaurant, afterwards. They make a wonderful gingerbread cake with pumpkin ice cream. Sally loves it. You really must try it."

Qigiq and Kandy waited, letting the room fill with silence.

Barry smiled. "The first time she tasted it she said, 'I could so drink this for breakfast.'"

Barry stared into space, holding the smile. Qigiq guessed he was remembering that moment. Or maybe he smiled like that when conniving to confuse police officers.

"So she didn't show on Tuesday night. And she didn't show up to class on Friday," Qigiq said.

"Correct," Barry said.

"And nothing in between," Kandy said.

Barry shook his head slowly, without moving his eyes from some point above Kandy's head.

"She's missing," Kandy said. "We know her whereabouts on Sunday night and Tuesday morning. After that, nothing."

Barry's eyes focused on Kandy's face for the first time.

"There's something else," Qigiq said. "A video of her has been posted to YouTube."

"Ah, social networking. Amazing what humans will spend their time doing when Bach and Glass are available."

"Have you seen this video?" Kandy asked.

Barry watched her face, shook his head and near as Qigiq could tell, showed no emotion whatsoever.

"Do you have broadband?" Qigiq asked, hoping it was the right way to ask the question.

"This building has had it for years."

"Have you lived here long?" Kandy asked.

Qigiq waited, he recognized fishing.

"Three years," Barry said. "I was fortunate to find a music publisher who engaged me to edit electronic scores. They are quite unusual, art in and of themselves, even beyond the sound they represent."

"Fortunate?" Qigiq said.

"As in a seven figure home with a large mortgage. And a lovely boat."

"Would that be *Firebird?*" Qigiq said.

Barry rotated his face toward Qigiq for the first time.

"Why yes. I wonder how you know that, but I remind myself that you are detectives and the State of California manages boat registrations."

"Why did you name it after a car?" Kandy asked, then burst out laughing.

Barry smiled for the first time. "You would be surprised how often I am asked that question. But of course my yacht is named after the Stravinsky suite from 1910. A breakthrough, the *Firebird*, I love it more each time I hear it."

Qigiq noticed the absence of the flute music he had heard earlier, and wondered when it had stopped.

"Do you have a computer we could use to show you the YouTube video?"

"Certainly," Barry said, standing up without using his hands, still fully naked but not seeming to care. "Please follow me."

He led them to the room where Qigiq had seen the big TV, pulled a keyboard from under a leather padded coffee table, and sat back on the matching couch with the device on his lap.

"Nice leather," Kandy said. "Lots of it."

"Well thank you—oh I'm so sorry, I was meditating and never asked your names. How rude of me."

"Detective Qigiq," Kandy said. "And I'm Detective Dreeson."

Barry nodded. "A pleasure to meet you both. Qigiq is an unusual name and a non-American sound. Where are you from?"

"Alaska," Qigiq said. "It's Inuit for *white hawk that flies in the sky.*"

Barry nodded. "What a wonderful name. I wish we could have met under better circumstances. But to your comment, there is no leather in this house. I abhor the terror humans put animals through. Everything here is overpriced synthetic. Please, have a seat and we will watch this video you speak of."

Kandy told Barry how to find the video and they watched it together in silence three times, with Barry glancing down at his smartphone every few seconds. When it stopped the third time on the *Don't Steal Music* message Barry jumped up and began pacing in a large circle, ignoring his state of undress.

"What an unusual work. Yes, that was Sally, or her twin sister, if she has one. Those mysterious eyes that never seem to focus, yet look inside of you all the same." He stopped and gazed out the window at the street below.

"Why do you say the video is unusual?" Qigiq asked.

"It is first class propaganda."

Kandy and Qigiq moved only their eyes to exchange glances.

"Someone has a political message he or she wishes to propagate. And nothing travels faster in American society than news of rape and murder. How incredibly inventive."

He didn't turn from the window, but Qigiq could see his reflection as the afternoon shadows passed across the building. His face showed excitement, as if he had discovered a new composer.

Kandy pursed her lips and pointed at Qigiq.

"Why do you say murder?" Qigiq asked.

Barry spun around looking confused. "Murder? Oh, as in nothing travels faster. Do you think Sally is alive, Detective?"

"We have no evidence that she's not," Qigiq answered, thinking about the knife in the hidden video.

"What do you think that video is trying to say?" Barry asked.

"I think he's trying to scare someone," Kandy said.

Barry nodded. "Yes, he's trying to scare everyone." More softly he added, "And using Sally to do it. Why? Why our sweet Sally?"

"Do you think it has something to do with her being a musician?" Kandy asked.

Barry stroked a beard he didn't have.

"No, I would think not. Imagine the—" he turned and faced the widescreen monitor, "one million two hundred and fifteen thousand people who have viewed this video. They have no way of knowing that girl is a musician. No, it's something else."

"The fact she's a woman?" Kandy asked.

"Perhaps," Barry said. "I haven't studied the piece carefully, but I would say the metaphor of rape is a key element, even though it's left to the viewer's imagination like an old school porn video. This stealing the author references is violating someone. But he doesn't make it clear who that might be."

"Record companies?" Qigiq offered.

"The video is silent on this point. Perhaps the creator just wants people to think about who they might be hurting when they steal."

"You mean this is an awareness campaign?" Kandy asked. "Like in a political race?"

"You might call it that. Quite unusual."

That word *unusual* bothered Qigiq. He didn't know why.

"And who does he want to make aware?"

"Everyone," Barry said. "File swapping is ubiquitous on the Internet. Music, movies, audio books, books themselves. Millions upon millions of files. The golden age of the perfect digital copy has brought with it a myriad of problems for our capitalistic society."

Qigiq could only think about the knife in the second video.

"Have you read the posts?" Barry asked. "I glanced at a few hundred while we watched the video. Most think this is an acting demonstration. But there was one. Did you see it? A poster calling himself *Freeisgood* wrote *What is being stolen? Information cannot be owned, information wants to be free.* Therein lies the crux of the problem. Because you see, there is much more to that famous quote from Mr. Stewart Brand than this poster understands. Would you like to hear it in its entirety?"

Qigiq thought the problem was to find Sally. Alive.

Kandy nodded.

"Let me think for a moment," Barry said. "The original comment was made in the year nineteen eighty-four. You do of course recall Orwell's novel, and his dire predictions of a highly controlled society? Hmm...I believe Brand said, 'On the one hand information wants to be expensive, because it's so valuable. The right information in the right place just changes your life. On the other hand, information wants to be free, because the cost of getting it out is getting lower and lower all the time. So you have these two fighting each other.'"

"Barry, would you mind if we searched your boat?" Kandy said.

Barry turned to her. "My boat? Whatever for?"

"We think that video was made on a boat," Qigiq said, pointing to the screen where the YouTube page sat frozen on its final frame.

Barry frowned and was quiet for nearly a minute.

"If you think it will help Sally."

Kandy said, "Barry, do you know anyone who might want to hurt Sally?"

His frown deepened. "She was such a loving girl."

Qigiq noticed his use of the past tense. "Think about it, will you? Someone chose her for this *awareness campaign,* as you call it. We need to know why. And if this is a solitary crime, or are we looking for a ser—" he almost said killer, "a series of crimes."

"I will think as you ask." He sat down on the floor again. "She had many friends at the conservatory. Perhaps her popularity made enemies. But this," he waved his hand at the big monitor, "doesn't seem to have anything to do with Sally. Why put this on YouTube? Unless you want to reach the world."

"A protest?" Kandy said.

Barry stood, walked back to the window.

"Like marching on Washington to draw attention to a cause?" He took a slow breath in and a slow breath out. "Unusual approach. But then, unusual makes the news these days. And spreads like wildfire before the wind via large technology companies. Facebook, Twitter, and hosts of others, use it to attract people so they can advertise to them. It's a wonderfully strange process of manufacturing attention, and then monetizing it."

"Have you seen the Chronicle today?" Qigiq asked.

"No. I haven't much use for popular media."

Qigiq dug inside his leather jacket and brought out the article he had torn from the paper. He passed it to Kandy, who passed it to Barry, who stood in front of the window and read the entire thing in less than thirty seconds.

When he turned toward them, his face was taut.

"Remarkable. Sally's fingers."

Qigiq could see his eyes grow shiny with dampness. If this was their man, he was a good actor. But sometimes they were. Often even. Especially the ones who wanted attention.

"Yes. We'll have a DNA report soon," Kandy said.

Barry dropped straight down into the Lotus position and steepled his fingers in front of his face. His eyes became dark orbs of blankness.

Qigiq tried. Then Kandy. But Walters wouldn't respond to more questions.

Kandy and Qigiq let themselves out, pulling the front door closed until the lock clicked. Kandy pushed her pistol deeper into the back of her pants and met Qigiq's eyes. They walked to his bike in silence.

"Not a reaction I expected," she said.

"He seemed distressed."

"Maybe. But that talk about propaganda and political agendas. Is that what you thought the first time you saw that video?"

He shook his head. "I thought a girl was being raped. Or tortured. I didn't know what to think about the *Don't Steal* stuff."

"Still don't," Kandy said. "Let's have the evidence gathering folks take a look at *Firebird*."

Qigiq compressed his lips on the left side of his mouth in a sort of half grin.

"What?" Kandy asked.

"They'll put crime scene tape all over it," Qigiq said.

She checked his eyes. "A big scene at the marina warns the other boats. Hell, and the perp too."

He nodded, zipping up his leather jacket.

"You want me to do it?" she asked.

"Karen knows you as a bikini bum."

She laughed. "I'll go at night. She won't be tanning."

"She's met me too," Qigiq added.

Kandy dug into her pocket and pulled out a stick of gum, held it up.

He shook his head. "Makes my teeth hurt."

"You get used to it." She popped the stick into her mouth. "Let's both go."

He thought about how he would approach *Firebird*.

"Midnight?"

~ 32 ~

***With a Bullet* launched itself** over the green white-capped waters of San Francisco Bay in the direction of the small town of Sausalito just north of the Golden Gate Bridge. Eddy had been anchored at a tiny beach near Pacifica down the coast most of the afternoon, bouncing Alicia's boobs harder and harder until she begged him to stop and meant it. Now he sipped a Heineken on the elevated white captain's chair of *Bullet* with his legs apart, her snuggled between them and driving. She liked to steer the boat when both engines were revving so hard they launched the hull over waves like a dolphin at play.

He glanced at the dash: 70 mph, 4:55 pm. That meant a Saturday crowd at Sushi Ran. Alicia yanked the wheel right and the 34-foot hull arched a smooth curve as if the waves weren't there. He grinned wide, a fast boat made him feel free, especially with a woman like Alicia naked and close.

"Ready for dinner?" he yelled into the wind in the general direction of her left ear.

She nodded vigorously and twisted the wheel back to the left. He glanced over his shoulder to make sure they weren't being overtaken, something she would never bother to do. To Alicia, life was there to grab. Something as cautious as checking a rearview mirror never even occurred to her. He loved her raw carelessness during sex, but in a four-ton watercraft—he enjoyed life too much to be ending it soon. And with Platter's latest moves he felt a soaring confidence it was about to get a whole lot better.

With one finger he nudged the wheel to the right until the bow pointed in the general direction of the guest docks.

"We'll be there soon. Do you want to get dressed?"

She shook her head hard, like a little kid that didn't want to go to bed, swatting him in the face with flying locks.

"Let me rephrase that," he said, smiling, though she couldn't see it.

"How about we slow down and you put some clothes on so I don't have to share you with anyone?"

He eased the throttles back slowly, letting the boat settle into a steady cruise at 30 mph. She hopped off the seat and spun around, threw both arms around his neck and pressed her wet red lips that had so recently been wrapped around his manhood hard against his.

"For you I get dressed, be your Asian whore for evening."

He laughed, ignoring the hint of truth in her fake accent. She had grown up in San Francisco and spoke English better than he did.

"You can stay on the boat if you like," he said.

She shook her head again.

"Then how about a dress? No panties." He infused his smile with the best leer he could muster.

"I have just the thing," she said as she hopped away and disappeared down steps into the forward cabin.

"Oh yes, you have just thing," he muttered. "Several of them."

Ten minutes later he idled the engines and drifted the boat sideways to a floating guest dock. Before he had it tied off, she returned wearing a snug green dress that seemed to glow like a lantern fish. He knew those fish had tiny organs that produced chemicals to make them light up. Some used it to attract mates, others to attract food. He smiled, wondering which he was.

He was glad she had decided no bra. And remarkably, her rubber flip-flops had heels. Not the spikes she usually wore, more of a platform. She was always adding height, wanting to be a tall slender dancer on broadway. But he didn't care if she were tall or short, he was crazy for her energy either way.

He tied off the bow and walked aft to loop the stern line over a dock cleat. She threw her arms around him and squeezed. He made a lame attempt to wrestle free, lifting her off the deck until she squealed with delight, then lowering them both to the cabin floor as he pretended to let her weight overwhelm him.

"Oh-oh, I give. Have you been eating your Wheaties?"

Sitting on top of him she said, "I name thee, Mount Alicia!"

"Mount Alicia? Sure," he said, rolling over and pinning her to the deck under his big body, her squirming starting to bring his tool back to life.

"Get off me Eddy, you big ox, you're crushing me," she yelled. But she was smiling.

He stood and picked her up in his arms like a groom ready to carry his bride across the threshold.

"Ally, you look fantastic."

When she saw his eyes she relaxed and laid her head on his shoulder.

"Oh, Eddy, you are such a silly white boy."

He placed her in the captain's chair, leaned over the seat on the port side, flipped open the glove box in the dash and withdrew a laptop computer.

"Eddy, you're not going to work *now!*" She stared at him with a big fake pout.

"No way, Babe. The marina has Wi-Fi. I'm going to pull up the menu for you."

He sat in the raised chair and faced her, the machine on his lap so she couldn't see the screen. It took only ten seconds to open Sushi Ron's website to the menu page.

"What are you in the mood for, sweetheart of all time? Fish, veggies, wine or saki?"

She smiled, her face lit by the soft gold of the evening sun on the water.

"Wine for sure."

"Let me see here." He clicked to the wine menu, and while reading it with one eye, brought up a chat window and entered his password SILVERBULLETONE.

"We have a Pinot from oh-five that sounds nice. Are you in the mood for red?"

He told the program to find Zeto.

"Red is okay. But do we have to get a Pinot?" She held her pout.

He grinned. "Of course not. After the day you've given me, you can have anything you want, Ally."

"Can I have *Bullet?*"

He frowned. "Wine Ally, wine. Besides, you wouldn't want to pay the dock fees on *Bullet.*"

She pouted.

Zeto answered the chat from a cellphone. Eddy wondered what happened to that five-thousand dollar cash advance.

Her pout morphed into a smile. "You could pay them for me."

He held his frown. "I might as well keep the boat then, huh?"

He typed Hello Mr. Zeto. How is the Invisible Hand?"

"So no Pinot. A Cabernet perhaps?" he said, smiling.

"They're so heavy. Can we get a Merlot?"

He read The Hand is working as planned. 20,546 postings so far: U.S., France, Japan.

"If you really want one," he said. "Let me take a look."

He typed Excellent news. Congratulations on fine work.

And read Thank you Mr. Blake. Your support for our strategy is appreciated.

"We have three, Ally. Two from California and one from France."

"Oh, let's get the French one. The French are so romantic."

He typed How fast is the news spreading?

"You know why people think the French are great lovers, don't you Ally?"

She frowned. "Because Paris is so beautiful, especially in the springtime. Not that I would know, you won't take me."

He read Adding 1,000 per minute.

"No, because most people have never been to China." He met her eyes and smiled.

She tossed her flip-flop with the high-heel at him.

"Oh, Eddy, you're just saying that."

He read The 1,000 should be 2,000 in less than 30 minutes.

He typed Impressive Mr. Zeto. Thanks for monitoring on the weekend.

Eddy rarely thanked anybody for anything; they were being paid, they should be working. But he felt great, and Zeto was doing a good job, sitting in New York babysitting on a Saturday night while he played with Ally. The least he could do was thank the guy. Then he remembered Zeto's stock options that he had promised to double.

"No I'm not Baby, you're fantastic. But if you're tired of hearing how wonderful you are, I'll shut up."

"Get the Merlot, Eddy. What's for dinner?"

He flipped the website to the menu.

"Tonight's special is a crab roll with seaweed and avocado. But I'm thinking about something juicy." He eyed her until she broke into a smile. "Like maybe a filet mignon, if they put that in a roll."

"Eddy, you're on the ocean. You should live in Wyoming, you eat so much meat."

"It just sounds tasty," he said. "What would you like?"

He read *No problem. We're all pleased the Hand is working as planned. Lili is managing the site measurements.*

"I want lobster, so you can watch me eat it like in that old *Flashdance* movie. It still gets hits on YouTube, you know. Would you like that, Eddy?"

He typed *ETA for one millionth customer?*

"I like what you like, Ally. You know that."

"Do they have Mahi?"

He glanced down the menu, watching the chat window for a response.

She hopped off the seat and stepped across the cabin.

He hid the chat window.

"Let me see that," she said.

"There," she pointed at the screen. "The sushi sampler. With edamame."

"Your wish is my command, doll face."

He opened the chat window and read *Before midnight PDT.*

He smiled. This was going great.

He clicked to order their meal, added the bottle of merlot, and entered his cellphone number. He put *With a Bullet at guest dock* in the comment section. That would speed things up. Then he typed *Excellent Mr. Zeto. Enjoy your evening,* and closed the program.

"I'm sending the order now, Ally. They'll call when our table is ready."

He opened a folder named TIHDEMO, took a breath, and launched the file he had made following Zeto's presentation. He watched it access the docks network, envisioning gamblers gathered around a craps table staring at dice, insisting they could see connections in random events.

He smiled...he was counting on them.

And he had just the guy to help already on the job.

He placed the laptop on the yacht's fiberglass dash and pushed it back under the long sloping windshield.

"What are we going to do while we wait?" he asked.

Alicia leaned across the steering wheel and stroked the iPod plugged into the dash until *Bullet's* eight speakers rumbled with slow rhythm. She stepped over and took his right hand and kissed the palm and each finger in turn.

Then while she panted in his ear she pulled his hand across her breast, down her side to her left thigh and up under the dress until his fingers touched her. She moved her hips slowly against his hand.

"Let's dance," she said.

~ 33 ~

At three minutes before midnight Qigiq walked across Embarcadero as the man inside the Walk light counted down from eighteen seconds. He strolled through the park in front of the marina to the light of a half-moon. Kandy wasn't visible. He reached *Delicious* and slowed to browse. No sign Karen had ever been there. The companionway hatch was secured with a dial combination lock. He stared at the floor of the cabin in the moonlight, trying to remember details of the videos. He wondered if Ferdinand had attempted a computer match of the deck patterns. He lifted his cellphone and took a picture under the marina lights.

Alone in the marina, he walked quickly, examining each boat on Ferdinand's list. *Pimp Squeak* was a large fishing yacht built by Riva Bertram replete with huge chairs that invited a shave and a haircut. Its towering fly bridge and outriggers suggested a giant mutant crab feeling for prey in the darkness.

A peek in the window of *Master Plan* revealed that it could sleep eight in its long forward cabin.

He paused beside *With a Bullet*, returned from its afternoon excursion, recalling his conversation with Bob. A black cable hung from the vertical post of the dock and trailed into the boat across the word DONZI in big capital letters: full electric, heat, air conditioning, refrigeration.

When he arrived at *Firebird*, he found Kandy sitting in the stern on the floor, her back against the engine compartment, low and out of sight. He reached into his pocket and slipped baggies over his shoes, the kind surgeons wore, then stepped aboard and crouched next to her.

"Been here long?" he whispered.

She held up her hand with all five fingers splayed outward.

"Anything interesting?"

"Hair on the floor of the head, in a corner. I picked up samples for DNA."

"Blond?"

She nodded.

"Prints?"

She shook her head. "It's been wiped down, probably by those boy gorillas you met. My flashlight shows a partial on the stove. Did Sally cook?"

He made a mental note to ask Robina. He ran his hand gently across the floor. It had a checkerboard pattern pressed into the vinyl that he didn't remember seeing in the video. He wondered if the pattern would show up in sunlight.

"Probably not," she said softly, watching his hand.

He crawled along the floor to the entryway to the forward cabin. The door had been folded and turned to the side.

"Was it locked?"

She shook her head. "Did Walters seem nervous to you?"

"Your question about the boat caught him off guard."

He removed a tiny tube from his pocket and turned on its lone LED. A cone of whiteness penetrated the dark cabin below. The head was all the way in the bow, sleeping berths along the port side and a stove and tiny dinette area on the starboard. He stared into the center of the cone, trying to clear his mind of preconceived notions so it would be open to anything that didn't quite fit.

Before descending he twisted around to see Kandy release the latches on the engine cover. He took a moment to survey the marina through the windshield. So quiet. He had expected a dozen rich folks partying on their yachts. But people who owned such boats probably had other options on a Saturday night. He stepped carefully down the polished wooden ladder.

He began his search in the head, looking in and around the chemical toilet boats were required to carry to keep human waste out of the waterways. His light showed the corner where Kandy had pulled the hair; she hadn't taken it all. Drawers lined with clever injection molded trays shaped to hold toothbrushes and bottles of shampoo and everything else the well-dressed sailor required were in abundance. Walters, or the gorillas, kept things sparkling clean.

He moved to the galley. A careful search for the knife he had seen in the second video yielded only stainless steel steak knives and a Hibachi that could hang from the stern. He wondered if Walters fished and went in search of a tackle box, but found nothing. He returned to open-mindedness.

In the floor between a bunk and the door of a refrigerator too small to hold a Thanksgiving Day turkey he saw a rectangular access panel. Most boats had them. But only three screws held this one in place. The fourth hole was empty. If he were to jump to conclusions, he would think someone had been in a hurry putting it back and either dropped the fourth screw, or ran out of time. He leaned closer. The screw heads had a six-pointed star pattern.

No tackle box yet. Still on the floor, he crawled back to the entryway and tapped quietly on the deck with one knuckle.

Kandy popped up from behind the upturned engine compartment. He leaned forward as far as he could.

"Do you have any tools?" he whispered.

She pointed. "Toolbox strapped to the engine cover."

"TORX screwdriver—about a T15?"

"I'll look," she said.

He heard the sound of velcro being separated and the snap of plastic.

"Sure do," she said. "Why do boats use this weird stuff?"

He whispered. "If that wasn't rhetorical, more torque than a Phillips or a flathead. But sometimes it's just for security."

"You work on too many motorcycles," she said, handing him the slender tool.

He removed the three screws and lifted off the panel in the floor. He pointed his tiny light inside. Gray water an inch deep covered the bilge. A small cylinder protruded above the water. He reached in with the screwdriver and lifted the rectangle beside it. A motor inside the cylinder whined. He dropped the float, pointed the light forward through the opening and saw the sides taper. Shuffling backward to put the cover in place he heard Ferdinand say, "Thorough." So he leaned his body over until the top of his head was about to go through the opening and pointed the light aft. He squinted and saw a shadowy rectangle lying in an inch of water. He wondered what anyone would put there.

He tapped the deck and waved Kandy forward.

"Did you see anything about this big," he held up both hands with crooked fingers to indicate a five-inch by ten-inch rectangle, "on the side of the main runners."

She frowned and pursed her lips. "Don't think so."

"Come look."

She crawled past him and bent her head to the opening.

"Where?"

"Aft on the port side. Two feet back."

"Dark wrapper. Doesn't look like the plastic toolbox."

"What do you think?" he asked.

"Black bubble wrap," she said.

"Part of a fire system?"

She sat up onto her heels in a full squat. "Down there?"

"Maybe to protect the forward cabin from an engine fire."

She dug in her pocket and popped a piece of gum. This time she didn't bother to offer one to him.

"Pretty weird. How would you service it?"

"Through this access port."

She looked at him with a twisted mouth. "Not real handy."

"Ask Walters?"

She chewed, her eyes narrow.

"He figured we wouldn't find it." She paused. "Remember how long he thought before giving the okay to search?"

"Warrant?"

She shook her head. "Too slow. We have his permission."

Qigiq peeled off the long sleeve shirt he was wearing while Kandy moved to the front of the boat. He stretched out on his left side and slipped his arm through the hole.

"Feels soft."

"What's holding it?" she asked.

"At least one zip tie...no...two. Hefty ones around a cable of some sort."

"Strapped in for heavy seas?"

He pulled his arm out and sat up.

"Too tight to shake loose. Doubt I can get my knife in."

Kandy put her face through the opening and came back up. She dug in her pocket and held a thin tube out for him.

"Burn through?"

"The engine cover's up. Don't smell gas," she said. "Try it."

He adjusted the flame on the lighter to make a tiny blowtorch and stretched out on the floor, his left hipbone pressed hard against the varnished, hardwood floor. He felt for the package, found the forward tie, and moved his fingertips along it until he found a place away from the package he could attack with the flame. He flicked the lighter. It lit on the second try. He pointed and counted to five. He held the lighter with his pinky and shook the package with the rest of his hand. It twisted partially free.

"Kandy, you're a genius. I didn't know you smoked."

"I don't, too dangerous. Karen gave it to me, said I should start. I'd look sexy with a cigarette. What do you think, Qu? Would I look sexy with a cigarette?"

He was reaching as far as he could with his left arm to get the flame into position for the second zip tie.

"Fifth amendment," he said with a grunt.

She laughed.

"Getting hot," he said.

"What?"

"My finger. It's getting hot."

He released and shifted the lighter in his hand. He flicked it three times before he saw light flicker in the hold.

"You're sure this is safe? Motorcycles don't have a bilge."

"I've done safer things," she said.

He struggled to extract his hand and passed her the lighter. He rolled over so he could use his right arm. It was a more challenging position, but his right hand was stronger. He grabbed the package and twisted down and up, down and up. On the fourth try it popped free.

"Not handy," he said.

She held the flashlight over the package. It felt like a roll of bubble pack, but the outer layer was sturdy black plastic, perhaps five-mil thick, that would withstand rough handling.

"Do we open it?" she asked.

He sat with his bare back against the ladder, both arms covered with bilge water that he could feel evaporating into the cool night air.

"Maybe not here," he said.

"Your place is close," she said. "Want to race?"

He smiled. "Not a fair contest."

"I'll swing by a café that can give us decent coffee. Give you a head start."

He nodded.

She went above, tossed the engine cover back together and left with the package.

He waved his arms around to dry them before pulling his shirt back on. He carefully replaced the three TORX screws in the floor cover, then thought about what to do with the screwdriver. He started up the ladder thinking he didn't want to pull that big cover to put the screwdriver back, but didn't want Walters to know they had been there either. On the second step his senses all fired; and he froze.

One row of docks over a shadow moved near *Pimp Squeak*. Qigiq lowered himself slowly below deck until his eyes were an inch above the dash. The shadow was wrapped in an overcoat with the collar up. Not so strange with the temperature near the bay now in the forties. The figure also wore a dark stocking cap, more unusual. And carried a small backpack.

Qigiq wondered if the person had been observing *Firebird*, saw Kandy leave, and concluded the boat was vacant. He wished now they had stood watch. Could it be Walters? The darkness and distance provided no answer.

Moving only his eyes Qigiq traced the path back to the park and across the boulevard to his bike. He didn't have to pass *Pimp*, but he had to cross over to the first row of docks and walk its entire length. If someone was watching, Qigiq would be visible every step of the way.

Had he already been seen? Why did it even matter? The guy might be meeting a woman, or have forgotten something on his boat. But he had disappeared; and no cabin lights glowed anywhere in the harbor.

Qigiq waited a full ten minutes and never saw another shadow. He questioned his night vision, wondering if he had really seen anything. He closed his eyes and conjured the shadowy image. It was clear, right down to the feet. He couldn't be certain, but he would bet he had seen dress shoes, not the dockers generally found in marinas.

Qigiq sighed. Of course, anyone could go out to dinner and swing by their boat. Or had an argument and been sent to the half-million dollar doghouse.

He decided to be cautious. His coffee would be cold and Kandy would beat him to the houseboat, but she knew the spare key was pinched under the stern cleat.

He slipped below and shone his light into the cupboards on the galley side until he found a box of fifty-gallon garbage bags. He was glad they were dark green. He stripped down to his synthetic underwear that wicked better than anything else he had ever tried and shoved the rest of his clothes into a garbage bag. Then he put that bag into a second one to waterproof it. He wrapped the end of the bags into a knot and moved toward the stern barefoot. He stared in the direction he had seen the figure, then went over the stern rail opposite from *Pimp*, on his belly, stepping carefully down to the swim platform then onto the big Mercury outdrives to lower himself silently into the waters of San Francisco Bay.

The chill of Alaska's winter wind permeated his body.

Holding the bag under his left arm, he kicked silently toward the next dock, his eyes riveted to the spot where he had seen the figure. His skin goose bumped from the cold, but he only needed to travel a hundred feet. He swam behind a long yacht named *Yes I Can* and under the dock where *Delicious* was moored. Here he turned ninety degrees and headed for shore. He took a long last look over his shoulder before climbing rocks up to the lot where he sat on the grass, swiped water off his body with his palm, stripped off his wet underwear, and slipped back into riding pants and shirt.

His skin was almost dry by the time he reached his bike, never once having gotten another peek at the mystery guest. Kandy was going to laugh her butt off at him for being paranoid.

A few minutes later air curving up into his helmet as he crossed the Golden Gate felt like it was making icicles of his wet hair. He wondered what the chill factor might be at 60 mph as he changed lanes to pass a mini-van on the inside that didn't seem to have the oomph to climb the bridge. Or maybe the driver was drunk and dead footing. He decided to move over an additional lane to buffer himself.

He pushed with his thumb to signal his intent and eased the bike to the rightmost lane. He passed the vista overlook at the north end of the bridge and leaned the bike into a long left sweeper that rolled uphill and turned back to the right near his exit. He thumbed again and leaned right for the single-lane downhill ramp that felt like a racetrack at highway speeds.

Halfway down the ramp his eyes followed a line toward the inside of the lane to the apex of the turn, that point where his tires would traverse the three inches of pavement closest to the inside shoulder. Though he was cold from the swim, his Guzzi was running strong and he was enjoying the feel of the bike's flight along the empty ramp. He saw no headlights and didn't hear a horn or the squeal of tortured rubber as a dark shape materialized two feet to his right. His leaned bike closed the distance. How could anyone have missed his guaranteed-to-be-seen LED taillights, the only technology on his Guzzi less than twenty years old? His automatic reaction stood the bike up and squeezed the front brake so the crazy person beside him could pass on the inside.

But the car slowed. Moved closer.

He noted it was black, or midnight blue, and wondered briefly if this is how professional racers trading paint at over a hundred mph felt. He squeezed the brake harder, touched the rear pedal, and felt the front shudder as he neared the limits of what the decades old suspension could handle.

The shape drew nearer.

The exit ramp tightened.

He knew from riding this route daily that to his left lay six feet of gravel shoulder and a steep grassy hill ending in a concrete drainage ditch along Lateral Road. He was thinking about how to ride down grass when cold metal pressed firmly against the outside of his right leg from knee to thigh.

Then accelerated.

As the car moved forward its fender caught his right hand forcing him to release the brake. Metal screeched against metal. He leaned hard on the left grip to remain upright and felt the bike shimmy across the fine stones of the shoulder.

The hill fell away.

As the bike danced on the slick dry grass of the downhill slope he focused to avoid slamming into that ditch at high speed. He pressed with his right toe. The rear wheel skidded. The bike dropped right. He pushed his body away from the mass of metal and landed on his right shoulder. Bright red flashed above him as his prized machine flipped into the air, while he fought like a fallen mountain climber to arrest his descent with heels and elbows.

~ 34 ~

He was standing in icy water up to his chest. Shivering. His vision filled with glaring white sand. He tasted salt. A blonde girl knelt on the beach facing him, waves alternately hiding and revealing shiny bare breasts. Her hair flowed left far into the sky, lifted by wind as her arms reached out to capture him in an embrace. She chanted two syllables over and over, but he couldn't understand them. Her eyes closed. A curved object rose between them; the sky grew darker and darker. Her voice chanted, the waves lifted and spun him around and around...

One eye cracked open and the images faded. He was on his back. It was dark except for flashes of red. He saw tiny bursts of light at the end of tubes in a giant cosmic lamp. His body shook.

"Qigiq, it's Kandy," he heard a voice say from far away. "The ambulance is here, we're taking you to University."

As if reading his mind the voice said, "Don't worry about your bike. I'll get it onto a flatbed."

He tried to smile, but couldn't feel his face.

He felt his body jostled. Moving with no effort felt like he was back dreaming. The tiny bursts of light became the interior roof of a truck. He didn't see the blonde-haired girl, but could hear her chanting.

When he opened his eyes again he was on his back on a firm white bed and a blurry image of Kandy sat across the room drinking from a white cup. He forced a smile.

She stood and crossed to the bed.

He turned his head toward her.

"Car pushed me," he said, his voice a dry crackle.

She nodded.

"Center of the turn. From the inside."

She nodded.

"No headlights."

She frowned. "Color?"

"Dark. Maybe black."

"Model?"

"Long hood. Front fender caught my bars. Heard scraping."

She nodded.

"Didn't see the driver," he said, and closed his eyes.

"That would be too easy." She patted his arm. "You want an update?"

He nodded, eyes still closed.

"Concussion. CT scan shows no internal bleeding. Your helmet has to retire. Hairline fracture in your ankle, maybe more."

His focus went to his left leg and he felt pressure from his knee down. He wiggled his toes.

"Yeah, your toes move. Doc says you'll have trouble putting weight on your leg for a while. Do you prefer a cane or a crutch?"

He smiled, and opened his eyes slowly. She hadn't moved.

"They've got it in a compression cast, he thinks that might be enough. If you're careful."

He tried to nod.

"Got to ask you something, Qu," she said. "I've been trying to figure it, but now you're awake, better you just tell me."

"Sure," he said softly.

"I find you lying on the grass next to a seriously twisted motorcycle. No big surprise, you crashed. But there's a pair of gray men's underwear in the grass and they're soaking wet. It hasn't rained here in months. And you're not wearing underwear. Now how does that happen?"

He smiled. It must have gotten through, because she smiled too.

"Marina. Saw someone. After you left."

Her brow creased over the white cup as she sipped.

"Swam under the docks. Clothes in a garbage bag."

"Underwear swim trunks, huh?" she said.

He smiled with just the corners of his lips. "Yeah." He rested.

"So who was it?" Kandy asked.

He shook his head; the right side ached.

"Business shoes, overcoat. Dock by *Pimp Squeak*. All shadows."

"Think you were seen?" she asked.

"I was low. Maybe my exit..."

She tossed her cup into the wastebasket beside his bed.

"Mysterious stranger. Mysterious crash. Related?"

"Big coincidence," he managed

She was quiet for a moment.

"Very big," she said. "Walters?"

"Saw us grab the package?"

She was quiet for a moment. Then, "We're getting closer to something."

Qigiq closed his eyes. His body didn't want to sleep so much as it didn't want to be awake. He took a long breath in, and forced them back open. "Package?"

"Waited for you, couldn't understand how I got to your place first. Backtracked, found you on the road. Didn't open it until you were stable here."

He nodded. His head felt wrong, like his helmet was too tight.

"They let me use an empty O.R. downstairs." She dug in her pocket for gum, unwrapped it, flipped it into her mouth in one motion. "Good thing, too. You're not going to believe what was in it."

"Sally," he whispered, the beach image of her in the dream flashing behind his eyes.

She stopped chewing and met his eyes.

"Now what makes you say that?"

"Three packages of Sally."

"The plastic wasn't like the others. No Amazon box, no delivery to a friend in Sally's address book."

"Walters is friendly," he said. "Special delivery."

"Qigiq, you amaze me," Kandy said. "The black plastic is from a painter's drop cloth. Inside was bubble wrap, just like I thought." She smiled. "Inside that, get this, blocks of dry ice on four sides of the contents."

The pain in his left leg displaced his tight helmet. Thoughts refused to assemble.

"Inside," he said. "Inside the ice, bag sealed with a *Don't Steal* sticker, and inside that bag...another finger." He took a slow breath.

"Close. Calf we think. Skin removed, like a filleted fish," she monotoned. "No *Don't Steal* message. And it was vacuum-sealed in thick clear plastic, like those fresh-never-frozen pizzas at the grocery store. Stay fresh for a long time."

Qigiq closed his eyes. Since he had first seen the black rectangle in the bilge, part of him had been hoping for something simple, like a few kilos of cocaine.

"How do we know it's Sally?"

"We don't," she said. "Pillar has it now. We'll have DNA as fast as he can do it. Someone raised the priority on our case."

"The power of the press," Qigiq said, managing a small smile.

~ 35 ~

Marie unlocked the heavy front door from the street while carrying a padded black bag over both shoulders like a huge backpack. It was so nice not to cramp her hands carrying a cello that she tried not to care about the hippo comments on the street. She stepped through the door quickly to make sure it didn't slam on her instrument, even though this was the cheaper "gigging" cello for jobs like the Sunday morning church service she had played an hour ago.

She stopped at the base of the stairs and peered down the hall. She hadn't checked her mail since finding that box the police had taken in exchange for a blue receipt—as if she wanted them to return it like a cello sent to the shop for restringing. She swallowed. She might have something in Saturday's mail. And it might be money from Dad.

She walked around the edge of the stairs and down the hall to the mailboxes. She stared at Minnel handwritten on a little piece of white paper and slipped into the slot of #6. She found the keys in the pocket of her black wool jacket and fumbled with them until a flat tin key was pointing at the lock. She saw Sally's fingers with their Very Berry tips holding the key and started shaking from her ankles up. She closed her eyes and hummed the cello part to Beethoven's Quartet #3 that she had just played. That calmed her enough that she could open them. She saw her own hand, and before her eyes could deceive her again she jammed the key into the lock and twisted.

She let her breath out, not realizing she had been holding it.

The mail box contained two pieces of mail. The smaller one was a postcard inviting her to an art opening next Sunday that she would surely be attending because she was playing duets with her friend Frances. The second was a white envelope with no return address. She ripped it open, read it, and wondered why so many banks wanted so much to give her a credit card when she didn't have any money. She slammed the box shut and dropped both items into a corner waste can before stomping up the stairs fighting a rising panic that Mom hadn't made Dad send the check this month.

Puffing at the top of fourteen stairs, she let herself in and plopped the big case onto her blue-ribbed sofa before plopping herself next to it, ignoring the dishes in the sink and the blankets in the corner. She hated sleeping and living in the same room. And eating, which made her think about lunch. She frowned. The room felt funny—like Mom had moved her furniture. She spoke aloud to comfort herself.

"Stop being silly, Marie. You're just shook up about that package."

She heard the hiss of rolling tires on the street below. That wasn't new.

She listened to the quiet, and began to shake again.

She stood and crossed to a corner table next to her tiny kitchen. The screen was dark, but her computer was purring like a tiny kitten had crawled inside and gotten stuck. She tapped the keyboard to wake it up.

A big black flag with a skull and crossbones was waving on the screen. Above, bold print welcomed *Hello, Pirate Marie,* and below declared *You have been caught with bootlegs. Now you will pay.*

Her eyes widened. She sat down. There was fine print under the *you will pay.* It said 40,325 illegal songs had been found on her machine. And they were being deleted.

Had she really downloaded all that?

"Why are you deleting my music?" she asked the waving flag.

She continued reading—Marie is a pirate, soon to be famous like Blackbeard and Captain Jack. Watch for her name and email on the Internet. A list of URL addresses was shown. It currently had 211 entries. While she watched, www.crackerjacks.com was added to the list.

"No!" she shouted at the skull.

She pointed at *crackerjacks* and clicked.

Her browser opened to a website with a blog in the center of the page. To the left was a list of media types: *CD, MP3, DVD, Blu-ray,* under the heading *HOW TO CRACK.*

She shrieked.

At the top of the blog was her face, the same icon that she used for chatting to identify herself to friends. Beside it was a note: *I, Marie, am a pirate. I had 40,325 songs before being caught. All of my songs have been destroyed and my name has been posted here as a warning to others who have tens of thousands of dollars of music on their hard drives that they haven't paid for. We are coming to get you too...*

She was shaking again—but not thinking about Sally. She was thinking about her face on websites next to the word *pirate.* And what her dad would think. And would he make her go back home to Texas?

She wanted to close her eyes, but she turned back to the pirate flag and continued reading.

Do not unplug this machine or it will become inoperable. Only music files are being destroyed, and they weren't yours anyway, were they?

Across the bottom of the screen an electronic banner scrolled: *Don't Steal Music—Don't Steal Music,* interspersed with tiny Jolly Rogers waving as they moved.

She held the table with both hands and tried to force herself to stop shaking, which only made it worse. Tears formed in her eyes that she didn't bother to wipe away. She tried to think of who would do this to her. She wasn't a pirate. She didn't steal things. All she did was listen to a few songs.

A little voice whispered that 40,325 wasn't *a few.*

She reached for the wall plug as the count ticked down from 19,241 to 19,213. She loved music, and her whole library was disappearing. She stared at the word *inoperable,* and drew her hand slowly back to her lap.

She watched the count drop and wished she could call Sally; she always knew what to do. There had to be a way to fight back. They couldn't just go inside her computer and delete things. That didn't seem right. It must be illegal.

She dug in the drawer for the cheap cellphone her dad would only let her use on Sunday because he had a deal for free minutes. She scrolled through the address book looking for someone she could tell and stopped and stared at Sally's number. Without thinking, she pressed dial.

A sleepy voice said, "Hello?"

Marie thought she would be okay, but she started sobbing.

More awake now, the voice said, "Hello? Hello? Who is this?"

"Hi," Marie squeaked out. "It's me, Marie."

The line was silent.

"Marie? From New York?"

"Yes." Marie sniffled moisture back up her nose. "I'm sorry."

"That's okay, Marie. What's wrong?"

"Robina, is that you?" Marie asked.

"Yes. Calm down. You didn't get another package did you?"

Marie's voice shook. "No, thank heaven, no. But something got into my computer."

"Got into?" Robina said. "You mean like a virus?"

"I, uh, I guess so. It's deleting my files," Marie said.

"Do you use a virus scanner?"

No response.

"You have a backup, right?"

Marie started sobbing again. "Not for my music files. They're too big," she managed to force out.

"Your music files? That's funny. I got a notice too, when syncing my iPod."

Marie calmed a bit with the news that she wasn't alone.

"Did it delete your music?"

"I don't think so. It just told me there was a charging problem with my iPod and had me enter the serial number. They're sending me a new one."

"A new iPod?"

Marie sat down and saw the file count drop to 9,315. She pressed keys to grab a picture of her screen. The machine clicked.

"Let me send you a picture."

"Okay."

Marie dragged the picture into an email and addressed it. She typed *When I got home from my job today, this was running on my computer.* She clicked send.

"It deleted my music and put my picture on the Internet. Says I'm a thief." She tried not to, but started sobbing.

"Easy, Marie. Let me look. I've never heard of anything like what you're talking about. Maybe it's a scam."

Marie heard a *bing* over the phone.

"Opening now," Robina said.

Marie sat quietly, trying not to sniffle.

"I've never seen anything this outrageous. Is your machine okay?"

"It can send email," Marie said. "But the waving flag is still on the screen. Over five thousand files to go."

"You mean it's running right now?"

"Yes."

"Stop it." Robina shouted.

"I don't know how," Marie said.

"Unplug your computer."

"It says right on the screen that I might wreck it if I do that."

"Let me read this," Robina said. After a few seconds she added, "Do you believe it?"

"I don't know. I'm not so good with computers. I play cello."

"Let it go and see what it does. How much music did you have?" Robina asked.

"40,352 files according to this virus."

"Even more than me," Robina said.

"I have loads of spare time, when I'm not practicing I mean."

"Boyfriend?" Robina asked.

"Boys don't like me. I eat too much."

"Screw 'em," Robina said. "Let's see what this virus is going to do. We need as much info as we can get, then I'll call Danny."

"Who's Danny?"

"Sally's boyfriend. He knows about technology. And if he can't help, I'll talk to Professor Walters."

"Thanks, Robina. I just don't know what to do."

"Don't worry, we'll figure it out."

"Did you see those blogs? It put my name on the Internet." Marie started sobbing again.

"There are only a couple of hundred. We can take them down, one by one."

Marie squinted through her tears. "It's up to four hundred and fourteen now." She scrolled the little window up and down. "I bet people have already seen me. I don't want them to think I'm a thief."

"Don't worry, Marie, no one will think you're a thief. Record companies have been ripping us off for years with overpriced CDs. You listening to a few songs isn't hurting anyone."

Marie's screen flashed bright red. White letters said she should have paid $39,948 for her songs. Then it showed how the money would have been distributed. Some went to Amazon for distributing the songs, some to the

174

record company for promotion and marketing, some to the musicians who played on the recording, some to the arranger and engineer, and some to the songwriter who might not even be in the band.

She frowned. That was a lot of money.

The last line of text, displayed in a cursive script like a little man was inside her computer handwriting on the back of the monitor said *Artists can only create if their creations are respected.* Under that in big block letters it said DON'T STEAL MUSIC OR MOVIES OR BOOKS. And in smaller letters: *The authors did the work—You don't work for free, they shouldn't have to either.*

She swallowed. Had she really cheated people?

"Marie, what's happening?"

"It finished. The screen has more warnings. It shows how the money goes to different people in the music business."

"Send me a screenshot," Robina said.

Marie set about snapping the screen and sending the email.

"What should I do next, Robina?"

"What were you going to do before you found the pirate flag?"

"Have lunch and practice."

"Why don't you do that. I'll call Danny to see if he can help."

"But the blogs?" Marie said. She didn't want her Dad to see her name next to the word thief.

"I'll find out how we take them down."

"The list was under the flag, but now it's gone."

"Have lunch Marie, you'll feel better. Let me call Danny," Robina said.

Then the line went dead.

~ 36 ~

Danny was practicing a hungarian-gypsy scale with his PRS guitar tuned down a half step when he heard the opening riff of *Purple Haze*. He reached for his cellphone with his right hand.

"Danny," he said, his left hand continuing to play.

"It's Robina. I've got a weird computer thing."

His hand stopped.

"Define weird."

"Free iPods and music-deleting viruses."

He spun the volume knob on his guitar to zero and leaned it against the wall. He took a step backwards and began pacing.

"You have my attention."

"I'm syncing my music this morning and I get a message that my battery is failing. But instead of sending me a free battery, it says I get a whole new iPod."

"Is there a catch? Like you have to send yours in first, and then you never see the new one?" Danny asked.

"No. I just had to fill out a form."

"Uh-oh. Phishing. Collecting your info. You'll never see the iPod."

"That's what I thought. But all they asked for was my serial number."

"Why would they phish for serial numbers?" Danny said, mostly to himself.

"And get this. I'm supposed to have the new one in two business days."

"You're right. Weird. They want the batteries off the market fast. Did you give them your serial number?"

"You bet I did," Robina said. "I've dropped my iPod a bunch of times, it's scratched to hell. Plus they let me pick a new color. I'm getting a pink one."

"Wow, a new color. Then for sure I'd get one." He laughed.

"Thin ice, buster. It's weird though," she said.

"This happened while you were syncing?" Danny asked.

"Yeah."

"That's how they knew what model you have," he said.

"Oh, cause it was connected. Sure."

"I'd say wait and see if the new one shows up. If not, they can't do much with a serial number," he said.

"Guess not, huh?"

"So, you called me to brag about your new toy? That's so unlike you, Robina," he said, laughing again.

"Knock it off, Danny, this is serious. I just told you about the iPod because I think it might be related to this other thing."

"And that would be?" he said, dropping to his butt next to the guitar.

"Sally's friend in New York called me."

His eyes saw an Amazon box. And its content. "You mean the girl who got a package like we did?"

"Yeah. Marie. She called me a couple of minutes ago, all freaked out."

"Another delivery?"

"Thank God no," Robina said. "It's so weird. She calls me all freaked out and says that a virus is eating her music files."

Danny tried to imagine what that would look like. "Never heard of such a thing."

"Me either. But she sent screen shots. Check your email."

Danny got up and headed to his bedroom. He stepped over a pair of basketball shoes and pulled open the top drawer of a desk. He flipped the front edge of the drawer down and the top of his laptop up.

"Got it," he said. "Hmm, not Windows."

Seconds ticked away.

"Wild. It's like the old hacker days you hear about. Remember that movie with Angelina Jolie when she was like nineteen? Did it really destroy her music files?"

"She says it did."

"Damn."

"At the bottom, there's a list of blogs. Marie said it put her name and picture out to hundreds of sites."

"No way. Let me check."

He read the URLs shown in the window and picked *www.freehotmusic.net*. It opened to a blog page with an entry only one minute old. But it wasn't Marie, it was someone named Anthony who looked like an accountant right down to black plastic eyeglass frames.

"I don't see Marie, Robina. How long ago did all this happen?"

"Just before I called you. Within the last half-hour for sure."

Danny scrolled backwards in time looking for other posts.

"Check this, Ro. Here's a post from someone calling himself Sixgun: What's this crap about pirates admitting they're stealing music? Are you people all on drugs? Why don't you just sign your soul over to the RIAA?"

"Who?"

"The Recording Industry Association of America. They protect copyrights on songs and go after violators. Remember those lawsuits?"

"Oh yeah, them."

"I'm scrolling back and there's one, two, three...seven...fourteen...there. Marie right? Pudgy blonde chick?"

"Hold the sexist commentary," she said.

"Oops, sorry. Didn't realize this was a data-free zone."

"Danny!"

He laughed. "Sorry, Ro. I was just describing what I saw. So, is that her?"

"Yeah. Does it say something about 'I'm a pirate'?"

"Reads like a confession. But you know something?"

"You secretly dig fat chicks?"

"Now who violates political correctness?"

"Oh, is this a data-free zone?" She laughed in his ear.

"You know I dig Sally," Danny said.

They both got quiet.

"Sorry," she said.

"Let's move on. What I was about to tell you is these pirate confessions, they're identical. Except for the number of music files. Anthony had 17,431, David had 54,677, Monica had 9,541, Kim had 31,988. But everything else about the posting, except for the picture, is the same."

"So it's a bot?" she asked.

"A bot? You're using big words there, Ro."

"Trying to impress you, Danny. Maybe have your first child." She laughed again.

"Looks to me like this virus uses a canned confession and stuffs in the name, the picture and file count. There are hundreds of confessions on this one blog alone."

He scrolled backward through the postings looking for pirates.

"I've got one here at eight o'clock last night. Nothing before that."

"I told you this was weird."

"Totally and inexplicably," Danny said.

"Can you take her posting down?" she asked.

"Hmm. This one only lets the poster delete. I'll send a note. No, better yet, tell Marie to send a removal request. I'll put the details in email for you."

"Thanks," she said.

"Oh man. Did you know Marie's email address is up here?"

"Her email? No way. She'll freak if she gets messages from strangers."

"Yeah. And half of them will be zealots who think she deserves jail time."

"Can we help her?" Robina asked.

"About the only thing she can do is request the post be removed. She'll have to search for them though. It'll take time."

"Think of a better way, Danny," Robina said. "Please."

"She could just wait. Looks to me like a whole lot of people are in this boat. Someone will figure out how to block the virus, and maybe post code that will automatically remove you from all the postings at once."

"How long will that take?"

"To post a fix? They're probably working on it now. I wouldn't doubt something will be up today, or tomorrow at the latest."

"So I tell her to wait, and we'll let her know when there's a fix?"

"Sure, do that. Also tell her not to read email from anyone she doesn't know. There's no telling what kind of viral junk screwballs will send her. Just delete it unread."

"Good idea."

"Holy ghost of Jimi. I don't believe it," Danny said.

"What what?" Robina squealed into the phone.

"You at your computer?" Danny asked.

"No, I'm out on the concrete steps we call a front porch."

"Go look at your computer. Your name just popped up at the top of freehotmusic. And this pic looks like your mug to me."

She screeched, "What?"

Danny heard shoes pounding on stairs while Robina yelled, "Goddamn son-of-a-bitch virus-writing hackers, fuck them, fuck them, fuck fuck fuck them." Her rant became the long scream of her team scoring a touchdown in the final minute.

He pulled the phone away from his ear.

"Goddamn thing is deleting my music!"

"Easy, Ro. Tell me what you see."

"A fucking Jolly Roger flapping like a burning flag in the hands of a demented junkie at a peace rally!"

"What's the file count?" Danny asked.

"The what? Oh...uh...17,541. Down from 38,921."

"Wow."

"It's deleting my precious music and all you can say is 'wow'?"

"Sorry. You were dead right." He gulped, thinking about Sally. "You were right, this is truly weird."

Danny looked at his machine and opened his music player. Along the bottom it said he had 84,767 songs. What was he going to do if he lost them all?

"Got to go, Ro. I'll call your cell if I figure anything out."

"Oh, thank you Prince Charming. Bailing out when things get tough."

"Weird," he said.

He stared at his machine for five seconds before turning off the wireless connection to the Internet. Then he shut the machine down. Then he unplugged it from the wall. He started to close the drawer and decided to be safe. He flipped the laptop over and removed the battery. He wanted the files that were on that disk drive and he wasn't going to let any weird virus into his machine until he had a backup. That meant this month's, and maybe next month's, beer money was going for the biggest USB flash drive he could find. His red guitar leaning against the wall caught his eye. He felt the weight of the battery in his left hand and suddenly wondered how many hours the girls and guys who recorded those eighty-four thousand songs had practiced.

~ 37 ~

Kandy's left boot squeaked each time she placed it on the hospital's tile floor. She slowed as she turned into the corridor for Room 2305, trying to make it be quiet. The door was closed. She pressed her ear against its smooth surface, then pushed the door open with two fingers and peeked inside. Qigiq appeared to be asleep, or maybe resting from pain meds. She slipped into the room and sat facing the foot of his bed.

"Your boot still squeaks," he said with a soft dry voice.

She grinned. "You're paying attention."

"Not much else to do except complain about the food."

"You must be thinking about going home."

"I'm thinking about Sally," he said. "When the leg doesn't stop me from thinking."

"What did the doctor say?"

"He hopes tonight. Says he's tired of listening to me complain about not working. Says I should be rejoicing that I'm alive and can walk."

"Typical doctor, only sees the silver lining," she said. "Need anything?"

"A ride home?"

She smiled. "Soon as the doc says."

Qigiq groaned.

Her bikini gum-pack phone buzzed at her waist.

"Incoming," she said, and stepped away from the bed to the window. She glanced at the display on the long side of the phone. "Robina."

She put the phone to her ear. "Dreeson."

"Hello? Is this Kandy? It's Robina. You won't believe what happened. It's so weird. I told Danny, and he said he's never seen anything like it."

Kandy tried to imagine something weirder than receiving a roommate's fingers in an Amazon box. "What is?"

"It says 'Don't steal music' across my computer screen. And Qigiq isn't answering his phone."

Kandy crossed the room and stood next to Qigiq's bed. She took the little phone from her ear and pressed its speaker button, then placed it on the pillow next to Qigiq's head.

"Could you say that again?" Kandy said.

"Sure. A virus invaded my computer. It trashed my music files and now says 'Don't steal music' across my screen like an electric sign at the subway."

Qigiq's eyes opened wide. He blinked hard.

"Anything else?" Kandy asked, knowing a witness never said everything on the first pass.

"Oh yeah. It trashed Marie's computer too."

"Marie?" Qigiq mumbled.

"Sally's friend in New York that also received an Amazon package," Kandy said.

"That's right," Robina said through the speakerphone. "And before this happened, I got a weird message that I qualified for a new iPod because my battery had failed."

Qigiq frowned, making the back of his head hurt.

"Is it still on your computer?" Kandy asked.

"Nope, it's gone. But I captured pictures so you can see what it looked like."

"Thanks, Robina. Very helpful."

"I have a couple of pics from Marie too."

"Are they the same as on your computer?" Kandy asked, watching Qigiq to see how his strength was holding up.

"Yep. And you know what else this thing did?"

Qigiq raised his eyebrows. Kandy laughed softly.

"What's that?" Kandy said.

"It posted my name and picture to a bunch of music trading sites and says I'm a pirate."

Qigiq met Kandy's eyes.

"A pirate?" he said.

"Like, you know, it says I stole thousands of songs and other people better beware, that this virus thing is coming to get them too."

"Are you home?" Kandy asked.

"Yeah, I'm watching my computer to see if anything else weird happens, and practicing for my performance on Tuesday."

Kandy whispered 'Walters' to remind Qigiq of the Tuesday student recitals.

He shifted his head on the pillow.

"Robina. Do you have any pictures of Sally in a bathing suit?" Kandy asked.

"A bathing suit? Uh, sure. I think. She was always hanging around boats. I'll look."

"Thanks. I'll stop over tonight."

"That's great. This is too weird for me."

Kandy watched Qigiq, who was watching her put the phone away.

"A virus?" he said.

"Yeah, spreads from computer to computer."

He nodded. "Aren't there programs to protect against those?"

"Most of them. But every time there's a new one, the programs have to catch up. This sounds like a new one."

Qigiq's eyes closed but he said, "So we wait for an update?"

"That's one way," Kandy said. "Unless we can find out where it's coming from."

"Don't steal. What are the odds?" he asked softly.

She watched. The drugs were making him tired. But she answered anyway.

"Zero."

~ 38 ~

As he awoke Qigiq felt softness against his back and appreciated how good it felt to be in his own bed before thoughts of who would want to run him off the road and why pressed against his mind. His left foot protruded from under the covers because the compression cast made his leg warm. Through the doorway he could see golden light from an east-facing window stripe the kitchen floor. That convinced him it was now Monday morning.

While summoning energy and directing it to his feet to make them begin the day, he heard the high-rpm whine of a car engine revving and falling, revving and falling. Someone driving a twisty road…fast.

He glanced at his immobilized ankle and wondered how long it would be before he could shift a bike again. He loved riding the California hills. A quick darkness passed over him as thoughts of being relegated to a bed, or the cage of a car, passed through.

The engine sound grew louder and was suddenly gone.

He forced himself up and lowered both feet to the floor. The throbbing in his leg didn't improve, but didn't get worse. He tapped the top of the clock. It said in an eerily human voice that reminded him of a newscaster, "The time is seven thirty-two AM. Outside temperature is fifty-one degrees."

He struggled into an old pair of black jeans cut open from the ankle to the knee and pulled on a dark blue sweater. He bent over to pick up the single crutch lying on the floor, and took a deep breath. He lifted himself with his good leg and stomped to the bathroom. He was standing when someone pounded on his front door.

He made his way slowly, peeked through the curtain and saw Kandy at the edge of the front deck staring in the direction of the morning sun. She was wearing boots and a black T-shirt under her leather jacket again. He wondered if she had multiple sets of the same clothes, or just did laundry often. He unlocked the door and poked his head outside.

"Hey," he said. "You're working early."

"Lots to do," she said. "Everyone's back in the office. Maybe we can get some answers."

"You want coffee?" he asked.

"You have it hot?" she said.

"Not yet. Just got up."

"Then no thanks. We'll get it on the way."

He noticed the pronoun.

"*We* just got out of bed. I imagine you already ran five miles this morning?"

"Ten, but who's counting? We have an appointment at eight. Glad you're dressed."

Her eyes ran down his body to his bare feet.

"Almost," she said. "I'm not disturbing anything am I? You didn't have Lolita over last night to ease your pain?" Her right cheek twitched toward a grin.

"Inuit tribal custom," he said. "Embrace virgin to heal bone fracture."

She shook her head. "You never know. Some of those old home remedies really work."

He stepped away from the door and she came in.

"This place we're going. Do I need to take anything?"

"It's chilly. You might want a coat."

© © ©

Ten minutes later Qigiq sat in the passenger seat of Kandy's Mini wearing his lined leather riding jacket. The crutch rested on the dash between them and reached almost to the rear window.

"Do I get to know our destination?" he asked.

"A surprise," she said. "There's a gift for you on the back seat."

He twisted around and stretched to retrieve a yellow manila envelope. It was sealed with a metal clasp and had no markings on it anywhere.

"It's not addressed to me."

"Trust me."

He squeezed the clasp. Inside he found four sheets of paper. The first two looked like computer screens. He saw *Don't Steal music* and the word *pirate* repeated over and over. He also saw a warning to not shut down the computer while the virus was working. Only they didn't call it a virus. Way down in legal fine print was a reference to *Smith*.

The second picture was another computer screen, this one with a red background. The *Don't Steal* message repeated along the bottom like a stock ticker.

"These are from that virus Robina called about?" he asked.

"Yeah. She captured those from her computer. I want to show them to Ferdinand, see what he can figure out."

He moved the second page to the back and saw a picture of Sally in a yellow bikini standing arm in arm with Robina in a blue bikini with white polka dots. Except for the diminutive size of their suits, the picture could have been from the 1950's.

"Body shot for Karen to ID?"

"Yeah," Kandy said. "Check the next one."

Qigiq flipped to the last page and saw Sally and Robina in the same swimsuits, only they had turned around and were looking back over their shoulders at the camera. Sally was the curvier of the two. He could see why men liked her.

"I'll find Karen," Kandy said. "Let's hope for warm and sunny this afternoon."

Qigiq returned to the screenshots and studied them.

"Who could write something like this?"

"Any good hacker. But why? And how does it get in? Does everyone have it? Am I going to wake up tomorrow and find it's deleted my poodle photos?"

"You collect illegal poodle photos?"

She grinned. "I'm just saying, does it only pick on music?"

"Or does it only pick on illegal music. How could it know that?" He paused and felt the uneasiness of someone being reminded that there's a whole lot he doesn't understand. "How about getting into a computer? Is that easy too?"

"Not sure, Ferd territory. Maybe it left tracks. Maybe we can trace it. Apparently the blogs are getting complaints about violation of privacy."

"Steal music that has a clear retail value," Qigiq said. "And scream violation of privacy when someone, uh, something, deletes your stolen files?"

Robina said to me, "'Computers make life weird.' She has a point."

The car arched along a long curve after the bridge exit with a wall not four feet from Qigiq's window. He preferred the feeling of a leaned bike.

"No hint on where we're going?" he asked.

"Surprise," she said.

He massaged his left leg where it disappeared into the cast. The device was cutting off circulation, but the doc had said, "Nah, it won't do that."

When she reached Valencia and 15th Kandy sliced into an on-street parking place between a massive Toyota SUV and a lifted GMC pickup truck. Qigiq felt incredibly small. He opened the door and the lower edge scraped the sidewalk. He turned to apologize to Kandy and saw a long hood shoot past.

He stared after the car.

"You see something?" Kandy said.

"That car. The hood."

She looked down the street. "Mercedes. You see the driver?"

"Just the back of a hoodie. Plate was short. Maybe didn't have numbers."

"You want me to catch it?"

"Just a feeling," he said, and twisted the crutch over his head and onto the concrete, popped the seatbelt and crabbed out the half-open door backwards. Kandy stood by holding his crutch, forcing her lips together so she wouldn't laugh.

He rolled to his side, got his good leg under him and held the open car door to stand. Kandy handed him the crutch and led down the sidewalk for half a block. Qigiq kept glancing up the street, wondering about that car.

She stopped.

He looked up at a sign directly above his head, but it was a foot thick and he couldn't see either side from below. He looked at Kandy, who had no expression he could read.

"You're having fun aren't you?"

Her mouth opened into a wide grin.

"C'mon," she said.

She reached for the handle of a glass door. He saw the number 412 flash by as she swung it open. He hobbled through and was greeted by the lovely unmistakable smell of gasoline and rubber. Before him sat four rows of shiny motorcycles.

"You're torturing me. Is that it?" he said, trying to be lighthearted but feeling a lead lump inside, knowing he couldn't ride these machines right now for any amount of money.

"This way," she said, waving her hand.

Qigiq took a deep breath and sighed. He had been postponing facing the reality that his bike had been converted to scrap metal.

A lean gray-haired man who looked like his face had been chiseled from bronze came around the corner. Qigiq guessed he was over sixty, maybe over seventy. But he moved like he had just come from gymnastics class.

"Well, hello. You are right on time. This is your friend?" he asked.

"Qigiq, I'd like you to meet Mr. Grojini."

The man said, "Mr. Grojini is my father. He's dead. I'm Loris." And held out his hand.

Qigiq smiled. "Nice to meet you, Loris." He balanced on his crutch. Loris had a grip like a man who knew how to hold a wrench: firm but not tight.

"You want to see what that cat dragged in?" Loris asked.

He led them through an archway to a narrow room lined with perhaps thirty motorcycles along the left wall and four mechanic's stations along the right. Several of the bikes looked almost new, their red or green or silver paint blaring from the line of much older, rusty bikes. Qigiq guessed maybe half would start.

Loris had moved quickly and was standing by the fourth bay gesturing with both hands.

Qigiq hobbled over. His bike was missing both wheels and the front fork. The engine had been used for a plow. He knew any insurance adjuster in the world would total it.

"This very nice Guzzi. Has taken hard tumble. Instruments crushed, fork twist. But the motor, she is good." He frowned. "Only one problem."

After the litany of tragedies, Qigiq tensed to think what might represent a problem.

"Only one?" he asked, trying to sound cheerful.

Loris smiled. "Looks worse than is," he said. "But." He held up a finger, stepped to the bike and pointed to the tubes running from the headstock. "The frame she is twist. We have choice. We twist back." As he said this he made fists with both hands and a wringing a towel motion. "But she not so strong. Second, we cut," he made a slicing motion with his hand in front of the engine, "and put on state-of-art front from Aprilia." He frowned. "Easy to do. But then," he looked sad and shrugged his shoulders, "She not Guzzi, though nice bike."

Qigiq felt Kandy watching him. "Is there a third choice?"

"Best choice, we look and find frame with fork. Maybe from fire, or rear end collision. Then we," he held his hands far apart like he was lifting a barrel, "take engine and move to new chassis. That be very very nice bike, all Guzzi." He smiled widely, revealing a partial gold tooth in his upper row.

"That's possible?" Kandy asked.

Loris shrugged. "We must find frame first."

Qigiq reached out and brushed dried mud from the side of the green gas tank. Loris disappeared and returned with a damp rag and wiped off the tank. It was scratched down to raw dark steel. Qigiq moved in close to examine the scratches.

Kandy leaned in next to him. "You think?"

"Worth a try. I might have an ounce of luck left," Qigiq said.

Loris interrupted. "So, the frame?"

"Let's look," Qigiq said. "We can always use a less *Guzzi* solution later."

Loris grinned. "Yes yes, good way to begin." He headed for the showroom, motioning them to follow. "We closed Monday. But for Kandy, I open. Come, I show you."

Qigiq looked at Kandy, who looked away at a calendar showing a topless girl holding a big wrench next to a red Ducati. "Nice bike," she said, and followed Loris.

Qigiq brought up the rear. As he reached the showroom Loris was rolling a silver bike out of the fourth row. It looked like an alien insect from a planet with curved gravity. The seat, the motor, headlights, frame, everything tilted forward like it wanted to slide onto the front wheel.

Loris pointed to the left side. "We add peg."

Qigiq tried to catch Kandy's eyes, but she was staring where Loris was pointing.

"Come try," Loris said. He looked at Qigiq.

Qigiq moved around to the left of the bike. The side of the tank said Aprilia, and below that *Mana 850.*

Kandy still hadn't looked up.

"We have seat adjusted low," Loris said.

"I've never mounted with a crutch."

Loris smiled. "Stand on right foot. Put crutch in left hand." Loris stepped up to help Qigiq place the tip. "Put weight here and throw good leg over."

Qigiq managed to get halfway onto the seat.

"Yes, that is good."

He held the crutch out to Loris, who shook his head. "No no, you must be independent." He pointed at what looked like a chrome beer can strapped to the frame."

Qigiq worked the tip of the crutch into the can.

"And here," Loris pointed out a U-shaped bracket tucked beside the seat. He pulled a black rubber ring up and over the crutch to secure it. "Don't forget rubber, is safer." Loris grinned.

Qigiq stood the bike up under him, imagining the roar of the motor and wind. He turned his head and laughed at the crutch running the length of the motorcycle between his cast and the engine.

"Is good, no?" Loris said.

"Very good," Qigiq said. "But I can't shift."

"Is Mana, eight-fifty cc, ninety-degree V-twin. Good power like Guzzi. You will love."

Qigiq repeated, "But I can't shift."

Loris frowned. He looked at Kandy who was studying the crutch mounting bracket.

Loris said. "Is Mana." He motioned at Kandy.

Qigiq twisted his head to meet Kandy's eyes.

"Shifts itself," she said. "Three modes: Touring, Sport, Rain." She pointed at the bar. "No clutch."

In his confusion to mount, he hadn't noticed the absence of a lever on the left grip.

Loris spread his arms again. "Big power. You will love."

Qigiq was stunned. He had thought about a scooter, but this was a full-blown motorcycle, lightweight and powerful. If it could shift itself, he sure as hell would learn to ride it. Except.

"I can't afford a new bike."

"Loaner. Insurance rental," Loris said. "You must have to do job."

Qigiq nodded slowly. "Whose idea was this?"

Loris said, "You have nice friend," not quite answering the question.

Qigiq caught Kandy's eye. Her face was almost shy. Not a look he had ever seen on Kandy Dreeson.

"Yeah, she's quite a partner," Qigiq said.

Loris smiled widely, showing off his gold tooth. "You two be very very happy with Mana. Good bike. All Italian. I get paperwork." He disappeared into the back cavern.

Qigiq blinked, then re-found Kandy's eyes.

"Thanks, Detective," he said.

"You're welcome, Detective."

He smiled. "I'll need a new helmet."

She punched his arm, momentarily helping him forget the pain in his leg.

He saw an image dance across the glass of the front window.

"Kandy, out front."

She spun around. The window was empty.

"Same hoodie. I swear," Qigiq said.

She was at the front door in three strides and through it in five.

~ 39 ~

They sat at the Good Egg Café on Embarcadero in fifty-five degree air because there had been no wait for an outside table. Ten feet away, Kandy's Mini was parked in front of a silver Mana sporting a custom crutch mount.

Qigiq said, "A farthing for your thoughts."

Kandy's crooked grin preceeded, "Spending big today?"

"Saving for a new bike."

Her eyes drifted up the street. "I was on that sidewalk in what? six, seven seconds, and no one. Completely empty."

He spread jelly on a corn muffin. "Maybe my mind was playing tricks. Or that hoodie ducked into a passing car."

She swirled a spoon through oatmeal and raspberries. "Fingers. Erased songs. Body parts. Someone tries to kill you. Now we're being followed. It's Monday morning. First package showed up last Wednesday. Adds up to what?"

"And the names on those blogs," he said, digging into his back pocket for the rumpled piece of paper. "You really think someone tried to kill me? Or send a warning?"

She chewed. "Kill you."

His leg stopped aching as he felt icy water pump through his veins.

"Could have been a warning."

She shook her head. "No way."

"You're convinced?"

"A warning would include a message. You know, *stay away from my woman*, or maybe *get out of town*. If it was a warning, where's the message?"

Qigiq thought about it. He smiled. "Replace your Moto Guzzi?"

"Exactly. You know what I think?"

"No. But if you tell me I'll buy breakfast."

Her grin returned. "I think you saw someone at the marina. Or that someone thinks you did. And they can't have a witness that places them there."

He bit a muffin. "You think I saw the perp?" He remembered the shadow figure by *Pimp*.

"Or a professional—someone whose livelihood depends on a reputation for keeping things clean. No one likes a messy murder."

Qigiq stopped chewing. "Kill me to protect his reputation?"

"Sure. You die in an accident, a motorcycle accident no less. No one cares about a crazy biker that runs off the road in a high-speed turn. They conclude you were riding too fast, probably even breaking the law. Look at that, a cop breaking the law...tsk tsk." She shook her head. "He protects himself, he protects whoever hired him, he keeps his reputation. Sounds like an easy decision to me."

"Not a drunk who didn't see my cool taillight?" He didn't buy it either, but he was still adjusting to the idea that he was important enough that someone would try to kill him.

"Not a chance," she said. "Not the way you describe a car with no headlights slowing down so it could push you off the road. A drunk would have shot straight past, or driven off the road on top of you."

He took notes on his wrinkled paper.

"What about the gas tank?" he asked.

She shrugged. "We can try a match. Might yield a manufacturer. I wouldn't get my hopes up."

"I'd rather find a scratched car with green and white Italian paint on the left front fender."

"Swell, how?"

"Well, if my partner would get a paint match and manufacturer, I could call around to the body shops in the area and see if they have a job that fits our specs."

"On it," she said.

"So someone wants to kill me because we found that package on Walters' boat?"

She shook her head. "We were meant to find that package. There's no reason I can think of to put something in dry ice and store it unless you plan to use it, or want it to be found. We just weren't supposed to find it so soon. Not while your mysterious shadow was still in the area."

"Meant to find it? So we're being led somewhere."

"By a ring in the nose," she said. "That's what I think."

"Someone who wants to get famous by killing people."

"My first guess," she said, scraping a spoon around the bottom of the bowl. "Why else all this wacky Internet stuff? Our psycho is being very public."

He clicked his teeth together while thinking about the word *public*.

"Ferdinand next?"

She nodded. "After you buy."

© © ©

They took the elevator to the fourth floor and found the young assistant who protected the entrance to the rooms where sensitive testing was performed. She frowned when they asked for Dr. Pillar.

"He won't be available until after lunch."

Qigiq tried to read her soft eyes, wondering how best to persuade her to open a file.

Kandy took a step closer to the counter and glanced at the girl's lab coat.

"Margie, we're working on a murder investigation and need the DNA test results ASAP. Bobby told me they would be ready this morning."

The young girls dark eyebrows shot up at someone referring to the great Dr. Robert M. Pillar as "Bobby."

"You can see him around one-thirty."

"That's hours from now," Kandy said. "Would you please just pull the file and tell us if the results are ready. It won't take but a second."

"I don't know who's allowed to see the file," Margie said.

"This is our case. I can give you the case ID and you can check it against our names and badge numbers," Kandy said. Then she smiled the softest, sweetest smile Qigiq had ever seen her features conjure and said, "It would really help us out, murderers are tough to catch."

The girl stood frozen reminding Qigiq of his computer when it was busy doing something. He forced himself to remain motionless so he wouldn't break the magic Kandy was building.

"What was your name?" Margie asked.

"Kandy. Kandy Dreeson. Detective," Kandy said, holding out her hand and gently shaking Margie's.

The girl turned and waved her badge at a sensor. Qigiq heard locks click just before she pushed open double glass doors.

"Bobby?" Qigiq said.

"Shh," Kandy whispered, digging for gum.

"I didn't know you two were so close."

She started chewing. "Neither does Bobby."

Qigiq crutched his way to the water cooler and lowered himself into a foam-coated chair to sip water and wait.

The girl returned in five minutes and placed a folder on the counter.

"You can't take this, but you can look at it," she said, staring at Kandy like a fan admiring a rock star.

He watched Kandy lean over the desk, reading what were probably Pillar's notes to himself. Her brow furled into ruffled ridges every few seconds. She flipped back through pages, searching. She stopped and read. Flipped some more. Read. She glanced over at Qigiq, her face looking like she had been forced to chew something besides Juicy Fruit.

Kandy straightened, closed the file and gave Margie a huge smile.

"Thank you, Margie. That was very helpful. I'll call Bobby after lunch to follow up."

Margie's shoulders relaxed. "Glad I could help you, Detective Dreeson."

Kandy headed for the outer door and remained silent while they waited for the elevator.

The doors binged, slid apart, Kandy stepped on. She held the button as he avoided the crack with his crutch tip.

"What's up?" he said softly.

"All the parts are Sally."

He nodded.

"But—"

He watched the number three light as the elevator moved.

"The time of death of the fingers is Tuesday night around midnight. And—" she stopped again.

He wished she wouldn't do that, but he knew she was struggling with new information. He focused on the throbbing in his leg to give his mind something to do.

"The time of death of the package we found on *Firebird*. Between two and four."

"That's what Ferdinand estimated," he said.

She shook her head.

"No. Ferd said maybe Tuesday night based on wave action and shadows and models. Pillar says two to four p.m. *Wednesday*—the day the package arrived at Robina's, based on blood absorption. He had to make temperature assumptions though, with the dry ice packaging."

He felt coldness in his lower spine. "She was alive between Tuesday night and Wednesday afternoon?" He coughed. "After..."

"Yeah, that's what it means," she said.

"Someone wanted Sally to suffer."

"Sadistic prick." She paused. "There's a big problem here."

He didn't ask.

She said, "Ferd's calculations are based around the moon shadows in that first movie."

"Is it possible he had her captive from two a.m. Tuesday morning, all the way through to Wednesday afternoon?" he asked.

"And then he killed her." Her gum cracked from the pressure. "That prick."

"You're repeating yourself," he said, trying to lighten her mood. "Twelve hours. Certainly possible."

"Prick," she said.

He remained quiet, his thoughts rumbling. "Or..."

The elevator stopped at the first floor. The doors opened. No one was waiting for it.

"Or what?" she said.

"Or our assumptions are wrong: the dry ice calculation; the moonlight."

She led the way to their office, kicking a trash can and chairs that were blocking the path, so he could get through the corridor with the crutch. Once inside, she closed the door.

"Not moonlight?" she said, staring at him.

"Uh, yeah. Well, maybe this isn't possible. I was just thinking that the video could have been taken in sunlight and then modified using special effect computers like Hollywood has. To throw us off when we analyzed timing."

She continued staring, but said nothing.

Qigiq lowered his butt to the chair and leaned his crutch against the wall.

"You might be a genius," she said.

He blinked, and smiled. "Let's go ask Ferdinand."

"He'll be pissed," she said.

"Pissed? Why?"

"Because he's the computer genius, and you thought of it first."

"Tell him it was your idea," Qigiq said.

"Not moonlight?" Ferdinand said. "What an unusual idea, Detective Kandy. But yes, it is possible to filter video to create the pale low-contrast of a moonlit night. I believe that was done for the bridge scene in the movie version of Peter Pan decades ago. I must have another look at that video." He crossed the lab to a black desk supporting a flat display large enough to be mounted on the wall of a sports bar.

"But first, we must look at this."

Qigiq and Kandy followed.

Ferdinand sat and started what he called the Chop movie reconstruction, but it was larger, and unfortunately, clearer than the one Qigiq had seen earlier.

"I have enhanced the data. Do you notice anything?"

Kandy stood behind Ferdinand holding her chin in her hand.

Qigiq leaned on his crutch. "It's sharper. Like you focused it."

"Yes. It is much better now. So good in fact," he tapped at the computer's keyboard, "We can select a section and bring it to life."

While they watched, the picture twisted and zoomed.

"We use data from many frames to improve the quality of solid objects," Ferdinand said.

Qigiq saw the knife rotate and zoom towards them. Then it stood still as frames zipped past in the background. Simultaneously, the detail of the knife improved until he could see *Excalibur* etched into the blade in extravagant letters that he associated with the middle ages.

"How do multiple frames do that?"

"Once we align the geometry," Ferdinand said, "and make assumptions about the noise inherent in video and compression, we can use the hundreds of pictures of the knife to create a single composite that uses data from all of them.

"It looks like a photograph," Kandy said.

"Exactly, a video camera takes thirty photos every second."

"And we know this is the murder weapon?" Qigiq asked.

"No," said Ferdinand. "We know it is the mutilation weapon."

Qigiq stared at the image, wondering how many different models Excalibur made.

As if reading his mind, Ferdinand said, "I have compared this knife to the Excalibur catalog. This is the Kingfisher. If you look carefully, you can see near the handle the etched image of a Belted Kingfisher. Note the neck feathers, and the long beak."

"A bird?" Kandy said.

"Brightly colored. Likes to dive for fish."

"So we know exactly what model knife was used?" Qigiq said.

"Absolutely," Ferdinand said. "But we know much more."

Qigiq looked at Kandy, who shrugged.

Ferdinand shook his head and smiled. "And you call yourselves detectives. Watch my friends." On the big screen, Ferdinand brought up a list of retail stores within a hundred miles of San Francisco. "Excalibur provided me with a list of their dealers. We are fortunate they do not sell their knives over the Internet."

"You want us to check out these dealers?" Kandy asked.

"Oh, my dear girl, no," Ferdinand said. "This is what computers are for."

He brought up another list.

"Here you see every Kingfisher knife, part number K54F5129, sold within the past six months by any of these dealers. Of course, I had to obtain certain legal documents before the stores would release their sales. But a murder investigation motivates judges, especially with movies like that." He pointed to the screen where Sally's ear was being removed.

"So we know where the knives were sold," Qigiq said. "That's great."

Ferdinand's big eyebrows crawled closer together as he said, "You have a low bar for greatness, my good man. Not only do we know where they were sold, but thanks to computerized purchasing via plastic cards, and the power of the Patriot Act to encourage banks to release names—we know *who* bought those knives."

Kandy said. "Ferdinand, you're amazing."

"Thank you, Detective. I try to be thorough."

"How many?" Qigiq asked.

"The Kingfisher is a popular knife among sportsmen. There have been 514 knives sold in the past six months within this radius." He drew a circle with his finger over the map on the screen.

"That's a lot of people to interview," Qigiq said. "We'll need help."

Kandy nodded.

"Not if this is correct," Ferdinand said.

"More magic?" Kandy asked.

Ferdinand huffed a big breath. "Science, Detective. Magic is for childhood birthday parties."

"But you're so good, it looks like magic."

Ferdinand smiled. "Well yes, sometimes lady luck smiles in our direction."

"What are you two talking about?" Qigiq asked.

"Naturally, I cross-referenced the list of knife purchasers with the owners of the boats."

"And?" Kandy said. "And?" Qigiq added.

He pointed to a window in the upper right corner of the big screen with a blue background. "And," Ferdinand said, "there is only one name common to both lists."

Qigiq read *Edward G. Blake.* A man who owned a Kingfisher knife and a boat with a Pendum radar. He turned his head and met Kandy's eyes.

"*With a Bullet,*" they said to each other.

"That is the boat the computer suggested." Ferdinand took off his thick glasses. "I hope you are able to locate that knife."

Qigiq couldn't remember ever seeing Ferdinand without glasses. He looked younger, though still like a college professor.

Ferdinand rubbed the bridge of his nose between his index finger and thumb.

"You must find this person soon."

"With you on the case, his ass is ours," Kandy said.

Ferdinand tried not to grin, but failed.

"Detective Kandy, when you have his ass, kick it please."

Kandy laughed. Qigiq joined her. Ferdinand shook his head at them.

"Now, let us discuss this moonlight problem you bring me." Ferdinand moved across the room to a computer he had placed next to Sally's machine. Hers was downloading music files and showing the name and byte count for each song.

"What's it doing?" Qigiq asked.

"Running a Sally simulation," Ferdinand said. "I have it downloading music from the sites she visited, and, as much as possible, in the styles she liked."

Ferdinand stepped to the side. "Now, here is the original video."

Qigiq watched the rape play out. The video was dark, mostly grays, except for Sally's hair showing a bit of the blondness he had seen in the bikini pictures.

Kandy opened the envelope with the four pictures she obtained from Robina.

"We have these," she said. "And digital originals."

Ferdinand examined them, one after the other, for what felt like minutes.

"These of Sally and the other girl will be helpful. I can measure hair color and perhaps design a filter to adjust to the color we see in the video, assuming sunlight as the source. We will see what that might reveal. But what are these?"

"Screen captures from two different computers, one here in San Francisco, the other in New York City. We're not sure, but it looks like some kind of virus."

Ferdinand eyebrows shifted again. "Virus? Well, we shall see." He studied the pictures carefully.

Kandy pointed. "Marie lives in New York City. It deleted music files and posted her name to a series of blogs."

"How unusual," Ferdinand said.

"The other is from Robina, Sally's roommate here in San Francisco. This one offered a free iPod, claiming hers had a defective battery. Both knew Sally. Both received Amazon boxes."

Ferdinand studied the second picture. "Have you talked to the manufacturer?"

"Not yet. We wanted to get your opinion on what might be happening before making inquiries."

"Wise," Ferdinand said. "I will look at the moonlight question later. Tell me all you can about these viruses the girls are getting."

"According to the blogs," Qigiq said, "there are thousands of people having their music deleted and identity publicized, often including email addresses."

"Violation of the Right to Privacy Act," Ferdinand said.

"But we have no idea how many free iPod offers are being made," Kandy added. "We only know about Robina."

Ferdinand studied the printouts. "You say thousands have been posted to blogs?"

"Yes," Kandy said. "We compiled a list by searching for the pirate language."

"I'll do more sear—" Ferdinand said stopped short.

He turned his head toward Sally's machine and snapped his eyes back to the paper in his hand, then back to the machine. "This cannot be happening."

Qigiq's eyes flicked to the computer and saw a Jolly Roger waving. His shoulders tensed like there were gangsters at the door, but he had no idea what to do.

"We must capture it," Ferdinand said.

Kandy looked at Qigiq and mouthed "Capture?"

"Quickly," Ferdinand said, as he raced his bulk across the room, returning with a laptop under one arm and a handful of cables trailing behind him.

Qigiq stepped backward and watched Ferdinand's hands move in a blur. The cover came off Sally's machine and a connector went into a long slot, which was then connected via a fat cable to the laptop.

"We must learn precisely what this processor is doing," Ferdinand said.

In less than a minute Ferdinand was staring at a display on the laptop and mumbling, "Bus traffic normal. This sector labeled Smith has fragmented into a huge number of child programs. Difficult to track."

Qigiq assumed Ferd was talking to himself and pulled Kandy aside.

"Ferdinand is going to be busy. What do you think?"

"Search *With a Bullet* before Mr. Blake gets to it...if it's not too late."

He nodded. "What about visiting Apple?" He tapped the picture offering the free iPod.

"If it's a real recall, we drop it. But if it's not...."

He rolled his lips tight together. "I could ride down and talk to them."

"Good idea. Get some fresh air; it'll be warmer down there. I'll go see *Bullet*—with a warrant." She smiled. "When you get back, we'll talk about Blake."

"Um, since we have permission," Qigiq said. "Would you mind checking to see what kind of knife Professor Walters prefers?"

~ 40 ~

The crutch drew glances from motorists as the Mana 850 shifted smoothly under him.

Kandy had been right, ten minutes out of San Francisco the cool air blowing into his helmet began to warm. His left leg stretched along the side of the bike hurt on big bumps, but was otherwise fine.

He tensed as a dark sedan pulled up close on his left. A glance told him a retiree was joyriding. Unable to shake the feeling that every dark car was danger, he eased his way to the leftmost lane and opened the throttle. If they couldn't catch him, they couldn't run him down.

He passed a major interchange and much of the traffic turned east toward the San Francisco Airport. He continued south past a highway numbered 92. Shortly, he arrived in Cupertino at a circular road named Infinite Loop. He didn't know much about computers, but he did know that an infinite loop was something a program could be caught in that made it keep doing the same thing over and over. Like some of his college buddies did with girls.

He located visitor parking and entered the building with a big number one out front.

A young girl with dark hair sitting behind a desk so high it almost hid her from sight looked up.

"May I help you?"

"I'm Detective Qigiq from the San Francisco Police Department." He held out his badge. "We're investigating a homicide. Could I talk to someone who would know about iPod failures and how replacements are being handled?"

The young girl frowned. "Um. Do you have an appointment?"

"No. I don't even know who I should see."

"Well, I don't know how I can help you if you don't know who you want to see."

"May I speak with the CEO?"

The girl's face froze. "No one can do that without an appointment."

"How about the President, can I see him?" he asked.

"Apple doesn't have a President." She stared at him.

He slipped his badge back into his leather jacket. Standing there on a crutch holding a motorcycle helmet probably wasn't helping his efforts to see an executive. He thought about who in a huge company would control a warranty claim.

"Maybe the vice president in charge of Customer Support?"

She lit up. "That would be in our marketing department." She dialed the phone and chatted into it.

His good leg grew tired so he backed up and lowered himself onto a long cushioned couch.

The girl stood and called to him.

"I'm sorry, she's not in today."

Other than testing the Mana, he hadn't accomplished anything. He was about to give up when the blog postings came to mind.

"Who's in charge of your web site?"

"That's in our marketing group too. Let me see which vice president."

The girl ducked behind her counter. Qigiq could see the top of her head and hear a computer bleep from time to time. Soon she was on the phone again; he heard the words "detective" and "San Francisco."

She stood with a big smile. "They're sending someone down."

"Thank you," he said, grateful she had made something happen.

He unfolded the free offer page. There was nothing about pirates, or stealing, or even music. Just *Your iPod has a defective battery* and instructions on how to get a new one. He wondered why they would send an entire iPod if it just needed a battery.

A blonde woman who looked like she surfed for a living entered through inner glass doors opposite the ones Qigiq had used. Tan and lean, she said simply, "Hello, Detective. You are a lucky man. Mr. Templeton happened to be between meetings and thought it would be interesting to meet a real detective. He's a big fan of Harry Bosch."

Qigiq smiled.

"You know Harry? Mr. Templeton has all his novels."

"Never met him," Qigiq said, letting the quizzical look on her face go unanswered. "But I'm grateful Mr. Templeton is available. What does he do here?"

"He's Vice President for Customer Relations, including responsibility for much of the website, the parts that aren't handled by the Marketing Department."

"My name is Qigiq," he said.

She smiled. "I'm Brenda, Mr. Templeton's assistant."

She walked over to a computer on the counter by the dark-haired girl and started typing.

"How do you spell kajeek?" she asked.

"Q-I-G-I-Q."

She turned around and pressed a white sticky badge to his leather jacket with fingernails the Italian red of a Ducati. He hoped it didn't have glue that was going to be difficult to remove.

"Please follow me," she said.

They passed through a series of glass doors, each one magically opened by her badge, until they were outdoors. As she walked and he limped along the sidewalk he realized they were surrounded by buildings that themselves were surrounded by a loop of road. While feeling free and comfortable outside, he was actually in a secure area.

They passed through more glass doors and up an elevator to the fourth floor and a corner office overlooking the secure grass he had just passed. She tapped on an open door.

"Detective Qigiq here to see you," she said.

She waved him in.

"Hello, Detective," said a short man with round gold-rimmed glasses standing behind a business desk. He wore a white shirt open at the collar and blue jeans. "I'm Tom Templeton. It's a pleasure to meet one of San Francisco's finest."

Qigiq had a short internal debate as to whether or not he should explain that he was one of Fairbanks' finest on loan, but decided it might confuse things.

"Thanks for seeing me," Qigiq said. "We have a situation that involves Apple and I wasn't sure where to start." Qigiq noticed rows and rows of paperbacks on a bookshelf behind Templeton. If those were all detective novels, Brenda hadn't been kidding.

Tom frowned. "Involves us?"

Qigiq said, "iPods."

"Generally it's a good idea to start with the Public Relations department.

But Brenda mentioned something about our website. Please sit down." Tom motioned to two wheelless chairs facing his desk.

Qigiq maneuvered into one and leaned his crutch against the other. He left his jacket on.

"I realize you don't have much time, so I'll come right to the point. Is Apple currently offering a free iPod replacement for units with defective batteries?"

"Not that rumor again. Is this about batteries overheating, or exploding? There was a ridiculous story running around years ago about exploding laptops and cellphones. No substance to any of it."

"This is quite recent," Qigiq said. "Over the weekend."

Tom frowned and sat, elbows on his desk, fingers steepled before him like a monk in prayer.

"A few days ago? I haven't heard about it. Not a whisper."

Qigiq wondered if he had heard about the pirates or the *Don't Steal* messages. Or maybe even seen the videos of Sally. First things first. He dug out the picture of the iPod offer, pressed it flat on Tom's desk, then pushed it across to him.

"Are you familiar with this?" he asked.

Tom picked up the paper and read, including the fine print along the bottom that said this offer was only valid for the original owner and was not transferable. It also said it only applied to specific models and serial number ranges. Then it listed the Apple trademark and logo copyright notice like every other ad that needed to protect such things.

"On the surface, this looks like an Apple piece. But I'm not aware of any program that would provide a replacement iPod. We do, of course, repair failed products under warranty and provide a new unit at our discretion."

"Could this offer be from somewhere else in the company?" Qigiq asked.

"It shouldn't," Tom said. "This is my jurisdiction. I'll check with Operations though, to see if such a program is underway, or possibly active in test markets."

"Thank you. But if this isn't Apple, who else would make such an offer?"

Tom shrugged. "Could be a competitor phishing for customers and sending out their own music players to iPod users. You know, seeding the market, trying to get people to switch and say how much better their product is than an iPod. Have you seen any of these supposedly free iPods?"

Qigiq hadn't heard if Robina's had arrived.

"Not yet." He pushed a second sheet of paper across the table. "The girl who gave us this just signed up yesterday. So perhaps it will arrive soon. That's the form she had to fill out."

Tom again read the document carefully. Qigiq wondered if he had gone to the same thoroughness school as Ferdinand.

"Only a serial number?" Tom said. "No address, proof of purchase, nothing that would show she's the original owner."

"Couldn't that be determined from sales records?" Qigiq asked.

"Only if the customer registered the iPod after purchasing it, which I'm afraid only a minority take the time to do, even though we make it very easy. Otherwise, we have no idea who bought which device."

"Then how could they know where to send the replacement?" Qigiq asked.

Tom just said, "This is not the way Apple does things."

The way he said it made Qigiq think of a religion, or something like Scientology—not quite a cult, and vaguely undefinable.

"We would surely require proof of purchase. And if we were going to do an exchange, we would do it through our retail stores so that we could check ID." He shook his head again, more emphatically. "I can't imagine giving away new devices without an exchange program. If there are defective units out there, we want them out of circulation."

"So you're ninety-nine percent certain this isn't Apple?"

"At least," Tom said. "I'll check with Operations to be certain."

Qigiq dug in his pocket and handed across his card. Tom was probably right, which didn't help at all.

"Do you have time for one more question?" Qigiq asked.

Tom turned and looked at a big bright computer to his right.

"I have a meeting in three minutes."

Qigiq took that as a yes.

"Apple uses a *Don't Steal Music* sticker on its iPod products, doesn't it?"

"Sometimes…in some markets. We understand there is an entire economic food chain that needs to be fed. Including, perhaps especially, the listener." He smiled.

"Heard anything unusual about those stickers in the last three or four days?"

Tom frowned. "Those were used a long time ago."

"So nothing new in the past few days?"

Tom shook his head, and looked at his wrist watch.

This was a big bomb to drop on a guy who had less than two minutes to deal with it, but Apple should know, and the information was hugely public. Qigiq stood, using Tom's desk for support. He peeled off a Post-it note from a stack on Tom's desk and grabbed a thin gold pen from a holder. He wrote down the URL of the first YouTube video, an address he had accessed so many times it was stuck in his memory, possibly forever. He handed the slip to Tom.

"Someone is using *Don't Steal* stickers with your logo in what we believe is a homicide. Check out this video. It was posted on YouTube late last week."

"A homicide?" Tom said, with equal parts disbelief and interest. "I'll look at it right after my meeting."

"If you have any ideas, please call me," Qigiq said.

"I certainly will, Detective. Thank you for stopping by. And if I may ask, what happened to your foot?"

"Twisted my ankle in a gopher hole," he replied, wanting to skip the motorcycles-are-dangerous conversation.

Brenda graciously led him back to the main entrance and gave him a key ring with a tiny iPod she called a Shuffle attached to it. He grinned, realizing there really was a free giveaway, you just had to talk to a vice president who liked detective novels.

He secured his crutch to the shiny Mana and leaned against the saddle to check email on his phone. None. He smiled, realizing that the little computer he held in his hand had been designed right here in one of these buildings.

A numeral three glowed beside the voicemail icon. The first message was from Loris. No luck on a new frame for his old Guzzi, but not to worry, the world was large.

The second was from Kandy. "Calling from *Bullet*. Yes there's a Kingfisher. Yes there's blood on the blade. Yes it's on its way to Pillar." A pause. In a softer voice, "Too easy though. Toolbox. Right on top. No effort to conceal. Heading to *Firebird*. Later."

Qigiq's leg throbbed. He shifted weight off of it. Why leave the weapon on the boat? Crime of passion? Not the Kingfisher from the video, but a matching one to throw them off the trail?

He closed his eyes and flipped through Ferdinand's close-up images: knife, small etching of a bird, the unusually ornate word. Unmistakable, though hardly unique with hundreds sold in only six months. Why leave it lying around? Toss it over the side in the middle of the ocean. Did the perp really believe they would never find the boat?

The voicemail number was now a one. He tapped it.

A breathy voice with unusual articulation, like a foreigner struggling with English said, "Hello, Detective. Did your riding skill allow you to survive our little mishap? Or were you just lucky? We shall soon know."

The pain in his ankle migrated up his leg as his chest tightened. He shook his head to clear it. His life had only been threatened twice—not something he could get used to. He studied the phone; the caller's number was blocked. He had heard that voice before, but couldn't place a name.

Or a face.

~ 41 ~

Harold sat shoulder to shoulder beside Lili at the counter of a coffee shop on Stevens Creek Boulevard. An open window let a sixty-eight degree California breeze stroke their cheeks. They each had a Grande Mocha sitting to the left of their respective laptops. A half-eaten chocolate chip muffin the size of a grapefruit sat between them.

"Is the Chinese site responding?" Harold asked.

"Yes. Updating like crazy."

He leaned left to see her screen. The count rolled upward like the progressive jackpot in a casino.

"Good."

The number stopped.

"Re-trigger your search. Data aggregators are defined by a time-indexed list; depending on when we check, we see different sites. Hard to track without the list and the math to traverse it."

Lili leaned and whispered, "No connection to us, right?"

"Nothing points back to Silver Platter." He watched her eyes. "Or you and me."

She studied him, her expression flat. "In case something goes wrong you mean?"

"Nothing is going to go wrong, Lili. Blake authorized this. He's the CEO. We're pawns in a tiny company doing what we're told. No one will come after us."

Her expression didn't change. "Is that why we're accessing on public Wi-Fi with machines that aren't registered to the company? Black-box laptops, running Linux no less. And watching websites that change every few seconds based on some weird algorithm you dreamed up?"

He broke off a chunk of the muffin. "No point in being careless."

"But nothing's going to go wrong?" she said with a little grin.

He stuffed the muffin into his mouth. "Hope not." He examined the numbers from the new post on her screen and whistled. "Over three million machines so far. There are boatloads of people listening to a whole-lotta music."

"Yeah, and on average every thief the Hand finds is being posted to forty-one blogs."

He chewed the muffin and shifted to glance at her screen.

"Can't be."

"What do mean, right there, average posts: 41." She pointed with the pale green-metallic nail of her right index finger.

"The user count is three-point-one million, and the total posts is only ninety million. That's an average of less than thirty posts per user."

"Why don't they match?" she said, leaning back with her mocha, "Mr. Nothing-will-go-wrong programmer on whom the company depends for its welfare."

He frowned. "An awfully good question for a manager."

"Your program can't divide correctly? I bet even a lowly manager like me could do that." She laughed.

Harold opened the calculator app on his computer and entered the numbers just to be sure he wasn't doing something stupid in his head.

"That's not how posts-per-user is calculated," he said. "For redundancy, every Hand sends user info first, *then* sends the number of posts it was able to achieve, before erasing itself. Since these are all natural numbers," he looked at her, "positive integers, no round off, we should be able to calculate the correct posts-per-user by dividing the totals."

"Sounds easy-peasy."

"But the numbers don't match; I'm betting reporting error. If every Hand posts forty-one times and there were three million of them, even management could figure out that's over a hundred and twenty million postings—not ninety."

"But there aren't," she said.

"Lili, your powers of observation astound me."

He reset his search and landed at a different website, this one in Denmark. The counts had risen as expected, but the average remained incorrect."

He stared at the numbers, contemplating how the hell they could be wrong.

Her voice tight, Lili said, "It's one thing to have a virus out there, even with our *insurance*. But Harold, you're telling me the Hand has a bug in it. Please don't tell me that."

"I'm not telling you anything, Lili. These things are hard to test in the lab. But I don't write many bugs."

She watched numbers pop up on his screen and reached over to steal a chunk of the muffin.

Harold rolled his lips between his teeth to help him think.

Twenty-eight seconds ticked past.

"OK. Hypothesis," he said.

"Confidence level?" she asked.

"Hmm. Ninety percent, based on zero testing."

"I feel all warm and fuzzy."

"The total posts are based on summing up the counts as reported by each copy of the Invisible Hand."

"Yes?"

"So if the count is low, either the math to add them up is broken. Highly unlikely. Or the Hands aren't reporting the posts correctly."

"Makes no sense, Harold. If each Hand sends a number, and the website adds them up, then the average must be correct. I'm missing something."

"Lili, you're right. The Hand sends user info, then sends the post count as a separate communication. If there's a bug so that sometimes it sends a user, but no post count, that would mean the user number is correct at three-point-one million, but the total number of posts is low because they're not all getting through. Thus the ninety million we see here, instead of the hundred and twenty we should be seeing."

"Uh, yeah, what you said," she said, sipping.

"I'm saying some of the Hands aren't reporting how many posts they did, but they *are* reporting that they found a user."

"Sounds like a bug." She laughed.

"Hypothesis number two: some users are pulling the plug on their machine after the Hand registers, but before it sends the posting count."

"How much time between those two actions?"

"Depends on the network, but could be several seconds. Reporting is done last, after all other work is complete. That's how we know the data we're looking at includes only successful postings. If the Hand fails, for whatever reason, it never reports."

Her eyes searched his face. "Awfully weird for people to be shutting down at just the right second."

"Yeah. Weird is a good word," he said, without looking up.

He continued to work his lower lip. "Unless..."

"Yes?" she said softly.

"Unless the reporting code didn't load," he mused.

"No way. None of the checksums would be right. The Hand would never even start up, knowing its own code was incomplete."

He looked up. "You're starting to get this."

She looked down at the remaining half of the muffin and blushed.

"It wouldn't launch," he said mostly to himself. "Somehow there are copies of the Hand out there that aren't reporting post count. It's as if there are two. Like there's been a mutation."

"Harold, computer viruses only mutate in science fiction."

"Unless they're programmed to," he said. "And this one isn't."

She leaned close. "You think there are two?"

He concentrated. "Maybe our insertion code has a bug and we let two go instead of one." He remembered Sarlin's dark hair flowing around her elfish ear while he watched her run the insertion scripts.

"And the second one is different?" she asked.

"Posting details must be turned off."

"How could that happen?"

He held his eyes pointed down at his laptop for several seconds.

"Best guess? Launch bug."

"How do we find out?"

"Can't. The machine I used to insert has been cleaned and—" he thought of Sarlin's warm wet kiss after he gave her the computer. "Uh, disposed of. If there was an error in the setup, we'll never know."

"Harold the Great makes a mistake on insertion? Now *that* is science fiction. The most important release of our technology ever, and you of all people blow it? Not likely."

Harold thought of Sarlin sitting across from him at that café in New York, her erect nipples pushing outward against Lycra. And the sweet smell of her, as she stood close, reading over his shoulder. He was normally too compulsively careful to make mistakes...

"You're right," he said, though he wasn't certain, a feeling he found profoundly uncomfortable. "Let's assume the insertion was up to my normal standards." He smiled. "We tested phantom launches in the lab hundreds of times, all perfect. But there's a mutation, or at least variation, out there that has posting turned off. It's reporting successful completions, but not updating the blogs or the count. How could that be?"

"Easy," she said instantly, turning her mocha upside down to drain the last drop of gooey chocolate from the recyclable paper cup.

This surprised him. "Easy? Even I don't think this one's easy."

"Sure it is," she said. "You're just focused on the computer side, and that's not how this happened."

"It's not? Hmm. Is management going to share with this lowly unworthy peon her brilliant insight?"

"Sure, peon. Someone did a second insertion."

He chewed his lip. Decided to replace it with what was left of the muffin.

"Another insertion with a different parameter list?"

"Seems like the simplest explanation to me. Isn't that what Sherlock always said?"

He smiled. "That's Occam's Razor. Holmes said, 'eliminate the impossible, and whatever is left, however improbable, is the correct answer.'"

"I was close." She grinned.

"You think someone has access to our launch system, and inserted another version of Hand?"

"I don't really think that, no. But it would explain these statistics." She waved her hand at their screens, each displaying a different site, but the same number: 3,721,440.

"Someone stole our technology," he said, more statement than question.

"Or it's an inside job."

He thought about how many people had both the access and knowledge to launch The Hand. "It's mostly an access issue," he said. "We made the launch program easy so the execs could understand what we can do."

"Not many people have access," she said.

"That we know about."

"So. You like my second insertion idea?" she asked.

"Oh yes." He had an insertion thought about Sarlin. Stopped himself. "It accounts for everything."

"Good enough to buy me another mocha?"

He turned to face her. She was smiling. "Oh goddess of insertion," he bowed slightly, "please allow this lowly peon to provide you with more of the delectable stimulant of our tribe, the genus mocha. And another muffin if you so desire."

He stood up from the stool. "You can even pick the flavor."

Lili sipped a piping hot mocha as they walked toward Platter's offices. Harold opened the white paper bag he was carrying and peeked inside.

"You eat things like this?"

"Cranberries and nuts are healthy," she said.

"Looks like little blotches of blood."

"Taste it before rejecting it?" she said. "You might like it."

His face twisted.

"You're such an adventurer, Harold." She laughed.

"Since you put it that way, I'll try it when we get back to the office and I'm close to a restroom."

"Oh ye of little faith. Would I steer you wrong?"

"You're management, Lili. By definition you steer wrong," he said, as evenly as he could.

She poked him in the biceps with her free hand and walked on in silence for half a block.

"Do you really like my second insertion theory?" she asked.

"Oh yes, Great Thinker of the hidden super-network connecting all consciousness, your multiple-insertion theory is the most profound I have heard in," he glanced at his watch, "the last seven minutes."

She punched him in the arm again, clearly trying for the same spot.

"I was wondering," she said. "If, let's call it SIT, is correct, should we try to track this second virus?"

Harold looked down at the muffin, debating whether he was hungry enough to eat blood. "SIT is interesting. And perhaps even correct," he said. "But an attempt to follow it would be dangerous. We're supposed to stay out of this, remember? If Platter is suddenly trying to track the demon virus...well, do the letters FBI mean anything to you?"

She nodded. "Good point."

They stopped to wait for the walk signal.

"But," he said.

She looked around to see if anyone was within earshot.

"But, you have a plan," she whispered.

He reached into the bag, broke a big chunk off the muffin, closed his eyes and stuffed it into his mouth. To his surprise the sweetness overruled the cranberries, and the nuts were actually pretty good. "What do you think, Lili? Inside job or has someone cracked our security and grabbed enough technology to launch their own virus?"

"You're eating my muffin prize," she said.

"A small price to pay to advance the project."

She frowned.

"So what do you think?" he asked.

"Inside job."

"Me too," he said, swallowing. "There are too many moving parts to get it right without our help."

"Which means?" she said.

The light changed and they started across the street.

He looked the muffin over, stole another chunk.

She punched him a third time.

He stepped to the sidewalk. "Which means someone with access was messing with the launcher. And either by accident, or on purpose, has released another version of the Hand."

"Can you find out?"

"Maybe," he said. "If I can locate the computer that did it."

"Then what? You send an antidote?"

"If we can learn enough about what was sent, I can rig something. The system giveth the Invisible Hand, the system can taketh it away. If we couldn't, the Hand would run forever. Might make for a good sci-fi novel; remember *Prey* by Crichton? Those little nano-bugs that got away and infected humans?"

She grabbed the bag, pulled the muffin out and started eating from the other side.

"So find it," she said.

"Easy for you to say, Miss Management. Hey, how about getting me access to every person's laptop and desk machine who has ever been disclosed on the Hand."

She stopped walking.

He realized she was gone, turned; saw her chewing in the middle of the sidewalk, backtracked.

"Are you serious? The investors, Mr. Blake, Legal all know about Full Disclosure, including The Hand."

"Yep," he said.

"You can't poke around in their machines. You'll get us both fired."

"Got a better idea?" he asked.

"Who else has access?"

He pointed. "You. Me."

She met his eyes, squinting. "Besides us."

"Lab techs can access subsystems. They would have to get together in a committee to reassemble the whole thing."

"How about other engineers?" she asked.

She saw the look on his face.

"I'm asking for completeness," she said. "I know you trust them."

He said, "I was thinking, Engineering is the same way. The right hand doesn't know what the left is doing."

She laughed.

"By design I mean," he clarified. "Only I assemble the complete system. I'm paranoid of this thing getting away from us."

"Me too," she said. "So you don't think any of these people have breeched our security?"

"Nope. I think someone we showed it to, someone high enough in the company to walk through our security like Brad Pitt going to an LA nightclub, was mucking around with it. And a virus got away." He scratched his chin. "That's my best guess."

"You don't think it was intentional?" she asked.

He eyed her hand. She looked down, then swung her arm up and handed it to him.

"A small price to pay," she said.

As he dug around in the bag he said, "I doubt it. What possible reason could someone inside the company have to release a Hand, when they knew we were doing it officially? Doesn't make sense. A mistake though? Yeah, I could see some exec showing off to his golfing buddy and inserting without even knowing it."

"In which case, we should find and eliminate it."

"That's one choice, cover the guy's ass. Or you could go to the board with your SIT and see what they want to do about it."

"You want me to tell the board we found a second virus that belongs to us?" she said. "But we don't know how it was inserted, we have no way to trace it, and no straightforward way to eliminate it? That sounds like early retirement to me."

He shrugged. "If you were on Silver Platter's board, wouldn't you want to know?"

"Yeah, I would want to know."

Her blue eyes searched. "But I wouldn't want to be me telling them."

~ 42 ~

Lili was three slides into her presentation before her voice stopped quivering. Harold watched from the stage left side of the conference table, opposite Simmons, the corporate legal dweeb. Blake sat at the head of the eight-seat table opposite the projection screen. The only other person in the room was his assistant Stacy acting as scribe, so the meeting would have official minutes.

Harold hated minutes because he couldn't control who would read the trivial summary created by an admin on the fly. To him it was a dangerous way to communicate technical material. But Blake insisted. Or maybe Simmons had convinced Blake it was necessary to cover their asses Enron style.

Now Blake wanted *daily* reports. Starting today. Before lunch.

Standing at the front of the room Lili held a laser pointer in her lowered hand. She spoke slowly and carefully.

"This graph shows the number of target machines that have been cleaned by copies of the Hand. Notice that it has been steadily increasing since the insertion on Saturday evening, currently at over four-point-one million machines."

Everyone listened quietly, even Blake, while Simmons right hand scribbled in a continuous stream, barely ever lifting the solid silver extra-fine point mechanical pencil he was using from the yellow legal pad.

"The reported average," she caught Harold's eyes for a split second, "for postings from these machines is forty-one. That's a better fan-out than we had predicted, so each copy is doing a good job of finding blogs to accept its postings. Of course we use the host machine and its owner's name, nothing connects to Silver Platter. In cases we can locate a picture associated with the owner's account, we also post that."

"So over 160 million of these posts currently carry the *Pirate* message?" asked Simmons.

Harold did the math in his head and nodded slightly.

Lili said, "Yes, that is correct." She went to the next slide.

"The green line is our prediction for machines found with illegal songs. You can see it is almost double our predictions."

"Excellent," Simmons said.

"Why?" Blake asked.

"Our estimates were crude. And conservative." Lili said. "It's not possible to know how many machines the Hand will infect, and how many of those will contain sufficient illegal music to trigger the postings. These results indicate there is much more illegal music than estimated by our model."

"Twice as many people steal as we thought," Simmons said, and whistled softly.

"So if we get them to stop," Blake said, "all the better for us."

Lili nodded. She waited for questions. None came, so she clicked for the next slide.

"This blue line shows average song sales per hour from the Silver Platter music website over the past four weeks. Our strategy, of course, is to identify pirates and make them public to generate an aversion to downloading in the broader consumer market. This could result in one of two things—people listen to less music, or they start paying for it through official music retailers like our custom SilverTunes web service, Apple iTunes, Amazon, and others."

"What's the punch line?" Simmons asked.

Harold's view of the guy dropped, even starting from the low opinion he held of lawyers. He shouldn't be interrupting Lili's flow, she would get to the conclusion after the proper setup.

"Statistically, it's too early to tell. We've had technology in the field for less than forty-eight hours."

Harold grinned at Lili. *Technology in the field* was a great way to describe a virus loose on the Internet. He wondered when she had come up with it.

"What have we got?" Blake asked.

Lili flipped to the next slide. A red line diverged from the average sales per hour beginning around noon Sunday. It hovered well above the line for the past three hours.

"Yes," Blake said.

"Take note of the vertical axis." She waved the red light of her pointer. "We're selling eight percent more than average."

"Eight percent in forty-eight hours? Very nice work, Lili," Blake said.

"Thank you, there were many people involved."

"It's your team." He turned to Stacy, "Stop." Her pen lifted from the steno book on her lap as if tied to a puppet string.

"Greg, this is the result we're after. If it holds, we'll need a press release. Properly timed, of course."

"I'll get someone on it," Simmons said while scribbling. "But I'm concerned that if we release news just as the media picks up on what's happening," he looked at Lili, "in the field, we'll draw attention to Silver Platter and create more problems than we solve."

"It's your job to worry," Blake said.

Harold noticed Simmons' face. He had thought these two guys were buds, hanging on the corporate yacht, drinking champagne at the company's expense and all that. But at the moment they looked like they were on opposing teams in the Superbowl.

"There is one thing, Mr. Blake," Lili said.

Harold's shoulders tensed.

Blake glanced at Stacy and held his palm up like a Don't Walk signal. Her pen didn't move.

"Is it important?" he asked.

She bit her lip. "It might be."

Blake nodded.

"Our posting average is inconsistent. It appears to be overestimating."

"Meaning?" Blake said.

"We're not sure. It could mean that some copies of the Hand are reporting a host, but then fail to report counts. So the cumulative blog post count is low."

"Why?" Blake said.

"Unclear. Users could be unplugging their machines despite the warning. Possibly a programming error. Network failures. An error in the algorithm that generates the timed sites. We have no way to examine what's happening in the field so long as we continue our anonymous-access only policy."

Blake nodded.

"We had better not lead anyone back here," Simmons said, his pencil finally still. "Not the authorities, and not some high school hacker that figured out our technology."

"There's another possible explanation for the data," Lili said.

Harold flicked his eyes to her face, then turned to watch Blake.

"And that is?" Blake asked.

"There's a second version of Hand technology out there set to no-post. We're calling this the Second Insertion Theory at this point. We have no hard evidence to support it, but it would explain the statistics."

Harold watched. Blake's eyes didn't move. He sat like a life-size Buddha statue in a garden for a full ten seconds.

"Probably a programming bug, wouldn't you say?" Blake said, apparently rhetorically, because he kept talking. "Does this affect our original plan?"

Harold wondered how Blake expected Lili to factor an unknown.

"If you mean, could this adversely effect sales growth, I would say that perhaps we are missing growth we could have if the postings were done correctly, but that the growth you see on this slide is real."

The statue nodded like an animatronic creature at Disneyland.

Harold grinned slightly, proud of Lili's tap dance.

"But," she said.

Harold sighed. Lili the perfectionist, wouldn't leave well enough alone.

"If the Second Insertion Theory is correct, we are in the dark. We don't know what this second copy is doing because we don't know how its parameters were set before it was inserted."

"I see," Blake said.

Harold wondered what he saw, because Lili had just said they had no idea what was going on.

"Keep tracking with our current approach. I'm not ready to risk involving Silver Platter in any visible way."

Blake stood. "Same time tomorrow."

He walked behind Simmons, patted him on the left shoulder, which made Simmons' jaw stiffen, nodded to Lili, ignored Harold and disappeared out the door.

~ 43 ~

Blake had been in the car less than five minutes when his cellphone buzzed. He groaned, took the call, and slowed the Mercedes to eighty so he could concentrate.

"Helen, please, can't we just do this ourselves? We both have good lawyers, we can iron out the wrinkles."

"I want the fucking house," Helen said, sounding small and tinny in his ear.

If it had been more of a *fucking* house instead of a *whining about what we don't have* house we might not be doing this divorce shit, he thought. But he said, "I understand you want the house. But there's millions in equity in it, and a huge loan. Don't you think I should at least get part of it?"

"Of course not, Eddy. You're the one that's been screwing those whores you prefer to your wife. Giving me the house is a small price to pay to free your dick."

He thought about his net worth, especially with the eight percent increase in sales this week already. He would be fine. But why should the bitch get the divorce *and* the house.

"So I keep the condos in San Francisco and Hawaii...and the yacht?"

"Of course not. I get half of those," she said.

His hands tightened on the wheel, compressing the leather under his fingers.

"You can't have that, and the whole house, and half of all the financial assets, Helen. How do you consider that fair?" he said slowly, forcing his voice to remain businesslike when he wanted to scream at the top of his lungs.

"Don't tell me about fair Mister Jump Any Twat."

She was angry again, and he was not making progress.

"How about if we let our lawyers meet and draw up something they think is reasonable under the law. Just to give us a place to start nego—, uh, talking?"

A little Japanese car with a loud muffler making it sound like an oversized eggbeater zipped past on the inside and cut him off with less than a car length to spare.

He gave the guy a one-finger salute and started to chase him. There was no way that little twerp could outrun his SL.

"Screw the law," she said. "I'll sue your ass and we'll see what the judge, or maybe even a jury, thinks about what you've done to me."

All he could think he had done was give her a life of luxury for almost five years. And for that, she wanted millions from the crazy appreciation of real estate in Silicon Valley and all his hard work building Silver Platter.

"Let's not go to court, Helen. We'll both waste money on lawyers and who knows how it will come out."

His speedometer needle hovered over the middle zero in 100. He was gaining on the guy fast, working his way through traffic with the help of five lanes of interstate.

"No, Eddy. I don't trust you for a single fucking tick of our anniversary clock. I'm calling my lawyer to draw up new papers. We'll see what the judge thinks."

His phone clicked dead.

That bitch.

His right foot pressed to the floor. The fine German transmission downshifted and hurled the car forward towards 150 mph.

He closed on the kid and was within ten car lengths when an idea lit up out of nowhere. He lifted his foot from the accelerator and coasted back to the legal speed limit, checking his mirrors.

No blinking lights.

The Japanese car pulled away. The driver's arm reached out the window and waved a return salute.

Eddy laughed. "My loony wife saved your ass kid. But thanks for the idea."

He had never told Helen about the house across the state line in Incline Village his accountant had suggested to save on income tax. He'd bet the millions Helen wanted to steal from him that getting divorced in Nevada was a better deal. Hell, between the sin cities of Vegas and Reno, Nevada was probably the king of chapel marriages *and* divorce.

So he'd be just like the kid in that crappy little car—if they couldn't catch him, they couldn't serve divorce papers, which would give him time to be first to file and serve the bitch on his terms. She would have to show up in Reno for the hearings. He laughed aloud. That would piss off her little Palo-Alto-loving ass, all the way to Reno to listen to a Nevada judge say she couldn't have the fucking house.

His smile widened. That was the answer: make this fun. He was letting her call too many shots.

He glanced at the fuel gauge: three-quarters tank.

First, make sure no one can find him until after his lawyer puts the paperwork in her greedy little hands. He remembered a novel he had read—who was that? He could rarely remember authors, only plots. But it came to him, the Deaver guy who wrote about the gimp that solved cases by analyzing dirt and shit. *Drive and pay cash and they can't trace you.*

He dug inside his jacket and pulled out his Prada wallet, flipped it opened and counted the hundreds. When he got to ten he stopped. Hell, he could live for a few days on a thousand bucks.

He pulled out his phone to call Mark Markay, supposedly the best divorce lawyer in Palo Alto if you were male. Eddy had been working with Mark to keep this thing out of court. Now he needed him to get it into court. The right court. With the right judge.

He thought about call records on cellphones, and that little GPS thing inside, and subpoenas, then pressed the power button and held it until the green light on the phone went dark. He smiled, remembering how he had rejected the dealer's offer for the satellite system that could track where his car was. No way he wanted anyone to know where he was at all times.

He exited the highway, made a careful U-turn when the green arrow came on and got back on headed north. He would wait until he crossed into

Nevada to contact Mark. It was after two o'clock and he would stay within the speed limit—keep a low profile. Maybe send a FAX from a shitty little hotel. It would have the sending number and the time of day, but would fall under client-attorney privilege. So long as the hotel didn't have his real name, and he paid in cash, and the clerk couldn't ID him, he'd be all right. He would park the Mercedes out of sight and change to the boating clothes he carried in the trunk.

There were lots of boats on Lake Tahoe.

~ 44 ~

Qigiq crutched onto the first floor of the station holding a white bag in his free hand. He glanced at the scratches in the pale green paint of the closed elevator doors, shut his eyes and listened to his leg, now stiff from the ride back from Cupertino.

It voted stairs.

He rotated in place and pushed a heavy bar with his back to enter the stairwell and make the slow climb to the fourth floor.

When he reached his office the door was not standing open, rare in the two months he had been working with Kandy. He smiled at a little piece of white cardboard with his name hand-lettered on it. She had made a big deal of making it so Qigiq could have his name on the door for his brief stay in San Francisco. He tapped the frosted glass softly with one knuckle so she wouldn't jump up and shoot him.

He saw a blurry head motioning him in.

He rattled the white bag as he limped through the door.

"I bear gifts from the gods of the great burrito who live in the cart on the wharf."

She smiled. "How did you know I was in the mood?"

"I figured being at the marina would remind you of Fisherman's Wharf, the cart and the smell of these."

"What a detective."

Her face returned to stone-like concentration.

"Something's not right," she said.

He lowered himself into the chair with his good leg.

"Pillar has the knife on rush." She glanced at the wall clock, a replica of a Dunlop racing tire with a silver hubcap for a face. "Preliminary within an hour."

"Sounds good. What's bothering you?"

"Blood on the knife—just one spot. How does that make sense? With the cutting we saw, either it should have blood everywhere, or the guy sterilized it and we find nothing."

"Rushed cleaning job?"

She shook her head. "Why rush? In fact, why keep it? Throw it over the side. Don't put it in a tool box."

Qigiq opened the bag, handed a sirloin across the desk and unwrapped his chicken.

"What if he's not done using it?" he asked.

Her hands stopped moving on the burrito wrap.

"You mean Sally was number one, and he's planning a sequel?"

"Sally was number one?" he asked.

"Shit."

"Yeah."

"The knife bugs me," she said, shifting in her chair. "I've been drilling down on Mr. With a Bullet. Owns the boat, condo near the ball park, house in Palo Alto, condo in Hawaii, beach house in Nevada, and is CEO of a company down in Silicon Valley called Silver Platter, LLC."

"As in...handed life on a silver platter?"

"As in gold record, music business, digital sales online. Their mission statement *Music by the people and for the people.* Want to guess what he drives?"

"Something dark and fast," Qigiq said through chicken and cheese.

"Black Mercedes 550 with the AMG mods." She looked up, "Fast car."

"No match for a Moto Guzzi," he said with a big smile.

She shook her head. "How's the leg?"

"Steady throb. But managed the steps."

She nodded approval of his self-imposed therapy.

"Got something for you." She spun a credit card size piece of plastic across the paired desks. He caught it.

"Get MynaTime from Apple's App store."

"Myna? That's a talking bird."

"It'll help you do therapy."

Qigiq studied the piece of plastic. "It knows what my therapist told me?"

She shook her head. "You tell it. Then it'll talk you through, step by step." She watched his face. "So you don't cheat the count."

"Me?" He tucked the card into his pocket. "Thanks." He dug the crumpled paper out of his back pocket and spread it on the desk. "So, Mr. Bullet's name is Edward Blake."

She nodded.

"What else do we know about Mr. Blake?" he asked.

"Not much. Maybe there's something on the knife, and it's his boat, but so what?"

"Ferdinand has a list."

"Yeah," she agreed. "Someone bought a knife with his credit card. He's married, has a full time assistant. How do we prove he bought it?"

"Not much is it?"

"Almost nothing in front of a jury," she said.

"Gut feel. With a Bullet?"

"That's our boat. But it's just a feeling. I'll get more pictures to Ferdinand to see if he can ID it better."

"What do you like next?" he asked as he realized there was a full coffee sitting next to his computer. It steamed as he removed the lid.

"We arrest Blake and non-torture him with a water board."

"Has that been approved in San Francisco?" he said.

"Not yet. The environmentalists think it's a waste of water."

He sipped. "Let me rephrase. What do you think we can get away with?"

"We might get a search warrant for the car and condo," she said.

He nodded. "That would alert Blake."

"Unfortunately."

"Unless."

She glanced up. Their eyes met over the tilted cup in front of his face.

"You want to go in quietly?" she asked.

He lowered the coffee. "It's very quiet in Alaska." He paused. "I like the condo. He lives in Palo Alto. If we could find something of Sally's, like a strand of hair, or her clothing..."

"Helpful. Not definitive."

"Then the water board," he said.

"We need a silencer for your crutch."

~ 45 ~

Qigiq thought about the height of twenty-eight stories as his ears popped. He was surrounded by dark polished wood and gold-tinted chrome while standing on thick plush carpet the deep red of a rose in moonlight.

And he was still in the elevator.

"Seems tall for an earthquake zone."

"Sure is," Kandy said.

He looked her way. "Comforting."

They had a search warrant, and if someone answered, they could use it.

"You're sure he's at work?" Qigiq asked, for perhaps the fifth time.

"That's what the men in blue tell me. They have a black Mercedes, license plate SIL. No visual on Blake, though."

The golden doors swished open to reveal a long corridor covered in deep red and purple tapestry suitable for a five-star hotel.

They turned left to locate two-eight, seven-eight.

"You think he got seventy-eight on purpose?" Qigiq asked.

"As in RPM?"

"Yeah."

She shrugged. "Could be the view, I'm not old enough to remember those." She huffed twice and knocked three times, hard.

Qigiq listened for movement inside the condo.

She knocked again.

He stepped a bit to the left.

She knocked a third time. "Now the hard part." She removed a card from inside her dark blue jacket and swiped it through the electronic slot. The door clicked. She turned the knob, pushed it open, scanned the interior once and walked in.

"Do I want to ask how you got that?" Qigiq said.

"Only if you want to know."

He stood outside the door as she held it open for him.

"Isn't every opening recorded on a computer somewhere?"

"Yeah," she said. "Courtesy check from the condo association. We want our owners to be happy when they return."

Qigiq stepped across the threshold and moved slowly left into a living area big enough for handball. Floor-to-ceiling glass on the outside walls made him feel like he was at the edge of a canyon looking down on a world of water and steel.

"A little crowded," he said softly.

Kandy moved straight down a corridor with doors on its right side.

"Three bedrooms, three baths," she said.

Qigiq's eyes passed over stone masonry around a fireplace filled with what looked like fresh birch logs.

"How many fireplaces?" he asked.

"I guess two. That one, and another in the master."

Qigiq whistled softly.

Kandy disappeared. He moved onto the carpet to keep his crutch quiet and strolled through the living room, trying to feel Blake's presence. He checked the corners where people often didn't clean well, but either Blake was a fanatic, or had a fantastic house cleaner. Perhaps both. There was a bronze sculpture on the coffee table at the center of a cushy three-piece sectional, every seat with a great view of the bay. It depicted two nudes in an embrace of pain or ecstasy. He looked closer. Both figures were female.

He crossed to a bookcase with half-glass, half-teak doors. He wondered if

Sally's fingerprints might be on one of the shiny book covers. The top shelf contained best sellers in paperback: Crais, Crichton, Gibson, stored in alphabetical order by author. Maybe Blake *was* a fanatic. The bottom row was all business: *How to Write a Business Plan, Elephants Can Dance, The Enron Story, The Tao of War.* In between were technical books for business people: *Understanding Opportunity in a Wired World, X-Gen Y-Gen How They Spend.*

Qigiq opened the zipper pocket on his jacket and removed black leather gloves. He slipped them on, then opened the cabinet with one finger. Below the business books were three drawers. He slid the first out quietly. It held large coffee-table books on deep-sea fishing stacked four deep. The one on the left had a picture of a sailing yacht drift fishing. He lifted it. Underneath was another with a powerboat and outriggers plowing through white-capped seas, spray flying from the bow.

Qigiq blinked.

Above the boat at the end of a white pole was a Pendum radar pod. The name on the stern said *Merry Mary,* but the craft looked exactly like *With a Bullet.* Qigiq wondered if Blake had seen the book and bought it because the cover looked like his boat, or if he had owned the book and took it to the yacht dealer and said, "Make me one like this."

The electronic release of the front door startled him.

He dropped the book and pushed the drawer closed without turning. He spun on the crutch and took the largest strides he could manage toward the kitchen. He saw twelve-inch slate tiles and slowed, looking for a walk-in pantry, or a door leading to an outside balcony.

He found a panel on the wall with buttons. Guessed. Pushed the bottom one.

He moved to the far side of the serving island in the middle of the kitchen and lowered himself to the floor, his back against the solid wood of the island. Vertical blinds powered by hidden motors slid across the huge expanse of windows, dropping the room into a deeper darkness than he had expected.

Kandy?

He heard the front door swish across the carpet.

He pulled out his cellphone and started a text message. Stopped. If her phone weren't muted...

A high-pitched voice called, "Yoo-hoo, Eddy. Is that you?"

Qigiq's throat tightened. The voice was both familiar and strange as it warbled a high singsong playfulness. He twisted to his right and poked one eye around the island to get a view of the hallway and saw—he blinked twice to be sure his eye was working in the darkness—Kandy racing toward the front door singing, "Eddy, you're early, Baby." He swallowed. She was wearing...hardly anything: just a black bra and skimpy panties. Her tan, toned body moved with the grace and power of a gymnast.

"Who the fuck are you?" a woman screamed.

"Where's Eddy?" Kandy said.

"What do you mean, where's Eddy? What the fuck are you doing in his condo, bitch?"

He couldn't see Kandy's face in the dark hallway, but he saw her step back.

"I'm where Eddy told me to be, Sweetie. And I'm right on time," Kandy said. "Monday is our day."

"Your day? Who the—?" The woman stared at Kandy in the dark. "Are you?" Long pause. "I'm calling Eddy."

Kandy put her hand on her left hip, looking like a pissed-off supermodel in her dressing room. He forced himself to concentrate on the evolving situation so he could provide backup.

"Be ready to tell him what you're doing here on Monday. Uninvited."

"I—" The girl stopped. Kandy didn't move. "Are you screwing Eddy?" the girl screamed.

"Why don't you ask Eddy."

Kandy changed hands so her right hip was jutting out.

Qigiq tried to look away but couldn't.

"He might not be happy about you spying on him."

"You bitch," the woman said. "You stay away from Eddy, he's—"

"Not your husband, girl. There's plenty of Eddy to go around," Kandy said.

Qigiq sincerely hoped the woman wasn't Eddy's wife.

He saw Kandy turn sideways, facing him, a moment before an Asian girl in a flying kick came into view. She was small, barely over five feet, and thin, wearing tiny pink shorts, flip-flop sandals and a tight top that didn't stop even dim light. The girl passed as Kandy ducked and swept her other foot away, bringing the girl's body down on the left hip. Hard.

"Don't get up, it will get ugly," he heard Kandy say as she put one hand around the back of the girl's neck and press her face to the floor.

The girl didn't move. But that didn't mean she wasn't going to. Qigiq figured Kandy knew this.

"Let's talk. Eddy told me to be here," Kandy said. "He gave me a card to let myself in. I thought he was at the door. Now that I know about you, maybe I'm not so interested in Eddy Blake anymore. So, what are you doing here?"

Kandy let go and stepped back. She squatted on the balls of her bare feet. The girl was still on the floor. Qigiq tried to stop the thought, but

Kandy's position reminded him of the erotic-dancing girls he had seen when busting up parties at clubs in Fairbanks.

"I meet Eddy here Tuesday and Thursday," the girl said. "I came by to relax, have a drink and pick up my clothes. I didn't think anyone would be here."

"This your first time on a Monday?" Kandy asked.

The girl nodded.

"Eddy's time slicing. What's your name?"

The girl lifted her head and sat up a bit higher. "Alicia."

"Nice to meet you Alicia," Kandy said, holding out her hand, "I'm Rebecca."

Kandy helped the girl up.

"Sorry for the misunderstanding," Kandy said.

The girl's eyes stared openly up and down Kandy's body.

"I've seen you...that bastard...Saturday. But your name was Kandy."

Kandy shrugged. "Spur of the moment."

Alicia's eyes drifted then snapped back. "How do you stay in shape?" she asked softly. "And where did you learn to fight like that?"

"Marines," Kandy said.

Alicia reached out slowly and stroked Kandy's right bicep. "You like girls?" Alicia asked.

Kandy smiled slightly. "Not usually."

The two women disappeared toward the front door. Their voices became fainter, but Qigiq caught snatches about leaving Eddy and the condo to Alicia. Maybe let Eddy stay in the dark and stew over why Rebecca didn't show up today. Serve him right. Then he heard Alicia give Kandy a phone number; and the door click closed.

He let out his breath and struggled to his feet.

Two minutes later Kandy walked into the kitchen in black jeans and a blue jacket.

"You were in the Marines?" Qigiq asked.

"No," she said.

He nodded.

"We had better get out of here," she said. "She might be calling Eddy, who is calling security, who will have questions we'd rather not answer."

He shook his head. "I think you were very convincing. Black is definitely your color."

She met his eyes, but hers were little solid stones that told him nothing.

"It's a job," she said, and started laughing.

"While you were dancing with your new friend, I had an idea."

He motioned her toward a refrigerator and a stainless sink. When she was next to him he pulled out the freezer drawer along the bottom of the fridge. It was full of black packets eerily similar to the one they removed from *Firebird*.

"They might be steaks," he said.

She stepped back and took pictures. "Do you think he counts them?"

"You want to borrow one?"

"You're going to feel awfully silly calling a forensics team up here if those are grass-fed grade A."

Still wearing gloves, he squirreled his arm in deep and carefully removed a package from the bottom of a pile, trying not to disturb the layout of the top or the frost along the edges of the drawer. If Blake was watching his freezer, he might not notice. Unless he really was counting.

"You have evidence bags with you," he asked.

"In the car."

He pointed. "I'd like to see what we find in the trap under that sink."

© © ©

It took the forensics team less than half an hour to block off the condo and start looking for prints after their call. The first package was toes. The nails hadn't been painted Very Berry; they were metallic gold. Qigiq didn't ask about the other twenty-eight packages, except to learn none had been USDA approved. DNA analysis would take at least twenty-four hours.

"Circumstantial," Kandy said, sitting beside him on a kitchen stool, gazing out at the gray waters of San Francisco Bay.

"The guy has a woman's body in his freezer. We have to bring him in," Qigiq said.

"For questioning. But how do we book him? We have nothing putting him at the scene of the crime. We don't even have a scene of the crime."

He couldn't disagree. "What about your girlfriend?"

She smiled. "Cute, wasn't she? You Alaskan boys like little Asian girls. Just a quick kayak paddle across that strait up there."

He tilted his head and drew his eyebrows together.

She laughed. "Sure, question her. But you have to do it. She'll recognize me."

"Once Blake's in custody, would it matter?"

She shrugged. "Why complicate things?"

Qigiq gazed across the bay; his eyes landed on the spire of a cathedral in the distance. He said: "Blake and Sally?"

"Triangle. You're thinking Blake's wife is the doer?"

"Statistics would back me up."

~ 46 ~

Captain Jasik tapped a yellow wooden pencil that needed sharpening against the side of his head. The office was filled with the soft thud of wood against skull, dampened by short-cropped nappy hair. Qigiq had his left leg, complete with brace, stretched out beside Kandy, and was rotating it slowly from side to side.

They waited.

Jasik said, "Can you tie him to the girl?"

"Body parts in his freezer; photos of her and his boat," Qigiq said. "Visual exam says we have a match to the Amazon fingers; lab has us fast-tracked for DNA. " He paused, thoughts of a young girl butchered making him feel weak. "If Robina is correct, we found Sally Bellowi."

"And have Blake for abuse of a corpse," Jasik said.

"Uh, " Kandy mumbled. They both looked her way. "We've been calling it Eddy's condo, but county documents show it belongs to Silver Platter."

"So he doesn't own it?" Jasik said.

"Not technically. And access records from the electronic lock show a dozen key codes have opened that door in the past few weeks."

"And we don't know which codes were Blake," Jasik said. "Maybe all of them; maybe none. Do they have records?"

"Might, if they're deducting it as an expense for visitors, instead of putting them in a hotel." She paused. "Or might not. They could have a drawer full of cards that get used once then thrown away."

Jasik sighed. "You have the knife report?"

Kandy pulled out her phone. She tapped and swiped and tapped.

"Preliminary came in from Pillar minutes ago." She turned the device sideways to use the wider dimension of the screen. "Only one blood sample on the knife, B-positive. Doesn't match the victim. Pillar's opinion: 'the knife was carefully sterilized within the past forty-eight to seventy-two hours. Standard dirt and airborne particulate matter are not present.'"

Jasik's pencil tapped. "Is anyone involved in this B-positive?"

"Medical records indicate Blake is. We don't have types on Walters, Danny or Robina. Should I get them?" Kandy said.

Jasik nodded. "So Blake cut himself with his own knife on his own boat. You can't arrest him for that."

"Robina thinks Sally dated Blake," Kandy said.

"Thinks?" Jasik said.

"I showed her Blake's picture from the Silver Platter website. She said,

'Oh yeah, Sally used to go out on his boat. He likes to fish.'"

"You said 'dated,' Detective," Jasik said.

"Robina says last summer. Sally hadn't talked about him since they all went to Alcatraz on *With a Bullet*. That was Independence Day last year."

"So Blake's the ex-boyfriend."

"Looks that way, Captain," she said.

"Her body ends up in the boyfriend's freezer a year after they break up," Jasik said. "Took a long time for the wife to get jealous. This make sense to anyone?" He stopped tapping and crossed his right ankle over his left knee.

"She jilted him," Qigiq offered.

"I would expect a more immediate crime of passion from a CEO." He paused. "No, CEO's don't commit crimes of passion. They commit logical, elaborate, carefully planned financial crimes. Doesn't fit. Can't we get them closer together?"

"Karen, a girl who hangs out on a boat named *Delicious* docked in the same marina as Blake's, is confident she's seen Sally recently."

"Can she put Sally with Blake?" Jasik asked.

Kandy shook her head. "Said Sally was always by herself in a bikini and heels, carrying a yellow and white striped beach bag. She would pass *Delicious* and disappear onto one of the boats. Couldn't say for sure which one."

"We think *Firebird* or *With a Bullet*," Qigiq said.

"Why?"

"The owners," Qigiq said.

Jasik nodded. "Do we have the striped beach bag?"

The room was quiet. Kandy caught Qigiq's eye. He shrugged.

"It's missing," she said.

"The bikini?" Jasik asked.

"Missing," Qigiq said.

"Can we put Blake and Sally in the same place at any point in time?"

"Not since that Alcatraz trip," Kandy said.

"Would be nice to have a crime scene," Jasik said. He picked up the pencil; held it still. His face calm, he said: "Arrest him, or question him?"

Kandy shook her head. "We'd prefer you shadow him; bring him in, he gets motivated to destroy evidence. I'd rather we let him get careless."

"Looks like he's already careless," Jasik said.

"Careless enough for the DA?" Qigiq asked.

Jasik's face didn't change. "I'll locate manpower and put him on the watch list; keep him in the country." The pencil started moving. "Do we know where he is now?"

The three glanced at each other. The radiator under the window crackled as hot water warmed aging cast iron. Kandy shook her head; a cellphone bleeped; she looked down.

"Pillar. He's got a partial from the knife."

"Shall we guess?" Jasik said.

"Don't bother, he votes Blake; there are prints all over the condo we're assuming are his. We'll confirm ASAP." She paused, reading. "Pillar is asking for extra time with the body; wants to look for contamination that could give us a crime scene."

Jasik pressed his lips together. "What about the family; the funeral?"

"Sally's mother finally returned our calls; she *demands* the body be shipped to the East coast."

Jasik blew a stream of air. "Arrangements will have to be made, could take days. Maybe even a couple of weeks with an autopsy. We'll need to check for drugs, poison, that sort of thing. Lab tests take a long time."

Kandy nodded, her lips twitching toward a smile.

"We should have someone at the funeral," Qigiq said. "See who shows up."

Jasik nodded. "So the guy used his knife in the past forty-eight hours?"

"He had the boat out Saturday," Qigiq said.

Kandy scrolled through the report on her small screen. "Wait, there's more. Pillar has a ton of prints from the condo he believes are female, and a single partial that matches Sally's. It was on the back cover of a book."

"Which book?" Jasik asked.

"The *Kama Sutra*. Trade paperback edition."

Jasik shook his head.

"So maybe Sally's been in the condo," Qigiq said. "Can he say when?"

"No. And the other prints are probably Alicia's."

"Alicia?" Jasik said, raising an eyebrow. "And maybe that book isn't Blake's."

"Blake's mistress," Qigiq said. "Age twenty-seven. U.S. citizen. Teaches dance locally. Attends grad school at SF State and performs with a troupe called Anna and the Annadroids. Mother is Asian."

Jasik sat up and reached to his left toward a low bookshelf. "Seen this?" He spread the Chronicle across his desk so it faced them. It was opened to McGreen's column.

Kandy stood and stepped over Qigiq's outstretched leg to lean over the paper and start reading.

"No," she said.

Qigiq could only see the title: It's Two AM—Do You Know Where Your Music Is?

"Came out this afternoon," Jasik said. "At least he's whining about something besides police incompetence."

She read silently.

Qigiq wondered what the article said, but his cast kept him too far from the desk. Unless he stood up. He decided to wait for Kandy's summary.

"He hasn't figured out if this is related, has he?" she said.

Jasik said, "If he has, he didn't put it in that article. Maybe it was too much of a stretch."

"Or maybe the rape video is old news and he figures he'll get more mileage out of a new story," Qigiq said, not quite sure what he was talking about.

"Maybe," Kandy said, and pointed. "Here he attacks the federal government for lax security allowing a destructive virus to roam the Web unchallenged. Mentions how the billions spent on Internet snooping to fight the war on terror should prevent such an atrocity."

"How many music files do you think he lost?" Qigiq asked.

Jasik chuckled.

"He has numbers," Kandy said. "Estimates over five million people have experienced file loss."

"How do you think he got that?" Jasik asked.

She scanned the newsprint. "He called around to companies that make anti-virus software. So far only MacAfee admits they're working on it. Here: the five million estimate came from a consultant in L.A. who wrote a book called *e-Viruses: Protecting Your Assets.*" She continued reading. "McGreen named it the DoomTunes virus—claims it will scare people away from buying downloadable music at all. Also claims most people don't bother to back up their music files."

"Or anything else," Jasik said.

"Ferdinand said it only deleted songs that had been illegally copied," Qigiq said.

"How could it know that?" Kandy asked.

Jasik leaned forward and tapped the paper with his pencil. "If you read further, you'll see that McGreen claims hundreds of people have written to the paper saying their music files have been deleted. He conveniently doesn't mention whether or not they owned those files."

"So if they don't buy downloadable music, what are they going to do?" Qigiq asked.

Kandy said, "McGreen recommends getting external storage and backing up your music. Or, get this, purchase only CDs so that you always have a master copy available."

"Are music sales going to go down or up?" Qigiq asked.

Jasik shrugged. "I'm sure McGreen has no frigging idea."

Kandy looked up at him, and smiled.

"What happens when he makes the connection with the *Don't Steal* video?" Qigiq asked.

"Are we certain there is one?" Jasik said. "Missing girl, mysterious videos, then suddenly the DoomTunes virus attacks pirates and discloses their names. Yes, it uses the *Don't Steal* message, but that could be copycat behavior. Maybe that's why he didn't mention it."

"And," Kandy said. "The cops getting calls to ask if free iPod offers are legit, even though Apple denies any such program exists."

"I don't think McGreen has seen the second video," Qigiq said. "He'd be on us every minute if he had seen that mutilation himself."

"So what do we do with this guy?" Jasik said, tapping the Chronicle.

Kandy sat down. "Ignore him."

"He won't go away," Jasik said.

She shrugged.

Qigiq shifted to reorient his body in the hard wooden chair using only his right leg. The chair slipped and screeched against the tile. Jasik and Kandy looked his way.

He smiled and said: "Or we use him to help us."

~ 47 ~

Kandy twisted around in her seat to look out the back window and swooped the Mini into a parking spot barely big enough for a golf cart.

"Smooth," Qigiq said across the crutch.

"Practice," she said.

"Why a Starbucks?" he asked.

"He likes their coffee."

"Feels wrong; awfully public."

"I think he doesn't want to be seen at the office talking to cops. Ruin his reputation for hating us." She laughed.

"He can claim we entrapped him at a coffee shop?"

"Exactly," she said. "No security to protect him. We just walked up, flashed our badges, and made him grant us an interview."

"Funny way to do business."

She smiled. "Qu, here in the lower forty-eight we do business any way we can when there's a dead girl in a freezer."

He nodded, his face grim, his mind seeing an engraved bird.

They found a corner table for four at 9:47 Tuesday morning. Kandy sat toying with a Grande Vanilla and Qigiq stared into black decaf. Caffeine could make him twitchy, and he was already twitchy from replaying videos in his head.

The place was filled with crowd noises and the grinding of espresso machines lofting the aroma of a dozen variations of coffee. Qigiq breathed slowly to relax, actually enjoying the bustle of the long room and the dozens of voices—almost like the roar of pounding surf when he parked his Guzzi at Half Moon Bay and stared towards Japan.

"Think he'll go for it?" Qigiq asked. "There's not much in it for him."

"The warm fuzzies if it works. Gets to criticize us if it doesn't. Might be a fair trade in his mind."

Qigiq wiggled his stocking covered toes to loosen his leg.

"It'll feel good when that comes off," Kandy said.

"You mean like taking your boots off being the best part of snow skiing?"

She grinned and tapped the business-size envelope lying on the table between them.

"Why would anyone want to kill her?"

"As many reasons as there are killers. All of them just a failure of the imagination to find a better way to solve a perceived problem—or fill an emotional need that has grown stronger than logic."

"Failure of the imagination?" She tapped the Grande with her fingertips. "Never thought of it that way. I figure it's me who doesn't have the imagination—I can't seem to think like this perp."

"Sawing off fingers with a fishing knife? Who could?"

A round balding man with a full black beard showing dabs of gray pushed through the door and swiveled his head around like he was caught in a fire and looking for a way out.

"McGreen," she said. "I'll go get him. He'll want me to buy."

Qigiq watched Kandy walk over and introduce herself. Seeing them side by side, his eyes even with her lips, he realized the guy couldn't be more than about five-foot-six. They joined a line of people waiting for a mid-morning fix. Monday had been full of surprises; he hoped Tuesday would be a day of answers.

"Qigiq, this is Mr. McGreen," Kandy said, as the two approached the table.

"Call me Aaron. And please don't get up, I see you've been injured," the man said, reaching across the table.

His hand was full and round like his body, its back dark with hair like his beard. But his grip was firm.

"Thank you for meeting us, Aaron," Qigiq said. "I'm from Alaska and it's a rare privilege to meet a first-class journalist from a famous city with a leading paper like the Chronicle."

Aaron smiled. "Well, you're one of the few people who probably won't complain about how cold it is in San Francisco."

Qigiq smiled back. "This isn't cold, nothing's even frozen. Please, sit down."

Aaron pulled out the chair opposite Qigiq. "You'd be surprised how many visitors are astonished at the temperature when the sun drops and the fog moves in. They seem to believe that all of California is a Beach Boy's song."

Kandy took the chair between them.

Aaron sipped from a big glass of brown liquid with white foam spilling over the lip as his eyes flicked back and forth between Qigia's face and his cast.

"I was injured in a motorcycle accident," Qigiq said. He watched a familiar attitude descend on Aaron's thick features. "Do you ride?"

Aaron blinked, not prepared for the question.

"Uh, not since my misspent youth when I rode a little Kawasaki 175 over to a particular girl's house who loved motorbikes," he said with a big smile. Qigiq thought he saw joy in the man's face. Then he frowned. "Too much traffic around here, I don't feel safe even walking in this city."

"I was fine until someone purposely ran me off the road in a fast right-hand sweeper."

Aaron's eyes widened. "Who would do such a thing?"

Qigiq read him as genuinely surprised that anyone would be so cruel.

"The person who has Sally Bellowi."

He saw Kandy lean away from the table slightly to open the space between the three of them. She lifted her glass to hide her expression behind the Grande.

Aaron's eyebrows knitted together, forming a long dark line over his eyes. Qigiq noticed they were brown, and moving.

"Bellowi? That girl on YouTube? Robina's roommate?" he said, and coughed.

Qigiq nodded.

"Why would anyone go after you, Detective?"

"Because I saw someone on a boat dock. I believe that person abducted Sally."

"Can you identify him?" Aaron said.

"Perhaps," Qigiq said. "But I can't find him."

"Ah, a *him*," Aaron said, smiling like he had just extracted information from a recalcitrant prisoner.

"Maybe a him, we have nothing conclusive. But you can help," Qigiq said.

Aaron lowered his glass carefully. His eyes glanced to Kandy's face, then back to Qigiq.

"Qigiq is an unusual name," he said.

"Inuit. White hawk flying in the sky," Qigiq said. "Reminds me to try to see the whole picture."

Aaron nodded, his eyebrows relaxing. "How could a journalist possibly help?"

Kandy leaned forward, "We need to find someone who has seen Sally recently. The last we have is a week ago Sunday when she was with her college boyfriend. Then Tuesday morning with Robina."

"I certainly haven't seen her," Aaron said.

A smile slowly curved Kandy's lips. She opened the envelope on the table and slid out three sheets of paper. She spread them in front of Aaron.

"This is Sally going boating, from the front and back. We have reason to believe she was kidnapped onto a boat. The third picture is a close-up from a college photo before a concert."

"And?" Aaron said.

Qigiq leaned in, twisting to get both elbows on the table. He slid his left leg closer; it bumped Kandy's chair.

"Wouldn't it be helpful if someone wrote an article about Sally and the video with the don't-steal message? And printed her pictures with contact information for anyone who has seen her?"

"Ah, the Chronicle."

"And perhaps speculate," he continued, "about how the don't-steal video might or might not be related to the strange happenings with missing music files."

Qigiq saw the hook set a little.

Aaron looked up. "You think a missing girl has something to do with the DoomTunes virus?"

Kandy pressed her lips together, smiling only slightly.

"It might," Qigiq said. "The pirate and don't-steal messages aren't so different really."

Aaron's head pumped in agreement.

"Amazing. And it all started here in San Francisco."

Qigiq could see Aaron collecting journalism awards in his mind. He dug into his jacket for his phone, looked up to meet Kandy's eyes. She nodded.

Qigiq said, "You won't want to print pictures of this, partly because it's no longer posted anywhere. But a lab at MIT analyzed the noise in the YouTube video."

"Noise?" Aaron said, lifting his foaming cup.

Qigiq started the rape video playing and turned his phone towards

Aaron.

"Look at the very bottom of the picture."

Aaron craned his neck forward and stared at the small screen.

"There's fuzzy stuff."

Kandy said, "It's an encoded message."

Aaron's eyes flashed to her face and back to the little screen. Qigiq was confident he was thinking about how to use this.

"The message decodes to another video," Qigiq said.

"Sounds fishy." Aaron leaned back and took a long drink of his coffee.

"The MIT people are confident of their findings," Kandy said. "Would you like to see it?"

Aaron nodded.

"Will you write the article and include Sally's pictures?" Qigiq asked.

"Is this a bribe?"

"Just a question," Kandy said, smiling.

Qigiq started the video and held out his phone. He watched Aaron carefully, wondering if he had already seen the video on the MIT site and was playing dumb.

Aaron squinted, leaned closer. Beneath his beard and around his eyes Qigiq saw his already light skin go pale. His head bobbled like it was loose. His left hand came up to his mouth and he leapt from the chair. As he ran through the coffee shop he slammed into the back of a tall guy in a green sweater, kept running, tripped over a chair leg and spun 360 to stay upright, then disappeared into the crowd in the direction of the restrooms.

Kandy said. "Did he play for the 49ers? He's pretty good open field."

Qigiq laughed. "Can we trust him?"

"We can trust him to do what's best for his career. I say he ties it all together for tomorrow's edition *and* prints at least two pictures."

"You're on," he said, "Lunch. Only one picture, and no mention of the second video."

She reached her right hand across the table and they shook.

~ 48 ~

Kandy slipped her black car west through slow moving traffic on Marina Boulevard like a barracuda swimming around rocks.

"Thanks for driving, I like the bike a lot but," Qigiq wiggled the crutch resting between the dashboard and rear deck, "street parking on hills is sketchy."

"Maybe we should get you a high-tech one: polished aluminum with a neoprene grip and retractable claw foot." She huffed her low laughter.

"I'll stick to Mother Nature. A million trees can't be wrong."

They slipped through a yellow light straight to an on ramp and climbed. Traffic was moving just below the 50 mph speed limit as they rolled onto Highway 1. They slowed to pass through the inactive toll booths for the Golden Gate, and squirted onto the bridge. Three lanes were open heading north. Kandy took the middle.

"What did you think of Mr. Aaron McGreen?" she asked.

"He was more agreeable in person than one might think from reading his column," Qigiq replied. "And he seemed cautious."

"Meeting with two detectives? The President of the United States would be cautious."

She downshifted and slowed.

"You think we did okay?" he asked.

"Yeah. I like the way you opened with your bike crash. Playing the sympathy card." She laughed.

"I wanted him off guard. Maybe shock him into understanding this isn't a story in a newspaper. There was a beautiful young musician. And now she's dead."

"You didn't tell him that."

"I figured it would make matters worse if this became a highly public murder rather than a missing-persons case before we're ready."

"And boy, are we not ready," she said.

He turned his head to watch her laugh and saw the passenger window of the car in the next lane roll down. The sun cast the interior in shadows, but he could see that the passenger seat was empty. He also saw a driver in a black sweatshirt and tan gloves wearing a full ski mast and goggles holding a handgun behind a huge silencer.

Qigiq threw his right arm out and around Kandy's neck and yanked her towards him, pulling her torso across the center console. He twisted hard and laid his body on top of hers as his left leg shot fireworks from the ankle to mid-thigh.

Both front side windows exploded.

"What the hell?" Kandy yelled. But she kept the wheel steady with her left hand.

The headrest on Qigiq's seat burst into a hundred particles, filling the car with dark foam dust.

Qigiq hadn't heard gunshots.

"Brake," he whispered into her ear, not knowing why he was being quiet.

Kandy jammed the brake pedal down hard.

The car's nose dove from the drag of screeching tires, the ABS holding it straight. A hole appeared in the upper right corner of the windshield surrounded by a spiderweb of cracks. A dozen horns blared behind her. Kandy wriggled out from under Qigiq and popped her head up. She pushed him with her right elbow and grabbed the shifter. An instant later both front wheels were smoking.

The car in the leftmost lane was accelerating away.

"You'll never catch him," Qigiq said.

"This is personal," Kandy called back. "What was it?"

"Maybe an older BMW 6-Series. But it could have been Japanese— Lexus...Acura."

"Hold on," she said. "I don't have spoilers on this thing to impress tuner boys."

She reached under the dash with her right hand.

He heard the engine wail like a thousand sirens on steroids as the seat pressed hard against his back. He fought to keep his head upright and flailed his arms in an attempt to reach the grab rail. He couldn't see much through the glare in the cracks and the wind roar through shattered windows made speech impossible. He turned to see Kandy bring a pair of aviator sunglasses to her face.

Unbelievably she was closing on the dark car in front of them. He wondered how fast they were moving because the traffic around them appeared to be parked.

She closed to within ten car lengths then slowed to match the pace of the shooter's car.

"He's got a gun," Qigiq shouted. Just to remind her.

She didn't reply, but held the distance between the two vehicles constant.

He craned his neck left. The needle was rotated off the right side of the white dial. He tried to recall the highest number on her speedometer, because it was shaking too much to read it.

"What now?' he yelled.

She reached over her right shoulder, patted her back and pointed at the roof.

He dug out his cellphone and pressed the speed dial for dispatch. He watched the face of the phone until it said he had a connection.

Kandy changed to the leftmost lane, slamming the door into his right shoulder.

He shouted at the phone. "Officer needs assistance. Hot pursuit. Suspect armed." He heard a mush of static in his ear.

The car shuddered like a jet at takeoff. He laced the fingers of his right hand around the door handle and squeezed.

He guessed at the question that might have been in the static and said,

"Highway 1, four miles north of Marin Exit, heading north." He heard more static and hung up.

"Maybe," he yelled in Kandy's direction.

He looked up to watch the vehicle in front motoring smoothly along. They followed it for almost five miles, which took slightly over two minutes.

Without warning the gap between them shrunk. Kandy got to the brakes. Qigiq watched the black car U-turn in the middle of the freeway. A white SUV blasted its horn and swerved onto the right shoulder.

Qigiq pressed against the seat back and stared. The sedan was accelerating directly toward them with an arm stretched out between the outside rearview mirror and the car's body. The arm ended in a pistol.

"Gun!"

He saw fire flare from the barrel and heard a loud crack. No silencer. He didn't feel pain or see anything shatter.

The Mini launched into reverse, then the front end spun to the left until it faced south. Smoke emerged from the wells around the front wheels. His nostrils told him he was at a race track.

Qigiq leaned forward to retrieve the roof light from the glovebox and glanced at the outside mirror. The BMW was gaining.

"Hold on," she said.

This time he got both hands around the safety bar in front of the shotgun seat before the engine went banshee and the little car made like a bottle rocket. He held his eye on the mirror and saw the BMW grow smaller. He heard two more cracks, but no glass shattered and the tires all kept rolling.

He looked up and instantly wished he hadn't.

They were accelerating fast into oncoming traffic, heading south on the north side of the freeway, blazing a trail for the masked driver behind them. A red Volvo wagon went to Qigiq's left toward the shoulder, but a gray pickup truck on lifts went to his right, searching for space between the Mini and the concrete divider. As Kandy accelerated, each car came closer and closer to crushing them before swerving off. He thought of lane-splitting on his motorcycle, and how baby-buggy safe it felt compared to this.

Kandy pumped the brights switch with one finger.

He managed to get the light onto the roof, then reached over and put his left hand down the back of Kandy's pants. She didn't flinch as he pulled out her mini-38. He twisted hard to his right until he could get his left arm through the shattered glass in the passenger's door. He got his right hand up and gripped his left forearm as hard as he could, fighting for a tiny bit of stability.

"Too much traffic," he yelled, but held focus on the BMW.

Kandy slammed on the brakes.

The BMW grew closer. Fast.

He squeezed. The little gun cracked and spit; he saw no damage. Fired again.

"He stopped," Qigiq yelled without turning from the window.

Kandy U-turned. A Kenworth truck with sleeper cab towing a long six-axle trailer passed behind them, air horns blaring.

Kandy pulled onto the shoulder and rolled forward in second gear.

"What's he doing?" she asked.

Qigiq stuck his head through the hole in the door's glass and studied the highway. The sun threw shadows across the concrete.

"He's backing up lane one."

She accelerated and shifted.

"You see him?" he asked.

"Yeah. Do you see the gun?"

"No."

They followed for a quarter mile, then the BMW backed fast across the gravel shoulder and up a hill covered with grass that reached to the door handle.

"He's off the highway," Qigiq said. "Stopped on a hill to the right, below a copse of pine."

She stopped, letting the car idle.

Qigiq saw the driver's window open slightly. The long fat silencer popped into view just above the rearview mirror.

"Gun," he said.

They both ducked below the dashboard to avoid being a target. Face to face like teenagers in the back seat of daddy's Ford, Qigiq realized he was perspiring. He heard a single soft sound. Then nothing.

"I hope we're out of range," he said into her left ear.

She nodded. "Did you hear it land?"

He shook his head, then raised an eye slightly to peek over the dash. He saw another flash from the fat barrel and ducked.

"Firing from the car. Has position on us."

"How would you handle this in Alaska?" she asked.

"Avalanche from above." He smiled.

"Hear anything?" she said.

They both listened to tire noise from passing cars, but no more shots.

"Reloading," she said.

He nodded. "Thoughts?"

"Backup arriving about now would be nice," she said. "Think we can get above him?"

Qigiq shifted his body until he could see over the door with one eye.

"If there's a road on the other side of that hill. Or backup shows up with an SUV. But the moment we move, he takes off and we never see him again."

"So, we wait?" she said.

"I don't have a better suggestion."

"Stay with the car," she said. "If he leaves, follow. I'll flank him."

He glanced down at his cast and imagined a clutch pedal.

"Careful, there's not much cover."

She eased the driver's door open halfway and waited. No shots.

"Kandy," he whispered, and held her gun out to her. She took it and smiled before she slithered out of the car like her body was a fluid being poured through the opening.

He heard muffled gravel crunch as she moved. He kept a careful watch on the barrel hovering above the BMW's rearview mirror. He could make out a silhouette sitting low behind the steering wheel and wished for a good hunting rifle.

He moved his right arm and started the stopwatch in his wristwatch.

He looked up the hill for Kandy, being careful to keep his head low so his gaze wouldn't give her away. All he saw was waving grass two feet high. He breathed slowly and tried to think. There the guy sat and all they had to do was take him.

The stopwatch said one minute and eight seconds. How long since he had called for backup? Five minutes maybe, but they had been driving fast. Backup was coming from the city...

Then he realized his backup call might not have been intelligible with so much wind in the car. He pulled out his phone. No service. He reached under the dash for her radio. It wouldn't turn on. He wondered how many bullets had passed through the car.

He imagined the arrival of a SWAT team and a helicopter.

He saw her move from the cover of the trees and start down the hill through the grass twenty yards behind the car. She was exposed and he wanted to scream at her to wait. He grabbed his phone and started to dial, then stopped, remembering he didn't have service.

"Kandy, what the...?" he said softly.

He watched as she skidded down the hill, not even laying low in the grass.

She reached the left rear of the car. She put one hand on it and moved slowly toward the driver's door with her butt pressed against the fender, gun in her left hand, low and pointing at the ground.

He fought confusion. Kandy was one of the best he had ever worked with, but this was crazy, even by her standards.

Unbelievably, she tucked her gun into the back of her pants, walked to the driver's door and yanked it open. Qigiq saw a torso in a dark shirt and ski mask sitting stock still behind the wheel.

She waved her left arm in a big circle. She wanted him to come up.

Qigiq guessed the driver was dead, another murder-suicide crime of madness. He worked his way along the highway, sinking and sliding. Placing his good foot on the grass just beyond the road's edge, he used the crutch to vault over the shallow drainage ditch. He hopped, then started the climb to the BMW, moving his good foot up and bringing the crutch along.

He was breathing hard by the time he reached Kandy. She had an expression halfway between a grin and a sneer.

"What do we have?" he asked as he approached the front of the long sweeping hood.

"A prepared criminal."

He positioned himself against the open driver's door to counter the hill and looked closely at the body behind the wheel.

"Sense of humor," he said.

"Clever." She poked the arm. The dark sweater dented under her finger. "Blow-up doll. Made us think he," she paused, "or she, was standing guard."

"While walking away."

Kandy nodded and motioned him around the car. "I saw rubber seams on the neck and knew we had been had." A twisting line of matted grass showed where someone had crawled from the passenger door to the edge of the conifers at the top of the hill.

"Why not ambush us?" Qigiq asked.

She shrugged. "Maybe didn't like the odds. Wanted to get a head start before reinforcements arrived."

"And we don't know who we're looking for, or what they're wearing."

"I called the plate in while you were waddling up here. It's registered to a mint green Toyota Prius. Last year's model."

He sighed. "And the car?"

"Stolen this morning from a dealer's lot in Mountain View. Could be why he picked an older model: no computer key, but still plenty fast." She paused, her eyes roving across the car like she wanted to buy it. "We might get a print."

He shook his head. "I have a very clear image of a butter tan gloved hand holding a big gun."

"Might get lucky and find a bullet."

"Since when did you become the optimist on this team?" he said, trying for a smile he didn't feel. "The shots passed through your windows, within inches of my head I might add, and into space. They're probably six feet under on a hillside."

Their eyes met, but neither spoke.

"The first shot was on the bridge," she said.

"Maybe we could have a team of divers scour the bottom of the bay?" They laughed.

"We know someone wants to kill us," he said.

"Or you."

His leg was tired, so he leaned against the trunk and nodded, while feeling that uneasy sensation of being hunted he couldn't shake.

"What does he think I saw?"

"Are you sure the driver was male?" she asked.

"You think a woman would use a blow-up doll?"

"All the time," she said. "They're cuddly."

She huffed her low laugh and started down the hill.

~ 49 ~

They drove with the roar of the wind through blown-out windows back to Qigiq's houseboat. Kandy pulled to a stop beside his rented bike.

"I'll get another car. You want me to pick you up for the concert, or you going to ride?"

Qigiq leaned his head out the window. The sky was the deepening blue of impending dusk, but cloudless.

"Ride. The fresh air might help me make sense of this case."

She nodded. "Starts at seven."

He was careful stepping onto the boat, thinking about the air-filled doll and the level of premeditation it implied.

He went to the living room and removed a framed picture of a house in the snow and a gray patterned cloth from an electric keyboard. He pulled a padded bench out and sat down, stretching his left leg straight. The machine took a moment to come alive. On a shelf to his left he ran his finger down the spines of a stack of books and pulled out an urtext edition of Bach Inventions. They were only two parts, but that was enough for Bach, and as much as he could handle. Opening the book to number 14 he played a B-flat scale with his left hand, then his right, then the two together. He played the invention slowly, letting the tones penetrate his bones and brain to free his thoughts, like meditating in the snow.

He stopped and dug into his back pocket for his notes. He spread the page flat and read it over three times, letting the details of videos, bike accidents, fingers and ears and dry ice and knives fill his mind. Then he started playing again from the beginning.

The third time through the conversation with McGreen intruded. He pondered what the journalist might publish the following day, and would it help or hinder their investigation?

He played slowly, trying to connect a gunshot on Highway-1 to Sally's fingers. He lifted both hands from the keyboard. Were they related? Maybe what he had seen at the marina was a drug deal and had nothing to do with Sally's murder. He swallowed. There, he had finally used the word *murder*, at least in his mind. No more missing persons. Sally was clearly dead. Killed in such a way that a DNA rape kit was useless. And still he had little idea of who or why.

He played the left-hand part, feeling the low pitches resonate in his floating home. Maybe that marina sighting *was* a drug deal. Dealers turned to violence quickly to protect themselves and their business.

His mind swirled. According to Walters, Sally was a musician with many interests. Certainly drugs floated in musical circles. Could she have been involved in a deal gone bad? Had she been tortured so a kingpin could send a message to his troops? Were the videos somehow that message?

He made notes on the wrinkled paper. Perhaps Kandy could add insight. Had anyone questioned Robina about Sally's drug habits? And there was the guy Sally called Mony. He remembered Robina singing that silly song in Peggy's restaurant.

Perhaps.

He shifted on the bench. Pain heated his left ankle, reminding him he hadn't done his therapy exercises. And of Kandy's gift.

He reached to the bookshelf for his laptop, and placed it on top of the piano. Using the gift card, it took only a minute to purchase the program she had mentioned.

He typed the exercises the therapist had insisted he do each morning and evening. With his hands on the edge of the piano for balance, he moved his foot as the computer voice spoke.

"Flex and hold for five seconds...relax...flex and hold for five seconds, relax..."

He marveled at the crazy things engineers could make technology do.

"Rotate your toes to the right...hold for ten seconds..."

He froze.

That voice.

The threat message left on his voicemail.

The caller had used a computer to speak for him.

Or her.

~ 50 ~

Qigiq approached the tollbooths at the south end of the Golden Gate, and slowed to let the FastTrack machine read his code.

He felt traffic press in behind him.

He checked his mirrors for warnings of another attack. A marina passed to his left; the highway became a four-lane boulevard. His eyes tracked, watching drivers with cellphone earbuds and drivers with a burger in one hand. Two cars in a hurry changed lanes with no signals. A red Camaro accelerated through a yellow light. Everything looked normal, but he felt more exposed than ever, more exposed than riding alone in winter hundreds of miles from assistance. He twisted the throttle.

Minutes later he pulled up behind the conservatory and was pleasantly surprised to find they had an entire row of narrow parking spaces labeled: *Motorcycle Parking Only.* Only two were in use. One held a blue Yamaha cruiser with two big pistons, and the other a bright green sport-bike that leaned forward like a predator insect ready to pounce. He parked one space beyond the predator.

As he was working his way to the front door of the hall he noticed Kandy step out of a black sedan that was twice as long as her Mini. She wore a black skirt above her knees, and a lavender blouse under a black jacket that had gray fur at the shoulders. And heels. He stood and watched for a moment as she crossed the parking lot, admiring how her body always seemed to know how to move, no matter the circumstances.

She glanced up and waved.

He waved back and noticed far behind her a tall thin college girl on the arm of a guy in a tailored suit that looked gray under the mercury lights. The guy was older, maybe 35, maybe 45—her father maybe, or brother...or maybe not. He would have to remember to ask Robina if she knew them.

He turned his attention to his one-step at a time routine and raced Kandy to the top. She overtook him with five steps to go.

"You see the guy following me through the parking lot?"

He nodded. "Good tailor."

"He's with Veronica."

"That's Veronica?" He glanced over his shoulder at the thin girl. "Know anything about him?"

"Nothing. Figure we talk to Robina, or maybe Veronica directly if we can pull her away after the concert."

Kandy handed a young man with fresh acne and a borrowed suit the two tickets Robina had provided. He tore them in half, returned the stubs, and pointed to the left side of the hall. They let themselves be towed along by the crowd to row fifteen and two seats next to the aisle. Qigiq remained standing, waiting for the row to fill so he wouldn't have to play jack-in-the-box.

He studied the room.

A sign under a small balcony in the back limited occupancy to 548. Tall thick curtains in dark blue framed the stage where a lone piano sat sideways, its lid open to the audience like Mick Jagger shouting. A gold logo on the side said *Steinway & Sons.*

Kandy sat beside him tapping her phone. She held it toward him.

"Veronica with Sally and Robina."

He examined the picture, then looked around for the pricey suit. He found it ten rows back on the far side of the main aisle. The man was seated and talking into a cellphone the size of a Milky Way miniature while his eyes shifted around the hall as if he were trying to locate someone. His free hand scribbled on a narrow notepad like a cop writing a ticket. The girl next to him was almost his height. She wore a lace sweater over a tight dress in a color Qigiq would name Moonlight Maroon Metallic. She was slender in a barely-there sort of way, her straight black hair touching her shoulders.

"How tall is Veronica?"

Kandy scrolled back through pages of text.

"Robina said almost six feet. Let's call it five-eleven."

"The guy is close to the same height, but heavier. She'd blow away in a stiff breeze."

Kandy didn't turn around. "What have you got?"

"Business exec, accountant, lawyer. A little geeky. Starting to gray. Spends time outdoors, maybe works out, but not regularly. Probably trying to keep his gut down so he can hang with dolls like Veronica."

"You don't approve," she said, rising to allow an elderly gentleman to pass into the row.

He shrugged. "I'm sure Veronica is a wonderful girl."

"But not your type?" she teased.

"She's younger than my Guzzi," he said. "And would blow off the back in a cross-wind."

Kandy chuckled. "But Robina wouldn't?"

He gave her the evil eye.

"Moving on," she said. "Vi should be here." She held up the phone with a picture of a redhead with freckles that Qigiq would guess wasn't more than fifteen.

"That's Violet?"

"The sweet little flute player we met who is jealous of Veronica's boyfriends."

Qigiq studied the picture then tried to find a matching face in the crowd. He heard a cellphone, but it wasn't the one he was holding.

Kandy dug in her pocket and came up with her bikini phone and a pair of ear buds. She stuck one into her ear.

"Blocked number," she said, stood and handed him the second bud.

Qigiq plugged it into his ear and resumed his search for the freckled face.

"Hello," Kandy said softly.

"You bitch," a woman's voice screamed. "You lousy lying bitch."

"Who are you calling?"

"You, Rebecca. You said you wouldn't tell Eddy. I'm going to get you for this."

Kandy met Qigiq's eyes. "Oh, hi Alicia. It's nice to hear from you."

"Don't play cute with me, bitch. You know damn well why I'm calling."

Kandy's voice remained soft and even. "No, I really don't. What's wrong?"

"What's wrong? You told Eddy I was at the condo yesterday. And you sweet-talked him into dropping me. That's what's wrong!"

"Alicia, I haven't talked to Eddy since I saw you."

The phone was silent.

"Alicia?"

"You really didn't tell him?" Alicia said, her voice shaking.

"No. Why did you think I had?"

"Because he didn't show up. It's Tuesday. Eddy's horny. He always shows up."

"I kept our bargain. I haven't told him a thing. Not a word."

"Did you see him yesterday?" Alicia asked.

"No," Kandy said. "I decided not to wait around for a messy conversation. And he hasn't called to find out why I wasn't there. You know, like maybe I was in a car accident."

Alicia snorted. "Eddy wouldn't. He'll wait for you to grovel."

The phone was quiet.

"He'll be waiting a long time," Kandy said.

"You're telling the truth? You haven't seen Eddy?"

"No Alicia, I haven't seen him. I'm done with the condo." She paused. "Would you like to meet for lunch? No reason we can't be friends now that Eddy's all yours."

There was no hesitation. "Sure, it'll be fun."

"Tomorrow? One-ish?"

"Green's?" Alicia said.

"See you there." Kandy ended the call, looked at Qigiq, who handed her the ear bud.

"Not keeping his regular schedule," Qigiq said.

"I'll see what I can find out tomorrow." She lifted her arm and smiled. "Alicia likes my biceps."

"When do we interview Mr. Blake?" he asked.

"His assistant says he hasn't been in all day. Plainclothes are watching his office, house and the condo in San Francisco. Nothing."

The house lights flashed so Kandy sat down and Qigiq lowered himself into the aisle seat, which squeaked as he tilted backwards.

"Think Blake's running?"

"Or wiling away his time trying to kill us," Kandy said.

The hall dropped into darkness as golden lights brightened the stage. Robina glistened in a long gown the color of a pool of deep water at midnight—not black, not blue—as she floated from the wings. She carried a violin under her left arm and a bow in her right hand, walked to center stage and lifted the instrument to her chin. Qigiq thought of that mark on her neck she had told him about.

The stage lighting faded, leaving her a bright iridescence in a single spotlight, her hair wrapped high on her head, making her inches taller.

Robina stood like an artist's model for seconds, elbow lifted, her bow poised over the strings.

He felt the audience collectively holding its breath in silence, and realized he too had stopped breathing.

~ 51 ~

Harold walked along De Anza Boulevard shortly after 7:00 pm on a Tuesday that felt like a blue Monday as four lanes of traffic moved and stopped, moved and stopped. His eyes burned from tracking the Hand all day—many thousands of machines. Countless thieves. He stepped off the curb and checked the white box under his arm to make sure the fingers were level. Silver Platter's engineering group had celebrated both the release of their Hand technology and the month's birthdays, including his, with a big cake shaped like a hand that served thirty people.

Lili had given him the leftover pinky and fourth finger.

He stomped up three flights and let himself into his apartment on the top floor. Humans were oblivious to the noise they made, so he didn't like his ceiling being someone else's floor. He crossed the living area to the kitchen and placed the box on the counter. He should eat supper, but cake sounded better. He peeked and figured there were at least four Harold servings.

He opened a drawer and grabbed a butter knife, then a Corona from the fridge. Beer and cake wasn't everyone's favorite food combo, but it was high on his list.

He heard a voice and stopped.

He heard it again, muffled, like a speaker under a blanket.

Carrying the beer bottle, he passed through the kitchen and out the other side into the only bedroom. His home computer sat on a glass topped desk in the corner, asking for attention. He took a long swallow, let the coolness cascade down his throat, then read the message. Someone had sent an urgent email and a series of chat requests.

He frowned and said, "Open Message."

The voice recognition system responded. The message contained an ink drawing of a lone figure in a small boat floating on a dark fog-filled river with the jagged outline of a treeless ridge behind. Across the picture white calligraphy said *Happy Birthday Haro*.

Sarlin had been playing with her computer. He was her hero now, though she pronounced it more like Haro, and so had given him a new nickname. All because she thought Harvey was an ugly sound.

"Scroll."

She had no idea how close she had come to the truth. And he was going to keep it that way.

The email rolled forward.

Please meet tonight at 8:00pm. I know it is your birthday and you will celebrate. But I have gift for you.

His lips tingled with the memory of her mouth at that New York subway entrance. How had she found out it was his birthday? Maybe he told her they would have a cake.

What would she give him?

She was right, he *should* be going out to celebrate. But Lili didn't think it was a good idea for them to be seen outside the office after business hours. And what passed for friends in his world worked as much as he did. So his celebration was going to be a little personal tracking of the Hand from his private machine—the thing he cared about most in the world at the moment.

But first.

He typed: *Thank you. See you at 8:00 sharp. Trying to guess your gift.* He clicked Send, and went back to the kitchen for cake, his mind alternating between its sweetness, and memories of Sarlin's petite body and what it might be like to touch.

A half-hour later he sat down in front of the computer.

"Open Chat."

The computer thought it was 7:58, so he went to the fridge for another beer. When he returned, a request for chat glowed on the screen.

"Accept."

A chat window opened but showed only black. He moved his face close to the screen and squinted, but still couldn't see anything. He started to type, but a bright spot began to glow. He leaned back and flicked off the lamp.

He saw another spot of yellow, just to the right of the first. He tapped a key to raise the volume on his speakers.

Nothing.

He waited. Soon a third spot of yellow appeared. And a fourth.

That sexy little Asian girl was lighting candles.

He smiled.

At candle twelve, he could see she was squatting barefoot and wearing a shiny black robe. As she lit more candles, he became aware of bright blue embroidery on both sleeves, and reds and green over her breasts. And his growing desire to possess her. He counted as she worked; twenty-seven candles encircled her.

She stood in the center and placed her palms together as if in prayer.

"Beautiful," he said.

The audio must have been active because she brought an index finger to her lips to shush him. She bent low and extended an arm into the darkness around the candles, returning with a violin and bow.

His tastes ran toward techno-rap and thrash metal, but it would be a treat to see her play.

She held both the violin and its bow in her left hand. With her right, she untied the cloth belt holding a robe that he'd bet had a name like sarong or something. She removed her right arm from the robe and let half of it drop away.

He swallowed hard. She was nude underneath and had revealed her right breast and hip and thigh.

"Sarlin—"

He had imagined her, and what he would do, a thousand times...

She held her finger up to shush him again and leaned in so close to her camera he could only see her lips.

"I am a girl of the Tao," she whispered, "who has studied the harmonious ways of the Plain Girl. We understand how important birthday is, and know what man wants...is not what he needs. Now please be quiet, I have Yin energy for you."

She lifted the violin and began to play the traditional happy birthday song at a tempo so slow it melted from his speakers. What beautiful tone, and what a lovely body.

His left hand reached for the beer while his eyes remained glued to the screen, covering and re-covering every inch of her from her tiny toes to the curve of her bare shoulder. He turned up the sound. So glorious an instrument playing such a simple tune. Then he realized he should be recording.

When she reached the final *to you* she held the last note for a long long time, then bowed deeply.

He watched her breast shift with gravity. Felt more desire. Then other feelings intruded he didn't understand.

He applauded.

She held her finger to her lips.

She moved the instrument and bow to her right hand and lowered the left side of the sarong to her waist.

He swallowed hard at the sight of her breasts, small, upturned and dark at the tips, doing something to him that a thousand pictures of women on the Internet had never done. She lifted the violin and played long notes that sounded like wind carving through a cave.

Or an animal calling for her mate.

She turned slowly in the center of the circle of candles, letting the dancing light flicker across her body. He devoured every curve, watching the lines of her neck and shoulder shift with the effort of playing, and without even knowing he was thinking about it, longed to see what was under the material draped from her waist to the floor.

She played faster, as if a record were speeding up, bending with the effort as she drove energy into the instrument. Turned away from him, she played a pounding rhythm that set an anchor note and climbed and climbed in pitch, only to drop down to set the anchor again.

With each drop she stood on the balls of her feet and slammed her heels against the floor beneath her, adding a drum-like thump, and causing the robe to inch downward. She played and played, faster and harder, louder, two notes at a time, the energy filling his ears, her raw beauty filling his eyes, until she held a high note for the longest time, shaking the bow until her body vibrated with the effort and the sarong shimmied and fell to the floor.

She stopped facing directly away from him, completely nude—her back expanding and contracting with the effort of breathing. He didn't move, his hand wrapped around a Corona bottle next to his computer that he didn't feel. He felt only a hypnotic trance, and realized his breathing was synchronized to hers.

He made no effort to change anything.

She began happy birthday again, slowly, as if Bach himself had written it for a religious ceremony. And she rotated in place, like the Earth was turning beneath her feet.

He was afraid to blink, not wanting the dream to collapse. He thought of her in a little apartment in the huge expanse of New York City, standing in a circle of fire, playing the most beautiful birthday song he had ever heard. Turning ever so slowly...

She lowered the violin, holding it just below her breasts.

She whispered, "Happy Birthday, Haro," and bowed deeply.

He memorized every inch of her.

Then she knelt and blew out the candles as she had lit them, one after another around the circle until his screen went black.

He sat motionless, images of her sound and body swirling through him, creating sensations he didn't know existed. He blinked and saw the black square on the computer. He wondered if he had fallen asleep and dreamt her. But his storage was nearly full. He opened the file and was about to press *Play*.

He wanted her like he had never wanted any of the others.

But how?

He watched, marveling in her calm expression and luscious nakedness.

But a recording could be discovered. And would connect him to her. And she knew his face, and what they had done that day. He reached out and hovered his finger over the Delete key, took a deep breath—and pressed.

The screen glowed *Are you sure?*

He hesitated. He could watch ten thousand times and it would never be enough.

He wondered how many hits on YouTube that video might get. How many people would send it to someone for a birthday?

He thought about anonymous postings. And how they could be cracked.

He clicked OK and watched while the machine destroyed the recording. Before the delete completed, Chat popped up and startled him. He hoped Sarlin was returning for an encore.

But the request was from Lili.

He frowned.

Lili didn't usually work late. She preferred to come in early.

He clicked Accept.

Oh Harold, so glad I caught you. I know it's your birthday, but I found something you have to see. I don't know what to do. Come back to the office? Please? And Happy Birthday! :-)

Something drastic had gone wrong with the Hand. What else would cause a Lili panic?

Hi Lili. If you need me.

He was suddenly hungry.

Do I have time to eat first?

Her reply was immediate.

Come right away. I'll buy dinner after you see this.

The world was turning in odd ways: Sarlin's performance, now a dinner invite from Lili. His 28th year on the planet held promise.

On my way!

Harold eyed the cake as he dashed through the kitchen and squatted to lace up black tennis shoes. He took two stairs down at a time and jogged to Silver Platter. Only one traffic light of five was red. He was mouth breathing when he walked down the hall towards Lili's little office at the far end.

It was empty.

He pulled out his cellphone and dialed her extension. It rang once then auto-transferred.

"Hi, Harold. I'm in the QA lab, way in the back."

"Be right there."

Her being in Quality Assurance edged his *Something has gone wrong with Hand* meter up into the red. He pushed through the lab door and walked past racks of machines at a speed-walker pace. The top of her head was visible above a monitor in the corner.

"Thanks for coming so fast," Lili said.

"Must be bad if you're hiding."

"I don't want anyone else to see this."

His throat tightened, worried he had missed something fundamental in the design of the Hand that was rising up from the lake at Loch Ness.

"Watch," she said.

He stood behind her as a movie played on YouTube. It showed a girl's face either in agony or ecstasy, he couldn't quite tell which.

"Video?"

"Yeah. A special video."

"She's not that special," he said, smiling. "You're much prettier."

She spun around in her roller chair and stared at him over glasses she only wore for long stints at the computer.

He shrugged. "I'm just saying."

"Pay attention, Harold, this is serious. See that line along the bottom?"

He leaned over with his hand on the back of her chair and felt the sizzle of her nearness. There was a strange scent in the air floating above the usual aroma of hot plastic.

"Yeah. Some kind of noise in the signal."

"That's what it's supposed to look like," she said.

He frowned. "Supposed to?"

"If we decode that signal and reassemble it, we get this."

His eyes widened as he watched a second video.

"Is that real or Hollywood special effects?"

"I don't know," she said. "That's why I had to show it to you."

"*Don't Steal Music?* Uh...sort of like the Hand finding pirates."

She leaned away from the monitor where a movie showed a jagged-edged knife against a finger.

"Awfully coincidental," she said.

"Where the hell did you get these?"

"Carl in marketing found the first one during the routine search we do every week for new postings about music piracy. I panicked when I saw the noise at the bottom, and personally tracked down the other one on an MIT lab site. Well, it used to be at the lab. Now it's roving the peer-to-peer servers."

"You panicked? Is this connected to the Hand in some weird way?"

She shook her head. "No, not at all."

His insides relaxed for the first time since seeing Sarlin's bare shoulder.

"That's good. I thought for sure you found a crashing bug in my software."

She stood and faced him. He noticed her lipstick was crooked. Cute, but something was very wrong, Lili didn't ever have crooked lipstick.

"The Hand is fine. This is..."

Her eyes drifted into space somewhere north of his left shoulder.

"Lili, what is it? You said this movie was sandwiched into the noise in the first one. A weird place to put a video, but it's no big deal. There are a hundred ways to do it."

Her gaze didn't move. "Maybe. But this is one of ours."

He stepped back. Some days, he hated pronouns.

"How can it be ours? I haven't ever worked on video encoding. We're exclusively audio."

"That's true," she said.

"Someone here is working on cryptographic hash functions independent of my audio work? That's idiotic. The two problems are closely related."

"Not here," she said as she rotated and slumped back into her chair.

The movie ended with a flickering display of a *Don't Steal* message that irritated his eyes in the dim light of the lab. He saw an equation in the flicker expressing an inequality of a set of functions. He blinked and it was gone. But it left a feeling he had seen that expression before. He closed his eyes...

Game theory.

Something about equilibrium.

He rolled the words *not here* over in his mind like they were a sculpture he was bidding on at auction. Platter had only this one-floor building, and fewer than fifty employees: tiny by any standards. He leaned his butt against the desk and faced her.

"I'm not following you, Lili."

She looked up.

"You have to promise not to tell anyone about this." She met his eyes. "Ever."

"About what?"

"This wasn't supposed to happen." She squeezed the sides of her head with two hands. "I don't know who else to turn—" She looked up fast, her entire face taut. "Really, I didn't tell you, you don't know."

She was blabbering. Lili didn't blabber.

"Lili, please just tell me. Between us."

She turned away and spoke at the monitor. "Blake wanted insurance. He was never confident that Full Disclosure, even with the Invisible Hand technology, could save Silver Platter. So he set up a second team."

Throwing corporate dollars at another team while Harold worked seven-day weeks because they couldn't afford more engineers?

"That bastard."

"He set up a project for tagging video, figuring that if the music market didn't work out, maybe video would because people steal movies too."

"Another team," he mumbled, still contemplating the enormous cost.

"Why do people steal stuff, Harold?"

He frowned at the back of her head, thinking of that bastard Blake in his flashy Mercedes wasting development money.

"So we can have jobs trying to stop them." He laughed.

"No, really. They know they don't own the stuff they copy."

"Lili, do you know why a male dog licks its balls?"

"Harold, that's disgusting."

"Not to the dog." He chuckled.

"Ugh. No, I don't."

"Because he can."

She spun around and peered at him, unblinking.

"People steal if they think they can get away with it," he said. "Look at the electronic detection used by clothing stores across the malls of America. Why are those necessary?"

She chewed her upper lip with her lower teeth. He thought it was a pretty fair chipmunk imitation, but didn't say so.

"Because," she said. "There are enough people who steal merchandise that surveillance systems are cost-effective."

"Spoken like a true business geek. And you're right. Now where are those detectors for people illegally copying files from the Internet?"

"There aren't any. That's why we built Full Disclosure."

"Exactly. If there's no penalty for taking without paying, lots of people will take, not everyone mind you, but many. Case in point, falling revenues from music sales. Culprit: online copying. It's not like people are actually listening to less music."

She pursed her lips. "You mean people behave just because they're afraid of getting caught?"

"Some people," he said.

"That's disgusting. Haven't they read the Bible? Don't they understand how an economy functions? There has to be payment for work performed and benefit received, or the whole world collapses."

"I think it's fair to say, as someone who has read the Bible and understands economics, you, Lili, are in the vast minority."

They were quiet. He watched her stare at the desktop. Not the computer desktop on the monitor, but the scratched surface of the desk holding it.

"You said there was another team?"

She nodded.

"And you managed it for Blake?"

"Only sort of."

"How can you 'sort of' manage?"

She turned her face up again to meet his eyes and smiled ever so slightly.

"We outsourced it."

"The whole project?"

"Yes."

"Sounds expensive," he said. "We could use that money here."

"True, but now we have a video play. It's not very far along, but it's based on a dynamic tag that changes with every frame. And there's a prototype tool for test encoding."

"Dynamic tags? Like the Hand?"

Her smile vanished and she looked down.

"Yes, they've seen our design documents."

"And they're trying to apply my work to video without even talking to me?"

"Blake wanted a separate team starting from a clean sheet of paper."

"Reading my documentation is *not* a fucking clean sheet of paper," he said, his voice echoing in the empty lab.

"You know, he wanted fresh eyes on the problem."

Harold tapped his knuckles repeatedly against the top of the desk. He felt violated, like someone had stolen his furniture. And his car. And girlfriend.

"And where did you find this brilliant team that is doing research for us by stealing my work?"

"China."

He stopped rapping his knuckles.

"Don't tell me. Now you have a security leak?"

Her eyes turned to the stopped movie. "Not sure. All I know is these two videos are on the Internet. And it looks to me like they came from our test tool."

"Can you show me this tool?"

Her head flopped left and right. "It's not installed anywhere in this building. I only run it at home."

"You're sure these came from it?"

"I'm not sure yet, but I know that encoding to the last visible line is an option with the tool. And stuffing one video inside another is exactly what our demo does. I have to take the first video home, and see if the tool can extract the second one. If it can, then this is our encoding for sure."

He rolled his tongue over his teeth and thought hard.

"Prove it when you get home, after you take me to dinner." He smiled. "But let's assume that yes, these videos were built with our test tool. Who has access?"

"No one," she said. "I mean, I do, but that's it."

"Whoa, Lili," he held both palms out. "You have a copy, a bunch of people in China have copies, maybe some testers have a copy."

"No testing in the U.S.," she said.

"So maybe these weird movies aren't from the U.S."

Her lips worked against each other, making her lipstick more crooked. "Not from the U.S.?"

"Let's start over. A software company in China has a copy."

She nodded. "Takana Consulting in Beijing. They're doing the development."

"Any idea how good their security is?"

"We surveyed their procedures once."

He paced behind her chair.

"So maybe a China connection. Who else has access?"

"Just me," she said.

He stopped behind her. "Did you post these videos Lili, and now you're trying not to take heat?" he asked calmly.

She spun around in her chair. "Harold! Of course not."

He laughed. "Just teasing, Lili, trying to lighten the mood."

"You're not funny." Then a smile, "Even if it is your birthday."

"So, an insider at Takana, or someone in the U.S., has a copy of the software. Who could that be?"

"Takana delivers a physical package once a month: source code, test files, running versions. I put them in the vault."

"That's supposed to protect us if they go out of business, right?"

She nodded slowly.

"Have they ever missed one?"

She shook her head.

"Have they ever been late? Like one went missing and they had to send another?"

"They arrive with full tracking. We've never lost one."

"Never one lying around where it could be stolen? Like that intern in Ohio who let the tax information go missing from his car? Or in the UK where the data on all those kids was stolen?"

"Nope. We get a package, I open and verify that the content is readable, and put it in the vault."

"Do you do a test compile and run the program?" he asked.

"Sure, but the disks contain compiled versions too. And I scrub the machine when I'm done."

"So anyone with access to our vault who can push a disk into a computer could run the test tool?"

She rubbed her forehead with the fingertips of her left hand.

"Uh, yeah, that's true."

"Any special machinery required?" he asked.

She shook her head and waved an arm at the QA lab.

"It'd run on any machine in here."

"Who has access to the vault? I know I don't," he said.

"Besides me? The board of directors, and Stacy, Blake's assistant." She put her forehead against her arms and dropped her head to the desk in one motion. "I don't get it Harold, why would anyone want to use our software to post such horrible movies?"

The possible answers to that question were legion and they all started stampeding through his mind at once. He took two deep breaths.

"Let's hold off on why, Lili, and see if we can figure out how. If I accept for the moment that our security hasn't been violated, there are only three choices. Those movies were made in China, inside this building, or outside this building."

"Wow, thanks Harold, that helps a lot," she said, sitting up. "I would never have thought of that."

"You're not being nice to me just because it's my birthday, are you?"

She forced a smile. "Sorry. I'm just so scared. That movie..."

He saw her shoulders shudder as her eyes glistened with tears: phase one of breakdown.

"Process of elimination. If it was made in China, we'll never find it, not without the FBI or someone helping us. If someone took the disk out of the vault and left, well, we'd have to search the whole planet."

"So we look in here?" she asked, incredulous.

"Think about it, Lili. If...what do you call this thing?"

"DOG," she said.

He squinted at her. "You call it DOG?"

She shrugged. "Year of the...and all that. It stands for Dynamic Optics Generator, though it's more of a remapping."

"Okay," he continued. "If someone wanted to use DOG and not get caught, where's the best place to hide it?"

It took her a moment. Then she said softly, "Right here. Where it's just one more project. And legal too, because Platter owns it. Anywhere else, it'd be stolen property."

"Bingo. So all we have to do is find it."

"On one of two hundred machines?" she asked. "Oh, that'll be easy."

"Piece of cake." He smiled. "No pun intended."

She shook her head but grinned.

"No really," he said.

"But why would it still be here?"

"Is there an un-installer for DOG?"

"I don't think so. Like I said, the project isn't very far along."

"And even if there is, would whoever did this know enough to run it?"

"You really think we can find it?" she asked, in a sort of breathless pant that Harold liked a lot.

"If we do, it'll confirm you, uh, we have a problem. Here's what we do..."

First they scrubbed the storage of a machine and installed a fresh version of the operating system. Then they wrote a script to make a list of every file on it. Lili got DOG from the vault, installed and ran it on the fresh machine, and made a second list. The difference between the two lists was 1045 files that constituted DOG. Finally, they started a search across the 200 machines for any of the 1045 files...and went out to dinner.

After three beers each, a steak cooked medium, a free birthday dessert of a chocolate log and two scoops of vanilla that seemed oddly erotic, many thoughts of Sarlin's nude body, a careful study of Lili's body whenever she wasn't looking, and a too brief birthday kiss on his cheek, Harold opened the door to the QA lab for Lili.

She watched over his shoulder while he checked the log file.

"Machine number 168 has a hundred of the 1045 files. Someone tried to clean up after using it," he said.

"When?"

"The installation was a week ago Sunday. Don't know when the cleanup attempt happened."

She squeezed his shoulders with both hands so hard it created a burning sensation in his bones.

"Oh, Harold, Harold."

He put his right hand over her left and patted it.

"Put the package back in the vault, scrub our test machine, and don't talk to anyone until we figure out what's going on."

"What about number 168?" she asked.

"Never heard of it," he said.

~ 52 ~

Robina played beautifully with an occasional slip, which was quite understandable given the week she had just lived through. A Bach suite, then Beethoven arranged for solo violin by someone other than Beethoven, and ending with a piece by a student composer named Samual Beler that seemed to be devoid of any rhythm Qigiq could find. The melody, though, was a haunted, drifting thing. It filled him with the same void as the first time he had gone out alone in a sea kayak—and lost sight of land.

The pianist who followed was Beler the composer, who played Chopin and Shostakovich admirably if a bit mechanically. Then Robina joined him for two piano sonatas of Beethoven: numbers 12 and 21, both of which Qigiq thoroughly enjoyed. The last piece was a violin sonata by Beler himself that meandered as if it were the thoughts of a lonely madman.

The audience was applauding at the second curtain call when Kandy said, "You listen to this stuff don't you?"

"The classics have a lot to offer," he said. "But they take some getting used to."

"Needs a drummer," she said with a grin. "But I like the sounds Robina made—so intense."

He nodded. "Intense is a good word for her. There's nothing like live music. No speakers. A kind of purity in the vibration of wood."

"And steel," she said. "Can't do much without steel-making technology."

They rose and joined the crowd drifting toward the rear of the hall. Qigiq watched the man with Veronica. His cellphone was out of sight now and she had one hand around his bicep. In heels, she was two inches taller, though he was about three of her wide. As they reached the end of the aisle, Qigiq planning his descent, Violet stepped up behind them.

"Hi Kandy, I want you to meet Margo."

"Hello, Margo, nice to meet you. This is my partner Qigiq," Kandy said.

A stocky girl a full head taller than Violet with a round face and short black hair cropped in a straight line nodded. She was wearing dark everything: boots, jeans, sweater, coat. It gave the impression of a spy striving to be invisible in the night.

"Don't you just love Robina?" Violet said. "She plays heavenly."

"I really enjoyed her phrasing in the Beethoven, but I didn't understand the Beler Sonata," Qigiq said.

Violet stopped smiling.

"I like her intensity," Kandy added.

Vi bopped up and down like a toy. "Oh yeah, she's super intense. You going wait to meet her?"

Kandy's eyes flicked to Qigiq's for a moment.

"Sure," she said. "Will you show us the stage door?"

"This way," Vi said, zipping down the steps like a puppy running outside to piddle.

"I'll catch up with you," Qigiq said.

Kandy grinned. "You got it." She disappeared, parting the crowd at the same pace as Vi.

Margo didn't move. "Curious name."

"Inuit. I'm was born in Alaska." He prepared himself for a question about cold.

She nodded. "You ever feel like a minority?"

They drifted forward with the crowd, passing through heavy doors into the evening darkness and carefully down marble stairs, impeding a wash of bodies on either side. Margo moved at his pace, making the bodies give him sufficient space as he reached forward with the black tip, feeling like a pole vaulter about to be launched.

"Once in awhile," he said.

"Sometimes they pull away like you're a leper," Margo said. "But sometimes they get so close it's as if you're not there, don't even deserve a bit of real estate on the planet."

Qigiq had felt both in his life. "And sometimes they ask you to leave point blank."

Margo studied his face, nodded slowly. "Why?"

He had contemplated that question a thousand times since leaving the village. Just not lately.

"Because you're not sufficiently like them. Not of their tribe. So you become an unknown. Unpredictable. An outsider." He paused. "And always second class."

By the time he reached the street Kandy was out of sight. He worked his way left through dresses, jeans and suit coats with Margo parting the crowd. They found the group gathered at the entrance to a narrow alley, Veronica pointing at the sky, her date pretending to listen. Violet smoked with one hand, eyes dancing repeatedly in Veronica's direction. Kandy was gazing up the alley.

Margo said, "Thanks for the chat," drifted to Violet and lit a cigarette off hers.

He reached the group just as a door opened in the distance and Robina stepped out. She had let her blond hair drape over her shoulders and was wearing tight black jeans with heeled boots so high she had to swivel to walk. Her sleeveless purple sweater closed asymmetrically across the front. Her gloved left hand held a box, her right, a violin case. A tiny pink iPod clipped to her right shoulder like a military stripe connected to white, swaying wires. Qigiq wondered what kind of music she would listen to after making so much of her own.

Kandy said, "Qigiq, this is Veronica and her friend Maximilian." She grinned her right-side grin.

Qigiq shook hands with Veronica. Her fingers were as long and thin as the rest of her body, her grip spun-glass feathery.

Max extended his hand.

"I love him like a million bucks," Veronica said, squeezing his arm.

Max had a firm handshake and a wide smile under a small black mustache.

"Only because she's never seen a million bucks," he said.

Violet jumped up and down. "Here she comes...here she comes."

Margo ignored the outburst and dragged on her cigarette.

Robina waved her violin case in greeting from halfway down the alley. Qigiq released the crutch and waved back with his left hand feeling warmly energized by the evening's music and the passions of youth surrounding him. As Robina lowered the case, he saw a brilliant flash of yellow light grow like a giant sunflower from her right side. Her body flew left as the sound of a gunshot reached his ears. His eyes reflexively slammed shut as wind pushed past him. When he opened them Robina was lying on her side in a field of wood splinters, the alleyway now filled with gray smoke.

Not moving.

Violet screeched a high-pitched squeal that didn't help him think.

Kandy touched his left arm. "Call. I'll help her."

He nodded, yanked out his cellphone and pressed 911, reported there had been a blast less than thirty seconds ago, one victim seriously injured, and their location. He gave his name and badge number and said he would call back with the victim's status as soon as possible.

"We have to secure the site, keep people away from her," he said to the group.

Veronica stared at him with wide round eyes and a closed mouth.

Violet screamed again.

Qigiq looked at Margo, who turned, put her left arm around Vi's waist from behind and her right hand over the girl's mouth.

"I'll help your friend," Max said from beside Veronica, and jogged off in Kandy's direction.

Qigiq looked over his shoulder to see the departing crowd turn toward the alley and begin to descend on Robina. Unless there was another way in that he couldn't see, they were going to impede the rescue crew. He moved as swiftly as the crutch would allow toward Robina, striving to stay ahead of the crowd. When he got there, Max stood blocking the alleyway, holding his arms outstretched like a guard at a crosswalk.

"Thanks, Max," Qigiq said, as he moved past.

"The least I can do for a beautiful young girl."

Kandy was kneeling beside Robina, who was on her back, her head twisted to the left, a pool of blood behind it. Kandy had removed her jacket and was holding one sleeve hard against Robina's upper right arm, the other sleeve tucked around her head.

"Blown against the wall," Kandy said. "Head is bleeding badly, maybe spinal injury...can't move her."

"The arm?"

"A mess above the elbow. I don't see where it came from. There's no damage to that wall." She indicated the wall opposite where Robina lay by wagging her head. "What was it?"

"Doesn't look like a gunshot." He examined the alley. Both walls were untouched except for a splash of blood where Robina's head had made contact. The cobble alleyway was undisturbed, not a single brick out of place. Between bricks? He would look later.

He dialed 911 again.

Kandy saw him. "Unconscious: respiration 15, heart rate 99. Pale. Pupils respond to light."

Qigiq relayed the info to the emergency operator, and was glad to hear about the eyes. Maybe Robina's brain would be okay.

"Five to six minutes," he said to Kandy. He heard a scuffle behind him and saw a crowd of fifty people pressing against Max.

Qigiq moved to the right, leaned against the wall and turned his crutch sideways, holding the tip out to Max. With his other hand, he held up his badge. Max grabbed the crutch on the first try and moved to the far side of the alley. It was crude, but they had a "Do Not Cross" police line.

"Please make room," he called out. "Paramedics arriving in five minutes."

The crowd shifted but didn't know how to arrange itself. Grumbling grew louder and Qigiq saw half a dozen people holding cellphones as far above their heads as possible. Flashes lit the walls of the narrow alley. He heard Vi's scream pierce the air and wondered how she had escaped Margo. He turned to see Kandy bent over with an ear to Robina's lips.

A siren bleeped its way through a nearby intersection. Moments later the walls of the alley flashed red and white. The crowd had grown in the intervening minutes, and he had made no progress at creating a path for the emergency personnel.

"Please make room, the ambulance is here," he called out.

That caused fifty heads to swivel, but no one moved. He felt the crutch drop to the ground and looked over to see Max pushing people away from the left building with a sweeping right arm, making a walkway along that side. He was moving slowly, but making progress and the crowd began to understand. He heard voices far in the back and stretched tall to see what was happening. The crowd was also moving away from the left wall in the back. It took a moment to realize that Margo was mirroring Max's crowd-control efforts.

Three EMTs crossed the sidewalk with a gurney and med bags. They moved unimpeded into the narrow aisle Margo had created and passed Max just as he and Margo met in the middle. The crowd was quiet; the only sound now the hammering of boots on cobbles. Qigiq pulled his crutch out of the way as the team arrived at a full sprint.

Kandy stepped away. Two men and a woman dropped down to Robina. An IV was inserted, monitors attached, and a flat board maneuvered under her with barely a jostle. They lifted her onto the gurney without a word, then lifted the gurney itself to eliminate the vibration of wheels on stone, and glided down the still open aisle. They couldn't have been there for more than forty-five seconds. Qigiq was still leaning against the wall holding his crutch when he heard the rising pitch of the siren.

Kandy walked up. "San Francisco Medical Center. Dave said she'll probably go right to surgery."

He raised an eyebrow.

A smile tried to find her face but failed. She tapped above her left breast. "Name tag."

The crowd drifted toward the spot where the ambulance had been parked, as if there were more to see.

"I'll call the bomb squad," she said.

He stuffed the crutch under his left arm and hopped around in a half circle to stare at the dark spots on the stone.

"What do you think?" he asked.

She was quiet. He normally took comfort in her quick comebacks, so the silence now made him uneasy, like they were both looking into a deep well and neither could see the bottom.

Finally she said, "MO is new. But I have to believe it's related to Sally."

"There's no evidence."

"They were roommates," she said. "What are the odds two random grabs would pick roommates?"

"How many people live in San Francisco?" he asked.

"You're not going to go Fermi on me are you?"

He grinned, but it was half-hearted. "You don't like the way Enrico Fermi estimated answers?"

"Go ahead, I want to see what you get."

"Say 500,000 people in the city. Half women, but two-thirds are married. Leaves about 80,000 singles. How many in their twenties? Maybe a third? Call it 30,000. How many have a female roommate? Most. Call it 25,000. So one chance in 25,000 the killer picks the roommate."

"Long odds," she said.

He nodded. "They have to be related."

"What if they're not?" she asked.

"Ferdinand will cover that angle. He won't accept the roommates argument."

Max returned with Veronica. Her eyes were red, wide and wet.

"Can we help?" Max asked.

"We need to notify her family," Kandy said.

"Her mom's in New York," Veronica said, in a calm voice, as if she were on a stage.

"Anyone else?" Kandy said.

Veronica said, "She never talked about her dad."

"You don't have a number for her mother do you?"

Veronica shook her head. "It's in her cellphone. She called home every week."

"Thanks, Veronica. Maybe you can go visit Robina tomorrow, after she's had time to stabilize," Kandy suggested.

Veronica nodded and pulled Max away with her.

"Odd couple," Qigiq said.

"Well-to-do businessman has cute music student in need of financial assistance on the side: the standard sugar daddy win-win. There are even websites where you can advertise."

He met her eyes, not knowing if she was serious.

"Someone always gets hurt," he said.

"That has nothing to do with money or age."

His thoughts turned to Robina. "Hospital duty or bomb squad?"

Her eyes shifted to where Robina had fallen.

"You're good with data," she said. "I'll take the hospital."

He nodded and lowered himself to the cobblestones, his back against the concert hall. He stretched his left leg carefully but pain rushed between his toes and knee anyway.

He waited alone in the cool alley trying not to jump to conclusions. He had hoped Sally was an isolated case. Now they might have a serial killer on their hands. But the methods were so totally divergent. *The targets*, a voice in his head whispered. *It's about the targets.* But nubile women were overrepresented as homicide victims, so that didn't narrow things. And sex crimes were often committed by someone known to the victim. Was this such a crime? Who knew both Sally and Robina?

Or was it something else entirely?

The cold from curved cobbles penetrated his cotton pants, pushing a chill into his spine. Those videos. The perp showing off. But they seemed more than mere bravado, though he couldn't say what.

He stared down the empty alley.

Where had those packages in Blake's freezer been going?

Rumbling from the street echoed into the alley. He looked up. A tall figure in a long coat and a smooth helmet floated along the sidewalk. The sound became metallic chatter before stopping abruptly as the figure leapt and a skateboard flipped into the air. The rider caught it in one hand and walked toward him.

Light seeping into the alley from a streetlamp on McAllister Drive turned the figure into a young man who hadn't shaved in days, then it became Danny.

Qigiq waved.

"Vi called me," Danny said.

"Robina's on her way to the medical center. They're taking her to surgery."

Danny dropped his board, wheels down, and straddled it. He sat and faced Qigiq.

"Vi said someone shot her."

Qigiq shook his head. "More like an explosion. Specialists are on the way. I'm guarding the site so it doesn't get contaminated."

Danny twisted his head around. His eyes stopped on the dark spot spread across the two stones where Robina's head had rested.

"Is that blood?"

Qigiq nodded. "The blast tossed her sideways. She fell hard."

Danny was quiet, except for rocking the board across two stones—clap-clap back, clap-clap forward.

"Is Sally dead?" Danny asked.

The hair on the back of Qigiq's neck stood tall. No information had been released; Danny was probing.

"I can't say officially, Danny. The final lab results have to be verified. But we think so, yes."

He pushed his lips out like he was going to blow up a balloon. The clap-clap stopped.

"Is Robina dead?"

"She was unconscious when the ambulance took her away, but she was very much alive."

Danny took off his helmet and placed it gently to his right. It was metal and the olive paint was scratched, possibly the real thing American troops used in World War II, except it had a leather pouch taped to the top. A white wire wiggled out of the pouch, down the side of the helmet, turned under and went inside.

"Can I see her?"

"I'm heading over soon as we get this roped off. You want a ride?"

Danny nodded and stared into space.

A cart being dragged over cobblestones broke the silence of the evening. Ferdinand approached, wearing his long white lab coat and towing a stack of electronic equipment.

Qigiq worked his way to his feet.

"Hello, Ferdinand. I didn't expect you personally."

"When I heard the source of the explosion was unidentified, I wished to see for myself."

"Thanks for coming. Here's what I know..." Qigiq recounted what he had seen, leaving out any speculation whatsoever.

Ferdinand nodded occasionally, but asked no questions. And eyed Danny.

Qigiq said, "Danny is," he hesitated at the present tense, "a friend of both Sally and Robina. Danny, this is Ferdinand."

Danny looked up from his seat on the skateboard, his long shadow from the streetlamp spilling up the alley across the bloodstained stones.

~ 53 ~

Eddy caressed the leather-wrapped steering wheel as he held five hundred horsepower in check on Lakeshore Boulevard along the shore of Lake Tahoe. He didn't believe the lake was really six thousand feet deep, but the morning sun peeking over the Sierra Nevada Mountains turning white caps to gold was relaxing him like a hot rocks massage.

Hiding from Helen was fun. No cellphone calls, no screaming matches, just the rush of wind past his ears and the crash of waves on sand on a hump-day morning. He turned left as he passed the Hyatt Regency casino and a quarter mile later turned right into a strip mall meant to look like an alpine village. He stopped the Mercedes in front of a glass door with *Box and Mail* in gold script. Pounding rhythm and a guy singing through his nose greeted him as he pulled the door open. The girl behind the counter smiled, showing two perfect rows of teeth that could win a prize for her orthodontist. The volume dropped. He walked toward the counter until he could read the name tag perched high on a Victoria's Secret assisted breast.

"Hello Martina, can I send a fax from here?"

"Sure." She pointed to the corner. "We charge by the page. It's more if I send it for you."

"Thanks, I'll do it."

He found a scratched machine in the corner on a square wooden stand. Graffiti scribbled on the top and sides of the beige plastic with multi-colored Sharpies recounted the minutes people doodled away while waiting for their faxes: Jimmy loves Bobbie, phone number, tree, outline of mountain peaks and a drawing of a bunny with a leather biker jacket and head scarf like something out of Beatrix Potter meets the Hells Angels.

The button labeled ON was sticky when he pressed it. He pulled three sheets of paper from inside his jacket: the handwritten proposal he had been discussing with Mark all last evening before going to the casino for blackjack practice.

He stuffed the pages into the machine and punched Markay's office fax number on more sticky keys, hoping Mark could get a package delivered to Helen today. The first page peeled slowly in. He leaned against the wall and watched Martina. She was young, maybe too young to go to the casino with him, but he liked the way her jeans curved. Rustic living in the mountains was fine, but without a woman to keep him company he almost wanted to go back to work.

The last page slid into the waiting slot.

"You ever go to the casino?"

She turned from her work to make sure he was speaking to her.

"Sure. But it's not much fun."

He didn't understand. He thought casinos were a blast: music, drinks, floor shows, gambling, a little fondling of waitresses. Hell, he could even make money if he tried hard and had a little luck.

"No fun? You should go with me."

She didn't giggle and turn away, just met his eye.

"Why's that?"

"We'd have a good time."

He noticed her eyes were blue, and when she blinked, they didn't move around, but stayed right on his face.

"I lose money fast. That's why it's no fun," she said, and turned back to her work.

He lifted his three sheets and a confirmation printout from the machine and folded them the long way so they would fit back into his pocket.

"You can lose my money," he said.

She half-turned and watched him from the corner of her eye, but kept moving papers around on a bench.

"Really. I don't mind." And he was serious. He wouldn't mind losing a couple big ones to watch her peel those jeans off in the three-story house in Incline Village he thought of as his cottage.

"How about you start by paying for the fax?" she said.

He gave her a big grin and peeled a fifty-dollar bill from a folded wad he kept in his pants.

"Will that cover the three pages?" he asked.

She took the fifty. "Including all applicable taxes." She smiled the double-row smile again.

"Keep the rest for the tables tonight."

She gave him that laser beam stare, like she had superman powers and was seeing through his clothes. Her eyes were gentle in a pale white face with no makeup that he could see. But that look made him uneasy.

"Meet at the casino?" she asked.

He figured this was a test. "Would you like to have dinner first?"

The laser-smile again. "You like fondue? There's a real authentic place right down the street." She pointed at the wall.

"Fondue it is. Seven?"

She nodded.

His turn to test. "Meet at the restaurant?"

She nodded again. "I know the owner, I'll make reservations."

He nodded and tried to match her high-wattage smile.

"What name?" she asked.

He kept smiling, "Martina."

"Hmm, Mister Mysterious," she said, but the smile didn't fade.

He stopped at the door and turned. She was holding him in that tractor-beam gaze.

"Seven."

She said, "Why does a man who drives a Mercedes send his own faxes?"

He held her eyes. "Because he wants to."

She said, "Fondue," and lifted her right index finger to touch her tongue, then wrapped her lips around it as if removing a chocolate covered strawberry from a skewer.

Outside, the finger-and-lip show made him think about Alicia's tight body wrapped around him. He had missed their regular Tuesday afternoon rendezvous, and hadn't called her. He wanted his disappearance to be complete: no mistakes that might let Helen find him with her damn papers. But Alicia was going to be bitchy; he had better find a nice gift.

He strolled through the little village on a wood plank walk elevated a foot above ground level. At the corner, a breakfast menu was scribbled in colored chalk on an easel beside a Dutch door. Next to it sat a row of bright green and black metal newspaper dispensers. He read headlines until he found the Chronicle. Its lead story jumped at him: *Killer Targets Music Fan.* He went back to Martina for enough quarters to convince the machine to give him a copy.

He found a corner table and flipped the paper open. The only other customer was a kid at the counter in clothing three sizes too large carrying a dark blue backpack with a hose sticking out of it trying to put moves on the waitress. The thin girl had full boobs under a black stretch top with a chili pepper on it, but not the fine shape of Martina.

He ignored them and read. He was half-way through, amazed this Aaron McGreen had uncovered so much new info, when he realized the stretch-top girl was standing next to his table. He looked up into dark eyes surrounded by dark eyeliner surrounded by straight dark hair.

"Would you like to order?" she said, in a soft sweet voice he wouldn't in a hundred years have put with her face.

It required seconds to shake the story from his mind.

"Uh, yeah. Do you have a menu?"

She pointed toward the counter.

"Just the blackboard up there. Oh, and the one on the sidewalk."

He squinted at the blackboard, its rows of handwriting hard to read for anyone not seated at the counter.

"How about two eggs, over easy, with toast. Wait, waffle?"

She shook her head, her long black hair swaying, trying to keep up.

"Pancakes?"

"Blueberries or bananas?" she asked.

"Both, no toast. Bacon, coffee, black. And could I have a glass of water, it's dry up here."

She smiled and went away.

He found his place in the middle of the article. McGreen claimed he had confidential sources who said the missing girl had been brutally murdered. He tied the murder to movies on YouTube that were somehow magically encoded one inside the other. Eddy turned seven pages to find the rest of the article. Here it printed URLs that linked to the movies, but he had split the valley on a whim and didn't have a computer. Then it claimed the murder and the movie's *Don't Steal* message were connected to what the author called the DoomTunes virus that was destroying music files and posting messages describing the offenders as pirates.

Now there was a leap of consciousness only a journalist could make.

Eddy had ordered the release of the software himself, and according to Volker's data, it was deleting files as planned. But an Amazon-box missing girl and *Don't Steal* stickers echoing the message of the Hand? Movies on YouTube? Huge surprise.

He hated surprises.

His breakfast arrived as he finished the article. The food smelled like it had come from grandma's country kitchen. What unbelievable luck he was having. Maybe he would let Martina bet big tonight. That usually got girls excited, especially ones who had never done it before.

He washed a mouthful of fluffy pancake down with black coffee and browsed articles. He turned the thin paper and a full-page ad from Apple confronted him. It consisted of a giant Apple logo, with a business letter printed inside it. He read carefully.

Dear iPod Owners:

It has come to our attention that some customers may have received online offers for free replacement iPods because a problem has been identified with your present unit. Please be advised that these offers are not from or associated with Apple Inc. in any way. We suggest that you do not provide information, about either your iPod or yourself, to anyone claiming to offer you a free device, and that you report any such offers to the Better Business Bureau in your area or contact the iPod hotline at 1-866-555-5488.

There are no known defects or recalls on iPods. However, if you are experiencing problems with your iPod, please contact Apple Service, or visit the Apple store in your area for repair or replacement under your original warranty agreement.

We thank you for your continued business.
Best Regards,
Customer Support Group
Apple Inc.

He whistled softly and checked the date on his alligator-strapped Longine. Wednesday morning. Less than four days. He was suddenly anxious for another Volker sales report.

He reread the letter and wondered where else they had published it: *New York Times, Chicago Tribune, L.A. Times?* A smile parted his lips as he turned the page. Minutes later, he was popping the last bit of bacon into his mouth when another article caught his attention. A single column story not six inches high—*Student Mysteriously Injured At Concert.* He read carefully: violin student leaving an evening recital injured in a blast of unknown origin. Shattered upper arm required surgery. Head injury, coma, critical condition at San Francisco General Hospital. No names released.

He tapped his finger against the page softly, the tick tick tick working on him like a meditation.

He turned in his seat. The kid was making small talk about how many weeks before it might snow and was she looking forward to the season and what kind of board was she planning on riding this year.

Eddy scanned the room and saw what he wanted on the back of the cash register, an orange bumper sticker that said Free Wi-Fi.

"Excuse me," he said.

The kid stopped talking and the girl looked his way. He held up his coffee cup. When she came around with the pot he said, "You have free Wi-Fi here?"

"Yeah. We've had it for a long time."

"Would you introduce me to your friend?" he said, indicating the kid at the counter with his right thumb.

Her dark eyebrows moved together like magnets attracting each other.

"Uh, sure, I guess. What's your name?"

"Bill Wilkins," Eddy said.

She held out her hand, "I'm Kathleen. Why do you want to meet Eddie?"

He smiled. What were the odds? "I need to access the net and I'm wondering if he has a computer in that backpack."

"Oh yeah. He always has it. But can't you access with your phone?"

Of course he could. But then he wouldn't be invisible would he?

"I need to see a video, my phone is too small."

She nodded and turned around. "Hey Eddie, Bill here needs to get on the net. Think you can help him out?"

Eddie boy responded as if the Pope had just issued a written request for his services in gold ink, hopping off the stool and pulling a slim laptop out of his backpack by the time he reached the table.

"Nice to meet you, Bill," he said, extending his right hand. "My name's Eddie, but the guys call me Cub."

The young man's hand was thin, almost like a woman's, but his grip was firm. He leaned over and had the laptop up and running in seconds, then sat down next to Bill. Kathleen stepped back and stood behind the boy, but didn't leave.

"What do you want to see?" Cub asked.

Blake flipped back through the Chronicle to the middle section where the lead article picked up and pointed with his left index finger.

"These URLs. This article says something about a murder in San Francisco."

They both looked at him, their faces wide with alarm. That single word gave their friendly little project new weight, like they were suddenly on an important case, even though they had no idea who Bill was.

"A murder?" Kathleen said.

"Sources say it's a murder. You know when they use anonymous sources though, it's hard to know what's really going on," Blake said.

Kathleen and Cub nodded together as if they were controlled by a single puppeteer. Cub typed in the first URL and pushed the machine to the center of the table so they could all watch.

Blake stared hard at the *Don't Steal* message wondering what the odds were that a video would contain the concept he had chosen for the Hand. The coincidence made him uncomfortable. Coincidence was worse than surprise.

The movie cut to a blonde girl tossing her head side to side.

Blake choked on his coffee and couldn't stop. He turned away from Cub and Kathleen and hacked hard four times before his throat cleared.

"You okay?" Kathleen asked.

"Wrong pipe," Blake gasped in a whisper, which was the truth. But the reason he had choked was because he knew the girl. She had been on his boat...he thought back...not this summer, last. Oh, he remembered, the wild ones. She and her student friends made him find a private beach so they could skinny dip and listen to the strangest music he had ever heard blasting over *With a Bullet's* sound system—like violins playing upside down in the clouds. What a surreal day, topless girls prancing around in a sort of bacchanal fertility ritual with just him and another guy. They drank and watched and the girls gave them suntan lotion massages when the mood struck them. And that night, Sally, yeah, that was her name. He remembered, docked back at the marina, everyone else had left but she wanted a nightcap. He never had time to open the bottle. That started a torrid summer romance where one of them was always unavailable. Yeah, she got around. And now he was watching the little nympho flop like a landed fish.

Kathleen moved closer and closer to the screen until Blake could barely see around her hair drooping onto the keyboard.

"What's going on?" she said. "It looks like..."

Yeah, it looked like that to Blake too, especially the motion.

"Somebody's doing her," Cub said.

"And she doesn't like it," Kathleen said. "I think he's raping her."

Blake leaned back and sipped his coffee. Glimpses of Sally on screen wouldn't let him shake the fish image as he thought about how that video got to YouTube. And when. He had released software only days ago. Time to be very careful.

Cub's voice brought him back to the café.

"You want to see the other video?"

Blake saw that the first had stopped with text on the screen. Yes, he very much wanted to know what was in that second video, but he wasn't sure he wanted these kids to know with him.

"I want to see it," Kathleen said, standing back from the screen. She turned to Blake, "Can I borrow your paper?"

He folded it so the article was on top and handed it to her.

"What the hell is going on in San Francisco?" she said as she started reading.

In less than a minute Cub had the second video playing on the laptop.

They watched.

The video had barely started when Cub said, "What is this fucking *Don't Steal* crap, like that's going to stop people from downloading?"

"I told you it wasn't right," Kathleen said.

Cub lowered his eyes. Clearly he didn't like upsetting Kathleen.

A knife entered the screen. "Oh my God," Kathleen said, dropping the paper and bringing both hands to her face.

Blake recognized a serrated fishing knife. He had one. They were great for cleaning fish.

Then the knife sliced off the girl's index finger and blood pulsed onto the floor around her.

Blake leaned forward, not believing, looking for an edit, or the telltale of a special effect.

Kathleen screamed until she ran out of breath. Then she gasped and screamed again.

Cub's eyes flashed to Kathleen, like he thought he should do something, and back to the screen so he wouldn't miss anything. Blake stood up and put a hand on Kathleen's shoulder to comfort her, but kept his eyes glued to the movie. Kathleen twisted to shake his hand off, and ran towards the kitchen.

"Is this real?" Cub asked.

"Don't know," Blake said. "You've seen as much as me. I just saw the article a couple of minutes ago."

He heard Kathleen start a fresh scream.

"Stop that," he said, gesturing at the computer. "You better go to her. If you want advice, try to hold her. If she fights you off, let her scream and hit you, but don't leave. No matter what she says, she doesn't want to be alone."

Cub stared at Blake, unmoving. The movie voice talked about stealing. Cub turned and slammed the cover closed.

"Thanks, Mister," he said, and dashed towards a new scream, his baggy pants making him look like a clown running from a bull.

Blake sat down and retrieved the paper from the floor. He slowly arranged and folded it until it was back to new. He sipped coffee trying to think, but it was cold and he knew Kathleen wasn't going to be coming out to warm it up. He remembered Sally, her body, energy, incredible enthusiasm—about everything. The boat ride, the sunshine, music, stripping, touching, devouring him.

He thought about a student injured by an unexplained explosion.

He thought about an old buddy who once said, "Security is about confusion."

He thought about coincidence. And surprise.

He thought about Volker, and wondered where sales stood.

He folded a pair of twenties and slipped them under the laptop. Then he lifted the screen and studied the image of a gloved hand holding a knife. He opened a new browser window, went to craigslist for San Francisco, and posted an ad for a yacht for sale, noting that it was in good working condition and had performed well so far this season. He wondered absently if Helen would see the ad, thought about how fast he wanted to move, how much risk he could tolerate, and set the asking price at $550,000.

He stepped outside.

The sun in a cloudless blue sky had made the black paint on his Mercedes warm to the touch. He bleeped the locks and opened the driver's door, aching to know how sales were doing. He wouldn't likely hear from Mark on the divorce papers for hours. Then Helen had to have them in her hand before he could even consider going back to California. He stepped away from his car and swung the door closed. Re-entering the Box and Mail he looked for Martina, but found an empty room. He walked to the counter and dinged a little silver bell like his third grade teacher had on her desk to restore order.

Martina strolled from the back and flashed her big smile.

"Couldn't stay away?"

"Could. Just didn't want to," he said, returning the smile. "Is there a pay phone around here?"

"A pay phone," she said flatly. "The man drives a Mercedes, but sends his own faxes, and doesn't own a cellphone?"

"Battery's dead."

"Hmm. Your car isn't smart enough to charge a cellphone?"

"Had them take that feature out to keep it light. Corners better."

She nodded, still smiling.

"I believe the casino has pay phones for people who are so broke they need to call collect to a nice person who will come and save them."

"Good idea. Thanks." He turned to go. As he reached the door he glanced back over his shoulder. She was fonduing the index finger of her left hand and hitting him with the eye lasers.

~ 54 ~

The Hyatt Regency Casino wasn't like the fairway-sized betting arenas in Las Vegas. Slot machines sat in four rows to Eddy's right and gave way to gaming tables. A long granite hotel registration counter looking like it had been chipped out of the nearby Sierras sat to his left. Smoke filled and comfortable, the place was small and personal without being claustrophobic. Straight ahead four phones were mounted to the wall in a row. He stopped by the desk to procure change then headed to the most distant phone.

"Silver Platter, may I help you?"

"Stacy, it's Eddy. How are things going?"

Long pause.

"Who may I say is calling?" Stacy said.

"What th—" He stopped. Drummed his fingers against the top of the phone. "Bill Wilkins, calling for Mr. Blake."

"I'm sorry, Mr. Blake is unavailable right now. May I have him return your call?

He looked for the number of his pay phone, found it on a paper tab in the upper right.

"530-555-1717. I'll be here for ten minutes."

"Yes, Mr. Wilkins. I'll have him call you as soon as possible."

He pressed the receiver button down with his left hand and tapped the Bakelite handset against the chrome face of the big phone. Who could be at the office that would make Stacy so nervous? Helen. The bitch was probably there looking for him. He hung up the phone and leaned against the wall next to it. He aimlessly scanned the casino, surprised that dozens of elderly white-haired ladies were yanking slots before noon on a Wednesday. He noticed a waitress in black stockings and a short skirt that revealed just the right amount of leg strolling among the old women. He waved, but she didn't look his way. He took two steps in her direction and realized that Murphy's Law would make the phone ring the moment he stepped away. He took two more small steps and swung his arms overhead.

Nothing.

As he turned to go back to the phone he noticed a pair of dollar machines to his right, close enough to the phone to hear it ring. He walked to the nearest, slid a twenty in, and started playing as fast as the machine would spin. He had only lost five dollars by the time the stockings walked up and asked if he'd like a drink.

"A Ku martini, please."

Her face was blank, as if he hadn't spoken.

"Ku Soju. Do you have it?"

"Not sure. I'll check. What would you like if we don't?"

"Your phone number," he said, smiling and listening for the phone.

She pressed her lips together, trying to hide a grin.

"Anything else?" she asked.

"What do you like to drink in the morning?"

"Mimosas." She held up a hand and moved her fingers. "Fresh squeezed."

"Excellent. That's my backup."

She shook her head and walked away. He watched closely, thinking she was using more wiggle than she had around the old ladies.

He turned to his bandit and was up seven dollars when she returned holding a tray with a tall orange drink in the middle. He tipped her a five and lifted the drink from the cork tray.

She gave him the suppressed grin again, held his eyes for a brief moment as she turned her body to leave, then walked in the direction of the old ladies.

He reached for the red plastic swizzle to stir the drink and noticed something dark, like it was dirty. He turned the swizzle back and forth and saw a number written along its length in black. He laughed softly, a girl with style.

He looked closer. It read *1-888-fuck-off.*

Bitch. She sure didn't know class when it slapped her on the ass.

He sipped the foamy orange juice off the top with one hand and bet the max with the other. He was up twenty-two dollars when the phone rang industrial and purposeful midst the bubbly jingle of slot machines.

He picked up the receive, "Hello."

"Hello, Mr. Blake. Sorry I couldn't talk before. There was a man standing at my desk with a package for you, insisting he must put it into your hands directly. He's been in the parking lot all morning."

"Nice work, Stacy. Where is he now?"

"I had him escorted out of the building, but he's still in his car."

Helen had been serious. She was going to sue him, the bitch.

"Anything else?"

"Your wife called eleven times yesterday. And four this morning."

"She's persistent. I'll have my lawyer ask her to stop calling you."

"That's not necessary, Mr. Blake. She's always polite."

He tried to think of the last time Helen had been polite to him. Probably before he bought *Bullet.*

"Anyone else?"

"Yes, a Detective Dreeson is trying to reach you, wants to set up an appointment."

A detective *and* a bond server? Helen was digging in for a fight.

"Did Dreeson leave a card?"

"She hasn't been here, she called. But she left a number for the SFPD."

"The police?" he asked before thinking about it. "Not a private eye?"

"She said she was with the homicide division of the San Francisco Police Department, and asked that you please call her at your earliest convenience."

Eddy racked his brain. Why would Helen want the Frisco cops involved? Maybe the condo, it was in the city, but the company shielded it. And the boat. He felt a chill thinking she might know something he didn't about property rights within the city limits. Then the word hit him.

Homicide? What the hell did that have to do with a divorce? Unless Helen was claiming he beat her up. He chewed his lower lip. He didn't like being confused.

"Give me her number. I'll call and set something up. Also, tell Volker I want to see up-to-date numbers right after lunch."

"Ms. Volker was here earlier looking for you. She said to let you know national numbers are up eleven percent from last week."

Eleven was better than eight.

"But she also said there are regional phenomena she can't explain. Let me quote her: 'Sorting by zip code reveals that major cities are up more than the national average with San Francisco leading sales, up twenty-one percent from last week, followed by Chicago and New York, both near thirteen percent."

Didn't make sense to him either.

"Can I talk to Greg?"

"I haven't seen Mr. Simmons this morning. He was here last night when I left though."

Eddy hung up and drifted back to his orange drink and the twenty-two dollars he had won on his slot machine. He played slowly, trying to think about the trouble a detective in San Francisco might cause him, but his mind kept drifting back to the *Chronicle*, and the sales numbers, and he couldn't help but smile as the machine took his cash.

~ 55 ~

Qigiq stared at the gray block wall of the theatre where Robina had played the night before. He leaned on the crutch under his left shoulder and sipped black coffee from a Starbucks container. Kandy was standing with her back to him looking at the opposite wall.

"What time is Ferd coming?" she asked.

"He said ten-thirty. He's not late yet."

The morning light cast the alley in long dark shadows in the direction opposite they had been the night before.

"I don't see a damn thing," she said.

"Neither do I. But I saw a ball of flame. It had to come from somewhere."

"The windows are too high." She pointed up. "And narrow. I checked the inside, doesn't look like they've been open for years." She pointed down. "No basement windows to get a shot in low."

He nodded, though she couldn't see him because they were facing opposite sides of the alley.

"How about from below?" he asked. "Like those Bouncing Betty land mines that shoot up from the ground before they go off."

Together they studied the cobble walk where Robina's body had lain twisted minutes after playing her Tuesday evening recital.

"Not even a chunk of mortar missing," she said.

"Maybe a small grenade."

Kandy looked straight up between the two buildings. A narrow strip of gray-white fog illuminated from above filled the space with a dim yellow glow.

"Could it have been fired from above?"

"I'd expect a lot more blow on the cobble stones. Dropped?"

"Yeah," she said. "You mentioned grenade, and it made me wonder if the perp could have dropped an improvised device that had a sensitive altitude trigger set to go off four feet above the ground."

He looked up, brought the cup up high, then back down.

"How about timing? He could know precisely how long it would take to fall four stories. If the timer was triggered by the drop, a little counter could have set it off."

"Yeah."

They stood in silence, eyes scanning the area that Ferdinand's team had spent hours analyzing.

"How about accuracy?" she asked.

He crutched a few yards toward the stage door that Robina had used.

"The alley isn't very wide. She was walking at maybe two or three miles per hour. A four story drop would take a second or so. He could have eyeballed it."

He looked up and down the cobble walk, and at the buildings on either side. "Or, he had a marker. Say, when she passes a particular cobblestone. I don't see any obvious dots, but he could have just picked one stone out with a scope and had the timing planned."

She nodded, and turned. "Here comes Ferd."

Ferdinand was making his way along the alley with a large flat case like painters used to carry canvases. He wore a tan cylindrical hat with huge earmuffs.

"Are you cold?" Kandy asked.

"I'm from Alaska," Qigiq said.

"Hello my friends. Thank you for meeting me here." He was breathing hard as he walked up and shook their hands. "It is a brisk morning, but is good fresh air."

Qigiq was about to question the freshness of air in San Francisco when Ferdinand opened his big case.

"I have done some studies. I thought they would be more easily analyzed if we met here."

"Thanks for hitting the street with us," Kandy said.

Ferdinand smiled widely inside his big hat.

"I do not get out enough." He placed a two-by-four foot drawing down on the pavement. It showed an overhead view of both buildings and the location of Robina's body in the alley.

"We found no residue from the explosion anywhere," he began.

Kandy's face tilted towards Qigiq. He shrugged.

"No residue?" she said. "How is that possible?"

"Precisely the correct question my friend," Ferdinand replied. "I have asked myself this many times in the past twelve hours. If the projectile came from above, then there must be residue on the ground."

Ferdinand went up the alley, then turned and walked along in Robina's footsteps.

"If the shot came from the right, then its velocity would carry it into that wall." He pointed with his left hand. "And it could not have come from her left, because she fell to the left. Very confusing."

Kandy said, "We considered a drop from above."

Ferdinand nodded. "Yes, possible. However, a solid object dropped from that height would be traveling well over one hundred miles per hour. Some part of it would surely have reached the ground. Yet we find nothing."

"Bouncing Betty?" Kandy asked.

"A trip mine? Yes, this would account for the known facts. But——" He looked at the ground and spread his hands like he was smoothing a tablecloth on a dinner table. "We find nothing. Not a hole, or a loose stone."

Kandy rolled one lip over the other like she was smoothing lipstick.

"What if," she said, "there was a device between two stones. When it was triggered, it leapt upward."

"Good, yes," Ferdinand said. "But no one saw such a device leap from the ground. And to make such a leap, we should find micro-scratches on the stones. Again we find nothing."

Qigiq smiled. "You win, Ferdinand. It didn't come from above, below, left or right. What aren't you telling us?"

"It is only a hypothesis," he said, stroking his beard with his big right hand.

Kandy leaned her back against the wall and studied the area, starting from the stage door.

"All ears," she said.

"We found residue on her clothing. I suspect there is more on her body, but she was in surgery before we were able to obtain samples for analysis. The right side of her sweater was covered with residue. And the guitar case."

Kandy frowned. "Guitar?"

"The black case she was carrying. It was destroyed."

"Violin," Qigiq offered.

"Ah, well, string family," Ferdinand said with a big smile. "It too is covered with residue. So the device could not have been hidden inside the case."

"So?" Kandy said.

"This bomb was high explosive RDX. Perhaps C-4 compound."

"Hi-tech," she said.

Ferd nodded. "My hypothesis is that it was planted on her body."

"Planted?" Qigiq said, wondering how and where.

"You see, the residue on the fragments of the guitar case was on the upper side by the handle. So I believe the explosion began above her hand."

"She was wearing a bomb?" Kandy asked.

"Yes, I think so."

"How much C-4?" Qigiq asked. "How small could it be?"

Ferdinand said, "Based on your description and the damage, but no residue, perhaps an ounce." He held his right hand up and made a little square about a centimeter on each side.

"Inside the sweater?" Kandy shook her head. "No, it was sleeveless. Those gloves?"

Qigiq nodded, touched his arm. "She was wearing long leather gloves to her elbow."

"But how?" Kandy asked.

"It is only a hypothesis," Ferdinand said. "But a properly shaped charge inside the glove, it could have been very small and still hurt her greatly."

Qigiq was quiet as his thoughts turned to an unconscious Robina in a hospital bed with a giant bandage covering the side of her head.

"So we don't look for a weapon," Kandy said. "We look for a maker of small bombs."

"This is what I think has happened," Ferdinand said. "But it is only a hypothesis."

He returned to his big case and pulled out a second drawing, placing it over the first. It showed eight sketches of boats and radar towers with ruled lines intersecting at acute angles, covered with handwritten notes.

"I have undertaken a study of your suggestion, Kandy, that the movies were shot in the daytime and later modified to look like nighttime recordings."

"It is only a hypothesis," Kandy said, with a wink at Qigiq.

Ferdinand smiled broadly and continued.

"First, an analysis of the white level does indicate that they more closely match a dimmed daylight spectrum than they do moonlight. This is not conclusive, but it also does not disagree with your proposition."

He lowered his big frame to his knees on the stone alley in front of the diagram.

"Further, the shadow angle indicates that the light source, in this case the sun, must be nearly overhead. Therefore, I limited my searches to the daylight hours of 10:30 am to 4:00 pm, a range I think more than generous."

Kandy squatted beside Ferd. Qigiq stood behind her.

"This is our best match. I wanted you to see the theoretical position, drawn in blue, with the position from the movie, in gray."

"They're really close," Kandy said.

Ferdinand raised an eyebrow under his floppy hat.

"Really close is not a scientific term, Detective."

Qigiq suppressed a grin.

"Is it closer than the moonlight match you had?" Qigiq asked.

"Much," Ferdinand said. Then, apparently realizing *much* wasn't a scientific term either added, "All eight samples exhibit less than half the error of our prior analysis. But this one," he pointed to the lower left corner, "matches almost exactly. Less than one-tenth the error."

"What time of day?" Qigiq asked.

"Early afternoon."

"Which boat?" Kandy said.

"One oddly named with a prepositional phrase: *With a Bullet.*"

Kandy turned her face up towards Qigiq, who met her eyes.

"How confident are you?" Qigiq asked.

Ferdinand moved first to one knee, then to his feet, with clear effort.

"This is not proof, Detective. However, it strongly suggests that the two movies I have been analyzing were both taken a week ago yesterday between one and three in the afternoon on the deck of the Donzi-built yacht called *With a Bullet* in the Pacific Ocean off the coast near Half Moon Bay, less than a hundred miles from San Francisco."

"Admissible?" Kandy asked.

Ferdinand shrugged, "The geometrical analysis is quite complicated and requires assumptions regarding how wave action affects the movement of a particular hull. A good defense attorney would shoot holes in it, and the details would likely be lost on a jury."

"But you're sure?" Kandy said.

Ferdinand nodded. "Yes, very." He gathered up his posters and slipped them back into the case. He rubbed his hands together as if warming them over a fire.

"It is quite cold in San Francisco."

"Colder than your lab, Ferd?" Kandy asked.

Surprisingly, Ferd smiled. "Ah, yes, my lab. What would you do without my lab, Detective Dreeson?"

He reached into the case, extracted a third large board, and handed it to Kandy. She held it in both hands like an oil painting. It was a three-dimensional graph with yellow and blue dots spread along an axis from the lower left corner towards the upper right. A rainbow of color spread across the graph, lighter in the upper right, more distinct in the middle. A black dot labeled *this one* resided about a third of the way up the chart.

"For me?" Kandy said. "Ferd, you shouldn't have. I didn't even know you painted."

Ferdinand smiled. "Art is my secret passion, but this is a plot of the components of paint. Your friend Mr. Grojini delivered to me a piece of bent metal he said was once a fuel tank for a motorbike."

Qigiq's eye widened. He had been too busy to think about his Guzzi.

"Grojini brought you my gas tank?"

"Yes. It is badly damaged." Ferdinand glanced down at Qigiq's leg. "You were quite lucky to walk away."

Qigiq's ankle ached from standing on cold stones. He was glad to be in one piece, but he didn't feel lucky.

"And?" Kandy said.

"And Detective, you are looking at the *and.*"

Kandy stared at the big chart. She turned to hold it out for Qigiq. It looked like a plot of colored raindrops on a dry sidewalk.

"You found paint on the gas tank," Qigiq said.

Ferdinand nodded vigorously, making his hat ears flop.

"And somehow, you matched it to something. That's what this is, a plot of the match."

"Exactly, Detective. I've found the paint."

Kandy said, "The paint."

"Yes. The paint that was used to paint the car that hit the motorbike."

"And you can tell us what auto manufacturers use it?" Qigiq said.

"Only European companies. It is a very special black with a great deal of tiny metal flakes in it. I dare say you were accosted by an expensive automobile."

"Which European companies, Ferd?" Kandy asked.

"Mercedes and Ferrari."

"How many black Ferraris are there in the world?" Kandy asked.

"I could perhaps find that out if you need to know," Ferdinand offered.

She shook her head. "I was just thinking, most are red, or maybe silver. So we're probably looking for a black Mercedes."

"Yes, that is what the chart says," Ferdinand said.

Kandy stared at the big board. "It does?"

"Surely. Each dot represents a color, the gradients show how I've mathematically aged the color."

Kandy frowned at the chart. "Nice."

"So what are we looking for?" Qigiq asked.

"A Mercedes coupe less than two years old."

"You're kidding," Kandy said.

"Not at all."

"How many can there possibly be in the Bay Area?" she asked.

"If we include locations within a hundred miles of the city, there are one hundred and eight," Ferdinand said.

"I was hit by one of those cars?" Qigiq asked.

"That's what the paint says. Of course, the car wouldn't have to be within a hundred miles. That was a reduction assumption on my part."

Ferdinand's lips slowly curved into a bigger and bigger grin.

"What?" Kandy said, her eyes dashing between the chart and Ferd's face.

"It is only a hypothesis," Ferd said.

"Out with it," Kandy shouted. Then laughed.

"The gas tank that Mr. Grojini brought to me was quite badly damaged."

Kandy nodded slowly.

Ferd continued, "So one can only assume..."

"There was damage to the car," she said.

"Correct."

"And if there was damage, the perp will try to get it fixed before we can find him."

Ferdinand nodded. "You are doing well, Detective."

"So you contacted the body shops in the area and asked if they're working on a black Mercedes?" she said.

"No," Ferdinand said.

The ache in Qigiq's ankle was growing sharper. He hoped it was only the cold stones.

"Could we go somewhere warm?" he said. "My ankle isn't liking this alley."

"Sure," Kandy said, handing the big chart back to Ferd.

They walked slowly toward the street.

"So Ferd, if you didn't call the body shops, what did you do?"

"I thought that the body shop owner might be a friend of the Mercedes driver and so not tell us they were working on his car."

"Good thinking," Qigiq said.

"And maybe tell him we were looking."

"You think he'll repaint the entire car?" Kandy asked

Ferdinand was quiet while they walked. "No, I don't think so. If he changes the color, then everyone knows something has happened to that car. If he repairs it before anyone sees the damage, they are no wiser. I think he will simply repaint the damaged fender."

"You're scheming, aren't you Ferd?"

He chuckled. "Yes, Detective, I have an idea. But we are still working on it."

"Is it a secret?" she asked.

"No, it is very simple. If the repair shop is going to make the car like new, well then..."

"They'll need paint," Qigq said, limping along beside Ferdinand as they neared the mouth of the alley where it opened onto the sidewalk.

"And there are probably very few suppliers of exotic paint," Kandy said. "Call them all and see who delivered that particular paint to a repair shop in the past few days. How many shops did you find?"

Ferdinand turned toward her and held up his index finger. His lips pulled together to form the word "One," but his voice disappeared into the piercing report of a gunshot.

The corner of the stone building three feet above their heads shattered, showering cement fragments down like heavy sleet.

Qigiq spun on his good foot, leapt toward the alley onto his injured ankle and slipped. He landed hard on his left hip. Kandy grabbed Ferd's arm and was pulling him into the alley when a second shot exploded a foot closer than the first. Qigiq rolled to get out of Ferdinand's way and slammed his back against the wall. Kandy left Ferd ten yards up the alley and ran up beside Qigiq with her weapon low in her right hand.

"What have we got?" she whispered.

"Shooter's in an apartment diagonally across the intersection," Qigiq said. "Third floor, above the traffic light in our line of sight. That's guessing based on where the building was hit. I haven't seen a thing."

"Ferd's calling for backup."

He nodded. "No way to exit the alley. It's exposed."

"I'm going through the recital hall."

"It'll be locked."

"I'll knock," she said, and headed off at a full sprint.

Kandy was fast. Still, Qigiq figured it would take her two or three minutes to get through the building, onto the next street, then come up behind the apartments. He and Ferdinand would be completely unprotected if the shooter moved in line with the alley. He peeked between two corner blocks where the mortar indent gave him an inch of protection. Nothing was moving, no reflections. He turned and looked up the alley. Ferdinand was sitting on the ground with his back pressed to the wall where Kandy had left him. Kandy was gone.

The shooter likely had a rifle, maybe even sniper equipment. It would be folly to face that firepower directly. Qigiq crawled on one knee, dragging his crutch until he reached Ferdinand, who had lost his hat and was breathing hard.

"Let's get out of here, Ferd," he said. He leaned on his crutch to stand and positioned himself against the wall. The scientist struggled to all fours, then to a knee, and finally with one hand on the wall and the other gripping Qigiq's wrist, he stood. Qigiq helped him down the alley until they reached the stage door for the concert hall. He pulled hard. The big door swung open slowly. He leaned out to see around Ferdinand. The alley was empty.

"Hurry, Ferdinand. We have to get out of this alley. There's no cover."

Ferdinand nodded, but his eyes were glazed as he stepped toward the doorsill. Qigiq pushed to help him move faster, took a last look down the alley and stepped up with his good leg.

He heard a shot as wood splinters rained down, but he didn't stop moving. The door stood open behind him. He instinctively reached out to close it, but a hand gripped his shoulder and pulled him into a dark hallway.

"Leave it," Ferdinand said. "He can't make the angle from the street."

They moved through the hall until reaching the back of a stage facing hundreds of empty seats. Qigiq kept moving until he found a chair where he could see both the main room and the hallway, sat down and flipped open a nylon pack strapped on the inside of his crutch. He withdrew a Glock and was glad Kandy had suggested he keep one with him.

Nothing moved—not in the empty hall that seemed to echo the wail of Robina's violin; nor in the alley visible through the doorway.

He watched, alert, silent, waiting for the seal to come to the hole in the ice.

The first change he saw was the wall of the building across the alley shifting color between gray and red tint, gray, blue tint. Then Kandy stepped slowly through the open doorway, her weapon held low in her right hand. She paused inside the door, her back to the wall, waiting for her eyes to meet the darkness.

"We're backstage," he called out.

She walked down the hall, slipping her weapon behind her.

"Fireworks are over," she said. "They're trying to find bullets, but lead against stone? Not much hope."

"How about the one in the door?"

"Wondered why the door was shattered, I opened it so carefully." She smiled. "I'll have them look."

She pulled out her phone and typed.

"Find anything?" Qigiq asked.

"No shell casings, no footprints. Not even an open window. The guy disappeared like a Vegas magician."

"So he knew we were coming," Qigiq said.

"How?" Kandy said. "*We* didn't know we were coming until Ferd called this morning."

Ferdinand, who had been sitting quietly beside Qigiq, stood.

"He saw you leave yesterday. Since your first priority was the victim, you didn't stay to examine the site. A simple educated guess says you would be back. He didn't know when. However, he surmised soon, because you wouldn't want the site to become contaminated."

"You think he guessed?"

"Yes, Kandy. I think he analyzed the situation and concluded you would return today. Perhaps even this morning. And he was correct."

She smiled. "So he wasn't after you, Ferd?"

Ferdinand was quiet for some time.

"I hadn't considered that. He would have no way to know that I planned to be here. I didn't decide to come until I finished the paint analysis early this morning."

"He was probably after me," Qigiq said. "Fortunately, third time wasn't charming."

He shuffled to his feet and leaned on the crutch.

"Think we can find that paint?"

"We haven't talked to all the suppliers yet, but we do have one confirmed delivery." Ferdinand dug into his pants pocket and pulled out a Post-It note folded in half. "The address."

"You scribbled it on a sticky note?" Kandy teased. "So thorough."

"It is a preliminary report," Ferdinand said with a smile. "A full report will be produced when we have finished contacting all suppliers." He passed the paper to Qigiq.

Kandy laughed.

Qigiq glanced at the note. "Cupertino. Coincidence, Apple is in Cupertino."

Ferdinand looked at him like a professor about to ask a hard question, and said: "I don't believe in coincidence. It's unhealthy in a scientist."

"Eddy Blake is down there, too," Kandy said.

They were silent for a moment.

Ferdinand said, "With a Bullet."

~ 56 ~

Kandy turned right onto Embarcadero Boulevard and cruised along the bay with minutes to spare. The sun was doing a good job burning off the fog she had seen from the alley, and her automatic felt secure against her back. Being shot at wasn't bothering her nearly as much as not catching the shooter. This time there hadn't even been a weird trick with a blow-up doll.

Just nothing. Not even a footprint.

How long had he planned it? Was it the same sleazebag who hit Sally and Robina? She hated having to guess what they were dealing with—a serial psycho, a copycat, something new under the sun—making it impossible to take action.

She touched the brake pedal, eased off, and changed lanes, downshifting to pass a lulling maroon mini-van whose driver held a pink cellphone to her left ear in violation of California law. She flipped the radio to KCSM and a Bill Evans piano solo. Too light. She switched to satellite radio and a blues station throbbed out a scorching guitar solo by Robben Ford. Better. She accelerated through the light just before it hit yellow and made another right onto Howard.

Two minutes later she walked through the front door of Seven, a boutique restaurant specializing in not specializing, unusual for San Francisco. A huge white-faced train-station clock hanging behind a shiny black bar claimed it was thirty seconds past 1:00 pm and WED.

She peeled off her waist-length leather jacket and slung it over her left shoulder, letting it hang from one finger to reveal a tight sleeveless top in plain olive green. She wore a fat black leather belt with a perfectly round chrome buckle the size of a silver dollar—the vintage ones, not the wimpy new ones that could pass for a quarter. She scanned the bar without moving her head and saw three guys under thirty, all wearing suits that broadcast financial district, hovering around a table. Three steps in their direction revealed Alicia seated at a table for four, looking up and smiling at the guys. She noticed Kandy and raised her hand far above her head to wave. Alicia was wearing a version of the outfit she had worn to the condo on Monday: heels, bare legs, shorts just below her crotch (in black), and spaghetti straps holding a speck of luminous blue cloth over braless breasts. Her jet black hair hung straight down on either side of a golden face, revealing it each time she looked up.

"Hi, Rebecca, glad you're here. These guys didn't believe I was waiting for someone."

Six eyes danced up and down Kandy's body, each trying to answer two questions. Was Alicia a friend, colleague, or lover? And what were their chances of making it with this new girl? She could tell the blond guy in the middle concluded "lovers" as the interest in his eyes faded. The other two were drooling.

"Hi, Alicia, nice to see you again."

Alicia stood, elbowed one guy out of her way and wrapped her arms around Kandy in a big hug.

"I'm really glad you came. I'm so worried."

In her heels, Alicia stood eyeball-to-eyeball with the shortest guy: a dark-haired former wrestler, judging by the thickness of his neck. Maybe he now coached kids on weekends.

Alicia spun.

"Guys, this is my friend Rebecca. She kicks ass, so be careful."

The guys chuckled, but inched back half a step.

"Rebecca, James, Brad, Roger." She pointed at each one with her blue and white index fingernail. "They work around here and offered to buy lunch. I told them the girl talk would be too boring." She smiled at the men. "Maybe next time, guys." She gave a little wave with just her fingers. "Bye bye."

Brad, the blond guy who had given up, appeared reignited by Alicia's banter. He smiled and gave a slight bow before following the other two away from the table.

Alicia grabbed Kandy's right hand in her left and sat down without letting go. Kandy pushed a black chair back with her knee and sat across from her.

"I'm really really worried," Alicia said. "Eddy has never ever missed a date."

Alicia's long nails would make fair weapons, but her skin was soft. She gripped Kandy's hand like she was keeping herself from drowning.

"How long have you been dating?" Kandy asked.

Alicia frowned. "Three months."

"And you've been meeting at the condo all that time?"

Alicia shook her head. "Of course not. We had to get to know each other first. We didn't have sex for two whole weeks after we met. And we didn't start meeting at the condo until...," she scrunched her face, "maybe eight weeks ago."

"So Eddy has been reliable for eight weeks?"

"Like the fucking atomic clock in that mountain in Colorado." She laughed a high-pitch squeal. "Tuesday and Thursday afternoons. He shows up around one-thirty, and likes to leave by four so he can get back to his office. You know, to deal with anything that happened while he was gone.

Oh, except for China."

Kandy waited, but Alicia didn't continue, so she said, "China?"

"Yeah. He had to travel to China once. I missed two in a row, a Thursday and the following Tuesday. It sucked."

"How so?"

"You know. Eddy's reliable," she laughed. "Ready for action when he gets to the condo. I like that in a man." She smiled, parting lips painted a bold red just dark enough to be subtle against her Asian complexion.

"He didn't take you to China?" Kandy said, slowly removing her hand from Alicia's and reaching for the menu.

"Oh, I knew you were in a hurry so I ordered for us," Alicia said. "I hope that's all right."

"Sure, but I'm not in a hurry."

Alicia's lips parted in a small smile. "You don't have to tell me, I can tell by the way you move. No, he wouldn't take me. Trade secrets and all that macho man's business shit. Besides, my grandmother came from Vietnam, though she's really Chinese." She waved her hand. "Whatever, I don't know a thing about the place and only speak ten words of Chinese."

Kandy nodded and filed info to think about later. Did she really give people the impression she was always in hurry?

"So what are we having?"

"It's a surprise," Alicia said. "I hope you like it."

Kandy smiled and shook her head. Alicia the take-charge girl. She wondered how a CEO-type handled her.

"What am I going to do?" Alicia asked.

"Have a pleasant lunch?"

Alicia gave Kandy's hand a little slap. "You know what I mean. Eddy didn't show up. And he hasn't called."

Kandy thought about how to phrase her next question. Men were thin-ice territory for girls, and she barely knew Alicia.

"Are you okay if he doesn't call?"

Alicia leaned back and sipped dark cola through a straw, holding it with both hands. Kandy would bet it contained no sugar, but lots of caffeine.

"Well, yeah. I'm okay. But I like having him around."

"Is there someone else?"

Alicia's dark eyes met Kandy's and didn't move. Finally she said, "Isn't there always?"

Kandy shrugged. "Just wondered if Eddy is your one and only."

Alicia grinned. "Eddy? No way. Johnny G is my one and only. Eddy...he's good to me. Not just the sex. He even came to see me dance once."

A waitress arrived with four plates of food and two cola drinks. Kandy tasted hers, Diet Pepsi.

"I got lamb and chicken, and this great little salad," Alicia pointed. "And these rolled butternut squash things that are fantastic. What do you think?"

"I think we have plenty of food," Kandy said, reaching for one of four lamb chops stacked in a row like fallen dominoes.

"You haven't seen me eat," Alicia said. "Dancers burn tons of calories."

Kandy tried to imagine how much food could be stuffed into that small body.

"So, Johnny G's your boyfriend."

Alicia had just stuffed a rolled butternut wrap into her mouth, the whole egg-roll sized thing, and was delicately forcing the tail end between her lips. She nodded and held up a finger for Kandy to wait.

Finally she said, "Johnny's the best boyfriend a girl could have."

"And Eddy?"

Alicia swallowed.

"He's sugar-daddying me through grad school. Man is it expensive. I guess that makes me his mistress, or a whore, or...an opportunistic businesswoman." She flashed a high beam smile.

Kandy thought while chewing.

"How do you keep them apart?"

Alicia flicked her hand left and right.

"Easy. Eddy during the day, Johnny at night."

"Brilliant simplicity." Kandy smiled.

Alicia's lips pursed around the straw and the level in her glass dropped precipitously.

"It works great. Johnny parties late, so he sleeps in. And Eddy has a wife. You knew he was married, right? Her name is Helen. I think he hates her because she's trying to get as much money out of the divorce as she can." She sipped. "Any woman would do the same."

Kandy decided a fairness-in-divorce discussion wouldn't help find Eddy.

"Where do you think he is?"

Alicia put her drink on the table. Her lips slid across each other like they were lubricated. "I don't know. He's never done this before. He might be with his wife trying to patch things up." She caught Kandy's eye. "But he could still call and tell me. To just not show up is beyond rude."

Kandy nodded, letting Alicia fill the space.

"Besides, I was horny. I'm still horny. He better show up tomorrow."

Kandy smiled.

Alicia stared, her face a frowning mask of angry tension that slowly broke into a grin, then outright laughter. "Well, I am," she said. "And Eddy's okay."

"I never found out," Kandy said truthfully. "But I'll bet he's better than okay."

Alicia's dark cheeks turned a little red.

Kandy continued. "I'm a little confused. What about Johnny?"

"Only available at night. Doesn't have breakfast until five o'clock in the afternoon."

Kandy nodded. "He makes you wait until midnight, huh?"

"Midnight? Hell, if he doesn't drink too much, he might be good by two in the morning. Before that, forget it."

"Makes for a long day for the graduate student," Kandy said.

Alicia burst out laughing. "Well, a girl has to have what she has to have." She reached for a domino lamb chop. "Will you help me find Eddy?"

"What can I do?"

No hesitation. "Call him, find out where he is. Maybe he'll slip up, and we can figure out where he was yesterday."

Kandy nodded slowly, wondering how she was going to call a guy she had barely met who stored body parts in his freezer.

"I don't know if he'll take my call."

"Sure he will. Remember to grovel. Beg him to forgive you."

Kandy forked salad onto her small plate. She met Alicia's dark eyes.

"I'm not really the begging type."

Alicia pumped her head up and down like she was listening to rock music. "I know. That's why I think it will work. Eddy's ego will blow up like a hot-air balloon with that burner thing blasting if he thinks he can get even a macho chick like you to grovel."

"Have you considered being a Fortune-500 strategist?"

Alicia laughed, "I hate politics."

"I'll give it some thought."

"Pleeeeez?"

Kandy sipped her drink, no straw, and met Alicia's eyes. The girl looked so sincere she could move to Hollywood.

"How do I reach you?" Kandy asked.

"Same cell."

"Has Johnny met Eddy?"

The color faded from Alicia's face. Even her lips grew lighter.

"Oh my god, no. Johnny would kill him."

"What's he like?"

"Johnny's cool. He's almost three of me."

Kandy grinned.

"No really. We did a test in a hot tub once, you know like Archimedes and the gold crown."

Kandy laughed. "You like math?"

"Math? No way. But I like gold and I read a story about this Greek dude. I remember it was called *The Law of Upthrust.* No way I was going to forget a word like that."

Kandy almost choked laughing.

"Why don't you just forget Eddy? There are plenty of fried fish."

"I don't like him blowing me off. I need to know what happened."

"Just wait, he'll call."

Alicia nibbled at the right side of her lower lip, covering a tooth in lipstick.

"You're not so sure?" Kandy asked.

"I'm afraid he's tired of me."

"He do anything to give you that idea?"

She shook her head. "No, the last time was great."

"When was that?"

"On the boat Saturday. I love sunshine."

Kandy thought maybe Alicia should get a boyfriend who got out of bed before 5:00 pm if she liked sunshine, but said, "Saturday? I thought you were Tuesday, Thursday?"

"We are, but Eddy asked me for last Saturday. Said having me twice a week wasn't enough."

Kandy shook her head. "Stop worrying, Alicia. I'll try to find him. What do you want me to say when I do? That you're pining away for him and squirming in your chair waiting?"

Alicia threw a crumpled napkin across the table.

Kandy caught it with her left hand.

"You better not, Rebecca. He can't know that."

~ 57 ~

They caught up on the drive to Cupertino, Kandy filling Qigiq in on her conversation with Alicia, and he bringing her up to date on Robina's condition: unconscious, but stable. She turned past an eight-foot high fence topped with razor wire into the gravel lot for Kline's Bodywerks, and said: "Pillar sent results; the DNA matches across the board, including her cello.'"

He sighed. "Okay, now we know. Any more thoughts on the sniper?"

"You mean besides that he wants us, or at least you, out of the way?"

"Something's been bothering me."

"Besides a pain in the leg?" she said with a smile.

"I know I haven't been in San Francisco very long—"

"Uh-oh. You miss the permafrost?"

"Just saying I don't know how things work down here exactly, but if we were in Alaska, I'd be dead by now. How can this character miss three times?"

"Didn't completely miss."

He looked down at his leg, wrapped tightly and still not able to support his weight.

"A car is a blunt instrument, hard to control. Plus, he was trying to make it look like an accident. How do you account for the other two?"

She glided forward to a curb, shut off the engine and turned to face him.

"We were lucky on the bridge. You saw his weapon come up and pulled me out of the way."

"And this morning?"

She rubbed her chin. "I'd say he had been waiting a long time, knew we were in the alley, but couldn't see into it from his position. So he had to remain vigilant from the time he saw us enter, and he got tired so his shot was high. Or, maybe he showed up after we did, became alert when Ferd arrived, and we surprised him when we left as a group. Or, he set his scope for the cooler morning temps, Ferd showed and delayed us and he didn't compensate properly as the day warmed. Slightly less dense air caused him to overshoot."

"Point taken."

"Maybe we should get out of the area, go see the Arctic."

"That won't help crack this case," he said, looking straight out the windshield at the front of a steel building. It was light blue with a huge garage door in the center and a standard door to its right.

"You were seen at the marina, puts you at risk. Eddy saw me on *Delicious*. We could have another team take over."

He was quiet, his left hand tapping the crutch stretched along the length of the car between them.

"We still can't be sure it's me he's after. I was only alone that first time, could have been a warning."

"A guy runs you off the road to warn you? About what?"

"Not sure, but if he wanted me dead, he should have pulled out at an intersection and let me T-bone his car."

"So maybe he doesn't want you dead."

Qigiq was quiet. He watched the front of the building; no one entered or left.

"I'll think on that, Kandy. Maybe he's trying to arrange for me to be unable to testify. Which I can't anyway, because I didn't see him clearly."

"He doesn't know that."

"Wish he'd call so I could tell him." He turned toward her.

Her face was pulled together in the slight tension of concern.

He tried to stop, but started laughing. "I'm wondering if we're dealing with an amateur. Someone who doesn't handle weapons regularly."

The interior was silent except for their soft breathing.

"Let's find this mysterious black car," she said, popping her door open with one finger.

They entered through the small door into a front office no bigger than an average bedroom where three desks hid under stacks of pink, blue, green and white papers. Three printers lined the side wall, one of which held green paper with sprocket holes along both edges. Kandy knocked on the nearest desk with her knuckles and they waited. She knocked again. She crossed the room and looked through a door whose top half was glass.

"To the shop?"

Qigiq nodded and followed her into a huge room with giant floor-to-ceiling movable walls dividing it into a series of stalls. The first three contained a yellow Mustang, a blue Camry and a silver 3-series BMW respectively. The remaining stalls were unlit and Qigiq couldn't make out the vehicles, though two clearly held pickup trucks.

Kandy walked along the stalls calling, "Hello, anyone here?" She paused at the silver BMW and waited for Qigiq, who was carefully planting the tip of his crutch between oil spots. When he arrived, Kandy pointed at the passenger's side. Blue pants spotted with dark oil and a pair of black work boots protruded from under the silver car.

"Hello?" Kandy called.

Soft metallic sounds, like a wrench being moved, answered.

They waited.

Kandy jumped back at a loud Brrrp! Brrrp! and turned to Qigiq.

"Pneumatic wrench," he said.

"Right. Should have expected it."

They listened to two more long Brrrp! sounds, followed by a thud, as if a hammer had been dropped onto concrete.

"Hello," Kandy tried as the Brrrping echoes faded.

The legs bent, pulling the body out from under the car. A woman wearing blue mechanic's work gloves, a once-white shirt, and a blue headband looked up at them. Her face was evenly coated with gray around black rubber goggles with bright yellow lenses. Her dark hair was pulled back and held in a ponytail. She didn't speak.

"Hi," Kandy said. "Sorry to bother you, we'd like to speak to someone about a car that was here for repair." She reached inside her jacket and pulled out her badge.

The woman stood up while staring at Qigiq's cast. She stepped over and looked at Kandy's badge.

"No bother. This machine isn't cooperating. Is there something wrong with a car we fixed? Don't tell me someone's gone to the police?"

Kandy shook her head. "No, nothing like that. We're following up on a hit-and-run."

The woman pulled off her right glove and held out her hand, "Hi, I'm Kline. Jane Kline. Would that be Stacy's parking lot scrape-and-go."

Kandy shook her hand, sneaking a glance at Qigiq.

"What did Stacy tell you?" Kandy asked.

"You're after a black Mercedes, right?"

Kandy nodded.

"She said one of their corporate cars was sideswiped in a parking lot over the weekend. We finished it yesterday. Painted it myself. That metallic they use is a bitch to blend. Had to paint the whole fender."

She took off her other glove and tossed the pair on the silver roof.

"You want to see it?" she asked.

"If it's not too much trouble," Qigiq said.

"Be careful of your stick," Jane said. "This floor has more oil than Saudi Arabia. Got to avoid lawsuits, customers in the work area and all that." She smiled, her white teeth gleaming midst the gray dust on her face. She motioned with her head. "It's back in the paint bay."

They passed the Mustang, a Ford pickup, and three empty work areas before coming to a mini airplane hanger built inside the larger steel building. She took them in to where a black Mercedes sat alone, surrounded by lights in rows across a curved ceiling. They were all off.

Jane flicked a switch and two rows of bright bulbs came on.

"This is where I paint. Dust free, ventilated, temperature controlled, drying lamps. I can put exotic paint on in here and ensure a perfect finish."

Qigiq walked to the left front fender. The black paint was so shiny it looked wet. The reflection of the crutch in his left armpit made him feel old.

"Is this dry?" he asked.

"Yeah. I was just keeping it in the bay until they pick it up."

"When did it come in?" Kandy asked.

"Stacy dropped it off first thing Monday, said it was no hurry. Personally, I've never met anyone with a car like this that wasn't in a hurry. This bay wasn't busy so we got right on it."

"Was there much damage?" Kandy asked.

Jane waved her toward a desk in the corner that had a roll top cover made of white plastic. She yanked the handle. The plastic screeched as it slid up to reveal a wide screen monitor and a computer keyboard.

"We keep track of everything for insurance purposes." She tapped the keyboard and the monitor came to life. She touched the screen to open a data base. In the Customer Name field, she typed "Silver Platter."

Qigiq pursed his lips, fighting the desire to jump to conclusions about the owner of *With a Bullet.*

Within seconds Jane had a picture on the wide screen of a California license plate that read "PLAT."

"We shoot the license plate of the car we're working on. I have the vehicle ID too, but showing a customer his plate and damage photos usually ends any what's-that-expense-for discussion." She touched the screen and it divided itself into four quadrants, each containing a picture of the Mercedes from a different angle.

"Here you can see the length of the scratches. Notice they're high on the fender, like maybe a four-wheel-drive pickup grazed it going into a parking spot. Or the side of a mini-van. Something waist high." She switched to four new pictures. "These are close-ups of the damage. The insurance company will ask us why we didn't just buff them out. But once the clear coat is penetrated and the damage reaches the color layer we have to repaint. And right here," she pointed with a dirty finger and a short nail, "there's a slight indention of the fender. Not much, but there was an impact, not just scraping."

Qigiq felt his Guzzi sliding sideways under him, his instincts fighting to keep it upright, the bars twisting, turning the front wheel and tossing him down the embankment. He blinked, cleared his throat, and with effort refocused his attention on the pictures.

"How severe was the impact?" he asked.

She twisted her lips in thought. "Hard to say, it's not much of a dent. The other guy almost missed the fender I'd guess. Probably saw it too late."

"So you think this was in a parking lot?" Kandy asked.

"Stacy said they found the car damaged on Monday."

"Whose car is it?" Kandy asked.

"It's from an executive pool."

Qigiq wondered what kind of company had a pool of six-figure Mercedes coupes.

"Is that common in California?" he asked.

"What, outrageously expensive cars for the wunderkind business boys to play with? That's not the least of it, you should see their houses," Jane said.

She brought up a third set of four pictures.

"Check this out, ten-times magnification."

Qigiq studied the gash on the screen. A legend drawn over the picture showed it to be less than a centimeter wide. It was gray, and had a ragged edge along the bottom, but the top was smooth, almost as if it had been drawn with a pencil.

"Notice the color," Jane said.

Kandy moved in close to study it, then stepped out of the way.

"I don't see color," Kandy said.

"Right. It's just gray," Jane said.

"Was it hit by a gray car?" Qigiq asked. He felt a wide strap tighten around chest. Perhaps this wasn't the Guzzi-smacking car after all.

"That's what I thought," Jane said. "Didn't think there was much chance of finding the other car. Besides, Silver Platter couldn't care less; they'll just let the insurance company deal with it. But I was curious, so I scraped off the top layer with an X-Acto knife. It was slow work, but I got lucky. This section," she pointed to the gash Qigiq had been studying, "didn't cut through the clear coat. So what we're looking at is layers, like bands of rock in the Painted Desert of Arizona. Metal, then primer, black, clear coat, and on top a super-thin layer of paint from the other vehicle."

She looked from Kandy to Qigiq, apparently wanting one of them to ask. For their part, they were waiting for the punch line like patrons at a comedy club.

Qigiq spoke first. "Were you able to identify the color?"

"Sort of."

They waited.

"Our paint-matching computer says it's white, but can't find it at any of our suppliers. DuPont, Diamond, DuraMix, 3M. Nothing." Jane tapped the screen and it filled with hundreds of one-inch squares of different shades of white. "That's our color in the center and," she waved her hand, "all of these are close matches."

"But none match exactly?" Qigiq asked.

Jane nodded.

"What if it's old?" Qigiq asked.

"The computer automatically ages," Jane answered.

Qigiq smiled. Right in front of him was *the* car. They had found it.

"Do you still have the paint?" Kandy asked.

"Sure," Jane said. "The insurance guys will want it."

"If we brought you a paint sample," Qigiq said. "Could your computer tell if it matched yours?"

"You mean if you scraped a little paint off the side of a suspect vehicle, could we match it? Sure, but we still wouldn't have a supplier or manufacturer. And it'd have to be from the color layer under the clear coat."

"If we provided the model of vehicle and the year, would that help?" Kandy said.

"Oh yeah, unless it's too old. Records only go back so far."

Qigiq nodded. He was confident paint from his bike would match. There wasn't any clear coat, he had had it painted the original *polizei* white, probably custom paint mixed for the Italian police.

"We'll get you a sample right away, Jane." He shuffled over to shake her hand. "We really appreciate the effort you put into this. Can you hold the car for a few days?"

"Sure, have to let the paint dry." A big grin set her white teeth shining against her dusty face. "Got to have a little fun when you can."

Back in the Mini, Kandy put the key in the ignition but didn't turn it.

"How did you get hit by a parked car?"

"Funny," he said.

Kandy turned and stretched her right arm between the seats to reach in the back. She returned with a copy of the Chronicle.

"So what do you think of our friend Aaron's fiction?"

"He did exactly what we asked. Even told readers how to find the movies."

"So I win?"

He turned his eyes toward her, moving his head only slightly. Nodded.

"That was too easy," she said, "tossing the paper into the back seat. "But I'll enjoy my free lunch anyway. Tomorrow?"

"Sure. Any fallout yet?"

"The blogosphere is having a writing marathon. I don't know how anyone is getting real work done. Most think the chop video was faked: must have been raised in Hollywood. And there's a growing consensus that record companies are secretly behind the disappearing music files. No evidence, just the observation that music publishers will benefit if people stop stealing music; so therefore, they must be the perpetrators. Interesting logic."

"I wouldn't call that logic," Qigiq said.

She laughed through her nose.

"No one claiming responsibility for the, what did McGreen call it, the DoomTunes virus?" Qigiq asked.

"Let me see if I have email from Ferd yet." She scrolled through a long list on her phone with her middle finger. She was the only person he knew with two cellphones, a big one and little one. "Bunches. Ferd has a team checking each lead. So far the so-called authors can't describe how it works. He thinks it's kids wanting the Greatest Hack of the Year award."

"What do you think?"

"I think we should find out about this car. We know it hit you, we know it's registered to Silver Platter, we know their CEO owns *With a Bullet,* and has strange stuff in his fridge. That spells Person of Interest in bright letters."

She turned the key.

He spoke slowly. "Yes, but *Firebird* and Walters? He's a strange cat with a stranger package on board. Bothers me he knew Sally so well. And nothing points to DoomTunes."

"Silver Platter is in the music business. It fits if we squint."

She started the car and they drove in silence to the other side of Cupertino, past the Apple campus, down Mariani Avenue into an industrial park where all the buildings were two stories tall and surrounded by moat-like parking lots.

"Why did Apple bother with that letter?" he asked.

"Protecting assets. I bet iPods are big business for them. And you scared that VP; he didn't like the word homicide and Apple being used in the same sentence."

Kandy passed a low sign that said *Silver Platter LLC* over a round silver disk. She turned right into the parking lot.

Qigiq looked at the Silver Platter website on his phone.

"These people sell music."

"Them and a hundred others, including monoliths like Amazon, Apple and independents like Bandcamp. What's special about Platter?"

Qigiq scrolled the web page. "They claim to have an exclusive client list, and a premium service for guiding you to music you'll like. Some sort of automated recommender based on your personal demographics including, get this, the car you drive and where you shop for groceries. 'Like having a close friend in the music business.' I wonder how well it works."

"Sign up. See what they recommend for you. Probably something from the sixteenth century." She laughed.

"That century wasn't so bad, though they didn't have pianos yet. Wait. This service isn't available yet. Website claims, 'Coming This Summer'."

Kandy slowed to a crawl as she passed behind two clones of the car they had seen at Kline's.

"Check those," she said.

Qigiq stared at a quarter of a million dollars of automobiles.

"Vanity," Kandy said.

Qigiq read two license plates that spelled VER TER.

"I wonder where the fourth car is?"

Kandy slipped the Mini into a slot a dozen spots away.

"Blake hasn't been in for my calls. What's your vote? Wait, come back later, or walk in?"

Qigiq shifted, and leaned his back against the car door.

"Call, see what they say. Then go in, find out if they're lying."

She nodded and dialed her cellphone.

Qigiq's mind drifted to the events at the marina Saturday night. The black brick in *Firebird*. Did Walters plant a decoy? Was someone framing him? Or was he framing Blake?

Qigiq couldn't see a connection.

He thought about a million-dollar apartment. Could they be working together?

The shadow. Did that person think Qigiq could identify him? Made sense, since the accident was immediate, as if he had been followed. Eliminate, or scare?

He wondered if the driver of that Mercedes knew he was a detective. Maybe figured him for just another boater. And why take a Mercedes from the Silver Platter lot and return it damaged? More dots that didn't connect.

Kandy hung up.

"Stacy says he hasn't been in all day."

"Sorry, I wasn't listening, did you talk about the car?"

Kandy shook her head. "Saving it for face-to-face."

Qigiq opened the door and put his right foot on the black asphalt. As he got out his eyes locked onto the Mercedes coupes fifty feet away. He wondered who needed such machines. Kandy's door slammed. He took a step toward the building. A car entering the parking lot caught his eye.

Her footsteps scratched across the pavement.

"Kandy."

She stopped ten yards away.

Qigiq watched a black Mercedes sweep through the lot and into a parking place between the other two. It was the same make, model and color, but it was dusty, as if it had been on the road for days. Qigiq inched slowly backwards to the Mini and rested against its front fender.

The driver was talking on a cellphone and gesturing wildly with his free hand. His jacket looked dark gray through the tinted window of the coupe. He talked for two minutes, then pounded on the steering wheel with both hands, his left still holding the phone, smiling like a running back during a touchdown dance. The door of the Mercedes swung open fast; he jumped out and slammed it. His right hand slipped into a trouser pocket and the car lights flashed.

Kandy's voice was soft from behind Qigiq.

"Eddy Blake, born Edward Gerald Blake the second, Madison, Wisconsin. Six feet, 183 pounds, 37 years old. Business Computing Bachelor's, University of Wisconsin at Madison on ROTC program. MBA Stanford. Vice President of Sales for Hewlett-Packard before becoming

CEO of Silver Platter when it was founded eighteen months ago."

Qigiq watched the man stride across the lot. He possessed the square jaw Hollywood prefers, and days of dark growth, creating a *Raider's of the Lost Ark* meets Armani look. He was whistling.

"Has a kind of power, doesn't he?" Qigiq asked.

"Yeah, in addition to money and the tennis-player physique. Might be why girls like him."

"Shall we?" he said.

They were stopped immediately inside dual glass doors that opened into a small lobby with dark orange carpet and a row of awards on the wall. A gum-chewing girl with wispy blond hair greeted them.

"Who are you here to see?"

"Edward Blake," Kandy said.

She chewed and frowned.

Kandy dug out Juicy Fruit and joined the chewing.

"Do you have an appointment?"

"No. But we've been trying to reach him for several days," Kandy said. She flipped open her badge and held it in front of the girl's green eyes that grew in size as she read.

She picked up a phone and spoke into it too softly for them to hear. She replaced the receiver.

"I'm sorry, he's not in."

"Yes he is," Kandy said. "We followed him into the building. Would you like to make that phone call again?"

The girl's brain froze, unsure how to handle an aggressive police officer who knew she was lying. She blinked and picked up the phone, but didn't dial.

Kandy said, "Tell Mr. Blake a friend of Alicia's is here to see him."

~ 58 ~

Harold smiled at his workstation computer whose camera was sending his face three thousand miles to the thin laptop he had given Sarlin. She smiled back, her oval head framed by the inside of the Starbucks where they had met and the bodies of people vying for caffeine. His office door was closed to the four-inch gap he used to let others in the company know he was coding and shouldn't be disturbed. If they really needed him, they could send a chat message.

The purple shirt hugging Sarlin's body he had found online at Victoria's Secret, guessing lucky at the size. Over it, a tiny violin carved from red onyx hung at the end of a gold chain. He had located it on a site called *fineviolins.com* that offered same-day shipping. He watched her smile, but his vision blurred periodically with memories of his birthday present.

They were typing so neither would be overheard.

"When will you be coming to New York?"

"The moment I get travel approved. I'm arranging for a field test follow-up." He smiled again. "You know, that test you helped me with the day we met." He thought about how he had used her to insulate himself last Saturday, and if it would come back to haunt him.

"Soon, Haro."

The words were just pixels on his screen, but he could feel the yearning in her voice reach inside him, and twist.

"Maybe next week, Sar, but not before. The company requires a full-week lead time on a flight. Blake has been out of the office. He has to sign my request."

"Fly fast, Haro. I wait for you."

He heard a soft female voice whispering his name, "Harold. Harold. I need you. Can I come—"

He hid the chat window and spun around in his chair. The silhouette of a woman's nose protruded slightly through the crack in the open door. Below it her lips were moving.

"Give me a second to finish," he called out.

He turned back to his workstation and typed.

"Sorry, Sar, work interruption. Same time tomorrow?"

"I have violin lesson tomorrow, Haro. I will be late."

"I'll wait. Play well."

He shut down chat and turned around. The face in the opening was licking its lips.

"Now that you've ruined my flow, you might as well come in," he said.

The door eased open slightly and Lili's face entered the room.

"I'm really sorry to interrupt, I know how you work. But this is, this is, this..."

"Come on in, Lili, have a seat. What the hell is going on now?"

She stepped into his office and closed the door. She stood holding the knob, her back against the doorjamb.

"Blake is back," she whispered.

He noticed her face: pale like she had been reading Stephen King on her lunch hour again. She was wearing blue jeans (tight all the way to her ankles), low black heels, and a long-sleeve pullover in a camo pattern of grays and pink.

"Uh, Lili. Camouflage is supposed to make you blend in with your surroundings. If you don't want to be seen, I'd lose the pink."

"Harold, stop it. This is serious."

"What is?"

"Blake. He's back."

"Acknowledged. I have received your transmission."

"Ooooh...you remember what I showed you?"

He nodded. "Videos from that project in—"

She fixed him with an evil stare. "Don't say it," she whispered.

"Uh...a place that rhymes with Dinah," he finished.

"Well, there are two detectives in the lobby waiting to see Blake."

"And we know this how?"

"Lonnie told me."

"Is that 'Lonnie the receptionist, worshipper of biker boys,' Lonnie?"

"You know who I mean. She called and whispered that detectives from San Francisco came in not two minutes after Blake showed up. One of them claims to know Alicia."

"Blake's squeeze?"

"Yes."

"And you think this has something to do with, uh...the woof-woof project?"

"She's Asian."

"Who?"

Lili scowled at him. "Blake's *squeeze.*"

He rocked his head back and forth. "Awfully tenuous connection, Lili."

"I haven't told Blake about that video yet. The one made with D—, uh, woof-woof."

He laughed. "Sorry. I don't know how you say that with a straight face."

"It wasn't my idea. I'm just a manager." Her lips curved into the slightest smile. "What should I do?"

"Tell him first chance you get. He just got back, he'll understand why you waited to talk in person. It's way too sensitive to put in an email and create a data trail."

Her head bobbed.

"Okay, I'll tell him at the sales update. No, after the update, one-on-one."

"Good plan."

"But what about now? Those detectives."

"They're probably here about his divorce.'

"Blake is getting divorced?" she said.

"Lili, can you even see the loop from way out there? He's been screwing around on his wife for years. Rumor has it she's fed up and is taking him for every dime."

"Just rumor though?"

"Yeah. I sure hope she doesn't mess with Platter."

She continued to lean against the door as if holding it closed could keep bad things out of the room. She pinched her lower lip with her eye teeth.

"Want to see something?" he asked.

She didn't move, but switched to pinching her upper lip.

"Come sit down. Maybe this will help."

She took small steps across the floor and sat in his guest chair—the uncomfortable one with straps for a seat.

He faced his computer and started typing. The screen went black.

"Watch," he said.

"It's blank."

"Give it a minute to connect."

The screen filled with four pictures. She stared at them uncomprehending. He waited, suppressing a grin.

"Harold, those are security cameras."

"Correct on your first guess. You should be on game shows."

"I mean, those are—" she leaned closer to the screen.

A fragrance wafted over him that he could get used to.

She whispered, "Those are *our* security cameras."

"Bingo. Blake's office in the lower left. The camera in the hallway pointing at his office door is next to it. The lobby is over there," he pointed to the upper right corner.

"Oh my god," she gasped. "You cracked our security?"

"Didn't have to; it's well documented if you're on the team that specified the system. Blake, me, and that guy Del he met at school. Remember him? All special ops, top secret, made us meet at night. Never did tell me his last name."

She shook her head.

"Don't look if you don't want," he said.

"I shouldn't."

"But you want to. Let's see what happens. The detectives are already in his office. Note the door is closed."

"What do you think they're talking about?" Lili asked.

"Hard to say. We didn't put audio in because Blake said it was too big of an eavesdropping risk. How paranoid can you get?" He laughed, twice. "They look friendly, and Blake has his it's-just-business game face on. Did Lonnie say what they wanted?"

"No. They just insisted on seeing Blake."

"The woman is doing the talking," he said. "How do you read Blake?"

Lili squinted.

"Do you have zoom? I can't see his face clearly."

The image in the lower left grew closer, rotated, and moved to Blake's face.

"They can't see the camera move, can they?"

"Relax Lili, these are casino-grade security cameras designed so you can't tell what they're doing by looking at them. If you could, the bad guys would figure out how to track them."

"Do they make noise?"

"The optics move, but they'll never hear it over the HVAC system."

She stared at Blake's face on the screen.

"I'd say he's annoyed that they're wasting his time."

They waited. And watched.

"He's agreeing to something," she said. "Can you tell what he said?"

"I'm not a lip reader, but my guess is 'I know Sally.' Who's Sally?"

"No idea," she said. "The guy with the cast is pulling something out of his jacket. Get a close-up?"

They watched as the detective unfolded paper from of his jacket and handed it to the woman. She stood and pressed two pages of newsprint flat on the desk in front of Blake. Blake's eyes danced over the article.

"He's seen it before," Lili said. "He's not surprised. And he's trying to act cool."

Harold zoomed the camera toward the papers.

"Oh my God," Lili erupted out of her chair. "That's the article about the two videos. It came out yesterday. I knew it. I just knew something was wrong."

They watched as the woman used Blake's computer to show both movies all the way through. The three watched in silence.

"Harold, did you see his reaction?"

"He must play poker."

"That's what I mean, he barely twitched. That's inhuman. I bet he's seen them before too."

The woman returned to her seat. Harold readjusted the camera to Blake as he leaned forward to place both elbows on his desk. They saw him jump back, like he had touched something hot. His face contorted as he spoke.

"I got that," Harold said. "He said, 'she's dead?'"

"Dead? Are you sure?"

"Hell no I'm not sure, but that's what it looked like. Just look at him."

They watched Blake study the article as if seeing it for the first time. He didn't speak. His head slowly turned to face his computer screen, where the last frame of the second movie remained. He turned towards his visitors and spoke.

"Can you tell what he's saying?"

"No, he's talking too fast," Harold said. "Like he's telling a story. Both of the detectives are listening. It's not a conversation."

The guy with the cast produced more documents. Handed them directly to Blake.

"Now what's he got?" Lili asked.

"A picture," Harold said. "Looks like...no, that would be stupid." He moved closer to the screen. "Yeah it is. It's a refrigerator. He's flipping to the next picture. Same fridge, but the freezer is open. Looks like it's full of steaks."

They watched Blake flip to a third picture.

"Oh God," Lili said, and turned away with her hand over her mouth. She dropped to her knees and grabbed the plastic wastebasket from the corner.

Harold's eyes flashed from the picture on the screen to Lili and back. In the picture, one of the packages had been unwrapped and placed on a table. There was a white outer wrap that wrinkled like plastic, next to white blocks that looked like chunks of snow, and part of a foot with all five toes.

"Lili, are you okay?"

Her head nodded, but she remained on the floor.

"Blake is shocked," Harold said. "He's got his palms out, denial style. I've seen him do the same thing when a customer traps him at a meeting. It looks real, but the guy is a master actor, so I can't be sure. He's flipping through the pictures again. This time shaking his head and talking."

Harold watched. Lili moaned like she had a headache.

"The woman is reading aloud from a sheet of paper. Blake is leaned back in his chair. His face looks tired, but I think he's scheming. His eyes keep moving around the room, like he's searching for an exit."

"Why?" Lili asked, still bent over the wastebasket.

"I think they're negotiating, the woman and Blake. Way too fast though, I can't make out any words."

Lili crawled across the floor and slipped back onto the chair. She was even whiter than when she came in.

"They're reaching a conclusion," she said. "See how relaxed Blake is? He's regaining control of the situation just like he does in meetings."

They watched Blake pick up the beige handset of his desk phone.

"Lili, is your extension 4466?"

"You know it is, Harold. You use it every time you want me to buy cappuccinos."

"Blake just dialed it."

Her eyes flashed.

"What? Shit. I mean, shoot. I've got to get—"

Lili leapt toward the door, yanked it open, and ran through as best she could in heels.

Harold watched Blake wait with the receiver to his ear, his eyes moving slowly from the photos on his desk, to the two detectives, to the long window running down the right side of his office, then back to his desk. Harold launched his chat client and waited.

Blake's mouth started moving. A moment later a chat request from Lili popped up.

He wants me to give them a tour. Come help?

He typed back: "Sure, where?"

Blake was talking.

Harold waited. No message.

Shortly he saw Lili's image appear in the lower monitor as she walked down the hall towards Blake's office. He stared at the way her bottom moved in heels, blinked, and saw Sarlin's face.

He moved his eyes back to Blake's office camera.

Lili entered Blake's office, shook hands and led the detectives away. She brought them down the hallway directly toward the security camera.

He guessed the lab, closed the link to the cams, and stood up.

~ 59 ~

Qigiq followed a young engineering manager named Lili Volker down a carpeted hallway while trying to make sense of the conference with Eddy Blake. He had met criminals before, even murderers. But Blake's reaction had been a confused mess of recognition and surprise that fit no profile Qigiq had ever seen. The meeting disturbed him more than the ache in his left ankle, and less than the three attempts on his life.

Volker turned right and led them through double doors into a large dark, cold room purring with fans. Row upon row of tall black racks made him think of a prison for computers.

"This is the heart of our business," Volker said. "These machines are online twenty-four seven, ready to sell and deliver digital content directly to the consumer. Well, most of them. Some are used for testing."

"What's special about how you do it?" Kandy asked.

"We have a private catalog of new acts that is exclusive to us because we help them be heard. The huge music aggregators don't do much to help people find music they'll enjoy. They mostly move the latest hits to teenagers, and more recently tweeners, age nine to thirteen. We have personal profiles that go far beyond what our competitors offer to help customers find music that touches their soul."

"I thought music companies were all based in Los Angeles," Kandy said.

A male voice came from behind them.

"Most are, but that's a historical anomaly from decades back when all the big recording studios were in LA."

Qigiq turned to see a young man in a plain black T-shirt that said SILVER PLATTER ENGINEER over a picture of a red location pin from a Google map. His not-quite-blond hair reached to his ear lobes.

"With computer-based tools bands can record anywhere, so there's not much reason to be in LA. On the other hand search, marketing and sales are now fully digital and based on advanced Web technologies. This gives big tech companies like Google and Yahoo located here in Silicon Valley the edge. Plus Apple, the manufacturer of all things "i", is here. That's why we're here, to be close to the source of new, relevant technology."

Volker said, "This is Harold Zeto, Chief Architect of our media products. Harold, I'd like you to meet Detectives Kandy Dreeson and Keyjeek."

They shared the American one-shake business greeting. Qigiq noticed Zeto had a solid grip, though he was a skinny six feet and stooped at the shoulders.

"What's this new technology for?" Qigiq asked.

"The Internet allows sharing of files. We're trying to work out how entertainment media, all media really but the big money is in entertainment, will be sold. There are many issues," Zeto said.

"What kind of issues?" Kandy asked.

"Convenience is primary. Customers have to be exposed to new media and have a chance to buy it before forgetting they want it." He smiled, "And once they have it, it has to go where they go: cars, the beach, airplanes, skiing, backpacking."

"You're talking about advertising?" Qigiq said.

Harold glanced at Lili. She nodded.

"Advertising is only part of it. Sure there are ads, TV, billboards, that old school stuff. More important are the email programs targeting ads directly to the inbox of potential customers, and social networking sites where people instantly share their opinion with hundreds, or even thousands, of their friends: Twitter, Facebook, Google-plus, Tumblr, Goodreads, Bandcamp the list goes on and on. And of course there's the little screen everyone now carries on his or her cellphone."

"You do this here?" Kandy asked.

Volker jumped in. "Some of it. Some we do with partners. Of course, everything happens electronically as if we were all one big company."

"What's secondary?" Qigiq asked.

Lili frowned.

Zeto answered. "Theft. Illegal download sites. Digital vaults. Customers sending entire albums to their friends, sharing media property in direct violation of the license agreement they digitally signed at the point of purchase. This has all become commonplace. People don't care who owns media; they ship it around like it costs nothing to produce and they are gods of a Hollywood where copyright was never invented."

"Don't steal music you mean?" Qigiq asked.

Zeto smiled, but the Volker girl's face faded to an eggshell white.

"Or movies or ebooks or photographs. But here at Silver Platter, our focus is music, yes."

"Is there really that much stolen?" Kandy said. "Aren't most people honest?"

"I wouldn't know how to define honest," Zeto said, "but I assure you there are enough people who think nothing of taking whatever music they can get their hands on that estimates of revenue loss run to tens of billions of dollars per year. Consider, for example, that whatever single is number one in the U.S. is stolen five million times *per day;* or put another way, illegal downloads outnumber legal sales of the song by about twenty to one."

Qigiq held his crutch with his left hand and waved his right at the room.

"All of these machines sell music?"

Zeto's mouth started to open, but Volker got there first.

"Yes, but they also allow our customers to create complex personal profiles based on lifestyle decisions that our intelligent matching engine uses to suggest new music for them."

"New music you sell them?" Kandy said, smiling.

"Exactly. More important though, new music they will enjoy so they keep coming back to us," Volker said.

The group strolled along the rows of machines. Qigiq watched hundreds of LEDs flash red, green, yellow, in the darkened room.

"How do you keep them from stealing it?" Kandy asked.

Volker and Zeto exchanged glances. Zeto spoke.

"We try to provide a service that is so useful to our customers that they wouldn't want to step outside of it to manage their music."

"Why not just put stolen music into your wonderful software?" Kandy asked.

Qigiq saw Zeto look to the Volker woman again.

"They can't," he said. "Our system recognizes pirated song files."

Qigiq stretched out his hand and touched the smooth front of a wide thin black computer. It was warm.

"Sounds complicated."

"It is," Zeto said. "It all started with the Microsoft watermarking patents years back. That motivated many people, including us, to work on marking and tracking media files so that information about where they originated could be maintained. There's a problem though."

Kandy's eyebrows lifted.

"Plastic: in the form of audio CDs. They carry music completely unmarked and unprotected. Sort of like leaving the digital key in the ignition of your expensive import and parking it downtown with the doors open." He grinned. "However, music sold directly over the Internet doesn't have that problem." He waved at the stacks of computers. "These machines can mark and deliver over half a million songs per minute."

Qigiq caught Kandy's eye. He wondered what her digitally experienced head was concluding.

"All this to make money on music?" Kandy asked.

"The ultimate goal," Zeto said, "is to allow digital artists to control sale of their wares. Painters set the price of their paintings, and the price of reprints made from those paintings, based on size, quality, signature, frame and whatever else they want. But in the digital arena, massive theft of unprotected works has resulted in the failure of the capitalistic economic model—meaning simply, no business can compete with free and easy. Average citizens willing to steal music sets the price at zero. Technology companies help people steal by making illegal sites searchable. The illegal sites make money by showing advertising to all those people who come for free wares. At Silver Platter we are working to make stealing music hard and risky. Therefore, Adam Smith's Invisible Hand—"

Lili's face turned toward Zeto.

"...can work to produce maximum benefit for the community. I ask you, why should Mozart played by the London Symphony cost the same as synth-pop from the latest estrogen queen? Only because the cost of plastic disks and channel distribution dominated the cost of delivery." He waved at the computers. "With, these, that's in the past."

The room was quiet for seconds.

"Maybe Tim Berners-Lee, the scientist who invented the World Wide Web, said it best in his lecture about Web standards and DRM. That's Digital Rights Management, technology to protect digital assets. He said, 'The W3C community is currently exploring Web technology that will strike a balance between the rights of creators and the rights of consumers.'"

"Do you work with video at all?" Kandy asked.

Zeto pursed his lips like he was thinking about a hard math problem.

Qigiq saw Volker shiver.

"We focus on audio delivery: music, lectures, books," she said. "However, the technology under development could theoretically be applied to movies or other forms of time-based digital information."

Kandy nodded.

Qigiq wondered what exactly she had said.

"Is all your development done here?" he asked.

Volker nodded. "Yes. Everything running on these machines was developed here in Cupertino, designed by Mr. Zeto."

Harold smiled as their eyes turned towards him.

"So this entire building is engineering development?" Kandy asked.

Zeto coughed.

Volker shot a glance his way. "Only a third is engineering. Web design, marketing, finance, human resources and accounting are all housed here." She motioned and led them back toward the lobby. Qigiq noticed a dark-haired man sitting in Blake's office engaged in energetic discussion. He seemed familiar, but was too far away for careful study. At the front door, Qigiq smiled at the young receptionist while the girl glared at Kandy.

In the parking lot he pulled a wrinkled paper from his back pocket and scribbled on it with half a pencil.

"So, Blake knew Sally."

"In the Biblical sense," Kandy added. "Ah, the beauty of summer romance." She huffed her laugh as she popped the car locks open.

Qigiq spoke across the car's low roof. "He claims not to know Walters." He scribbled another note.

"I have this recorded if you want it."

"That's okay, writing helps me remember. What did you think of his reaction to the freezer photos?"

"Looked like shock to me," Kandy said.

"Good actor?"

"Brad Pitt couldn't pull that off." She pulled open the car door. "Unless he prepared. I called Stacy a bunch of times, he knew we were coming."

"He sure looked surprised," Qigiq said.

"Not by the videos. Did you see his eyes check to see if we were watching him while the movies played?"

Qigiq nodded. "It was like he knew what was coming and wanted to see our reaction to his reaction."

She rolled her lips inward. They sat in silence. She broke it.

"He didn't hesitate to tell us he knew Sally, and had sex with her on his boat. Like he wasn't trying to hide their relationship."

Qigiq drew two circles on his paper and doodled a motorbike in the lower right hand corner.

"That surprised me. I thought he would deny it. If he killed her, why make it easy for us by revealing a connection? Especially a romantic one."

Kandy tapped the wheel with both index fingers in a staccato machine gun rhythm.

"Damn good question, Mr. Qigiq. Maybe he knows we can find witnesses, so why not appear cooperative."

"Thank you, Ms. Dreeson, but the polygraph bothers me more. Much more."

"That he agreed to take it?"

He twisted in his seat to face her. "That he seemed eager. As if it would clear him."

"Odd. Especially since he wouldn't talk about where he was this week."

"What about Miss Volker?"

She hesitated. "Young manager, wet behind the ears. Smart though."

"Seem nervous to you?"

"Jumpy. I figure she was afraid that egghead Zeto was going to say the wrong thing to outsiders."

"Yeah. Like something she was hiding," he said.

Kandy dug into the back pocket of her black pants. "You mean something like this?" She unfolded a single page of paper and handed it to Qigiq.

He studied it carefully. "This is an invoice to Silver Platter."

"For consulting services rendered."

"Do I want to know where you got it?" he asked, squinting at the fine print along the bottom of the page.

"It fell into my pocket as we passed Stacy's desk."

"I'll watch my wallet," he said. "This refers to a project called D.O.G."

"No idea."

"What did you find interesting?"

"The location," she said.

"Mantong, China?"

Kandy dug around inside the front of her jacket and pulled out a small silver square. She handed it to Qigiq. There was a white Apple logo on the front. He turned it over.

"It says, 'Designed by Apple in California.'"

"Keep reading."

He examined the bottom, turned the square over and back. Finally he found it, "Made in China."

"Right."

"Kandy, lots of things are made in China. Maybe everything is made in China."

"True. But iPods are made in China. And Volker tells us all Platter work is done here in Cupertino; then suddenly an invoice from a Chinese company shows up."

"I don't get it," he said.

"Me either, but it doesn't feel right."

They were quiet for a full minute. Kandy reached forward and started the car.

"How did you get your car fixed so fast?"

"I didn't," she said.

He twisted his head around to look at the blood red and gray leather seats. He leaned toward his window and saw the checkered motif on the rearview mirror.

"This isn't your car?"

"Rented. Doesn't have a turbo, or the nitro push."

He shook his head.

"I like having familiar wheels. In case I have to chase anything."

"You're crazier than a motorcyclist," he said with a laugh.

They were quiet again. The thrum of the idling engine filled the air.

"Did you see the guy with Blake as we left?" Kandy asked.

"Yeah."

"Look familiar?"

"I was going to ask you the same thing," he said.

"Was he at the concert?"

Qigiq closed his eyes and ran faces through his head. Came up with a distant guess.

"Max? But Max had a mustache. Darker hair. And a tan. This guy was pale."

"You can buy a tan in a bottle; ever read that book *Black Like Me?*" She took a long breath. "Maybe my imagination. Or the lighting. Or he has a brother."

She dug into her jacket, handed Qigiq an article clipped from a newspaper. She talked while he read.

"The French are pressuring Internet service providers to disconnect people who illegally copy media. According to that, they tried a similar thing years back, but this time are specifying the technology that has to be used; the government thinks the ISPs are being lazy about stopping thieves."

"Sounds like a government crackdown version of the McGreen DoomTunes virus."

"Yeah. Connected?" she said.

"Is DoomTunes connected to the French crackdown connected to the YouTube movies connected to our murderer?"

"Farfetched, huh?"

"Not more than body parts in baggies stuffed in a freezer and the bilge of a boat owned by men who were known to have banged the deceased."

She grinned her half grin. "Getting frustrated, Detective?"

"Yeah...and my leg hurts."

"We should talk to Walters."

He nodded. "Let's eat first."

She slipped the car into gear. "You want to pay off the bet now?"

<h2 style="text-align:center">~ 60 ~</h2>

They walked along Steuart Street with the cool water of the San Francisco Bay to their right after dining at a French restaurant called the Brickyard, whose name made Qigiq think of a race track in Indianapolis rather than food. It was after 6:00 pm, the light softening toward darkness, and he didn't feel any closer to making the connections that would lead to an arrest.

"I should bet you lunch more often if I win a free dinner," Kandy said. "The French have a way with food."

"I thought the ceiling was going to collapse," Qigiq said.

"You mean those bricks? They've been arched like that for a hundred years."

"Always a first time."

They turned right at Market toward the water. To their left, four youths in oversized pants flipped skateboards under their feet, jumping against steel railing leading down to an outdoor sculpture. One leapt from the side of the fountain and Qigiq saw his silhouette against the bright bulb of a streetlamp. He was wearing a helmet with the small visor of the U.S. military in World War II.

Qigiq tapped Kandy's shoulder.

"Doesn't Danny have a helmet like that?"

They stopped and watched the young man go up steps on his board, waddling like a penguin.

"That *is* Danny."

She started in the direction of the skate crew.

Qigiq was staring at Market Street. He didn't move.

She took six steps and must have realized he wasn't with her, because she turned around.

"There's a car following us," he said. "It's circling."

Kandy looked over her shoulder at the boys in the park that filled the corner of Market and Embarcadero.

"Let's disappear," he said.

They descended the steps in the direction of the skaters until they were just low enough that they could still see the road. In less than a minute, a black car came into view.

"Mercedes," she said.

"Same model?" he asked.

"Looks like it from here. Did you get the plate?"

"I don't think there is one."

"No plate," she said. "Where are the cops in this city?"

The black car inched along the four-lane road and turned right, traveling opposite the direction they had walked.

"How did you see it?"

He tapped his knee. "I'm sensitive to black. Saw it twice since we left the restaurant. That was the third time."

"A charm. Could be rotating. Waiting to pick someone up," she offered.

"Like us?"

She smiled. "You're paranoid."

"Doesn't mean they're not—"

She punched his arm.

They headed toward the skaters. Qigiq looked over his shoulder every ten seconds. As he was about to twist around for the third time, the skater Kandy thought was Danny slid down a long metal railing that leveled off at the bottom. As he left the rail, he jumped and rotated into a somersault.

"That's amaz—" Qigiq began.

A ball of yellow light flared from Danny's head and contorted his body higher, spinning it twice before it hit the concrete feet first. Without the board, his rubber-soled feet gripped, hurtling his body forward in a face-first slide across cement.

"Holy crap!" one of the boys yelled. All three ran towards Danny.

Kandy yanked out her cellphone; it rang in her hand. She glanced down. "It's the hospital," she said, and lifted the phone to her ear.

Qigiq made a 911 call for an ambulance. He wasn't sure it would be needed, but Danny, if indeed it *was* Danny, hadn't moved.

Kandy was talking so Qigiq made his way toward the boys. The one who had yelled was kneeling beside the body.

"Is he conscious?" Qigiq asked.

The boy turned to see who was asking. His own face was white, his lips quivering.

"No, but he's breathing," the boy said.

"I called an ambulance."

The boy's eyes widened. He looked down at Danny, then back to Qigiq. The two boys standing ran; the kneeling boy hesitated.

"It'll be okay," Qigiq said. "Let's just take care of Danny."

"It's illegal to skate here."

"Did you see the flash?" Qigiq said.

The boy nodded.

"Know what caused it?"

The boy shook his head.

"Does Danny use pyrotechnics as part of his tricks?"

The boy shook his head again.

Danny's body was on its right side, his head rolled back as if he were gazing at the stars. Qigiq could see his chest rising and falling. He looked back at Kandy, who was still on the phone. He lowered himself with his right leg until he could sit on the concrete. Then he slid across the ground to Danny. Carefully, he felt the wrist for a pulse and watched the second hand sweep across the faux tachometer on his watch.

Kandy walked up.

"Respiration twenty-five, pulse ninety-one. Unconscious," he said.

She nodded. Stared at him.

"Qigiq."

He looked up.

"Robina's in trouble. Stopped breathing. They put her on a machine and took her into surgery. That call was from the guard on her room."

Qigiq took a long slow breath in, and a long slow breath out.

"Do you have a flashlight?" he asked.

She shook her head.

The guy kneeling reached his hand across Danny and held out a key ring. Qigiq took it. There were two car keys, an electronic key fob and a round rubber disk. Qigiq squeezed the disk and a single white LED glowed. He nodded in the boy's direction, lifted Danny's left eyelid and moved the light across it. The pupil contracted and relaxed. He started to lift the right eyelid when a hand wrapped around his wrist.

"What are you doing?" Danny slurred.

"You were unconscious," Qigiq said.

"My leg hurts," Danny said. "What happened?"

"You crashed big time, bro," the other boy said. "I've never seen anything like it. A huge flash of fire."

"Fire?"

"Yeah, shot out of your head, man."

The green helmet was still in place, but scorched black. Danny's left hand reached up, the fingers moving over the top.

"It's hot," he mumbled.

Kandy squatted above Danny's head.

"My iPod's gone," he said.

Kandy and Qigiq met eyes.

"You had an iPod on your helmet?" Kandy asked.

Danny moaned before answering. "Yeah. Duct taped it to the top, keeps the wires out of my way. And I never fall on it." He rolled onto his back and groaned.

"Be careful," Kandy said, supporting his head with two hands. "You could have a neck injury. An ambulance is on the way."

"Ambulance? Shit. Kevin, we gotta get out of here before the cops show up. They hate skaters."

"The cops are already here," Kandy said.

Danny moaned again, and lowered his arm.

"Tell us about your iPod?" Qigiq asked. "If you're too sore, it can wait."

"I just got it," he said. "They're giving them away free."

Kandy's face stiffened. "They?"

"A consumer rights group is replacing defective iPods."

Sirens whined into silence as an ambulance pulled up on the Market Street side of the park. Three EMTs headed toward them.

Kandy leaned forward. "Danny. Do you know if Robina got one too?"

Danny turned his head side to side in slow motion, testing his neck.

"Sure. She turned me on to it."

~ 61 ~

Eddy burst into the corner conference room saying nothing as he strode to the far end of the long table, kicked the chair back and dropped into it. Mark had insisted he return to California so his bitch wife couldn't file a bullshit abandonment suit, and promised to put papers in her whiny little hands no later than 1:00 p.m today. Which meant he would miss fondue tonight with Box-and-Mail Martina, and that finger-sucking move that held so much promise. Now detectives had invaded.

He felt perspiration under his arms.

A man must have priorities to be successful.

He glared first at Harold, then at Lili, as if they were the ones who had been fifteen minutes late.

"Where's Greg?" Blake asked.

Lili cleared her throat. "Stacy said he couldn't stay for the meeting. She didn't tell me why."

"Fine. We don't need legal for this. What do you have?"

Lili turned on the projector connected to her tablet computer, dimmed the lights, and hoped she could summarize data fast enough for Blake.

"Sales are growing slightly less than one percent every twenty-four hours. Our revenue is low in absolute terms, averaging $53,000 a day, but this is more growth than we've seen in the past six months, even with the twenty-eight additions we've made to our private catalogue."

Blake didn't react.

Lili flicked to the next slide.

"While it's unreasonable to expect these growth rates to continue, for the sake of discussion I've projected them out six months. Silver Platter would become profitable fourteen weeks from today."

Blake put his elbows on the table and steepled his fingers in front of his lips. He remained silent.

Lili tapped the screen. The next slide displayed bar graphs of week-to-week growth in each music area by genre. Pop and Country tied for the largest change at 15%.

"How do we make this continue?" Blake said.

Lili glanced at Harold and back to Blake.

Harold cleared his throat. "The Hand is spreading rapidly. We've passed the two million mark for machines that have been cleaned. The blogosphere is ranting that someone figure out how to stop this thing."

"Will they?" Blake said.

"It's only a matter of time, Mr. Blake," Harold said. "The Hand is exceedingly difficult to detect, and even if detected it's ephemeral, making it hard to understand. But there are smart hackers everywhere. Someone is going to find it."

"And?"

"When they do, they'll release software, either for free or for sale depending on who finds it, that will block us. Of course, we can modify our technology to circumvent whatever they build, but until we know how they've blocked us, I can't begin working on it."

Blake nodded. "You care to guess how long before we're blocked?"

Harold rubbed fingertips across his lips.

"Weeks. Perhaps as much as two months. That's a guess; there's no data to base it on. The Internet hasn't seen a virus that delivers like we do—tiny pieces encoded into thousands of files. In my opinion, they won't block the delivery. They'll just detect when we start up, and shut us down." He paused. "If the academics take interest, they might stop us sooner."

"So our delivery mechanism is safe?"

"In my opinion, yes," Harold answered. "However, if they find our proxy audio driver and remove it—" He shrugged. "Game over. Still, it's a race. Once a fix is posted, everyone won't get it instantly even if the big dogs like Microsoft distribute it themselves."

Blake nodded and waved his hand.

Lili changed slides and continued.

"Individuals are requesting that blog sites remove the information we've posted about them. So far, most hosting sites have refused to accept the burden of figuring out which requests are valid. Some have tried to block our posts. As you know, the Hand uses SPAM-creation technology repeatedly until it succeeds, so it's unlikely they'll be able to block much without a good deal of time and effort."

"Anything else?"

"Um, yes," Lili licked her lips. "At least one lawsuit has been filed by an individual against a hosting site. That site removed the offending information, but the lawsuit hasn't been dismissed."

"Isn't it a little hard to sue when the posting came from your own machine?" Blake asked.

Neither Harold nor Lili commented.

"None of this traces back to us, correct?" Blake asked.

Harold nodded. "Correct. If someone cracks the encrypted tracking information embedded in the music files, they'll find a fabricated audit trail that leads to peer-to-peer machines. Not here."

"Good." Blake stood up.

Lili's face blanched and she met Harold's eyes. He nodded.

"Uh, Mr. Blake, there is one more thing," Lili said.

Blake sat back down.

"A problem?"

"I'm not sure. Something strange has happened. It's DOG."

Blake sighed. "That's just research." He looked at Harold and back to Lili.

"Harold helped me verify some technical details. He's not familiar with the project."

"Probably time he is," Blake said. "What's the problem?"

Lili replaced the last slide with a movie of a blonde-haired girl writhing on the floor.

Blake's face stiffened, his lips pressed firmly together.

"Where did you get that?"

"From a URL published in the San Francisco chronicle," Lili said. "Notice the jittery line at the bottom."

Blake nodded.

Lili stopped the video. "That noise is information encoded with our DOG prototype software."

"It can't be," Blake said flatly.

Lili stepped back. She turned to her tablet and changed the movie to the one she called the *Knife Video*. She touched play and turned to watch it so she wouldn't have to see Blake as she spoke.

"This is the movie that can be decoded from the lines of noise in the first video."

Blake stood and leaned on the table with both hands.

"This is insane!" he said, slowly and clearly. "No one, but no one, has access to that software."

Harold remembered the list Lili had given him. It was short, but it wasn't no one.

"We used the DOG prototype for the decoding test," Harold said. "This is the movie that resulted. We compared it frame by frame to the one at MIT referenced in the Chronicle. It's exactly the same video, every frame, every pixel. I think there can be no doubt that both were processed with DOG."

Blake dropped back into his chair. "Explanation?"

"The software is in our vault. Someone could have stolen it," Lili said. "I've checked security records, all known access in the past thirty days has been by authorized personnel."

Harold added, "According to Lili, this software is shipped from China to California every month for backup. Someone could have intercepted it and made a copy. It isn't encrypted, which is risky."

"Or someone in China is fucking with me," Blake said.

The *Knife Movie* continued to play. Lili stared at the big screen for a handful of seconds, reached over and turned the projector off.

Blake stared out the window and said, "Show me the access list."

Lili handed him a single sheet of paper.

"The time and date of every access are shown, unless someone knows how to get the safe open without leaving a record."

"That's supposed to be impossible," Blake said.

Harold pushed his tongue out slightly and squeezed it with his teeth.

Blake stood and crossed to the window. He stared out at the parking lot with his hands behind his back.

Lili looked at Harold, who shrugged.

"Is there any kind of unique code encrypted into those videos?" Blake asked without turning from the window.

"Does DOG have that capability?" Harold asked.

"The specification calls for file watermarking, but it's not in the prototype," Lili said.

Blake spoke to the window. "Is there a way to find the computer that made those videos?"

Lili jerked upright and turned white.

Harold watched her eyes, then pointed at himself. She nodded, barely moving her head.

"Most any machine could do it, the installation isn't difficult." He paused. "However, I think I know where these were made."

"And where might that be, Mr. Zeto?" Blake said to the glass.

"One of the spare machines in our music-server farm."

Blake turned one-eighty, slowly like the beam of a lighthouse, and leaned against the windowsill.

"What makes you think that, Harold?"

Harold blinked at the use of his first name.

"Whoever did it didn't clean up properly. I found a handful of files from the DOG prototype on a lab machine. These are temporary files created while DOG is running so the uninstaller doesn't remove them. DOG should clean them up itself, but it's an early prototype and handy but non-critical features like deleting garbage files aren't implemented yet."

He paused. Blake said nothing.

Harold continued, "There's absolutely no reason those files should have been on the farm. We've never installed or tested DOG in our lab here. I've only known about it for a few days."

Blake nodded slowly, his lips pursed, his eyes focused somewhere in the next county.

"I see," he said.

Lili sat down in slow motion and clicked her computer off. She was barely breathing.

Blake didn't move from the window.

"Did the detectives enjoy their tour?"

Lili moved only her eyes to meet Harold's. He pointed at her.

"They seemed to," she said. "They asked questions about our business and how it works and why we need so many computers. They seemed satisfied with our answers, especially the woman."

"Did they give you contact information?"

"The woman gave me her card," Lili said.

"Harold, do you think you can explain what DOG is, and why we're developing it, without talking about specifics that would help a competitor?"

"Yes. The detectives weren't very technical."

"We could ask them to sign an NDA?" Lili said.

Blake's lips curved slowly into a smile that didn't seem comfortable on his face.

"I'm not sure we can ask officers of the law to agree to non-disclosure terms, Ms. Volker. You might try, though it will be an interesting day if we have to sue them for breach. NDA or not, go see them and have Harold explain what he has. Cooperate with their investigation, but play it smart. Let them draw their own conclusions."

"Yes, Sir," Lili said.

"And keep me informed every step of the way."

"Absolutely," she said.

"Reveal only the DOG prototype and the one computer where files were found. Not a hint of any—." He inhaled slowly. "Other projects. They are all trade secrets."

"Of course, Sir," Lili said.

Harold nodded slowly, his hands flat on the table as if he were trying to make it levitate.

Blake walked casually toward the door, his shoes swishing the carpet. He pulled it gently closed behind him.

Lili sat holding her right hand in her left, the thumb stroking the back of the opposite hand.

Harold said softly, "Holy Toledo, Lili. Did he just tell us to do what I think he told us to do?"

She bit her lip and didn't answer for a long time.

"I think so."

~ 62 ~

The boss must be happy; the man wanted fifty more.

That trip to San Francisco was paying off like a rigged horse race. Not only the gravy job he could have handled when he was fourteen, but the story of that missing girl in a newspaper left behind by a hurry-up guy in a sweater. Manna fell from YouTube heaven; blondie writhing on the floor hotter than Britney and Beyoncé going at it.

A simple thing to hang out, follow people...and presto: *smokescreen.*

But fifty? So he had scored little ones—the Nano thing with the touch screen and some tiny Shuffles—from a dozen different street vendors. He got all available colors and loaded them with trashy music, as if he were running a door-to-door business selling iPods like Hoover vacuums. In case anyone asked.

But they hadn't.

He had breezed through security for first class in Beijing with his black carry-on holding two changes of clothes and the little machines sewn into the lining so they looked like part of the bag's structure on X-ray. The girl who read the passport that declared him Jonathan Farley, home town Miami, Florida, though he was flying to Wisconsin, had even given him a big smile like she wanted to go to America in his suitcase.

Upon arrival, he rode a stubby green and white shuttle bus to long-term parking and retrieved a metallic gray all-wheel drive Subaru Outback wagon. It wasn't flashy; he preferred the invisibility of the mundane. He paid cash for three days of parking and drove northwest on back roads through Waunakee and Dane to a Lodi post office box that contained a slender package from the boss. He slipped it inside his jacket and zipped the pocket closed, then pointed the wagon west toward Black Earth. One stop at a fast food drive-thru, cash, and a few more hours delivered him to a hunting cabin at the end of a dirt fire road unsuitable for standard automobiles.

After lighting a fire in the stove he slit the package open. A tiny SIM memory chip wrapped in bubbles slipped out. He sat on the maroon couch that opened into a bed and pushed it into his computer. A window popped open on the screen, displaying only a question mark. He typed.

Fear or respect yield the same outcome.

The window closed. Another replaced it, displaying two question marks. He pressed return.

A third window displayed three question marks. He entered his 21-digit private encryption key. A video opened to its first frame.

Damn he loved security.

He clicked play and watched traffic flow past on a nameless road. The bottom row jittered and danced. He stopped it and fed the movie file into a decoding program called *unbark*. In less than a minute he had a second video. He started it playing. A list of handwritten names and address scrolled slowly up the screen like the credits at the end of a movie. He now had fifty names and addresses, two of which were designated *special*.

"So we're moving out of San Francisco," he said to the fire. "No more following cops." He opened the steel and glass door and flipped the memory chip into five hundred degree flames like a tiny UFO making its last flight. "Too bad, she was hot."

He watched the plastic disintegrate to ash.

He enjoyed talking to fire. It clarified the strategy in his head, and never got bitchy or talked back.

"Round one—easy. Follow the motorbike to the friends; direct attention toward the YouTube wacko that did the missing girl. Brilliant, eh Boss?"

He crossed the dusty wood floor to the opposite wall where a plastic sink and a half-height refrigerator separated by three feet of countertop made a kitchen. The fridge provided a cold Heineken and promised four more. He returned to the worn sofa and stared at his computer.

He closed the fifty-addresses movie and a new window popped up with four question marks. He typed.

Attacking with Fire. All warfare is based on deception.

Another window appeared with lines of text. He opened his notebook and began to decipher these using a codebook. Within minutes he had a list of a hundred PayPal accounts and their passwords.

He sharpened a kitchen knife and carefully slit his carry-on bag, in case the boss ordered another trip to China. He removed a blue Nano and a silver Shuffle and placed them on the kitchen counter. He pulled a package from the cabinet above the fridge and unrolled a black nylon bag to reveal a series of X-Acto knives, screwdrivers, three types of pliers, and a very small hammer. With these he opened the Nano and inserted a blob of gray clay smaller than a dime. He pushed a tiny circuit into the back of the clay and wired it to the Play/Pause button, then set the timer for thirteen minutes, with a variation range of eleven.

By the time he finished the Nano, the beer had been gone for nearly thirty minutes. He opened another before starting on the Shuffle. It was both easier and harder: easier because it didn't contain the complex circuitry of a video display, harder because it was so incredibly small. He pried with a triangular blade. Got lucky. The case opened perfectly. He wired in his addition. Pressed Play. Verified the timer.

With the specials ready he faced the mundane effort of packaging. Forty-eight would be easy, but care was required for the others. He splashed the large plastic packing bubbles on both sides with liquid, packed the player carefully, and included a bottle.

Hours later, with fifty packages stuffed into his carry-on, he opened road maps on his laptop. Starting with Chicago, he selected cities at least a hundred miles apart. These might not be the cities he would ultimately use, because he liked to improvise along the way, but it gave him a general lay of the driving landscape for the next twenty-four hours.

He pulled out the sofa bed and adjusted the airflow control on the fire. Before lying down he retrieved his Beretta from under a floor panel and tied a clear fishing line through the spiral back of his codebook to the strap on his wristwatch. He placed the codebook and revolver under his pillow and stretched out to stare at the center beam on the ceiling.

"Jonathan Farley is ready Boss."

~ 63 ~

Qigiq sat hunched over on a low stone wall staring at an outdoor art piece that looked like heating ducts dancing as the whine of a siren faded in the direction of Market Street. He tried to let the sound of traffic soothe the sense of waste washing over him. He hoped Danny wasn't hurt, but couldn't stop thinking about Robina being tossed sideways like an unwanted doll.

Kandy stood with her back to him staring at the space where the ambulance had been.

"It's still here," she said.

He glanced up the street. A black Mercedes coupe disappeared behind a bus made to look like a cable car.

"Same one?"

"Can't be sure," she said, "but that's where I'd place my money."

"Following us?"

"Doing a lousy job if he is."

"He? Did you get a look?"

"No, but women don't drive that shitty." She grinned and pulled her phone from her black jacket. "Walters?"

"Sure."

She tapped the phone, held it to her left ear, unwrapped a stick of gum with the other hand and chewed with her lips pressed together.

"No answer."

"Machine?"

"Yeah. Generic outgoing message, 'Your call is important, blah blah blah, if you're a student currently enrolled in one of my courses, please send email to the college.'"

Qigiq stood and situated the crutch under his arm. He leaned on it and flexed his leg at the knee until his shin was parallel to the ground, then extended it straight. He repeated the motion three times.

"Done with your workout?"

"It's a little stiff from sitting on concrete."

"Where to?"

A heavy sigh escaped him. "I'd like to search Robina's apartment before anyone else gets there."

Kandy made a call downtown that took less than a minute.

"We'll have the OK shortly. Let's head over."

They walked the two blocks back to the car in silence. Kandy pulled up to the exit gate of the Howard Street parking garage and waited for the arm to lift.

"Watch for the black coupe," she said.

"Have been."

She passed through and stopped at the sidewalk, then slipped smoothly into traffic heading west on Howard. They traveled a few blocks and reached the huge Moscone Conference Center.

"Anything?"

"Not behind us," he said.

"I haven't seen him cross."

"Think he's gone?"

She drove for the better part of a minute.

"No. I think he wants something from us—or you."

"He must know, or guessed, that we visited Kline's. Why continue to use the Mercedes?" He heard Janet Kline's voice saying she would try to keep the car to let the paint dry. "Or *a* Mercedes."

Kandy cracked her gum. "Wants us to know he's around. Figures we'll recognize that car."

Qigiq shook his head. "You have weird criminals down here."

Kandy flicked the Mini right onto 11th Street, right on Mission, right on 10th and finally right again onto Minna.

"One way streets will make it harder," she said.

She drifted to the curb a half block past the entrance to Robina's apartment, switched off her lights and waited, her eyes glued to the outside rearview mirror on the street side. Qigiq watched the intersection with 11th ahead. They sat for almost three minutes.

"Nothing," he said.

She drove around the block again, this time going all the way to Market Street, and stopped just past the entrance to the apartment. She looked down at her phone. "We have the warrant."

"How do we get in? It'll be empty."

"You hope it's empty," she said.

They climbed stone steps from the sidewalk. The main door to the four apartments was unlocked. Kandy flew up the stairs while Qigiq did the one-step rumba with his crutch. By the time he reached the upper landing the apartment door was open.

"What about prints?" he asked.

"It'll take hours to get a crew out here and properly dust the place." She leaned against the wall of the hallway. "And we just did it last week."

"So you want to look around?"

She nodded.

"We could wear gloves," he said.

Kandy removed thin leather driving gloves from her jacket. Qigiq did the same.

"Try not to smudge anything," she said, pushing the door open with one finger.

The apartment was dark, save for a streak of streetlamp pushing its way between faded rust curtains.

"Lights on?" she asked.

"Do you think this place is being watched?"

"They'll see the flashlights anyway."

He shrugged.

She flicked the wall switch and a lamp at the end of the sofa came on.

Qigiq felt a wall of *déjà vu* press against him as he remembered walking into this apartment when Sally was only a missing person.

Now she was gone.

And Robina was in critical condition.

"Only a week," he said.

She faced him. "Not even, it's only Wednesday night. Robina called last Thursday morning. Things are happening fast." She looked around. "We're not keeping up." She drifted slowly towards the bedroom.

He crossed the living area and stared at the tiny kitchen with a dinette table for two, yellow walls and a floor of black foot-square tile. The counters were clean and the sink empty, making him wonder if Robina had even been living here. He tried to imagine the trauma of seeing your roommate, his mind paused...and lover, dismembered in a YouTube video. His gaze traveled past a refrigerator that reached only to eye level and rattled as it cooled. A pale green plastic wastebasket filled to the brim sat beside it.

His eyes stopped on a brown cardboard box at the top of the waste heap. As he walked closer, he thought of the Amazon boxes with fingers inside. This one didn't have the word Amazon on the side, but it did contain big clear bubbles of plastic. He lowered himself to his right knee by holding the crutch with two hands and looked for an address label. Strangely, he smelled a fragrance too subtle to be trashcan deodorizer. Tilting his head and moving closer he found an address label on an open flap and saw Robina's name. The return address was P.O. Box 13229, Chicago, IL. No zip code. He inched closer to read the postmark.

"Dumpster diving?"

"Something smells good over here," he said.

"Didn't know you were into girly trash. What else do you do up there in the land of no night?"

"Postmark says this box was shipped from Columbus, Ohio."

"Land of Victoria's Secret," Kandy said.

He twisted his face to see her.

"You're serious?"

She nodded.

"It's awfully small," he said.

"You don't shop at Victoria's much, do you Qu?"

"And it smells sweet and heavy, like perfume."

She frowned.

"Women's perfume? Maybe J Lo Deseo?" she said.

He rotated his body and sat on the floor. His knee wasn't enjoying the hard tile.

"Can you smell it from over there?"

"No, but there's a brand new thirty-milliliter bottle on Robina's dresser with plastic wrap beside it the same shape as the bottle. The three gowns she decided not to wear to the recital are still lying on her bed."

"Mail order perfume. Then why does this box bother me?"

"Because it's right on top of the garbage, which means she just opened it. The perfume was in it." She paused. "But why is the smell so strong? The bottle was sealed in shrink-wrap."

"The bottle wasn't cracked?"

"No. Why spray packing material with perfume?"

"To cover the smell of something else."

"Such as?" She smiled.

"The brand new iPod Robina told Danny about that contained an explosive a dog might sniff out."

"You should be a detective," she said.

"Think there's anything to this post office box in Chicago?"

"Not a chance. Probably doesn't even exist."

"There might be a print," he said.

"Want to bet? I could use another free dinner."

He shook his head.

"I'll have Ferd look anyway," she said. "Want to see what I found?"

Qigiq followed her to the bedroom. Three gowns, red, green, black, lay in a row on a lavender quilt, as if Robina had been staring at them deciding which to wear. Along the side of the bed were six pairs of black heels, all strikingly similar.

Kandy pointed at a bottle. "Deseo means desire." She gestured to the computer. On the screen was a list of folders sorted by date. "Robina took pictures by the hundreds."

"What would the younger generation do without digital toys?" he said.

"Useful toys," Kandy said. "Check this."

The screen filled with a huge color picture of three girls lying face down on black and orange beach towels. Both the water and the sky were so blue

Qigiq felt he could see into the screen. Only one girl had the telltale strap of a top.

"Recognize anyone?" Kandy asked.

"Sally's in the middle."

"Yep."

"Veronica on the left, and Vi on the right."

"Agreed. Robina probably took the picture."

"When?"

"July of last year according to the file date, like Eddy told us."

"Eddy Blake?"

"Watch."

The girls crossfaded to a yacht at anchor. An onshore wind had swung it around so the stern faced the beach. *With a Bullet* was clearly visible.

"Robina took this?" he asked.

"Not sure, but the file is consecutively numbered from the last one."

"So the four girls are on a beach, and the boat is close enough to swim to."

"Sounds like fun to me," Kandy said. "There's more."

The boat became Sally and Veronica waist deep in water. Both were topless.

"The water must be cold," he said.

Kandy ignored him.

The next picture showed three girls running out of low surf. The only clothing was Vi's black bikini bottom.

"Any more of the boat?" he asked.

"Coming up."

He watched five more pictures of the girls frolicking on the beach, including one of all four together, the camera apparently on a timer and sitting in the sand judging from the angle. Robina wore a green bikini bottom.

The next picture was again the boat at anchor. This time, he could see shadows in the cabin gazing out through the windshield. The boat was under power and heading for the camera.

"What's your guess?" he asked.

"Two guys, like Eddy sort of remembered. My bet, that's Eddy behind the wheel, but I sure can't ID him, too much reflection. The second guy could be anybody. Could even be another woman."

"Should we take these to Ferdinand?" he asked.

"Sure, I'll make copies. But wait," she held up a finger. "There's more."

The next picture showed a naked Sally with both feet on the stern ladder.

"What's that?" he asked.

Kandy studied the picture. "What's what?"

"Her left arm, the biceps."

Kandy zoomed. "Bruises?"

"In a row," he added.

"You're thinking someone grabbed her?"

"Grabbed and squeezed a little hard."

The next two pics showed Veronica, and finally Vi ascending the ladder.

"Hold that one," he said.

Robina had moved closer to the boat and part of the cabin was visible.

"Eddy on the right?" he asked.

"For sure, though a jury won't buy it."

"And the left?"

"Too dark. I'll have to stretch my imagination."

"Can you stretch it to Max?"

"No mustache complicates my thorough analysis." She laughed. "Leaner. Could even be a woman with short hair. How about other people at Silver Platter? Board member. Zeto, Lili in a big sweatshirt. That lawyer. Eddy's golf buddy. His proctologist?"

He laughed. "Think Eddy can identify the shadow for us?"

"I think he can," she said, "But I also think his memory will fail."

They watched a dozen more pictures go by in silence.

"Wait, back up," Qigiq said.

Sally was diving off the bow. Robina, or someone, had leaned far over the side of the boat to take a picture, and hands were holding her by the waist to prevent her from falling over the rail. The water was just smooth enough to generate a reflection.

"Who do you see?" he asked.

"Robina topless. And a funhouse reflection of something that might be human."

Qigiq could make out a tousled head of damp hair and part of an arm.

"Enough for an ID?"

"Ferd territory," she said. "But I'd guess, hmm..."

Qigiq switched off the room light, hoping to see the watery reflection more clearly. He walked around Kandy and reached up to pull the curtains closer together to block the light from the street. His hand stopped. He peered through the two-inch slit.

"We have company."

"An expensive German car?"

He nodded. "You're clairvoyant."

"Who's driving?" she asked.

"Can't tell. Parked across the street. Positioned to watch both your car and the front door."

"I want to go look." She pushed the chair back and stood. "I'll get these pictures to Ferd later."

"Is your car unlocked?"

Her eyes ran down and up his leg.

"What are you thinking?"

"I'm thinking I'll limp out to the Mini while you watch the Mercedes. Maybe provide a distraction."

"There's a 9-mm under the passenger seat. Give me two minutes before you go out the front door."

"It'll take that long for me to get down the stairs."

"Leave the lights." She moved up and down the center hallway then poked her head back in. "I'm going out the back, there's a fire escape."

He nodded, but she was already gone.

At the bottom of the stairwell he stopped. Two narrow bands of glass ran the length of the front door. But the glass was old and thick and distorted so he could see that the Mercedes hadn't moved, but couldn't see Kandy. He glanced at his watch to satisfy himself that two minutes had passed. He pushed the door open and held the Mercedes in his peripheral vision, watching for movement as he descended five stone steps. Kandy's car was directly to his right, the Mercedes to his left and across the street. He stopped when his crutch touched the sidewalk and reached into his jacket pocket, not because he needed anything, but because he wanted to examine the Mercedes.

He tried to hear the car running—too far away.

He glanced to his right and located the Mercedes in the reflection from the near-vertical rear window of the rented Mini. Nothing moved. He started for Kandy's car at a brisk step, crutch, step, crutch. Less than halfway to the car he saw movement by the Mercedes. He glanced over his left shoulder and saw Kandy standing beside the driver's door, gun extended, flashing a badge. The glare from a streetlamp prevented seeing through the windshield, so he never saw the driver's reaction.

An injured-hyena screech filled the air and blue smoke erupted from the rear wheels. The Mercedes rocketed forward, swerved and pointed its grille directly at him. He lurched toward the Mini as the sound of squealing tires and a brash horn joined the hyena. A quick glance revealed a blue pickup truck sliding down the street as the Mercedes crossed in front of it. Loud thumps told him the Mercedes had made its way onto the sidewalk, close enough that the roar of exhaust could be heard.

Qigiq dropped the crutch and threw himself onto the hood of Kandy's car. The Mercedes flew past his feet, shattering the wooden crutch as it fell towards the sidewalk. Splinters bounced off the Mini and rained down on his back. With his left cheek pressed to the still warm hood and both hands gripping the left front fender, he watched the Mercedes twist back onto the street and accelerate away. He spun to look for Kandy and ducked as the pickup roared by in a blue flash. As he lifted his head, he saw the truck make a fast right turn at the corner.

Ford.

"Are you all right?" Kandy shouted as she sprinted across the road.

"Don't think I was hit."

She ran around the front of the car and stopped briefly to examine the remains of his crutch.

He felt her hands grab his left shoulder and drag him off the hood, supporting him as she did so.

"Get in fast."

He hopped on his right leg along the sidewalk. She flung the passenger door open and stuffed him into the car. He was still struggling to drag the door closed when the Mini took off.

"Did you get a look?" he asked.

"Six-six. Blonde. Blue eyes. Nice teeth. Scar on the left cheek."

"What?"

"Slouched body in a ski mask through a dark window," she said.

The Mini arched a low trajectory around the right corner onto 11th Street. Kandy slapped a light onto the roof and set a siren going. As they approached Market, they saw the pickup run a red light with its horn blaring and head north on Van Ness. By the time they worked their way through the tangle of cars in its wake, the truck was out of sight.

Kandy accelerated, then slowed at an alleyway so they could look right and left, then accelerated, and slowed at the next street to look, making Qigiq feel like he was on an industrial-strength hobbyhorse. Hayes, Grove, Fulton yielded nothing. To the left up McAllister, a man stood in the street. Kandy turned and gunned the little engine.

As they approached Qigiq saw a big man with a full dark beard leaning against the trunk of a black Mercedes, smoking the second half of a cigarette. Kandy pulled up behind the coupe.

Qigiq bent forward until his forehead was pressed to the dashboard and felt beneath the seat. His fingers touched a small wooden box. Inside he found a Ruger 9-mm lying in blue velvet. He flipped the safety off.

She nodded and opened her door, held out her badge and let the man see her gun.

He blew smoke upwards and met her gaze.

"Too late, officer," the man said. "Bastard took my truck. Some prick in a ski mask waving a Magnum. Would of broken the little shit into pieces except for that barrel."

"What's the plate number?" she asked.

"Back off," he said. "B-A-K-O-F-F. California."

Qigiq grabbed his cellphone to call in a search.

"How long ago did he leave?" she asked.

The man stood and looked at his watch.

"Less than three minutes. But he has plenty of power." His eyes fell on the little Mini. "You'll never catch him."

She stuck her head into the Mini. "Chopper."

Qigiq nodded.

"I should have crushed the dick when he pulled in front of me," the man called out.

She stood and fought the urge to agree. Had he smacked the Mercedes they'd likely have the driver in custody now.

"Only natural to avoid a collision," she said.

"Yeah. Just shot across the road; never looked. And sure as hell didn't signal."

She went back to check the man's license and verify he was the owner of the missing pickup. A quick search of the Mercedes revealed a full water bottle and a pair of binoculars with a Nascar logo on one side.

"Got the chopper," Qigiq called from inside the car.

The man, whose name was Fred Grant according to the registration for the BAKOFF plate, sat on the trunk of the Mercedes and smoked.

Kandy headed for her car.

"They found the pickup," Qigiq said, as she hopped behind the wheel. "Patrol car is already there. No sign of the driver, keys in the ignition."

"Where?"

"Waterfront, Pier 47, near Lou's."

"A million people down there," she said. "Anyone see the driver get out?"

"No one who's talking."

A San Francisco police cruiser pulled up behind the Mini. Qigiq was glad to have them take over the details.

"Now what?" Kandy said.

"Want to go see the pickup?"

"Not really, we'll get a report. I think the guy was improvising, he almost hit Grant's pickup trying to get away from me."

"You think Grant was an accident? Or a plant?"

"You mean they choreographed the dancing autos back there that almost ran you down. Could be, but why?" she asked.

"Misdirection." He paused. "Or a fourth try."

She shook her head. "Doubt it. He had no idea when I would show up, couldn't time the truck. I think it was improv." A pause. "Now what?" she asked again.

"We still have to talk to Walters."

She pulled out her phone and dialed.

Qigiq stared at the back of the plateless Mercedes. Two officers were talking to Grant, who had lit another cigarette.

"Hello Professor Walters, Detective Dreeson. Fine, thank you. No, we haven't, we're still looking. Could we talk with you?"

Grant moved his hands, palms flat, indicating the path of the Mercedes, his truck and the near collision.

"Yes, tonight. Now if it's convenient, we can be there in ten minutes...rehearsal later? We'll be brief...thank you, professor."

Grant's hands were describing the chase, twisting and getting closer and closer together. One officer was taking notes.

"We're on," she said.

"You're missing the show" He nodded out the windshield.

Kandy looked up, Grant was contorting his body and moving both hands like a street mime. She smiled. "He'll be telling that story for a long time." She fired up the engine and pulled out.

They drove in silence to Walters' apartment. Kandy parked in the same spot she had a few days before. She got out and looked up at the building.

"Do you have an umbrella?" Qigiq asked from inside the car.

"Umbrella?"

"Cane, tree branch, hockey stick? My crutch had an accident."

Kandy popped the rear hatch open and leaned in. He pushed open the passenger door with his right foot and hopped out. He tried walking carefully. The pain started immediately so he leaned against the roof with his elbow, but he smiled, glad he could walk even a little.

Kandy slammed the hatch and came around the rear fender carrying what looked like a broom handle without the broom. She held it out horizontally with both hands.

He said, "Your broom needs its 25,000 mile service."

~ 64 ~

Frantic notes from a piano filtered through the door of Walters' second floor apartment. Kandy rapped three times. The music stopped. A moment later the door opened.

"Welcome Detectives," Walters said.

Kandy nodded and Qigiq shook Walters' hand. It was moist with perspiration. He was glad the professor was wearing jeans, though shirtless and shoeless.

"I'm sorry, I don't have much time. We're rehearsing this evening for a Saturday performance."

"Is that the piece you were playing?" Qigiq asked.

"That was the cadenza. It appears about two-thirds of the way through. Quite difficult, the left-hand rhythm is a bit counterintuitive."

"Who wrote it?" Qigiq asked.

"My composition students. Each semester we create a piece the way Tarantino and Rodriguez sometimes collaborate on movies, where each director does a scene of a larger whole. Books have been written that way too. *The Chopin Manuscript* comes to mind—I think fifteen writers contributed to it. Each of my six students is allowed up to five minutes and must fit his or her work into the overall arch of the piece."

"And the piano part?"

"A young woman named Violet wrote it. She hears unusual music, not well suited to piano. Still, I will give it my best shot, as they say."

Walters led them down the hall toward the room where they had seen him inverted. Along the way Qigiq glanced into a bedroom. A pair of suitcases sat on the bed, each half full of clothing. The back room was almost dark, lit only by four candles on a grand piano near the room's center. Walters seated himself and began playing a soft staccato run, rising and falling over and over.

"How may I help you?" he asked without breaking the smooth rhythm of the phrase.

"Are you going someplace?" Qigiq asked. "I noticed suitcases." He gestured towards the bedroom.

"China. I leave right after the concert."

"Do you go often?" Kandy said.

"Every year for the past fifteen, except one. I was ill four years ago and couldn't travel. We give concerts and meet on teaching curriculum. The Chinese are keenly interested in Western music."

Qigiq nodded. The room grew quiet except for the soft line from the piano.

"We found Sally," Kandy said.

"That's wonderful. How is she?"

Kandy turned only her eyes to catch Qigiq's gaze.

"She's dead," Qigiq said, watching Walters closely.

His left hand stopped and hovered over the keys. His body sagged as if he were a life-sized Gumby dropped onto the piano bench. He took a deep deep breath and straightened, then sagged again as he exhaled.

"What happened?"

"We don't really know," Kandy said. "We found her body."

Walters turned. He stared at Kandy.

"Part of it was on *Firebird*," Qigiq said.

Walters didn't move, just continued taking deep breaths.

"My Firebird?"

"Yes," Kandy said. "In the bilge."

"That's..." he didn't finish.

"We found the rest..." Qigiq puased. "Elsewhere."

Walters bowed his head as if in prayer.

"What madman would destroy such a creature?"

Qigiq assumed the question was rhetorical.

"Where were you a week ago Tuesday?" Kandy asked. "In the afternoon, say around two o'clock?"

Walters' eyes opened wide, but appeared not to be seeing anything.

"Composition class. We end at one-fifty."

"Then what?" she asked.

"I go to the Presidio, do my personal yoga practice in the park for an hour or so, then teach an outdoor yoga class at four."

"Did you teach that class eight days ago?" Qigiq asked.

"I teach every Tuesday if I'm in town. I volunteer at a local studio that is committed to spreading the benefits of yoga to anyone interested. There is no charge for the outdoor class." He looked up. "Surely you don't think I had anything to do with hurting Sally? That would be ridiculous."

Qigiq stared out the window at the blacktopped roof of the building next door. He had heard those exact same words from many a guilty party. Maybe even all of them.

"How do you think part of Sally ended up on your boat?" Kandy asked.

"I imagine it was planted there by someone who wishes to involve me in this affair. It is common knowledge, after all, that Sally and I...interacted. But that is hardly unusual. Even the great John Lennon had an affair with his assistant, May Pang. Proximity is a powerful aphrodisiac."

"Are you married, Professor?" Qigiq asked.

"In the technical sense. My wife lives in France. We have an amiable separation."

"Sally was your assistant?" Kandy asked.

"She helped organize concerts. It doesn't pay well, but whoever holds the position gets to meet visiting artists and travel with them to and from the airport and hotels. She liked being close to that kind of talent."

"How close?" Qigiq asked, wondering if he had stated his question correctly.

"You must have learned a bit about Sally by now," Walters said. "She would get as close as she wanted."

"Who has access to your boat?" Kandy asked.

"Anyone who can pass through the marina gate. Nothing on the boat is locked. The only key is for the ignition."

"Did anyone witness your visit to the Presidio?" Kandy asked.

"I imagine someone did, Detective, because there are many people in the park after lunch. However, none of them were known to me."

"So no one can corroborate—"

The window shattered. Shards of glass danced across the hardwood floor like glistening fireworks. A dark object bounced twice as it passed between Qigiq and Walters on its way to the far wall.

Walters leapt up and was out the door before Qigiq realized the object was a grenade. He raised his walking stick and pushed himself out of the chair. Halfway up he was tackled by Kandy, driving him forward towards the only door to the room. The collar of his jacket choked him as she dragged him to the door. He dog paddled with his arms to help slide himself across the smooth floor. When he cleared the doorjamb he rolled down the narrow hall towards the front door, his ankle screaming at him to stop. He caught a glimpse of Walters with his hand on the doorknob.

Kandy's face flashed into view as she dropped to a prone position. He struggled to pull himself into a ball as the wall behind him bulged outward like a giant ballon. Before he could close his eyes the wall shattered into a thousand projectiles of plaster. He covered his head with both arms and thought of Danny's helmet.

The floor beneath him shook as a freight train of sound roiled through his inner ear, followed immediately by the clattering of fragments falling around him. He opened his eyes to a gray dusk and rolled. A board wedged against his spine.

"Qigiq? You okay?" Kandy called.

"My parts are working."

"Walters is down," she said. "I'm going."

Watching her crawl through the dust, he noticed a strange pulsing glow, as if the airborne particles were electrified. He frowned and crawled toward the missing wall. It was on fire in half a dozen places: campfire-sized flames he knew would grow quickly. He squinted and looked through the hole in the wall to the shattered window. The roof next door was empty.

He heard moans he thought might be Walters and moved on his elbows in their direction.

"I'm sorry. I heard the glass shatter. That happened so many times in Iraq, I ran without thinking. I should have warned you."

"It's okay, Professor, we're fine," Kandy said. She slipped off her jacket and pulled her shirt over her head revealing a white Nike swish on the front of a deep purple sports bra. She rolled the shirt up. "Put your head on this. Gently. We don't know how hard you were hit, we just want to slow the bleeding."

Qigiq tapped Kandy's boot. She turned.

He said softly, "Fire extinguisher?"

She looked away.

"Professor. Fire extinguisher. Where?"

"A what? Fire? Oh, yes...it's..." His eyelids fluttered and he stopped speaking.

"Out," she said.

Qigiq looked over his left shoulder. The flames reached almost to the ceiling.

"Trying kitchen."

"I'll call," she said.

He elbowed himself left into the kitchenette. The yellow tile was strewn with lumber that looked like it had been broken in a karate demonstration. There were rows of white-doored cupboards along either side, and more above the stove and sink. He flipped them open fast. Rows of pans, wine glasses, ceramic bowls. He crawled and yanked. Beneath the sink he found a wastebasket. He dragged it and bottles of cleaning fluids out of the way, but found nothing stashed in the back. He grabbed the edge of the countertop and lifted himself to his right foot. He pulled open the high doors, working his way toward the stove. He turned and surveyed the small kitchen. Every cabinet door was open. He didn't want to, but he instinctively turned to check the fires. There were fewer, but they were larger.

He pulled open the refrigerator, grabbed a gallon of milk with his right hand and two green bottles he hoped contained mineral water with his left. Twisting his upper body to shove the door closed with an elbow, his eye caught a flash of red in the crevice between the refrigerator and the wall. He dropped everything on the counter and pushed the door back open to reduce the reach. He bent down, slamming one knee into a crisper bursting with carrot tops before he could get a hand on the red canister. He yanked it free, dropped the glass bottles and pulled the pin with his left hand as he stood. He hopped to the wall, pointed the hose on the side of the extinguisher, and squeezed.

The tank sputtered then hissed a stream of white foam onto burning beams. He moved four feet to his right, took two steps closer and directed the stream along the jagged edge where charred wood was falling through a hole. The can sputtered and bubbles dribbled from the plastic nozzle.

He watched the three fires he hadn't been able to reach grow. He was about to go back for the milk when he heard a siren. Dropping the empty canister, he hopped over to Kandy.

"Conscious?"

"No. His head is bleeding, I hope that's the medics."

"And firemen," he said, pointing with his thumb.

Heavy footsteps thudded on the stairs, moving fast. Medics and three people in black firefighting suits burst into the room. Two medics knelt beside Walters, two firefighters headed for the flames, and a third pointed at Kandy.

"Time for you two to get out of here."

Kandy put an arm under Qigiq's left shoulder and they raced toward the door, coughing from the growing smoke in the room.

In the car Qigiq was taking long slow breaths when Kandy caught his eye.

"How did he find us?" she asked.

"He knew we'd be at the Mercedes with Grant. Did he ditch the pickup, grab a ride, and get back in time to follow us?"

"You see a tail?"

He shook his head.

"I was watching. Didn't see anything either," she said.

"How could he have known we were going to see Walters? Bug on Walters' phone?"

Her head bobbed. "Possible. We visited last week."

They sat in silence, traffic struggling to squeeze through the one open lane on the street, the fire truck and ambulance blocking the other. A police car arrived. Qigiq noticed the medics coming out with Walters.

"Something bothers me," Qigiq said. "While we were talking to Walters, just before the explosion, I could see the roof next door clearly. There was no one on it, no place to hide. Where did the grenade come from?"

She hopped out of the car, slammed the door and stuck her head back through the open window. "Give me a minute."

He watched her step over the fire hose and walk around the engine, still wearing only a purple stretch bra, black jeans and boots. A firefighter lost his grip on the hose as she walked past, and struggled to pick it back up. She held out her badge to get past another man and stopped between the two buildings to stare up at the second floor where smoke flowed from Walters' windows. She was back in less than a minute.

"There's a rappelling rope hanging from the roof of Walters building right across the center of the window where the grenade came in.”

“Did you see anyone at the window?” Qigiq said.

She shook her head. “I don’t think he came down. I think the grenade was at the end of that rope and he let it swing like a pendulum, knowing the rope would guide it to the window.”

“Special mechanism to let it go at the right time?” he asked.

“Something like that. Swing and run. We’ll get a look when the macho firemen decide to let me through, but we’ll be lucky to find a couple of footprints.”

“How long would it take to rig that line?”

“If he had pre-planned and knew exactly what he needed to do? Seconds.” she said.

“Would have worked for any room in Walters’ place, wouldn’t it?”

“Any large window, which open to the biggest rooms.”

“What about Walters?” Qigiq asked, watching car drivers passing slowly behind Kandy try to ogle both her and the burning apartment without hitting the fire engine.

“Think he rigged this? Automatic release. That would explain how he got out so fast.”

“Dumb to get hurt. He could’ve been killed.”

She shrugged. “Fuse timing was off.”

Qigiq pulled the box from under the seat and took the 9 mm from his jacket and placed it carefully inside. “He looked surprised. Maybe more than us, since we’re sort of getting used to being shot at.”

“Hang on to that,” she said, pointing towards the pistol. “This keeps up, you’re going to need it.”

He studied the dark metal against the blue velvet lining of the box, picked up the gun, checked the safety and stuffed it back inside his jacket.

“Best to always be ready,” he said softly, “just like during an Alaskan winter.”

“Always.” She frowned. “He *always* seems to know where we are...” Her eyes turned glassy, like she was thinking about a Mai Tai on a remote island. “Do you think?”

She hopped in and backed up a car length, spun the wheel and drove up on the curb with the right two tires, shut it off, and disappeared to the rear. Qigiq watched in the mirror as she crawled under the car. He heard clunks, like she was tapping the frame with a water pipe. He waited, wondering why she had suddenly decided to work on the car out here, and feeling the unusual weight of the 9 mm in his jacket pocket. He needed a proper holster.

And a new crutch.

"That bastard," emerged from beneath the Mini, followed by the scraping sound of metal on metal, and the shuffling of jeans on pavement.

She appeared at his window. He cranked it down.

"You're dirty," he said.

She brushed dust and rust particles off her tush and turned around. Dirt and stones were embedded in the exposed skin from her neck to her waist. He reached through the open window and gently brushed them away with the flat of his hand.

When he finished, she spun and handed him a black square the size of a brownie. He looked up at her face, smudged with soot from the fire. He could see the uncommon presence of fatigue in the corners of her eyes.

"The prick slipped a GPS transmitter onto my car. He knew exactly where we were. Might even have guessed our destination and beat us here."

"When?"

"While we were inside Robina's place no one was watching the car." She paused as she turned the box round and round in her hand. "Or when Danny's helmet exploded. He was cruising around the block and knew we were busy. The car was in the parking garage."

"So you think it was today? He didn't plant it before you picked the car up?"

Her lips pressed each other. "You mean like he knew I was going to get this car?" She laughed. "Not a hard guess, huh?"

He smiled. "Either way, he's been tracking us."

"Yeah. Implies the hit was against us, not Walters."

"Hit on Walters? Interesting thought, Detective. Could he know something that would explain that package on his boat?"

"He said Sally was his assistant."

~ 65 ~

Qigiq held his cup of black coffee with both hands, warming his fingers from the morning ride in. Thursday. Exactly one week since Robina's first-ever motorcycle ride to Peggy's for breakfast. And now? Now he felt like the case was growing larger, and his head was getting smaller.

He sat in the back beside Kandy's fighting staff, which stood in the corner of the ten-by-ten room that held three people and the readout from a polygraph machine. Two officers had been questioning Eddy Blake in the room next door for over forty-five minutes, while Peter Hopkins marked the readout and answered Kandy's stream of questions.

"How much longer?" she asked for the third time.

Peter chuckled. "Patience your strong suit, Detective?"

She twisted like she was trying to scratch an itch in the middle of her back.

"Getting stiff sitting in these fine handcrafted plastic chairs you have."

"Wouldn't want you to get too comfortable. You might stay longer," Peter said. He put a small check mark beside a squiggly line on the polygraph's paper readout.

"What's your opinion now?" she asked.

"Same as twenty minutes ago. Blake is mostly telling the truth." He brought up copies of the polygraph readout on his computer screen. "See the pattern where he verifies his name and address. That's baseline. Most of the answers stay like that. He claims he was with this Alicia person, still telling the truth. And you said she corroborates his story, but won't testify because she's afraid of her boyfriend. We can subpoena her if things go that far."

He tapped the keyboard and changed the charts.

"He says he doesn't know anything about the freezer. True. He says he didn't cut the girl with the fishing knife. True. He says he knew he had the knife on the boat. True. Even says he cut himself with it when he found it in the toolbox, which isn't where he normally keeps it. All true, near as this machine can tell."

"So he's not our man," Qigiq said.

"Didn't say that. This isn't a hard science. It's PDD, Psychophysiological Detection of Deception. Sometimes it even works. Remember Wonder Woman's Magic Lasso?"

Kandy looked at Qigiq. He shrugged.

"Comic book character," she said, smiling.

"The Lasso forces its captives to tell the truth. William Marston modeled it after a lie detector. Did you know he worked on blood-pressure-based deception detection when he was at Harvard? That was before he created Wonder Woman."

"Wonder Woman? You detector guys go in for the strong dominant type?" Kandy said.

Peter didn't comment, but he smiled.

She continued, "How about this time?"

"Well, your man Blake is a good poker player. He could be beating the machine like Aldrich Ames did. He was a CIA agent who spied for the USSR. He beat the detector in 1986, and again in '91."

"So if Blake is beating the machine, what good is it?" she said.

"None...but I don't think he's beating it. I think he's telling the truth."

He used a mouse to scroll a huge graph across the screen left to right.

"Let's go back a few minutes." He pointed to the top. "This is a stereo audio recording of the voices in the interrogation room, so you can hear his answers for yourself. These graphs below are synchronized recordings of physiological parameters—skin response, heart rate, respiration and a few others. Listen."

He clicked a big Play button and the voice of the first interrogator came from a pair of speakers on either side of Peter's wide display.

"Did you know Sally Bellowi?"

"Yes," answered Blake's voice.

"How well did you know her?"

"She was one of a bunch of college girls I'd take out on the boat from time to time. I dated her for a month or two."

"Dated?"

"You've never dated a girl?" said Blake.

"Please just answer the question."

"We went to concerts; she was crazy for all kinds of music. Dancing, restaurants up and down the peninsula, boating, sightseeing."

"Did you have sexual relations with her?"

"Is my wife going to use this against me?"

"I've told you before," entered a woman's voice, "this isn't about your wife. She does not have access to these records. So unless you tell her, she won't know this meeting ever happened." A long sigh. "And besides, the State of California does not care about consensual sex in divorce matters."

"Mr. Blake. You may refuse to answer if you wish," said a new voice.

"That the lawyer?" Kandy said.

Peter nodded. "Yeah. Name is Simmons. Corporate guy. Came in with Blake."

Qigiq sipped his coffee.

"They're not giving me options," Blake said.

Peter pointed to the computer screen.

"See how gently these lines move. Almost flowing. The truth."

"So," the first interrogator said, "did you?"

A long pause and slow tapping, perhaps a fingernail on a table.

"Yes, I had sexual relations with Sally Bellowi many times over the summer. She was a kind sweet girl—but wild as they come."

"Still telling the truth," Peter said.

"Please, Mr. Blake," Simmons interjected. "Once this material goes into a record, it's difficult to control who can access it, or when. You have every right to remain silent."

"Why did you stop seeing her?" The female interrogator asked.

A hesitation.

Simmons said. "A response is not required by law. I advise you to end this meeting now."

"She got too close," Blake said.

Qigiq looked up at Kandy. She was picking one fingernail with another.

"Too close?" the woman asked.

"She started screwing guys, um...I didn't want anything to get back to my wife. You know, give her ammo."

Qigiq scribbled with his tiny pencil on the corner of the paper from his pocket. It was torn along the left side.

"How did she feel about your breakup?" a man's voice said.

"Eddy, c'mon," Simons pleaded. "Stop this nonsense. They're recording your answers along with a polygraph. There's no way this is helping you. And it's the kind of PR disaster that could destroy millions of Silver Platter's valuation, all over a college kid."

"Like they all do. Didn't want to stop," Eddy said. "Kept calling and teasing me with places we could go, things we might do. For months."

"Things?" The woman's voice.

"You know, things you do in your birthday suit."

"Mr. Blake, as your corporate legal advisor, you must terminate this conversation. Do not discuss specifics," Simmons said.

"He's telling the truth, isn't he?" Kandy asked, watching the little lines wiggle across the screen.

Peter nodded.

"Would you mind telling us about these things?" the man asked.

"Do you really think that's necessary?" Simmons said.

Blake laughed. "No, I wouldn't mind, but you might. You'll have to X-rate your tape."

"Please, one example," the woman said. "For calibration purposes."

"She wanted to do it in a cell in Alcatraz. You know, sneak away during a tour."

"I see." The woman's voice.

"She wanted to climb to the top of a Golden Gate tower, which we all know is not only hard, but dangerous and illegal. Said she wanted to do it up there, closer to the stars."

Silence.

"Blake, stop." Simmons said, "A comment like that hits the media, Silver Platter will never go public. Cease and desist, or I'm calling Terry to get a board vote to have you removed."

Blake laughed. "Calm down, Greg. I'm having fun. We're trying to help these fine officers."

"The truth?" Qigiq asked.

Peter nodded. "In my opinion."

"He's showing off," Kandy said, meeting Qigiq's eyes.

"Would you like more?" Blake asked.

"Mr. Blake, revealing more information serves absolutely no purpose," Simmons shouted.

"If you wish," the woman said.

"She wanted to sit on my lap, you know, with it inside her, while she played some Bach piece she was crazy about on her cello. She played beautifully right up until the moment she climaxed in this really intense part of the music. Then her rhythm went haywire. It was quite moving."

Silence.

A deep sigh. Qigiq guessed it was the lawyer.

"Thank you," the man said. "Mr. Blake, did you kill Sally Bellowi?"

"Of course not."

"Still the truth?" Kandy asked.

"Didn't flinch," Peter said. "If he killed her, he's a good actor."

"Do you know a friend of Sally's named Robina?"

"Roommate."

"Watch," said Peter. "I saw this go by before."

"Did you also have sexual relations with Robina?"

"No, never," Blake said.

"Maybe," Peter said.

"Did you know that Robina is in the hospital?" the woman's voice asked.

"I read about an accident in the Chronicle. Was that Robina?"

"Do you usually read the San Francisco Chronicle?"

"Only occasionally. I read the San Jose Mercury News. It has better technology coverage."

"But you read it recently?"

"There were stories about the music industry, which is what we do."

"The truth," said Peter, "but he's getting nervous." He pointed to the fifth squiggle from the top.

"Do you know how she was injured?" the woman asked.

"Only what I read," Blake said.

"That line is more active," Peter said, pointing. "He knows something."

"How well did you know Robina?" the man asked.

"She was on my boat a few times. Once I started in with Sally, she insisted I not see her friends."

"Did you find that strange?"

"Mr. Blake, they're asking for speculation. Do not answer," Simmons interjected.

A pause.

Blake said, "Sally could be possessive in a sort of free bird kind of way. Besides, it was fine with me. I don't like being seen with women I'm not married to."

"Back to the truth," Peter said.

"Can we feed in questions," Qigiq asked.

"Sure. The interrogators are on a text system."

Qigiq scribbled on his paper and handed it to Peter, who typed into his computer, then switched from playback to live.

"...this boat you refer to."

"It's named *With a Bullet*. You know, from the Billboard Magazine charts. A song going up the charts gets a bullet symbol. I use it for fishing mostly."

"Fishing?" the woman said.

Blake laughed. "Yeah, fishing." He wiggled his hand toward her. "You know, big silver beasts swimming in the ocean. The record company execs I entertain love it. The girls were an afterthought. They really dig being out on the water though, freedom from the concrete jungle, turns them on. It was Sally who insisted I upgrade the sound system. Better than what most people have in their living rooms."

"More honesty," Peter said.

"Let's change the subject, Mr. Blake. You're in the music business, correct?"

"The technology side, yes. We sell digital music, like lots of other people."

"Watch," said Peter.

"Have you ever heard of DoomTunes, Mr. Blake?" the woman's voice asked.

A slight pause.

"He's nervous," Peter said.

"DoomTunes?" Blake repeated.

"Old trick to buy time," Peter said, "repeating the question, pretending he's thinking. Look at the fourth graph, it's going crazy."

"No, never heard of it," Blake said.

"Three lines abnormal. Outright lie," Peter said.

"Never?" said the man. "It's been in the Chronicle. Are you sure you haven't seen any articles about it?"

"Must have missed it," Blake said.

"Lie lie lie," Kandy said, standing to get a better look at the monitor.

"So you wouldn't know anything about what it does?" the man asked.

"Is it a product I should know about?" Blake asked.

Peter said, "He's trying to redirect the conversation."

"Yes, I think you should know about it," the woman said. "It's a virus spreading on the Internet. It deletes music files from unsuspecting customers."

"That's crazy," Blake said. "Who would create something like that?"

"He's very nervous, though he's got a great poker face for the TV camera," Peter interjected. "He knows about the virus."

"Do you have any idea how a virus like that might work, Mr. Blake, since you're in the music technology sector?" the woman asked.

"Just a reminder, Mr. Blake. Trade secrets," Simmons said.

Silence. Then Blake's voice.

"I'm the CEO. I cut deals, make things happen. I don't know how this DoomTunes thing you're talking about could even get into the Internet, let alone delete files. Someone should stop it."

"What a jerk," Kandy said. "Look at those graphs. They're all over the place."

"Correct, Detective," Peter said. "Your boy knows more than he's saying."

Qigiq stood and reached for the staff.

"How do we find out what it is?"

~ 66 ~

Qigiq and Kandy shuffled along the hall and grabbed two cups of coffee from the kitchen. He had been listening to Blake answer questions for over two hours and was now more confused than ever. Blake seemed to know nothing about Sally since he stopped seeing her over a year ago; although he admitted to the occasional "dip in her love pool" throughout that autumn. And if he secretly knew about the murder, the lie detector wasn't showing it, even though her body had been found in his condo. Qigiq knew that some people who practiced meditation could beat a polygraph. But then why did it show him lying later in the interview when the talk turned to technology? An interview he agreed to voluntarily.

The whole thing seemed upside down.

They turned left at a T-intersection of hallways into a low security wing. The paint was pale yellow here, but the doors remained gray steel with bulletproof glass. A dull ache throbbed in his ankle, a new pain he took as a sign of recovery. He blocked it and Blake from his mind to focus on the pending meeting. Lili Volker from Silver Platter had called and asked to speak to them immediately and confidentially, declining to produce even a hint of a reason.

Kandy stopped in front of a conference room barely large enough for a round table and four chairs. The door was closed. Through the glass Qigiq saw Volker and her geek sidekick from the demo. Kandy tapped on the glass with the nail of her right pinky, managing not to spill her coffee. The two figures inside looked up. She waited for Qigiq to open the door.

"Hello again," Kandy said.

Lili stood and offered her hand.

"Thank you for seeing us on short notice."

Kandy smiled. "Your call was mysterious. Detectives hate that."

Harold said, "Sorry for being vague. We're dealing with trade secrets in a cutthroat industry."

Qigiq wondered about his choice of words.

They all sat, Kandy directly across from Harold, Qigiq to her left, across from Lili.

"Would it be possible," Lili said, "for us to sign a mutual non-disclosure agreement? I have a simple form here." She produced documents from a bright brown leather case hanging from her chair by a long shoulder strap.

Kandy turned to Qigiq.

"I don't see how we can," he said. "If anything you tell us is material, it will have to be made public in court."

Lili shoved the papers back into her briefcase.

"That's what we thought," Harold said, "but Mr. Blake asked us to try."

"Blake?" Kandy said.

Lili cleared her throat.

"Yes, Mr. Blake, our CEO, instructed us to convey certain information to you as soon as possible. That was yesterday afternoon. We tried to reach you last night without success."

Qigiq remembered dodging a grenade and spraying foam on a fire.

"Sorry," Kandy said. "We were tied up."

"Mr. Blake personally asked you to convey this information?" Qigiq said, leaning forward.

Lili nodded. "He insisted."

Harold opened a thin gray laptop and placed it in the center of the table facing Qigiq and Kandy.

"You may have seen an article about DoomTunes in the San Francisco chronicle," Lili said.

Kandy's eyes snuck a peek at Qigiq, who met her glance without changing expression or moving his head.

"The article reported on an Internet virus that has been deleting the song files of music users and making names public."

They nodded.

"It also said a woman named Sally Bellowi is missing, and contained links to two movies." Lili paused and licked her lips. "The article reported rumors that she had possibly been murdered."

"We saw the article," Kandy said, her features expressionless.

Lili cleared her throat again.

"We're technology people, so we have no experience in dealing with this kind of thing. I apologize if this presentation is overly technical. We just want to be clear about what we've found."

They waited.

Harold played the first video.

Lili narrated. "Notice that this movie contains a jittery line along the bottom that appears to be noise in the signal. Most people simply ignore it."

Not Ferdinand, Qigiq thought. That flickering line bothered him a lot.

"Well...it isn't noise," Lili continued. "It contains another signal, made to look like noise, but intended to securely and secretly convey information."

"What kind of information?" Kandy asked.

"Another movie, of any size and frame rate desired," Lili said.

"A film within a film?" Qigiq asked.

"Exactly," Lili said.

"So there's something in those flashing dots?" Kandy asked.

"Yes," Lili said. "This movie."

Harold started the second movie playing. They all watched until the knife appeared on the screen next to Sally's index finger. Harold touched a key to freeze the playback.

"That's the second movie referred to in the article?" Kandy asked.

"Yes," Lili replied. "It can be decoded from the first. If you know how."

"You figured this out?" Qigiq asked.

Lili turned to Harold. They appeared to communicate without speaking.

"We didn't exactly have to figure it out," Harold said.

Kandy frowned, but remained silent.

Harold cleared his throat.

"You see, the technology required to encode the second movie into the noise line, and to decode the noise into a complete movie, was developed by Silver Platter as part of our cryptography project."

In the quiet, the fan on Harold's laptop started to hum.

"I thought you only did music," Kandy said.

"Commercially, yes," Harold said. "But we also have a research project going on with an outside firm."

"Outside," Qigiq said, stretching the word.

Lili jumped in.

"We only work on music in Cupertino. But we have a research project called DOG, as in 'Year of the DOG,' with a team in China."

Qigiq's tilted his eyes toward Kandy. She was staring at the still frame in the video.

"China?" she said softly.

Lili answered, "Yes. Our CEO wanted to keep the video work separate from the music so it wouldn't become a distraction. He also wanted to learn how to leverage the lower cost of development in China."

"Which is a myth," Harold added.

Lili stared at him for a moment. "And we want to prepare for the evolving Chinese digital delivery market."

Kandy nodded.

"This DOG thing?" Qigiq said. "What's it like?"

"It's custom software," Harold said. "But it can run on any standard desktop computer."

"And who has access to it?" Kandy asked.

"The full list is confidential," Lili said. "However, Mr. Blake told me to say that it includes the team in China, which is five, the executives of Silver Platter and me." She glanced to her side. "Mr. Zeto has only known for two days."

"So fifteen, maybe twenty people," Kandy said.

"At most."

"Why did Mr. Blake want us to know about DOG?" Qigiq said.

Lili took a deep breath and let it out slowly.

"He told us that if criminals had used the DOG prototype to make these videos, we should let you know because it might assist your investigation. Naturally, we do not want our competitors to know what we're working on, or how far along we are, so we hope to keep the name Silver Platter out of any public forum."

"Not to mention the negative publicity," Kandy said. "Anything else?"

"Mr. Blake also hoped you might help us find our security leak. No one should have access to DOG, yet clearly someone does."

Qigiq studied the still frame on Harold's laptop. It showed a gloved hand, the fishing knife, Sally's palm.

"How confident are you that these videos were made using your technology?"

Lili's neck twisted toward Harold, who answered without hesitation.

"It's difficult for me to imagine that someone could have independently developed precisely the technology that our team in China engineered, based as it is on my audio work here in California."

"So you're saying?" Kandy said.

"These movies were made with copies of our software, far beyond any reasonable doubt," Harold said.

"Here in California?" Qigiq asked.

Their faces stiffened. Lili swallowed hard.

Harold turned in his chair and lifted a black bag onto the table. He unzipped three sides and flipped the padded cover back to reveal a black box the size of a serving plate, but an inch thick.

"I am reasonably confident this computer made both videos," Harold said.

Qigiq examined the long rectangle. It had a row of colored LEDs, and female receptacles on what was probably the back. It didn't look anything like his laptop.

"Where?" Kandy asked.

"In our test lab," Lili said. "It's server number one hundred and sixty eight."

Qigiq remembered the massive rows of computers they had seen on the tour.

"These movies are from your test lab?" Kandy said. She hesitated. "Do you have any idea who made them?"

Lili's eyes darted nervously to Harold and back to Kandy.

"We don't know. We can only estimate when they were made."

"What can you tell us, Harold?" Qigiq said.

Harold jerked slightly at the direct question.

"Um, this machine contains remnants of a DOG install. The files were created exactly two weeks ago, so the movies could have been made any time after that, but we can't pinpoint when because there were no movie files found on this machine."

"Remnants?" Qigiq said.

Harold nodded. "Scratch files that are created the first time a movie is made. Whoever did the installation apparently didn't know how to remove them."

"What was in them?" Kandy asked. "These remnant files."

"Intermediate calculations needed before the noise insertion can take place."

"Why doesn't DOG delete them?" Qigiq asked.

Kandy looked Harold's way and smiled.

"It will if it becomes a product," Lili said. "But right now it's only a prototype, so the clean-up routines aren't operational."

"Who would know that?" Kandy asked.

"That the prototype doesn't clean up?" Lili said. "Anyone working on the project directly, or carefully reading the monthly status reports."

Qigiq picked up one side of the boxy computer. The bottom was a smooth black metal panel.

"So you think this machine made the movies because it contains remnants of a few files that are a side effect of running DOG?" he asked.

"No," Harold said.

Everyone stared at him.

"The existence of the files confirms that DOG ran on this machine, probably for the first time, two weeks ago."

Qigiq nodded slowly and picked up his coffee cup from the table.

"It's the content of the files that convinced me," Harold added.

Three blank stares waited for more.

"It was a bit of a hassle, but I had DOG remake the movie you saw on YouTube. During processing, I interrupted the software manually at the exact point that these particular files would be accessed."

Qigiq sipped from his paper cup. The edge was getting soggy.

"Everything matched," Harold said.

Kandy relaxed against the back of her chair and crossed her left ankle over her right thigh.

Qigiq leaned forward to point at the laptop. "So the files you discovered were created when this movie with the knife was inserted into the movie of Sally's face. Not just any random movies, this precise pair?"

"That is correct," Harold said.

"What is this machine normally used for?" Kandy asked.

Lili coughed. Harold turned to her.

Lili said, "It's used for testing new versions of software, which means unless there is a tech running a test on a pending release, it isn't used for anything."

"Who would know this machine was available?" Kandy said.

"Anyone familiar with our test lab procedures."

Qigiq stared at the dark box, remembering the hundreds he had seen at Silver Platter. He brought his left elbow to the table and scratched his forehead. "You told us there were over two hundred machines in that room."

Lili nodded.

"How many for testing?"

"Varies," Lili said. "Usually fifty. Sometimes as many as a hundred."

Kandy asked, "How would someone walking into the room know which machines were available? Could they tell just by looking at the front panel?"

"Probably not," Harold said, "unless the machine was off. Then its panel would be dark. If it were running a long test, it would look like any other machine."

Qigiq frowned.

"You have to know how to check the test log," Lili said. "It's an internal website that shows the status of every machine in real time."

"Who has access?" Qigiq asked.

Lili's forehead furled in thought. "Lab techs, most of Engineering, including Harold and me. Department managers. Executives."

Conversation ceased for nearly thirty seconds.

"Can we keep this machine?" Kandy said, gesturing at the box with her left hand.

Lili nodded. "Mr. Blake told us to give you our full cooperation. If you want the machine, we'll just need a receipt."

"Um..." Harold said.

Eyes turned toward him.

"Sorry, but with so many machines in our lab, a handful of keyboards are electronically allocated as needed. So we don't know which keyboard was used to make the movies...might even have been the one Lili and I used to run our tests."

© © ©

Kandy carried the padded bag containing the flat computer. Qigiq followed three steps behind. They entered the elevator; he pressed 4 with his borrowed fighting stick, and they rode upward in silence. A bell pinged and the doors slipped open. Ferdinand walked into the elevator with his head down in thought, and would have rammed Kandy if she hadn't stepped aside.

"Hello," she said.

His head jerked up.

"Ah, Detectives. I was on my way to see you. We must talk."

"We have something for you," Kandy said, lifting the black bag in her arms.

Ferdinand's right eyebrow danced as he examined the bag.

"Yes, well, perhaps some privacy." He backed out of the elevator without removing his gaze from the bag. "I have results that disturb me."

"Something disturbs you?" Kandy said. "Why Ferd, are you losing your touch?"

"Hardly, Ms. Dreeson. The data is momentarily confusing."

"Momentarily," she said slowly, smiling.

Ferdinand unlocked the door to his lab and relocked it behind them, making Qigiq wonder who Ferdinand wanted to keep out.

He led them to an empty table in the back. Kandy lowered the bag gingerly and placed it on the flat surface.

"Come, look at this," Ferdinand said.

They followed him through a door to a smaller room that contained a pair of tables with thick-walled clear boxes built on the top. Big gloves protruded into the boxes like dismembered arms. Ferdinand approached the second box and inserted his hands into the gloves. He pointed with a blue rubber-coated finger.

"The fragments on the left were found in Robina's clothing from the explosion by the theater. Those on the right are scrapings from Danny's helmet and shirt."

"I thought you were *Electronic* Evidence Recovery."

"That is correct, Detective Kandy."

"Then why are you sifting through bomb fragments?"

He frowned at her. "Because I personally examined the scene, and because the bomb, as you call it, contains residue that indicates an electronic device was involved. I have been asked to determine its nature from these," he waved a blue rubber hand, "scraps."

"Is that what you're disturbed about?" she said.

"Heavens no. The materials match the chips used to build mobile music players, just as you described Danny was using when the explosion occurred."

Qigiq wondered how it was possible to determine anything so specific from ashes.

"iPods are exploding?" Kandy said.

"Not exactly."

She pursed her lips and pulled a stick of gum from her back pocket.

"There was an integrated circuit, a chip if you will, in both of these explosions that isn't used in any iPod."

Qigiq's ankle urged him look around for a chair, but the only one available was a rolling stool under the worktable.

"What kind of chip?" Qigiq asked.

"I cannot identify a part number or manufacturer. However, based on the crudeness of the material, I would guess a cheap timer chip."

"Cheap?" Kandy asked.

"Yes. But cost wasn't a factor. It was chosen because there are so many millions fabricated each day we will be unable to trace its source."

"That's what you find disturbing?" Kandy said.

"No, Detective, that is a simple fact of life."

Kandy shrugged.

"There's something else?" Qigiq asked.

"The explosive. I've attempted to match the compound to known compounds that are powerful in small quantities, such as TNT and C-14."

"You found something so common we can't trace it?" Kandy offered.

"Tsk, tsk Detective, this is not your lucky day. No, I found a compound similar to C-14, but the ratios are incorrect. No one manufactures it."

Qigiq shifted his weight, trying to get comfortable. "Home grown?"

"That is my suspicion. But this material could not be made in one's kitchen."

"Someone has a friend in the military," Kandy said.

Ferdinand removed his arms from the blue gloves and spun in place like a chubby top.

"Not the U.S. military," he said.

"A connection to rebels who operate an explosives lab," Qigiq said. "Could be anywhere: Afghanistan, China, Pakistan."

"Precisely, Detective," Ferdinand said. "Precisely."

"This helps us how?" Kandy said, leaning to gaze into the clear box.

Qigiq added, "And money to pay rebels."

"Yes, Detective," Ferdinand said. "And the trust of the rebels; they will not sell to just anyone." He spun his stool. "Now tell me, Detective Kandy, what is this package you have for me?"

~ 67 ~

Qigiq and Kandy stood outside Captain Jasik's closed office door facing each other. Through the wavy vertical lines in the half-glass they could see him moving behind his desk, a black handset pressed to his ear. Kandy leaned against the wall, standing on one foot, the other knee bent to put her boot flat against a yellow wall that had so many marks new ones would never be noticed. Qigiq leaned on his borrowed staff with both hands.

"Do you want to agree on what we're going to tell him, or play it by ear?" Kandy asked.

He shrugged. "If the polygraph is right, Blake isn't our man on the Bellowi killing. But her body was in his freezer. And there's his reaction to the Robina and DoomTunes questions."

"Jasik will laugh at the polygraph," she said.

"Stop it, you're building my confidence." He peered through the glass, Jasik was still on the phone. "What would you like to do?"

"Arrest Blake and make him talk. He knows something. Whatever it is might help."

"Think the Distract Attorney will agree?"

"No, I think arresting a CEO will get ugly. The guy probably has enough money for a bus full of lawyers waving harassment lawsuits."

"And your friend Alicia says he was with her during Ferdinand's time window."

"That's an estimate. And she could be lying."

Qigiq sighed. He saw a blurry image of Jasik's arm lower the receiver and heard the word, "Damn," emerge from the office.

"You first," Kandy said with a big grin.

Qigiq tapped on the door with his knuckles.

"Enter."

"Enter," Kandy mouthed silently.

Qigiq pushed the door open and hobbled into the Captain's office with Kandy in tow.

"Welcome Detectives, please sit down. I hope you have good news for me."

"We have more information, but not clarity," Qigiq said.

Jasik's eyes moved from one to the other as if he were deciding whether to barbecue the chicken or the steak first.

"There's no time for clarity, we need action. The chief just got a call from the DA in New York City."

Kandy's eyes shifted to their leftmost corner.

"Do you know about New York?" Jasik asked.

"Ferdinand believes the DoomTunes virus was inserted from a public network there," Kandy said.

"I wasn't referring to a stupid computer hack."

"A body-parts package was delivered to a friend of Sally Bellowi," Qigiq said. "We're not sure it went through the mail, but Kandy filed forms with the feds just in case. Nothing else points to New York."

"It does now," Jasik said as he let a pair of fax pages flutter to his desk. "Let me save you the reading. A girl is dead, early twenties, explosion, no sign of a perp, just kaboom." He spread his fingers like he was trying to flick something off the tips. "Someone with sharp eyes at NYPD saw the Chronicle article about the girl injured after the concert. Put one and one together."

Qigiq reached for the documents and started speed reading.

"How close is the MO?" Kandy asked.

"Sounds identical."

"When?" Qigiq asked

"DOA twenty minutes ago. Hit by a taxi. Witnesses say she was walking along the sidewalk, there was a bright flash and she toppled off the curb into its path."

Qigiq checked his watch.

"They're three hours ahead of us," Jasik said.

"We just came from EER," Kandy said. "Ferdinand thinks he has a unique signature for the explosive."

Jasik studied her face like an artist preparing to sketch a model, reached slowly for a pen and dragged a tablet from the corner of his desk. He tore off the top page.

"Go ahead," he said.

"The compound isn't commercially manufactured with the component ratios he found. He thinks it's coming from a paramilitary lab in the East, based on mineral traces from dirt used as an inhibitor."

"Terrorists are killing American girls on U.S. soil," Jasik said. It wasn't quite a question.

"There has been one attempt against a male," Qigiq said. "Mild concussion and a stiff neck."

"How's that?" Jasik said.

Kandy shifted in her chair. "He was wearing a helmet."

Jasik frowned.

Kandy pointed at the ceiling. "Explosion was above him."

He shook his head. "What is going on, Detectives?"

Qigiq dug a crumpled piece of paper out of his back pocket.

"There are moving parts. In Danny Merkel's case, he was wearing a World War II helmet that belonged to his grandfather, with a music player taped to the top."

Jasik leaned back, his elbows resting on worn leather arms, fingertips pressed together over his chest.

"To keep the wires out of his eyes," Kandy interjected. "He doesn't use Bluetooth."

Jasik's eyebrows lifted.

"Wireless technology," Kandy said.

Qigiq pressed his paper flat on Jasik's desk.

"New York is the third explosion. But there's also Bellowi, the girl dismembered by the fishing knife."

"And these are related?" Jasik asked.

"Two explosions were people known to Bellowi," Qigiq said. "And the videos of her included a *Don't Steal Music* message. The DoomTunes virus is showing up everywhere deleting music files, warning people not to steal music, and posting personal information with a picture to a huge list of websites. Ferdinand has identified over a hundred so far." He paused. "Then, there's the independent offer for free replacement iPods."

Jasik spoke slowly. "How is this related to terrorist explosives?"

"We believe explosives were carried by an iPod music player in the two cases in San Francisco. Apple has publicly and proactively denied offering free replacement players for defective units. Based on Danny's description, the free offer goes directly to customers, just pops up on their machines."

"That sounds like another virus to us," Kandy said.

"Has anyone seen this free iPod offer?" Jasik said.

"Danny saw it," Kandy said, "but can't make his machine do it again. Robina saw it; she described it to Danny before he knew anything about it; and gave us screen shots."

Jasik leaned forward, moving his elbows to his desk.

"The New York incident?" Jasik said.

Kandy's lips pressed tight together and moved left and right before she spoke.

"Have they searched the victim's apartment?"

Jasik shrugged and pressed his speaker phone on. Waited. Voice mail answered.

"Hello, Chief. I have the detectives covering the San Francisco explosions sitting in my office. We believe the New York incident might be related. If we can speak directly to the officer leading the investigation in New York, we could have an answer for you quickly. Thank you."

"When he calls, what do you want to know?" Jasik asked.

"Did they find a box from Victoria's Secret in the victim's apartment?" Qigiq said.

"And look for a bottle of Deseo by J Lo perfume," Kandy added. "The bottle is shaped like a diamond in the rough."

~ 68 ~

The ripping sound made him tense his shoulders as Qigiq removed the fat velcro straps holding the foam cast to his leg. He lifted the leg gently with both hands and placed it across a flat chair he kept for visitors. Very slowly he rotated his ankle to the left, back to straight up, then to the right. He waited a handful of heartbeats, then flexed his toes toward his knee. They moved only an inch. He pressed them toward the wall.

"One of us should go to New York," Kandy said from across the facing desks.

"They'll find the box and Deseo. Do you think there's more?"

She rolled an unopened stick of gum around her fingers like a magician about to make a quarter disappear.

"Might find something to make sense of this." She looked up to meet his eyes. "And it might be safer there."

Neither spoke. His ankle cracked.

"Maybe," he said, and winced before letting his ankle relax. "Want to review?"

She glanced up at the tire clock.

"Sure, but I have to work out before heading to Valente's. You're going, aren't you?"

He nodded. "For sure." He tried to breathe deeper. "I know they tried. It's just..."

"The brain is nothing to mess with," she said.

He dug the paper out of his pocket and spread it on the desk. From the center drawer he extracted a clean sheet and wrote as he spoke.

"Sally goes missing."

"Ferdinand finds a strange board inside her computer."

"With an unknown fingerprint."

"Danny, Robina and Marie (in New York City) receive Amazon boxes."

"Rape movie shows up on YouTube."

"Ferdinand decodes the knife movie."

"MIT team decodes and posts the knife movie."

"DoomTunes shows up, deleting files and posting identity information."

"Package found on Walters' boat."

"Kandy muscles Alicia."

He looked up and grinned.

She shook her head. "You haven't seen muscle."

"We find Sally's body in Blake's freezer."

He inhaled. "Mrs. Blake doesn't set foot in the condo; says it's Eddy's *man cave*. Do some guys really own a place like that for fishing?"

"Sports fishermen are crazy; ever see a tiny bass boat with 350 horsepower hanging on the back? But I think Helen Blake has been looking the other way for a long time." She paused. "And ole Eddy's in the CEO boys club. Could just be a 'Mine is bigger than yours' show. Or..."

"She's lying," Qigiq said, wrote *Helen and the man cave*, and moved on.

"McGreen writes the article we asked for, tying the Don't Steal stories together."

"Blake disappears for two days."

"Free iPod offer shows up on Robina's computer. We start getting 'Is this legit?' calls."

"Apple advertises public denial and warns users to protect private information."

"iPod explodes after Robina's concert."

He paused. "And we were there. Two officers to protect her."

Kandy made a fitzing inhale sound with her lips, but said nothing.

"Another iPod explodes. Danny's helmet saves him."

"A third explodes in New York City; a girl dies falling into traffic."

"Did I miss anything critical?"

"You didn't mention Blake's polygraph."

He lowered his leg to the floor with both hands.

"What do you make of that? Is the whole thing useless?"

She tapped her wrapped gum against the desktop.

"Those questions about Robina make me wonder what he left out. And the way he reacted to DoomTunes, now that we know Platter technology was used to make those videos. Better add those to your pocket list too."

"A lot of arrows point at Silver Platter."

She nodded and unwrapped the gum she'd been playing with.

"And at Eddy Blake."

Qigiq was quiet, his eyes running up and down the new list.

"What do you think of Mr. Zeto?"

She sucked her lips in and pressed them together with her teeth, blew out a slow breath, and slid the gum into her mouth.

"Geeky guy who seems to know everything. I find him hard to read even though he answered our questions. He's certainly smart enough to build DoomTunes."

"Could he build an iPod bomb?"

"If not, he'd go web surfing and come up with a dozen people who could in less than ten minutes." She leaned back to stretch.

He nodded. "Seems secretive."

"Yeah. He's got all that patented trade-secret stuff in his head they're trying to turn into a bazillion dollars. Might just be how he operates."

Qigiq sat quietly.

"You skipped something," she said.

He ran his finger down the list like he was checking to be sure he had picked up everything at the grocery store.

"What's that?"

"Motorcycle accident, Magnum on the highway with a blow up doll, sniper, Mercedes on the sidewalk. Oh yeah, and a burning building."

He smiled and scribbled. "The Mercedes paint. Maybe it's time to get a carry gun."

She leaned to her right and pulled open the bottom drawer. She returned with a 38 revolver and placed it on the desk between them.

"It's been hot-rodded," she said, "to reduce response time and improve accuracy. Makes for a simple gun that will go off only when you want it to. And titanium...huge improvement over the department stuff."

He reached across and picked it up, rolling it around first in one hand and then the other.

"About as heavy as the toolkit on my Guzzi. Where do I put it?"

"Keep things simple, maybe the inside pocket on your leather jacket. But leave the zipper open. When you need it, you'll need it right away."

"No holster?"

"Up to you. I don't like shit strapped to my body. Inhibits movement."

He met her eyes. "Thanks. Hope I don't need it."

"Me too."

The loudest sound in the room was gum against Kandy's teeth when the phone jangled.

She reached for it.

"Detective Dreeson...hi, Ferd...yeah he's here. You want him? OK. Sure, I'll let him know. That's it, just the partial? A curved partial? Thanks. You bet."

Qigiq waited as Kandy replaced the receiver on a black desk phone that had probably been in continuous use for twenty years.

"Ferdinand to the rescue?" he said.

"Partial print on the power button of that machine Zeto gave us. Says he only got the perimeter. Someone else used the button after this print was left."

"Who?"

"Don't know."

"Why'd he bother to call?"

"Because the partial matches the print on that weird eavesdropping board inside Sally's computer."

Qigiq reached over to update the list of events on his paper.

She cracked her gum twice.

"And because it's not Blake's."

~ 69 ~

He had slept for only three hours before the excitement of the deliveries invaded his dreams. So he loaded up the fifty boxes and set off like an excited paper boy with a news flash. The first package went into a blue box on the corner of First and Lake in Chicago. The dark water of Lake Michigan made him think about taking a ferry, but he slept poorly on boats. He chose South Bend, Indiana, for the second drop for no good reason other than it was a college town and he might see hot girls frolicking in the park or returning from a drunken night out. He didn't have time for them with the boss breathing over his shoulder, but looking inspired him.

He dropped boxes faster then: Bryan, Toledo, the college town of Bowling Green and Columbus. The last got his first phase-2 special. He tried not to smile when closing the door on the mailbox, but he couldn't help it. Dropping that package felt like sending his little kid off to school, the thud when it hit the bottom the bus door closing. He hummed *The Things We Do for Dough* to that tune by 10 cc and laughed.

He drove southwest all night and most of the day, and was becoming drowsy even though the spinning wheels of the Subaru were keeping him in daylight. He reached Tennessee with ten packages to go. But the two that counted had been expressed on their way long ago. He pulled into a Starbucks advertising free Wi-Fi on the door, glanced over his shoulder into the back seat and considered dropping all ten here and finding a nearby hotel. The thought of a soft bed wrestled with his need for quality execution; he was a professional after all. He dragged the black bag off the back seat, and locked the car.

He waited behind eight other patrons, seven of whom ordered caffeine, before a freckle-faced girl wearing a gray sweater with red hair curled upwards on both sides of her face looked at him.

"Hi, what can I get for you?"

"Large double latte," he said, slipping a ten-dollar bill across the counter.

"Name?

"Jon, no 'h,'" he said.

She looked up and smiled. He wanted to kick himself in the ass for giving her something to remember. He must be more tired than he thought.

She waited until he held out his hand and counted his change back for him, stroking the side of his palm with hers for each bill and coin.

"There you are, Jon, no 'h.' Thank you for stopping at Starbucks."

She held his eyes. Hers were a deep shade of green he didn't think he had ever seen before. One thought of the packages in his bag ended the conversation.

He waited until a dark-haired girl called "Jon," and walked over to pick up his drink. He migrated to a table intended for two, but with only one chair, and sat down. He sipped the hot drink for a couple of minutes, watching the coffee crowd move through the room, wondering why all Starbucks seemed to be too small. Were they trying to make the place feel exciting, or was it simply a dollars per square foot equation?

When the latte was half gone, and he was convinced no one had followed him, he zipped open the case and removed a black laptop. He hooked up to the free Wi-Fi network and went to www.craigslist.org for the city of San Francisco. In quick succession he clicked: post to classifieds, for sale, boats. The site reminded him his ad would expire in seven days. He smiled, took a sip from the latte and thought about how different his world would be when those seven days had passed. He typed a title.

50 ft Yacht. Perfect condition.

Then he entered the price the boss had agreed to, plus the bonus for finishing the project before the weekend.

$1,550,000

Then the message the boss would be looking for.

Ideal yacht for business or pleasure. Like new. Two exquisite custom staterooms unique in the industry. Will deliver anywhere in the continental United States within seven days.

The latte was cold. He reread, checking for typos. He hated receiving messages from people who were so careless they didn't even let their computers correct spelling for them. He set the contact to the anonymous email address provided by craigslist and submitted the ad.

"You have a yacht?" a woman's voice said.

He spun around, angry that someone had been able to approach unnoticed. The redhead stood near, smiling. The light gray sweater she had been wearing behind the cash register was gone, revealing a shiny dark green blouse stretched tight over what he guessed were 36's that were either cold or excited.

"No, my boss has a yacht. I'm just helping him with advertising."

"Will you take me for a ride on it?"

He tried not to imagine her in a tiny green bikini with a thong bottom, but he failed.

"I'd love to, but it's in California."

"I've never been to California."

She was standing next to him, her 36's inching closer to his eyes with each word she spoke.

"Wish I could take you," he said. "But I'm heading south to Texas. What's your name anyway?"

"Becky with a 'b,'" she said. "I've never been to Texas, either."

"There's no yacht in Texas."

"That's okay. We'll find something to do."

She was close now, so close he had to be careful not to bite her.

"Becky with a 'b,' I've got to be getting back to work. Thanks for stopping over."

He thought she would back away, but she didn't move. He lifted his eyes and saw her pouting. She was also blocking his view of the restaurant and its patrons, which was making him nervous. He turned back to his laptop. He had to wait for the craigslist email to confirm the posting, or the boss wouldn't get the message.

She was so close he could feel heat on the side of his body.

"Can you at least give me a ride home? It's closer than Texas."

He needed her to go away before he would open email. That wasn't something she could see.

"How close?" he said.

"About ten miles, but it's all country road. You can drive fast if you want."

"Sure. Give me a minute to finish here." He thought about those other ten packages and the message he had just posted confirming they had been delivered. They weren't armed, but they were part of the plan.

Sloppy.

She hadn't moved.

"Go get your purse and sweater. Weren't you wearing a sweater before?"

She smiled. "You did notice me. I thought so. I'll be right back," she said as she lightly touched his shoulder with fingertips that he hadn't noticed until now had green painted nails.

She turned and pranced through a door marked Employees Only.

He opened the email address he had set up twenty-four hours before, found the message from craigslist, clicked the link, published the posting, closed the laptop, dropped it into its bag, and walked out without looking back.

~ 70 ~

With Kandy at martial arts practice, Qigiq opted for take-out Moo Goo Gai Pan and a Coke on his upper deck, which was also the roof over his floating living room. He watched the sun drop behind the foothills and tried not to think about Sally's case and the hairball it had formed in his mind. Chewing slowly, he focused instead on how the technology he was learning about had interconnected millions, including those who would dismember a music student.

He sipped soda from a large red paper cup and wondered about the explosion in New York. Would NYPD find the perfume? He thought about Captain Jasik and what it must be like waiting for detectives to find enough evidence to make an arrest, all the while feeling the hot breath of the Chief and the media and the DA.

It sounded claustrophobic.

He blew across his chopsticks and cleared his mind by letting it wander, releasing thoughts as they entered in a sort of water-treading meditation. Robina's face appeared, standing tall in her dark gown, her violin screaming anguished music.

What must it feel like to draw such beauty from a steel string?

He placed the cup down on the roof and stopped eating, knowing he would be hungry again soon but not caring. He descended a short ladder to the main deck and went inside to find his only suit. He could fold the charcoal jacket and strap it to the bike, but he would wear the pants. They would cover most of his riding boots.

He removed his cast and walked carefully back and forth across the room, surprised to find his leg enjoying the freedom though throbbing like crazy. From the tiny drawer of his nightstand he lifted a dark leather sheath with a long thin bloodstain on the outside, and a knife on the inside. He pulled it out with his left hand and squeezed the ivory handle carved by his grandfather from the tusk of a walrus, an animal the man had killed with simple technology: a spear and a kayak. It was a good knife, and Qigiq had used it many times growing up to prepare animals for food. He held it close to his chest and thought of his grandfather, and his father, and the life in the wilderness they had led before so-called civilization invaded Alaska when he was ten.

He strapped it above the ankle and felt the warmth of home ease into his sore leg.

The freedom in his leg insisted that he ride, so he pulled his leather jacket over a white shirt and blue tie with thin gold stripes. The titanium lump Kandy had given him thudded against his chest. He zipped the jacket and massaged the bump until it didn't poke his ribs, then limped toward the bike with helmet in hand.

© © ©

By the time he guided the bike into the parking lot off Mission Street he felt cold and as alone as a kayak fisherman lost at sea. The lot was nearly full, so he slipped the bike into a corner between a gray Audi and an almost matching steel trash bin. He waited and watched. If he had been followed, he couldn't detect it. He scanned carefully, looking for dark fenders that matched the one burned into his memory, but found nothing.

Kandy's heavy-metal loan presented a small problem. He placed the gun on the bike's gas tank and switched jackets. He strapped his helmet and riding jacket to the seat and slipped the gun into his left pants pocket. It felt out of place and threatened to drag his trousers lower, but it didn't show much under the suit coat.

He limped across the gravel parking lot with great care, happy that his ankle worked so long as he didn't bend it. When he arrived at the front of the building, he saw double doors closing behind two men and two women. He followed. A small black sign with white letters slipped into slots directed him to Ms. Robina Kidner. Once inside he hung toward the back of the room and watched. Criminals occasionally attended to see the result of their work, though in his experience, they preferred the cemetery to the funeral home.

Without speaking to anyone he worked his way slowly to the opposite side of the room to stand in line. The attendees were mostly young adults he assumed were student friends or music colleagues. He didn't see anyone who might be her parents, and wondered if they hadn't been able to travel to the west coast on such short notice, or worse, didn't care. As he approached the casket, he heard her telling him about Sally the day he had given her a motorcycle ride. He smiled inside thinking of her excitement that day. Then he remembered the sound of her voice singing *You make me feel, Mony Mony...so...Mony Mony...good.*

He thought about rich men.

He blinked damp eyes and stepped up. The face looked cool and plastic in a way she never was when alive, though beautiful, even with the gray eyeshadow she preferred applied by the funeral home. He vowed in a silent conversation with her to find out who had made this happen, and bring them to justice. Then wondered what justice would mean for a young girl like Robina. The odd weight in his left pocket intruded on his thoughts and he moved on, stopping toward the corner by a huge bouquet of yellow daisies. They made him wonder if she had a favorite flower.

He saw Kandy enter wearing a black suit. Her hair too was jet black, and asymmetric, below her ear on the right, and above it on the left. She wore long earrings that dangled in a straight line, and gold-rimmed glasses. Qigiq didn't know if she was in disguise, or this was just how she dressed for a funeral. She caught his eye and nodded, not moving her lips, as she drifted toward the back of the line to pay her respects.

As Kandy moved away from the door Veronica and Vi passed through it together. Wearing dark green and black dresses respectively, they looked even thinner than in the frolicking photos on Robina's computer. Qigiq watched them survey the crowd. Veronica wore wide sunglasses with dark lenses, maybe part of her glamour image along with the fuzzy scarf and alligator handbag. More likely, she had been crying.

Kandy arrived at his side.

"I only know Veronica and Violet," she said.

"Is Danny out of the hospital? I'd expect him to be here."

"He's been released, but I don't know how he's feeling. He's listed as a pallbearer for tomorrow." She tapped a two-page program in her hand.

"Are their friends from the concert here?"

Kandy looked up, eyes scanning the room. "I don't see Margo or Max. The girls seem to be sticking close together."

Qigiq watched the two make their way through the line until they stood arm in arm beside Robina, tears streaming down their faces, Veronica a head taller. Neither spoke.

"I think they've been crying a lot," Kandy said. "Can you imagine, two friends in a week, under such brutal circumstances? A car accident would be bad, but that video..." She leaned closer to his ear. "The guard from Robina's hospital room has been reassigned. How do things look here?"

"The Director was a bit shocked; but he understands why we need to be here, and what we're looking for."

The girls approached.

"Thanks for coming," Vi said through a sniffle.

They nodded, almost a bow, together.

"Can you find out who did it?" Vi asked.

"We're trying very hard," Kandy said.

Vi's round wet eyes stared at her.

"We won't give up."

Veronica's red-painted lips began quivering. "Why?"

"We'll figure that out too."

"Some bastard did it," Veronica said. "Some guy wanted her and couldn't have her. No one could have her, she was free." Large tears slid out from behind the sunglasses.

Qigiq wondered if Veronica was talking about Robina, or Sally, or perhaps both of her friends. He had the good sense to keep his mouth shut.

Kandy touched Veronica's elbow softly and slowly turned her towards the door.

"Let's go powder our nose."

Vi remained but turned stoic. Only the damp look in the green eyes under the glowing red of her bangs indicated anything was amiss.

Qigiq offered his arm and guided her to pictures of Robina starting from when she was a babe in arms, through a series of her holding a violin at age five, and seven, then ten, fifteen, up through her last concert and the deep blue dress. It was a beautiful display of a wonderful life.

"Do you like it?" Vi asked in a quiet voice.

"It's a lovely tribute. Did you do it?"

She nodded. "Veronica and Margo helped. We put it together this afternoon."

"That was very kind of you. And brave."

She shrugged. "We didn't know what else to do. It's so unfair."

Before Qigiq could comment on the fairness of life, Kandy and Veronica came through the doorway. He watched their approach and ached inside for the girls. He wished he had a way to comfort them, knowing his best contribution was to find the person behind this.

Kandy pulled him aside until her back was to the girls.

"You notice anything about Veronica?"

He looked over Kandy's shoulder. Veronica was talking softly with Vi.

"She's awfully thin," he said.

"Her right eye," Kandy said.

Qigiq studied the right side of Veronica's face. Then the left.

"Does she have an asymmetric face?"

"Not last time I saw her."

He looked more closely. Veronica turned her face up to view a picture in the shrine the girls had built and he saw puffiness in her right cheek. Darkness around her eye was almost completely covered by the sunglass.

"She's injured?" Qigiq said.

"I got a look while she lifted the glasses to adjust her makeup."

"Accident?"

"Claims she was carrying the poster boards for the display and tripped coming out of her apartment. Slammed her face into a banister."

Qigiq nodded. "That would do it."

They stood side by side listening to the murmur of voices. Qigiq watched a distraught Veronica struggling to stop crying, and failing.

"Do you have your car?"

"Borrowed a department tugboat."

"Got a helmet I could borrow?"

She turned to face him. "Sure, for racing, required safety equipment. It's a small though. You'll never fit that head into it."

He smiled slightly, even that making him uncomfortable.

"The trunk's open. Grab it if you want," she said.

"Thanks. I might not need it. We'll see."

Qigiq crossed diagonally to the shrine where Vi stared at the pictures as if she could make Robina come back by wishing. He tapped Veronica on the shoulder and motioned her away.

"How are you feeling?"

"I miss her so much." She dug into an alligator handbag that wasn't much larger than her cellphone, and was bulging with wads of white paper.

He touched her forearm.

"Do you like motorcycles?"

She sniffed and lifted her face to him, the strangeness of the question interrupting her grief for a brief moment.

"They make cool sounds, but I've never been on one." She paused and met his eyes, making him stare into big dark lenses. "Robina said she rode with you once."

He nodded. "Yes, she did. It was her first ride." He held his gaze on the glasses and thought about people who would destroy such youth and beauty. "I thought maybe you would like a ride later. As a tribute to Robina. We could share the thrill she found in the open air, and dedicate the ride to her."

He couldn't see well through the dark lenses, but he thought she was blinking her eyes.

"Tonight?"

"Anytime you like, but tonight would be fine. I have the bike, and a helmet you can use."

"Won't it be cold?"

"You can wear my coat."

Veronica turned and gazed for a long time at Robina's body lying between huge stacks of flowers. Her lips never stopped quivering.

"Yes...for Robina. Where should we go?"

"The Golden Gate?"

She paused before saying, "You mean like up the Stairway to Heaven for Robina?" She hesitated, her face frozen. "Okay, that would be super."

"Stay here as long as you like. There's no rush."

"Let's go now. I'm coming back in the morning."

"Do you want to tell Vi?"

Veronica turned and looked for Vi. She found her talking to two tall guys on the far side of the room.

"I'll meet you at the front door," she said, turned, and walked across the carpet with long steps.

He watched her slender body sway for a moment, then made his way around the periphery to the door, down the hall and out to the parking lot. He found Kandy's sedan parallel parked along the wall and popped the trunk. A black sport helmet was there with a dark shield. He carried it back to the front door of the funeral home and leaned against a white beam to rest his leg.

In less than a minute Veronica came through the double doors still wearing her sunglasses. She looked down at the black helmet in his hand then lifted her head. He thought she was making eye contact because she had stopped walking, but he could see nothing through the lenses in the evening light.

He held out his arm and she took it in silence. They walked slowly across the uneven gravel, her ankles wavering with each step on a heel less than a quarter inch on a side. His left leg limped along. At the bike he freed his riding jacket.

"How tall are you?"

"Five eleven without heels," she said.

He slipped the jacket over her dress. The arms fit okay, but it was three sizes too large around her waist. He zipped it up, folded it, then used the belt to synch it snug. She tucked her scarf in around the collar.

"Leather feels good," she said, her fingers stroking the front of the jacket.

He wished he had more riding gear for her, boots in particular. And pants. He hated seeing girls ride in high heels, and here he was doing it himself. He put her helmet on the seat and picked up his own so he could show her how to hold it and pull it over her head.

"You'll have to take your glasses off," he said.

She looked at him for a few seconds, then slowly inched them off her face with two hands and handed them to him. Her eye socket was a deep blue in the moonlight and seeing her straight on he could see the swelling in her right cheek bone.

He kept his mouth shut.

He held her helmet upside down so she could grab hold of the straps. She moved it gingerly into place and he raised the visor. Her little face inside was trying to smile. He buckled first her strap, pulling it snug under her narrow chin, then his own.

"For Robina," he said.

"For Robina," she echoed softly, her voice muffled by the helmet. She touched both of his shoulders. Gave him a slight hug.

When she released him he slipped her glasses into his suit coat and buttoned it. He felt naked without riding leather, but was glad she was inside a good coat. He was also glad he had removed the 38 from its pocket. He walked around the right side of the bike and swung his weak leg over, then straightened the machine. He looked over his left shoulder. She was staring at him. He flicked the passenger pegs down, pointed to her left foot and the left peg. She put the arch of her high heel on the peg and swung her right leg across the seat like mounting a horse. Though she was very light, the load on his left leg injected pain into his ankle. Without prompting she scooted her body up close to his back and wrapped both arms around him, her bare knees squeezing.

"You've never ridden?" he asked.

She shook her head and banged her helmet into his.

"I've seen motorbikes in the movies. Am I doing it right?"

"You're doing fine."

He pressed the starter, held the bike up with his right leg, stretched his left to the special peg, and pulled across the parking lot, tires crunching gravel. In ten minutes the road climbed onto the Golden Gate Bridge where he slowed to let her take in the panoramic sight of the city lights behind them, and the dark waters of San Francisco Bay two hundred feet below. And think about Robina, as he was currently doing.

Such waste. And no reason in sight.

He heard a faint sound on the wind and realized she was singing. He made out: *And as we wind on down the road, our shadows taller than our soul.*

He pulled off at the vista on the north end of the bridge and stopped the bike where they could see across the bay to the forty-eight story TransAmerica Pyramid that no longer had anything to do with TransAmerica. He remembered reading that the odd shape was a clever design response to zoning restrictions that limited floor space. He marveled at man's desire to be high in the air.

He marveled at man's capacity for destruction.

"It feels like flying on a magic carpet," she said into his ear. "I see why Robina loved it." Her body shook against his back. "I miss her so much," she whispered.

He felt her crying. He felt powerless. He felt he was failing. He felt he should have protected Robina. He took a deep breath in. He felt that if he thought hard enough, and tried hard enough, maybe, just maybe, he could protect the next one.

"Why?" she said, between sobs.

How he wished he had that answer.

"Are you warm enough?" he asked.

"My legs are cold."

He fired the bike with his thumb and made a slow circle through the curved parking lot, passing a handful of tourists out to see the city through coin operated telescopes. He saw the white back-up lights of a maroon Volvo wagon come on in his left rearview mirror. He cruised until he reached the on-ramp, then let the bike breathe as he swept onto the freeway, giving the Volvo no chance to follow.

Just in case.

~ 71 ~

Harold was asleep in the first class seat he had scored on delta.com, using all the points he could scrounge together from his six credit cards for the upgrade, when the aging DC-10 dropped onto runway number four on Friday morning at 6:11 am Eastern Daylight Time, only eight minutes late. He felt wheels rolling under him, and was surprised to realize he was already on the ground in New York City.

He had dreamed of a cave of twisty passages filled with thousands of candles hidden between stalagmites casting spear-shaped shadows onto wet curved walls. At each turn the light changed color—lavender, pink, green. Sarlin's voice echoed with a lone violin, calling him to find her as he stumbled, chasing a shifting light in the distance...always in the distance.

He came further awake with a bit of sadness. The dream had felt so warm, his longing so real. Then was shocked to realize he had an erection. He twisted his head to look and was relieved to find the other passengers monkeying with their under-seat luggage, just the way the announcement had told them not to. He sighed and tried to blink himself awake. Only 3:00 am in California. Sometimes he stayed up late working, but he never dragged himself out of bed at such a ridiculous hour.

He made his way with a backpack and a single duffle bag through the airport looking for food, decided on Starbucks as a known entity and ended up with a large coffee, two muffins that reminded him of Lili, and a banana. He resisted the urge to pull out his laptop and connect because it would slow down eating, so he watched the hundreds of people crowding the gates, even though it wasn't yet 7:00 am local time. He caught himself watching a slender redhead tucked into skin-tight white pants that reminded him of ski underwear, but his usual interest in her shape and performance skills had been replaced by a vision of Sarlin in the same outfit. She was doing something to him, and the growing obsession created tension in his gut like a noise in the woods when camping alone.

He swallowed the last of the second muffin and decided he could carry the coffee and eat the banana while walking out to find a taxi. What he found was a long line of people standing between fat blue ropes and dozens of taxis loading them like livestock being hauled to slaughter. Thirty minutes and three twenties got him to the Juilliard School at Lincoln Plaza. He followed her emailed directions and walked twelve blocks through an area he didn't trust until he stood in front of a block of buildings jammed together like a scene from *Sex and the City*. He moved his watch three hours forward. It wasn't yet 8:00.

He wanted to surprise her, not ruin her day.

He debated.

He sat on stone steps in front of her building and pulled out his laptop. As he expected, the air was full of wireless networks from nearby apartments, and almost half of them didn't require a password. He picked *ThisOnes4You* and started the messaging software, hoping she was logged in trying to contact him in California before heading off to school.

Her icon indicated inactive.

A tan Lexus drove past, splashing noise into the suburban-like quiet. He stared down at her icon and willed it to glow. He flipped into email to see if he had missed anything from work, but the inbox was empty. He sent Sarlin an email to chat him right away, hoping she was busy reading her own email. Anyone else he could text, but her parents refused to let her go near a cellphone because they insisted the radiation would affect her *qi* energy and ruin her playing.

He had waited ten minutes when his head nodded forward and his laptop almost slid down the steps. He put it away and went to the main door. The knob was black, with a thumb latch. He pressed and shook.

It opened. Somehow he thought all of New York would be locked. He climbed three flights of stairs until he stood in front of a cream painted door. A pink post-it note had three names pencilled on it; the second was S. Li.

He tapped the door gently with a single knuckle and listened. He tried a second time and heard rustling from inside, followed by a high-pitched Asian language. He hoped it was Sarlin speaking Vietnamese, but he couldn't tell.

He moved forward until his mouth was within an inch of the door.

"It's Harvey from California," he said softly.

"Who it is?" a woman's voice said.

"It's Harvey—"

The door flung open and Sarlin stood facing him wearing white panties and a yellow T-shirt with light blue sequins around the sleeves. A tiny blue rabbit hovered over the left breast and beneath dark eyes opened wide like someone had pinched her bottom.

He smiled.

She threw herself against him, both arms closing around the back of his neck, her cheek pressed firmly against his, forcing him backwards. He caught his balance by colliding his backpack with the door to the facing apartment.

She whispered, "Oh, Haro, you came see me all away from California. I'm so happy."

He smiled and hugged her with his free arm. She let go and stood back to look him over, holding his right hand in her left.

"Let's go inside," he suggested.

She trotted into the apartment towing him behind her like a child with a toy boat.

"Are your roommates here?"

She stopped in the middle of a living room where the sofa was extended into an unmade bed. He could see down a small hallway into a bedroom with two twin beds made up smooth as an army barracks, but no occupants.

"They at school. I leave soon."

Her leaving wasn't what he had hoped for. Suddenly his duffle felt heavy, so he dropped it.

"Can I stay until you get back? I flew all night and came here from the airport. I don't have a hotel yet."

She put a finger to her lips and crunched her brow.

"You stay. I leave note."

She dashed into the kitchenette off the living area and began pulling out drawers. He saw her run to the front door, open it and add a second pink Post-it note below the first one.

"I back for lunch," she said. "We eat together." She smiled.

He forced his eyes up from the little bumps on her T-shirt and returned the smile. She grabbed his duffle with two hands and dragged it across the floor toward the corner. He tossed his backpack on the unmade bed.

"I tried to get you on your computer."

She stopped dragging and frowned again.

"It not work."

"Your computer doesn't work?"

"But it's okay. Wait."

She ran on the balls of her feet like a dancer into the back bedroom, emerging less than a minute later with white ear buds flowing from beneath her black hair into a tiny silver iPod.

"I have iPod now, listen to music on walk to school."

He flashed to an Asian suitor who could speak to her without the English barrier, giving her gifts.

"That's great. Where did you get it?"

"Came in mail with perfume. Here."

She stepped up close, stood on tiptoe, and tilted her head to the left so he could sniff her neck. He smelled something wonderful, but wasn't sure it was perfume.

"Free?"

She nodded her head fast. "Before computer break, it offer me free iPod. I say yes." She smiled, still on tiptoe so their eyes were closer, not level, but closer.

"Then your computer broke?"

She continued nodding. "Yesterday."

She looked over his shoulder like there was someone coming.

"Oh-oh. I'm late."

She spun on her toes and ran toward the back room again. Harold watched, thinking she looked even better than in his imagination. He sat on the edge of the bed and fatigue instantly crawled up the center of his thighs.

She trotted back into the room before he could formulate thoughts about why anyone would give away iPods and why a brand new computer hadn't lasted even a month. She stopped in front of him in the same yellow shirt and a pair of black silk pants so tight and shiny he was reminded of the hood of a Mustang GT he once stared at for ten full minutes at a car show. Looking down, he saw she had slipped on black sandals with heels. Looking up, he figured she was maybe five percent taller. He shifted his weight to stand, but she pressed down on his shoulder with one hand and lifted his chin with the other before pressing her lips tight against his for what felt like an hour.

"I be back fast fast."

She turned and walked the way slender women move in high heels. In the kitchen, she pulled a large flat bag out of a drawer that had four brightly colored stuffed animals dangling from its single strap. She grabbed a rectangular nylon case from the corner, slipped it on like a back pack and disappeared through the door with a blown kiss.

Harold's lips were on fire, the way hot sauce felt when he put on too much. He let himself fall backward onto the bed, then dragged his body up with his elbows. He took off his long sleeve pullover and draped one of its arms over his eyes to block the daylight. He began to make a mental note to figure out what was wrong with her computer and get to the bottom of the iPod gift, but the *Cave Girl of the Candles* returned, and he was asleep.

Harold registered the sensation of his eyelids fluttering. He floated between blackness and a deep gold seeping in from below. Then he felt the hard surface under him and recalled an unmade sofa bed. He dragged his right arm up and pulled the shirt off his face. Instantly he was transported to a land of blazing red that made the space behind his eyes hurt. He rolled over and faced the wall. His body was sticky with drying sweat and a lump of blanket under his butt had produced a numb spot.

He reached down to massage it.

He remembered he was in Sarlin's New York apartment. He smiled at her smile, her hair, her little nips, her slender legs, her joy in seeing him, her scorching goodbye kiss and her cute butt. Suddenly, the red-eye flight was worth the pain in his head. He rolled over, forced one eye open far enough to find his shirt and slip it on, rolled back, pressed his face to the mattress, took a deep breath and sighed—the smell of her was everywhere.

He unlaced his boots and pushed them under the foldout couch. He was about to raid the fridge when he realized he had appeared in the middle of her morning routine, otherwise she would never have left the apartment looking like a bum lived there. He held the sheets to his face and breathed her scent in one more time before straightening the covers and lifting the iron stand back into the couch, tripping over his boots as he pushed. He found sofa cushions and three hand-embroidered silk pillows stacked in the corner and arranged them symmetrically.

He went to the kitchen and quickly learned that small Asian woman might be small because they don't eat much. He managed a bowl of Cheerios, fat-free milk and toast with butter and apricot jam. He slipped a twenty-dollar bill under the cereal—he would be the provider. While chewing the toast, he thought about finding a hotel before she got back and decided to wait. It'd be wild fun to stay in the apartment. There was so much of *her* here, and he wanted to absorb every ounce.

On the other hand: roommates.

He stepped to the bathroom and stood while viewing the cumulative effect of three women: pinks and greens and oranges, all fluffy and odorous, from the cover on the toilet seat to fringe along the top of the shower curtain. He felt like an earthling beamed to a distant planet to study an alien culture.

He wandered to the back bedroom to look for the laptop. A couple of drawers in a scratched dresser held undergarments he would love to see her wear, but no computer. He went back to the living room but the only furniture besides the bed was a row of music stands with folding chairs.

He was feeling stupid for not asking where she stored it, returned to the kitchen, checked the cabinets and on a whim, opened the refrigerator. He bent over and behind three rows of Chobani greek yogurt with active cultures was the rectangle of a laptop, a light at the corner pulsing in sleep mode. He shook his head, not knowing which was worse: her putting it there, or him thinking she would.

He pulled the machine out, knocking over a yogurt that bounced off the floor but didn't open. He carried it to the sofa and unzipped his pack to get a power supply—not wanting to guess where she might keep hers—then lifted the screen.

Her desktop was a picture of a room with a ring of candles, making the computer appear three-dimensional. The rust-colored carpet made him realize it was the same room that he was in now, and the candles were the very ones Sarlin had lit for his birthday.

She said the machine had stopped working yesterday, but it seemed to be working now. He reached for the keyboard and stopped just before his fingertips made contact. Whatever was wrong might still be running.

He dragged out his own laptop and a cable. Connecting the two machines with the high-speed wire let him start the debugger on his computer and probe hers. The graphic display of the memory told him exactly what had happened in one glance: the Invisible Hand. Music files had disappeared; she concluded the machine was broken.

His eyes flicked back and forth between the memory layout and the picture of unlit candles. Two things bothered him, and his subconscious was struggling to put them into words so his left brain could engage. First, why the hell was the Hand on this machine? He had given Sarlin a legal account at Silver Platter.

Roommates.

And had the Hand posted her identity? He frowned, wanting to know if her picture was on the machine. But first...

Yes, the Hand was still running.

How was that even possible? He had tested its self-erase function personally. If his code remained active on a machine where real computer scientists hung out...

He scrolled slowly through the inside of her machine watching. He took a snapshot and compared it to saved maps he had from testing.

They differed.

He blew a fast stream of air up from his lower lip.

He asked for details.

The program dutifully drew orange highlights around a dozen changes. This Hand had a different graphics file, randomly deleted songs instead of removing them all, and didn't post results to blogs.

He poked around until he could open the graphics file and his screen filled with an offer for a free iPod, claiming his was defective. He leaned against the back of the sofa—Lili's Second Insertion Theory was right. Here was a new version, not the one he and Sarlin had released. Someone else had access to the Constructor. But an iPod offer? His stomach felt hollow as he realized he had never tested two versions roaming the Web at the same time.

His machine bleeped and popped open a high-priority alert window. He read it without moving. Lili.

Must talk to you ASAP. Something has happened.

He looked at the two computers and wanted to pursue Hand #2 to find out what it was doing. Lili was right, something had happened. He pulled out his cellphone and punched her number.

"Volker."

"Hi Lili, Harold."

"Oh my God, oh my God, Harold, I have to talk to you."

"Lili, calm down, you are talking to me."

"Where are you? We have to talk?"

"You said that, Lili. I'm in New York for a three-day weekend."

"New York!" she screamed. "You can't be. Oh my God. What are you...never mind. We have to talk."

"I'm with you Lili. So talk."

He could hear hair swish over the handset as she flicked her head back and forth, likely making sure no one was close enough to hear her. She dropped her voice to a whisper.

"Harold. Have you seen the Times? In New York, I mean. There's an article. Is it...I mean...could it be...uh...shit, I mean shoot...is it okay to talk on these?"

"No Lili, it's not. If this is about trade secrets, Del specified we need to use a scrambled line. Hang up, put your chip in, and I'll call you back."

"OK, OK. Oh Harold, I don't know——"

"Say goodbye Lili. And stay by the phone."

"OK, OK. Bye Harold. Bye."

She hung up.

He found his scrambler chip in a tiny zipper pocket inside his backpack, right where it was supposed to be. He opened the phone, positioned it carefully and snapped the back closed. He powered the phone off and restarted it, watching for the scrambler notification. Then he dialed Lili's number.

"Volker."

"Got your chip in?"

"Yes."

"Okay, we're secure. Now, what is this about?"

She sniffled. "I just saw an article in the Times online. A girl in New York has been killed by an exploding iPod. Or at least that's what they think, no one knows for sure."

"An iPod?"

"She was walking down the street and there was a flash and she fell off the curb into traffic. I don't know what to do."

"Why do you have to do anything? I don't understand."

"The article says a free-iPod offer might have something to do with the explosion. And get this: they're even guessing someone is punishing music pirates."

Harold touched his computer and reopened the graphics he had seen earlier.

"I still don't get it, Lili. What does this have to do with us? We're not sending anyone iPods."

"I know, Harold. But that offer. They have a screenshot in the Times."

"What about it?"

"It looks like a Hand window to me." A silent pause. "Are we out of control?"

You are, he thought, but she was technically his boss.

"Lili, what do you mean, 'it looks like a Hand window?'"

"I mean the window size and location. And it pops up out of nowhere."

"So what if it's ours?" he said.

"So what? Then we're somehow connected to people dying. What's gone wrong, Harold?"

"Hold on a minute, Lili. We're not shipping bombs. Someone might be, and maybe they even used our software; but *we* didn't do it."

"We put the Hand out there to delete songs."

"That's a long way from causing bodily harm." Perhaps it was the word bodily, but he thought of Sarlin. "Lili, where's this article?"

"Home page of nytimes dot com. Everyone is speculating; the blogs are ranting; facebookers are afraid to play their songs. There's a twitter tag, let me look...here, go follow #musicterror. It's a big mess and we're right in the middle of it. This, after those horrible DOG movies."

"Who knows, Lili?"

"Knows what?"

"Knows we're behind the virus that is deleting files."

"And the one offering the free iPod," she insisted.

He looked at the two machines sitting in front of him like a pair of puppies waiting to be petted.

"Maybe. Who?"

The line was quiet for almost thirty seconds.

"I don't think anyone outside the company knows. The article never mentions us."

He breathed easier. If the company name got in the papers, he'd *never* make money from his stock options.

"Not to be crass, Lili, but what's happening to sales?"

More silence.

He waited.

"You didn't just ask me that," she said.

"I did. Just because there's madness somewhere in the world doesn't mean we get to stop doing our jobs."

Shuffling of paper. Tapping on a keyboard.

"Hour to hour comparison from two weeks ago. Up twenty-seven percent. I can't believe you care about this."

His brain stopped like it had been sprayed with liquid nitrogen. Two words were visible through the frost: *Sarlin, iPod.*

"Lili, did the article mention perfume?"

"Yes. The iPods are delivered with it."

"What kind?"

"What kind of...oh, let me look."

He stood and started pacing back and forth behind the computers.

"J Lo. Something called Deseo."

He stopped.

"You sure?"

"Of course I'm sure. I'm reading from the Times website."

His heart started banging to get out of his chest.

"Does it say anything specific about the bomb?"

"You mean the iPod?"

"Uh, yeah, I guess that's what I mean."

"One of three incidents was confirmed as an iPod exploding. The other two are speculation, but they found the shipping box and perfume."

He took long strides until he was in the bathroom.

"What's a Deseo bottle look like?"

"You want to know what the bottle looks like? What does that have to do—"

"Please Lili, humor me. Look it up on the web and describe it."

"Wait a second. Here. The catalog says 'encased in a dazzling aquamarine and golden diamond bottle.' Does that help?"

He opened the medicine cabinet and saw pill bottles from *Walgreens*. Below the sink he found Cottonelle toilet tissue and Puffs boxes.

"Harold?"

"Yeah?"

"What are we going to do?"

He turned the corner into the little bedroom in back. There were two four-drawer dressers. Both of them were covered with bottles of stuff.

He walked up to the first chest and scanned from bottle to bottle with his eyes, not touching anything.

"There isn't anything to do," he said. "We already showed the detectives what we found on those videos. They even have the machine."

"But this free iPod. It could be our software," she said.

"It's not the one I released in New York. It can't be."

"But shouldn't we tell someone?"

"What, Lili? That we released the Internet virus deleting millions of files around the world? Think Blake will approve that?"

He moved to the second chest, it was a bit lower. He was careful, checking one bottle at a time, keeping track of where his eyes had been.

Her voice was quiet. "No, he would never approve that. It just seems like we should tell those detectives everything and help them figure out what's going on. People are dying, Harold. Young people, like you and me."

And Sarlin, he thought. And Sarlin.

"There."

"What?" she said.

"Uh, nothing. There isn't much we can say Lili, without making everything we do public. That would destroy the company and everyone's jobs. For what? Because you think might-maybe-perhaps this free iPod thing has something to do with our technology?"

He picked up the Deseo bottle and took it with him to the living room. He sat on the sofa and stared at the computers.

"We don't really have proof of that, do we?" he said.

"Well, no, but it sure looks like ours. And those movies are ours, so maybe this is too."

"We'll have to figure out a way to verify the free-offer software. Sound like a good next step?" he said.

"Yes. If we can verify it's ours, I'll talk to Mr. Blake."

"Okay, Lili. I've got to go, I'm three hours ahead of you. I'll let you know if I find anything."

"Thanks, Harold. Enjoy your weekend. Please call right away if you find anything at all. I'm so worried."

"Bye, Lili." He hung up.

"Oh, it's ours all right," he said to the empty music stands.

His mind flashed to the cave girl beckoning him, waving her fingers like she was playing a harp, her body exploding into a giant flame.

He glanced at his watch, almost noon. He had to separate Sarlin from that free iPod. His head jerked back and forth as if he expected to find her in the apartment. His eyes landed on the computers. He decided to leave them running so he could track more later. She told him on his last visit where she went to school, but all he could remember was "not Juilliard."

He stared at the music stands.

Of course.

How many could there be?

He raced back to his laptop, put in the address of the apartment he was standing in and asked for music schools in the area.

Manhattan School of Music. That was it.

He told Google to show directions.

Almost three miles.

The image of Sarlin walking out of the apartment rose in his eyes. How did she get there in heels? A bicycle?

He grabbed a jacket from his backpack, verified he had his wallet and phone and ran down the stairs two at a time, not stopping until he was standing in the middle of the street. There wasn't much traffic so he turned and ran north until he reached a cross street. He stood in the middle of the intersection like a cop directing traffic until he saw a cab coming from his left.

He stepped into its path.

The cab driver stuck his head out the window and screamed at him in a foreign language. He ran up to the driver's door and handed him a hundred-dollar bill he kept as backup cash.

"Manhattan School of Music, West 122nd Street. There's another hundred if you can get there in less than five minutes."

The man stopped yelling, crumpled the bill into his pocket and started the cab rolling slowly. Harold yanked the door open and jumped in the back where a white-haired woman in a gray coat sat with both hands on a cane.

"I'm sorry, Ma'am, I don't mean to trouble you, but I have a serious problem."

She turned to run her eyes up and down his body.

"Boy, if you have a a hundred dollars to give a cabbie, it can't be too serious."

"Did you read the paper today," he said. "About the girl who was killed by the explosion."

"Oh yes, I saw that. Crazy gadgets these kids carry."

Harold tried to keep his voice slow and even.

"Well, my girlfriend got one yesterday just like it, and she doesn't know it's dangerous."

"Did you hear that, driver," she said, raising her voice and tapping the cane against the back of the front seat. "Step on it, you get to be a hero and save this young man's girl. And get paid for it to boot."

The cab accelerated and passed a VW bus on the right. The bus driver honked long and hard.

"Is she pretty?"

Harold smiled. "Yes Ma'am, she's very pretty. And plays the violin."

"Oh, a music student is she? So many in this town."

He nodded.

"Well, I hope she can make a decent living. Life can be hard on artists. I know my grandpappy could never sell his paintings."

"She doesn't have to worry about money, Ma'am. I'm an engineer."

"In New York?"

"No Ma'am, I live in California. A place called Silicon Valley."

The cab turned hard to the left through a yellow light. Two more horns blared.

"Oh, those girls shouldn't do that to themselves. Wait until they get to be my age."

He thought about explaining the difference between silicone and silicon.

"Coming up on your left," the driver said.

Harold dug out his other hundred and passed it up between the seats.

The cabbie waved his hand.

"One's enough. Keep it for your girl."

Harold thought maybe New York wasn't as bad as people said.

The cab screeched to a halt.

He jumped out, yelled, "Thank you," to the driver, and "Thank you, goodbye Ma'am," before he dashed through traffic to the entrance, up steps and into a corridor.

He stopped cold.

A long hallway with rows of doors on either side faced him. He needed a main office. He walked down the hall until a bald man stepped through a doorway.

"Excuse me, could you tell me where the office is?" Harold asked.

"Surely. Which office would you like? Admissions is that way, Finance is that way, and Concert Management is upstairs."

"I need to find a student who is attending classes right now."

"Hmm, well. Perhaps you should try Admissions. They have access to schedules."

"Thank you."

Harold turned and headed in the direction the man had pointed.

His phone rang.

"Haro?" A voice said softly.

"Sarlin, oh thank heaven. Where are you?"

"At my home. But you not here. I go to neighbor to call you."

"'I'm at the Manhattan School looking for you."

She giggled. "Really?"

"Yes, really. Sarlin, dear Sarlin, do you have that iPod you showed me this morning?"

"Yes, Brahms is playing in my other ear."

His mind saw a fireball vaporize her, the apartment and both computers.

"I'll explain when I get back. But please, turn it off and get as far away from it as you can."

"But why, Haro? I like it so much."

"Please Sarlin. Just for a few minutes. Put it as far away from you as possible. And turn it off. I'll buy you a brand new one in any color you want. Or a Touch so you can get email from the café."

"Okay. For you. Hurry back."

If she only knew how he had hurried over.

"I'll be there in ten minutes," he said. "Promise you'll get away from the iPod, right away. No listening to the rest of Brahms, OK?"

He heard a soft sigh.

~ 72 ~

Harold sat on the closed sofa bed watching Sarlin learn to operate her new toy. She giggled every time it reacted to the touch of her fingertips. He was amazed such a simple device could give her so much pleasure, but his mind was on the little silver iPod she had stowed in the bottom drawer of a heavy wooden dresser, just like he had asked. She had even closed the bedroom door.

That was the easy part. Now he felt like a tightrope walker halfway between two skyscrapers...like that French guy in *Man on Wire*. He couldn't leave a bomb in her apartment, but he couldn't very well take it onto a plane.

"Look Haro, it say find network."

She was holding the Touch out for him to read. It had found the same networks he had located from the front steps earlier. His eyes drifted down her black slacks, one leg over the other, the top one dangling a shoe by the toe strap. He noticed for the first time her toes were painted the same deep red as the violin necklace she wore.

"Can I join?" she asked.

He pointed. "See those locks. You can't join those, they need a password. You can join any of the others."

She frowned as she read down the list, then broke into a wide smile.

"I'll join PoodleNet."

He watched the machine hook up and update her email.

"Try to send me an email," he said.

Her face tensed as if she were playing a particularly difficult passage, the tip of her tongue protruding from the side of her mouth.

He knew the right thing was to call Qigiq and have him send a team who had the technology to deal with bombs. That move would put him at the center of a thousand questions, most of which he didn't want to answer. How did he know Sarlin? Why was he in town just now? They wouldn't believe the birthday story even if he were willing to tell them, and if they started asking about how she got the iPod and examined her computer...

His laptop burped its incoming email sound. He glanced at Sarlin without turning his head. She was grinning and bouncing up and down on the sofa like she had to go to the bathroom. He leaned forward and opened the message.

Hello H, I am so much fun having. Thank you for new Touch.

He clicked *reply* and leaned to his left so she couldn't read the screen.

Hello Sarlin, I will think of Touching you every time I read your email.

He pressed send and closed the window before leaning back. She looked down at her little screen and waited.

He could rent a car and drive to California, maybe put the thing in the trunk in an ammunition case, something solid he could get at a pawnbroker for cash. But he'd have to explain why he needed a week off. And if he drove fast like those *Cannonball Run* guys racing coast to coast, he'd be stopped.

And asked questions.

And searched.

She was frowning. Her toy hadn't yet retrieved its email. He wondered if he could do an anonymous drop of the iPod at a police station without anyone seeing him. That seemed unlikely in a place as dense as New York. He cursed silently. He wanted to be close to Sarlin's lovely body, not solve problems.

He had to get that thing out of the apartment.

He felt a tap on his left arm and turned. She reached across him and wrapped her soft fingers around his right wrist and pulled his hand toward her. She interlaced her fingers with his and looked up. Her face was relaxed, not smiling, not frowning, but open...and kind, he thought. She unlaced her fingers and pulled his hand to her left cheek, tilting her face into it. Her eyes drifted closed. She licked her lips and dragged his hand down across her throat and the red violin pendant he had sent her and down between her small breasts and finally directly over her left one. He listened to her breath, feeling his body fill with a kind of swirling tension. He could feel her heart pump under his hand. He leaned forward and kissed her.

His head clouded. He didn't move, or want to move, or think. The touch of her lips, full, wet, soft, filled him, and the train of problem-solving logic that filled his brain at all waking hours peeled away until he lost track of time or place.

The first sensation that returned was the hot hardness of her nipple pressing into the palm of his hand, then of an insistent alert sounding from his laptop. He peeked at the screen with one eye. A high priority mail alert was flashing. He moved away, touching her leg with his left hand to maintain physical contact, and leaned forward.

The message was from Sarlin. He laughed.

"How did you do that?"

She held up her Touch.

"I write. Then take your hand."

"And you pressed send while I was kissing you."

383

She looked down at her lap.

"Very clever," he said.

She met his eyes.

"You not mad?"

He shook his head.

"Of course not. Should I read it?"

Her eyes glowed above her smile. He opened the message.

Dear my Hero, I like you kissing me. Kiss again.

He turned back to find her looking down at her lap again. Her cheek was slightly red, he hoped from the kiss. He took a deep breath.

"Do you have to go back to school today?"

She nodded.

He forced himself not to swear, thinking it could break the building connection.

"Now, right?"

She nodded ever so slightly.

He got up and walked around the two computers to her feet. He knelt down and slipped her shoe on and buckled the narrow strap around her ankle. His fingertips grazed her anklebone and sizzled.

"I can do that," she said.

He looked up. Her dark eyes were wide and her back stiff.

He smiled. "I want to, Sar. Is it ok?"

Her head moved slowly up and down.

He retrieved the other shoe from the floor, helped her switch legs, gently strapped it on, then lifted her up to her feet.

"I'll be here when you get back."

She smiled and bear hugged him with her cheek turned against his chest. He started to hug her back but she released him and raced to the door.

He stretched out on the sofa and checked his watch. Not yet one o'clock on a Friday off work. Two computers stared at him, both running software from his hands. Well, not off, he was sort of working; he was always sort of working. Pretty much everything he did was to help Silver Platter make it big. He considered options, pulled out his cellphone and dialed. The number rang unanswered, not even a machine. He dialed again: a young woman's voice.

"Hello."

He sat up.

"Uh, yes, hello. Is Detective Qigiq available?"

"Sure."

He glanced down at his phone to verify he had dialed the Detective's home number. He put the phone back to his ear and listened. The woman was talking, maybe with the phone still in her hand.

"Keejee. A guy wants to talk to you." A pause. "Who's calling please?"

He hesitated. He was about to push a big ball over the edge of a steep hill and he didn't want to end up like those Zorbing dudes in New Zealand trapped inside an out-of-control air-ball as it slammed into a giant rock.

"Hello hello, are you there?" the girl asked.

"Uh, yes. This is Harold Zeto from Silver Platter. I met with Detective Qigiq yesterday. I have more information for him."

He heard her voice call out, sounding distant through the phone. Then a clatter.

"Hello, Harold, I didn't expect to hear from you so soon."

"I ran into something unusual and I'm not sure what do to about it. After we met yesterday, I took a red-eye flight to New York to visit a friend. When I got here she showed me an iPod she got in the mail. The strange thing is, it was free."

"Did she win it?" Qigiq asked.

"No. And I saw an article in today's *Times* where a girl was killed by an explosion. The article said it might be related to the Pod Murders."

"Pod Murders?"

"That's how it referred to iPods exploding."

"I appreciate your calling, Harold. Did the iPod come packaged with anything else?"

"Yeah. My friend demoed it for me. Some kind of perfume by J Lo, you know, the movie star pop singer."

He heard Qigiq breathe.

"Harold, you have a bomb on your hands. Where is it now?"

"A dresser in the back room. I figured if it exploded, that was the best thing I had to contain it."

"Good. Can you stay out of the apartment?"

"Well, that's the thing. There are three girls living here and I don't think they have anywhere else to go. They're college students on visas. I mean, I hate to get them mixed up in police business. For all I know, their families will pull them out of the U.S. if they hear about this, and they'll never get an education."

"Three college girls?" Qigiq said.

"They're music students here in New York."

The line was quiet long enough for Harold to become concerned.

"That's why I called. I was hoping you could get it out of here without involving them, or me for that matter."

"I could have NYPD pick it up on an anonymous tip, but they'll want to search the premises."

"I could move it."

"Not safe," Qigiq said.

"She's been using it for a couple of days. Nothing has happened. How do we know this one is a bomb?"

"The perfume. All three of the explosions included the Deseo."

"Oh yeah, that was the name." Reality registered. "All of them?"

"Yes, Harold, just those three. Eleven people who received iPods contacted us. None received the perfume and the devices turned out to be harmless."

Harold sidestepped across the living room until he was in the kitchen, as far from the bedroom as possible. "You really think it's a bomb?"

"Absolutely. Please stay away from it, and keep the girls away from it."

"They're not here right now."

"How long do we have?"

"My friend won't be back for a couple of hours. Maybe they're all on the same schedule."

"Can you stay there and keep everyone away from it?"

"Sure," he said, realizing too late he wasn't sure what he had just agreed to.

"Let me see what I can do."

Harold ended the call and stared at the fridge, wondering if it would be a better spot for the bomb. No, he wasn't going to touch it. He carefully returned to the sofa and stretched out. He closed his eyes and watched mental simulations of the bedroom door being blown off and tossed through the opposing wall and into the kitchen.

His next mental image was of a rubber mallet pounding against the inside of a chalk-colored skull. The skull exploded in a shower of white powder as he opened his eyes to green striped wall paper. The pounding continued. He rolled, stumbled off the sofa and stood. The pounding grew louder. He made his way to the door and wished for a peephole before cracking it open.

The largest Afro-American male he had ever seen faced him. He wore a gray XXXL hooded sweatshirt and black jeans with the inseam between his knees. Black boots with big round toes containing titanium, according to the label on the side, protruded from the jeans. He held what looked like a small Army tank in his right hand like a big suitcase. For such a huge man, he spoke softly.

"Hi. You Harold?"

Harold nodded slowly.

"Kandy says you have a package."

Harold's mind thought Candy, Candy...do I know a Candy? This is

Sarlin's apartment. I'm in New York. Then the right neurons fired.

"Qigiq's partner. Sure, come on in."

"Uh-uh. You come out." A big finger pointed. "There's a package in there."

Arguing seemed like a foolish idea, so Harold stepped through the doorway.

The man placed the machine on the floor and Harold read the side.

iRobot 510 PackBot.

"Who are you?"

"Today, my name is PodMan. Let's go."

The man turned and danced down the stairs like a running back. He was waiting for Harold at the front steps. He motioned and started strolling down the street, Harold half-jogged to keep up.

"We're going to put your package in the containment vessel that's piggybacked on my little friend Moro up there. I checked all the apartments and no one answered. You picked a good time of day."

PodMan turned toward the street and almost ran Harold over. He opened the side door of a tall gray van and stepped inside.

Harold stopped at the curb. The interior looked like a command post for a Halo team. Or a mobile TV production unit.

"Come in Harold, close the door. You know the layout, and we don't have much time."

Harold ducked into the van and slid the door shut, dropping the interior into near darkness. He took an empty seat in front of a pair of big flat displays.

PodMan picked up what looked to Harold like a game controller.

"Where?"

"Bedroom. Bottom drawer of the tall dresser."

He saw the monitors come alive with a video image of the open door to Sarlin's apartment. The door came closer as the robot began moving.

"Direction?"

"To the right." The image swung like a kid with a GoPro camera on his bicycle helmet. "That door on the side is the bathroom. The door that's closed leads to the bedroom."

In moments the machine was to the door. He watched a gripper hand reach out, spin the knob and push. Then the images shifted as it looked around.

"That one in back?"

Harold nodded, realized his mistake. The man's eyes were on the displays. "Yes. Bottom drawer. I don't know where in the drawer, I didn't put it there."

The pictures followed as the machine climbed up on the first bed, dipped down, and climbed onto the second. From there it peeked over the side and reached for the bottom drawer. PodMan had it work back and forth between two knobs to get it open.

The drawer was full of lingerie and shirts. Moro's hand started moving things around.

"There's a white wire," PodMan said.

The wire led Moro to the tiny music player.

PodMan stopped, the image of the player ten times life-size on the screen.

"The entire front is a Play button," PodMan said.

Harold agreed.

"OK, Moro. We go for the narrow side."

The gripper moved into the drawer, lifted a bra out of the way and dropped it to the floor. Went back in and positioned on either side of the iPod. In slow motion, the gripper closed.

Nothing bad happened.

Still in slow motion, the arm lifted the tiny device from the drawer, dragging the white wires behind. As it came out, the earbuds caught and dragged along a pair of peach panties.

"Buy her a new pair," PodMan said, as the image swung and Moro lowered panties, wires and iPod through a five-inch opening in the thick box on the robot's back, then rotated a knob to close the hole.

"We're half-way," PodMan said.

Moro's head spun until the monitors showed the kitchen. The robot moved back to the front door, stuck its head out, and twisted to look in the hallway.

"All clear," PodMan said. "Check the street."

Harold pulled open the side door and stuck his head out, feeling like he was doing exactly what Moro had just done. "Two women, walking away from us."

"Current distance?"

Harold counted cars, multiplied by ten. "About seventy feet."

"Give me a hundred," PodMan said.

Harold waited. The two women stopped and faced each other, talking. "They've stopped at car eight."

"Tell me if they head this way, Moro's coming home."

Harold swiveled his eyes between the two women on the street and the monitors showing Moro's descent down the stairs. The women were still talking when Moro's grip reached for the knob to the front door.

"Distance?"

"No change."

"How about you go chase them?" PodMan said.

Harold turned to look at him, but the man was staring at the screen and Moro was moving through the door. If the women saw Moro, they'd probably want to pet it.

Harold jumped out of the van and slid the wide door shut. He turned up his collar, looked down at the ground and banged on the side of the van with his fist. As he hoped, the noise caused the two women to look up.

He dropped his eyes to the sidewalk and strolled toward the women with both hands shoved deep into the pockets of his jeans. They watched. The one on the right lifted her eyes, and maybe saw Moro. Harold couldn't be sure because the robot was behind him. He walked a little faster and lifted his face to stare at the women.

That worked.

Whoever he was, they didn't want to know what had just gone on in that van. They turned and started walking. He clomped on the sidewalk extra loud so they would know he was still coming until they turned right at the corner, both twisting their necks to see if he was following them.

After they disappeared, Harold spun around and saw Moro rumbling down the sidewalk toward the back of the van. If there had been a tree, he would have hidden behind it. Instead he stepped between a green Ford and a blue Honda, ducked and waited.

The sound of Moro's motors reached him for about a minute and stopped. He looked up. PodMan was stepping out of the van. He ran back.

"Tell Kandy PodMan has a gift for her, let's hook up."

He nodded. "I'll call her right away."

"Thanks, Harold." The big man reached out and they shook hands like partners after a heist.

Harold watched the truck pull away. Unlike Moro, it had no markings. He lifted his phone and hovered his finger over Dreeson's number. He ran back up the four flights and found the door standing open. He crossed the living room to his dual computer work area, moved the power cord from Sarlin's machine to his, and sat down.

He opened his debugger. Blake had told him to tell the detectives whatever they wanted to know, but that had been regarding the DOG research going on in China. What would Blake want him to do with this? It was Platter technology, and awfully close to the software he and Sarlin had released. He couldn't imagine Blake wanted cops nosing around Cupertino. The boss could tap dance a good story about how fingerprinting legal music files was security for the customer, but it wasn't the whole truth.

He thought about calling Lili, she could ask Blake directly if she didn't freak out first. Or he could tell the detectives and hope they would protect their source. He knew about information wanting to be free though...Blake would eventually find out. He went to the fridge and rummaged around for the Coke he had seen earlier behind the low-sodium soy sauce. The top hissed as he pulled, making him think of an explosion. He paced the small living room and thought hard about the future. Halfway to an empty can he sat down and studied his probe again. There was no mistaking the footprint. He dialed.

"Dreeson."

"Hello, Detective, this is Harold Zeto. I have a message for you from PodMan."

She laughed. "So today's he's PodMan? Descriptive if not creative. What did the big guy have to say?"

"He said to tell you he has a gift for you. And, I quote, 'let's hook up.'"

"Good news, thanks."

"He doesn't waste time."

"His creed is: 'Why go slow if you can go fast?'"

"He wasn't here long."

"Where is here, Harold?"

"I gave you the address."

"I mean, why are you there?"

"A girl I know lives here."

"You have a girl in New York? The commute must be tough."

"I'm learning to use red-eye flights." He tried to laugh but the exploding skull intruded.

"How did you find our exploding friend?"

"Times article scared me."

He heard tapping in the background.

"Anything else?"

He stared at his probe. The system appeared to be deadlocked. He should have tested multiple copies active simultaneously, but he never even considered it.

"The free offer, the way it came in."

"How's that?"

"Looks like a virus rather than standard SPAM."

"You saw it?"

He swallowed a mouthful of Coke, hard.

"I analyzed Sarlin's machine, that's my, uh, the girl I know. There was something weird running, but I couldn't identify it before it went away."

He put himself on red alert. He was lying and must remain perfectly consistent. He reminded himself: *She's a detective.*

"That's weird," she said. "It was still running even though she already had the iPod? Must have been days."

Two, he thought.

"I can't tell for sure when it showed up. It might have been inside for a long time before making the offer. You know, waiting for a trigger of some type. Hard to tell how these things work until you can take them apart."

"My friend Ferd complains about viruses all the time. He's trying to isolate the free offer too."

Harold wondered how long it would take a competent computer scientist to associate DoomTunes with the free offer. He had done it in seconds, but he knew exactly what to look for. It bothered him that someone named Ferd was also looking. He didn't think Dreeson would have dumb friends.

"Has he had any luck? Maybe I could help him?"

"Thanks for the offer, Harold, I'll let him know. And thanks for calling us on the iPod, we appreciate your help."

He hesitated. "I appreciate your not sending a bunch of cops over and scaring my friends."

"My pleasure. I don't like having cops hanging around either, makes me nervous." She laughed a kind of little steam engine huffing sound. "Enjoy your weekend."

He terminated the call and mentally reviewed what he had said, wanting to kick himself for saying "free offer." But he had covered it well enough.

Then he leaned back against the couch and smiled at the thought of the cops calling him in to help analyze viruses he had written.

~ 73 ~

Kandy pulled in beside Qigiq's rental bike, which reminded her to get her helmet back. The seat was damp. She carried a small pink box under one arm, walked the length of the dock and looked over his houseboat. Friday, yet the entire marina was quiet. She glanced at her phone, 12:03 pm, and tapped three, pause, three times on his back door. Feet shuffled across the floor inside.

The door swung open.

Kandy stared at the blueish-purple spreading around Veronica's right eye. She wore a white T-shirt the length of a micro-dress with a big red oval logo on the chest. Kandy couldn't tell if she was wearing anything else.

"Oh hi," Veronica said. Then she called out, "Keejee, it's for you," turned and trotted across the kitchen linoleum, leaving the door open for Kandy.

"Hi," Kandy said to the retreating figure.

She stepped into the kitchen and closed the door. The aroma of coffee was strong in the room, but a glance told her there was less than a cup left. She dropped the box on the table and walked over to start another pot. Before she got it going, Qigiq drifted in wearing jeans and a flannel shirt, barefoot. He was holding a half-empty green mug.

"Hello, Detective," he said. "To what do I owe the pleasure?"

Her eyes ran over him.

"We've got the loaded iPod moving"

"Harold's?"

She nodded. "Marco the Magnificent got it for us. It'll be set up later today."

Qigiq put his cup on the table and sat down facing her.

"What do you think it will tell us?"

A shower started running.

"Is she doing okay?" Kandy asked.

"Torn up badly about her friends. Tries to hide it by being cheerful."

"What about that eye?"

He shook his head. "Still sticking to the story about the bannister."

Kandy watched the coffee drip, pointed to the box on the table.

"Apple strudel. Has fruit in it." She laughed.

He smiled. "What a partner." He snapped the tape holding the top closed, pulled out a long pastry with white stripes dribbled across the top, and took a huge bite.

"You going to the cemetery?" she asked.

He nodded.

"Need a ride?"

He shook his head. "I'll take the bike."

"How about your friend?"

"Vi is picking her up in a couple of minutes. They've been on and off the phone all morning." Qigiq eyed the coffee pot, now dripping furiously. "Anything new on the bomb?"

Kandy pulled the pot out of the machine and poured two cups, carried them over.

"Marco said the case had been opened by someone who knew how to do it—not a scratch, then epoxied closed. He's getting it set up."

"Set up?"

"Friend with a virtual reality system." She glanced at her phone. "Ferd should be able to access in a few hours."

"Impressive," he said, finishing the strudel. He eyed the box. "Want one?"

"Not so hungry today. Bombs, music players, random deaths…"

He broke a new pastry in half slowly.

"With one to examine, maybe Ferdinand can help."

She looked up, but her face didn't glow with hope.

"Might figure out who's making them," he said. "And where. Find the source. How many thousands of names has this DoomTunes thing posted? How can we stop someone mailing to that list?" He stared at the wall. "And why is a terrorist's explosion so small? Doesn't seem designed to kill. That New York girl fell in front of a taxi."

"Warning? Induce fear? Of what?" She paused. "You think they're random?"

He stopped chewing.

"No. Their ages are too close."

"Sally and Robina are connected. And Danny," Kandy said.

"Three of five, if this last one is really a bomb."

"Sixty percent," she said. "Zeto knows one of the five. Seem strange to you?"

"All of this is strange to me. Computers connected to other computers that move names and pictures around without people even knowing it." He sipped the fresh coffee. "How many people know Zeto has a girl in New York?"

"I'll find out."

"He liked that Lili girl," Qigiq said. "Did you see his eyes?"

She nodded. "He for sure likes the way she looks."

"Likes the way who looks?" Veronica asked as she walked into the kitchen with a gentle sway like she was flowing down a modeling runway. Her nearly six-foot frame was draped in black to below the knee. She was wearing sunglasses again.

Qigiq said, "A woman who works over at Silver Platter."

"Is she cute?" She turned to Kandy. "Is this all right? I got it in town this morning."

"It's perfect," Kandy said. "I think most guys would say she's cute."

Veronica's head turned to Kandy then back at Qigiq. He couldn't see her eyes.

"Can I meet her?"

Kandy stifled a laugh and looked down at her coffee.

There was a light tap at the door.

"That's Vi," Veronica said. Then, as if realizing where she was going for the first time, silent tears appeared on her cheeks.

Qigiq stood and Veronica stepped forward and gave him a little hug. Then she turned to Kandy and waited for her to stand up to get a hug too.

"Bye," she said, turning and opening the door.

Qigiq caught a glimpse of Violet in black slacks before the door swung closed.

~ 74 ~

Watching the coffin being lowered into a rectangular hole reminded Qigiq how unfairly the world turned. While his face remained calm, his mind flipped through the circumstances that brought him to this graveside, flashed to an image in which he was stabbing the shadowy perp repeatedly with his ivory-handled knife, then to the quiet contemplation of a young girl's soul, whatever and wherever it might be.

He stood through the service, the lowering, a small chorus singing a requiem, the tossing of soil, more prayer. He watched faces in the crowd, recognizing many from the funeral home. Margo drifted over and stood beside him, but didn't speak. Professor Walters mingled with a group of three girls and two boys that were likely from his class. Veronica and Vi took turns holding each other with Max standing behind them like a watchful bodyguard.

His eyes settled for a moment on a slender section of shaven hair on Danny's head where he had been treated. Danny's eyes stared a hundred miles away, blinking erratically, but dry.

Qigiq tried to imagine losing two beautiful friends in the space of a week.

He tried to imagine a lover turned killer.

He tried to imagine each face disassembling a tiny music player and filling it with explosives.

He imagined faces that weren't there: Blake, Zeto, even the young girl Lili, all of whom had complete access to Silver Platter technology.

He tried hard to connect all the dots in the paper in his pocket.

The crowd drifted away until only he, Kandy and men waiting to finish their job remained. Finally he turned and Kandy followed until they reached his bike parked on the grass behind her rented Mini. He watched the gravediggers begin their work.

"What now?" Kandy asked.

"I wish I could take a knife to the perp."

"Now look who's Action Jackson. I thought that was my job."

"Correct on all counts." He sighed. "Frustration makes me feel impotent."

She smiled with narrowing eyes.

"Let's go see Ferd. Maybe he'll have something for us."

Qigiq tapped the pink box strapped to the back of the bike seat. "I brought a bribe."

© © ©

They stood behind Ferdinand watching a computer monitor where robot arms handled a tiny iPod deep underground somewhere in New York City. The mechanical fingers scaled Ferdinand's movements so he could make tiny adjustments easily. The device had been separated into two parts, and Ferdinand was removing the internals like an astronaut fixing the space station with NASA's Dexter robot.

"Must you be so quiet?" Ferdinand said.

Qigiq looked at Kandy and they both shrugged.

"We thought you wanted silence," he said.

"It makes me nervous, I keep waiting for an outburst," Ferdinand said. "Say something."

Qigiq laughed.

Kandy said, "Sure Ferd. How did you like the strudel?"

Ferdinand stared into a binocular eyepiece that showed him a 3D version of what was on the monitors. "This piece has held my interest for several minutes. And in those minutes, I find interesting things."

They waited.

"You're quiet again," Ferdinand said.

"I thought you were going to thrill us with your brilliance," Kandy said.

"It may thrill you to know that this was assembled by a professional."

"Meaning?" Kandy said.

"Meaning he or she has selected integrated circuits that are so widely available we have no hope of tracing them. And has assembled them brilliantly. A timer resets when the Play button is pressed. If that timer expires before the machine is stopped, it merely short circuits and overheats, setting off the charge."

"That's brilliant?" Kandy asked.

"Ah, Detective. You see, each time the button is depressed, the timer resets to a random number that I believe gives the machine ten to sixty minutes of play time. It is possible that a person could use it for days, even weeks, before finally setting it off."

Qigiq thought of Robina, and how long she might have been listening to her iPod before walking down the alley to meet her friends.

"What about the charge?" Kandy asked.

"It is as we hypothesized from the residue. This material wasn't made by an industrial firm, at least not in the United States or European Union."

"So where was it made?" Kandy said.

"Asia. Possibly Pakistan. I will try, but cannot promise to get closer."

Qigiq dropped his gaze away from the monitors to the floor and frowned.

"Ferdinand, what do you mean by a professional? You don't think this was done by the perp?"

"Possible," Ferdinand said. "But I would suggest that the person who did this work was contracted. It is carefully done, with not the tiniest fingerprint in sight. He loves his job. It is not the work of a crazed madman."

"You can tell that by looking through a microscope?" Kandy said.

"I am only providing my opinion. This could have been done by a widowed schoolteacher because knitting grew boring."

"Ha." She said, and glanced at Qigiq. "But I take your point. So where does that leave us? We can't search Asia."

"Nor would it be fruitful even if you could," Ferdinand said. "This person is smart enough to be far away from his or her suppliers by now."

"You think it might be a woman?" Qigiq said.

Ferdinand leaned away from the scope's eyes and rubbed his own.

"The work is delicate. It would best be done by the hands of a young Asian woman." He interlaced his fingers and bent them backwards until the knuckles cracked. "Or a man who is a fanatic for detail."

"Is it possible that the assembler didn't know what they were for?" Kandy said.

"You mean working to a specification without knowing that the material is an explosive?"

She nodded.

"I think that unlikely, Detective. However, it is a thought I had not considered."

Kandy smiled.

"Does the music player itself tell us anything?" Qigiq asked.

"It has a standard serial number and could likely be tracked to when and where it was manufactured," Ferdinand said.

"Which would tell us absolutely nothing," Kandy said.

"Correct, Detective."

"Could we find out where it was sold?" Qigiq asked.

"If it were sold through a retailer, yes."

"But if it was sold for cash on the street in Beijing, after being stolen from a factory, or a truck, or even a little girl riding her scooter to work, we find nothing," Kandy said.

"Much more likely," Ferdinand agreed.

"So Ferdinand, what do we conclude?" Qigiq said.

Ferdinand rocked his big body in the wheeled office chair. It squeaked in rhythm.

"We conclude that we have a serious national problem. There are an unknown number of these in the mail system. We must find and stop them."

The room was quiet except for the squeak of the chair. Qigiq broke the silence.

"We could ask the Post Office to help us."

"Federal entity," Kandy said. "FBI jurisdiction. They already have everything we know about the other packages; I filed that info as we obtained it. No idea when they'll get to it, but anything in the mail spells FBI."

"You might have to turn the entire case over to them," Ferdinand added. "And this package won't help; there isn't anything special about it."

"The perfume?" Qigiq said.

"A popular variety. Perhaps thousands of bottles ship every day. Maybe tens of thousands," Ferdinand said.

"You know Deseo is popular, Ferd? I didn't know you were so hip," Kandy said.

Ferdinand scoffed, "Research, Detective." He brightened. "Perhaps you could try it sometime."

Kandy laughed and crossed her arms over her chest.

"So that leaves us where?" Qigiq asked.

"I will try to find the source of the explosive, and continue to look for fingerprints, though I am not optimistic."

"How about the perfume?" Qigiq said.

They watched Ferdinand and waited.

"Any chance we could find where it was purchased? Maybe even by whom?" Kandy asked.

"The bottle in New York might bear a lot number," Ferdinand said.

"Any luck with Robina's bottle?" Qigiq asked.

"Still waiting. But we can't hope for more than a retail store; and only if we are very lucky."

"Might be able to interview a clerk," Kandy said. "Maybe our pro left a memory in some pretty little girl's head."

"I believe we call that a long shot," Ferdinand said.

"I'll have Marco contact Zeto and grab that bottle." Kandy turned and faced a window set high in the wall. She sighed.

"There is one more thing," Ferdinand said.

Qigiq watched her, but she didn't respond. "What's that?" he asked for both of them.

"I have been studying the computer Mr. Zeto gave you."

Kandy turned slowly in place.

"We have achieved the Free iPod offer on it."

"How the hell?" she said.

"We had it run a test script from the Silver Platter laboratory that Ms. Volker provided. It made the machine download music from all over the Internet, over one hundred thousand songs."

"And the iPod offer showed up?"

Ferdinand nodded.

"Did you ask it to send one?" Kandy said.

"We didn't get that far. You see, when it gave us the free offer, we tried to analyze the code running on the machine."

"Tried?" Qigiq said.

"Yes. We connected a second machine and attempted to peek into it."

"I'm not liking your choice of words here, Ferd," Kandy said.

"Do you remember there was a virus that showed up on Sally's machine while in our laboratory? It deleted illegal songs, then accessed the local address book and posted the owner's picture to blogs?"

"The Chronicle calls that DoomTunes," Kandy said.

Ferdinand smiled. "Journalists do like to overstate the situation."

"So what about it?" Kandy asked.

"It is difficult to be certain, because we were only able to probe for seventy-two seconds before the virus realized we were there and deleted itself."

"It realized you were there?" Qigiq said.

"Oh yes. I believe it was performing self-timing operations, so when we took away machine cycles, it knew something unusual was happening...and it just went away."

"A computer can do that?" Kandy said.

"Were you able to learn anything?" Qigiq asked.

Ferdinand nodded slowly. "We learned something I am highly confident is true, yet I have no explanation for why it should be."

Qigiq and Kandy looked at each other, back to Ferdinand, and waited.

Ferdinand stopped rocking and stood. He began pacing between the microscope eyes and the window Kandy had been staring through.

"You see, my friends. These two things, this DoomTunes and the free iPod offer, are entirely independent. They arrived on the Internet separately, at different times, I see nothing to correlate them."

"Please tell me, Ferd," Kandy said.

He stopped pacing and met her eyes. He was frowning.

"These two so-called viruses, which seem to arrive by magic and not by any traditional viral infection path."

"Yes?" she prodded.

"They're related. They share the same internal structure."

"The same structure?" Qigiq echoed.

"They came from the same place?" Kandy asked. "Or is one a mutant of the other?"

"Common origin," Ferdinand said. "I see no possibility that two independently developed pieces of software could be so similar in the way they use data."

"Huh?" Kandy said.

"There's no chance it just happened." Qigiq said.

"Precisely. It would be more likely for the Earth to spontaneously implode."

Qigiq studied Ferdinand, who wasn't smiling.

"So we're looking for a hacker who deletes music files and kills people?" Kandy said.

"Or a team," Ferdinand said. "It's unlikely the person who wrote the software also performed the hardware modifications. Software and hardware skills are rarely in the same individual."

"How so?" Kandy asked.

"Hardware people tinker and gamble, trying to keep their designs ahead of others. Software people are compulsive anal retentive organizational fanatics who worship Apollo, the god of order. Of course, I'm generalizing."

"Of course," Kandy said, kicking the base of Ferdinand's spare chair to roll it into the one stream of sunlight entering the room. She dropped into it. "How do we find these jerks?"

"Since DoomTunes and the free offer are clearly from the same source, try to locate the hacker who created them. He or she likely had contact with the bomb maker, and can, therefore, provide a path to his lair."

"Lair?" Kandy said, smiling at Ferdinand.

"What about the movies?" Qigiq asked.

"They are clearly tied to the viruses by the *Don't Steal* message. And I suspect were created by this hacker's software."

"And we know where that software was written," Kandy said. "Zeto showed it to us."

"Did he write it?" Ferdinand asked.

She shook her head. "No, claims it was outsourced to the Chinese."

"But he said it was based on his audio work," Qigiq said.

Silence.

Ferdinand broke it. "Another tie to Asia."

Kandy said. "There's still no connection to DoomTunes."

"What if we go look?" Qigiq said. "Or better yet, have Ferdinand look."

"Do we have enough for a warrant?" she asked.

"A confirmed connection to movies of fingers being severed. That would be enough in Fairbanks," Qigiq said, beginning to pace, favoring his ankle.

Kandy waved her index finger toward the robot hands. "What do we do about little surprises arriving in the mail?"

"How many have we examined?" Qigiq asked.

"Six. Seven counting the one in New York," Ferdinand said, poking his thumb in the direction of the same hands. "Out of the eleven that contacted us, only six were willing to let us dismantle them."

"And the three we missed," Kandy said. She pressed her lips together as if to keep from screaming.

"Let's offer a reward," Qigiq said.

"Reward?" Kandy echoed.

"Yes. Let's buy them back for more than the price of a new one. Try to get them out of circulation before they explode."

"Very good idea, Detective. We could study the little machines. Perhaps we will find a clue. I have a technology acquisition budget that could be used. How will we tell the entire country quickly?"

Qigiq and Kandy looked up at the same time. Qigiq glanced down at his watch. Kandy was already standing.

"McGreen," they said together.

"Thanks, Ferdinand," Kandy yelled over her shoulder as she headed for the door. Qigiq hobbled after her. When they reached the first floor, Kandy held her right hand straight up and closed it into a fist. "McGreen or the judge?"

Qigiq lifted his arm and counted, "One, two, three."

He held out two fingers. She had her fist closed.

"Rock smashes scissors. I'll take McGreen," she said.

"It's Friday afternoon. The judge is going to be mighty annoyed with us."

"Show him pictures from Robina's funeral. And that girl in New York lying at the curb in a heap."

"He won't like it," Qigiq said.

"You trying to win a popularity contest, Keegee?" She laughed, and disappeared down the corridor through frosted glass doors before he could suggest an alternative.

He headed for the courthouse using a wooden cane with a ninety-degree handle at the top he had found at a Goodwill store. Going without support the previous night at the funeral home had been a bad idea, so he was back in his cast and felt numb, like he had an old boot at the end of his leg without a foot in it. At the courthouse he supported his weight against the back wall of an elevator that took him to the fifth floor and the office of his honor Franklin Jonister. He had met Jonister on only two other occasions, each related to a search warrant he needed, and needed right away.

"Is the judge in?" he asked the judge's long time assistant.

She looked him up and down, and stared at his cane for a moment.

"Don't think he'll take pity on you just because you hurt your foot."

~ 75 ~

Qigiq spent an hour in the judge's office showing the movies of Sally, explaining how they had been made with Silver Platter video technology being developed in China, and carefully outlining why Ferdinand believed the DoomTunes and Free-iPod viruses were related to each other. He then described three explosions, and the iPod Zeto had discovered in New York. He ended with a request for a warrant to search Silver Platter without warning. He was asking for a raid. He knew it; the judge new it.

The judge shuffled through Zeto's statement for the fourth or fifth time, but said nothing. He scrubbed through the movies, examining seemingly random parts of each. Finally he said, "When would you perform this...inspection?"

Qigiq thought fast. They would want free run of the building, and maybe Volker as a guide.

"First thing tomorrow. It's a Saturday, the building should be empty."

The judge nodded. "You've described two of the strangest crimes I've seen in my time on the bench. And yet you think they're related."

"The technology points to Silver Platter. We believe someone there, or someone who has access to their technology, is behind all of this."

"But you have nothing tying this, um, DoomTunes, to Silver Platter or anywhere else."

Qigiq cleared his throat. "We're going on what little we know about the structure of the software. EER believes it's related. We hope to demonstrate that conclusively with our search."

"We cannot violate a company's trade secrets, Detective. Or harm them with negative publicity. Start-up companies in Silicon Valley live and die by public relations."

Qigiq considered for a moment.

"Saturday morning is ideal; most employees will be absent and we can cover our work with a story of a security check. Assuming Ms. Volker cooperates."

"And she is?" the judge asked.

"The Engineering manager who gave us the tour, and who came to us with the DOG video technology."

The judge nodded, exhaling upward as if he were smoking a fine cigar.

"OK, Detective. I'll contact our colleagues in Cupertino. Avoid involving the city in a wrongful search litigation, if you would."

On his way out Qigiq removed a slip of paper from his pocket. Her florid handwriting was difficult to decipher, but he needed to commit the directions to memory before getting on the bike. San Francisco remained a puzzle to him—so many one way streets.

His brain wanted to sit on the beach and stare at waves to mull over the case. Instead, he forced it to focus on the blue sedan in front of him and the white van to his right. He checked his mirror and saw a gray pickup truck, then the image of Veronica's black eye.

He blinked it away.

He made the first two turns correctly, but missed the turn onto Larkin. Three red lights and a hundred slow-moving cars later he backed the bike to the curb in front of number 452. Straddling the idling machine, he dug in his pocket for the note. It clearly read *third floor,* but this building appeared to have only two beneath a peaked roof. He switched the bike off and bent forward to place the key on top of the front tire. Then he stepped off to the right, taking his cane along. He stopped on the sidewalk in front of a yellow house crammed between a tan one on the left and a pale pink one on the right, looking for a way to a third floor he couldn't see. He patted the lump that was Kandy's loan and walked toward the pink house. The yellow building was tight against it—no way to squeeze between the buildings to a rear entrance.

He heard the familiar rumble of an Italian V-twin and reached into his pocket.

"Hi, Kandy."

"Alicia called. Eddy contacted her. The girl is ecstatic."

"He still in town?"

"Supposed to meet her tonight."

"Want me to do anything?"

"Will let you know. She's texting updates."

He slid the phone into his jeans. Blake seemed to be falling back into his standard routine—not the acts of someone on the run. His mind went to the squiggles of the lie detector, and heard Peter telling stories of beating it.

He studied the buildings again, wondering if there were a West Larkin, or South Larkin and he was in the wrong place entirely. His pocket vibrated and rang like a desk phone from World War II.

Unidentified caller.

"Hello."

"You never sent me my picture."

He couldn't place the female voice.

"Your picture?"

"Yeah, you promised to email it to me so I could see my butt."

He smiled.

"Sorry, Karen. I got busy with the case I told you about."

"Apology accepted. Send it now, I'll wait."

He shook his head, but lowered the phone and flipped back through pictures until he found one of Karen lying on *Delicious*. He entered her Delicious34 email address.

"On it's way now."

"Thanks, Qigiq, you're the best. But that's not why I called."

He walked slowly back to his 850 and leaned against the seat.

"I'm standing on the back of *Delicious* cooking. I bet you didn't think I could cook. Well, I'm not really *cooking;* I'm grilling burgers on a hibachi that hangs over the stern. And yes I'm wearing my red bikini."

"I'll bet your burgers are delicious," he said.

"Ha ha. Anyway, remember you told me about *Firebird* and that musician guy. Well, he's down here tonight."

He recalled talk of a trip to China. "Professor Walters is at the marina?"

"Yeah. I saw him load a bunch of suitcases earlier."

"What's he doing now?" Qigiq said.

"Being naked. He's in that flower yogi position on his swim platform, staring up at the sky. Once in awhile he waves his hand around and sprinkles dust over the water. I can see it float in the wind."

Qigiq imagined the man he had seen upside down sitting on a swim platform.

"And get this," Karen continued. "There's a girl with him."

"Do you know her?"

"Maybe. Don't know a name. She's standing behind him playing the flute. Weird haunting stuff that makes my skin feel funny."

"Is she a redhead waif, a little over five feet?"

"Oh my god, how did you know?"

"I'm a detective." Her laugh, full of innocence and joy, reminded him of Robina. "Will you let me know if they set sail?"

"Sure, but that's not why I called."

"Are you going to tell me why you called, or is it a secret?"

She giggled. "Okay, yeah. Let me flip the burgers." The phone was silent, but not for long. "You know that boat *With a Bullet* you were interested in. I know you never told me that, but I saw you snooping around."

He waited.

"Well, the guy who owns it just got on board and there was a woman waiting for him."

She made him wait again.

"Are you going to describe the woman, Mr. Detective?"

Qigiq figured Alicia and Eddy. "Hmm...not sure. How about you tell me?"

"Well, you know, the guy looks like he used to be an athlete but doesn't keep up like some of us do, if you know what I mean."

Qigiq remembered Karen lying on the deck. Yes, he knew.

"And the woman is down here in heels and a dress. Can you believe that? On a boat? A dress? I mean...I could understand a sexy miniskirt for an evening cruise. But this outfit looks like she's planning to negotiate the sale of oil fields to the Arabs."

"Is she Asian?" Qigiq ventured.

"Nope, got you. Lilly white, dark hair. Cut short. Not a strand out of place."

"Thanks, Karen. Anything else hiding up your sleeve?"

She giggled again. It was a nice friendly sound.

"You bet. I wouldn't call you to talk about a bunch of boring people hanging out on their expensive boats grilling sirloin burgers."

"So what's going on?"

"The naked guy is chanting in some weird language. Eerie. Reminds me of a movie when something really intense is about to happen in the dark."

Qigiq tried to figure how a chant was going to help find the killer. And why Walters had lied to him.

"And guess what?" Karen said.

"You're going to surprise me again?"

"Sure am. I recorded him with my phone. Want me to email it to you?"

"Yes, please. I bet you have something up the other sleeve too."

"You know it. That bitchy looking Arab dealer is fighting with the guy. Something nasty is going on over there."

"How are your burgers?" Qigiq asked.

"Oh shoot." He heard metallic scuffing and laughter. "Well, they don't call them charcoal burgers for nothing."

"So, Karen. Care to guess what the argument is about?"

"Same as all of them: sex and money. I can't make out the words, but the faces say they don't like each other at the moment."

"Since you're such a keen observer of the human animal, what do you think? Is the woman his wife's lawyer, his wife, or his girlfriend?"

"Oh, wife for sure. She lords it over him like only a wife can. If he hasn't been screwing around on her I'll lick whipped cream off the entire deck of *Delicious*."

Qigiq wondered how she could read body language from so far away.

"Thanks. You've been very helpful. Is there a third sleeve?"

"Yeah, yours. When are you going to come by and tell me about the case? You can take more pictures of my bikini if you want. And I'll make you a burger."

He remembered her smile. "That's very generous. When we wrap this up, I'll stop by the marina."

"Don't wait long, I love play-by-play."

He put his phone away and walked up six shallow steps to knock on the dark-varnished door of the pink house. Nothing. He tried the knob and it turned in his hand, allowing him into a foyer the size of a phone booth with a door in front of him and a stairway to his right. A pink sticky-note on the wall had *2&3* scribbled on it with a red marker. A curved arrow pointed up. He started up a narrow stairway with no handrail, twisting his body sideways to make room for the cane.

The steps turned ninety degrees to the left twice before he arrived at a door numbered *2* and another pink note with a *3* and an arrow pointing up. There were no more stairs, just a red plastic button on the end of a cord hanging from the ceiling. He pulled the cord and a wooden ladder swung down, turning on a light above. He made his way up one wobbly step at a time. At the top a closed door covered with cracked white paint had a florid *3* drawn on it with a black marker.

He knocked.

The door swung open to reveal Veronica in a black robe embroidered from chest to knee. He recognized the shape of a yellow dragon down her left sleeve before she tossed her arms around his neck.

"Oh, Keejee, I'm so glad you're here."

He held her sobbing body with one arm and used the cane to steady them with the other, wondering how long she had been crying. They moved together through the door until he could swing it closed with his foot. He smelled soy sauce and sandalwood incense.

"What's for dinner?" he asked, trying to pull her away from memories.

She stepped back and managed a tiny smile between streams of tears.

"I picked up Chinese on my way home from school. I only went to one class. I hope that's okay?"

He wondered if she meant the food, or her skipping classes on the day of Robina's funeral.

"I love Chinese. What did you get?"

She sidestepped to a counter with two hot plates and lifted a big wooden spoon from inside a silver pot. "This is snow peas in creamy white wine sauce. I thought you might like wine." She moved her spoon to the other pot. "And this is Happy Family." She sniffled and wiped her left eye with the back of her hand. "It has beef, shrimp, chicken, pork and vegetables."

"Sounds terrific."

She smiled, padded across the faded beige tile in her bare feet and opened a refrigerator not much larger than the gas tank on his Guzzi. She pulled out a half-bottle of white wine and two glasses, and pushed the door closed with her elbow.

"Come, sit," she said, leading him from the makeshift kitchen toward a living room smaller than the bedroom on his houseboat.

The only thing dividing the kitchen from the living area was the introduction of maroon carpet. The roof slanted down to the left to meet a tan sofa. Through a door at the back of the room he saw a small bedroom and bath. If she and Vi shared this place, they either slept real cozy in the back room, or one used the living room.

Directly across from the couch was the time proven college bookshelf, cement blocks and a long board. This one, however, supported a computer whose screen must have been a couple feet across, sitting in front of a window with a deep blue shade drawn. She must have seen him looking.

"That's our entertainment center. It plays music, movies in HD, and we can video chat to our friends all around the world. I love it so much. Watch."

She picked up something the size of a gum pack and pointed it at the computer. The machine came on with a list of the things she had just described. She selected music and navigated through what seemed like thousands of albums. She picked one entitled *The Joni Letters* and jazz piano accompanying a female vocalist singing *I wish I had a River* filled the room.

"Could I ask you something?" he said.

She turned to him, holding the remote. The robe wasn't tied and hung slightly open, revealing a two-inch strip of her from neck to belly.

She said quietly, "Sure, is something wrong?"

"No. I just wondered, did you buy all that music?"

She turned to the screen, then back to him, the silky robe flowing slightly behind her movements.

"Oh, you mean, did I just copy it from the Internet, like that Doom thing trashing everyone's songs?" She shook her whole head from side to side, her straight black hair lagging, her breasts moving slightly beneath the silk. "No. I bought it all. Daddy gave me an account to get as much as I want. He says music is good for the soul."

Qigiq wondered if she meant her father. He decided not to ask.

"Wise words."

They ate Chinese on the couch and watched a strange movie called *Sex and Lucia* in which the heroine disappeared into a wormhole on an island that looked back in time. The threads of the story were coming together by the time the green tea ice cream she had pulled from her tiny fridge melted in his mouth. Only the fortune cookies remained.

"You first," she said.

"Ladies before gentleman."

She looked at him and grinned but didn't move.

"Age before beauty, eh?" he said, and she burst out laughing. "Okay, wise girl, I'll go first."

He cracked the pale cookie like an egg and pulled out the little slip of paper. Without looking at it, he handed it to her. She flattened it before reading it aloud.

"Your lucky number is 03 55 22 48." She looked up. "My birthday is the 22nd. See how lucky you are." She turned the paper over and frowned, her lips quivered. "Everyone is the age of their heart." Her lips parted in a big smile. "See, I told you."

He felt old. And useless. But only said, "How about yours?"

She opened her cookie, glanced at the number, and flipped the paper over. "Be open to change." She looked up with a raised eyebrow and met his eyes, her face serious. They stared at each other.

"Are you going to eat that?" he said.

She punched him in the arm with her left hand and handed it to him.

"They're great with ice cream," he said, using half a cookie as a spoon to scoop up the light green mush he had made by stirring vigorously.

After the movie ended she used the remote to tell the computer to play music that sounded like someone had tuned the Grand Canyon.

"What's this?"

"R. Carlos Nakai playing the Native American flute. I find it haunting and relaxing, and it makes me..." Her voice drifted away like the canyon music.

She nudged him off the couch and dragged it open to a full size bed in a single motion. Then she pushed him back down on it and stretched out, the left side of her face on his shoulder. Her fingertips, with nails painted in black and gray, toyed with the top button of his shirt until it popped open, then moved down to the next one.

"Don't you think it's much too soon?" he said.

Her index finger circled the second, still unopened, button.

"You're the first man I have ever met who could even think the words *too soon*." She lifted herself onto an elbow to study his face. "Is that your way of saying you don't want me?"

Qigiq thought back over a decade to what he knew about life when standing at a window in his dorm room, watching snow fall from a black sky, thinking about being two decades old. He felt certain it was less than this young woman.

"Never say never," he said, sounding like another fortune cookie.

She smiled and continued to twirl her finger. Without warning she rolled away and popped to her feet. "I'll be right back," and she disappeared into the tiny bedroom.

Qigiq thought about how long it had been since a woman wanted to take his clothes off. Maybe he was working too hard, feeling a need to be competent in a world that moved so fast answers couldn't catch questions. He reached into a pocket, found his cellphone, and pressed Kandy's number.

"Hey," she said.

He spoke barely above a whisper, "Can you do me a big favor?"

"Sure. When?"

"Now. Four-five-two Larkin. My bike is out front. I'm on the third floor in an attic apartment. Walk up and ride it away without being recognized. Key is on top of the front tire. Park out of sight."

"Are you okay?"

"Yeah. Following a long-shot hunch."

The phone was quiet for a few seconds. "Sure. On my way."

"Thanks, Kandy."

He lowered the phone just as Veronica pranced in with her arms holding her black robe closed. She turned off the overhead light, leaving only the blueish-white glow of the computer screen. She waved her remote and the screen changed to a movie of a flickering foot-high candle, flooding the room in orange.

"Veronica."

She put a finger to her lips. "Shhh." She swayed with the flute music, the curves of her slender body shaping the draped black material, floating shadows in his direction as she passed between the sofa and the screen.

She danced…and danced.

Slowly she lowered the robe to her waist, then her knees, finally the floor. She was wearing pale green lingerie with matching stockings that reached to mid-thigh, and dancing on the balls of her feet. As she moved she lowered her body in a slow motion twirl until she was on all fours and crawling toward him.

He studied the large dark splotch around her right eye.

"Veronica," he said slowly, trying to break the trance that was hypnotizing the room.

"Shhh. If you won't taste, you look."

She raised herself onto the bed and up to her knees, never ceasing the fluid motion so perfectly synchronized with the music she could have been playing the native flute with her body. He heard a motorcycle start, its engine revving up and down, creating counterpoint with the flute and Veronica's swaying arms. Then in one long rumble it faded into the distance.

She pulled off his right boot and slid to her knees. She took his foot in her hands and pressed both thumbs deep into his sole. The sensation moved along his spine as if the bottom of his foot were hot-wired to his brain. Without meaning to he let out a low sigh as tension building for days released from his shoulders. His eyes drifted across her back to the candle. Kandy had told him it was only millions of colored dots on a screen, but he found it comforting.

He tried to read the expression on Veronica's shadowed face, but her bruised eye socket monopolized his eyes.

~ 76 ~

Loud raps rattled the front door.

Veronica jumped up and stumbled into the TV.

Qigiq spun off the bed, grabbed his cane and jacket, leaned close to her ear and whispered, "Expecting anyone?"

She shook her head slowly.

"Your robe," he said, and headed for the back room. Along the way he flicked the living room lights on with his elbow and picked up his right boot. Once inside, he swung the bedroom door closed, leaving only a tiny crack.

She scooped her robe from the floor and shut off the candle movie. She headed for the door and had the robe halfway on when three more raps shook the tiny apartment.

Qigiq surveyed the back room for a way out. The slit of light from the door showed a single bed, a floor chest and a closet with a louvered folding door. Over the chest was a narrow window covered by sheer white curtains.

"Who is it?" she said through the door.

As she touched the knob the door burst open, pushing her backwards. A man stepped in and grabbed her by the upper arm. He dragged her through the kitchen and tossed her on the bed without saying a word.

"Why so rough?" she said.

Qigiq tried to make out the man's features through the crack and thought he saw the hint of a smile. He retreated deeper into the room and dug into the jacket for Kandy's revolver. The light through the crack evaporated as the living room lights were switched off.

"You haven't seen rough," a man said.

Qigiq tried to place the voice as he inched his way back to the crack. A tearing sound broke the silence. When he reached the door he saw the man wrapping black tape around Veronica's wrists and the bed frame.

"Not now. Please stop," she said faintly.

He opened her robe and pulled her left stocking from her leg, stuffed it into her mouth and crossed it with a piece of tape. She kicked him with her naked leg and he laughed. He spun more tape around her ankles with one hand, the spool making a rip, rip noise with each loop. He pulled it taught around the bed frame, leaving her thin body stretched.

Then Qigiq saw a knife.

"You slut. Up here with that cop. You're not staying pure for me. You're as bad as that bitch Sally. Worse...she didn't go for cops."

Veronica tossed her head against the mattress and tried to scream, but only a soft buzzing made it through the stocking. Her robe was open and her legs pulled so tight Qigiq could see muscles in her thin thighs, and ribs pushing up against her skin. But mostly he saw wide dark eyes lost in terror.

The knife, long and serrated, reached down and under her bra.

His cellphone vibrated against his leg.

The man's wrist flicked upward, slicing through the material, exposing breasts and dark hard nipples.

She tried again to scream.

Ninety-percent of his messages were from Kandy; he pulled the phone out and held it behind the door so the light wouldn't be visible.

The man laughed so low in his throat it was almost a gurgle.

"Now what are we going to do with a slant-eye slut giving her sweet womanhood away when she knows it's mine? We were having a fine time, but you...she wanted that bastard Blake, and a stupid rock-and-roll kid. And you? *You* fuck a cop. Not even a white man of pure lineage."

A text message read: Vi left a note. She's running off with her professor. I'm worried about her. Please help me. —Margo

The point of the knife reached up to Veronica's right elbow and slowly down toward her shoulder, the tip piercing the skin, leaving a tiny ribbon of blood behind. She was so frozen with fear she didn't move as it curved toward her neck. The man had one knee on the bed. Qigiq figured the bedroom door was in his peripheral vision.

He felt the gun in his right hand, touched the trigger, took a long breath in, pulled the door open and lunged into the living room in a single motion.

"Stop, police," he shouted, feeling like a television cliché, but knowing most people froze when hearing those words.

The man turned his head slowly in the direction of Qigiq's voice.

"Well, well, the bastard is still here. Now who rode your little motorbike away?" The man's eyes studied Qigiq in the near darkness. "Why aren't you out arresting Blake? There's enough evidence for a blind judge to convict him of killing Sally."

"Move the knife away."

"No, I'm not going to do that. If you shoot me, hell, my arm might twitch." He moved the knife lower until it rested on the left side of Veronica's throat. "Might even cut her badly. The ambulance would never get here in time. Difficult to explain, Detective."

Qigiq moved to his right so the bullet would drive the man's body away from the bed. He watched the knife hand; a human body could spasm when pierced by a bullet. He tried to see the face. Close-cropped hair. Clean shaven. Glasses he hadn't seen before.

The knife pressed harder against Veronica's skin.

"Better stop, Detective, this knife could slip."

"As could my finger...Greg. And when it does, it will slip more than once. Or do you prefer Max?" He paused, watching the knife. He said it as flatly as he could, "You were jealous of Blake."

"That prick. I have the ideas. I run the company. And he gets the fat-cat CEO package. But once the law removes him, I'll get the job. I'd have the girl too, if she hadn't turned out to be a slut like her friend here."

"Why the explosions? Why hurt innocent people?"

The knife hadn't moved, and neither had his pistol.

"I haven't the faintest idea what you're talking about. Sally was many things, but innocent was not one of them."

"You're the first murderer I've ever known to use correct grammar when torturing a victim."

"I'll take that as a compliment. It's the legal training. And call me Greg, we're all friends here." He cut an inch down Veronica's throat. "Aren't we, honey?"

"Back away," Qigiq said.

"Or what, Detective?"

Greg Simmons' left hand, hidden by his body, came up under his right armpit. Qigiq recognized the fat cylinder of a silencer beneath the biceps, the barrel aimed at the middle of his chest. He assumed it was attached to a Magnum.

"Tell you what, lover boy. Put that little snot nose gun down and I'll let you watch my honey and me have some fun. We like to have fun, don't we, honey?"

Veronica squirmed and tried to shake her head, but didn't get far against the knife.

"Hurry, Detective. I waited for that motorcycle to leave for eons and my patience is thinner than the condoms I use on this bitch."

Qigiq bent down slowly, struggling with his left leg, watching Simmons' body for any sign of motion. He released the gun on the carpet.

"Good move, Detective. Stand up and back against the wall. Slowly."

Qigiq stood and hopped on his good leg until his back pressed against the wall.

"Now watch an expert perform subtraction."

Simmons moved the knife to Veronica's right and pulled the tip down along her tender underarm flesh. The gun's muzzle never moved. Veronica's nostrils flared and she screamed, but it came out like a scraping sound in the distance.

Qigiq waited, avoiding Veronica's eyes. He watched the silenced barrel, willing it to waver, just for an instant.

"The tender spots are the best," Simmons said. He lowered the knife to Veronica's chest and moved the tip to her right nipple. He pressed it down gently. Her chest was heaving, but as the tip pressed she exhaled, trying to make her body thinner to escape the pain.

Glass shattered into the room from behind the big computer. Simmons' face jerked toward the noise. Qigiq dropped to his right knee, found the ivory handle in his cast with his left hand and dove onto his right shoulder as Simmons' gun spit. Dust flew from the hole blasted in the wall above him. He continued rolling and came up on his left knee, releasing the knife before a second shot was fired.

The ivory spun until the blade entered Simmons' throat at the Adam's apple. Its tip exited the left side of his neck under his ear and stopped. Blood pulsed into the air as his body jerked and fell out of sight on the far side of the bed.

Qigiq found the revolver with his right hand, then Simmons' fishing knife lying on Veronica's bare chest with his left. He reached to the top of the bed and cut Veronica's hands free with a single stroke. As she sat up he saw Simmons' left hand rise over the edge of the bed.

The silencer spewed bright light.

He grabbed Veronica with both arms and pulled her body with him as he rolled off the bed toward the floor, pointed his right arm at the mattress, guessing where Simmons' body might be on the other side, and fired.

Qigiq heard gurgling, like someone screaming underwater.

A shadow flitted on the far wall.

412

Simmons struggled to his knees, the Magnum wavering in his left hand.

Qigiq tried to lift the pistol, but Veronica's writhing body pinned his arm to the floor.

The room flashed and thundered as blood erupted from Simmons' head, covering the mattress and Veronica's back, and driving Simmons into the bed. Veronica lay twisted across his leg, her feet still taped to the foot of the bed. He worked free, pressed the knife handle into her hand and jumped up over the bloodstained sheets.

Simmons was face down on the floor, his left arm twisted behind him, the silenced magnum trapped in his fingers. Thick blood was forming a pool on the maroon carpet around his head. Qigiq stared at the body, fighting the urge to empty the revolver into it, which would only make his report that much more difficult to write. He turned toward the computer and watched Kandy crawl through the broken window, smashing shards of glass out of her way with the muzzle of her weapon and the elbow of her jacket. He examined Veronica's wounds while she cut her ankles free, grabbed clean towels from the bathroom, and applied pressure.

Once fully into the small apartment Kandy called for assistance, gave the address and hung up. She knelt down beside him.

"She okay?"

"I think so. Bleeding is way down," he said.

Kandy touched his shoulder. "Next time, please tell me what you're up to?"

He sighed. "I thought if we planned it, everything would be stiff, and he wouldn't go for it."

"You had *me* thinking it was real. I'm sure you fooled him."

Veronica's large eyes filled with tears. "You don't like me?"

He shifted to his good leg.

"Yes, Veronica, I like you. And I had to find a way to protect you."

"You don't really like me. I thought..." She scooted her bottom backward across the floor until she reached the wall, leaned against it, and began sobbing.

He reached and touched the darkness by her right eye with the back of his hand.

"I had to get you away from him."

She looked up. The water in her eyes made him wonder about the things he did to protect innocent people from madmen.

© © ©

The ambulance arrived in four minutes. Veronica wanted to dress, but they needed access to the wounds on her arms and chest, so she and Kandy quickly packed a bag before a male and female EMT guided her carefully down the narrow stairs wearing her black robe over jeans and pink flip-flops.

As they followed the EMT's Qigiq said, "Karen called before I entered Veronica's apartment. Vi is at the marina, playing flute on Walter's yacht. Then while Simmons was torturing Veronica a text message arrived. I thought it might be from you, but it was Margo saying that Vi was running off with him."

"The Coast Guard will help us out," Kandy said, tapping her phone. "For Violet's sake, let's make sure they don't go sailing."

"Based on Karen's description, I'm betting a wake for Sally and Robina."

They stood on the sidewalk and watched as the techs loaded Veronica into the back of a mostly white truck with enough lights for a rock show.

"Think she'll be okay?" he asked.

"Eventually," Kandy said. "Guns freak people out, as do near death experiences. But she's tough as a wildcat."

"In wildness is the preservation of the world."

She grinned. "You're quoting."

"Thoreau."

Kandy pulled her weapon from the back of her pants, checked it over, and put it back.

"Nice shot," Qigiq said.

"Close range, easy. The hard part was getting to that damn window." She pointed up where the third floor wasn't even visible from where they stood. "I had to go up the back fire escape, realize you weren't in the bedroom, think about crashing through that window, decide against it, go back down, up the fire escape next door, onto their roof and then to the side window.

"Glad you arrived when you did."

She smiled with her right cheek.

"Nice throw," she said. "You've done that before."

He turned toward the street where the ambulance was pulling away quietly but brightly.

"Hunted with a knife before I could afford bullets."

"Teach me to do that sometime?"

"Sure."

They stood listening to the sounds of San Francisco evening traffic. An occasional car horn disturbed the steady drone of tires on pavement. A motorcycle moved in the distance.

"Italian twin," he said. "Ducati."

"You can tell from here?"

"Unique valve system. Distinct exhaust note."

Kandy turned and sat down on the steps. Qigiq paced slowly with his cane, letting the adrenaline seep out of his body.

"Something he said bothers me."

"Dead men tell no tales." She laughed.

"When I asked about the bombs, he claimed complete ignorance."

"He's a lawyer, they have a patent on ignorance."

He smiled in spite of the uneasy feeling intuition was brewing in his stomach.

"I don't think he was lying."

"Based on..."

"His blank eyes. The guy was a completely functional madman. Holding that knife to her throat, he could have been negotiating a business deal with the Chinese."

She flipped a stick of gum into the air and caught it with her teeth before pulling it into her mouth. She watched him pace.

"You're not going to tell me he didn't kill Sally."

He stopped to face her. "He kept telling Veronica she was as much of a slut as Sally. And claiming Sally wanted Blake. Blake not deserving the CEO job."

"So he kills Sally?"

"Another jealousy murder for the books. That made framing Blake and taking control of the company a double win."

She cracked her gum.

Qigiq shifted his weight to his right leg.

"Two birds with one serrated knife," she said. "Which leaves us where?"

"Getting a warrant for his residence. By the way, Judge Jonister agreed. Ferdinand is going into Silver Platter tomorrow morning."

She sighed. "You want me to get a judge out of bed to get a warrant to search a dead man's house? He's going to love that."

"Maybe I'm wrong and we'll find evidence that ties Simmons to the explosions. He was an executive at Platter, he surely had access to the technology." He paced in silence, staring at his feet; feeling like this whole San Francisco sabbatical was maybe too little too late. Computer technology was far beyond his ability to predict what criminals would do with it.

She watched him for a full minute; then stood.

"Look at the bright side. Sally's killer is dead. Veronica's safe. And we're standing here talking about it. A decent day's work." She smiled. "And finally some action. I'll go see the judge. Your bike is on the opposite side of the block." She tossed him a key. "After they show up to rope this off, think about the two fingerprints we have. I think they're Simmons', but what if they're not? Talk tomorrow."

He watched her stride north in the darkness, thinking that a woman out alone might not want to be on these streets if her name wasn't Kandy Dreeson.

~ 77 ~

Qigiq sat on the stretched-cloth seat of a folding chair on his upper deck. The morning sun warmed his black sweatshirt with the double bar 'R' logo of Roland Musical Instruments on the front while he thought that Saturday wasn't feeling like a day off. He had slept poorly, waking to dream after dream of Simmons pushing the knife into Veronica's throat while a silenced bullet moved towards him in slow motion, his left leg refusing to function. In one, Simmons had fallen after the knife pierced his windpipe, but only to his knees. He then turned the Magnum and put three shots into Veronica's head.

He was tired, worried, and trying to fill out a report on his laptop to summarize the events of the past sixteen hours. Needing to recall them in detail was only worsening the visions. He heard a shuffling of feet behind him, and turned to see Veronica climbing the ladder.

The ER doctor at San Francisco General had released her after stitches in each arm and, he could barely comprehend this, two in her right nipple. There was no way she could return to her apartment, now a blood-soaked crime scene. She might not be able to go back ever. So he had honored her request to visit his little floating piece of rental real estate. He didn't mind sleeping on the couch, it reminded him of being twenty himself, traveling North America on two wheels and sleeping wherever the road ended.

She stood next to him in bare feet, her skin golden in the morning sun, wearing dark pants of a magic material that clung to her body below one of his blue work shirts, which was large enough to allow her bandaged arms freedom of movement. She held a plate with a strudel and a cup of coffee in one hand, and his cellphone in the other.

"You have to eat something," she said.

"Sure, Veronica," he said, taking the plate from her hand.

"And you had a phone call." She held up the phone and pressed a button to make Kandy's name light up.

He took the phone and laid it on the deck. "I'll call her back soon as I eat. How's that?"

She gave him half a smile, then lowered herself to the deck and sat cross-legged facing him.

"Keejee, did you mean what you said?"

He took a bite of strudel. It was getting dry, but sweet as ever.

"About what?"

"You know...about liking me."

"Of course. You're a kind, wonderful person. I like you a lot."

She slapped his leg. "You know what I mean."

He sipped at the coffee. She stared up at him.

"You'll be happier with a guy," he swallowed, "or girl...your own age."

"I can make my own choices," she said. "I'm way past eighteen."

Qigiq pondered briefly if two years constituted way past.

"And I'm *way past* thirty."

"So?"

How was he supposed to answer that? She wasn't looking for logic, this was that Venus talk.

"Veronica, if I were fifteen, even ten, years younger, a team of Budweiser Clydesdale's couldn't keep me away from you."

She smiled broadly; then tried to force her mouth back to serious. She failed, gave up, and let the smile make her face glow.

"Oh, Keejee." She hopped up, hugged him gently around his neck with her bandaged arms, lowered one hand to the zipper of his jeans and rubbed while whispering, "If you ever let yourself go like the biker boys on TV, you come find me." She patted away, bare feet slapping the hard deck.

He stopped himself from turning to watch her go, saw the phone lying under his chair and reached to pick it up. He pressed callback.

"Dreeson."

"What do we have?"

"Simmons was certifiable. This place is big, expensive, and weird."

"Want me to guess?"

"Let me send you pictures. Remember that movie *A Beautiful Mind?* The one about the brilliant mathematician who started seeing government agents that didn't exist. Remember the room where he taped up hundreds of magazine articles and swore they contained secret messages?"

"Haven't seen it."

"Well, this place is like that, except they're not magazine articles. Remember the account that posted the videos? Zeto called it the Fibonacci series. There's a number like that under every picture. Goes up to over a quarter million. Check the photos."

Qigiq lowered the phone and found her email message. There were five pictures of a room painted light blue. It contained a double bed covered by a white spread. The spread had two life-size nudes of Sally printed into the material, one lying on her back reading, the other lying face down, perhaps sleeping. Both were taken from directly above her. The walls were covered with cork board that was covered with all things Sally. Music programs, hundreds of pictures with and without clothing, panties and bras and stockings in white, green, black, red, pink, a violin with a scribbled note stating the date on which she played it and a large poster of her and Simmons standing side-by-side, perhaps naked, in waist deep water. He zoomed on the picture and saw that the right wall was covered with printouts of email messages. He couldn't read them, but he'd guess they were all from Sally. Under one message was the handprinted number 89. He raised the phone back to his ear.

"Hi, Kandy. Are we sure Simmons did this himself?"

"His prints are on everything. And we didn't find anyone else's in the room except for a few of Sally's: on the violin, the waistband of the panties, some of the photographs. Speaking of prints, did Ferd call you?"

"No, I haven't heard from him today."

"They ran Simmons' prints: definitely him on the eavesdropping hardware in Sally's computer. Eighty-five percent for the print on the button of that computer Zeto gave us."

"So you think he made the movies?"

"As sure as I'm ever going to be. His computer here has the original footage prior to editing. There are versions of the final movies on it, too. If I keep looking, I bet I find the camera."

"Anything else in that room? Looks like all Sally from the pics."

"It is. Every item refers to her in some way, right down to taxi receipts and concert tickets. Even old-fashioned locks of hair...not all from her head. And the printouts include emails she wrote to other people, including Blake. I bet that board in her computer was copying email and sending it to Simmons. Want to guess her pet name for Blake?"

He closed his eyes and let the sun turn them orange inside. They had Sally's killer.

If only it could bring her back.

He heard Robina's gentle voice singing a song.

He said, "Mony."

"You must be a detective. There's another bedroom just like that one, only dedicated to Veronica. It's about a third done; the remaining walls are blank. Has a life-size oil of her. Nude. Either Simmons was a good painter, which I doubt, there aren't any materials or art books here, or he commissioned the work. We can probably find the painter."

He was quiet, thinking about how close Simmons had come to taking Veronica away too.

"Qigiq. It's good we got this guy. Who knows how many women he might have attacked."

"What about—"

"The iPods? Negative. There's nothing here about any of the four known bomb targets. No pictures, names, New York addresses. Nothing about iPods, nothing on bomb building. I looked for the files Ferd told me I might find if the DoomTunes technology had been used. Negative on that too."

"Do you think he outsourced the bombs?"

"Still looking. I've got more stacks of notebooks here than a stationery store—all scribbled by hand. Scanning as fast as I can. After months of back and forth Sally dumped him and he went berserk—especially because she pursued Blake, just like he said. No doubt Simmons was framing Blake. There are pages and pages of clues he considered leaving for us. You'll like this, he was concerned about making it so easy we wouldn't believe it. And was pleased with himself when he hit upon the idea to use Platter technology to make videos."

"Walters?"

"Hated him because Sally liked him, which may explain that package we found on *Firebird*. I must say, he wasn't fond of you either, though after missing a couple of times, I can see respect filtering into his prose."

"So Simmons was trying to kill me?"

"At first he wanted to scare you off the case. Later, he was missing on purpose and planned to stop trying to kill you after we arrested Blake, to point the finger at Eddy."

"Why was he foolish enough to have a journal?"

"The inside cover says, *If I am gone, this is what really happened,* and it's even signed: Gregory Simmons J.D."

"His ego didn't want to be misunderstood after death?"

"That's one way to put it."

"Could it be a plant?" he asked.

She laughed. "Is everyone from Alaska suspicious? It's in long hand. We'll have to verify samples, but my gut says, yeah, it's his. There are long rants about the stupid decisions Blake was making that were running the company into the ground and ruining Simmons' chance at millions. Want to hear one?"

"If it's not too long."

He heard pages being flipped.

"From last month. 'Today, Blake authorized Zeto to move forward with the Invisible Hand project. While I think the technology is relevant and the timing good, it is beyond folly to develop it in the U.S. This should be outsourced to our Chinese partner like D.O.G. to minimize legal exposure.'"

"What's an Invisible Hand?"

"The diary never says. I'll ping Ferd, ask him to add it to his search."

"Any idea where Blake is now?" he asked, letting his eyes rest on the waves in the bay.

"We've got two men on him. Last report, he was at his house in Palo Alto."

"How long since they had a visual?"

"I'll check. Talk later."

He put the phone back under his chair and returned to the report. He was up to the point where Simmons pounded on Veronica's door when his phone buzzed.

"Qigiq."

"Hey, Ferd doesn't answer his cellphone," Kandy said.

"Think he's out of range?"

"In Cupertino? That should be impossible."

"You worried?"

"Ferd is an awfully diligent guy, he wouldn't be out of touch by choice. Other thing. No visual on Blake since last night."

"You mean he hasn't left the house?" He squinted at the sun. "Got to be at least ten."

"Ten fourteen. Our guys didn't see him leave."

"Now I'm nervous."

"Me too. Should we go get him?"

"I'd feel better. What do you want to do about Ferd? It'll take me an hour to get down there," he said.

"Forever if something's wrong."

Qigiq's phone started squeaking like a wagon wheel in need of grease.

"Kandy, my phone is chirping."

"Look at it," she said.

Qigiq lowered the device. A little bubble icon with a red dot was pulsing. He returned it to his ear.

"There's a blue bubble."

"Video chat. Hang up and activate it, see who's trying to reach you."

"Thanks. Call you right back."

Qigiq tapped *End Call* and touched the blue bubble. The screen went black, then filled with a close-up of Ferdinand's bearded face.

"Hello, Detective," Ferdinand whispered.

"Uh, hello Ferdinand."

"We have a development here at Silver Platter."

"Did you find anything?"

"Oh yes, plenty. DoomTunes came from here, which implies the free offer did also. I was looking through backups when a strange occurrence interrupted us." His head turned away, and back. "Ms. Volker is here with me."

Qigiq waited.

"The building's security system has been turned on. And strangely, Ms. Volker's codes no longer work. What concerns me is that this system is two-way. None of the doors will open outward—a clear violation of fire code."

Qigiq stood up on his deck.

"You mean you're trapped?"

"Yes, that is indeed what I mean. No phone lines work, and cellphones appear to be blocked within this building."

"Where are you?"

"The test lab. I believe you saw it on your tour. I am using an Internet-based chat sys—"

The screen went black.

"Ferdinand? Are you there?"

Veronica came up the ladder behind him.

"Why are you yelling? Is everything okay?"

"I have to leave," he said.

"I'm going with you."

"No, you can't; I'm riding to Cupertino. Something's gone wrong."

"I'm going with you."

He shook his head.

She nodded hers.

He suddenly wondered if Simmons was the only threat; if she would be safe alone; if leaving her alone was exactly what someone wanted.

"You're hurt."

"I can ride."

He considered. Reconsidered. Considered again.

"Spare leathers are in the closet off the kitchen."

She turned and ran.

He touched Kandy's name.

"Kandy, that was Ferdinand on Internet chat. He and Lili are trapped inside the lab at Silver Platter."

"Inside? That's impossible. Just walk out."

"The security system has locked the doors in both directions. And Lili's codes won't work."

"Why would they have that?"

"My guess, to trap people trying to steal trade secrets. While we were talking, his screen went black and didn't come back. What would cause that?"

"Connection went down. Could be a dozen reasons."

"He said the phones were out. Maybe he lost power."

"Checking the Web...no reported outages in Cupertino," she said.

"Perhaps just the building."

"This is not good, Qu. And something else is making me nervous."

"Go ahead," he said, as he worked his way down the ladder.

"I put our finance team on chasing Eddy's money to see if he was in trouble. He's not; he's loaded. But they found something funny. Four-figure sums going to PayPal, like he's buying a whole bunch of stuff from eBay. Total is over half-a-million so far."

"To where?"

"A hundred PayPal accounts."

"Are they related?" He opened the closet door and tossed his riding pants onto the bed.

"Maybe. We're tracking the last login to each of those accounts. Over half have been accessed from Internet service providers in the Wisconsin area."

"He likes cheese?" He slipped his jacket on over the sweatshirt. The revolver was still there.

"The money transferred to those PayPal accounts over the past forty-eight hours; that's why they jumped out."

"I'm not getting it," he said as he wiggled into leather pants and realized Veronica was on the other side of the room watching him, looking like a supermodel wearing black paint.

"And it's being pulled out. Starting yesterday."

"From a bunch of accounts?" he asked.

"Yes."

"Big coincidence."

"Very big," she said.

"So you think one guy is driving around Wisconsin making withdrawals?"

"Yes. And he's being paid for something worth over half-a-million dollars."

"Delivery of specially prepared iPods?" He zipped his jacket to his pants and grabbed his helmet. Veronica led into the kitchen and opened the door.

"I think Blake has a munitions guy mailing these things from the Midwest," Kandy said. "Remember Columbus, Ohio?"

He stopped on the deck and ran his eyes over the leather on Veronica's body.

"Victoria's Secret," he said. "Can we locate this person?"

"I'll get the Wisconsin folks on top of uncovering addresses for these withdrawals. If this guy keeps logging in to move PayPal money, we might get lucky."

"Meanwhile, I ride to Cupertino and free Ferdinand?"

"Too slow. I'll call the locals and send them over."

"Anything on our friend Blake?" he said, walking down the dock with Veronica hopping along beside him.

"Yes. He's gone. They searched the house. His Mercedes is in the garage, so he has another car."

"Or he's on a train, or a plane. Or maybe even in a taxi. They're tough to trace if he pays cash."

"Shit," she said.

He agreed. "I'm heading down now."

~ 78 ~

Qigiq tucked close to the gas tank and rode hard for half an hour, thankful that Saturday morning traffic wasn't in his way. Veronica held tight and made no complaint as he pushed the speed limit down a beautiful piece of concrete five lanes wide. In other circumstances he would have enjoyed the rolling hillsides and sunshine. Today he only saw concrete not disappearing fast enough beneath his front wheel as the digital speedo of the rented bike sat at nine-zero. Given the optimistic nature of speedometers, he hoped he was doing at least eighty.

A green sign with a white silhouette of an airplane indicated the turnoff to San Francisco International Airport. A vague idea formed. He slowed carefully, worked his way to the rightmost lane, and pulled onto the shoulder. Veronica hopped off and removed her helmet, her straight black hair falling over her face. He felt a crazy urge to kiss her rise, then subside. He remained straddled over the bike and pulled out his phone.

He scrolled back through the calls he had received most recently until he found the one he thought was Zeto's. He pressed callback.

"Hello Mr. Zeto, this is Detective Qigiq. I hope I'm not interrupting anything."

"Uh, oh, hi Qigiq." Zeto was panting like a jogger. "That's okay, did the iPod help?"

"Yes, a great deal, thank you. We have an emergency and I'm afraid I need another favor."

Qigiq heard a deep sigh over the phone.

"The timing isn't real great. Can it wait for fifteen minutes?"

"I wish it could, Harold. Are you aware that the security system at Silver

423

Platter will lock people in?"

The line was quiet. A car passed in the nearest lane, it's turbulence shook the bike.

"I was on the security committee," Zeto said.

"The double-lock protects your trade secrets from getting out?"

"Exactly."

"What can you tell me about the system?"

More silence. No one drove past. Qigiq felt like he was trapped in the eye before a three-day winter storm.

"This is highly confidential," Harold said. "Late in the project Blake stopped inviting me to meetings with his security consultant. I wanted to know what they were up to, so I did a little secret hacking. Found out stuff I'm not supposed to know." He paused. "Blake will fire me."

"Harold, Lili and my friend Ferdinand are trapped inside. The police are heading over to try to get them out."

"No, don't."

"Don't what?" Qigiq said. He turned to check on Veronica. She was leaning against the street side of the bike, waving at the boys who shouted at her as they drove by. He'd guess she was pretending cheerful again, and thinking about Robina.

"Don't try to break in, it can set the system off," Harold said.

"Meaning?" Qigiq looked at his watch. He had been stopped for four and half minutes.

"No one can know I told you," he said. "I have to be able to be trusted with confidential information or I won't be able to work in Silicon Valley."

"Harold. What will happen to Lili if the system is set off?"

"She'll die."

"Could you repeat that? I'm standing by a noisy highway."

"The building is wired to self-destruct if Spore gets a go order."

"Spore?"

"You know, like the defense system bacteria use in adverse conditions."

"How does it get a go order?" Qigiq said slowly.

"I'm going to be in so much trouble."

"Harold...Lili is trapped."

"OK, OK. Once Spore is activated, it will go to destruct if its perimeter security is breached. The explosives were designed by Blake's expert to be untraceable. If Spore decides it's under attack, they explode and burn so the insurance company will pay for the fire."

"Destroying all records of what is going on at Silver Platter?"

"Uh, yeah, something like that."

"Including the Invisible Hand?"

Silence.

"Forget it," Qigiq said. "How else can Spore be activated?"

"I hacked Blake's encrypted email to find this. He doesn't know I know." A long pause followed by a sigh. "OK. Spore watches craigslist for an oil painting called *The Silver Bullet* to go on sale for a hundred and thirteen thousand dollars. It has to be a signed original by Susan Rothenberg, which of course, doesn't exist."

"Your computer watches the list?"

"The Spore security system does, yeah. It's a computer on its own uninterruptible power source."

"And when it sees this ad?"

"It starts a countdown that can only be stopped with another code. I heard Blake and Simmons have the code, I could never find it. Oh, the designer might have it too."

Qigiq looked at his watch again, almost ten minutes.

"Who's the designer?"

"A guy named Del. Never met him, as part of our security cloak. I know he was in the Central time zone though, because we had to shift our meeting schedule."

"Hold for a minute, Harold."

He tapped Veronica on the shoulder. She jumped and spun around.

"Call Kandy. Tell her do not, under any circumstances, attempt to enter the building with force. It's wired with explosives. Got it?"

Her head bounced like a bobble-head toy and she pulled a thin razor of a phone from the leather suit.

"Hi, Harold. Sorry, had to get a message to Cupertino. Please tell me that Rothenberg ad is not on this list you mentioned."

"Looking."

Qigiq stared at the mini-tachometers in his watch, feeling like it was running in time lapse.

"Fuck no. The message is up there. Posted...forty-three minutes ago."

"How much time do we have?"

"It's a two-hour countdown. Poor Lili."

Qigiq heard a girl's voice ask Harold what was wrong.

"Harold, where's Blake?"

"I have no idea. I'm in New York. I haven't seen him since a meeting at the office last Thursday."

"Help me, Harold, please. I have to find him. You just told me that Lili has an hour and seventeen minutes to live."

"Give me a second."

Qigiq heard rustling of cloth and a screech that sounded like a bed spring. A minute passed before Harold returned.

"I can find his cellphone...I think. Maybe."

"You can what?"

"His company smartphone is just like mine. When we got them, I messed with the GPS stuff. I've got a little app that will send me the coordinates of his phone in email. I just have to trick him into loading it."

"The phone knows where it is?" Qigiq said.

"By the cell towers or a GPS chip. It's pretty easy, really."

Traffic zipped past. Qigiq looked around for a cell tower but didn't see one.

"Trick him how?"

"The phone will notify him when I try to load the app. I'll have it masquerade as a sales update. Blake is super interested in Silver Platter's sales."

Qigiq wondered how to be effective in a world where a cellphone knew where it was and an app could pretend to be anything it wanted.

"Please try, Harold, and try fast."

"You got it, I'll call you back."

Qigiq hung up and put one hand on his bike to steady himself. He thought of Ferdinand and Lili trapped inside of a huge firebomb.

He felt a tap on his shoulder.

"Are you okay," Veronica said softly.

He shook his head.

"No, sweet Veronica, I am definitely not okay. The world is being buried in shit and my shovel is too small."

He punched Kandy's number and gave her the update. She wanted to get the guys who dealt with IEDs out there and see what they could do, and try to get a message to Ferd. He explained what little he knew about the self-destruct mechanism and Harold's tracking effort.

Back on the bike with blue light flashing he headed south as close to 100 mph as Camrys, Chevys, and pickup trucks would allow. The 850 pulled strong, but he wished for the familiar stability of his Guzzi. He also wished he could have left Veronica on the boat, her presence was making him careful. But if someone were watching...

Ten minutes later, as he was passing a long reservoir on his right, he felt the cellphone in his jacket vibrate. He exited at State Route 92 and pulled onto the gravel shoulder. With the bike running beneath him, he dug out the phone.

There was a voice message.

He peeled off his left glove and tapped the phone.

"Qigiq, this is Harold Zeto. He went for it. I don't think he even read it, just accepted it. So long as he doesn't turn the phone off, I'll have coordinates for you. He has a chip, so these are accurate GPS updates from a satellite."

Zeto's recorded voice stopped and Qigiq heard a scraping and tapping noise in the background.

"I've sent you a map of his latest position in your email. It's a snapshot. I'll update it manually every minute. Please tell me when Lili's safe."

Qigiq fumbled with the device until he found Harold's email. He tapped an icon and the picture opened to a map of the very road he was parked on. A red pin showed Blake less than five miles away. He gave thanks that Harold was an engineer. Next to the red dot a rectangular cartoon bubble read *Heading north on 280.* The dot was north of 92, partway back to San Francisco. And the picture was four minutes old. He sighed. They had raced past each other going in opposite directions.

He held the phone up so Veronica could read over his shoulder and pointed at the screen.

"Harold is sending maps," he said.

She nodded.

"Can you watch them?"

"Sure."

"You have to take your glove off. It needs to feel your finger."

"OK." She jabbed him in the ribs with her fingertips. "Let's go, he's getting away."

Qigiq smiled inside his helmet; she sounded like someone who should stop watching television. The tiny joy vaporized, replaced by the word Spore, and the loud ticking of a giant clock.

He checked traffic and pulled onto the road. In less than a minute they had reversed direction and were heading north on the five-lane interstate. As he dodged cars, he thought about where Blake might be heading, and why. Ferdinand's search had alerted someone—someone willing to blow up a building to destroy evidence.

"North on this road," Veronica screamed in his ear.

"Are we catching him?" After asking he realized she didn't have the information she needed to make that assessment. She only had Blake's location on the map, not their own.

"How fast are you going?" she yelled.

He looked down, the digital speedo showed 96. If he assumed a five percent error, he was going just over 90.

He held up his left hand: four fingers, five fingers, then touched his finger and thumb together to make a zero.

She screamed. "Zeto says seventy-eight."

The five-miles map was minutes old. Plus the time it took him to turn around. Closing at twelve mph meant nearly an hour to catch him. Lili and Ferd only had an hour. Qigiq checked his mirror and pulled out to pass a tall bus spewing dark fumes in his face. He considered options—couldn't think of any. If Blake's car didn't stop, he wasn't going to catch him in time.

He saw a sign with a silhouette of an airplane flash by. He curved right behind a white stake truck and in front of a blue Mustang, concentrating to avoid a high-speed crash, asking the same question over and over.

How did Blake fit?

~ 79 ~

Eddy Blake looked down at his right hand. It was shaking. He tried to force himself to relax in the plush back seat of the pewter Town Car he had hired to pick up Franky Thompson in his neighbor's driveway. It had been laughably easy to sneak low across his backyard, wait for the right moment, jump the fence and stand at the neighbor's barbecue pretending to grill steaks for a party. Now the car was moving, he hadn't seen anyone tailing him, and only one man knew what he was doing. Given how things had evolved, he should be happy.

But he wasn't.

Platter sales had just started ramping up, and now this incredible complication from too much explosive and bad luck. A fucking taxi—how was he supposed to predict that? He wanted to frighten people, not kill them.

He ran his palm across his newly shaven head. Considering he had done it himself, he looked pretty good. More important, he didn't look like Eddy Blake shaker-and-mover, he looked like a white rapper, from the magnetically attached emerald on his left earlobe to the oversized sneakers he had purchased to use if this ever happened.

And it had.

He looked at his phone and reread the text message for the tenth time, still having a hard time believing.

Hey Boss, THREAT LEVEL BLACK. I was visiting Mr. Paypal right away as we agreed. Traveling. Never more than one at a stop. The last bank was staked out. Something is very wrong. Respond soon. Need to trash this phone.

Eddy didn't understand how. A hundred accounts, a hundred names, a hundred different email addresses, a hundred tiny transactions. It seemed impossible for the cops to track. But there was no way he could let the delivery man talk, even if it was going to cost him another half-mill. He had immediately sent back a response he had hoped never to need.

Get Elvis out of the building.

He looked up and stared out the windshield. They were approaching a Fiat the size of a bathtub moving like a turtle. The Town Car hit a bump and Eddy lurched sideways. As his butt hit the seat his mind lit up. They hadn't tracked the PayPal accounts.

They had tracked him.

Shit.

That meant they could be tracking...

He stared at the phone in his hand. He pressed and held the power button until its screen went black. He wondered if it was really off, or still connected to a satellite or something. He flipped it over and stuck a toothpick in the side to release the SIM chip. Then he remembered that screen telling him about a sales update.

How the hell could he be so stupid?

The car eased past the Fiat and curved onto I-380 East. He had decisions to make. He stared at the chip. No Eddy, you can't use this phone again. He broke the little chip in two like a fat potato chip and tossed the first half out the window, counted to fifteen, then tossed the other half.

"Driver, could I borrow your cellphone?"

The drivers eyes, light blue under a black cap and over a gray beard, studied Eddy in the rearview mirror.

"Twenty bucks," Eddy said. "Mine won't connect."

The driver nodded so slightly Eddy thought maybe the car had hit another bump. But he held up a small clamshell phone and traded Eddy for a crisp twenty.

Eddy made one decision. If the cops were smart enough to hunt through his finances and find PayPal accounts, they were smart enough to find With a Bullet. He just hoped they weren't fast enough. He dialed a number from memory having learned the hard way never to record a mistress's phone number in any device.

"Hi Alicia, it's Eddy."

"You bastard. You stood me up," Alicia screamed.

"Sorry, honey. I really was tied up, and I'm working like crazy to finish the paperwork for the divorce. I've got my lawyer finalizing things today."

"Oh, Eddy, really?"

He could almost hear her smile.

"Yes, really. But I didn't call to talk about her. I know it's not our day. But can you meet me?"

"On Saturday again? Really?"

"Yes, really. Alicia. I'm not a mirage."

"Well. I have plans."

She was going to punish him now, then make him beg. The game had begun. But he didn't have time for the game.

"Please break them, Ally. Get to Bullet as fast as you can. I'm already in the car. I'd sure hate to have to go fishing without you."

"You expect me to drop everything and be your little slut when you snap your fingers."

He heard fingers pop twice through the phone. More game. "Alicia, I'm sorry I missed our appointment. Things are a little hectic right now. I've got balls in the air." And in a vice, he thought. "But seeing you is at the very tip top of my list. If you could change your plans, and meet me on the boat, I will do everything in my power to make it worth your effort."

"Oh, Eddy. I'm on my way. Wait till you see the new bikini I bought. It's even hotter than the leopard."

Her smile was back. And something better than the leopard must really be good. For a moment he wanted to go see it.

"I can't wait to see it, Ally. And you."

He caught the driver's eyes on him in the mirror as he clipped the phone shut.

"Will the twenty cover it?" Eddy asked.

A nod.

"How much longer?"

"Have you at the terminal in less than ten minutes, Sir."

~ 80 ~

Veronica's helmet smacked the back of Qigiq's as he studied a road sign for upcoming I-380 East. A split in the highway meant a decision.

"Kandy's calling," Veronica shouted.

He slowed. "Which way?"

No response.

He moved over one lane, rode briefly behind a red truck, then moved another to pull in front of a dark blue van with big yellow letters on the hood that included the word Airport written backwards. He accelerated to create space behind, then pulled onto the shoulder. Veronica handed him the phone.

He pointed up at big green highway signs and asked Veronica, "Which way did he go?"

She lifted her face shield with one finger. "Zeto didn't say." Then she stepped off the bike in one smooth motion.

He slipped the phone under his helmet even as he worried why Zeto hadn't updated him.

"Hi, Kandy."

"Rebecca just got a call from Alicia. Eddy wants her to meet him at the boat."

"Why call Rebecca?"

"Wanted some girlfriend advice on whether she should show, or stand him up like he did her."

"So Eddy's heading for the boat."

"That's what Alicia says. He called her just minutes ago."

His phone made a blurping sound.

"Hold on a second."

Qigiq handed the phone to Veronica, hoping the message was from Zeto.

She tapped the screen and held it in front of her face. "Zeto says he's lost Blake. Hasn't been able to track location for almost ten minutes. His hippo...uh, hypothesis, Blake has turned off phone. Last known location: I-280 North three miles south of the 380 interchange."

Qigiq checked the signs. Just about where he was now standing. Veronica handed him the phone. He slipped it back under his helmet.

"Message from Zeto. Lost Blake. Zeto thinks he turned his phone off ten minutes ago. Don't know if he went North or East from here."

"Any idea what he's driving?" Kandy asked.

"Never got close enough for a visual."

Neither spoke.

Qigiq watched Veronica pace on the shoulder like a black cat in a cage, and listened to traffic whiz past. His mind seemed to be stalled. He hoped his subconscious was working overtime.

Kandy broke the silence. "Qu, if you were going to blow Silver Platter, what would you do next?"

"Leave the country."

"Me too."

"But we don't know if Blake armed the system," he said.

"We have to assume something."

"How's Ferd?" he heard himself ask.

"He's building a room within a room bunker using office partitions to protect the two of them if there's a blast. And he's making breathing apparatus from the compressed air used to blow dust off computer keyboards."

"How did you reach him? I thought the power was off."

"It is. He's sending Morse code with a flashlight to a demolition expert the locals brought in."

Qigiq imagined Ferd working feverishly to protect Lili.

"How would you get out?" he asked.

"Drive, float or fly. Blake's in a car and moving. He has a boat where he's meeting Alicia. And his last known location is ten miles from an airport."

"That narrows it down," he said. He saw Veronica pull off her helmet and shake out her hair. She pulled its shiny blackness back into a ponytail and wrapped something around to hold it. Without the hair he saw her face as if for the first time. Her eyes were spaced far apart, the right one still blackened, her cheekbones high and visible. She barely looked like the person in the green lingerie. Something clicked in his stalled head.

"Think he plans to take Alicia and the boat to Mexico?" Kandy asked. "Californians do it all the time."

"I think the boat is a decoy. He's on his way to the airport under an assumed name, in a rented vehicle we can't track, wearing a disguise we won't be able to see through."

The phone line was quiet.

He added. "Grandfather of the ivory knife, 'Run where you cannot be seen.' He meant forest, snowstorm, within a herd of caribou."

"I'll ask the Coast Guard to sit on With a Bullet and meet you at the International terminal. After I call for backup."

"What are we going to do when we get there?" he asked.

But the line was dead.

~ 81 ~

The long car pulled to the curb under a sign for Alaska Airlines just past two guys in blue pants checking baggage on the street. Eddy paid the driver with two hundreds, flipped the hood up on his black sweatshirt, and dragged his backpack behind him as he stepped out. What a ridiculous piece of luggage, but it fit with his cloths and the antique 1888 silver dollar hanging from a silver chain around his neck. More important, his delivery man had cleverly designed the sections to be padded with packets of $100 bills, each a centimeter thick. The cash was not new; but it was official right down to the purple paper band holding a hundred of them together. By making the wall of the backpack two centimeters thick, it was able to hold fifty packs. A half-million dollars hidden in a ten-pound backpack that also held a couple pair of underwear and sunglasses.

Eddy smiled. He was traveling light and fast. He dug for the sunglasses and slipped them on. Hip musicians always wore sunglasses.

The driver lifted a black roll-on from the trunk and placed it on the sidewalk. He smiled at Eddy and touched his hat.

"Have a good day, Mr. Thompson."

"Thanks for the ride, enjoy your day man," Eddy said, and reached for the wheeled case that also had two-centimeter thick walls made of money. A million in cash between the two, yet not a cent visible. It'd take hard work and a sharp knife for TSA to find even the first bill. And motivation.

He needed to avoid motivation.

Thinking of the money reminded him that Elvis was traveling. He owed the delivery man another half-million to forget that together they had almost won state in high-school wrestling, dodged the cops in fast cars, and chased girls who seemed keen on blow jobs. They had worked together on and off over the years as the delivery man learned about security from both sides of the law, and Eddy's needs for such knowledge grew.

Like the need to have a pre-planned getaway in case bad things happened.

Eddy looked up and down the sidewalk for anything unusual: too many cops, a group gathering, guys yakking on walkie-talkies like they were clearing the way for the President. Nothing struck him except that he was looking around attracting attention. He slouched and took long easy strides toward the door to the huge SFO International terminal.

The cold air hit him and he took a long slow breath to feel it fill his insides. Without a phone in his pocket for the first time in a decade he felt like Alicia had cut his dick off. He needed the Internet. If that money wasn't where he had promised it would be, the guy would move to protect himself like the fighter he was, reacting to the threat of the moment.

Eddy turned right.

He passed a small shop where a bored-looking Hispanic woman sat surrounded by junk food. He passed hundreds of travelers waiting in lines. He stopped at a public Internet access machine, but it wanted a credit card. He had cards matching his three passports, but he hesitated to add risk. Even his pre-paid card would leave digital breadcrumbs some geek could probably track.

He kept walking.

Gift shop. Big gift shop. In the distance.

He stepped up his pace and forced himself to slouch inside the big shirt while crossing a couple hundred feet of hard gray tiles. Inside the shop he sought out the electronics section.

"Hi, may I help you?"

He turned around to a thin young woman in a deep blue skirt that almost reached her ankles.

"Oh yeah you can, let me count the ways," he said, speaking slowly.

Her eyes darted to his dark glasses and away and back again. She blushed.

"I'm looking for an Internet access device," he waved his arm that wasn't holding the back pack. "Gotta get me Wi-Fi soon, check out some tunes."

"This is the Museum store. We mostly sell artwork."

"Oh, baby," he looked her up and down, "I don't need art, I need tech. Unless you're on sale." He gave her a big smile.

Her face brightened. "Try the ZoomShop."

"The Zoom? What's a zoom, girl-with-no-name girl?"

"I"m Zelda. But my friends call me Zel."

"Well hello, Zel, call me Franky, and take me to your Zoom leader."

Zel looked over her shoulder. There was one customer at the counter talking to an overweight clerk. The rest of the place was empty.

"I'm not supposed to leave."

"That's cool, Zel. But you say it like you're going to show Franky the land of Zoom anyway."

She lowered her eyes and blushed again.

"That's great, girl. Let's go. Is your Zoom near or far? Take me there, maybe I'll write a tune for Zel Zoom when I get back."

She stepped closer. "You write music?"

He started moving out of the store and she followed.

"All the time Zel, my belle. I gotta make tunes like you watch the moon. A big light glows in me all the time. Makes me rhyme. Sometimes I wish I could change it, ya know, just to be more normal, a bit more formal. But Franky is who he is, baby Zel."

She led him across the wide aisle and around a corner. In a few moments they were standing in front of a vending machine.

"Here's the ZoomShop, Franky. I gotta get back. If Mrs. Moth notices I'm gone, she'll get me in trouble."

"Mrs. Moth? Does she like light bulbs?" He smiled.

"Oh, Franky. How long are you here in San Francisco?"

"All the time, Zel. Just leaving now for a little trip to the islands; hear some real music made from the heart."

Her eyes danced to his face and away again. She ran up and kissed him on the cheek.

"Come back and buy some art, Franky. Let me hear that song you're gonna write for me."

She watched his face

He gave her another wide smile. "Franky will fill you with song when he returns on the big bird from paradise. Thank you for the kindly Zelicious guidance."

She spun and dashed away double time like cops were chasing her.

Instead of him.

He looked at the big vending machine full of gadgets. He could buy a cellphone, iPod, headphones, even a digital camera. He studied his reflection, slouched a little more. If the cops talked to Zelda the man she described wouldn't match anything anyone knew about Eddy Blake, would it Franky?

The machine wanted a credit card. He could do it, but he sure didn't want to.

He shifted on his feet and glanced over the top of his shades.

No one was within fifty feet. The delivery man had advised: keep your options open until the last minute. If they can't predict you, they can't catch you. So he could still turn around, get a rental car and hide in Vegas. Or even take the train up to Reno and do a little gambling. They might look in Reno though, because his Incline place was nearby. Or he could continue on the path he was on.

He felt the weight of the pack dig into his left shoulder. Get out now, or hide and get out later? Would they close the border in such a way that he couldn't slip through? Would the delivery man fumble and tell them something they could use?

Now won.

He lowered his pack and pulled out a large gray wallet. It contained a passport and three credit cards for Franky Thompson. It hid passports and six credit cards for two mystery men he hoped he wouldn't need.

MasterCard. Zoom land was safer than an airport Internet terminal anyway. Franky bought an iPod. So what?

He pressed a letter and a number to select his purchase.

A robot arm whirred and moved to retrieve an Apple iPod Touch that looked a lot like his discarded phone, then lowered it with a subtle clunk. He hoped the damn thing was charged. He grabbed it from the bin and looked around at the glass cases showing off old shit like an art museum; he needed a place to hide in the open.

He strolled back toward Zel's store, waved the box as he passed, got a big smile in return. He worked his way along a forty-foot display case to a corner café situated directly across from the security entrance to the international gates.

Perfect.

He purchased a cup of coffee and a twisted pastry using cash and found a white table with cheap chairs away from the one couple eating lunch. He could see the corridor and a hundred people zigzagging back and forth waiting to get through the detection machines. If uniforms started gathering, they would be easy to notice.

He bit the pastry, unwrapped the dozen layers of pretty plastic crap that Apple puts around its products, and finally got the Touch in his hand.

Nothing.

He messed with more plastic and wires, keeping one eye on the wide aisle to his left between him and the gate agents, and the other on the security line. Seemed like just another day at the airport: no special personnel running around with his picture on a handout, or extra guards standing at attention eyeing travelers.

He plugged the little transformer into a receptacle in the floor and the device glowed. It found sfo free wifi. Ten seconds later he logged into the first bank's web page and started a fifty-thousand dollar transfer. He waited for confirmation then moved on to a second bank and second account.

He stared at Franky's reflection in the tiny screen.

He sipped coffee through a plastic lid.

The banks would take days to get this done, but the transfer notifications should keep the delivery man calm. He took the penultimate bite of the pastry and moved his eyes behind the dark glasses, scanning, searching. They landed on the ass of a skinny chick walking past wearing something that looked like biker leather. His groin tensed. Man he'd like to do her. He suddenly missed Alicia, wished he didn't have to leave her behind. But some things just had to be.

The girl turned and he saw her profile.

His jaw froze. She had been topless on his boat.

And the buff babe with her...holy crap! That polka dot bikini with Karen on the deck of Delicious. The candy girl Alicia wanted to lick.

He pulled his face deep into the hood of his sweatshirt like a startled turtle and lifted the coffee cup almost to his nose. The guy with them had been in his office. And that had been her with him looking different with her clothes on: detectives from San Francisco with computer movies, pictures of his condo, packages. Now they were at the airport.

No coincidence was that big.

He shifted slightly left in his chair. They were scanning the security line.

The delivery man had been right, keep the options open. He hadn't purchased a ticket yet, so he could still choose any destination he wanted. Or, backtrack, rent a car, drive to a safe place in the desert and wait. Or...

He finished the pastry and licked his fingers slowly, one at at time.

Step one—get out of sight.

He disconnected from the network, switched the new device to face-forward video so it would act like a rearview mirror, and hoisted the backpack to one shoulder. Still seated, he turned slowly away from the trio, watching them on the tiny screen.

They didn't look his way.

He stood slowly, remembering to hunch forward, grabbed his roll-on, and moved carefully between the tables. The camera told him the Kandy woman noticed the motion, glanced his way, then turned back to the group.

His heart pounded like he was back at school in the middle of a wrestling match. He forced himself to breathe and...move...slowly. He turned left, walked fifty feet and shifted the camera.

They had moved closer to the security line, and a uniformed employee was talking with them from behind a rope. They weren't looking his way. The tension in his chest dropped half-a-notch. He walked slightly faster.

"Hi."

He turned. Zelda was standing in front of the museum store like a street barker, smiling at him.

Options. Plane. Car. Could he still get to the boat, or would they have it covered too?

"Hey, Zel gal. How's the artsy business?"

She scowled. "Slow and boring. When's your flight?"

Options.

He held up his iPod to take her picture and checked behind him. No change.

She smiled.

He tapped the screen so it would make its picture taking noise for her, and snap a picture of the detectives.

"Not sure, Zel. Been thinking. Lots of places to go, but no one to go with, ya know?"

Her lips started to smile, but stopped, like they weren't sure they were supposed to.

He moved closer, slipped the device into his pocket but left it on.

"What time you done working?"

Her head spun to the woman behind the counter in the rear of the store. "I'm supposed to stay until five." She turned back. "But it's really slow today."

"Do you have a car, Zel gal?"

She shook her head. "I take the train to the city."

Train? He hadn't thought much about trains. Cash for mileage. No credit cards. No security.

He moved close and whispered. "Do you think the bad bag lady in back will let you fly away now?"

Zel frowned. "She won't like it. Extra work for her. We don't get paid much."

"But she'll get all the commission," Eddy said.

She grinned. "We only get them on a few of the big art pieces. We don't sell many of those."

Eddy moved closer, pulling his roll-on, until their shoulders touched.

"Can we bribe her a mite? Your cousin just arrived on a bumpy flight and you'd love to show him the city while there's still loads of light."

"I don't have a...oh," she smiled. "Hi, cuz," she said, not whispering. "How was your flight?"

"Great, Zel." He reached out his right arm and gave her a hug. Her body shook like she was frightened, then relaxed a little. He whispered, "How much should we offer for her coffer?"

Without removing herself from the mini-hug she said, "She'll want my wages. Twenty, maybe thirty dollars."

Eddy reached into his left pocket and came back with a roll, twenties on the outside. He peeled a pair and pressed them into her hand.

"Pay off witchy woman, and join me for dinner, Zelicious?"

She looked directly at his glasses, probably trying to see his eyes. She didn't answer, but grabbed the twenties and spun out of his arm to dash away.

Eddy inched into the store and stood close enough to the entrance that his camera could see out. The detective and the leather chick were still talking to the security guy, but Kandy of the polka dots was now scanning the crowd. She was good, barely moving a muscle.

But she was scanning all right.

~ 82 ~

Qigiq shook Jack Spinner's hand and thanked him. The security manager had electronically circulated photos of Blake to all checkpoints, and put his entire team on notice that they had a presumed psychopath trying to escape through their airport.

But it had yielded nothing.

He turned around to see Kandy scanning the giant room that seemed big enough to host a soccer game if the registration desks were removed. He heard her gum crack. Veronica stood next to him pulling the zipper on her riding suit up and down nervously, first revealing a lavender bra, then hiding it.

He didn't know what to do either. They weren't even sure Blake was in the airport. It had just been the best guess. The Coast Guard had the boat covered, but if Blake decided to stay on the highway...

He thought about Lili and Ferdinand. Break out and the building explodes. Wait inside and the building explodes. What kind of paranoid mind would construct such a thing? He walked across to the café seating and dropped into a chair. There must be something he should be doing, he just couldn't formulate a plan. Veronica sat next to him, Kandy across, so she could continue to watch the terminal.

Kandy's gum popped.

Veronica traded zipper swishing for rocking on her plastic chair, the leather squeaking with each move.

He tried to see Veronica's eyes behind her dark glasses, then he tried to stop thinking. He never had any ideas when trying to think.

His bike sitting out at the curb came to mind. Would they tow a bike?

"What if he's not here?" Veronica asked.

Silence.

"Anything from Zeto?" he said, hoping for help.

Kandy's phone played its race car. She put it to her right ear. "Dreeson."

Qigiq watched her faced, hoping for good news.

"Three?" She licked her lips. "When?"

She leaned back, his eyes followed. "Can you figure where?"

Her eyes flashed to Qigiq.

"Thanks, let me know if you can get me closer." She clicked off.

"Eddy accessed his banks over the Internet, moving fifty thousand at a time to offshore accounts: Caymans, Switzerland."

"That's not a big number," he said.

"Times ten it is. I bet it's for the guy in Wisconsin we picked up."

"Hush money?"

She nodded. "There's more. Our finance guys have the network girls helping. They tracked the access."

"We know where he is?" Veronica chimed in.

Kandy shook her head. "Nope. We know where he was. He was on the sfo-free-wifi network. Registered a transaction twelve minutes ago."

"Then?" Qigiq said.

"He got on a plane and is taxiing toward a foreign country, is heading back to the highway, hiding in a restroom stall, standing in a security line, sitting in a corner watching us. But he can't be far, the network only covers the airport terminals."

"Big airport," he said.

She stood, so he did too.

Qigiq heard a thin buzzing sound, like a mosquito caught in his ear.

Veronica looked down at her hip. "It's Vi." She lifted a tiny device to her ear.

Kandy stared at Veronica, who talked softly to Vi, who apparently wasn't happy Veronica was still on the houseboat.

Qigiq watched Kandy stare, her face a frozen mask.

"Qu—" Kandy began.

"Vi wants to go sailing," Veronica whispered. "She's mad the Coast Guard stopped them."

He waited.

"Alicia called Rebecca," Kandy said. "Wanted to know if she should go to the boat."

He nodded, but she wasn't looking at him.

"Which means Blake called her," she continued.

"Right. That's why we sent the Coast Guard to watch With a Bullet."

She turned to face him. "That means her phone has the number he called from."

"But he turned his phone off," he said. "That's why Zeto lost him."

Kandy pulled a phone out of her pocket.

"When? When did Blake turn his phone off? Before or after he called Alicia?"

"I...uh." He thought about it. Everything seemed to be happening at once. "I don't know," he finally managed.

"Give me a minute." She took five steps away from the table.

Veronica spoke to her phone. "Kandy and Qigiq are both here and we're in a public place. Please don't worry."

Qigiq moved to the chair Kandy had just vacated so he could survey both the giant terminal and the security line. Maybe Blake would show up. He tried to imagine each man moving past as Blake in elaborate disguise. A woman? He had to consider that. Many were too short. He carefully analyzed the others.

Kandy walked back to the table and stood beside Veronica.

"Jackpot."

"I gotta go, Vi. I'm fine, really. Bye." Veronica slipped her slender phone away.

"Alicia's phone captured a caller's number she didn't recognize," Kandy said. "I just called." She paused. He could see her mouth trying not to move. She had something.

"Blake has a second phone. We can track its location," he said.

She shook her head. "Not the Mega Lotto. It's the personal phone of

Peter, the chauffeur at Top-Hat Limo."

"And he remembers Blake?"

"Franky Thompson was the name. But yeah, it's Blake. Picked him up with a Town Car a block from Blake's residence. Dropped him right out there." She pointed across the wide terminal to the departure doors. "Alaska Airlines."

"Good memory."

"It gets better." She placed her phone on the table and tapped speaker.

A male voice said, "Yes, I remember him because he was dressed like a street kid, said he was a rapper slash musician slash producer in L.A. But he seemed more like a businessman from one of the computer companies out here. He asked to use my cellphone, even paid me for it, after he took the card out of his and tossed it out the window. Not something I see every day. He was wearing all black, big sweatshirt, and unlaced basketball shoes. Reminded me of a middle-aged guy having a big time mid-life crisis. Trying to dress young and hip."

"So we're looking for a six-foot tall fifteen-year-old rapper?" Qigiq said.

Kandy smiled. "Got something else."

She fussed with the screen of her phone. The voice came back.

"He had a backpack. I remember because usually college kids have backpacks and this guy was mid-thirties and clean-shaven. No tattoos that I could see. And a black roll-on; I got it out of the trunk. He kept the backpack with him protective like. And...oh, yes...not so unusual, but he paid me with two hundred dollar bills. Let me keep the change."

"Think he's still here?" Qigiq asked.

Veronica frowned. "Why come to the airport if you're not going to fly somewhere?"

"I'll email this recording to Spinner so he can get it to his security people," Kandy said, touching the little screen.

"So we assume he's in the airport," Qigiq said.

"And Spinner's people have the security entrances."

"Unless he's already inside," Veronica tossed in.

"Ticket agents. Think he bought a ticket? Or checked luggage?" He stared out at rows and rows of counters and hundreds of people waiting in line.

"Take hours to check the video," Kandy said. "Checked bags? Too easy to track. I think he's carrying everything with him, and using a different name."

"He could already be on a plane," Veronica said.

"In that case, we watch the bank accounts and get Interpol to issue a red notice," Kandy said.

Qigiq nodded. He knew she was right, but it felt like failure.

"If he were famous, he'd be easy to find," Veronica said.

Qigiq and Kandy looked at each other, then at Veronica.

"You know. We could follow his fan-sightings on Twitter."

The table was silent.

"Think Spinner'll go for it?" Kandy asked.

"I'll ask him." Veronica disappeared in a flash of swaying black leather.

They turned around. She was waving to get Spinner's attention, who was standing next to a conveyor belt feeding an X-ray machine with colorful baggage.

They watched Veronica dance from one foot to the other while talking non-stop to Spinner.

"What's a Twitter?" Qigiq asked.

"Online service for posting tweets," Kandy said.

Qigiq nodded. "Of course."

She laughed. "Micro-blogging broadcast technology that uses the Internet and SMS for instant communication."

"Much clearer. Thanks."

They saw Spinner reach for the radio on his belt as Veronica spun on a toe and headed back toward them, her straight black hair flying in the self-made breeze.

"Your attention please," Spinner's voice said from the overhead speakers. "We've just been informed that the famous DJ Slim Slam is at the airport, and as a thank you to his San Francisco fans..."

Veronica ran up to the table. "Can I borrow a smartphone?"

At the moment Qigiq felt like his phone was smarter than him, so he handed his over. Veronica started poking around. "I want to load a Twitter client that can search."

"...Mr. Slam is offering a free weekend for two at his crib in Los Angeles to the first fan who spots him, and tweets the message, "I slammed SF with Slim," followed by his correct location."

"A contest?" Qigiq asked no one in particular. He watched Spinner, who was still holding the radio.

"Slim is wearing his signature black hood and carrying two pieces of black luggage. Look carefully, he'll be hiding." A pause. "Slim says...slam now."

The public address system fell silent.

Veronica sat down and stared at the phone in her hand. "Get ready."

Qigiq watched Kandy, who had reached around her back and was shifting her pistol.

They sat in silence for a few seconds.

Qigiq said, "How will we kno—"

"I slammed SF with Slim," Veronica read. "He's entering the glass bridge heading for the elevated A-train with a hot babe in a blue dress. Send me my weekend, Slam!" She looked up. "Posted by ronnyS."

Kandy jumped up. "Inside or outside?"

"Outside," Qigiq said, thinking the bike could help him move.

Kandy took off at a dead run.

"Follow her, you can watch Twitter," Qigiq said. "I'll try to catch up." He touched Veronica's arm. "Try to let Spinner know what's happening."

Veronica took off running, reminding him of that movie with a woman as a cat.

He stood and limp-hopped fast toward the main door, his ankle not registering pain. He pushed through glass doors to his motorcycle sitting undisturbed next to the curb, but blocked in by triple-parked traffic. He slammed his helmet on, touched the gun in his pocket with one hand and the knife in his boot with the other, started the bike and sliced between cars.

The glass bridge from the main terminal to the train station was above and behind him, and he saw no way to get to it except through the terminal. To catch Blake he'd gladly ride through an airport, but the crowds were thick. He accelerated around the drop-off traffic circle toward the parking garage.

He jumped the curb onto the sidewalk and flashed past the entry gate to the garage. At the far end of a long row of cars he accelerated onto a circular ramp and leaned the bike hard to carve upward in a long spiral turn that lasted for two floors.

He shot into daylight and the top parking lot right next to train tracks, but separated by a low wall to stops cars. He apologized silently to Mr. Grojini, pulled up to the wall, lofted the front wheel, and powered the back wheel up like it was a boulder in the outback.

Metal screeched across concrete as he launched onto a four-foot wide walkway beside the train track, losing most of his exhaust system in the process. He turned left toward the train station and accelerated. Steel rail flashed by to his right as the wailing of the unleashed motor roared between his knees.

In seconds he entered the station through the train tunnel. The rails turned and the path beside them narrowed. The train's single headlight glared at him, but the train was sitting still, taking on passengers.

He slowed, bounced along the crossties, twisted the bars to jump the glistening rail, and slithered down steel. He aimed the 500-pound bike at a glass door labeled DANGER ELECTRIC RAIL KEEP AWAY on the inside, ducked, shattered the glass and shot up a down escalator onto the boarding platform.

A hundred heads turned at the crackling exhaust in the enclosed area. One of them was a man in a black hood with his arm around a slender girl in a blue dress, and a backpack over his right shoulder. Qigiq pointed the bike straight at the face he recognized as Eddy Blake in dark glasses.

Blake didn't move, he just slipped the backpack on like he was going for a hike.

The bell for door-closure warning on the train chimed three times.

Qigiq slid the bike to a stop ten feet from Blake, knowing that if Blake ran, the bike was the only way he could catch him.

Blake ran.

Directly toward him.

Qigiq felt the gun against his chest. No time.

He accelerated.

Blake sidestepped with unexpected quickness and wrapped both of his arms around Qigiq, pinning his elbows, lifting him from the bike, and tossing him the way a garbage man tosses a trashcan.

Qigiq landed hard on his left knee, tried to roll with the force and ended up on his back in time to see Blake lift the fallen bike like a toy, jump on and twist the throttle. The rear wheel smoked as it spun against floor tiles and the engine filled the station with the ear-splitting wail of unmuffled combustion.

Kandy sprinted from the glassed-walled bridge that stretched across six lanes of roadway.

The rear of the bike fishtailed toward the train.

Kandy grabbed the extended handle of a black roll-on that a girl in a blue dress had been towing. She dragged it forward fast.

Veronica grabbed the girl in the blue dress and pushed her to the pavement.

The bike thundered forward.

Pedestrians ran in a dozen directions.

Kandy spun the bag in a full circle, lifting it off the ground like an Olympic hammer thrower.

And let go.

The wheels caught the mirror of the bike and twisted the bars left. The bike leapt and tossed Blake into the air to the right. The side of the roller bag ripped across the shattered mirror and a stream of cash trailed as it flew in the direction of the train.

Someone screamed, "Money!"

A crowd descended on Blake.

The girl in the blue dress tried to stand. Veronica grabbed a handful of hair and pulled her down.

Qigiq tried to get up, but his left leg failed.

Blake lifted himself to his knees then lunged forward like a sprinter coming out of blocks. He took two steps before colliding with Kandy's foot. Blake doubled over and landed on his back, gasping.

The bike lay on its side, grumbling low and harsh, like it was angry.

Kandy said, "Edward Blake, you have the right to remain silent..."

Blake gasped for air.

Qigiq crawled toward them, arriving as Kandy finished the Miranda warning. Blake was still struggling to breathe when they rolled him to his side and cuffed his hands together below his backpack.

Qigiq watched Blake's eyes carefully. They were tight, the eyes of a wolf on hearing the steel door of a trap slam shut.

"Blake. The Spore security system has been activated," Kandy shouted over the crowd noise.

Those eyes revealed that Blake recognized the word.

"You figured it would be empty on Saturday," Qigiq said. "But there are people inside the Silver Platter building, including your employee Lili Volker." He waited until Blake met his eyes. "How do we stop it?"

Blake turned his head and coughed. He wasn't breathing normally, but he was breathing.

"Stop what?" Blake said.

Kandy squinted. She grabbed his shoulders and dragged him to his feet.

"Hey?!" Blake said, trying to shake her loose.

A voiced yelled, "These are hundred dollar bills."

Qigiq heard feet shuffle behind him and a dozen voices talking at once. He struggled to his feet.

Kandy marched Blake away from the growing crowd.

"Hey, Franky. Where are you going?" a girl's voice called after them.

Qigiq limped beside Blake and talked fast. "The security system at Silver Platter. We know it can destroy the building. We know a Craigslist's ad about a painting activated it." Qigiq had no idea how, but he was sure that's what Zeto had said. Qigiq glanced at his watch. "We have less than thirty minutes to stop it."

"Good luck," Blake said.

"And," Kandy said. "We have the IP address of the computer that did the posting."

Qigiq checked Kandy's face, wondering how much she was extrapolating.

Blake's head twisted to face her. He looked back over his shoulder. "Hey, that's my money," he screamed. "Get the hell away from it."

"Care to guess where that machine is located, Mr. Blake?" Kandy asked.

He tried to stop but she pushed him out of the depot and down to the tracks, forcing him forward and away from the airport buildings.

"You can't know that," he said.

That was enough for Qigiq.

"Zeto told us how you built Spore to be remotely activated."

"Zeto doesn't know how to activate Spore."

Qigiq smiled. Blake was admitting much by his denials. He put his hand on Blake's shoulder.

"Sure he does, Eddy, my friend. Zeto's a top-notch engineer. Hacking your computer after you cut him out of Spore was child's play. Only you don't keep shutdown instructions on your computer." Qigiq had a wild guess he hoped was close. "You keep them in your head."

They reached the far side of the tracks where a low cement wall below a steel railing divided them from a two-story drop to asphalt.

"Eddy, tell us how to stop Spore," Kandy said.

"You're both crazy," Blake replied.

Qigiq stepped back, guessing what Kandy was up to. He reached inside his jacket and lifted out the pistol. Blake's eyes flashed to the gun, then back toward the terminal where a hundred people were ravaging his money, then to Qigiq's face even though Kandy was talking.

"We don't have time for bullshit, Eddy. We know you paid your guy in the midwest to plant explosives. We know you fed him addresses. We know you built an illegal security system. And we know two more people are about to die at your hands."

Kandy released the handcuffs and stepped back. "Run, Eddy."

Blake looked from one to the other. "You can't do this."

"If they die, Eddy," Kandy said, "You'll be there to meet them."

"You're crazy," Eddy said again.

Qigiq nodded slowly. "In Alaska, we'd let you freeze to death in a snow storm." He looked over the wall. "But you could accidentally fall resisting arrest."

Blake stepped to his left, Kandy moved with him. He moved right, Qigiq pointed his gun at Eddy's heart.

"You can't do this."

"Of course we can," Kandy said. "You won't be around to tell your side of the story. And the people up there are too occupied to remember anything."

Blake put both hands on the railing and looked back over his shoulder, maybe wondering if he could jump and survive.

"Eddy," Qigiq said softly. "Zeto told me very clearly that only two people can stop Spore. You and your legal guy Simmons. Simmons is dead."

Qigiq blinked as he said Simmons name. He glanced at Kandy. "If I am gone."

Her face was blank for a moment, then she nodded.

"Talk, Eddy," she said. "Or jump, because if you don't talk, we have no use for you."

Eddy stared at the ground a couple of stories below.

"Time, Eddy. Time. That snow storm is moving in," Qigiq said.

He turned to look back at Qigiq, then directly at Kandy.

Qigiq knew he was a CEO weighing options and after effects. Admit to Spore, or let it explode and see where the chips would land when the lawyers all got in a courtroom.

"No."

Kandy grabbed Blake, yanked the backpack off with two hands and tossed it to Qigiq. Blake tried to swing at her but she grabbed his wrist, twisted it up hard behind his back, slapped a handcuff around it, yanked it away from his body and locked it to a railing stanchion.

"My car," she said. "Meet you in the terminal."

And she ran.

Qigiq stepped across the tracks as fast as he could move.

Eddy yelled, "What the hell are you doing? You can't leave me here. That's my property!"

Qigiq shouted over his shoulder, "Watch out for trains, Eddy."

Inside the station half a dozen people were on their knees scrambling for loose hundred dollar bills, while others ran both toward and away from Blake's ripped luggage. The train sat silent, Emergency Stop blinking on an electric sign over the open doors. Two men in security uniforms were trying to restore order.

Qigiq found Veronica and the girl in the blue dress standing together near the entrance to the glass-walled bridge. They were talking to Spinner. A tall dark-haired woman, also in uniform, stood beside him.

"He's all yours, Mr. Spinner," Qigiq said, handing over the backpack. He turned to Veronica. "Downstairs quick. We're meeting Kandy."

The three of them started across the bridge as fast as he could move using Veronica for support.

"Veronica, what's a Craigslist?" he asked.

"A website where you post classified ads for free. Everyone uses it to sell stuff. Some post themselves to find relationships. You can even list things you want and people show up to sell it to you."

Sounded like a flea market to Qigiq.

They reached the escalator. He motioned for the girls to go first, then stepped on with his right foot. He felt small and incapable looking out over the huge terminal teaming with thousands of travelers. Lili and Ferdinand. Spore. Robina. A girl in New York whose name he didn't even know. And all he had was a hunch about a dead madman.

He checked his watch. Twenty-three minutes.

Assuming Zeto was correct.

He stepped off the moving staircase and turned to watch the street. Kandy's black car was just pulling up to the curb. She jumped out, popped the hatch, stuck her head inside, and came running in his direction with a satchel. He found a long bench and sat down. His leg was throbbing and his left shoulder had started to stiffen. Veronica and her friend in the blue dress were examining something in a glass case that looked like bleached driftwood.

Kandy plopped on the bench beside him, reached in the satchel and came out with a leather bound book as thick as a pair of Gideon Bibles.

"That's his journal?" he said.

"The most recent one. What are we looking for?"

"Zeto only said, 'Blake and Simmons have the codes to stop Spore.' Could be anything. But do you think it's another posting to this Craigslist thing, since that's how you turn it on?"

"Symmetry makes sense," she said. "But who knows? Maybe they wouldn't consider that secure." She grabbed her cellphone, dialed and put it on speaker.

He glanced down. Twenty-one minutes. His spine tightened. For some reason he remembered the bike was still running. He picked up the journal and started scanning pages.

"Hi, Harold," Kandy said. "I have Simmons' journal. What am I looking for to stop Spore?"

Harold's voice came through the small speakers in the phone. "Never found out when I tried to hack it: too many layers, nothing on Blake's machine. They might use the Craigslist mechanism simply because they had it built and tested. It would be double effort to do something different for shutdown."

Qigiq flipped pages, getting comfortable with the handwriting. Searching for "Craigs."

"What are you doing?" Veronica asked.

Qigiq looked up. The two girls had drifted over.

"Looking for a code," he said.

"In that huge thing?" the girl in the blue dress asked.

"Oh, Zel, this is my friend, Qigiq. He rides motorcycles."

The girl smiled and held out her hand. Qigiq shook it. "Yes, in this huge thing."

"What kind of code?" Zel asked.

"To turn off a security system in a building."

"Oh, like when I open the museum shop in the morning?"

He nodded. "Kandy, nineteen minutes."

"Look for Spore," Zeto said. "He might use the code name for the system."

Veronica moved closer to Qigiq, her leg rubbing his arm as she looked at the book.

"When?" she asked.

Kandy and Qigiq looked up at her.

"When what?" Zeto said through the speaker.

"When was it built? My apartment is super old and has this four-digit thingie I have to remember to set. I made it tones." She sang, "fa do ti re."

"When did Silver Platter move in?" Kandy asked.

"Only been there...uh...thirteen months," Zeto said. "The security system was installed before Blake let us move in."

Qigiq flipped to the last entry, which was only three days old. He backed up until he was just over a year back, put the book between them and held a page vertical.

"Thanks, Harold," Kandy said. "Later."

She worked from the page backward and Qigiq worked from the page forward.

"I want to help," Veronica said. "Zel too."

"Read over our shoulders. Look for Craigslist, Spore, shutdown, security, anything that might have to do with disabling the system."

The two girls ran around behind the bench and four people silently read as fast as they could, flipping pages every few seconds, Qigiq and Veronica moving forward in time, Kandy and Zel moving backward.

"There, there," Zel yelled and pointed. "It says Spore."

"Blake insists on installing Spore," Kandy read aloud. "It's inconceivable to me that such a system is legal, even to protect trade secrets. And the possibility of an accident is real. But Blake is going ahead without consulting the board. I've advised him he's on shaky legal ground, in writing."

Kandy's eyes scanned. She flipped a page back and forth. "That's all."

Qigiq didn't really want to know, but he looked. "Fourteen minutes."

"Confirms Simmons knew about Spore," she said. "Let's give it five more. Then I'm going up to kick the shit out of Blake."

"Cut his dick off," Veronica said.

Qigiq swallowed hard, and started reading as fast as he could—afraid to go too slow, but afraid to miss critical information.

Pages swished as they were turned.

His eyes scanned: coming, cars, situation, static, disclosure, attention, later, meeting postponed, time, cash reserves, third patent filing, Sally. He choked, flipped the page: tomorrow, secular music, canned response, sales adjustment, Cra—.

"There," Veronica yelled. "Craigslist."

Qigiq put his finger on the page and backed up a few lines.

"Blake gave me confidential information so two parties would have it in case of emergency. Maintain plausible deniability. It goes here, and nowhere else. Craigslist. For Sale: Bootleg copy of Elvis performing with Jimi Hendrix at the Joplin Mansion. Memphis."

Veronica pulled out Qigiq's smartphone that she was still carrying.

"What do think, Kandy?" Qigiq asked.

Kandy leaned over and read the text for herself.

"I have the Memphis Craigslist," Veronica said.

They turned to face her.

"It says to post the message to Memphis." She shrugged. "You know, Elvis. Where else would you post it?"

Qigiq shook his head.

"Try it," Kandy said.

Veronica typed quickly into the small device as if playing a video game. She held the phone out in front of their faces.

"Check it for me. I don't want to make a mistake."

Qigiq read it. Kandy read it. They each went back and forth between her typed message and the writing in Simmons' journal.

"Be sure you get the punctuation right," Zel said. "Computers are picky."

They checked again.

"We need a colon after For Sale," Qigiq said.

Veronica fumbled with the device, held it out again.

"Looks good," Qigiq said.

"Sent," Veronica said. "Now we wait for the email confirmation."

Qigiq looked at her. She must have seen his confusion.

"Craigslist will send an email confirming our ad. It should show up in a second." She smiled at Qigiq. "I used your address."

His phone made a muffled ringing sound.

Veronica tapped at the phone. "I replied. I'll check the ad to make sure it's right. It should be up in a few seconds."

Qigiq looked ahead a few pages in the journal, didn't see another reference to Spore. He turned to Kandy.

"How will we know?"

Kandy's phone indicated an incoming text message.

Detective Kandy, good news. Power has returned and the doors have unlocked. We are exiting immediately—Ferdinand.

She slouched against the bench. "Spore is off. They're exiting the building."

Qigiq's eardrums were nearly pierced by the sound of Veronica and Zel screeching and jumping up and down like demented cheerleaders who had just won a free trip to Daytona Beach with the varsity football team. A couple hundred people turned to see what was happening.

His entire body released tension and he slid low on the bench next to Kandy. His heart rate slowed. Without thinking he looked as his watch.

"Nine minutes."

Kandy nodded slowly.

"What do we do with Blake?" he asked.

"Cut his dick off," Veronica said.

"Yeah!" Zel agreed.

Qigiq turned to Kandy. "You can use my knife."

~ 83 ~

"Mr. Zeto, are you actually proposing that we make you, a programmer, CEO of this company?"

Harold faced the two largest investors and only remaining board members of Silver Platter. Through the window behind them he could see the parking lot, now mostly empty because Terry McTyme had sent everyone home while they figured out what to do next. Blake had been arrested on Saturday. It was only Monday. Not much time to digest reality.

"Yes," he said simply, so there could be no confusion.

Terry fidgeted with an expensive fountain pen. Roberts stared at Harold, his lower jaw moving like a cow chewing.

"Gentleman," Harold continued. "Last week our corporate counsel was killed in a confrontation with a police detective while resisting arrest for the torture and murder of a young coed. Apparently, he was attacking a second victim when he was shot to death."

He held their gaze. Neither responded.

"Two days ago, our CEO was arrested on multiple counts of conspiracy to commit murder. He hatched a scheme, using Silver Platter technology without the approval of this board, to sabotage iPods and ended up killing and injuring innocent music fans."

He paused, leaving plenty of air space for them to talk if they wanted to.

"Not to be immodest, but I'm the person who designed and coded most of the technology that forms the foundation of this company. I would have a hard time being worse than the two men who have recently departed this board."

"But we need an MBA type. Someone with a business background to lead the company," Terry said.

"Mr. McTyme, I've been leading this company for two years. Blake had no idea what we needed to do in the current music environment."

"Still," Terry said, shuffling the financial documents he was holding as if they were crucial to the decision, "I don't see how the investors would ever accept you."

"You gentlemen hold a good deal of the investor stock. If you two agree, they will likely follow, since none of them want to get anywhere near the scandal currently surrounding this company."

"Don't remind me," Roberts said. "Our investment is worth zilch right now."

"As are my stock options. But it doesn't have to stay this way. We could also threaten them if you like."

"How's that?" Terry McTyme asked.

"The investors believed in us, so I'm not going to make ultimatums and put you in a more difficult position. But you could tell them that the two options are one: make Zeto CEO and see what he can do, or two: find a new CEO and move forward without Zeto because he has refused to stay."

"Would you really leave if we got another CEO?" Roberts said.

Harold shrugged. "Depends on the CEO. But if you don't use me, you'll lose six months to a year while the new guy figures out where we are and where we might go. Whereas..."

"Yes?" Terry said.

"Whereas, you can hire me into the package Eddy Blake had. No hassles, no lawyers, just give me his package. If he's convicted, he forfeits all stock under Platter's contract agreement anyway. I have that clause in my contract, too. So you give me Eddy's package on top of the options I already have. You issue nothing new. No dilution."

Roberts leaned back and sighed.

Terry said, "What about our technology? Who handles that with you in the CEO seat?"

"Lil...Ms. Volker can handle the management. I already consult with her regularly. We'll need to hire people to carry my coding load, but our technology is advanced enough to buy us a year, maybe two. The technology is the least of our problems."

Roberts turned toward Terry as if he hadn't been paying attention.

"I'm not happy about the way Eddy stuck us with the company."

"He sure did," Terry said. "So Mr. Zeto, where do we go?"

"We have audio fingerprint implant and detection technology and the patents filed for it. The obvious choice is to go to the big Hollywood companies: Disney, Warner, Sony. Sell them on the idea of tagging their files instead of putting free music out there like they've been doing for years with the audio CD format."

"Slow, tough sell," Roberts said.

"I agree. Better if we gave it to them," Harold said.

"For free?" Terry said.

"Yes, very free. As in license to use with no royalty."

"Then what?" Roberts said.

"Then we urge the government to follow France's lead and make Internet Service Providers responsible for preventing the movement of illegal content. As I'm sure you're aware, the core problem is simply that the beautiful, robust architecture of the Internet makes it trivially easy for anyone to steal in large volume. Coupled with consumer's general disregard for copyright law, the world has a disaster on its hands. So we sell software that detects copyrighted content direct to the ISPs so they can slow the illegal movement of data. Or at least comply with the evolving legal landscape."

"Possible," Terry said. "No guarantee though, and it could take a long time."

"I agree," Harold said. "Plus, smart people will figure a way around it, so it might never grow to the level we need."

Roberts sighed, and slid lower in his chair.

Harold let the room be silent for a few moments. Then he said, "But I have another idea."

"Which is?" Terry said.

"Which is unique and innovative and won't do me much good unless I'm CEO," Harold said with a big smile.

"So you want us to sign NDAs so you can tell us this big idea?" Roberts said.

"I already work here. I can't sign an NDA," Harold said. "However, I'd be a lot more comfortable if I felt you were close to giving me the job."

Terry looked to Roberts, who shrugged and said, "I don't have the time or energy for a CEO search. Let's give him a six-month trial and see what happens."

Terry turned to Harold, "Is that acceptable to you?"

Harold nodded. "Sure, with the standard golden strings attached. We can do a lot in six months."

Roberts brought a hand to his chin and nodded agreement.

"Okay, let's do it," Terry said. "So, Mr. Zeto, what do you have for us?"

"We package our detection technology and sell it to end users."

"What? Why would thieves buy technology to detect bootlegged music? That's nuts."

"Thieves won't, but honest people will. People who want to know their machines are legal, and their kids' machines are clean."

Both investors were quiet. Terry spoke first.

"It might work."

Harold said, "We create a new product category, like a virus detector. You remember McAffee before it became Intel Security, market cap $400 million; or Norton, market cap over $600 million. Only our software doesn't block viruses, it identifies and blocks downloads of illegal music."

"There are quite a few honest people out there," Roberts said.

"And they'll pay to keep what they consider the dark side of the Internet off the computers in their homes," Harold said. "That's why we license the fingerprinting technology to the big boys for free. They want to know where their music is and how it got there and we'll help them track it. Parents want to know they're not going to get hit with an RIAA lawsuit because little Timmy has been downloading boatloads of heavy metal and explicit rap again."

"It'll never work," Roberts said. "The crackers will undermine our software the minute we release it."

"You mean like the way new viruses are released all the time?" Harold asked.

"Exactly."

"That's the beauty of it."

The investors looked at him with blank stares, then at each other, and back to him.

"It's an ongoing battle between the crackers and us, so our customers need continuous updates. We sell recurring subscriptions and create new updates for download whenever necessary."

"New category," Terry said. "That means we're number one by definition."

Harold nodded.

"And each new threat and update release provides another burst of PR, building our brand at no cost to us," Terry added.

"That's the general idea," Harold said.

"This is a much better business model than Eddy was feeding us," Roberts said.

Terry looked directly into Harold's eyes. "Will it work, Mr. Zeto?"

Harold met his gaze, then turned to Roberts.

"I believe there are enough moving parts to this problem that it will work long enough for us to create an exit event, most likely sale of the company to an eight hundred pound gorilla like Google, or Microsoft. Or possibly a media giant like Sony."

"That's as long as we need," Roberts said, smiling for the first time in the entire meeting.

"One more thing," Terry said. "What about these trips to New York you've been making?"

Harold hesitated before speaking, choosing his words carefully.

"I'm done commuting to New York. Silver Platter LLC is my priority, once I have the job."

Terry stood, and shook hands with Harold.

"Congratulations, Mr. Zeto, as the new CEO of Silver Platter, please move forward with your plan as quickly as you can. I understand this is a new category, so the market is currently zero, but any projections you can share would be appreciated."

Roberts and Terry departed the room together, leaving Harold to contemplate what he had just gotten himself into. He put his elbows up on the conference table and stared out the window, absently counting cars as they passed, imagining each one as a cranberry muffin. He was at fifty-four when someone tapped on the door.

"Come in."

"Mr. Zeto, I followed up with the San Francisco Conservatory like you asked. They are pleased with the audition tape you provided."

"That's great, Stacy. Thank you for making the calls for me."

"There is a problem, though," she said, then chewed on her lower lip.

He looked at her standing next to the conference table in a teal-colored sweater that looked as if it were shedding, noticing for the first time that her blonde hair reached all the way to the tips of her breasts.

"What kind of problem?"

"To reserve the violin slot for the candidate they require full payment for the first year by the end of this week. And you should know it's non-refundable, even if the candidate fails to maintain an adequate Grade Point Average and is forced to leave the Conservatory."

He reached into a zippered pocket on the thigh of his pants and came back with a nylon wallet. From an inside sleeve he pulled out a blank check folded four times that he carried for emergencies. He pressed it flat on the table with his palm, trying to remove the creases.

"How much?"

She consulted the note in her hand. "Fifty-three thousand, two hundred and fourteen dollars."

"Do you have a ballpoint?" he asked.

She reached to the collar of her sweater and pulled out a pen that had been clipped inside.

He held the pen, feeling the warmth it had absorbed from her body, pressed a thin rectangular button at the end, and began to write.

~ 84 ~

Qigiq lay stretched flat, his bare back pressed against the roof of the houseboat, a forearm between his face and the sun, staring up at the jumping second hand of his MotoGP commemorative wristwatch as it counted off 540 seconds.

That close to losing Lili and Ferdinand.

He took a deep breath and blew it at the watch face.

A jealous madman obsessed with note taking...and a young cellist named Sally.

He reached around and pulled a rumpled sheet of paper out of the back pocket of his jeans. His eyes slowly scanned the list of items accumulated since the morning he and Robina had shared a Guzzi ride to Peggy's...

Eddy Blake hired his buddy Del, who hit on the idea of delivering IEDs to friends of a missing girl; thus, misdirecting the explosion investigation toward her abductor. And inadvertently, back toward Blake, who had an affair with her the year before. To make it happen Del had tailed him and Kandy; he remembered feeling the shadow at the motorcycle shop, thinking it was the man who had run him off the road. It wasn't. Two men had been following him; something else he had never considered. He and Kandy led Del to Sally's apartment, her roommate, her boyfriend Danny. And he, the visiting detective from Alaska, had fallen for the scheme, searching for one criminal, not two.

Qigiq lowered his arm and grinned at the sun. Poor Eddy hadn't a clue that the target of Del's misdirection had been Greg Simmons: a man sitting in his own boardroom planting clues to incriminate Eddy for Sally's death.

His smile faded.

Not poor Eddy. The man deployed IEDs, including one to Zeto's girlfriend.

The last bit clicked into place.

The duo switched to random targets.

A young woman in New York. An iPod. A passing taxicab.

This phase depended on timing: the media following the DoomTunes virus closely, music player explosions igniting the press, social networks erupting in a frenzy of conjecture.

People connecting dots that weren't there.

Terrorists Punish Bootleggers headlines.

Exactly what Eddy wanted: fear in the marketplace. Fear he hoped would drive people to trusted download providers like Silver Platter.

It too had worked. Lili said Platter's sales were up nearly fifty percent.

All this in an effort to increase profit at a tiny startup company so it could go public; make a few people wealthy; then in all likelihood fade into oblivion.

He closed his eyes and studied the red light flowing through his eyelids, dreading the paperwork he was supposed to be doing at this very moment.

Dreading visiting Sally's gravesite, though he knew he had to soon to tell her what they had found, and that her killer was dead.

Dreading the hundreds of times he would think of a young girl in New York being blown into traffic.

Dreading...

He thought about Robina's joy as she hopped off his Guzzi, and ordered a pile of burnt bacon sky high, and sang that silly song for him.

Mony Mony.

Made him think of money. And greed. And the lengths some people—

His cell phone rumbled.

"Qigiq here."

"Oh, Kee-jee. She's talking, she's talking."

"Hi, Veronica. Who is?"

"Vi and me are at the hospital. I heard it, I heard it, I know I did."

"Hospital?" Flashes of her bruised left eye filled his head. Had they missed? Was someone else beating her up. "Are you okay?"

"Me?" The line crackled during a long pause. "Of course I'm okay. What are you...oh Kee-jee. She didn't open her eyes, but I heard it, I heard it."

"Heard what Veronica?"

"Robina. Her lips moved and I heard what she said, so I know she's going to be okay."

He felt Robina's slender body behind him on the bike and the squeeze of her thin arms. Saw her lying in the alley."

"What did she say, Veronica, that has you all excited?"

"Well, me and Vi, we were being real quiet so we wouldn't disturb her. You know when people are in a coma all kinds of things can happen. Their spirit moves around the room and can see and hear everything."

"Is that so?"

"Oh yeah. So we were being real super still and just sort of connecting with our minds begging her to come and talk to us. And, you know, we asked her not to be mad about that fake funeral you arranged because it might bring the killer to the cemetery. That wax face was really good; it totally convinced me. My heart was so broken. But when you told me yesterday she was alive..."

The phone grew quiet. He heard the girls whispering. He remembered the shock on the Director's face when he asked him to stage a funeral. And it had worked. Sally's killer had come to the cemetery. But Greg Simmons as Max had been calm and supportive of Vi and Veronica, appearing innocent; maybe because he actually was innocent of hurting Robina. Qigiq wondered if that had been the first moment his subconscious suspected Max. And why later, he had felt the need to stay close to Veronica.

When they didn't speak, he said again, "Are you okay?"

"Yes, yes. We're so happy you got him."

More quiet.

"What did she say, Veronica?"

More whispering, this time for nearly a minute.

Then they hummed a theme he knew well.

He listened. And smiled.

Finally the two girls shouted together.

"Beethoven!"

ABOUT THE AUTHOR

Joe Klingler became fascinated with computers while completing an engineering degree, after which he spent a decade computer-analyzing medical images and writing academic papers. Years developing software for editing and special effects drew him to Silicon Valley and the art of storytelling. The interplay of people and the technology they build their lives around continues to intrigue him. *Mash Up* was inspired by a colleague who wore a *Napster* T-shirt to the office in the days of the Metallica lawsuit. Joe currently resides in California.

If you enjoyed this novel, please consider writing a brief review at Amazon.com. Your assistance in helping reach new readers is appreciated immensely.

To occasionally receive news on book releases, previews, discount promotions and more, please join *Joe's Readers* at
www.joeklingler.com

Made in the
USA
Columbia, SC